AMERICAN SCIENCE FICTION

FIVE CLASSIC NOVELS 1956–1958

AMERICAN SCIENCE FICTION

FIVE CLASSIC NOVELS 1956–1958

Double Star • Robert Heinlein
The Stars My Destination • Alfred Bester
A Case of Conscience • James Blish
Who? • Algis Budrys
The Big Time • Fritz Leiber

Gary K. Wolfe, *editor*

THE LIBRARY OF AMERICA

Contents

Online Companion

THE LIBRARY OF AMERICA has created an online companion to this volume. For more on 1950s science fiction and these works and writers, including jacket art and photographs, additional stories, author interviews, new appreciations of the novels by Michael Dirda, Neil Gaiman, William Gibson, Nicola Griffith, James Morrow, Tim Powers, Kit Reed, Peter Straub, and Connie Willis, and more, go to loa.org/sciencefiction.

DOUBLE STAR

Robert A. Heinlein

To Henry and Catherine Kuttner

I

IF A man walks in dressed like a hick and acting as if he owned the place, he's a spaceman.

It is a logical necessity. His profession makes him feel like boss of all creation; when he sets foot dirtside he is slumming among the peasants. As for his sartorial inelegance, a man who is in uniform nine tenths of the time and is more used to deep space than to civilization can hardly be expected to know how to dress properly. He is a sucker for the alleged tailors who swarm around every spaceport peddling "ground outfits."

I could see that this big-boned fellow had been dressed by Omar the Tentmaker—padded shoulders that were too big to start with, shorts cut so that they crawled up his hairy thighs as he sat down, a ruffled chemise that might have looked well on a cow.

But I kept my opinion to myself and bought him a drink with my last half Imperial, considering it an investment, spacemen being the way they are about money. "Hot jets!" I said as we touched glasses. He gave me a quick glance.

That was my initial mistake in dealing with Dak Broadbent. Instead of answering, "Clear space!" or, "Safe grounding!" as he should have, he looked me over and said softly, "A nice sentiment, but to the wrong man. I've never been out."

That was another good place to keep my mouth shut. Spacemen did not often come to the bar of Casa Mañana; it was not their sort of hotel and it's miles from the port. When one shows up in ground clothes, seeks a dark corner of the bar, and objects to being called a spaceman, that's *his* business. I had picked that spot myself so that I could see without being seen —I owed a little money here and there at the time, nothing important but embarrassing. I should have assumed that he had his reasons, too, and respected them.

But my vocal cords lived their own life, wild and free. "Don't give me that, shipmate," I replied. "If you're a ground hog, I'm Mayor of Tycho City. I'll wager you've done more drinking on Mars," I added, noticing the cautious way he lifted his glass, a dead giveaway of low-gravity habits, "than you've ever done on Earth."

"Keep your voice down!" he cut in without moving his lips. "What makes you sure that I am a *voyageur?* You don't know me."

"Sorry," I said. "You can be anything you like. But I've got eyes. You gave yourself away the minute you walked in."

He said something under his breath. "How?"

"Don't let it worry you. I doubt if anyone else noticed. But I see things other people don't see." I handed him my card, a little smugly perhaps. There is only one Lorenzo Smythe, the One-Man Stock Company. Yes, I'm "The Great Lorenzo"— stereo, canned opera, legit—"Pantomimist and Mimicry Artist Extraordinary."

He read my card and dropped it into a sleeve pocket—which annoyed me; those cards had cost me money—genuine imitation hand engraving. "I see your point," he said quietly, "but what was wrong with the way I behaved?"

"I'll show you," I said. "I'll walk to the door like a ground hog and come back the way you walk. Watch." I did so, making the trip back in a slightly exaggerated version of his walk to allow for his untrained eye—feet sliding softly along the floor as if it were deck plates, weight carried forward and balanced from the hips, hands a trifle forward and clear of the body, ready to grasp.

There are a dozen other details which can't be set down in words; the point is you have to *be* a spaceman when you do it, with a spaceman's alert body and unconscious balance—you have to live it. A city man blunders along on smooth floors all his life, steady floors with Earth-normal gravity, and will trip over a cigarette paper, like as not. Not so a spaceman.

"See what I mean?" I asked, slipping back into my seat.

"I'm afraid I do," he admitted sourly. "Did I walk like that?"

"Yes."

"Hmm . . . Maybe I should take lessons from you."

"You could do worse," I admitted.

He sat there looking me over, then started to speak— changed his mind and wiggled a finger at the bartender to refill our glasses. When the drinks came, he paid for them, drank his, and slid out of his seat all in one smooth motion. "Wait for me," he said quietly.

With a drink he had bought sitting in front of me I could not refuse. Nor did I want to; he interested me. I liked him, even on ten minutes' acquaintance; he was the sort of big ugly-handsome galoot that women go for and men take orders from.

He threaded his way gracefully through the room and passed a table of four Martians near the door. I didn't like Martians. I did not fancy having a thing that looks like a tree trunk topped off by a sun helmet claiming the privileges of a man. I did not like the way they grew pseudo limbs; it reminded me of snakes crawling out of their holes. I did not like the fact that they could look all directions at once without turning their heads— if they had had heads, which of course they don't. And I could not *stand* their smell!

Nobody could accuse me of race prejudice. I didn't care what a man's color, race, or religion was. But men were men, whereas Martians were *things*. They weren't even animals to my way of thinking. I'd rather have had a wart hog around me any day. Permitting them in restaurants and bars used by men struck me as outrageous. But there was the Treaty, of course, so what could I do?

These four had not been there when I came in, or I would have whiffed them. For that matter, they certainly could not have been there a few moments earlier when I had walked to the door and back. Now there they were, standing on their pedestals around a table, pretending to be people. I had not even heard the air conditioning speed up.

The free drink in front of me did not attract me; I simply wanted my host to come back so that I could leave politely. It suddenly occurred to me that he had glanced over that way just before he had left so hastily and I wondered if the Martians had anything to do with it. I looked over at them, trying to see if they were paying attention to our table—but how could you tell what a Martian was looking at or what it was thinking? That was another thing I didn't like about them.

I sat there for several minutes fiddling with my drink and wondering what had happened to my spaceman friend. I had hoped that his hospitality might extend to dinner and, if we became sufficiently *simpatico*, possibly even to a small temporary loan. My other prospects were—I admit it!—slender. The last two times I had tried to call my agent his autosecretary had simply recorded the message, and unless I deposited coins in the door, my room would not open to me that night . . . That was how low my fortunes had ebbed: reduced to sleeping in a coin-operated cubicle.

In the midst of my melancholy ponderings a waiter touched me on the elbow. "Call for you, sir."

"Eh? Very well, friend, will you fetch an instrument to the table?"

"Sorry, sir, but I can't transfer it. Booth 12 in the lobby."

"Oh. Thank you," I answered, making it as warm as possible since I was unable to tip him. I swung wide around the Martians as I went out.

I soon saw why the call had not been brought to the table; No. 12 was a maximum-security booth, sight, sound, and scramble. The tank showed no image and did not clear even after the door locked behind me. It remained milky until I sat down and placed my face within pickup, then the opalescent clouds melted away and I found myself looking at my spaceman friend.

"Sorry to walk out on you," he said quickly, "but I was in a hurry. I want you to come at once to Room 2106 of the Eisenhower."

He offered no explanation. The Eisenhower is just as unlikely a hotel for spacemen as Casa Mañana. I could smell trouble. You don't pick up a stranger in a bar and then insist that he come to a hotel room—well, not one of the same sex, at least.

"Why?" I asked.

The spaceman got that look peculiar to men who are used to being obeyed without question; I studied it with professional interest—it's not the same as anger; it is more like a thundercloud just before a storm. Then he got himself in hand and answered quietly, "Lorenzo, there is no time to explain. Are you open to a job?"

"Do you mean a *professional* engagement?" I answered slowly. For a horrid instant I suspected that he was offering me . . .

Well, *you* know—a *job*. Thus far I had kept my professional pride intact, despite the slings and arrows of outrageous fortune.

"Oh, professional, of course!" he answered quickly. "This requires the best actor we can get."

I did not let my relief show in my face. It was true that I was ready for *any* professional work—I would gladly have played the balcony in *Romeo and Juliet*—but it does not do to be eager. "What is the nature of the engagement?" I asked. "My calendar is rather full."

He brushed it aside. "I can't explain over the phone. Perhaps you don't know it, but any scrambler circuit can be unscrambled—with the proper equipment. Shag over here fast!"

He was eager; therefore I could afford not to be eager. "Now really," I protested, "what do you think I am? A bellman? Or an untried juvenile anxious for the privilege of carrying a spear? *I* am Lorenzo!" I threw up my chin and looked offended. "What is your offer?"

"Uh . . . Damn it, I *can't* go into it over the phone. How much do you get?"

"Eh? You are asking my professional salary?"

"Yes, yes!"

"For a single appearance? Or by the week? Or an option contract?"

"Uh, never mind. What do you get by the day?"

"My minimum fee for a one-evening date is one hundred Imperials." This was simple truth. Oh, I have been coerced at times into paying some scandalous kickbacks, but the voucher never read less than my proper fee. A man has his standards. I'd rather starve.

"Very well," he answered quickly, "one hundred Imperials in cash, laid in your hand the minute you show up here. But hurry!"

"Eh?" I realized with sudden dismay that I could as easily have said two hundred, or even two fifty. "But I have not agreed to accept the engagement."

"Never mind that! We'll talk it over when you get here. The hundred is yours even if you turn us down. If you accept— well, call it a bonus, over and above your salary. Now will you sign off and get over here?"

I bowed. "Certainly, sir. Have patience."

Fortunately the Eisenhower is not too far from the Casa, for I did not even have a minum for tube fare. However, although the art of strolling is almost lost, I savor it—and it gave me time to collect my thoughts. I was no fool; I was aware that when another man is too anxious to force money on one, it is time to examine the cards, for there is almost certainly something illegal, or dangerous, or both, involved in the matter. I was not unduly fussy about legality *qua* legality; I agreed with the Bard that the Law is often an idiot. But in the main I had stayed on the right side of the street.

But presently I realized that I had insufficient facts, so I put it out of my mind, threw my cape over my right shoulder, and strode along, enjoying the mild autumn weather and the rich and varied odors of the metropolis. On arrival I decided to forego the main entrance and took a bounce tube from the sub-basement to the twenty-first floor, I having at the time a vague feeling that this was not the place to let my public recognize me. My *voyageur* friend let me in. "You took long enough," he snapped.

"Indeed?" I let it go at that and looked around me. It was an expensive suite, as I had expected, but it was littered and there were at least a dozen used glasses and as many coffee cups scattered here and there; it took no skill to see that I was merely the latest of many visitors. Sprawled on a couch, scowling at me, was another man, whom I tabbed tentatively as a spaceman. I glanced inquiringly but no introduction was offered.

"Well, you're here, at least. Let's get down to business."

"Surely. Which brings to mind," I added, "there was mention of a bonus, or retainer."

"Oh, yes." He turned to the man on the couch. "Jock, pay him."

"For what?"

"Pay him!"

I now knew which one was boss—although, as I was to learn, there was usually little doubt when Dak Broadbent was in a room. The other fellow stood up quickly, still scowling, and counted out to me a fifty and five tens. I tucked it away casually without checking it and said, "I am at your disposal, gentlemen."

The big man chewed his lip. "First, I want your solemn oath not even to talk in your sleep about this job."

"If my simple word is not good, is my oath better?" I glanced at the smaller man, slouched again on the couch. "I don't believe we have met. I am Lorenzo."

He glanced at me, looked away. My barroom acquaintance said hastily, "Names don't matter in this."

"No? Before my revered father died he made me promise him three things: first, never to mix whisky with anything but water; second, always to ignore anonymous letters; and lastly, never to talk with a stranger who refuses to give his name. Good day, sirs." I turned toward the door, their hundred Imperials warm in my pocket.

"Hold it!" I paused. He went on, "You are perfectly right. My name is——"

"Skipper!"

"Stow it, Jock. I'm Dak Broadbent; that's Jacques Dubois glaring at us. We're both *voyageurs*—master pilots, all classes, any acceleration."

I bowed. "Lorenzo Smythe," I said modestly, "jongleur and artist—care of The Lambs Club." I made a mental note to pay my dues.

"Good. Jock, try smiling for a change. Lorenzo, you agree to keep our business secret?"

"Under the rose. This is a discussion between gentlemen."

"Whether you take the job or not?"

"Whether we reach agreement or not. I am human, but, short of illegal methods of questioning, your confidences are safe with me."

"I am well aware of what neodexocaine will do to a man's forebrain, Lorenzo. We don't expect the impossible."

"Dak," Dubois said urgently, "this is a mistake. We should at least——"

"Shut up, Jock. I want no hypnotists around at this point. Lorenzo, we want you to do an impersonation job. It has to be so perfect that no one—I mean *no one*—will ever know it took place. Can you do that sort of a job?"

I frowned. "The first question is not 'Can I?' but 'Will I?' What are the circumstances?"

"Uh, we'll go into details later. Roughly, it is the ordinary doubling job for a well-known public figure. The difference is that the impersonation will have to be so perfect as to fool people who know him well and must see him close up. It won't be just reviewing a parade from a grandstand, or pinning medals on girl scouts." He looked at me shrewdly. "It will take a real artist."

"No," I said at once.

"Huh? You don't know anything about the job yet. If your conscience is bothering you, let me assure you that you will not be working against the interests of the man you will impersonate—nor against anyone's legitimate interests. This is a job that really needs to be done."

"No."

"Well, for Pete's sake, why? You don't even know how much we will pay."

"Pay is no object," I said firmly. "I am an actor, not a double."

"I don't understand you. There are lots of actors picking up spare money making public appearances for celebrities."

"I regard them as prostitutes, not colleagues. Let me make myself clear. Does an author respect a ghost writer? Would you respect a painter who allowed another man to sign his work— for *money*? Possibly the spirit of the artist is foreign to you, sir, yet perhaps I may put it in terms germane to your own profession. Would you, simply for *money*, be content to pilot a ship while some other man, not possessing your high art, wore the uniform, received the credit, was publicly acclaimed as the Master? Would you?"

Dubois snorted. "How much money?"

Broadbent frowned at him. "I think I understand your objection."

"To the artist, sir, kudos comes first. Money is merely the mundane means whereby he is enabled to create his art."

"Hmm . . . All right, so you won't do it just for money. Would you do it for other reasons? If you felt that it had to be done and you were the only one who could do it successfully?"

"I concede the possibility; I cannot imagine the circumstances."

"You won't have to imagine them; we'll explain them to you."

Dubois jumped up off the couch. "Now see here, Dak, you can't——"

"Cut it, Jock! He has to know."

"He doesn't have to know now—and here. And you haven't any right to jeopardize everybody else by telling him. You don't know a thing about him."

"It's a calculated risk." Broadbent turned back to me.

Dubois grabbed his arm, swung him around. "Calculated risk be damned! Dak, I've strung along with you in the past—but this time before I'll let you shoot off your face, well, one or the other of us isn't going to be in any shape to talk."

Broadbent looked startled, then grinned coldly down at Dubois. "Think you're up to it, Jock old son?"

Dubois glared up at him, did not flinch. Broadbent was a head taller and outweighed him by twenty kilos. I found myself for the first time liking Dubois; I am always touched by the gallant audacity of a kitten, the fighting heart of a bantam cock, or the willingness of a little man to die in his tracks rather than knuckle under . . . And, while I did not expect Broadbent to kill him, I did think that I was about to see Dubois used as a dust rag.

I had no thought of interfering. Every man is entitled to elect the time and manner of his own destruction.

I could see tension grow. Then suddenly Broadbent laughed and clapped Dubois on the shoulder. "Good for you, Jock!" He turned to me and said quietly, "Will you excuse us a few moments? My friend and I must make heap big smoke."

The suite was equipped with a hush corner, enclosing the autograph and the phone. Broadbent took Dubois by the arm and led him over there; they stood and talked urgently.

Sometimes such facilities in public places like hotels are not all that they might be; the sound waves fail to cancel out completely. But the Eisenhower is a luxury house and in this case, at least, the equipment worked perfectly; I could see their lips move but I could hear no sound.

But I could indeed see their lips move. Broadbent's face was toward me and Dubois I could glimpse in a wall mirror. When I was performing in my famous mentalist act, I found out why my father had beaten my tail until I learned the silent language of lips—in my mentalist act I always performed in a brightly lighted hall and made use of spectacles which—but never mind; I could read lips.

Dubois was saying: "Dak, you bloody, stupid, unprintable, illegal and highly improbable obscenity, do you want us both to wind up counting rocks on Titan? This conceited pip-squeak will spill his guts."

I almost missed Broadbent's answer. Conceited indeed! Aside from a cold appreciation of my own genius I felt that I was a modest man.

Broadbent: ". . . doesn't matter if the game is crooked when it's the only game in town. Jock, there is nobody else we can use."

Dubois: "All right, then get Doc Capek over here, hypnotize him, and shoot him the happy juice. But don't tell him the score—not until he's conditioned, not while we are still on dirt."

Broadbent: "Uh, Capek himself told me that we could not depend on hypno and drugs, not for the performance we need. We've got to have his co-operation, his intelligent co-operation."

Dubois snorted. "What intelligence? Look at him. Ever see a rooster strutting through a barnyard? Sure, he's the right size and shape and his skull looks a good bit like the Chief—but there is nothing behind it. He'll lose his nerve, blow his top, and give the whole thing away. He can't play the part—he's just a ham actor!"

If the immortal Caruso had been charged with singing off key, he could not have been more affronted than I. But I trust I justified my claim to the mantle of Burbage and Booth at that moment; I went on buffing my nails and ignored it—merely noting that I would someday make friend Dubois both laugh and cry within the span of twenty seconds. I waited a few moments more, then stood up and approached the hush corner. When they saw that I intended to enter it, they both shut up. I said quietly, "Never mind, gentlemen, I have changed my mind."

Dubois looked relieved. "You don't want the job."

"I mean that I accept the engagement. You need not make explanations. I have been assured by friend Broadbent that the work is such as not to trouble my conscience—and I trust him. He has assured me that he needs an actor. But the business affairs of the producer are not my concern. I accept."

Dubois looked angry but shut up. I expected Broadbent to look pleased and relieved; instead he looked worried. "All right," he agreed, "let's get on with it. Lorenzo, I don't know exactly how long we will need you. No more than a few days, I'm certain—and you will be on display only an hour or so once or twice in that time."

"That does not matter as long as I have time to study the role—the impersonation. But approximately how many days will you need me? I should notify my agent."

"Oh no! Don't do that."

"Well—how long? As much as a week?"

"It will be less than that—or we're sunk."

"Eh?"

"Never mind. Will a hundred Imperials a day suit you?"

I hesitated, recalling how easily he had met my minimum just to interview me—and decided this was a time to be gracious. I waved it aside. "Let's not speak of such things. No doubt you will present me with an honorarium consonant with the worth of my performance."

"All right, all right." Broadbent turned away impatiently. "Jock, call the field. Then call Langston and tell him we're starting Plan Mardi Gras. Synchronize with him. Lorenzo . . ." He motioned for me to follow and strode into the bath. He opened a small case and demanded, "Can you do anything with this junk?"

"Junk" it was—the sort of overpriced and unprofessional make-up kit that is sold over the counter to stage-struck youngsters. I stared at it with mild disgust. "Do I understand, sir, that you expect me to start an impersonation *now?* Without time for study?"

"Huh? No, no, no! I want you to change your face—on the outside chance that someone might recognize you as we leave here. That's possible, isn't it?"

I answered stiffly that being recognized in public was a burden that all celebrities were forced to carry. I did not add that it was certain that countless people would recognize The Great Lorenzo in any public place.

"Okay. So change your phiz so it's not yours." He left abruptly.

I sighed and looked over the child's toys he had handed me,

no doubt thinking they were the working tools of my profession—grease paints suitable for clowns, reeking spirit gum, crepe hair which seemed to have been raveled from Aunt Maggie's parlor carpet. Not an ounce of Silicoflesh, no electric brushes, no modern amenities of any sort. But a true artist can do wonders with a burnt match, or oddments such as one might find in a kitchen—and his own genius. I arranged the lights and let myself fall into creative reverie.

There are several ways to keep a well-known face from being recognized. The simplest is misdirection. Place a man in uniform and his face is not likely to be noticed—do you recall the *face* of the last policeman you encountered? Could you identify him if you saw him next in mufti? On the same principle is the attention-getting special feature. Equip a man with an enormous nose, disfigured perhaps with *acne rosacea*; the vulgar will stare in fascination at the nose itself, the polite will turn away—but neither will see the face.

I decided against this primitive maneuver because I judged that my employer wished me not to be noticed at all rather than remembered for an odd feature without being recognized. This is much more difficult; anyone can be conspicuous but it takes real skill not to be noticed. I needed a face as commonplace, as impossible to remember as the true face of the immortal Alec Guinness. Unfortunately my aristocratic features are entirely too distinguished, too handsome—a regrettable handicap for a character actor. As my father used to say, "Larry, you are too damned pretty! If you don't get off your lazy duff and learn the business, you are going to spend fifteen years as a juvenile, under the mistaken impression that you are an actor—then wind up selling candy in the lobby. 'Stupid' and 'pretty' are the two worst vices in show business—and you're *both*."

Then he would take off his belt and stimulate my brain. Father was a practical psychologist and believed that warming the *glutei maximi* with a strap drew excess blood away from a boy's brain. While the theory may have been shaky, the results justified the method; by the time I was fifteen I could stand on my head on a slack wire and quote page after page of Shakespeare and Shaw—or steal a scene simply by lighting a cigarette.

I was deep in the mood of creation when Broadbent stuck

his face in. "Good grief!" he snapped. "Haven't you done anything yet?"

I stared coldly. "I assumed that you wanted my best creative work—which cannot be hurried. Would you expect a *cordon bleu* to compound a new sauce on the back of a galloping horse?"

"Horses be damned!" He glanced at his watch finger. "You have six more minutes. If you can't do anything in that length of time, we'll just have to take our chances."

Well! Of course I prefer to have plenty of time—but I had understudied my father in his quick-change creation, *The Assassination of Huey Long*, fifteen parts in seven minutes—and had once played it in nine seconds less time than he did. "Stay where you are!" I snapped back at him. "I'll be with you at once." I then put on "Benny Grey," the colorless handy man who does the murders in *The House with No Doors*—two quick strokes to put dispirited lines into my cheeks from nose to mouth corners, a mere suggestion of bags under my eyes, and Factor's #5 sallow over all, taking not more than twenty seconds for everything—I could have done it in my sleep; *House* ran on boards for ninety-two performances before they recorded it.

Then I faced Broadbent and he gasped. "Good God! I don't believe it."

I stayed in "Benny Grey" and did not smile acknowledgment. What Broadbent could not realize was that the grease paint really was not necessary. It makes it easier, of course, but I had used a touch of it primarily because he expected it; being one of the yokels, he naturally assumed that make-up consisted of paint and powder.

He continued to stare at me. "Look here," he said in a hushed voice, "could you do something like that for *me?* In a hurry?"

I was about to say no when I realized that it presented an interesting professional challenge. I had been tempted to say that if my father had started in on him at five he might be ready now to sell cotton candy at a punkin' doin's, but I thought better of it. "You simply want to be sure that you will not be recognized?" I asked.

"Yes, yes! Can you paint me up, or give me a false nose, or something?"

I shook my head. "No matter what we did with make-up, it would simply make you look like a child dressed up for Trick or Treat. You can't act and you can never learn, at your age. We won't touch your face."

"Huh? But with this beak on me——"

"Attend me. Anything I could do to that lordly nose would just call attention to it, I assure you. Would it suffice if an acquaintance looked at you and said, 'Say, that big fellow reminds me of Dak Broadbent. It's not Dak, of course, but looks a little like him.' Eh?"

"Huh? I suppose so. As long as he was sure it wasn't me. I'm supposed to be on . . . Well, I'm not supposed to be on Earth just now."

"He'll be quite sure it is not you, because we'll change your walk. That's the most distinctive thing about you. If your walk is wrong, it cannot possibly be *you*—so it must be some other big-boned, broad-shouldered man who looks a bit like you."

"Okay, show me how to walk."

"No, you could never learn it. I'll force you to walk the way I want you to."

"How?"

"We'll put a handful of pebbles or the equivalent in the toes of your boots. That will force you back on your heels and make you stand up straight. It will be impossible for you to sneak along in that catfooted spaceman's crouch. Mmm . . . I'll slap some tape across your shoulder blades to remind you to keep your shoulders back, too. That will do it."

"You think they won't recognize me just because I'll walk differently?"

"Certain. An acquaintance won't know why he is sure it is not you, but the very fact that the conviction is subconscious and unanalyzed will put it beyond reach of doubt. Oh, I'll do a little something to your face, just to make you feel easier—but it isn't necessary."

We went back into the living room of the suite. I was still being "Benny Grey" of course; once I put on a role it takes a conscious effort of will to go back to being myself. Dubois was busy at the phone; he looked up, saw me, and his jaw dropped. He hurried out of the hush locus and demanded, "Who's *he*? And where's that actor fellow?" After his first glance at me, he had looked away and not bothered to look back—"Benny Grey" is such a tired, negligible little guy that there is no point in looking at him.

"What actor fellow?" I answered in Benny's flat, colorless tones. It brought Dubois' eyes back to me. He looked at me, started to look away, his eyes snapped back, then he looked at my clothes. Broadbent guffawed and clapped him on the shoulder.

"And *you* said he couldn't act!" He added sharply, "Did you get them all, Jock?"

"Yes." Dubois looked back at me, looked perplexed, and looked away.

"Okay. We've got to be out of here in four minutes. Let's see how fast you can get me fixed up, Lorenzo."

Dak had one boot off, his blouse off, and his chemise pulled up so that I could tape his shoulders when the light over the door came on and the buzzer sounded. He froze. "Jock? We expecting anybody?"

"Probably Langston. He said he was going to try to get over here before we left." Dubois started for the door.

"It might not be him. It might be——" I did not get to hear Broadbent say who he thought it might be as Dubois dilated the door. Framed in the doorway, looking like a nightmare toadstool, was a Martian.

For an agony-stretched second I could see nothing but the Martian. I did not see the human standing behind him, nor did I notice the life wand the Martian cradled in his pseudo limb.

Then the Martian flowed inside, the man with him stepped in behind him, and the door relaxed. The Martian squeaked, "Good afternoon, gentlemen. Going somewhere?"

I was frozen, dazed, by acute xenophobia. Dak was handicapped by disarranged clothing. But little Jock Dubois acted with a simple heroism that made him my beloved brother even as he died . . . He flung himself at that life wand. Right at it —he made no attempt to evade it.

He must have been dead, a hole burned through his belly you could poke a fist through, before he hit the floor. But he hung on and the pseudo limb stretched like taffy—then snapped, broken off a few inches from the monster's neck, and poor Jock still had the life wand cradled in his dead arms.

The human who had followed that stinking, reeking thing into the room had to step to one side before he could get in a shot—and he made a mistake. He should have shot Dak first, then me. Instead he wasted his first one on Jock and he never got a second one, as Dak shot him neatly in the face. I had not even known Dak was armed.

Deprived of his weapon, the Martian did not attempt to escape. Dak bounced to his feet, slid up to him, and said, "Ah, Rrringriil. I see you."

"I see you, Captain Dak Broadbent," the Martian squeaked, then added, "You will tell my nest?"

"I will tell your nest, Rrringriil."

"I thank you, Captain Dak Broadbent."

Dak reached out a long bony finger and poked it into the eye nearest him, shoving it on home until his knuckles were jammed against the brain case. He pulled it out and his finger was slimed with a green ichor. The creature's pseudo limbs crawled back into its trunk in reflex spasm but the dead thing continued to stand firm on its base. Dak hurried into the bath; I heard him washing his hands. I stayed where I was, almost as frozen by shock as the late Rrringriil.

Dak came out, wiping his hands on his shirt, and said, "We'll have to clean this up. There isn't much time." He could have been speaking of a spilled drink.

I tried to make clear in one jumbled sentence that I wanted no part of it, that we ought to call the cops, that I wanted to get away from there before the cops came, that he knew what he could do with his crazy impersonation job, and that I planned to sprout wings and fly out the window. Dak brushed it all aside. "Don't jitter, Lorenzo. We're on minus minutes now. Help me get the bodies into the bathroom."

"Huh? Good God, man! Let's just lock up and run for it. Maybe they will never connect us with it."

"Probably they wouldn't," he agreed, "since neither one of us is supposed to be here. But they would be able to see that Rrringriil had killed Jock—and we can't have *that*. Not now we can't."

"Huh?"

"We can't afford a news story about a Martian killing a human. So shut up and help me."

I shut up and helped him. It steadied me to recall that "Benny Grey" had been the worst of sadistic psychopaths, who had enjoyed dismembering his victims. I let "Benny Grey" drag the two human bodies into the bath while Dak took the life wand and sliced Rrringriil into pieces small enough to handle. He was careful to make the first cut below the brain case so the job was not messy, but I could not help him with it—it seemed to me that a dead Martian stank even worse than a live one.

The oubliette was concealed in a panel in the bath just beyond the bidet; if it had not been marked with the usual radiation trefoil it would have been hard to find. After we had shoved the chunks of Rrringriil down it (I managed to get my spunk up enough to help), Dak tackled the messier problem of butchering and draining the human corpses, using the wand and, of course, working in the bathtub.

It is amazing how much blood a man holds. We kept the water running the whole time; nevertheless, it was bad. But when Dak had to tackle the remains of poor little Jock, he just wasn't up to it. His eyes flooded with tears, blinding him, so I elbowed him aside before he sliced off his own fingers and let "Benny Grey" take over.

When I had finished and there was nothing left to show that there had ever been two other men and a monster in the suite, I sluiced out the tub carefully and stood up. Dak was in the doorway, looking as calm as ever. "I've made sure the floor is tidy," he announced. "I suppose a criminologist with proper equipment could reconstruct it—but we are counting on no one ever suspecting. So let's get out of here. We've got to gain almost twelve minutes somehow. Come on!"

I was beyond asking where or why. "All right. Let's fix your boots."

He shook his head. "It would slow me up. Right now speed is more essential than not being recognized."

"I am in your hands." I followed him to the door; he stopped and said, "There may be others around. If so, shoot first—there's nothing else you can do." He had the life wand in his hand, with his cloak drawn over it.

"Martians?"

"Or men. Or both."

"Dak? Was Rrringriil one of those four at the Mañana bar?"

"Certainly. Why do you think I went around Robinson's barn to get you out of there and over here? They either tailed you, as we did, or they tailed me. Didn't you recognize him?"

"Heavens, no! Those monsters all look alike to me."

"And *they* say *we* all look alike. The four were Rrringriil, his conjugate-brother Rrringlath, and two others from his nest, of divergent lines. But shut up. If you see a Martian, shoot. You have the other gun?"

"Uh, yes. Look, Dak, I don't know what this is all about. But as long as those beasts are against you, I'm with you. I despise Martians."

He looked shocked. "You don't know what you are saying. We're not fighting Martians; those four are renegades."

"Huh?"

"There are lots of good Martians—almost all of them. Shucks, even Rrringriil wasn't a bad sort in most ways—I've had many a fine chess game with him."

"What? In that case, I'm——"

"Stow it. You're in too deep to back out. Now quick-march, straight to the bounce tube. I'll cover our rear."

I shut up. I was in much too deep—that was unarguable.

We hit the sub-basement and went at once to the express tubes. A two-passenger capsule was just emptying; Dak shoved me in so quickly that I did not see him set the control combination. But I was hardly surprised when the pressure let up from my chest and I saw the sign blinking JEFFERSON SKYPORT —*All Out.*

Nor did I care what station it was as long as it was as far as possible from Hotel Eisenhower. The few minutes we had been crammed in the vactube had been long enough for me to devise a plan—sketchy, tentative, and subject to change without notice, as the fine print always says, but a plan. It could be stated in two words: Get lost!

Only that morning I would have found the plan very difficult to execute; in our culture a man with no money at all is baby-helpless. But with a hundred slugs in my pocket I could go far and fast. I felt no obligation to Dak Broadbent. For reasons of his own—not *my* reasons!—he had almost got me killed, then had crowded me into covering up a crime, made me a fugitive from justice. But we had evaded the police, temporarily at least, and now, simply by shaking off Broadbent, I could forget the whole thing, shelve it as a bad dream. It seemed most unlikely that I could be connected with the affair even if it were discovered—fortunately a gentleman always wears gloves, and I had had mine off only to put on make-up and later during that ghastly house cleaning.

Aside from the warm burst of adolescent heroics I had felt when I thought Dak was fighting Martians I had no interest in his schemes—and even that sympathy had shut off when I found that he liked Martians in general. His impersonation job I would not now touch with the proverbial eleven-foot pole. To hell with Broadbent! All I wanted out of life was money enough to keep body and soul together and a chance to practice my art; cops-and-robbers nonsense did not interest me—poor theater at best.

Jefferson Port seemed handmade to carry out my scheme. Crowded and confused, with express tubes spiderwebbing from it, in it, if Dak took his eyes off me for half a second I would be halfway to Omaha. I would lie low a few weeks, then get in touch with my agent and find out if any inquiries had been made about me.

Dak saw to it that we climbed out of the capsule together, else I would have slammed it shut and gone elsewhere at once. I pretended not to notice and stuck close as a puppy to him as we went up the belt to the main hall just under the surface, coming out between the Pan-Am desk and American Skylines. Dak headed straight across the waiting-room floor toward Diana, Ltd., and I surmised that he was going to buy tickets for the Moon shuttle—how he planned to get me aboard without passport or vaccination certificate I could not guess but I knew that he was resourceful. I decided that I would fade into the furniture while he had his wallet out; when a man counts money there are at least a few seconds when his eyes and attention are fully occupied.

But we went right on past the Diana desk and through an archway marked *Private Berths*. The passageway beyond was not crowded and the walls were blank; I realized with dismay that I had let slip my best chance, back there in the busy main hall. I held back. "Dak? Are we making a jump?"

"Of course."

"Dak, you're crazy. I've got no papers, I don't even have a tourist card for the Moon."

"You won't need them."

"Huh? They'll stop me at 'Emigration.' Then a big, beefy cop will start asking questions."

A hand about the size of a cat closed on my upper arm. "Let's not waste time. Why should you go through 'Emigration,' when officially you aren't leaving? And why should I, when officially I never arrived? Quick-march, old son."

I am well muscled and not small, but I felt as if a traffic robot were pulling me out of a danger zone. I saw a sign reading MEN and I made a desperate attempt to break it up. "Dak, half a minute, please. Got to see a man about the plumbing."

He grinned at me. "Oh, yes? You went just before we left the hotel." He did not slow up or let go of me.

"Kidney trouble——"

"Lorenzo old son, I smell a case of cold feet. Tell you what I'll do. See that cop up ahead?" At the end of the corridor, in the private berths station, a defender of the peace was resting his big feet by leaning over a counter. "I find I have a sudden attack of conscience. I feel a need to confess—about how you killed a visiting Martian and two local citizens—about how you held a gun on me and forced me to help you dispose of the bodies. About——"

"You're crazy!"

"Almost out of my mind with anguish and remorse, ship-mate."

"But—you've got nothing on me."

"So? I think my story will sound more convincing than yours. I know what it is all about and you don't. I know all about you and you know nothing about me. For example . . ." He mentioned a couple of details in my past that I would have sworn were buried and forgotten. All right, so I did have a couple of routines useful for stag shows that are not for the family trade—a man has to eat. But that matter about Bebe; that was hardly fair, for I certainly had not known that she was underage. As for that hotel bill, while it is true that bilking an "innkeeper" in Miami Beach carries much the same punish-ment as armed robbery elsewhere, it is a very provincial attitude —I would have paid if I had had the money. As for that unfortunate incident in Seattle—well, what I am trying to say is that Dak did know an amazing amount about my background but he had the wrong slant on most of it. Still . . .

"So," he continued, "let's walk right up to yon gendarme and make a clean breast of it. I'll lay you seven to two as to which one of us is out on bail first."

So we marched up to the cop and on past him. He was talking to a female clerk back of the railing and neither one of them looked up. Dak took out two tickets reading, GATE PASS— MAINTENANCE PERMIT—Berth K127, and stuck them into the monitor. The machine scanned them, a transparency directed us to take an upper-level car, code King 127; the gate let us through and locked behind us as a recorded voice said, "Watch your step, please, and heed radiation warnings. The Terminal Company is not responsible for accidents beyond the gate."

Dak punched an entirely different code in the little car; it wheeled around, picked a track, and we took off out under the field. It did not matter to me, I was beyond caring.

When we stepped out of the little car it went back where it came from. In front of me was a ladder disappearing into the steel ceiling above. Dak nudged me. "Up you go." There was a scuttle hole at the top and on it a sign: RADIATION HAZARD —Optimax 13 Seconds. The figures had been chalked in. I stopped. I have no special interest in offspring but I am no fool. Dak grinned and said, "Got your lead britches on? Open it, go through at once, and straight up the ladder into the ship. If you don't stop to scratch, you'll make it with at least three seconds to spare."

I believe I made it with five seconds to spare. I was out in the sunlight for about ten feet, then I was inside a long tube in the ship. I used about every third rung.

The rocket ship was apparently small. At least the control room was quite cramped; I never got a look at the outside. The only other spaceships I had ever been in were the Moon shuttles *Evangeline* and her sister ship the *Gabriel*, that being the year in which I had incautiously accepted a lunar engagement on a co-op basis—our impresario had had a notion that a juggling, tightrope, and acrobatic routine would go well in the one-sixth gee of the Moon, which was correct as far as it went, but he had not allowed rehearsal time for us to get used to low gravity. I had to take advantage of the Distressed Travelers Act to get back and I had lost my wardrobe.

There were two men in the control room; one was lying in one of three acceleration couches fiddling with dials, the other was making obscure motions with a screw driver. The one in the couch glanced at me, said nothing. The other one turned, looked worried, then said past me, "What happened to Jock?"

Dak almost levitated out of the hatch behind me. "No time!" he snapped. "Have you compensated for his mass?"

"Yes."

"Red, is she taped? Tower?"

The man in the couch answered lazily, "I've been recomputing every two minutes. You're clear with the tower. Minus forty-, uh, seven seconds."

"Out of that bunk! Scram! I'm going to catch that tick!"

Red moved lazily out of the couch as Dak got in. The other man shoved me into the copilot's couch and strapped a safety belt across my chest. He turned and dropped down the escape tube. Red followed him, then stopped with his head and shoulders out. "Tickets, please!" he said cheerfully.

"Oh, cripes!" Dak loosened a safety belt, reached for a pocket, got out the two field passes we had used to sneak aboard, and shoved them at him.

"Thanks," Red answered. "See you in church. Hot jets, and so forth." He disappeared with leisurely swiftness; I heard the air lock close and my eardrums popped. Dak did not answer his farewell; his eyes were busy on the computer dials and he made some minor adjustment.

"Twenty-one seconds," he said to me. "There'll be no rundown. Be sure your arms are inside and that you are relaxed. The first step is going to be a honey."

I did as I was told, then waited for *hours* in that curtain-going-up tension. Finally I said, "Dak?"

"Shut up!"

"Just one thing: where are we going?"

"Mars." I saw his thumb jab at a red button and I blacked out.

II

WHAT IS so funny about a man being dropsick? Those dolts with cast-iron stomachs always laugh—I'll bet they would laugh if Grandma broke both legs.

I was spacesick, of course, as soon as the rocket ship quit blasting and went into free fall. I came out of it fairly quickly as my stomach was practically empty—I'd eaten nothing since breakfast—and was simply wanly miserable the remaining eternity of that awful trip. It took us an hour and forty-three minutes to make rendezvous, which is roughly equal to a thousand years in purgatory to a ground hog like myself.

I'll say this for Dak, though: he did not laugh. Dak was a professional and he treated my normal reaction with the impersonal good manners of a flight nurse—not like those flat-headed, loud-voiced jackasses you'll find on the passenger list of a Moon shuttle. If I had my way, those healthy self-panickers would be spaced in mid-orbit and allowed to laugh themselves to death in vacuum.

Despite the turmoil in my mind and the thousand questions I wanted to ask we had almost made rendezvous with a torch-ship, which was in parking orbit around Earth, before I could stir up interest in anything. I suspect that if one were to inform a victim of spacesickness that he was to be shot at sunrise his only answer would be, "Yes? Would you hand me that sack, please?"

But I finally recovered to the point where instead of wanting very badly to die the scale had tipped so that I had a flickering, halfhearted interest in continuing to live. Dak was busy most of the time at the ship's communicator, apparently talking on a very tight beam for his hands constantly nursed the directional control like a gunner laying a gun under difficulties. I could not hear what he said, or even read his lips, as he had his face pushed into the rumble box. I assumed that he was talking to the long-jump ship we were to meet.

But when he pushed the communicator aside and lit a cigarette I repressed the stomach retch that the mere sight of tobacco smoke had inspired and said, "Dak, isn't it about time you told me the score?"

"Plenty of time for that on our way to Mars."

"Huh? Damn your arrogant ways," I protested feebly. "I don't want to go to Mars. I would never have considered your crazy offer if I had known it was on Mars."

"Suit yourself. You don't have to go."

"Eh?"

"The air lock is right behind you. Get out and walk. Mind you close the door."

I did not answer the ridiculous suggestion. He went on, "But if you can't breathe space the easiest thing to do is to go to Mars—and I'll see that you get back. The *Can Do*—that's this bucket—is about to rendezvous with the *Go For Broke*, which is a high-gee torchship. About seventeen seconds and a gnat's wink after we make contact the *Go For Broke* will torch for Mars—for we've *got* to be there by Wednesday."

I answered with the petulant stubbornness of a sick man. "I'm not going to Mars. I'm going to stay right in this ship. Somebody has to take it back and land it on Earth. You can't fool me."

"True," Broadbent agreed. "But you won't be in it. The three blokes who are supposed to be in this ship—according to the records back at Jefferson Field—are in the *Go For Broke* right now. This is a three-man ship, as you've noticed. I'm afraid you will find them stuffy about giving up a place to you. And besides, how would you get back through 'Immigration'?"

"I don't care! I'd be back on ground."

"And in jail, charged with everything from illegal entry to mopery and dopery in the spaceways. At the very least they would be sure that you were smuggling and they would take you to some quiet back room and run a needle in past your eyeball and find out just what you were up to. They would know what questions to ask and you wouldn't be able to keep from answering. But you wouldn't be able to implicate me, for good old Dak Broadbent hasn't been back to Earth in quite a spell and has unimpeachable witnesses to prove it."

I thought about it sickly, both from fear and the continuing effects of spacesickness. "So you would tip off the police? You dirty, slimy——" I broke off for lack of an adequately insulting noun.

"Oh no! Look, old son, I might twist your arm a bit and let you think that I would cry copper—but I never would. But Rrringriil's conjugate-brother Rrringlath certainly knows that old 'Griil went in that door and failed to come out. He will tip off the nosies. Conjugate-brother is a relationship so close that we will never understand it, since we don't reproduce by fission."

I didn't care whether Martians reproduced like rabbits or the stork brought them in a little black bag. The way he told it I could never go back to Earth, and I said so. He shook his head. "Not at all. Leave it to me and we will slide you back in as neatly as we slid you out. Eventually you will walk off that field or some other field with a gate pass which shows that you are a mechanic who has been making some last-minute adjustment—and you'll have greasy coveralls and a tool kit to back it up. Surely an actor of your skill can play the part of a mechanic for a few minutes?"

"Eh? Why, certainly! But——"

"There you are! You stick with ol' Doc Dak; he'll take care of you. We shuffled eight guild brothers in this current caper to get me on Earth and both of us off; we can do it again. But you would not stand a chance without *voyageurs* to help you." He grinned. "Every *voyageur* is a free trader at heart. The art of smuggling being what it is, we are all of us always ready to help out one another in a little innocent deception of the port guards. But a person outside the lodge does not ordinarily get such co-operation."

I tried to steady my stomach and think about it. "Dak, is this a smuggling deal? Because——"

"Oh no! Except that we are smuggling *you*."

"I was going to say that I don't regard smuggling as a crime."

"Who does? Except those who make money off the rest of us by limiting trade. But this is a straight impersonation job, Lorenzo, and you are the man for it. It wasn't an accident that I ran across you in that bar; there had been a tail on you for two days. As soon as I hit dirt I went where you were." He frowned. "I wish I could be sure our honorable antagonists had been following *me*, and not you."

"Why?"

"If they were following me they were trying to find out what I was after—which is okay, as the lines were already drawn; we knew we were mutual enemies. But if they were following *you*, then they *knew* what I was after—an actor who could play the role."

"But how could they know that? Unless you told them?"

"Lorenzo, this thing is big, much bigger than you imagine. I don't see it all myself—and the less you know about it until you must, the better off you are. But I can tell you this: a set of personal characteristics was fed into the big computer at the System Census Bureau at The Hague and the machine compared them with the personal characteristics of every male professional actor alive. It was done as discreetly as possible but somebody might have guessed—and talked. The specifications amounted to identification both of the principal and the actor who could double for him, since the job had to be *perfect*."

"Oh. And the machine told you that I was the man for it?"

"Yes. You—and one other."

This was another good place for me to keep my mouth shut. But I could not have done so if my life had depended on it—which in a way it did. I just had to know who the other actor was who was considered competent to play a role which called for my unique talents. "This other one? Who is he?"

Dak looked me over; I could see him hesitate. "Mmm—fellow by the name of Orson Trowbridge. Know him?"

"*That* ham!" For a moment I was so furious that I forgot my nausea.

"So? I hear that he is a very good actor."

I simply could not help being indignant at the idea that anyone should even think about that oaf Trowbridge for a role for which I was being considered. "That arm-waver! That word-mouther!" I stopped, realizing that it was more dignified to ignore such colleagues—if the word fits. But that popinjay was so conceited that—well, if the role called for him to kiss a lady's hand, Trowbridge would fake it by kissing his own thumb instead. A narcissist, a poseur, a double fake—how could such a man *live* a role?

Yet such is the injustice of fortune that his sawings and rantings had paid him well while real artists went hungry.

"Dak, I simply cannot see why you considered him for it."

"Well, we didn't want him; he is tied up with some long-term contract that would make his absence conspicuous and awkward. It was lucky for us that you were—uh, 'at liberty.' As soon as you agreed to the job I had Jock send word to call off the team that was trying to arrange a deal with Trowbridge."

"I should think so!"

"But—see here, Lorenzo, I'm going to lay it on the line. While you were busy whooping your cookies after *Brennschluss* I called the *Go For Broke* and told them to pass the word down to get busy on Trowbridge again."

"*What?*"

"You asked for it, shipmate. See here, a man in my racket contracts to herd a heap to Ganymede, that means he will pilot that pot to Ganymede or die trying. He doesn't get fainthearted and try to welsh while the ship is being loaded. You told me you would take this job—no 'ifs' or 'ands' or 'buts'—you took the job. A few minutes later there is a fracas; you lose your nerve. Later you try to run out on me at the field. Only ten minutes ago you were screaming to be taken back dirtside. Maybe you are a better actor than Trowbridge. I wouldn't know. But I know we need a man who can be depended on not to lose his nerve when the time comes. I understand that Trowbridge is that sort of bloke. So if we can get him, we'll use him instead, pay you off and tell you nothing and ship you back. Understand?"

Too well I understood. Dak did not use the word—I doubt if he would have understood it—but he was telling me that I was not a trouper. The bitter part about it was that he was justified. I could not be angry; I could only be ashamed. I had been an idiot to accept the contract without knowing more about it—but I had agreed to play the role, without conditions or escape clauses. Now I was trying to back out, like a rank amateur with stage fright.

"The show must go on" is the oldest tenet of show business. Perhaps it has no philosophical verity, but the things men live by are rarely subject to logical proof. My father had believed it—I had seen him play two acts with a burst appendix and then take his bows before he had let them rush him to a hospital. I could see his face now, looking at me with the contempt of a trouper for a so-called actor who would let an audience down.

"Dak," I said humbly, "I am very sorry. I was wrong."

He looked at me sharply. "You'll do the job?"

"Yes." I meant it sincerely. Then I suddenly remembered a factor which could make the part as impossible for me as the role of Snow White in *The Seven Dwarfs*. "That is—well, I *want* to. But——"

"But what?" he said scornfully. "More of your damned temperament?"

"No, no! But you said we were going to Mars. Dak, am I going to be expected to do this impersonation with Martians around me?"

"Eh? Of course. How else on Mars?"

"Uh . . . But, Dak, I can't *stand* Martians! They give me the heebie jeebies. I wouldn't want to—I would try not to—but I might fall right out of the characterization."

"Oh. If that is all that is worrying you, forget it."

"Huh? But I can't forget it. I can't help it. I——"

"I said, 'Forget it.' Old son, we knew you were a peasant in such matters—we know all about you. Lorenzo, your fear of Martians is as childish and irrational as a fear of spiders or snakes. But we had anticipated it and it will be taken care of. So forget it."

"Well—all right." I was not much reassured, but he had flicked me where it hurt. "Peasant"—why, "*peasants*" were the audience! So I shut up.

Dak pulled the communicator to him, did not bother to silence his message with the rumble box: "Dandelion to Tumbleweed—cancel Plan Inkblot. We will complete Mardi Gras."

"Dak?" I said as he signed off.

"Later," he answered. "I'm about to match orbits. The contact may be a little rough, as I am not going to waste time worrying about chuck holes. So pipe down and hang on."

And it *was* rough. By the time we were in the torchship I was glad to be comfortably back in free fall again; surge nausea is even worse than everyday dropsickness. But we did not stay in free fall more than five minutes; the three men who were to go back in the *Can Do* were crowding into the transfer lock even as Dak and I floated into the torchship. The next few moments were extremely confused. I suppose I am a ground hog at heart for I disorient very easily when I can't tell the floor from the ceiling. Someone called out, "Where is he?" Dak replied, "Here!" The same voice replied, "Him?" as if he could not believe his eyes.

"Yes, yes!" Dak answered. "He's got make-up on. Never mind, it's all right. Help me get him into the cider press."

A hand grabbed my arm, towed me along a narrow passage and into a compartment. Against one bulkhead and flat to it were two bunks, or "cider presses," the bathtub-shaped, hydraulic, pressure-distribution tanks used for high acceleration in torchships. I had never seen one before but we had used quite convincing mock-ups in the space opus *The Earth Raiders.*

There was a stenciled sign on the bulkhead behind the bunks: *WARNING!!! Do Not Take More than Three Gravities without a Gee Suit. By Order of——* I rotated slowly out of range of vision before I could finish reading it and someone shoved me into one cider press. Dak and the other man were hurriedly strapping me against it when a horn somewhere near by broke into a horrid hooting. It continued for several seconds, then a voice replaced it: "Red warning! Two gravities! Three minutes! Red warning! Two gravities! Three minutes!" Then the hooting started again.

Through the racket I heard Dak ask urgently, "Is the projector all set? The tapes ready?"

"Sure, sure!"

"Got the hypo?" Dak squirmed around in the air and said to me, "Look, shipmate, we're going to give you a shot. It's all right. Part of it is Nullgrav, the rest is a stimulant—for you are going to have to stay awake and study your lines. It will make your eyeballs feel hot at first and it may make you itch, but it won't hurt you."

"Wait, Dak, I——"

"No time! I've got to smoke this scrap heap!" He twisted and was out the door before I could protest. The second man pushed up my left sleeve, held an injection gun against the skin, and I had received the dose before I knew it. Then he was gone. The hooting gave way to: "Red warning! Two gravities! Two minutes!"

I tried to look around but the drug made me even more confused. My eyeballs did feel hot and my teeth as well and I began to feel an almost intolerable itching along my spine—but the safety straps kept me from reaching the tortured area—and perhaps kept me from breaking an arm at acceleration. The hooting stopped again and this time Dak's self-confident baritone boomed out, "Last red warning! Two gravities! One minute! Knock off those pinochle games and spread your fat carcasses—we're goin' to smoke!" The hooting was replaced this time by a recording of Arkezian's *Ad Astra*, opus 61 in C major. It was the controversial London Symphony version with the 14-cycle "scare" notes buried in the timpani. Battered, bewildered, and doped as I was, they seemed to have no effect on me—you can't wet a river.

A mermaid came in the door. No scaly tail, surely, but a mermaid is what she looked like. When my eyes refocused I saw that it was a very likely looking and adequately mammalian young woman in singlet and shorts, swimming along head first in a way that made clear that free fall was no novelty to her. She glanced at me without smiling, placed herself against the other cider press, and took hold of the hand grips—she did not bother with safety belts. The music hit the rolling finale and I felt myself grow very heavy.

Two gravities is not bad, not when you are floating in a liquid bed. The skin over the top of the cider press pushed up around me, supporting me inch by inch; I simply felt heavy and found it hard to breathe. You hear these stories about pilots torching at ten gravities and ruining themselves and I have no doubt that they are true—but two gravities, taken in the cider press, simply makes one feel languid, unable to move.

It was some time before I realized that the horn in the ceiling was speaking to me. "Lorenzo! How are you doing, shipmate?"

"All right." The effort made me gasp. "How long do we have to put up with this?"

"About two days."

I must have moaned, for Dak laughed at me. "Quit bellyaching, chum! My first trip to Mars took thirty-seven weeks, every minute of it free fall in an elliptical orbit. You're taking the luxury route, at a mere double gee for a couple of days—with a one-gee rest at turnover, I might add. We ought to charge you for it."

I started to tell him what I thought of his humor in scathing green-room idiom, then recalled that there was a lady present. My father had taught me that a woman will forgive any action, up to and including assault with violence, but is easily insulted by language; the lovelier half of our race is symbol-oriented— very strange, in view of their extreme practicality. In any case, I have never let a taboo word pass my lips when it might offend the ears of a lady since the time I last received the back of my father's hard hand full on my mouth . . . Father could have given Professor Pavlov pointers in reflex conditioning.

But Dak was speaking again. "Penny! You there, honey chile?"

"Yes, Captain," the young woman with me answered.

"Okay, start him on his homework. I'll be down when I have this firetrap settled in its groove."

"Very well, Captain." She turned her head toward me and said in a soft, husky, contralto voice, "Dr. Capek wants you simply to relax and look at movies for several hours. I am here to answer questions as necessary."

I sighed. "Thank goodness someone is at last going to answer questions!"

She did not answer, but raised an arm with some difficulty and passed it over a switch. The lights in the compartment died out and a sound and stereo image built up in front of my eyes. I recognized the central figure—just as any of the billions of citizens of the Empire would have recognized him—and I realized at last how thoroughly and mercilessly Dak Broadbent had tricked me.

It was Bonforte.

The Bonforte, I mean—the Right Honorable John Joseph Bonforte, former Supreme Minister, leader of the loyal opposition, and head of the Expansionist coalition—the most loved (and the most hated!) man in the entire Solar System.

My astonished mind made a standing broad jump and arrived at what seemed a logical certainty. Bonforte had lived through at least three assassination attempts—or so the news reports would have us believe. At least two of his escapes had seemed almost miraculous. Suppose they were not miraculous? Suppose they had all been successful—but dear old Uncle Joe Bonforte had always been somewhere else at the time?

You could use up a lot of actors that way.

III

I HAD never meddled in politics. My father had warned against it. "Stay out of it, Larry," he had told me solemnly. "The publicity you get that way is bad publicity. The peasants don't like it." I had never voted—not even after the amendment of '98 made it easy for the floating population (which includes, of course, most members of the profession) to exercise franchise.

However, insofar as I had political leanings of any sort, they certainly did not lean toward Bonforte. I considered him a dangerous man and very possibly a traitor to the human race. The idea of standing up and getting killed in his place was—how shall I put it?—distasteful to me.

But—*what* a role!

I had once played the lead in *L'Aiglon* and I had played Caesar in the only two plays about him worthy of the name. But to play such a role *in life*—well, it is enough to make one understand how a man could go to the guillotine in another man's place—just for the chance to play, even for a few moments, the ultimately exacting role, in order to create the supreme, the perfect, work of art.

I wondered who my colleagues had been who had been unable to resist that temptation on those earlier occasions. They had been artists, that was certain—though their very anonymity was the only tribute to the success of their characterizations. I tried to remember just when the earlier attempts on Bonforte's life had taken place and which colleagues who might have been capable of the role had died or dropped out of sight at those times. But it was useless. Not only was I not too sure of the details of current political history but also actors simply fade out of view with depressing frequency; it is a chancy profession even for the best of us.

I found that I had been studying closely the characterization.

I realized I could play it. Hell, I could play it with one foot in a bucket and a smell of smoke backstage. To begin with, there was no problem of physique; Bonforte and I could have swapped clothes without a wrinkle. These childish conspirators who had shanghaied me had vastly overrated the importance of physical resemblance, since it means nothing if not backed up by art—and need not be at all close if the actor is competent. But I admit that it does help and their silly game with the computer machine had resulted (quite by accident!) in selecting a true artist, as well as one who was in measurements and bony structure the twin of the politician. His profile was much like mine; even his hands were long, narrow, and aristocratic like mine—and hands are harder than faces.

That limp, supposedly the result of one of the attempts on his life—nothing to it! After watching him for a few minutes I knew that I could get up from that bed (at one gravity, that is) and walk in precisely the same way and never have to think about it. The way he had of scratching his collarbone and then brushing his chin, the almost imperceptible tic which preceded each of his sentences—such things were no trouble; they soaked into my subconscious like water into sand.

To be sure, he was fifteen or twenty years older than I was, but it is easier to play a role older than oneself than one younger. In any case, age to an actor is simply a matter of inner attitude; it has nothing to do with the steady march of catabolism.

I could have played him on boards, or read a speech in his place, within twenty minutes. But this part, as I understood it, would be more than such an interpretation; Dak had hinted that I would have to convince people who knew him well, perhaps in intimate circumstances. This is surpassingly more difficult. Does he take sugar in his coffee? If so, how much? Which hand does he use to strike a cigarette and with what gesture? I got the answer to that one and planted it deep in my mind even as I phrased the question; the simulacrum in front of me struck a cigarette in a fashion that convinced me that he had used matches and the old-fashioned sort of gasper for years before he had gone along with the march of so-called progress.

Worst of all, a man is not a single complexity; he is a *different* complexity to every person who knows him—which means that, to be successful, an impersonation must change for each "audience"—for each acquaintance of the man being impersonated. This is not merely difficult; it is statistically impossible. Such little things could trip one up. What shared experiences does your principal have with acquaintance John Jones? With a hundred, or a thousand, John Joneses? How could an impersonator possibly know?

Acting *per se*, like all art, is a process of abstracting, of retaining only significant detail. But in impersonation *any* detail can be significant. In time, something as silly as not crunching celery could let the cat out of the bag.

Then I recalled with glum conviction that my performance probably need be convincing only long enough for a marksman to draw a bead on me.

But I was still studying the man I was to replace (what else could I do?) when the door opened and I heard Dak in his proper person call out, "Anybody home?" The lights came on, the three-dimensional vision faded, and I felt as if I had been wrenched from a dream. I turned my head; the young woman called Penny was struggling to lift her head from the other hydraulic bed and Dak was standing braced in the doorway.

I looked at him and said wonderingly, "How do you manage to stand up?" Part of my mind, the professional part that works independently, was noting how he stood and filing it in a new drawer marked: "How a Man Stands under Two Gravities."

He grinned at me. "Nothing to it. I wear arch supports."

"Hmmmph!"

"You can stand up, if you want to. Ordinarily we discourage passengers from getting out of the boost tanks when we are torching at anything over one and a half gees—too much chance that some idiot will fall over his own feet and break a leg. But I once saw a really tough weight-lifter type climb out of the press and walk at five gravities—but he was never good for much afterwards. But two gees is okay—about like carrying another man piggyback." He glanced at the young lady. "Giving him the straight word, Penny?"

"He hasn't asked anything yet."

"So? Lorenzo, I thought you were the lad who wanted all the answers."

I shrugged. "I cannot now see that it matters, since it is evident that I will not live long enough to appreciate them."

"Eh? What soured your milk, old son?"

"Captain Broadbent," I said bitterly, "I am inhibited in expressing myself by the presence of a lady; therefore I cannot adequately discuss your ancestry, personal habits, morals, and destination. Let it stand that I knew what you had tricked me into as soon as I became aware of the identity of the man I am to impersonate. I will content myself with one question only: who is about to attempt to assassinate Bonforte? Even a clay pigeon should be entitled to know who is shooting at him."

For the first time I saw Dak register surprise. Then he laughed so hard that the acceleration seemed to be too much for him; he slid to the deck and braced his back against a bulkhead, still laughing.

"I don't see anything funny about it," I said angrily.

He stopped and wiped his eyes. "Lorrie old son, did you honestly think that I had set you up as a sitting duck?"

"It's obvious." I told him my deductions about the earlier assassination attempts.

He had the sense not to laugh again. "I see. You thought it was a job about like food taster for a Middle Ages king. Well, we'll have to try to straighten you out; I don't suppose it helps your acting to think that you are about to be burned down where you stand. Look, I've been with the Chief for six years. During that time I *know* he has never used a double . . . Nevertheless, I was present on two occasions when attempts were made on his life—one of those times I shot the hatchet man. Penny, you've been with the Chief longer than that. Has he ever used a double before?"

She looked at me coldly. "Never. The very idea that the Chief would let anybody expose himself to danger in his place is— well, I ought to slap your face; that's what I ought to do!"

"Take it easy, Penny," Dak said mildly. "You've both got jobs to do and you are going to have to work with him. Besides, his wrong guess isn't too silly, not from the outside. By the way, Lorenzo, this is Penelope Russell. She is the Chief's personal secretary, which makes her your number-one coach."

"I am honored to meet you, mademoiselle."

"I wish I could say the same!"

"Stow it, Penny, or I'll spank your round fanny—at two gravities. Lorenzo, I concede that doubling for John Joseph Bonforte isn't as safe as riding in a wheel chair—shucks, as we both know, several attempts have been made to close out his life insurance. But that is not what we are afraid of this time.

Matter of fact, this time, for political reasons you will presently understand, the laddies we are up against won't dare to try to kill the Chief—or to kill you when you are doubling for the Chief. They are playing rough—as you *know!*—and they would kill me, or even Penny, for the slightest advantage. They would kill you right now, if they could get at you. But when you make this public appearance *as the Chief* you'll be safe; the circumstances will be such that they can't afford to kill."

He studied my face. "Well?"

I shook my head. "I don't follow you."

"No, but you will. It is a complicated matter, involving Martian ways of looking at things. Take it for granted; you'll know all about it before we get there."

I still did not like it. Thus far Dak had told me no outright lies that I knew of—but he could lie effectively by not telling all that he knew, as I had learned the bitter way. I said, "See here, I have no reason to trust you, or to trust this young lady—if you will pardon me, miss. But while I haven't any liking for Mr. Bonforte, he does have the reputation for being painfully, even offensively, honest. When do I get to talk to *him?* As soon as we reach Mars?"

Dak's ugly, cheerful face was suddenly shadowed with sadness. "I'm afraid not. Didn't Penny tell you?"

"Tell me what?"

"Old son, that's why we've got to have a double for the Chief. They've kidnaped him."

My head ached, possibly from the double weight, or perhaps from too many shocks. "Now you know," Dak went on. "You know why Jock Dubois didn't want to trust you with it until after we raised ground. It is the biggest news story since the first landing on the Moon, and we are sitting on it, doing our damnedest to keep it from ever being known. We hope to use you until we can find him and get him back. Matter of fact, you have already started your impersonation. This ship is not really the *Go For Broke*; it is the Chief's private yacht and traveling office, the *Tom Paine*. The *Go For Broke* is riding a parking orbit around Mars, with its transponder giving out the recognition signal of this ship—a fact known only to its captain and comm officer—while the *Tommie* tucks up her skirts and rushes to Earth to pick up a substitute for the Chief. Do you begin to scan it, old son?"

I admit that I did not. "Yes, but—see here, Captain, if Mr. Bonforte's political enemies have kidnaped him, why keep it secret? I should expect you to shout it from the housetops."

"On Earth we would. At New Batavia we would. On Venus we would. But here we are dealing with Mars. Do you know the legend of Kkkahgral the Younger?"

"Eh? I'm afraid I don't."

"You must study it; it will give you insight into what makes a Martian tick. Briefly, this boy Kkkah was to appear at a certain time and place, thousands of years ago, for a very high honor— like being knighted. Through no fault of his own (the way we would look at it) he failed to make it on time. Obviously the only thing to do was to kill him—by Martian standards. But because of his youth and his distinguished record some of the radicals present argued that he should be allowed to go back and start over. But Kkkahgral would have none of it. He insisted on his right to prosecute the case himself, won it, and was executed. Which makes him the very embodiment, the patron saint, of propriety on Mars."

"That's crazy!"

"Is it? We aren't Martians. They are a very old race and they have worked out a system of debts and obligations to cover every possible situation—the greatest formalists conceivable. Compared with them, the ancient Japanese, with their *giri* and *gimu*, were outright anarchists. Martians don't have 'right' and 'wrong'—instead they have propriety and impropriety, squared, cubed, and loaded with gee juice. But where it bears on this problem is that the Chief was about to be adopted into the nest of Kkkahgral the Younger himself. Do you scan me now?"

I still did not. To my mind this Kkkah character was one of the more loathsome items from *Le Grand Guignol*. Broadbent went on, "It's simple enough. The Chief is probably the greatest practical student of Martian customs and psychology. He has been working up to this for years. Comes local noon on Wednesday at Lacus Soli, the ceremony of adoption takes place. If the Chief is there and goes through his paces properly, everything is sweet. If he is not there—and it makes no difference at all why he is not there—his name is mud on Mars, in every nest from pole to pole—and the greatest interplanetary and interracial political coup ever attempted falls flat on its face. Worse than that, it will backfire. My guess is that the very least that will happen is for Mars to withdraw even from its present loose association with the Empire. Much more likely there will be reprisals and human beings will be killed—maybe every human on Mars. Then the extremists in the Humanity Party would have their way and Mars would be brought into the Empire by force—but only after every Martian was dead. And all set off just by Bonforte failing to show up for the adoption ceremony . . . Martians take these things very seriously."

Dak left as suddenly as he had appeared and Penelope Russell turned on the picture projector again. It occurred to me fretfully that I should have asked him what was to keep our enemies from simply killing *me*, if all that was needed to upset the political applecart was to keep Bonforte (in his proper person, or through his double) from attending some barbaric Martian ceremony. But I had forgotten to ask—perhaps I was subconsciously afraid of being answered.

But shortly I was again studying Bonforte, watching his movements and gestures, feeling his expressions, subvocalizing the tones of his voice, while floating in that detached, warm reverie of artistic effort. Already I was "wearing his head."

I was panicked out of it when the images shifted to one in which Bonforte was surrounded by Martians, touched by their pseudo limbs. I had been so deep inside the picture that I could actually feel them myself—and the stink was unbearable. I made a strangled noise and clawed at it. *"Shut it off!"*

The lights came up and the picture disappeared. Miss Russell was looking at me. "What in the world is the matter with you?"

I tried to get my breath and stop trembling. "Miss Russell— I am very sorry—but please—don't turn that on again. I can't *stand* Martians."

She looked at me as if she could not believe what she saw but despised it anyhow. "I told them," she said slowly and scornfully, "that this ridiculous scheme would not work."

"I am very sorry. I cannot help it."

She did not answer but climbed heavily out of the cider press. She did not walk as easily at two gravities as Dak did, but she managed. She left without another word, closing the door as she went.

She did not return. Instead the door was opened by a man who appeared to be inhabiting a giant kiddie stroller. "Howdy there, young fellow!" he boomed out. He was sixtyish, a bit too heavy, and bland; I did not have to see his diploma to be aware that his was a "bedside" manner.

"How do you do, sir?"

"Well enough. Better at lower acceleration." He glanced down at the contrivance he was strapped into. "How do you like my corset-on-wheels? Not stylish, perhaps, but it takes some of the strain off my heart. By the way, just to keep the record straight, I'm Dr. Capek, Mr. Bonforte's personal therapist. I know who you are. Now what's this we hear about you and Martians?"

I tried to explain it clearly and unemotionally.

Dr. Capek nodded. "Captain Broadbent should have told me. I would have changed the order of your indoctrination program. The captain is a competent young fellow in his way but his muscles run ahead of his brain on occasion . . . He is so perfectly normal an extrovert that he frightens me. But no harm done. Mr. Smythe, I want your permission to hypnotize you. You have my word as a physician that it will be used only to help you in this matter and that I will in no wise tamper with your personal integration." He pulled out an old-fashioned pocket watch of the sort that is almost a badge of his profession and took my pulse.

I answered, "You have my permission readily, sir—but it won't do any good. I can't go under." I had learned hypnotic techniques myself during the time I was showing my mentalist act, but my teachers had never had any luck hypnotizing me. A touch of hypnotism is very useful to such an act, especially if the local police aren't too fussy about the laws the medical association has hampered us with.

"So? Well, we'll just have to do the best we can, then. Suppose you relax, get comfortable, and we'll talk about your problem." He still kept the watch in his hand, fiddling with it and twisting the chain, after he had stopped taking my pulse. I started to mention it, since it was catching the reading light just over my head, but decided that it was probably a nervous habit of which he was not aware and really too trivial a matter to call to the attention of a stranger.

"I'm relaxed," I assured him. "Ask me anything you wish. Or free association, if you prefer."

"Just let yourself float," he said softly. "Two gravities makes you feel heavy, doesn't it? I usually just sleep through it myself. It pulls the blood out of the brain, makes one sleepy. They are beginning to boost the drive again. We'll all have to sleep . . . We'll be heavy . . . We'll have to sleep . . ."

I started to tell him that he had better put his watch away—or it would spin right out of his hand. Instead I fell asleep.

When I woke up, the other acceleration bunk was occupied by Dr. Capek. "Howdy, bub," he greeted me. "I got tired of that confounded perambulator and decided to stretch out here and distribute the strain."

"Uh, are we back on two gravities again?"

"Eh? Oh yes! We're on two gravities."

"I'm sorry I blacked out. How long was I asleep?"

"Oh, not very long. How do you feel?"

"Fine. Wonderfully rested, in fact."

"It frequently has that effect. Heavy boost, I mean. Feel like seeing some more pictures?"

"Why, certainly, if you say so, Doctor."

"Okay." He reached up and again the room went dark.

I was braced for the notion that he was going to show me more pictures of Martians; I made up my mind not to panic. After all, I had found it necessary on many occasions to pretend that they were not present; surely motion pictures of them should not affect me—I had simply been surprised earlier.

They were indeed stereos of Martians, both with and without Mr. Bonforte. I found it possible to study them with detached mind, without terror or disgust.

Suddenly I realized that I was *enjoying* looking at them!

I let out some exclamation and Capek stopped the film. "Trouble?"

"Doctor—you hypnotized me!"

"You told me to."

"But I can't be hypnotized."

"Sorry to hear it."

"Uh—so you managed it. I'm not too dense to see that." I added, "Suppose we try those pictures again. I can't really believe it."

He switched them on and I watched and wondered. Martians were not disgusting, if one looked at them without prejudice; they weren't even ugly. In fact, they possessed the same quaint grace as a Chinese pagoda. True, they were not human in form, but neither is a bird of paradise—and birds of paradise are the loveliest things alive.

I began to realize, too, that their pseudo limbs could be very expressive; their awkward gestures showed some of the bumbling friendliness of puppies. I knew now that I had looked at Martians all my life through the dark glasses of hate and fear.

Of course, I mused, their stench would still take getting used to, but—and then I suddenly realized that I was smelling them, the unmistakable odor—and I didn't mind it a bit! In fact, I liked it. "Doctor!" I said urgently. "This machine has a 'smellie' attachment—doesn't it?"

"Eh? I believe not. No, I'm sure it hasn't—too much parasitic weight for a yacht."

"But it must. I can smell them very plainly."

"Oh, yes." He looked slightly shamefaced. "Bub, I did one thing to you that I hope will cause you no inconvenience."

"Sir?"

"While we were digging around inside your skull it became evident that a lot of your neurotic orientation about Martians was triggered by their body odor. I didn't have time to do a deep job so I had to offset it. I asked Penny—that's the youngster who was in here before—for a loan of some of the perfume she uses. I'm afraid that from here on out, bub, Martians are going to smell like a Parisian house of joy to you. If I had had time I would have used some homelier pleasant odor, like ripe strawberries or hot cakes and syrup. But I had to improvise."

I sniffed. Yes, it did smell like a heavy and expensive perfume—and yet, damn it, it was unmistakably the reek of Martians. "I like it."

"You can't help liking it."

"But you must have spilled the whole bottle in here. The place is drenched with it."

"Huh? Not at all. I merely waved the stopper under your

nose a half hour ago, then gave the bottle back to Penny and she went away with it." He sniffed. "The odor is gone now. 'Jungle Lust,' it said on the bottle. Seemed to have a lot of musk in it. I accused Penny of trying to make the crew space-happy and she just laughed at me." He reached up and switched off the stereopix. "We've had enough of those for now. I want to get you onto something more useful."

When the pictures faded out, the fragrance faded with them, just as it does with smellie equipment. I was forced to admit to myself that it was all in the head. But, as an actor, I was intellectually aware of that truth anyhow.

When Penny came back in a few minutes later, she had a fragrance exactly like a Martian.

I loved it.

IV

M Y EDUCATION continued in that room (Mr. Bonforte's guest room, it was) until turnover. I had no sleep, other than under hypnosis, and did not seem to need any. Either Doc Capek or Penny stuck with me and helped me the whole time. Fortunately my man was as thoroughly photographed and recorded as perhaps any man in history and I had, as well, the close co-operation of his intimates. There was endless material; the problem was to see how much I could assimilate, both awake and under hypnosis.

I don't know at what point I quit disliking Bonforte. Capek assured me—and I believe him—that he did not implant a hypnotic suggestion on this point; I had not asked for it and I am quite certain that Capek was meticulous about the ethical responsibilities of a physician and hypnotherapist. But I suppose that it was an inevitable concomitant of the role—I rather think I would learn to like Jack the Ripper if I studied for the part. Look at it this way: to learn a role truly, you must for a time become that character. And a man either likes himself, or he commits suicide, one way or another.

"To understand all is to forgive all"—and I was beginning to understand Bonforte.

At turnover we got that one-gravity rest that Dak had promised. We never were in free fall, not for an instant; instead of putting out the torch, which I gather they hate to do while under way, the ship described what Dak called a 180-degree skew turn. It leaves the ship on boost the whole time and is done rather quickly, but it has an oddly disturbing effect on the sense of balance. The effect has a name something like Coriolanus. Coriolis?

All I know about spaceships is that the ones that operate from the surface of a planet are true rockets but the *voyageurs* call them "teakettles" because of the steam jet of water or hydrogen they boost with. They aren't considered real atomic-power ships even though the jet is heated by an atomic pile. The long-jump ships such as the *Tom Paine*, torchships that is, are (so they tell me) the real thing, making use of E equals MC squared, or is it M equals EC squared? You know—the thing Einstein invented.

Dak did his best to explain it all to me, and no doubt it is very interesting to those who care for such things. But I can't imagine why a gentleman should bother with such. It seems to me that every time those scientific laddies get busy with their slide rules life becomes more complicated. What was wrong with things the way they were?

During the two hours we were on one gravity I was moved up to Bonforte's cabin. I started wearing his clothes and his face and everyone was careful to call me "Mr. Bonforte" or "Chief" or (in the case of Dr. Capek) "Joseph," the idea being, of course, to help me build the part.

Everyone but Penny, that is . . . She simply would not call me "Mr. Bonforte." She did her best to help but she could not bring herself to that. It was clear as scripture that she was a secretary who silently and hopelessly loved her boss, and she resented me with a deep, illogical, but natural bitterness. It made it hard for both of us, especially as I was finding her most attractive. No man can do his best work with a woman constantly around him who despises him. But I could not dislike her in return; I felt deeply sorry for her—even though I was decidedly irked.

We were on a tryout-in-the-sticks basis now, as not everyone in the *Tom Paine* knew that I was not Bonforte. I did not know exactly which ones knew of the substitution, but I was allowed to relax and ask questions only in the presence of Dak, Penny, and Dr. Capek. I was fairly sure that Bonforte's chief clerk, Mr. Washington, knew but never let on; he was a spare, elderly mulatto with the tight-lipped mask of a saint. There were two others who certainly knew, but they were not in the *Tom Paine*; they were standing by and covering up from the *Go For Broke*, handling press releases and routine dispatches—Bill Corpsman, who was Bonforte's front man with the news services, and Roger Clifton. I don't know quite how to describe Clifton's job. Political deputy? He had been Minister without Portfolio, you may remember, when Bonforte was Supreme Minister, but that says nothing. Let's put it symbolically: Bonforte handed out policy and Clifton handed out patronage.

This small group had to know; if any others knew it was not

considered necessary to tell me. To be sure, the other members of Bonforte's staff and all the crew of the *Tom Paine* knew that something odd was going on; they did not necessarily know what it was. A good many people had seen me enter the ship—but as "Benny Grey." By the time they saw me again I was already "Bonforte."

Someone had had the foresight to obtain real make-up equipment, but I used almost none. At close range make-up can be seen; even Silicoflesh cannot be given the exact texture of skin. I contented myself with darkening my natural complexion a couple of shades with Semiperm and wearing his face, from inside. I did have to sacrifice quite a lot of hair and Dr. Capek inhibited the roots. I did not mind; an actor can always wear hairpieces—and I was sure that this job was certain to pay me a fee that would let me retire for life, if I wished.

On the other hand, I was sometimes queasily aware that "life" might not be too long—there are those old saws about the man who knew too much and the one about dead men and tales. But truthfully I was beginning to trust these people. They were all darn nice people—which told me as much about Bonforte as I had learned by listening to his speeches and seeing his pix. A political figure is not a single man, so I was learning, but a compatible team. If Bonforte himself had not been a decent sort he would not have had these people around him.

The Martian language gave me my greatest worry. Like most actors, I had picked up enough Martian, Venerian, Outer Jovian, etc., to be able to fake in front of a camera or on stage. But those rolled or fluttered consonants are very difficult. Human vocal cords are not as versatile as a Martian's tympanus, I believe, and, in any case, the semi-phonetic spelling out of those sounds in Roman letters, for example "kkk" or "jjj" or "rrr," has no more to do with the true sounds than the *g* in "gnu" has to do with the inhaled click with which a Bantu pronounces "gnu." "Jjj," for instance, closely resembles a Bronx cheer.

Fortunately Bonforte had no great talent for other languages —and I am a professional; my ears really hear, I can imitate any sound, from a buzz saw striking a nail in a chunk of firewood to a setting hen disturbed on her nest. It was necessary only to acquire Martian as poorly as Bonforte spoke it. He had worked hard to overcome his lack of talent, and every word and phrase of Martian that he knew had been sight-sound recorded so that he could study his mistakes.

So I studied his mistakes, with the projector moved into his office and Penny at my elbow to sort out the spools for me and answer questions.

Human languages fall into four groups: inflecting ones as in Anglo-American, positional as in Chinese, agglutinative as in Old Turkish, polysynthetic (sentence units) as in Eskimo—to which, of course, we now add alien structures as wildly odd and as nearly impossible for the human brain as non-repetitive or emergent Venerian. Luckily Martian is analogous to human speech forms. Basic Martian, the trade language, is positional and involves only simple concrete ideas—like the greeting: "I see you." High Martian is polysynthetic and very stylized, with an expression for every nuance of their complex system of rewards and punishments, obligations and debts. It had been almost too much for Bonforte; Penny told me that he could read those arrays of dots they use for writing quite easily but of the spoken form of High Martian he could say only a few hundred sentences.

Brother, how I studied those few he had mastered!

The strain on Penny was even greater than it was on me. Both she and Dak spoke some Martian but the chore of coaching me fell on her as Dak had to spend most of his time in the control room; Jock's death had left him shorthanded. We dropped from two gravities to one for the last few million miles of the approach, during which time he never came below at all. I spent it learning the ritual I would have to know for the adoption ceremony, with Penny's help.

I had just completed running through the speech in which I was to accept membership in the Kkkah nest—a speech not unlike that, in spirit, with which an orthodox Jewish boy assumes the responsibilities of manhood, but as fixed, as invariable, as Hamlet's soliloquy. I had read it, complete with Bonforte's mispronunciations and facial tic; I finished and asked, "How was that?"

"That was quite good," she answered seriously.

"Thanks, Curly Top." It was a phrase I had lifted from the language-practice spools in Bonforte's files; it was what Bonforte called her when he was feeling mellow—and it was perfectly in character.

"*Don't you dare call me that!*"

I looked at her in honest amazement and answered, still in character, "Why, Penny my child!"

"Don't you call me *that*, either! You *fake!* You *phony!* You—*actor!*" She jumped up, ran as far as she could—which was only to the door—and stood there, faced away from me, her face buried in her hands and her shoulders shaking with sobs.

I made a tremendous effort and lifted myself out of the character—pulled in my belly, let my own face come up, answered in my own voice. "Miss Russell!"

She stopped crying, whirled around, looked at me, and her jaw dropped. I added, still in my normal self, "Come back here and sit down."

I thought she was going to refuse, then she seemed to think better of it, came slowly back and sat down, her hands in her lap but with her face that of a little girl who is "saving up more spit."

I let her sit for a moment, then said quietly, "Yes, Miss Russell, I am an actor. Is that a reason for you to insult me?"

She simply looked stubborn.

"As an actor, I am here to do an actor's job. You know why. You know, too, that I was tricked into taking it—it is not a job I would have accepted with my eyes open, even in my wildest moments. I hate having to do it considerably more than you hate having me do it—for despite Captain Broadbent's cheerful assurances I am not at all sure that I will come out of it with my skin intact—and I'm awfully fond of my skin; it's the only one I have. I believe, too, that I know why you find it hard to accept me. But is that any reason for you to make my job harder than it has to be?"

She mumbled. I said sharply, "Speak up!"

"It's dishonest! It's *indecent!*"

I sighed. "It certainly is. More than that, it is impossible—without the wholehearted support of the other members of the cast. So let's call Captain Broadbent down here and tell him. Let's call it off."

She jerked her face up and said, "Oh no! We can't do that."

"Why can't we? A far better thing to drop it now than to present it and have it flop. I can't give a performance under these conditions. Let's admit it."

"But—but—we've *got* to! It's necessary."

"Why is it necessary, Miss Russell? Political reasons? I have not the slightest interest in politics—and I doubt if you have any really deep interest. So why must we do it?"

"Because—because *he*——" She stopped, unable to go on, strangled by sobs.

I got up, went over, and put a hand on her shoulder. "I know. Because if we don't, something that *he* has spent years building up will fall to pieces. Because he can't do it himself and his friends are trying to cover up and do it for him. Because his friends are loyal to him. Because *you* are loyal to him. Nevertheless, it hurts you to see someone else in the place that is rightfully his. Besides that, you are half out of your mind with grief and worry about him. Aren't you?"

"Yes." I could barely hear it.

I took hold of her chin and tilted her face up. "I know why you find it so hard to have me here, in his place. You love him. But I'm doing the best job for him I know how. *Confound it, woman! Do you have to make my job six times harder by treating me like dirt?*"

She looked shocked. For a moment I thought she was going to slap me. Then she said brokenly, "I am sorry. I am very sorry. I won't let it happen again."

I let go her chin and said briskly, "Then let's get back to work."

She did not move. "Can you forgive me?"

"Huh? There's nothing to forgive, Penny. You were acting up because you love him and you were worried. Now let's get to work. I've got to be letter-perfect—and it's only hours away." I dropped at once back into the role.

She picked up a spool and started the projector again. I watched him through it once, then did the acceptance speech with the sound cut out but stereo on, matching my voice—*his* voice, I mean—to the moving image. She watched me, looking from the image back to my face with a dazed look on her own. We finished and I switched it off myself. "How was that?"

"That was perfect!"

I smiled his smile. "Thanks, Curly Top."

"Not at all—'Mr. Bonforte.'"

Two hours later we made rendezvous with the *Go For Broke*.

Dak brought Roger Clifton and Bill Corpsman to my cabin as soon as the *Go For Broke* had transferred them. I knew them from pictures. I stood up and said, "Hello, Rog. Glad to see you, Bill." My voice was warm but casual; on the level at which these people operated a hasty trip to Earth and back was simply a few days' separation and nothing more. I limped over and offered my hand. The ship was at the moment under low boost as it adjusted to a much tighter orbit than the *Go For Broke* had been riding in.

Clifton threw me a quick glance, then played up. He took his cigar out of his mouth, shook hands, and said quietly, "Glad to see you back, Chief." He was a small man, bald-headed and middle-aged, and looked like a lawyer and a good poker player.

"Anything special while I was away?"

"No. Just routine. I gave Penny the file."

"Good." I turned to Bill Corpsman, again offered my hand.

He did not take it. Instead he put his fists on his hips, looked up at me, and whistled. "Amazing! I really do believe we stand a chance of getting away with it." He looked me up and down, then said, "Turn around, Smythe. Move around. I want to see you walk."

I found that I was actually feeling the annoyance that Bonforte would have felt at such uncalled-for impertinence, and, of course, it showed in my face. Dak touched Corpsman's sleeve and said quickly, "Knock it off, Bill. You remember what we agreed?"

"Chicken tracks!" Corpsman answered. "This room is sound-proofed. I just want to make sure he is up to it. Smythe, how's your Martian? Can you spiel it?"

I answered with a single squeaking polysyllabic in High Martian, a sentence meaning roughly, "Proper conduct demands that one of us leave!"—but it means far more than that, as it is a challenge which usually ends in someone's nest being notified of a demise.

I don't think Corpsman understood it, for he grinned and answered, "I've got to hand it to you, Smythe. That's good."

But Dak understood it. He took Corpsman by the arm and said, "Bill, I told you to knock it off. You're in my ship and that's an order. We play it straight from here on—every second."

Clifton added, "Pay attention to him, Bill. You know we agreed that was the way to do it. Otherwise somebody might slip."

Corpsman glanced at him, then shrugged. "All right, all right. I was just checking up—after all, this was my idea." He gave me a one-sided smile and said, "Howdy, Mister Bonforte. Glad to see you back."

There was a shade too much emphasis on "Mister" but I answered, "Good to be back, Bill. Anything special I need to know before we go down?"

"I guess not. Press conference at Goddard City after the ceremonies." I could see him watching me to see how I would take it.

I nodded. "Very well."

Dak said hastily, "Say, Rog, how about that? Is it necessary? Did you authorize it?"

"I was going to add," Corpsman went on, turning to Clifton, "before the Skipper here got the jitters, that I can take it myself and tell the boys that the Chief has dry laryngitis from the ceremonies—or we can limit it to written questions submitted ahead of time and I'll get the answers written out for him while the ceremonies are going on. Seeing that he looks and sounds so good close up, I would say to risk it. How about it, Mister—'Bonforte'? Think you can swing it?"

"I see no problem involved in it, Bill." I was thinking that if I managed to get by the Martians without a slip I would undertake to ad-lib double talk to a bunch of human reporters as long as they wanted to listen. I had good command of Bonforte's speaking style by now and at least a rough notion of his policies and attitudes—and I need not be specific.

But Clifton looked worried. Before he could speak the ship's horn brayed out, "Captain is requested to come to the control room. Minus four minutes."

Dak said quickly, "You all will have to settle it. I've got to put this sled in its slot—I've got nobody up there but young Epstein." He dashed for the door.

Corpsman called out, "Hey, Skip! I wanted to tell you——"

He was out the door and following Dak without waiting to say good-by.

Roger Clifton closed the door Corpsman had left open, came back, and said slowly, "Do you want to risk this press conference?"

"That is up to you. I want to do the job."

"Mmm . . . Then I'm inclined to risk it—if we use the written-questions method. But I'll check Bill's answers myself before you have to give them."

"Very well." I added, "If you can find a way to let me have them ten minutes or so ahead of time, there shouldn't be any difficulty. I'm a very quick study."

He inspected me. "I quite believe it—Chief. All right, I'll have Penny slip the answers to you right after the ceremonies. Then you can excuse yourself to go to the men's room and just stay there until you are sure of them."

"That should work."

"I think so. Uh, I must say I feel considerably better now that I've seen you. Is there anything I can do for you?"

"I think not, Rog. Yes, there is, too. Any word about—*him?*"

"Eh? Well, yes and no. He's still in Goddard City; we're sure of that. He hasn't been taken off Mars, or even out in the country. We blocked them on that, if that was their intention."

"Eh? Goddard City is not a big place, is it? Not more than a hundred thousand? What's the hitch?"

"The hitch is that we don't dare admit that you—I mean that *he*—is missing. Once we have this adoption thing wrapped up, we can put you out of sight, then announce the kidnaping as if it had just taken place—and make them take the city apart rivet by rivet. The city authorities are all Humanity Party appointees, but they will have to co-operate—after the ceremony. It will be the most wholehearted co-operation you ever saw, for they will be deadly anxious to produce him before the whole Kkkahgral nest swarms over them and tears the city down around their ears."

"Oh. I'm still learning about Martian psychology and customs."

"Aren't we all!"

"Rog? Mmm . . . What leads you to think that he is still alive? Wouldn't their purpose be better served—and with less risk—just by killing him?" I was thinking queasily how simple it had turned out to be to get rid of a body, if a man was ruthless enough.

"I see what you mean. But that, too, is tied up with Martian notions about 'propriety.'" (He used the Martian word.) "Death is the one acceptable excuse for not carrying out an obligation. If he were simply killed, they would adopt him into the nest after his death—and then the whole nest and probably every nest on Mars would set out to avenge him. They would not mind in the least if the whole human race were to die or be killed—but to kill this one human being to keep him from being adopted, that's another kettle of fish entirely. Matter of obligation and propriety—in some ways a Martian's response to a situation is so automatic as to remind one of instinct. It is not, of course, since they are incredibly intelligent. But they do the damnedest things." He frowned and added, "Sometimes I wish I had never left Sussex."

The warning hooter broke up the discussion by forcing us to hurry to our bunks. Dak had cut it fine on purpose; the shuttle rocket from Goddard City was waiting for us when we settled into free fall. All five of us went down, which just filled the passenger couches—again a matter of planning, for the Resident Commissioner had expressed the intention of coming up to meet me and had been dissuaded only by Dak's message to him that our party would require all the space.

I tried to get a better look at the Martian surface as we went down, as I had had only one glimpse of it, from the control room of the *Tom Paine*—since I was supposed to have been there many times I could not show the normal curiosity of a tourist. I did not get much of a look; the shuttle pilot did not turn us so that we could see until he leveled off for his glide approach and I was busy then putting on my oxygen mask.

That pesky Mars-type mask almost finished us; I had never had a chance to practice with it—Dak did not think of it and I had not realized it would be a problem; I had worn both space suit and aqua lung on other occasions and I thought this would be about the same. It was not. The model Bonforte favored was a mouth-free type, a Mitsubishi "Sweet Winds" which pressurizes directly at the nostrils—a nose clamp, nostril plugs, tubes up each nostril which then run back under each ear to the supercharger on the back of your neck. I concede that it is a fine device, once you get used to it, since you can talk, eat, drink, etc., while wearing it. But I would rather have a dentist put both hands in my mouth.

The real difficulty is that you have to exercise conscious control on the muscles that close the back of your mouth, or you hiss like a teakettle, since the durn thing operates on a pressure difference. Fortunately the pilot equalized to Mars-surface pressure once we all had our masks on, which gave me twenty minutes or so to get used to it. But for a few moments I thought the jig was up, just over a silly piece of gadgetry. But I reminded myself that I had worn the thing hundreds of times before and that I was as used to it as I was to my toothbrush. Presently I believed it.

Dak had been able to avoid having the Resident Commissioner chit-chat with me for an hour on the way down but it had not been possible to miss him entirely; he met the shuttle at the skyfield. The close timing did keep me from having to cope with other humans, since I had to go at once into the Martian city. It made sense, but it seemed strange that I would be safer among Martians than among my own kind.

It seemed even stranger to be on Mars.

V

M R. COMMISSIONER BOOTHROYD was a Humanity Party appointee, of course, as were all of his staff except for civil service technical employees. But Dak had told me that it was at least sixty–forty that Boothroyd had not had a finger in the plot; Dak considered him honest but stupid. For that matter, neither Dak nor Rog Clifton believed that Supreme Minister Quiroga was in it; they attributed the thing to the clandestine terrorist group inside the Humanity Party who called themselves the "Actionists"—and they attributed *them* to some highly respectable big-money boys who stood to profit heavily.

Myself, I would not have known an Actionist from an auctioneer.

But the minute we landed something popped up that made me wonder whether friend Boothroyd was as honest and stupid as Dak thought he was. It was a minor thing but one of those little things that can punch holes in an impersonation. Since I was a Very Important Visitor the Commissioner met me; since I held no public office other than membership in the Grand Assembly and was traveling privately no official honors were offered. He was alone save for his aide—and a little girl about fifteen.

I knew him from photographs and I knew quite a bit about him; Rog and Penny had briefed me carefully. I shook hands, asked about his sinusitis, thanked him for the pleasant time I had had on my last visit, and spoke with his aide in that warm man-to-man fashion that Bonforte was so good at. Then I turned to the young lady. I knew Boothroyd had children and that one of them was about this age and sex; I did not know—perhaps Rog and Penny did not know—whether or not I had ever met her.

Boothroyd himself saved me. "You haven't met my daughter Deirdre, I believe. She insisted on coming along."

Nothing in the pictures I had studied had shown Bonforte dealing with young girls—so I simply had to *be* Bonforte—a widower in his middle fifties who had no children of his own, no nieces, and probably little experience with teen-age girls—

but with lots of experience in meeting strangers of every sort. So I treated her as if she were twice her real age; I did not quite kiss her hand. She blushed and looked pleased.

Boothroyd looked indulgent and said, "Well, ask him, my dear. You may not have another chance."

She blushed deeper and said, "Sir, could I have your autograph? The girls in my school collect them. I have Mr. Quiroga's . . . I ought to have yours." She produced a little book which she had been holding behind her.

I felt like a copter driver asked for his license—which is home in his other pants. I had studied hard but I had not expected to have to forge Bonforte's signature. Damn it, you can't do *everything* in two and a half days!

But it was simply impossible for Bonforte to refuse such a request—and I was Bonforte. I smiled jovially and said, "You have Mr. Quiroga's already?"

"Yes, sir."

"Just his autograph?"

"Yes. Er, he put 'Best Wishes' on it."

I winked at Boothroyd. "Just 'Best Wishes,' eh? To young ladies I never make it less than 'Love.' Tell you what I'm going to do——" I took the little book from her, glanced through the pages.

"Chief," Dak said urgently, "we are short on minutes."

"Compose yourself," I said without looking up. "The entire Martian nation can wait, if necessary, on a young lady." I handed the book to Penny. "Will you note the size of this book? And then remind me to send a photograph suitable for pasting in it—and properly autographed, of course."

"Yes, Mr. Bonforte."

"Will that suit you, Miss Deirdre?"

"Gee!"

"Good. Thanks for asking me. We can leave now, Captain. Mr. Commissioner, is that our car?"

"Yes, Mr. Bonforte." He shook his head wryly. "I'm afraid you have converted a member of my own family to your Expansionist heresies. Hardly sporting, eh? Sitting ducks, and so forth?"

"That should teach you not to expose her to bad company—eh, Miss Deirdre?" I shook hands again. "Thanks for meeting us, Mr. Commissioner. I am afraid we had better hurry along now."

"Yes, certainly. Pleasure."

"Thanks, Mr. Bonforte!"

"Thank *you*, my dear."

I turned away slowly, so as not to appear jerky or nervous in stereo. There were photographers around, still, news pickup, stereo, and so forth, as well as many reporters. Bill was keeping the reporters away from us; as we turned to go he waved and said, "See you later, Chief," and turned back to talk to one of them. Rog, Dak, and Penny followed me into the car. There was the usual skyfield crowd, not as numerous as at any earth-port, but numerous. I was not worried about them as long as Boothroyd accepted the impersonation—though there were certainly some present who *knew* that I was not Bonforte.

But I refused to let those individuals worry me, either. They could cause us no trouble without incriminating themselves.

The car was a Rolls Outlander, pressurized, but I left my oxygen mask on because the others did. I took the right-hand seat, Rog sat beside me, and Penny beside him, while Dak wound his long legs around one of the folding seats. The driver glanced back through the partition and started up.

Rog said quietly, "I was worried there for a moment."

"Nothing to worry about. Now let's all be quiet, please. I want to review my speech."

Actually I wanted to gawk at the Martian scene; I knew the speech perfectly. The driver took us along the north edge of the field, past many godowns. I read signs for Verwijs Trading Company, Diana Outlines, Ltd., Three Planets, and I. G. Farbenindustrie. There were almost as many Martians as humans in sight. We ground hogs get the impression that Martians are slow as snails—and they are, on our comparatively heavy planet. On their own world they skim along on their bases like a stone sliding over water.

To the right, south of us past the flat field, the Great Canal dipped into the too-close horizon, showing no shore line beyond. Straight ahead of us was the Nest of Kkkah, a fairy city. I was staring at it, my heart lifting at its fragile beauty, when Dak moved suddenly.

We were well past the traffic around the godowns but there

was one car ahead, coming toward us; I had seen it without noticing it. But Dak must have been edgily ready for trouble; when the other car was quite close, he suddenly slammed down the partition separating us from the driver, swarmed over the man's neck, and grabbed the wheel. We slewed to the right, barely missing the other car, slewed again to the left and barely stayed on the road. It was a near thing, for we were past the field now and here the highway edged the canal.

I had not been much use to Dak a couple of days earlier in the Eisenhower, but I had been unarmed and not expecting trouble. This day I was still unarmed, not so much as a poisoned fang, but I comported myself a little better. Dak was more than busy trying to drive the car while leaning over from the back seat. The driver, caught off balance at first, now tried to wrestle him away from the wheel.

I lunged forward, got my left arm around the driver's neck, and shoved my right thumb into his ribs. "Move and you've had it!" The voice belonged to the hero-villain in *The Second-Story Gentleman*; the line of dialogue was his too.

My prisoner became very quiet.

Dak said urgently, "Rog, what are they doing?"

Clifton looked back and answered, "They're turning around."

Dak answered, "Okay. Chief, keep your gun on that character while I climb over." He was doing so even as he spoke, an awkward matter in view of his long legs and the crowded car. He settled into the seat and said happily, "I doubt if anything on wheels can catch a Rolls on a straightaway." He jerked on the damper and the big car shot forward. "How am I doing, Rog?"

"They're just turned around."

"All right. What do we do with this item? Dump him out?"

My victim squirmed and said, "I didn't do anything!" I jabbed my thumb harder and he quieted.

"Oh, not a thing," Dak agreed, keeping his eyes on the road. "All you did was try to cause a little crash—just enough to make Mr. Bonforte late for his appointment. If I had not noticed that you were slowing down to make it easy on yourself, you might have got away with it. No guts, eh?" He took a slight curve with the tires screaming and the gyro fighting to keep us upright. "What's the situation, Rog?"

"They've given up."

"So." Dak did not slacken speed; we must have been doing well over three hundred kilometers. "I wonder if they would try to bomb us with one of their own boys aboard? How about it, bub? Would they write you off as expendable?"

"I don't know what you're talking about! You're going to be in trouble over this!"

"Really? The word of four respectable people against your jailbird record? Or aren't you a transportee? Anyhow, Mr. Bonforte prefers to have me drive him—so naturally you were glad to do a favor for Mr. Bonforte." We hit something about as big as a worm cast on that glassy road and my prisoner and I almost went through the roof.

" 'Mr. Bonforte!' " My victim made it a swear word.

Dak was silent for several seconds. At last he said, "I don't think we ought to dump this one, Chief. I think we ought to let you off, then take him to a quiet place. I think he might talk if we urged him."

The driver tried to get away. I tightened the pressure on his neck and jabbed him again with my thumb knuckle. A knuckle may not feel too much like the muzzle of a heater—but who wants to find out? He relaxed and said sullenly, "You don't dare give me the needle."

"Heavens, no!" Dak answered in shocked tones. "That would be illegal. Penny girl, got a bobby pin?"

"Why, certainly, Dak." She sounded puzzled and I was. She did not sound frightened, though, and I certainly was.

"Good. Bub, did you ever have a bobby pin shoved up under your fingernails? They say it will even break a hypnotic command not to talk. Works directly on the subconscious or something. Only trouble is that the patient makes the most unpleasant noises. So we are going to take you out in the dunes where you won't disturb anybody but sand scorpions. After you have talked—now here comes the nice part! After you talk we are going to turn you loose, not do anything, just let you walk back into town. But—listen carefully now!—if you are real nice and co-operative, you get a prize. We'll let you have your mask for the walk."

Dak stopped talking; for a moment there was no sound but the keening of the thin Martian air past the roof. A human being can walk possibly two hundred yards on Mars without an oxygen mask, if he is in good condition. I believe I read of a case where a man walked almost half a mile before he died. I glanced at the trip meter and saw that we were about twenty-three kilometers from Goddard City.

The prisoner said slowly, "Honest, I don't know anything about it. I was just paid to crash the car."

"We'll try to stimulate your memory." The gates of the Martian city were just ahead of us; Dak started slowing the car. "Here's where you get out, Chief. Rog, better take your gun and relieve the Chief of our guest."

"Right, Dak." Rog moved up by me, jabbed the man in the ribs—again with a bare knuckle. I moved out of the way. Dak braked the car to a halt, stopping right in front of the gates.

"Four minutes to spare," he said happily. "This is a nice car. I wish I owned it. Rog, ease up a touch and give me room."

Clifton did so, Dak chopped the driver expertly on the side of his neck with the edge of his hand; the man went limp. "That will keep him quiet while you get clear. Can't have any unseemly disturbance under the eyes of the nest. Let's check time."

We did so. I was about three and a half minutes ahead of the deadline. "You are to go in exactly on time, you understand? Not ahead, not behind, but on the dot."

"That's right," Clifton and I answered in chorus.

"Thirty seconds to walk up the ramp, maybe. What do you want to do with the three minutes you have left?"

I sighed. "Just get my nerve back."

"Your nerve is all right. You didn't miss a trick back there. Cheer up, old son. Two hours from now you can head for home, with your pay burning holes in your pocket. We're on the last lap."

"I hope so. It's been quite a strain. Uh, Dak?"

"Yes?"

"Come here a second." I got out of the car, motioned him to come with me a short distance away. "What happens if I make a mistake—in there?"

"Eh?" Dak looked surprised, then laughed a little too heartily. "You won't make a mistake. Penny tells me you've got it down Jo-block perfect."

"Yes, but suppose I slip?"

"You won't slip. I know how you feel; I felt the same way on my first solo grounding. But when it started, I was so busy doing it I didn't have time to do it wrong."

Clifton called out, his voice thin in thin air, "Dak! Are you watching the time?"

"Gobs of time. Over a minute."

"Mr. Bonforte!" It was Penny's voice. I turned and went back to the car. She got out and put out her hand. "Good luck, Mr. Bonforte."

"Thanks, Penny."

Rog shook hands and Dak clapped me on the shoulder. "Minus thirty-five seconds. Better start."

I nodded and started up the ramp. It must have been within a second or two of the exact, appointed time when I reached the top, for the mighty gates rolled back as I came to them. I took a deep breath and cursed that damned air mask.

Then I took my stage.

It doesn't make any difference how many times you do it, that first walk on as the curtain goes up on the first night of any run is a breath-catcher and a heart-stopper. Sure, you know your sides. Sure, you've asked the manager to count the house. Sure, you've done it all before. No matter—when you first walk out there and know that all those eyes are on you, waiting for you to speak, waiting for you to do something—maybe even waiting for you to go up on your lines, brother, you feel it. This is why they have prompters.

I looked out and saw my audience and I wanted to run. I had stage fright for the first time in thirty years.

The siblings of the nest were spread out before me as far as I could see. There was an open lane in front of me, with thousands on each side, set close together as asparagus. I knew that the first thing I must do was slow-march down the center of that lane, clear to the far end, to the ramp leading down into the inner nest.

I could not move.

I said to myself, "Look, boy, you're John Joseph Bonforte. You've been here dozens of times before. These people are your friends. You're here because you want to be here—and because they want you here. So march down that aisle. Tum tum te *tum!* 'Here comes the bride!'"

I began to feel like Bonforte again. I was Uncle Joe Bonforte, determined to do this thing perfectly—for the honor and welfare of my own people and my own planet—and for my friends the Martians. I took a deep breath and one step.

That deep breath saved me; it brought me that heavenly fragrance. Thousands on thousands of Martians packed close together—it smelled to me as if somebody had dropped and broken a whole case of Jungle Lust. The conviction that I smelled it was so strong that I involuntarily glanced back to see if Penny had followed me in. I could feel her handclasp warm in my palm.

I started limping down that aisle, trying to make it about the speed a Martian moves on his own planet. The crowd closed in behind me. Occasionally kids would get away from their elders and skitter out in front of me. By "kids" I mean post-fission Martians, half the mass and not much over half the height of an adult. They are never out of the nest and we are inclined to forget that there can be little Martians. It takes almost five years, after fission, for a Martian to regain his full size, have his brain fully restored, and get all of his memory back. During this transition he is an idiot studying to be a moron. The gene rearrangement and subsequent regeneration incident to conjugation and fission put him out of the running for a long time. One of Bonforte's spools was a lecture on the subject, accompanied by some not very good amateur stereo.

The kids, being cheerful idiots, are exempt from propriety and all that that implies. But they are greatly loved.

Two of the kids, of the same and smallest size and looking just alike to me, skittered out and stopped dead in front of me, just like a foolish puppy in traffic. Either I stopped or I ran them down.

So I stopped. They moved even closer, blocking my way completely, and started sprouting pseudo limbs while chittering at each other. I could not understand them at all. Quickly they were plucking at my clothes and snaking their patty-paws into my sleeve pockets.

The crowd was so tight that I could hardly go around them.

I was stretched between two needs. In the first place they were so darn cute that I wanted to see if I didn't have a sweet tucked away somewhere for them—but in a still firster place was the knowledge that the adoption ceremony was timed like a ballet. If I didn't get on down that street, I was going to commit the classic sin against propriety made famous by Kkkahgral the Younger himself.

But the kids were not about to get out of my way. One of them had found my watch.

I sighed and was almost overpowered by the perfume. Then I made a bet with myself. I bet that baby-kissing was a Galactic Universal and that it took precedence even over Martian propriety. I got on one knee, making myself about the height they were, and fondled them for a few moments, patting them and running my hands down their scales.

Then I stood up and said carefully, "That is all now. I must go," which used up a large fraction of my stock of Basic Martian.

The kids clung to me but I moved them carefully and gently aside and went on down the double line, hurrying to make up for the time I had lost. No life wand burned a hole in my back. I risked a hope that my violation of propriety had not yet reached the capital offense level. I reached the ramp leading down into the inner nest and started on down.

*   *   *   *   *   *   *   *   *   *   *

That line of asterisks represents the adoption ceremony. Why? Because it is limited to members of the Kkkah nest. It is a family matter.

Put it this way: A Mormon may have very close gentile friends—but does that friendship get a gentile inside the Temple at Salt Lake City? It never has and it never will. Martians visit very freely back and forth between their nests—but a Martian enters the inner nest only of his own family. Even his conjugate-spouses are not thus privileged. I have no more right to tell the details of the adoption ceremony than a lodge brother has to be specific about ritual outside the lodge.

Oh, the rough outlines do not matter, since they are the same for any nest, just as my part was the same for any candidate. My sponsor—Bonforte's oldest Martian friend, Kkkahrrreash—

met me at the door and threatened me with a wand. I demanded that he kill me at once were I guilty of any breach. To tell the truth, I did not recognize him, even though I had studied a picture of him. But it had to be him because ritual required it.

Having thus made clear that I stood four-square for Motherhood, the Home, Civic Virtue, and never missing Sunday school, I was permitted to enter. 'Rrreash conducted me around all the stations, I was questioned and I responded. Every word, every gesture, was as stylized as a classical Chinese play, else I would not have stood a chance. Most of the time I did not know what they were saying and half of the time I did not understand my own replies; I simply knew my cues and the responses. It was not made easier by the low light level the Martians prefer; I was groping around like a mole.

I played once with Hawk Mantell, shortly before he died, after he was stone-deaf. There was a trouper! He could not even use a hearing device because the eighth nerve was dead. Part of the time he could cue by lips but that is not always possible. He directed the production himself and he timed it perfectly. I have seen him deliver a line, walk away—then whirl around and snap out a retort to a line that he had never heard, precisely on the timing.

This was like that. I knew my part and I played it. If *they* blew it, that was their lookout.

But it did not help my morale that there were never less than half a dozen wands leveled at me the whole time. I kept telling myself that they wouldn't burn me down for a slip. After all, I was just a poor stupid human being and at the very least they would give me a passing mark for effort. But I didn't believe it.

After what seemed like days—but was not, since the whole ceremony times exactly one ninth of Mars' rotation—after an endless time, we ate. I don't know what and perhaps it is just as well. It did not poison me.

After that the elders made their speeches, I made my acceptance speech in answer, and they gave me my name and my wand. I was a Martian.

I did not know how to use the wand and my name sounded like a leaky faucet, but from that instant on it was my legal name on Mars and I was legally a blood member of the most aristocratic family on the planet—exactly fifty-two hours after a ground hog down on his luck had spent his last half Imperial buying a drink for a stranger in the bar of Casa Mañana.

I guess this proves that one should never pick up strangers.

I got out as quickly as possible. Dak had made up a speech for me in which I claimed proper necessity for leaving at once and they let me go. I was nervous as a man upstairs in a sorority house because there was no longer ritual to guide me. I mean to say even casual social behavior was still hedged around with airtight and risky custom and I did not know the moves. So I recited my excuse and headed out. 'Rrreash and another elder went with me and I chanced playing with another pair of the kids when we were outside—or maybe the same pair. Once I reached the gates the two elders said good-by in squeaky English and let me go out alone; the gates closed behind me and I reswallowed my heart.

The Rolls was waiting where they had let me out; I hurried down, a door opened, and I was surprised to see that Penny was in it alone. But not displeased. I called out, "Hi, Curly Top! I made it!"

"I knew you would."

I gave a mock sword salute with my wand and said, "Just call me Kkkahjjjerrr"—spraying the front rows with the second syllable.

"Be careful with that thing!" she said nervously.

I slid in beside her on the front seat and asked, "Do you know how to use one of these things?" The reaction was setting in and I felt exhausted but gay; I wanted three quick drinks and a thick steak, then to wait up for the critics' reviews.

"No. But do be careful."

"I think all you have to do is to press it here," which I did, and there was a neat two-inch hole in the windshield and the car wasn't pressurized any longer.

Penny gasped. I said, "Gee, I'm sorry. I'll put it away until Dak can coach me."

She gulped. "It's all right. Just be careful where you point it." She started wheeling the car and I found that Dak was not the only one with a heavy hand on the damper.

Wind was whistling in through the hole I had made. I said, "What's the rush? I need some time to study my lines for the press conference. Did you bring them? And where are the others?" I had forgotten completely the driver we had grabbed; I had not thought about him from the time the gates of the nest opened.

"No. They couldn't come."

"Penny, what's the matter? What's happened?" I was wondering if I could possibly take a press conference without coaching. Perhaps I could tell them a little about the adoption; I wouldn't have to fake that.

"It's Mr. Bonforte—*they've found him.*"

VI

I HAD not noticed until then that she had not once called me "Mr. Bonforte." She could not, of course, for I was no longer he; I was again Lorrie Smythe, that actor chap they had hired to stand in for him.

I sat back and sighed, and let myself relax. "So it's over at last —and we got away with it." I felt a great burden lift off me; I had not known how heavy it was until I put it down. Even my "lame" leg stopped aching. I reached over and patted Penny's hand on the wheel and said in my own voice, "I'm glad it's over. But I'm going to miss having you around, pal. You're a trouper. But even the best run ends and the company breaks up. I hope I'll see you again sometime."

"I hope so too."

"I suppose Dak has arranged some shenanigan to keep me under cover and sneak me back into the *Tom Paine?*"

"I don't know." Her voice sounded odd and I gave her a quick glance and saw that she was crying. My heart gave a skip. Penny crying? Over us separating? I could not believe it and yet I wanted to. One might think that, between my handsome features and cultivated manners, women would find me irresistible, but it is a deplorable fact that all too many of them have found me easy to resist. Penny had seemed to find it no effort at all.

"Penny," I said hastily, "why all the tears, hon? You'll wreck this car."

"I can't help it."

"Well—put me in it. What's wrong? You told me they had got him back; you didn't tell me anything else." I had a sudden horrid but logical suspicion. "He was *alive*—wasn't he?"

"Yes—he's alive—but, oh, they've *hurt* him!" She started to sob and I had to grab the wheel.

She straightened up quickly. "Sorry."

"Want me to drive?"

"I'll be all right. Besides, you don't know how—I mean you aren't supposed to know how to drive."

"Huh? Don't be silly. I do know how and it no longer matters that——" I broke off, suddenly realizing that it might still matter. If they had roughed up Bonforte so that it showed, then he could not appear in public in that shape—at least not only fifteen minutes after being adopted into the Kkkah nest. Maybe I would have to take that press conference and depart publicly, while Bonforte would be the one they would sneak aboard. Well, all right—hardly more than a curtain call. "Penny, do Dak and Rog want me to stay in character for a bit? Do I play to the reporters? Or don't I?"

"I don't know. There wasn't time."

We were already approaching the stretch of godowns by the field, and the giant bubble domes of Goddard City were in sight. "Penny, slow this car down and talk sense. I've got to have my cues."

The driver had talked—I neglected to ask whether or not the bobby-pin treatment had been used. He had then been turned loose to walk back but had not been deprived of his mask; the others had barreled back to Goddard City, with Dak at the wheel. I felt lucky to have been left behind; *voyageurs* should not be allowed to drive anything but spaceships.

They went to the address the driver had given them, in Old Town under the original bubble. I gathered that it was the sort of jungle every port has had since the Phoenicians sailed around the shoulder of Africa, a place of released transportees, prostitutes, monkey-pushers, rangees, and other dregs—a neighborhood where policemen travel only in pairs.

The information they had squeezed out of the driver had been correct but a few minutes out of date. The room had housed the prisoner, certainly, for there was a bed in it which seemed to have been occupied continuously for at least a week, a pot of coffee was still hot—and wrapped in a towel on a shelf was an old-fashioned removable denture which Clifton identified as belonging to Bonforte. But Bonforte himself was missing and so were his captors.

They had left there with the intention of carrying out the original plan, that of claiming that the kidnaping had taken place immediately after the adoption and putting pressure on Boothroyd by threatening to appeal to the Nest of Kkkah. But they had found Bonforte, had simply run across him in the street before they left Old Town—a poor old stumblebum with a week's beard, dirty and dazed. The men had not recognized him, but Penny had known him and made them stop.

She broke into sobs again as she told me this part and we almost ran down a truck train snaking up to one of the loading docks.

A reasonable reconstruction seemed to be that the laddies in the second car—the one that was to crash us—had reported back, whereupon the faceless leaders of our opponents had decided that the kidnaping no longer served their purposes. Despite the arguments I had heard about it, I was surprised that they had not simply killed him; it was not until later that I understood that what they had done was subtler, more suited to their purposes, and much crueler than mere killing.

"Where is he now?" I asked.

"Dak took him to the *voyageurs*' hostel in Dome 3."

"Is that where we are headed?"

"I don't know. Rog just said to go pick you up, then they disappeared in the service door of the hostel. Uh, no, I don't think we dare go there. I don't know what to do."

"Penny, stop the car."

"Huh?"

"Surely this car has a phone. We won't stir another inch until we find out—or figure out—what we should do. But I am certain of one thing: I should stay in character until Dak or Rog decides that I should fade out. Somebody has to talk to the newsmen. Somebody has to make a public departure for the *Tom Paine*. You're sure that Mr. Bonforte can't be spruced up so that he can do it?"

"What? Oh, he couldn't possibly! You didn't *see* him."

"So I didn't. I'll take your word for it. All right, Penny, I'm 'Mr. Bonforte' again and you're my secretary. We'd better get with it."

"Yes—Mr. Bonforte."

"Now try to get Captain Broadbent on the phone, will you, please?"

We couldn't find a phone list in the car and she had to go through "Information," but at last she was tuned with the clubhouse of the *voyageurs*. I could hear both sides. "Pilots' Club, Mrs. Kelly speaking."

Penny covered the microphone. "Do I give my name?"

"Play it straight. We've nothing to hide."

"This is Mr. Bonforte's secretary," she said gravely. "Is his pilot there? Captain Broadbent."

"I know him, dearie." There was a shout: "Hey! Any of you smokers see where Dak went?" After a pause she went on, "He's gone to his room. I'm buzzing him."

Shortly Penny said, "Skipper? The Chief wants to talk to you," and handed me the phone.

"This is the Chief, Dak."

"Oh. Where are you—sir?"

"Still in the car. Penny picked me up. Dak, Bill scheduled a press conference, I believe. Where is it?"

He hesitated. "I'm glad you called in, sir. Bill canceled it. There's been a—slight change in the situation."

"So Penny told me. I'm just as well pleased; I'm rather tired. Dak, I've decided not to stay dirtside tonight; my gimp leg has been bothering me and I'm looking forward to a real rest in free fall." I hated free fall but Bonforte did not. "Will you or Rog make my apologies to the Commissioner, and so forth?"

"We'll take care of everything, sir."

"Good. How soon can you arrange a shuttle for me?"

"The *Pixie* is still standing by for you, sir. If you will go to Gate 3, I'll phone and have a field car pick you up."

"Very good. Out."

"Out, sir."

I handed the phone to Penny to put back in its clamp. "Curly Top, I don't know whether that phone frequency is monitored or not—or whether possibly the whole car is bugged. If either is the case, they may have learned two things—where Dak is and through that where *he* is, and second, what I am about to do next. Does that suggest anything to your mind?"

She looked thoughtful, then took out her secretary's notebook, wrote in it: *Let's get rid of the car.*

I nodded, then took the book from her and wrote in it: *How far away is Gate 3?*

She answered: *Walking distance.*

Silently we climbed out and left. She had pulled into some executive's parking space outside one of the warehouses when she had parked the car; no doubt in time it would be returned where it belonged—and such minutiae no longer mattered.

We had gone about fifty yards, when I stopped. Something was the matter. Not the day, certainly. It was almost balmy, with the sun burning brightly in clear, purple Martian sky. The traffic, wheel and foot, seemed to pay no attention to us, or at least such attention was for the pretty young woman with me rather than directed at me. Yet I felt uneasy.

"What is it, Chief?"

"Eh? *That* is what it is!"

"Sir?"

"I'm not being the 'Chief.' It isn't in character to go dodging off like this. Back we go, Penny."

She did not argue, but followed me back to the car. This time I climbed into the back seat, sat there looking dignified, and let her chauffeur me to Gate 3.

It was not the gate we had come in. I think Dak had chosen it because it ran less to passengers and more to freight. Penny paid no attention to signs and ran the big Rolls right up to the gate. A terminal policeman tried to stop her; she simply said coldly, "Mr. Bonforte's car. And will you please send word to the Commissioner's office to call for it here?"

He looked baffled, glanced into the rear compartment, seemed to recognize me, saluted, and let us stay. I answered with a friendly wave and he opened the door for me. "The lieutenant is very particular about keeping the space back of the fence clear, Mr. Bonforte," he apologized, "but I guess it's all right."

"You can have the car moved at once," I said. "My secretary and I are leaving. Is my field car here?"

"I'll find out at the gate, sir." He left. It was just the amount of audience I wanted, enough to tie it down solid that "Mr. Bonforte" had arrived by official car and had left for his space yacht. I tucked my life wand under my arm like Napoleon's baton and limped after him, with Penny tagging along. The cop spoke to the gatemaster, then hurried back to us, smiling. "Field car is waiting, sir."

"Thanks indeed." I was congratulating myself on the perfection of the timing.

"Uh . . ." The cop looked flustered and added hurriedly, in a low voice, "I'm an Expansionist, too, sir. Good job you did today." He glanced at the life wand with a touch of awe.

I knew exactly how Bonforte should look in this routine. "Why, thank you. I hope you have lots of children. We need to work up a solid majority."

He guffawed more than it was worth. "That's a good one! Uh, mind if I repeat it?"

"Not at all." We had moved on and I started through the gate. The gatemaster touched my arm. "Er . . . Your passport, Mr. Bonforte."

I trust I did not let my expression change. "The passports, Penny."

She looked frostily at the official. "Captain Broadbent takes care of all clearances."

He looked at me and looked away. "I suppose it's all right. But I'm supposed to check them and take down the serial numbers."

"Yes, of course. Well, I suppose I must ask Captain Broadbent to run out to the field. Has my shuttle been assigned a take-off time? Perhaps you had better arrange with the tower to 'hold.'"

But Penny appeared to be cattily angry. "Mr. Bonforte, this is ridiculous! We've *never* had this red tape before—certainly not on *Mars*."

The cop said hastily, "Of course it's all right, Hans. After all, this is Mr. Bonforte."

"Sure, but——"

I interrupted with a happy smile. "There's a simpler way out. If you—what is your name, sir?"

"Haslwanter. Hans Haslwanter," he answered reluctantly.

"Mr. Haslwanter, if you will call Mr. Commissioner Boothroyd, I'll speak to him and we can save my pilot a trip out to the field—and save me an hour or more of time."

"Uh, I wouldn't like to do that, sir. I could call the port captain's office?" he suggested hopefully.

"Just get me Mr. Boothroyd's number. *I* will call him." This time I put a touch of frost into my voice, the attitude of the busy and important man who wishes to be democratic but has had all the pushing around and hampering by underlings that he intends to put up with.

That did it. He said hastily, "I'm sure it's all right, Mr. Bonforte. It's just—well, regulations, you know."

"Yes, I know. Thank you." I started to push on through.

"Hold it, Mr. Bonforte! Look this way."

I glanced around. That *i*-dotting and *t*-crossing civil servant had held us up just long enough to let the press catch up with us. One man had dropped to his knee and was pointing a stereo-box at me; he looked up and said, "Hold the wand where we can see it." Several others with various types of equipment were gathering around us; one had climbed up on the roof of the Rolls. Someone else was shoving a microphone at me and another had a directional mike aimed like a gun.

I was as angry as a leading woman with her name in small type but I remembered who I was supposed to be. I smiled and moved slowly. Bonforte had a good grasp of the fact that motion appears faster in pictures; I could afford to do it properly.

"Mr. Bonforte, why did you cancel the press conference?"

"Mr. Bonforte, it is asserted that you intend to demand that the Grand Assembly grant full Empire citizenship to Martians; will you comment?"

"Mr. Bonforte, how soon are you going to force a vote of confidence in the present government?"

I held up my hand with the wand in it and grinned. "One at a time, please! Now what was that first question?"

They all answered at once, of course; by the time they had sorted out precedence I had managed to waste several moments without having to answer anything. Bill Corpsman came charging up at that point. "Have a heart, boys. The Chief has had a hard day. I gave you all you need."

I held out a palm at him. "I can spare a minute or two, Bill. Gentlemen, I'm just about to leave but I'll try to cover the essentials of what you have asked. So far as I know the present government does not plan any reassessment of the relation of Mars to the Empire. Since I am not in office my own opinions are hardly pertinent. I suggest that you ask Mr. Quiroga. On the question of how soon the opposition will force a vote of confidence all I can say is that we won't do it unless we are sure we can win it—and you know as much about that as I do."

Someone said, "That doesn't say much, does it?"

"It was not intended to say much," I retorted, softening it with a grin. "Ask me questions I can legitimately answer and I will. Ask me those loaded 'Have-you-quit-beating-your-wife?'

sort and I have answers to match." I hesitated, realizing that Bonforte had a reputation for bluntness and honesty, especially with the press. "But I am not trying to stall you. You all know why I am here today. Let me say this about it—and you can quote me if you wish." I reached back into my mind and hauled up an appropriate bit from the speeches of Bonforte I had studied. "The real meaning of what happened today is not that of an honor to one man. This"—I gestured with the Martian wand—"is proof that two great races can reach out across the gap of strangeness with understanding. Our own race is spreading out to the stars. We shall find—we *are* finding—that we are vastly outnumbered. If we are to succeed in our expansion to the stars, we must deal honestly, humbly, with open hearts. I have heard it said that our Martian neighbors would overrun Earth if given the chance. This is nonsense; Earth is not suited to Martians. Let us protect our own—but let us not be seduced by fear and hatred into foolish acts. The stars will never be won by little minds; we must be big as space itself."

The reporter cocked an eyebrow. "Mr. Bonforte, seems to me I heard you make that speech last February."

"You will hear it next February. Also January, March, and all the other months. Truth cannot be too often repeated." I glanced back at the gatemaster and added, "I'm sorry but I'll have to go now—or I'll miss the tick." I turned and went through the gate, with Penny after me.

We climbed into the little lead-armored field car and the door sighed shut. The car was automatized, so I did not have to play up for a driver; I threw myself down and relaxed. "Whew!"

"I thought you did beautfully," Penny said seriously.

"I had a bad moment when he spotted the speech I was cribbing."

"You got away with it. It was an inspiration. You—you sounded just like *him*."

"Was there anybody there I should have called by name?"

"Not really. One or two maybe, but they wouldn't expect it when you were so rushed."

"I was caught in a squeeze. That fiddlin' gatemaster and his passports. Penny, I should think that you would carry them rather than Dak."

"Dak doesn't carry them. We all carry our own." She reached

into her bag, pulled out a little book. "I had mine—but I did not dare admit it."

"Eh?"

"*He* had *his* on him when they got him. We haven't dared ask for a replacement—not at this time."

I was suddenly very weary.

Having no instructions from Dak or Rog, I stayed in character during the shuttle trip up and on entering the *Tom Paine*. It wasn't difficult; I simply went straight to the owner's cabin and spent long, miserable hours in free fall, biting my nails and wondering what was happening down on the surface. With the aid of anti-nausea pills I finally managed to float off into fitful sleep—which was a mistake, for I had a series of no-pants nightmares, with reporters pointing at me and cops touching me on the shoulder and Martians aiming their wands at me. They all knew I was phony and were simply arguing over who had the privilege of taking me apart and putting me down the oubliette.

I was awakened by the hooting of the acceleration alarm. Dak's vibrant baritone was booming, "First and last red warning! One third gee! One minute!" I hastily pulled myself over to my bunk and held on. I felt lots better when it hit; one third gravity is not much, about the same as Mars' surface I think, but it is enough to steady the stomach and make the floor a real floor.

About five minutes later Dak knocked and let himself in as I was going to the door. "Howdy, Chief."

"Hello, Dak. I'm certainly glad to see you back."

"Not as glad as I am to be back," he said wearily. He eyed my bunk. "Mind if I spread out there?"

"Help yourself."

He did so and sighed. "Cripes, am I pooped! I could sleep for a week . . . I think I will."

"Let's both of us. Uh . . . You got him aboard?"

"Yes. What a gymkhana!"

"I suppose so. Still, it must be easier to do a job like that in a small, informal port like this than it was to pull the stunts you rigged at Jefferson."

"Huh? No, it's much harder here."

"Eh?"

"Obviously. Here everybody knows everybody—and people will talk." Dak smiled wryly. "We brought him aboard as a case of frozen canal shrimp. Had to pay export duty, too."

"Dak, how is he?"

"Well . . ." Dak frowned. "Doc Capek says that he will make a complete recovery—that it is just a matter of time." He added explosively, "If I could lay my hands on those rats! It would make you break down and bawl to see what they did to him—and yet we have to let them get away with it cold—for *his* sake."

Dak was fairly close to bawling himself. I said gently, "I gathered from Penny that they had roughed him up quite a lot. How badly is he hurt?"

"Huh? You must have misunderstood Penny. Aside from being filthy-dirty and needing a shave he was not hurt physically at all."

I looked stupid. "I thought they beat him up. Something about like working him over with a baseball bat."

"I would rather they had! Who cares about a few broken bones? No, no, it was what they did to his *brain*."

"Oh . . ." I felt ill. "Brainwash?"

"Yes. Yes and no. They couldn't have been trying to make him talk because he didn't have any secrets that were of any possible political importance. He always operated out in the open and everybody knows it. They must have been using it simply to keep him under control, keep him from trying to escape."

He went on, "Doc says that he thinks they must have been using the minimum daily dose, just enough to keep him docile, until just before they turned him loose. Then they shot him with a load that would turn an elephant into a gibbering idiot. The front lobes of his brain must be soaked like a bath sponge."

I felt so ill that I was glad I had not eaten. I had once read up on the subject; I hate it so much that it fascinates me. To my mind there is something immoral and degrading in an absolute cosmic sense in tampering with a man's personality. Murder is a clean crime in comparison, a mere peccadillo. "Brainwash" is a term that comes down to us from the Communist movement of the Late Dark Ages; it was first applied to breaking a man's will and altering his personality by physical indignities and subtle torture. But that might take months; later they found a "better" way, one which would turn a man into a babbling slave in seconds—simply inject any one of several cocaine derivatives into his frontal brain lobes.

The filthy practice had first been developed for a legitimate purpose, to quiet disturbed patients and make them accessible to psychotherapy. As such, it was a humane advance, for it was used instead of lobotomy—"lobotomy" is a term almost as obsolete as "chastity girdle" but it means stirring a man's brain with a knife in such a fashion as to destroy his personality without killing him. Yes, they really used to do that—just as they used to beat them to "drive the devils out."

The Communists developed the new brainwash-by-drugs to an efficient technique, then when there were no more Communists, the Bands of Brothers polished it up still further until they could dose a man so lightly that he was simply receptive to leadership—or load him until he was a mindless mass of protoplasm—all in the sweet name of brotherhood. After all, you can't have "brotherhood" if a man is stubborn enough to want to keep his own secrets, can you? And what better way is there to be sure that he is not holding out on you than to poke a needle past his eyeball and slip a shot of babble juice into his brain? "You can't make an omelet without breaking eggs." The sophistries of villains—bah!

Of course, it has been illegal for a long, long time now, except for therapy, with the express consent of a court. But criminals use it and cops are sometimes not lily white, for it does make a prisoner talk and it does not leave any marks at all. The victim can even be told to forget that it has been done.

I knew most of this at the time Dak told me what had been done to Bonforte and the rest I cribbed out of the ship's Encyclopedia Batavia. See the article on "Psychic Integration" and the one on "Torture."

I shook my head and tried to put the nightmares out of my mind. "But he's going to recover?"

"Doc says that the drug does not alter the brain structure; it just paralyzes it. He says that eventually the blood stream picks up and carries away all of the dope; it reaches the kidneys and passes out of the body. But it takes time." Dak looked up at me. "Chief?"

"Eh? About time to knock off that 'Chief' stuff, isn't it? He's back."

"That's what I wanted to talk to you about. Would it be too much trouble to you to keep up the impersonation just a little while longer?"

"But why? There's nobody here but just us chickens."

"That's not quite true. Lorenzo, we've managed to keep this secret awfully tight. There's me, there's you." He ticked it off on his fingers. "There's Doc and Rog and Bill. And Penny, of course. There's a man by the name of Langston back Earthside whom you've never met. I think Jimmie Washington suspects but he wouldn't tell his own mother the right time of day. We don't know how many took part in the kidnaping, but not many, you can be sure. In any case, *they* don't dare talk—and the joke of it is they no longer could prove that he had ever been missing even if they wanted to. But my point is this: here in the *Tommie* we've got all the crew and all the idlers not in on it. Old son, how about staying with it and letting yourself be seen each day by crewmen and by Jimmie Washington's girls and such—while *he* gets well? Huh?"

"Mmm . . . I don't see why not. How long will it be?"

"Just the trip back. We'll take it slow, at an easy boost. You'll enjoy it."

"Okay. Dak, don't figure this into my fee. I'm doing this piece of it just because I *hate* brainwashing."

Dak bounced up and clapped me on the shoulder. "You're my kind of people, Lorenzo. Don't worry about your fee; you'll be taken care of." His manner changed. "Very well, Chief. See you in the morning, sir."

But one thing leads to another. The boost we had started on Dak's return was a mere shift of orbits, to one farther out where there would be little chance of a news service sending up a shuttle for a follow-up story. I woke up in free fall, took a pill, and managed to eat breakfast. Penny showed up shortly thereafter. "Good morning, Mr. Bonforte."

"Good morning, Penny." I inclined my head in the direction of the guest room. "Any news?"

"No, sir. About the same. Captain's compliments and would it be too much trouble for you to come to his cabin?"

"Not at all." Penny followed me in. Dak was there, with his heels hooked to his chair to stay in place; Rog and Bill were strapped to the couch.

Dak looked around and said, "Thanks for coming in, Chief. We need some help."

"Good morning. What is it?"

Clifton answered my greeting with his usual dignified deference and called me Chief; Corpsman nodded. Dak went on, "To clean this up in style you should make one more appearance."

"Eh? I thought——"

"Just a second. The networks were led to expect a major speech from you today, commenting on yesterday's event. I thought Rog intended to cancel it, but Bill has the speech worked up. Question is, will you deliver it?"

The trouble with adopting a cat is that they always have kittens. "Where? Goddard City?"

"Oh no. Right in your cabin. We beam it to Phobos; they can it for Mars and also put it on the high circuit for New Batavia, where the Earth nets will pick it up and where it will be relayed for Venus, Ganymede, et cetera. Inside of four hours it will be all over the system but you'll never have to stir out of your cabin."

There is something very tempting about a grand network. I had never been on one but once and that time my act got clipped down to the point where my face showed for only twenty-seven seconds. But to have one all to myself——

Dak thought I was reluctant and added, "It won't be a strain, as we are equipped to can it right here in the *Tommie*. Then we can project it first and clip out anything if necessary."

"Well—all right. You have the script, Bill?"

"Yes."

"Let me check it."

"What do you mean? You'll have it in plenty of time."

"Isn't that it in your hand?"

"Well, yes."

"Then let me read it."

Corpsman looked annoyed. "You'll have it an hour before we record. These things go better if they sound spontaneous."

"Sounding spontaneous is a matter of careful preparation, Bill. It's my trade. I know."

"You did all right at the skyfield yesterday without a rehearsal. This is just more of the same old hoke; I want you to do it the same way."

Bonforte's personality was coming through stronger the longer Corpsman stalled; I think Clifton could see that I was about to cloud up and storm, for he said, "Oh, for Pete's sake, Bill! Hand him the speech."

Corpsman snorted and threw the sheets at me. In free fall they sailed but the air spread them wide. Penny gathered them together, sorted them, and gave them to me. I thanked her, said nothing more, and started to read.

I skimmed through it in a fraction of the time it would take to deliver it. Finally I finished and looked up.

"Well?" said Rog.

"About five minutes of this concerns the adoption. The rest is an argument for the policies of the Expansionist Party. Pretty much the same as I've heard in the speeches you've had me study."

"Yes," agreed Clifton. "The adoption is the hook we hang the rest on. As you know, we expect to force a vote of confidence before long."

"I understand. You can't miss this chance to beat the drum. Well, it's all right, but——"

"But what? What's worrying you?"

"Well—characterization. In several places the wording should be changed. It's not the way *he* would express it."

Corpsman exploded with a word unnecessary in the presence of a lady; I gave him a cold glance. "Now see here, Smythe," he went on, "who knows how Bonforte would say it? You? Or the man who has been writing his speeches the past four years?"

I tried to keep my temper; he had a point. "It is nevertheless the case," I answered, "that a line which looks okay in print may not deliver well. Mr. Bonforte is a great orator, I have already learned. He belongs with Webster, Churchill, and Demosthenes—a rolling grandeur expressed in simple words. Now take this word 'intransigent,' which you have used twice. I might say that, but I have a weakness for polysyllables; I like to exhibit my literary erudition. But Mr. Bonforte would say 'stubborn' or 'mulish' or 'pigheaded.' The reason he would is, naturally, that they convey emotion much more effectively."

"You see that you make the delivery effective! I'll worry about the words."

"You don't understand, Bill. I don't care whether the speech is politically effective or not; my job is to carry out a characterization. I can't do that if I put into the mouth of the character words that he would never use; it would sound as forced and phony as a goat spouting Greek. But if I read the speech in words he *would* use, it will automatically be effective. He's a great orator."

"Listen, Smythe, you're not hired to write speeches. You're hired to——"

"Hold it, Bill!" Dak cut in. "And a little less of that 'Smythe' stuff, too. Well, Rog? How about it?"

Clifton said, "As I understand it, Chief, your only objection is to some of the phrasing?"

"Well, yes. I'd suggest cutting out that personal attack on Mr. Quiroga, too, and the insinuation about his financial backers. It doesn't sound like real Bonforte to me."

He looked sheepish. "That's a bit I put in myself. But you may be right. He always gives a man the benefit of the doubt." He remained silent for a moment. "You make the changes you think you have to. We'll can it and look at the playback. We can always clip it—or even cancel completely 'due to technical difficulties.'" He smiled grimly. "That's what we'll do, Bill."

"Damn it, this is a ridiculous example of——"

"That's how it is going to be, Bill."

Corpsman left the room very suddenly. Clifton sighed. "Bill always has hated the notion that anybody but Mr. B. could give him instructions. But he's an able man. Uh, Chief, how soon can you be ready to record? We patch in at sixteen hundred."

"I don't know. I'll be ready in time."

Penny followed me back into my office. When she closed the door I said, "I won't need you for the next hour or so, Penny child. But you might ask Doc for more of those pills. I may need them."

"Yes, sir." She floated with her back to the door. "Chief?"

"Yes, Penny?"

"I just wanted to say don't believe what Bill said about writing his speeches!"

"I didn't. I've heard his speeches—and I've read this."

"Oh, Bill does submit drafts, lots of times. So does Rog. I've even done it myself. He—*he* will use ideas from anywhere if he thinks they are good. But when he delivers a speech, it is *his*, every word of it."

"I believe you. I wish he had written this one ahead of time."

"You just do your best!"

I did. I started out simply substituting synonyms, putting in the gutty Germanic words in place of the "intestinal" Latin jawbreakers. Then I got excited and red in the face and tore it to pieces. It's a lot of fun for an actor to mess around with lines; he doesn't get the chance very often.

I used no one but Penny for my audience and made sure from Dak that I was not being tapped elsewhere in the ship—though I suspect that the big-boned galoot cheated on me and listened in himself. I had Penny in tears in the first three minutes; by the time I finished (twenty-eight and a half minutes, just time for station announcements) she was limp. I took no liberties with the straight Expansionist doctrine, as proclaimed by its official prophet, the Right Honorable John Joseph Bonforte; I simply reconstructed his message and his delivery, largely out of phrases from other speeches.

Here's an odd thing—I believed every word of it while I was talking.

But, brother, I made a speech!

Afterwards we all listened to the playback, complete with full stereo of myself. Jimmie Washington was present, which kept Bill Corpsman quiet. When it was over I said, "How about it, Rog? Do we need to clip anything?"

He took his cigar out of his mouth and said, "No. If you want my advice, Chief, I'd say to let it go as it is."

Corpsman left the room again—but Mr. Washington came over with tears leaking out of his eyes—tears are a nuisance in free fall; there's nowhere for them to go. "Mr. Bonforte, that was *beautiful*."

"Thanks, Jimmie."

Penny could not talk at all.

I turned in after that; a top-notch performance leaves me fagged. I slept for more than eight hours, then was awakened by the hooter. I had strapped myself to my bunk—I hate to float around while sleeping in free fall—so I did not have to move. But I had not known that we were getting under way so I called the control room between first and second warning. "Captain Broadbent?"

"Just a moment, sir," I heard Epstein answer.

Then Dak's voice came over. "Yes, Chief? We are getting under way on schedule—pursuant to your orders."

"Eh? Oh yes, certainly."

"I believe Mr. Clifton is on his way to your cabin."

"Very well, Captain." I lay back and waited.

Immediately after we started to boost at one gee Rog Clifton came in; he had a worried look on his face I could not interpret —equal parts of triumph, worry, and confusion. "What is it, Rog?"

"Chief! They've jumped the gun on us! The Quiroga government has resigned!"

VII

I WAS still logy with sleep; I shook my head to try to clear it. "What are you in such a spin about, Rog? That's what you were trying to accomplish, wasn't it?"

"Well, yes, of course. But——" He stopped.

"But what? I don't get it. Here you chaps have been working and scheming for years to bring about this very thing. Now you've won—and you look like a bride who isn't sure she wants to go through with it. Why? The no-good-nicks are out and now God's chillun get their innings. No?"

"Uh—you haven't been in politics much."

"You know I haven't. I got trimmed when I ran for patrol leader in my scout troop. That cured me."

"Well, you see, timing is everything."

"So my father always told me. Look here, Rog, do I gather that if you had your druthers you'd druther Quiroga was still in office? You said he had 'jumped the gun.'"

"Let me explain. What we really wanted was to move a vote of confidence and win it, and thereby force a general election on them—but at our own time, when we estimated that we could win the election."

"Oh. And you don't figure you can win now? You think Quiroga will go back into office for another five years—or at least the Humanity Party will?"

Clifton looked thoughtful. "No, I think our chances are pretty good to win the election."

"Eh? Maybe I'm not awake yet. Don't you *want* to win?"

"Of course. But don't you see what this resignation has done to us?"

"I guess I don't."

"Well, the government in power can order a general election at any time up to the constitutional limitation of five years. Ordinarily they will go to the people when the time seems most favorable to them. But they don't resign between the announcement and the election unless forced to. You follow me?"

I realized that the event did seem odd, little attention as I paid to politics. "I believe so."

"But in this case Quiroga's government scheduled a general election, then resigned in a body, leaving the Empire without a government. Therefore the sovereign must call on someone else to form a 'caretaker' government to serve until the election. By the letter of the law he can ask any member of the Grand Assembly, but as a matter of strict constitutional precedent he has no choice. When a government resigns in a body—not just reshuffling portfolios but quits as a whole—then the sovereign *must* call on the leader of the opposition to form the 'caretaker' government. It's indispensable to our system; it keeps resigning from being just a gesture. Many other methods have been tried in the past; under some of them governments were changed as often as underwear. But our present system insures responsible government."

I was so busy trying to see the implications that I almost missed his next remark. "So, naturally, the Emperor has summoned Mr. Bonforte to New Batavia."

"Eh? New Batavia? Well!" I was thinking that I had never seen the Imperial capital. The one time I had been on the Moon the vicissitudes of my profession had left me without time or money for the side trip. "Then that is why we got under way? Well, I certainly don't mind. I suppose you can always find a way to send me home if the *Tommie* doesn't go back to Earth soon."

"What? Good heavens, don't worry about that now. When the time comes, Captain Broadbent can find any number of ways to deliver you home."

"Sorry. I forget that you have more important matters on your mind, Rog. Sure, I'm anxious to get home now that the job is done. But a few days, or even a month, on Luna would not matter. I have nothing pressing me. But thanks for taking time to tell me the news." I searched his face. "Rog, you look worried as hell."

"Don't you see? The Emperor has sent for Mr. Bonforte. The *Emperor*, man! And Mr. Bonforte is in no shape to appear at an audience. They have risked a gambit—and perhaps trapped us in a checkmate!"

"Eh? Now wait a minute. Slow up. I see what you are driving at—but, look, friend, we aren't at New Batavia. We're a hundred million miles away, or two hundred million, or whatever it is. Doc Capek will have him wrung out and ready to speak his piece by then. Won't he?"

"Well—we hope so."

"But you aren't sure?"

"We can't be sure. Capek says that there is little clinical data on such massive doses. It depends on the individual's body chemistry and on the exact drug used."

I suddenly remembered a time when an understudy had slipped me a powerful purgative just before a performance. (But I went on anyhow, which proves the superiority of mind over matter—then I got him fired.) "Rog—they gave him that last, unnecessarily big dose not just out of simple sadism—but to set up this situation!"

"*I* think so. So does Capek."

"Hey! In that case it would mean that Quiroga himself is the man behind the kidnaping—and that we've had a *gangster* running the Empire!"

Rog shook his head. "Not necessarily. Not even probably. But it would indeed mean that the same forces who control the Actionists also control the machinery of the Humanity Party. But you will never pin anything on *them*; they are unreachable, ultrarespectable. Nevertheless, they could send word to Quiroga that the time had come to roll over and play dead—and have him do it. Almost certainly," he added, "without giving him a hint of the real reason why the moment was timely."

"Criminy! Do you mean to tell me that the top man in the Empire would fold up and quit, just like that? Because somebody behind the scenes ordered him to?"

"I'm afraid that is just what I do think."

I shook my head. "Politics is a dirty game!"

"No," Clifton answered insistently. "There is no such thing as a dirty game. But you sometimes run into dirty players."

"I don't see the difference."

"There is a world of difference. Quiroga is a third-rater and a stooge—in my opinion, a stooge for villains. But there is nothing third-rate about John Joseph Bonforte and he has never, *ever* been a stooge for anyone. As a follower, he believed in the cause; as the leader, he has led from conviction!"

"I stand corrected," I said humbly. "Well, what do we do?

Have Dak drag his feet so that the *Tommie* does not reach New Batavia until he is back in shape to do the job?"

"We *can't* stall. We don't have to boost at more than one gravity; nobody would expect a man Bonforte's age to place unnecessary strain on his heart. But we can't delay. When the Emperor sends for you, you come."

"Then what?"

Rog looked at me without answering. I began to get edgy. "Hey, Rog, don't go getting any wild notions! This hasn't anything to do with *me*. I'm through, except for a few casual appearances around the ship. Dirty or not, politics is not my game—just pay me off and ship me home and I'll guarantee never even to register to vote!"

"You probably wouldn't have to do anything. Dr. Capek will almost certainly have him in shape for it. But it isn't as if it were anything *hard*—not like that adoption ceremony—just an audience with the Emperor and——"

"The Emperor!" I almost screamed. Like most Americans, I did not understand royalty, did not really approve of the institution in my heart—and had a sneaking, unadmitted awe of kings. After all, we Americans came in by the back door. When we swapped associate status under treaty for the advantages of a full voice in the affairs of the Empire, it was explicitly agreed that our local institutions, our own constitution, and so forth, would not be affected—and tacitly agreed that no member of the royal family would ever visit America. Maybe that is a bad thing. Maybe if we were used to royalty we would not be so impressed by them. In any case, it is notorious that "democratic" American women are more quiveringly anxious to be presented at court than is anybody else.

"Now take it easy," Rog answered. "You probably won't have to do it at all. We just want to be prepared. What I was trying to tell you is that a 'caretaker' government is no problem. It passes no laws, changes no policies. I'll take care of all the work. All you will have to do—if you have to do anything—is make the formal appearance before King Willem—and possibly show up at a controlled press conference or two, depending on how long it is before *he* is well again. What you have already done is much harder—and you will be paid whether we need you or not."

"Damn it, pay has nothing to do with it! It's—well, in the

words of a famous character in theatrical history, 'Include me *Out.*' "

Before Rog could answer, Bill Corpsman came bursting into my cabin without knocking, looked at us, and said sharply to Clifton, "Have you told him?"

"Yes," agreed Clifton. "He's turned down the job."

"Huh? Nonsense!"

"It's not nonsense," I answered, "and by the way, Bill, that door you just came through has a nice spot on it to knock. In the profession the custom is to knock and shout, 'Are you decent?' I wish you would remember it."

"Oh, dirty sheets! We're in a hurry. What's this guff about your refusing?"

"It's not guff. This is not the job I signed up for."

"Garbage! Maybe you are too stupid to realize it, Smythe, but you are in too deep to prattle about backing out. It wouldn't be healthy."

I went to him and grabbed his arm. "Are you threatening me? If you are, let's go outside and talk it over."

He shook my hand off. "In a spaceship? You really are simple, aren't you? But haven't you got it through your thick head that you caused this mess yourself?"

"What do you mean?"

"He means," Clifton answered, "that he is convinced that the fall of the Quiroga government was the direct result of the speech you made earlier today. It is even possible that he is right. But it is beside the point. Bill, try to be reasonably polite, will you? We get nowhere by bickering."

I was so surprised by the suggestion that *I* had caused Quiroga to resign that I forgot all about my desire to loosen Corpsman's teeth. Were they serious? Sure, it was one dilly of a fine speech, but was such a result possible?

Well, if it was, it was certainly fast service.

I said wonderingly, "Bill, do I understand that you are complaining that the speech I made was too effective to suit you?"

"Huh? Hell, no! It was a lousy speech."

"So? You can't have it both ways. You're saying that a lousy speech went over so big that it scared the Humanity Party right out of office. Is that what you meant?"

Corpsman looked annoyed, started to answer, and caught

sight of Clifton suppressing a grin. He scowled, again started to reply—finally shrugged and said, "All right, buster, you proved your point; the speech could not have had anything to do with the fall of the Quiroga government. Nevertheless, we've got work to do. So what's this about you not being willing to carry your share of the load?"

I looked at him and managed to keep my temper—Bonforte's influence again; playing the part of a calm-tempered character tends to make one calm inside. "Bill, again you cannot have it two ways. You have made it emphatically clear that you consider me just a hired hand. Therefore I have no obligation beyond my job, which is finished. You can't hire me for another job unless it suits me. It doesn't."

He started to speak but I cut in. "That's all. Now get out. You're not welcome here."

He looked astounded. "Who the hell do you think you are to give orders around here?"

"Nobody. Nobody at all, as you have pointed out. But this is my private room, assigned to me by the Captain. So now get out or be thrown out. I don't like your manners."

Clifton added quietly, "Clear out, Bill. Regardless of anything else, it is his private cabin at the present time. So you had better leave." Rog hesitated, then added, "I think we both might as well leave; we don't seem to be getting anywhere. If you will excuse us—Chief?"

"Certainly."

I sat and thought about it for several minutes. I was sorry that I had let Corpsman provoke me even into such a mild exchange; it lacked dignity. But I reviewed it in my mind and assured myself that my personal differences with Corpsman had not affected my decision; my mind had been made up before he appeared.

A sharp knock came at the door. I called out, "Who is it?"

"Captain Broadbent."

"Come in, Dak."

He did so, sat down, and for some minutes seemed interested only in pulling hangnails. Finally he looked up and said, "Would it change your mind if I slapped the blighter in the brig?"

"Eh? Do you have a brig in the ship?"

"No. But it would not be hard to jury-rig one."

I looked at him sharply, trying to figure what went on inside that bony head. "Would you actually put Bill in the brig if I asked for it?"

He looked up, cocked a brow, and grinned wryly. "No. A man doesn't get to be a captain operating on any such basis as that. I would not take that sort of order even from *him*." He inclined his head toward the room Bonforte was in. "Certain decisions a man must make himself."

"That's right."

"Mmm—I hear you've made one of that sort."

"That's right."

"So. I've come to have a lot of respect for you, old son. First met you, I figured you for a clotheshorse and a facemaker, with nothing inside. I was wrong."

"Thank you."

"So I won't plead with you. Just tell me: is it worth our time to discuss the factors? Have you given it plenty of thought?"

"My mind is made up, Dak. This isn't my pidgin."

"Well, perhaps you're right. I'm sorry. I guess we'll just have to hope he pulls out of it in time." He stood up. "By the way, Penny would like to see you, if you aren't going to turn in again this minute."

I laughed without pleasure. "Just 'by the way,' eh? Is this the proper sequence? Isn't it Dr. Capek's turn to try to twist my arm?"

"He skipped his turn; he's busy with Mr. B. He sent you a message, though."

"Eh?"

"He said you could go to hell. Embroidered it a bit, but that was the gist."

"He did? Well, tell him I'll save him a seat by the fire."

"Can Penny come in?"

"Oh, sure! But you can tell her that she is wasting her time; the answer is still 'No.'"

So I changed my mind. Confound it, why should an argument seem so much more logical when underlined with a whiff of Jungle Lust? Not that Penny used unfair means, she did not even shed tears—not that I laid a finger on her—but I found myself conceding points, and presently there were no more points to concede. There is no getting around it, Penny is the world-saver type and her sincerity is contagious.

The boning I did on the trip out to Mars was as nothing to the hard study I put in on the trip to New Batavia. I already had the basic character; now it was necessary to fill in the background, prepare myself to *be* Bonforte under almost any circumstances. While it was the royal audience I was aiming at, once we were at New Batavia I might have to meet any of hundreds or thousands of people. Rog planned to give me a defense in depth of the sort that is routine for any public figure if he is to get work done; nevertheless, I would have to see people—a public figure is a public figure, no way to get around that.

The tightrope act I was going to have to attempt was made possible only by Bonforte's Farleyfile, perhaps the best one ever compiled. Farley was a political manager of the twentieth century, of Eisenhower I believe, and the method he invented for handling the personal relations of politics was as revolutionary as the German invention of staff command was to warfare. Yet I had never heard of the device until Penny showed me Bonforte's.

It was nothing but a file about people. However, the art of politics is "nothing but" people. This file contained all, or almost all, of the thousands upon thousands of people Bonforte had met in the course of his long public life; each dossier consisted of what he knew about that person *from Bonforte's own personal contact.* Anything at all, no matter how trivial—in fact, trivia were always the first entries: names and nicknames of wives, children, and pets, hobbies, tastes in food or drink, prejudices, eccentricities. Following this would be listed date and place and comments for *every occasion* on which Bonforte had talked to that particular man.

When available, a photo was included. There might or might not be "below-the-line" data, i.e., information which had been researched rather than learned directly by Bonforte. It depended on the political importance of the person. In some cases the "below-the-line" part was a formal biography running to thousands of words.

Both Penny and Bonforte himself carried minicorders powered by their body heat. If Bonforte was alone he would dictate into his own when opportunity offered—in rest rooms, while riding, etc.; if Penny went along she would take it down in hers, which was disguised to look like a wrist watch. Penny could not possibly do the transcribing and microfilming; two of Jimmie Washington's girls did little else.

When Penny showed me the Farleyfile, showed me the very bulk of it—and it was bulky, even at ten thousand words or more to the spool—and then told me that this represented personal information about Mr. Bonforte's acquaintances, I scroaned (which is a scream and a groan done together, with intense feeling). "God's mercy, child! I tried to tell you this job could not be done. How could anyone memorize all that?"

"Why, you can't, of course."

"You just said that this was what *he* remembered about his friends and acquaintances."

"Not quite. I said that this is what he wanted to remember. But since he can't, not possibly, this is how he does it. Don't worry; you don't have to memorize anything. I just want you to know that it is available. It is my job to see that he has at least a minute or two to study the appropriate Farleyfile before anybody gets in to see him. If the need turns up, I can protect you with the same service."

I looked at the typical file she had projected on the desk reader. A Mr. Saunders of Pretoria, South Africa, I believe it was. He had a bulldog named Snuffles Bullyboy, several assorted uninteresting offspring, and he liked a twist of lime in his whisky and splash. "Penny, do you mean to tell me that Mr. B. pretends to remember minutiae like that? It strikes me as rather phony."

Instead of getting angry at the slur on her idol Penny nodded soberly. "I thought so once. But you don't look at it correctly, Chief. Do you ever write down the telephone number of a friend?"

"Eh? Of course."

"Is it dishonest? Do you apologize to your friend for caring so little about him that you can't simply remember his number?"

"*Eh?* All right, I give up. You've sold me."

"These are things he would like to remember if his memory were perfect. Since it isn't, it is no more phony to do it this way than it is to use a tickler file in order not to forget a friend's birthday—that's what it is: a giant tickler file, to cover *anything*. But there is more to it. Did you ever meet a really important person?"

I tried to think. Penny did not mean the greats of the theatrical profession; she hardly knew they existed. "I once met President Warfield. I was a kid of ten or eleven."

"Do you remember the details?"

"Why, certainly. He said, 'How did you break that arm, son?' and I said, 'Riding a bicycle, sir,' and he said, 'Did the same thing myself, only it was a collarbone.'"

"Do you think he would remember it if he were still alive?"

"Why, no."

"He might—he may have had you Farleyfiled. This Farleyfile includes boys of that age, because boys grow up and become men. The point is that top-level men like President Warfield meet many more people than they can remember. Each one of that faceless throng remembers his own meeting with the famous man and remembers it in detail. But the supremely important person in any one's life is *himself*—and a politician must never forget that. So it is polite and friendly and warmhearted for the politician to have a way to be able to remember about other people the sort of little things that they are likely to remember about him. It is also essential—in politics."

I had Penny display the Farleyfile on King Willem. It was rather short, which dismayed me at first, until I concluded that it meant that Bonforte did not know the Emperor well and had met him only on a few official occasions—Bonforte's first service as Supreme Minister had been before old Emperor Frederick's death. There was no biography below the line, but just a notation, "*See* House of Orange." I didn't—there simply wasn't time to plow through a few million words of Empire and pre-Empire history and, anyhow, I got fair-to-excellent marks in history when I was in school. All I wanted to know about the Emperor was what Bonforte knew about him that other people did not.

It occurred to me that the Farleyfile must include everybody in the ship since they were (a) people (b) whom Bonforte had met. I asked Penny for them. She seemed a little surprised.

Soon I was the one surprised. The *Tom Paine* had in her *six* Grand Assemblymen. Rog Clifton and Mr. Bonforte, of course —but the first item in Dak's file read: "Broadbent, Darius K., the Honorable, G. A. for League of Free Travelers, Upper Division." It also mentioned that he held a Ph.D. in physics, had been reserve champion with the pistol in the Imperial Matches nine years earlier, and had published three volumes of verse under the nom de plume of "Acey Wheelwright." I resolved never again to take a man at merely his face value.

There was a notation in Bonforte's sloppy handwriting: "Almost irresistible to women—and vice versa!"

Penny and Dr. Capek were also members of the great parliament. Even Jimmie Washington was a member, for a "safe" district, I realized later—he represented the Lapps, including all the reindeer and Santa Claus, no doubt. He was also ordained in the First Bible Truth Church of the Holy Spirit, which I had never heard of, but which accounted for his tight-lipped deacon look.

I especially enjoyed reading about Penny—the Honorable Miss Penelope Taliaferro Russell. She was an M.A. in government administration from Georgetown and a B.A. from Wellesley, which somehow did not surprise me. She represented districtless university women, another "safe" constituency I learned, since they are about five to one Expansionist Party members.

On down below were her glove size, her other measurements, her preferences in colors (I could teach her something about dressing), her preference in scent (Jungle Lust, of course), and many other details, most of them innocuous enough. But there was "comment":

"Neurotically honest—arithmetic unreliable—prides herself on her sense of humor, of which she has none—watches her diet but is gluttonous about candied cherries—little-mother-of-all-living complex—unable to resist reading the printed word in any form."

Underneath was another of Bonforte's handwritten addenda: "Ah, Curly Top! Snooping again, I see."

As I turned them back to her I asked Penny if she had read her own Farleyfile. She told me snippily to mind my own business!—then turned red and apologized.

*

Most of my time was taken up with study but I did take time to review and revise carefully the physical resemblance, checking the Semiperm shading by colorimeter, doing an extremely careful job on the wrinkles, adding two moles, and setting the whole job with electric brush. It was going to mean a skin peel before I could get my own face back but that was a small price to pay for a make-up job that could not be damaged, could not be smeared even with acetone, and was proof against such hazards as napkins. I even added the scar on the "game" leg, using a photograph Capek had kept in Bonforte's health history. If Bonforte had had wife or mistress, she would have had difficulty in telling the impostor from the real thing simply on physical appearance. It was a lot of trouble but it left my mind free to worry about the really difficult part of the impersonation.

But the all-out effort during the trip was to steep myself in what Bonforte thought and believed, in short the policies of the Expansionist Party. In a manner of speaking, he himself was the Expansionist Party, not merely its most prominent leader but its political philosopher and greatest statesman. Expansionism had hardly been more than a "Manifest Destiny" movement when the Party was founded, a rabble coalition of groups who had one thing in common: the belief that the frontiers in the sky were the most important issue in the emerging future of the human race. Bonforte had given the Party a rationale and an ethic, the theme that freedom and equal rights must run with the Imperial banner; he kept harping on the notion that the human race must never again make the mistakes that the white subrace had made in Africa and Asia.

But I was confused by the fact—I was awfully unsophisticated in such matters—that the early history of the Expansionist Party sounded remarkably like the present Humanity Party. I was not aware that political parties often change as much in growing up as people do. I had known vaguely that the Humanity Party had started as a splinter of the Expansionist movement but I had never thought about it. Actually it was inevitable; as the political parties which did not have their eyes on the sky dwindled away under the imperatives of history and ceased to elect candidates, the one party which had been on the right track was bound to split into two factions.

But I am running ahead; my political education did not proceed so logically. At first I simply soaked myself in Bonforte's public utterances. True, I had done that on the trip out, but then I was studying how he spoke; now I was studying what he said.

Bonforte was an orator in the grand tradition but he could be vitriolic in debate, e.g., a speech he made in New Paris during the ruckus over the treaty with the Martian nests, the Concord of Tycho. It was this treaty which had knocked him out of office before; he had pushed it through but the strain on the coalition had lost him the next vote of confidence. Nevertheless, Quiroga had not dared denounce the treaty. I listened to this speech with special interest since I had not liked the treaty myself; the idea that Martians must be granted the same privileges on Earth that humans enjoyed on Mars had been abhorrent to me—until I visited the Kkkah nest.

"My opponent," Bonforte had said with a rasp in his voice, "would have you believe that the motto of the so-called Humanity Party, 'Government of human beings, by human beings, and for human beings,' is no more than an updating of the immortal words of Lincoln. But while the voice is the voice of Abraham, the hand is the hand of the Ku Klux Klan. The true meaning of that innocent-seeming motto is 'Government of all races everywhere, by human beings alone, for the profit of a privileged few.'

"But, my opponent protests, we have a God-given mandate to spread enlightenment through the stars, dispensing our own brand of Civilization to the savages. This is the Uncle Remus school of sociology—the good dahkies singin' spirituals and Ole Massa lubbin' every one of dem! It is a beautiful picture but the frame is too small; it fails to show the whip, the slave block—and the counting house!"

I found myself becoming, if not an Expansionist, then at least a Bonfortite. I am not sure that I was convinced by the logic of his words—indeed, I am not sure that they were logical. But I was in a receptive frame of mind. I wanted to understand what he said so thoroughly that I could rephrase it and say it in his place, if need be.

Nevertheless, here was a man who knew what he wanted and (much rarer!) why he wanted it. I could not help but be impressed, and it forced me to examine my own beliefs. What did I live by?

My profession, surely! I had been brought up in it, I liked it, I had a deep though unlogical conviction that art was worth the effort—and, besides, it was the only way I knew to make a living. But what else?

I have never been impressed by the formal schools of ethics. I had sampled them—public libraries are a ready source of recreation for an actor short of cash—but I had found them as poor in vitamins as a mother-in-law's kiss. Given time and plenty of paper, a philosopher can prove anything.

I had the same contempt for the moral instruction handed to most children. Much of it is prattle and the parts they really seem to mean are dedicated to the sacred proposition that a "good" child is one who does not disturb mother's nap and a "good" man is one who achieves a muscular bank account without getting caught. No, thanks!

But even a dog has rules of conduct. What were mine? How did I behave—or, at least, how did I like to think I behaved?

"The show must go on." I had always believed that and lived by it. But why must the show go on?—seeing that some shows are pretty terrible. Well, because you agreed to do it, because there is an audience out there; they have paid and each one of them is entitled to the best you can give. You owe it to them. You owe it also to stagehands and manager and producer and other members of the company—and to those who taught you your trade, and to others stretching back in history to open-air theaters and stone seats and even to storytellers squatting in a market place. *Noblesse oblige.*

I decided that the notion could be generalized into any occupation. "Value for value." Building "on the square and on the level." The Hippocratic oath. Don't let the team down. Honest work for honest pay. Such things did not have to be proved; they were an essential part of life—true throughout eternity, true in the farthest reaches of the Galaxy.

I suddenly got a glimpse of what Bonforte was driving at. If there were ethical basics that transcended time and place, then they were true both for Martians and for men. They were true on any planet around any star—and if the human race did not behave accordingly they weren't ever going to win to the stars because some better race would slap them down for double-dealing.

The price of expansion was virtue. "Never give a sucker an even break" was too narrow a philosophy to fit the broad reaches of space.

But Bonforte was not preaching sweetness and light. "I am not a pacifist. Pacifism is a shifty doctrine under which a man accepts the benefits of the social group without being willing to pay—and claims a halo for his dishonesty. Mr. Speaker, life belongs to those who do not fear to lose it. This bill must pass!" And with that he had got up and crossed the aisle in support of a military appropriation his own party had refused in caucus.

Or again: "Take sides! Always take sides! You will sometimes be wrong—but the man who refuses to take sides must *always* be wrong! Heaven save us from poltroons who fear to make a choice. Let us stand up and be counted." (This last was in a closed caucus but Penny had caught it on her minicorder and Bonforte had saved it—Bonforte had a sense of history; he was a record keeper. If he had not been, I would not have had much to work with.)

I decided that Bonforte was my kind of man. Or at least the kind I liked to think I was. His was a *persona* I was proud to wear.

So far as I can remember I did not sleep on that trip after I promised Penny that I would take the royal audience if Bonforte could not be made ready. I intended to sleep—there is no point in taking your stage with your eyes bagging like hound's ears—but I got interested in what I was studying and there was a plentiful supply of pepper pills in Bonforte's desk. It is amazing how much ground you can cover working a twenty-four-hour day, free from interruptions and with all the help you could ask for.

But shortly before we were due at New Batavia, Dr. Capek came in and said, "Bare your left forearm."

"Why?" I asked.

"Because when you go before the Emperor we don't want you falling flat on your face with fatigue. This will make you sleep until we ground. Then I'll give you an antidote."

"Eh? I take it that you don't think *he* will be ready?"

Capek did not answer, but gave me the shot. I tried to finish listening to the speech I had running but I must have been asleep in seconds. The next thing I knew Dak was saying deferentially, "Wake up, sir. Please wake up. We're grounded at Lippershey Field."

VIII

O UR MOON being an airless planet, a torchship can land on it. But the *Tom Paine*, being a torchship, was really intended to stay in space and be serviced only at space stations in orbit; she had to be landed in a cradle. I wish I had been awake to see it, for they say that catching an egg on a plate is easy by comparison. Dak was one of the half dozen pilots who could do it.

But I did not even get to see the *Tommie* in her cradle; all I saw was the inside of the passenger bellows they fastened to her air lock and the passenger tube to New Batavia—those tubes are so fast that, under the low gravity of the Moon, you are again in free fall at the middle of the trip.

We went first to the apartments assigned to the leader of the loyal opposition, Bonforte's official residence until (and if) he went back into power after the coming election. The magnificence of them made me wonder what the Supreme Minister's residence was like. I suppose that New Batavia is odds-on the most palatial capital city in all history; it is a shame that it can hardly be seen from outdoors—but that minor shortcoming is more than offset by the fact that it is the only city in the Solar System that is actually impervious to fusion bombs. Or perhaps I should say "effectively impervious" since there are some surface structures which could be destroyed. Bonforte's apartments included an upper living room in the side of a cliff, which looked out through a bubble balcony at the stars and Mother Earth herself—but his sleeping room and offices were a thousand feet of solid rock below, by private lift.

I had no time to explore the apartments; they dressed me for the audience. Bonforte had no valet even dirtside, but Rog insisted on "helping" me (he was a hindrance) while going over last-minute details. The dress was ancient formal court dress, shapeless tubular trousers, a silly jacket with a claw-hammer tail, both in black, and a chemise consisting of a stiff white breastplate, a "winged" collar, and a white bow tie. Bonforte's chemise was all in one piece, because (I suppose) he did not use a dresser; correctly it should be assembled piece by piece and the

bow tie should be tied poorly enough to show that it has been
tied by hand—but it is too much to expect a man to understand both politics and period costuming.

It is an ugly costume, but it did make a fine background for
the Order of Wilhelmina stretched in colorful diagonal across
my chest. I looked at myself in a long glass and was pleased
with the effect; the one color accent against the dead black and
white was good showmanship. The traditional dress might be
ugly but it did have dignity, something like the cool stateliness
of a *maître d'hôtel*. I decided that I looked the part to wait on
the pleasure of a sovereign.

Rog Clifton gave me the scroll which was supposed to list
the names of my nominations for the ministries and he tucked
into an inner pocket of my costume a copy of the typed list
thereof—the original had gone forward by hand of Jimmie
Washington to the Emperor's State Secretary as soon as we
had grounded. Theoretically the purpose of the audience was
for the Emperor to inform me that it was his pleasure for me
to form a government and for me to submit humbly my suggestions; my nominations were supposed to be secret until the
sovereign graciously approved.

Actually the choices were all made; Rog and Bill had spent
most of the trip lining up the Cabinet and making sure the
nominees would serve, using state-scramble for the radio messages. I had studied the Farleyfiles on each nomination and
each alternate. But the list really was secret in the sense that
the news services would not receive it until after the Imperial
audience.

I took the scroll and picked up my life wand. Rog looked
horrified. "Good Lord, man, you can't carry that thing into
the presence of the Emperor!"

"Why not?"

"Huh? It's a *weapon*."

"It's a ceremonial weapon. Rog, every duke and every pip-
squeak baronet will be wearing his dress sword. So I wear this."

He shook his head. "They have to. Don't you understand
the ancient legal theory behind it? Their dress swords symbol-
ize the duty they owe their liege lord to support and defend him
by force of arms, in their own persons. But you are a com-
moner; traditionally you come before him unarmed."

"No, Rog. Oh, I'll do what you tell me to, but you are missing a wonderful chance to catch a tide at its flood. This is good theater, this is *right*."

"I'm afraid I don't follow you."

"Well, look, will the word get back to Mars if I carry this wand today? Inside the nests, I mean?"

"Eh? I suppose so. Yes."

"Of course. I would guess that every nest has stereo receivers; I certainly noticed plenty of them in Kkkah nest. They follow the Empire news as carefully as we do. Don't they?"

"Yes. At least the elders do."

"If I carry the wand, they'll know it; if I fail to carry it, they will know it. It matters to them; it is tied up with propriety. No adult Martian would appear outside his nest without his life wand, or inside on ceremonial occasions. Martians have appeared before the Emperor in the past; they carried their wands, didn't they? I'd bet my life on it."

"Yes, but you——"

"You forget that *I am a Martian*."

Rog's face suddenly blanked out. I went on, "I am not only 'John Joseph Bonforte'; I am Kkkahjjjerrr of Kkkah nest. If I fail to carry that wand, I commit a great impropriety—and frankly I do not know what would happen when the word got back; I don't know enough about Martian customs. Now turn it around and look at it the other way. When I walk down that aisle carrying this wand, *I am a Martian citizen about to be named His Imperial Majesty's first minister*. How will that affect the nests?"

"I guess I had not thought it through," he answered slowly.

"Nor would I have done so, had I not had to decide whether or not to carry the wand. But don't you suppose Mr. B. thought it through—before he ever let himself be invited to be adopted? Rog, we've got a tiger by the tail; the only thing to do is to swarm aboard and ride it. We can't let go."

Dak arrived at that point, confirmed my opinion, seemed surprised that Clifton had expected anything else. "Sure, we're setting a new precedent, Rog—but we're going to set a lot of new ones before we are through." But when he saw how I was carrying the wand he let out a scream. "Cripes, man! Are you trying to kill somebody? Or just carve a hole in the wall?"

"I wasn't pressing the stud."

"Thank God for small favors! You don't even have the safety on." He took it from me very gingerly and said, "You twist this ring—and shove this in that slot—then it's just a stick. Whew!"

"Oh. Sorry."

They delivered me to the robing room of the Palace and turned me over to King Willem's equerry, Colonel Pateel, a bland-faced Hindu with perfect manners and the dazzling dress uniform of the Imperial space forces. His bow to me must have been calculated on a slide rule; it suggested that I was about to be Supreme Minister but was not quite there yet, that I was his senior but nevertheless a civilian—then subtract five degrees for the fact that he wore the Emperor's aiguillette on his right shoulder.

He glanced at the wand and said smoothly, "That's a Martian wand, is it not, sir? Interesting. I suppose you will want to leave it here—it will be safe."

I said, "I'm carrying it."

"Sir?" His eyebrows shot up and he waited for me to correct my obvious mistake.

I reached into Bonforte's favorite clichés and picked one he used to reprove bumptiousness. "Son, suppose you tend to your knitting and I tend to mine."

His face lost all expression. "Very well, sir. If you will come this way?"

We paused at the entrance to the throne room. Far away, on the raised dais, the throne was empty. On both sides of the entire length of the great cavern the nobles and royalty of the court were standing and waiting. I suppose Pateel passed along some sign, for the Imperial Anthem welled out and we all held still for it, Pateel in robotlike attention, myself in a tired stoop suitable to a middle-aged and overworked man who must do this thing because he must, and all the court like show-window pieces. I hope we never dispense with the pageantry of a court entirely; all those noble dress extras and spear carriers make a beautiful sight.

In the last few bars he came in from behind and took his throne—Willem, Prince of Orange, Duke of Nassau, Grand Duke of Luxembourg, Knight Commander of the Holy Roman

Empire, Admiral General of the Imperial Forces, Adviser to the Martian Nests, Protector of the Poor, and, by the Grace of God, King of the Lowlands and Emperor of the Planets and the Spaces Between.

I could not see his face, but the symbolism produced in me a sudden warm surge of empathy. I no longer felt hostile to the notion of royalty.

As King Willem sat down the anthem ended; he nodded acknowledgment of the salute and a wave of slight relaxation rippled down the courtiers. Pateel withdrew and, with my wand tucked under my arm, I started my long march, limping a little in spite of the low gravity. It felt remarkably like the progress to the Inner Nest of Kkkah, except that I was not frightened; I was simply warm and tingling. The Empire medley followed me down, the music sliding from "Kong Christian" to "Marseillaise" to "The Star-Spangled Banner" and all the others.

At the first balk line I stopped and bowed, then again at the second, then at last a deep bow at the third, just before the steps. I did not kneel; nobles must kneel but commoners share sovereignty with the Sovereign. One sees this point incorrectly staged sometimes in stereo and theater, and Rog had made sure that I knew what to do.

"*Ave, Imperator!*" Had I been a Dutchman I would have said "Rex" as well, but I was an American. We swapped schoolboy Latin back and forth by rote, he inquiring what I wanted, I reminding him that he had summoned me, etc. He shifted into Anglo-American, which he spoke with a slight "down-East" accent.

"You served our father well. It is now our thought that you might serve us. How say you?"

"My sovereign's wish is my will, Majesty."

"Approach us."

Perhaps I made too good a thing of it but the steps up the dais are high and my leg actually was hurting—and a psychosomatic pain is as bad as any other. I almost stumbled—and Willem was up out of his throne like a shot and steadied my arm. I heard a gasp go around the hall. He smiled at me and said *sotto voce*, "Take it easy, old friend. We'll make this short."

He helped me to the stool before the throne and made me sit down an awkward moment sooner than he himself was again seated. Then he held out his hand for the scroll and I passed it over. He unrolled it and pretended to study the blank page.

There was chamber music now and the court made a display of enjoying themselves, ladies laughing, noble gentlemen uttering gallantries, fans gesturing. No one moved very far from his place, no one held still. Little page boys, looking like Michelangelo's cherubim, moved among them offering trays of sweets. One knelt to Willem and he helped himself without taking his eyes off the nonexistent list. The child then offered the tray to me and I took one, not knowing whether it was proper or not. It was one of those wonderful, matchless chocolates made only in Holland.

I found that I knew a number of the court faces from pictures. Most of the unemployed royalty of Earth were there, concealed under their secondary titles of duke or count. Some said that Willem kept them on as pensioners to brighten his court; some said he wanted to keep an eye on them and keep them out of politics and other mischief. Perhaps it was a little of both. There were the nonroyal nobility of a dozen nations present, too; some of them actually worked for a living.

I found myself trying to pick out the Habsburg lips and the Windsor nose.

At last Willem put down the scroll. The music and the conversation ceased instantly. In dead silence he said, "It is a gallant company you have proposed. We are minded to confirm it."

"You are most gracious, Majesty."

"We will ponder and inform you." He leaned forward and said quietly to me alone, "Don't try to back down those damned steps. Just stand up. I am going to leave at once."

I whispered back, "Oh. Thank you, Sire."

He stood up, whereupon I got hastily to my feet, and he was gone in a swirl of robes. I turned around and noticed some startled looks. But the music started up at once and I was let to walk out while the noble and regal extras again made polite conversation.

Pateel was at my elbow as soon as I was through the far archway. "This way, sir, if you please."

The pageantry was over; now came the real audience.

He took me through a small door, down an empty corridor, through another small door, and into a quite ordinary office.

The only thing regal about it was a carved wall plaque, the coat of arms of the House of Orange, with its deathless motto, "*I Maintain!*" There was a big, flat desk, littered with papers. In the middle of it, held down by a pair of metal-plated baby shoes, was the original of the typed list in my pocket. In a copper frame there was a family group picture of the late Empress and the kids. A somewhat battered couch was against one wall and beyond it was a small bar. There were a couple of armchairs as well as the swivel chair at the desk. The other furnishings might have suited the office of a busy and not fussy family physician.

Pateel left me alone there, closing the door behind him. I did not have time to consider whether or not it was proper for me to sit down, as the Emperor came quickly in through a door opposite. "Howdy, Joseph," he called out. "Be with you in a moment." He strode through the room, followed closely by two servants who were undressing him as he walked, and went out a third door. He was back again almost at once, zipping up a suit of coveralls as he came in. "You took the short route; I had to come long way around. I'm going to insist that the palace engineer cut another tunnel through from the back of the throne room, damme if I'm not. I have to come around three sides of a square—either that or parade through semi-public corridors dressed like a circus horse." He added meditatively, "I never wear anything but underwear under those silly robes."

I said, "I doubt if they are as uncomfortable as this monkey jacket I am wearing, Sire."

He shrugged. "Oh well, we each have to put up with the inconveniences of our jobs. Didn't you get yourself a drink?" He picked up the list of nominations for cabinet ministers. "Do so, and pour me one."

"What will you have, Sire?"

"Eh?" He looked up and glanced sharply at me. "My usual. Scotch on ice, of course."

I said nothing and poured them, adding water to my own. I had had a sudden chill; if Bonforte knew that the Emperor always took scotch over bare cubes it should have been in his Farleyfile. It was not.

But Willem accepted the drink without comment, murmured,

"Hot jets!" and went on looking at the list. Presently he looked up and said, "How about these lads, Joseph?"

"Sire? It is a skeleton cabinet, of course." We had doubled up on portfolios where possible and Bonforte would hold Defense and Treasury as well as first. In three cases we had given temporary appointments to the career deputy ministers—Research, Population Management, and Exterior. The men who would hold the posts in the permanent government were all needed for campaigning.

"Yes, yes, it's your second team. Mmm . . . How about this man Braun?"

I was considerably surprised. It had been my understanding that Willem would okay the list without comment, but that he might want to chat about other things. I had not been afraid of chatting; a man can get a reputation as a sparkling conversationalist simply by letting the other man do all the talking.

Lothar Braun was what was known as a "rising young statesman." What I knew about him came from his Farleyfile and from Rog and Bill. He had come up since Bonforte had been turned out of office and so had never had any cabinet post, but had served as caucus sergeant at arms and junior whip. Bill insisted that Bonforte had planned to boost him rapidly and that he should try his wings in the caretaker government; he proposed him for Minister of External Communications.

Rog Clifton had seemed undecided; he had first put down the name of Angel Jesus de la Torre y Perez, the career subminister. But Bill had pointed out that if Braun flopped, now was a good time to find it out and no harm done. Clifton had given in.

"Braun?" I answered. "He's a coming young man. Very brilliant."

Willem made no comment, but looked on down the list. I tried to remember exactly what Bonforte had said about Braun in the Farleyfile. Brilliant . . . hardworking . . . analytical mind. Had he said anything against him? No—well, perhaps—"a shade too affable." That does not condemn a man. But Bonforte had said nothing at all about such affirmative virtues as loyalty and honesty. Which might mean nothing, as the Farleyfile was not a series of character studies; it was a data file.

The Emperor put the list aside. "Joseph, are you planning to bring the Martian nests into the Empire at once?"

"Eh? Certainly not before the election, Sire."

"Come now, you know I was talking about after the election. And have you forgotten how to say 'Willem'? 'Sire' from a man six years older than I am, under these circumstances, is silly."

"Very well, Willem."

"We both know I am not supposed to notice politics. But we know also that the assumption is silly. Joseph, you have spent your off years creating a situation in which the nests would wish to come wholly into the Empire." He pointed a thumb at my wand. "I believe you have done it. Now if you win this election you should be able to get the Grand Assembly to grant me permission to proclaim it. Well?"

I thought about it. "Willem," I said slowly, "you know that is exactly what we have planned to do. You must have some reason for bringing the subject up."

He swizzled his glass and stared at me, managing to look like a New England groceryman about to tell off one of the summer people. "Are you asking my advice? The constitution requires you to advise me, not the other way around."

"I welcome your advice, Willem. I do not promise to follow it."

He laughed. "You damned seldom promise anything. Very well, let's assume that you win the election and go back into office—but with a majority so small that you might have difficulty in voting the nests into full citizenship. In such case I would not advise you to make it a vote of confidence. If you lose, take your licking and stay in office; stick the full term."

"Why, Willem?"

"Because you and I are patient men. See that?" He pointed at the plaque of his house. "'I Maintain!' It's not a flashy rule but it is not a king's business to be flashy; his business is to conserve, to hang on, to roll with the punch. Now, constitutionally speaking, it should not matter to me whether you stay in office or not. But it does matter to me whether or not the Empire holds together. I think that if you miss on the Martian issue immediately after the election, you can afford to wait—for your other policies are going to prove very popular. You'll pick up votes in by-elections and eventually you'll come around and tell me I can add 'Emperor of Mars' to the list. So don't hurry."

"I will think about it," I said carefully.

"Do that. Now how about the transportee system?"

"We're abolishing it immediately after the election and suspending it at once." I could answer that one firmly; Bonforte hated it.

"They'll attack you on it."

"So they will. Let them. We'll pick up votes."

"Glad to hear that you still have the strength of your convictions, Joseph. I never liked having the banner of Orange on a convict ship. Free trade?"

"After the election, yes."

"What are you going to use for revenue?"

"It is our contention that trade and production will expand so rapidly that other revenues will make up for the loss of the customs."

"And suppose it ain't so?"

I had not been given a second-string answer on that one—and economics was largely a mystery to me. I grinned. "Willem, I'll have to have notice on that question. But the whole program of the Expansionist Party is founded on the notion that free trade, free travel, common citizenship, common currency, and a minimum of Imperial laws and restrictions are good not only for the citizens of the Empire but for the Empire itself. If we need the money, we'll find it—but not by chopping the Empire up into tiny bailiwicks." All but the first sentence was pure Bonforte, only slightly adapted.

"Save your campaign speeches," he grunted. "I simply asked." He picked up the list again. "You're quite sure this line-up is the way you want it?"

I reached for the list and he handed it to me. Damnation, it was clear that the Emperor was telling me as emphatically as the constitution would let him that, in his opinion, Braun was a wrong 'un. But, hell's best anthracite, I had no business changing the list Bill and Rog had made up.

On the other hand, it was not *Bonforte's* list; it was merely what they thought Bonforte would do if he were *compos mentis*.

I wished suddenly that I could take time out and ask Penny what she thought of Braun.

Then I reached for a pen from Willem's desk, scratched out "Braun," and printed in "De la Torre"—in block letters; I still could not risk Bonforte's handwriting. The Emperor merely said, "It looks like a good team to me. Good luck, Joseph. You'll need it."

That ended the audience as such. I was anxious to get away, but you do not walk out on a king; that is one prerogative they have retained. He wanted to show me his workshop and his new train models. I suppose he has done more to revive that ancient hobby than anyone else; personally I can't see it as an occupation for a grown man. But I made polite noises about his new toy locomotive, intended for the "Royal Scotsman."

"If I had had the breaks," he said, getting down on his hands and knees and peering into the innards of the toy engine, "I could have been a very fair shop superintendent, I think—a master machinist. But the accident of birth discriminated against me."

"Do you really think you would have preferred it, Willem?"

"I don't know. This job I have is not bad. The hours are easy and the pay is good—and the social security is first-rate—barring the outside chance of revolution, and my line has always been lucky on that score. But much of the work is tedious and could be done as well by any second-rate actor." He glanced up at me. "I relieve your office of a lot of tiresome cornerstone-laying and parade-watching, you know."

"I do know and I appreciate it."

"Once in a long time I get a chance to give a little push in the right direction—what I think is the right direction. Kinging is a very odd profession, Joseph. Don't ever take it up."

"I'm afraid it's a bit late, even if I wanted to."

He made some fine adjustment on the toy. "My real function is to keep you from going crazy."

"Eh?"

"Of course. Psychosis-situational is the occupational disease of heads of states. My predecessors in the king trade, the ones who actually ruled, were almost all a bit balmy. And take a look at your American presidents; the job used frequently to kill them in their prime. But me, I don't have to run things; I have a professional like yourself to do it for me. And you don't have the killing pressure either; you, or those in your shoes, can always quit if things get too tough—and the old Emperor—it's almost always the 'old' Emperor; we usually mount the throne about the age other men retire—the Emperor is always there, maintaining continuity, preserving the symbol of the state, while you professionals work out a new deal." He blinked solemnly. "My job is not glamorous, but it *is* useful."

Presently he let up on me about his childish trains and we went back into his office. I thought I was about to be dismissed. In fact, he said, "I should let you get back to your work. You had a hard trip?"

"Not too hard. I spent it working."

"I suppose so. By the way, who *are* you?"

There is the policeman's tap on the shoulder, the shock of the top step that is not there, there is falling out of bed, and there is having her husband return home unexpectedly—I would take any combination of those in preference to that simple inquiry. I aged inside to match my appearance and more.

"Sire?"

"Come now," he said impatiently, "surely my job carries with it some privileges. Just tell me the truth. I've known for the past hour that you were not Joseph Bonforte—though you could fool his own mother; you even have his mannerisms. But who are you?"

"My name is Lawrence Smith, Your Majesty," I said faintly.

"Brace up, man! I could have called the guards long since, if I had been intending to. Were you sent here to assassinate me?"

"No, Sire. I am—loyal to Your Majesty."

"You have an odd way of showing it. Well, pour yourself another drink, sit down, and tell me about it."

I told him about it, every bit. It took more than one drink, and presently I felt better. He looked angry when I told him of the kidnaping, but when I told him what they had done to Bonforte's mind his face turned dark with a Jovian rage.

At last he said quietly, "It's just a matter of days until he is back in shape, then?"

"So Dr. Capek says."

"Don't let him go to work until he is fully recovered. He's a valuable man. You know that, don't you? Worth six of you and me. So you carry on with the doubling job and let him get well. The Empire needs him."

"Yes, Sire."

"Knock off that 'Sire.' Since you are standing in for him, call me 'Willem,' as he does. Did you know that was how I spotted you?"

"No, Si—no, Willem."

"He's called me Willem for twenty years. I thought it decidedly odd that he would quit it in private simply because he was seeing me on state business. But I did not suspect, not really. But, remarkable as your performance was, it set me thinking. Then when we went in to see the trains, I knew."

"Excuse me? How?"

"You were *polite*, man! I've made him look at my trains in the past—and he always got even by being as rude as possible about what a way for a grown man to waste time. It was a little act we always went through. We both enjoyed it."

"Oh. I didn't know."

"How could you have known?" I was thinking that I should have known, that damned Farleyfile should have told me . . . It was not until later that I realized that the file had not been defective, in view of the theory on which it was based, i.e., it was intended to let a famous man remember details about the *less* famous. But that was precisely what the Emperor was *not*—less famous, I mean. Of *course* Bonforte needed no notes to recall personal details about Willem! Nor would he consider it proper to set down personal matters about the sovereign in a file handled by his clerks.

I had muffed the obvious—not that I see how I could have avoided it, even if I had realized that the file would be incomplete.

But the Emperor was still talking. "You did a magnificent job—and after risking your life in a Martian nest I am not surprised that you were willing to tackle me. Tell me, have I ever seen you in stereo, or anywhere?"

I had given my legal name, of course, when the Emperor demanded it; I now rather timidly gave my professional name. He looked at me, threw up his hands, and guffawed. I was somewhat hurt. "Er, have you heard of me?"

"Heard of you? I'm one of your staunchest fans." He looked

at me very closely. "But you still look like Joe Bonforte. I can't believe that you are Lorenzo."

"But I am."

"Oh, I believe it, I believe it. You know that skit where you are a tramp? First you try to milk a cow—no luck. Finally you end up eating out of the cat's dish—but even the cat pushes you away?"

I admitted it.

"I've almost worn out my spool of that. I laugh and cry at the same time."

"That is the idea." I hesitated, then admitted that the barnyard "Weary Willie" routine had been copied from a very great artist of another century. "But I prefer dramatic roles."

"Like this one?"

"Well—not exactly. For this role, once is quite enough. I wouldn't care for a long run."

"I suppose so. Well, tell Roger Clifton—— No, don't tell Clifton anything. Lorenzo, I see nothing to be gained by ever telling anyone about our conversation this past hour. If you tell Clifton, even though you tell him that I said not to worry, it would just give him nerves. And he has work to do. So we keep it tight, eh?"

"As my Emperor wishes."

"None of that, please. We'll keep it quiet because it's best so. Sorry I can't make a sickbed visit on Uncle Joe. Not that I could help him—although they used to think the King's Touch did marvels. So we'll say nothing and pretend that I never twigged."

"Yes—Willem."

"I suppose you had better go now. I've kept you a very long time."

"Whatever you wish."

"I'll have Pateel go back with you—or do you know your way around? But just a moment——" He dug around in his desk, muttering to himself. "That girl must have been straightening things again. No—here it is." He hauled out a little book. "I probably won't get to see you again—so would you mind giving me your autograph before you go?"

IX

Rog and Bill I found chewing their nails in Bonforte's upper living room. The second I showed up Corpsman started toward me. "Where the hell have you been?"

"With the Emperor," I answered coldly.

"You've been gone five or six times as long as you should have been."

I did not bother to answer. Since the argument over the speech Corpsman and I had gotten along together and worked together, but it was strictly a marriage of convenience, with no love. We co-operated, but we did not really bury the hatchet—unless it was between my shoulder blades. I had made no special effort to conciliate him and saw no reason why I should—in my opinion his parents had met briefly at a masquerade ball.

I don't believe in rowing with other members of the company, but the only behavior Corpsman would willingly accept from me was that of a servant, hat in hand and very 'umble, sir. I would not give him that, even to keep peace. I was a professional, retained to do a very difficult professional job, and professional men do not use the back stairs; they are treated with respect.

So I ignored him and asked Rog, "Where's Penny?"

"With *him*. So are Dak and Doc, at the moment."

"He's here?"

"Yes." Clifton hesitated. "We put him in what is supposed to be the wife's room of your bedroom suite. It was the only place where we could maintain utter privacy and still give him the care he needs. I hope you don't mind."

"Not at all."

"It won't inconvenience you. The two bedrooms are joined, you may have noticed, only through the dressing rooms, and we've shut off that door. It's soundproof."

"Sounds like a good arrangement. How is he?"

Clifton frowned. "Better, much better—on the whole. He is lucid much of the time." He hesitated. "You can go in and see him, if you like."

I hesitated still longer. "How soon does Dr. Capek think he will be ready to make public appearances?"

"It's hard to say. Before long."

"How long? Three or four days? A short enough time that we could cancel all appointments and just put me out of sight? Rog, I don't know just how to make this clear but, much as I would like to call on him and pay my respects, I don't think it is smart for me to see him at all until after I have made my last appearance. It might well ruin my characterization." I had made the terrible mistake of going to my father's funeral; for years thereafter when I thought of him I saw him dead in his coffin. Only very slowly did I regain the true image of him—the virile, dominant man who had reared me with a firm hand and taught me my trade. I was afraid of something like that with Bonforte; I was now impersonating a well man at the height of his powers, the way I had seen him and heard him in the many stereo records of him. I was very much afraid that if I saw him ill, the recollection of it would blur and distort my performance.

"I was not insisting," Clifton answered. "You know best. It's possible that we can keep from having you appear in public again, but I want to keep you standing by and ready until he is fully recovered."

I almost said that the Emperor wanted it done that way. But I caught myself—the shock of having the Emperor find me out had shaken me a little out of character. But the thought reminded me of unfinished business. I took out the revised cabinet list and handed it to Corpsman. "Here's the approved roster for the news services, Bill. You'll see that there is one change on it—De la Torre for Braun."

"*What?*"

"Jesus de la Torre for Lothar Braun. That's the way the Emperor wanted it."

Clifton looked astonished; Corpsman looked both astonished and angry. "What difference does that make? He's got no goddamn right to have opinions!"

Clifton said slowly, "Bill is right, Chief. As a lawyer who has specialized in constitutional law I assure you that the sovereign's confirmation is purely nominal. You should not have let him make any changes."

I felt like shouting at them, and only the imposed calm personality of Bonforte kept me from it. I had had a hard day and, despite a brilliant performance, the inevitable disaster had overtaken me. I wanted to tell Rog that if Willem had not been a really big man, kingly in the fine sense of the word, we would all be in the soup—simply because I had not been adequately coached for the role. Instead I answered sourly, "It's done and that's that."

Corpsman said, "That's what *you* think! I gave out the correct list to the reporters two hours ago. Now you've got to go back and straighten it out. Rog, you had better call the Palace right away and——"

I said, "Quiet!"

Corpsman shut up. I went on in a lower key. "Rog, from a legal point of view, you may be right. I wouldn't know. I do know that the Emperor felt free to question the appointment of Braun. Now if either one of you wants to go to the Emperor and argue with him, that's up to you. But I'm not going anywhere. I'm going to get out of this anachronistic strait jacket, take my shoes off, and have a long, tall drink. Then I'm going to bed."

"Now wait, Chief," Clifton objected. "You've got a five-minute spot on grand network to announce the new cabinet."

"*You* take it. You're first deputy in this cabinet."

He blinked. "All right."

Corpsman said insistently, "How about Braun? He was promised the job."

Clifton looked at him thoughtfully. "Not in any dispatch that I saw, Bill. He was simply asked if he was willing to serve, like all the others. Is that what you meant?"

Corpsman hesitated like an actor not quite sure of his lines. "Of course. But it amounts to a promise."

"Not until the public announcement is made, it doesn't."

"But the announcement *was* made, I tell you. Two hours ago."

"Mmm . . . Bill, I'm afraid that you will have to call the boys in again and tell them that you made a mistake. Or I'll call them in and tell them that through an error a preliminary list was handed out before Mr. Bonforte had okayed it. But we've got to correct it before the grand network announcement."

"Do you mean to tell me you are going to let *him* get away with it?"

By "him" I think Bill meant me rather than Willem, but Rog's answer assumed the contrary. "Yes. Bill, this is no time to force a constitutional crisis. The issue isn't worth it. So will you phrase the retraction? Or shall I?"

Corpsman's expression reminded me of the way a cat submits to the inevitable—"just barely." He looked grim, shrugged, and said, "I'll do it. I want to be damned sure it is phrased properly, so we can salvage as much as possible out of the shambles."

"Thanks, Bill," Rog answered mildly.

Corpsman turned to leave. I called out, "Bill! As long as you are going to be talking to the news services I have another announcement for them."

"Huh? What are you after now?"

"Nothing much." The fact was I was suddenly overcome with weariness at the role and the tensions it created. "Just tell them that Mr. Bonforte has a cold and his physician has ordered him to bed for a rest. I've had a bellyful."

Corpsman snorted. "I think I'll make it 'pneumonia.'"

"Suit yourself."

When he had gone Rog turned to me and said, "Don't let it get you, Chief. In this business some days are better than others."

"Rog, I really am going on the sick list. You can mention it on stereo tonight."

"So?"

"I'm going to take to my bed and stay there. There is no reason at all why Bonforte can't 'have a cold' until he is ready to get back into harness himself. Every time I make an appearance it just increases the probability that somebody will spot something wrong—and every time I do make an appearance that sorehead Corpsman finds something to yap about. An artist can't do his best work with somebody continually snarling at him. So let's let it go at this and ring down the curtain."

"Take it easy, Chief. I'll keep Corpsman out of your hair from now on. Here we won't be in each other's laps the way we were in the ship."

"No, Rog, my mind is made up. Oh, I won't run out on you. I'll stay here until Mr. B. is able to see people, in case some utter emergency turns up"—I was recalling uneasily that the Emperor had told me to hang on and had assumed that I would—"but it is actually better to keep me out of sight. At the moment we have gotten away with it completely, haven't we? Oh, *they* know—somebody knows—that Bonforte was not the man who went through the adoption ceremony—but they don't dare raise that issue, nor could they prove it if they did. The same people may suspect that a double was used today, but they don't *know*, they can't be sure—because it is always possible that Bonforte recovered quickly enough to carry it off today. Right?"

Clifton got an odd, half-sheepish look on his face. "I'm afraid they are fairly sure you were a double, Chief."

"Eh?"

"We shaded the truth a little to keep you from being nervous. Doc Capek was certain from the time he first examined him that only a miracle could get him in shape to make the audience today. The people who dosed him would know that too."

I frowned. "Then you were kidding me earlier when you told me how well he was doing? How is he, Rog? Tell me the truth."

"I was telling you the truth that time, Chief. That's why I suggested that you see him—whereas before I was only too glad to string along with your reluctance to see him." He added, "Perhaps you had better see him, talk with him."

"Mmm—no." The reasons for not seeing him still applied; if I did have to make another appearance I did not want my subconscious playing me tricks. The role called for a well man. "But, Rog, everything I said applies still more emphatically on the basis of what you have just told me. If they are even reasonably sure that a double was used today, then we don't dare risk another appearance. They were caught by surprise today—or perhaps it was impossible to unmask me, under the circumstances. But it will not be later. They can rig some deadfall, some test that I can't pass—then *blooey!* There goes the old ball game." I thought about it. "I had better be 'sick' as long as necessary. Bill was right; it had better be 'pneumonia.'"

Such is the power of suggestion that I woke up the next morning with a stopped-up nose and a sore throat. Dr. Capek took time to dose me and I felt almost human by suppertime;

nevertheless, he issued bulletins about "Mr. Bonforte's virus infection." The sealed and air-conditioned cities of the Moon being what they are, nobody was anxious to be exposed to an air-vectored ailment; no determined effort was made to get past my chaperones. For four days I loafed and read from Bonforte's library, both his own collected papers and his many books . . . I discovered that both politics and economics could make engrossing reading; those subjects had never been real to me before. The Emperor sent me flowers from the royal greenhouse—or were they for *me?*

Never mind. I loafed and soaked in the luxury of being Lorenzo, or even plain Lawrence Smith. I found that I dropped back into character automatically if someone came in, but I can't help that. It was not necessary; I saw no one but Penny and Capek, except for one visit from Dak.

But even lotus-eating can pall. By the fourth day I was as tired of that room as I had ever been of a producer's waiting room and I was lonely. No one bothered with me; Capek's visits had been brisk and professional, and Penny's visits had been short and few. She had stopped calling me "Mr. Bonforte."

When Dak showed up I was delighted to see him. "Dak! What's new?"

"Not much. I've been trying to get the *Tommie* overhauled with one hand while helping Rog with political chores with the other. Getting this campaign lined up is going to give him ulcers, three gets you eight." He sat down. "Politics!"

"Hmm . . . Dak, how did you ever get into it? Offhand, I would figure *voyageurs* to be as unpolitical as actors. And you in particular."

"They are and they aren't. Most ways they don't give a damn whether school keeps or not, as long as they can keep on herding junk through the sky. But to do that you've got to have cargo, and cargo means trade, and profitable trade means wide-open trade, with any ship free to go anywhere, no customs nonsense and no restricted areas. Freedom! And there you are; you're in politics. As for myself, I came here first for a spot of lobbying for the 'continuous voyage' rule, so that goods on the triangular trade would not pay two duties. It was Mr. B.'s bill, of course. One thing led to another and here I am, skipper of his yacht the past six years and representing my guild brothers since the last general election." He sighed. "I hardly know how it happened myself."

"I suppose you are anxious to get out of it. Are you going to stand for re-election?"

He stared at me. "Huh? Brother, until you've been in politics you haven't been *alive*."

"But you said——"

"I know what I said. It's rough and sometimes it's dirty and it's always hard work and tedious details. But it's the only sport for grownups. All other games are for kids. All of 'em." He stood up. "Gotta run."

"Oh, stick around."

"Can't. With the Grand Assembly convening tomorrow I've got to give Rog a hand. I shouldn't have stopped in at all."

"It is? I didn't know." I was aware that the G.A., the outgoing G.A. that is, had to meet one more time, to accept the caretaker cabinet. But I had not thought about it. It was a routine matter, as perfunctory as presenting the list to the Emperor. "Is *he* going to be able to make it?"

"No. But don't you worry about it. Rog will apologize to the house for your—I mean *his*—absence and will ask for a proxy rule under no-objection procedure. Then he will read the speech of the Supreme Minister Designate—Bill is working on it right now. Then in his own person he will move that the government be confirmed. Second. No debate. Pass. Adjourn sine die—and everybody rushes for home and starts promising the voters two women in every bed and a hundred Imperials every Monday morning. Routine." He added, "Oh yes! Some member of the Humanity Party will move a resolution of sympathy and a basket of flowers, which will pass in a fine hypocritical glow. They'd rather send flowers to Bonforte's funeral." He scowled.

"It is actually as simple as that? What would happen if the proxy rule were refused? I thought the Grand Assembly didn't recognize proxies."

"They don't, for all ordinary procedure. You either pair, or you show up and vote. But this is just the idler wheels going around in parliamentary machinery. If they don't let him appear by proxy tomorrow, then they've got to wait around until he is well before they can adjourn sine die and get on with the serious business of hypnotizing the voters. As it is, a mock quorum has been meeting daily and adjourning ever since Quiroga resigned. This Assembly is as dead as Caesar's ghost, but it has to be buried constitutionally."

"Yes—but suppose some idiot *did* object?"

"No one will. Oh, it could force a constitutional crisis. But it won't happen."

Neither one of us said anything for a while. Dak made no move to leave. "Dak, would it make things easier if I showed up and gave that speech?"

"Huh? Shucks, I thought that was settled. You decided that it wasn't safe to risk another appearance short of an utter save-the-baby emergency. On the whole, I agree with you. There's the old saw about the pitcher and the well."

"Yes. But this is just a walk-through, isn't it? Lines as fixed as a play? Would there be any chance of anyone pulling any surprises on me that I couldn't handle?"

"Well, no. Ordinarily you would be expected to talk to the press afterwards, but your recent illness is an excuse. We could slide you through the security tunnel and avoid them entirely." He smiled grimly. "Of course, there is always the chance that some crackpot in the visitors' gallery has managed to sneak in a gun . . . Mr. B. always referred to it as the 'shooting gallery' after they winged him from it."

My leg gave a sudden twinge. "Are you trying to scare me off?"

"No."

"You pick a funny way to encourage me. Dak, be level with me. Do you *want* me to do this job tomorrow? Or don't you?"

"Of course I do! Why the devil do you think I stopped in on a busy day? Just to chat?"

The Speaker pro tempore banged his gavel, the chaplain gave an invocation that carefully avoided any differences between one religion and another—and everyone kept silent. The seats themselves were only half filled but the gallery was packed with tourists.

We heard the ceremonial knocking amplified over the speaker system; the Sergeant at Arms rushed the mace to the door. Three times the Emperor demanded to be admitted, three times he was refused. Then he prayed the privilege; it was granted by acclamation. We stood while Willem entered and took his seat back of the Speaker's desk. He was in uniform as Admiral General and was unattended, as was required, save by escort of the Speaker and the Sergeant at Arms.

Then I tucked my wand under my arm and stood up at my place at the front bench and, addressing the Speaker as if the sovereign were not present, I delivered my speech. It was not the one Corpsman had written; that one went down the oubliette as soon as I had read it. Bill had made it a straight campaign speech, and it was the wrong time and place.

Mine was short, non-partisan, and cribbed right straight out of Bonforte's collected writings, a paraphrase of the one the time before when he formed a caretaker government. I stood foursquare for good roads and good weather and wished that everybody would love everybody else, just the way all us good democrats loved our sovereign and he loved us. It was a blank-verse lyric poem of about five hundred words and if I varied from Bonforte's earlier speech then I simply went up on my lines.

They had to quiet the gallery.

Rog got up and moved that the names I had mentioned in passing be confirmed—second and no objection and the clerk cast a white ballot. As I marched forward, attended by one member of my own party and one member of the opposition, I could see members glancing at their watches and wondering if they could still catch the noon shuttle.

Then I was swearing allegiance to my sovereign, under and subject to the constitutional limitations, swearing to defend and continue the rights and privileges of the Grand Assembly, and to protect the freedoms of the citizens of the Empire wherever they might be—and incidentally to carry out the duties of His Majesty's Supreme Minister. The chaplain mixed up the words once, but I straightened him out.

I thought I was breezing through it as easy as a curtain speech—when I found that I was crying so hard that I could hardly see. When I was done, Willem said quietly to me, "A good performance, Joseph." I don't know whether he thought he was talking to me or to his old friend—and I did not care. I did not wipe away the tears; I just let them drip as I turned back to the Assembly. I waited for Willem to leave, then adjourned them.

Diana, Ltd., ran four extra shuttles that afternoon. New Batavia was deserted—that is to say there were only the court and a million or so butchers, bakers, candlestick makers, and civil servants left in town—and a skeleton cabinet.

Having gotten over my "cold" and appeared publicly in the Grand Assembly Hall, it no longer made sense to hide out. As the supposed Supreme Minister I could not, without causing comment, never be seen; as the nominal head of a political party entering a campaign for a general election I had to see people—some people, at least. So I did what I had to do and got a daily report on Bonforte's progress toward complete recovery. His progress was good, if slow; Capek reported that it was possible, if absolutely necessary, to let him appear any time now—but he advised against it; he had lost almost twenty pounds and his co-ordination was poor.

Rog did everything possible to protect both of us. Mr. Bonforte knew now that they were using a double for him and, after a first fit of indignation, had relaxed to necessity and approved it. Rog ran the campaign, consulting him only on matters of high policy, and then passing on his answers to me to hand out publicly when necessary.

But the protection given me was almost as great; I was as hard to see as a topflight agent. My offices ran on into the mountain beyond the opposition leader's apartments (we did not move over into the Supreme Minister's more palatial quarters; while it would have been legal, it just "was not done" during a caretaker regime)—they could be reached from the rear directly from the lower living room, but to get at me from the public entrance a man had to pass about five check points—except for the favored few who were conducted directly by Rog through a bypass tunnel to Penny's office and from there into mine.

The setup meant that I could study the Farleyfile on anyone before he got to see me. I could even keep it in front of me while he was with me, for the desk had a recessed viewer the visitor could not see, yet I could wipe it out instantly if he turned out to be a floor pacer. The viewer had other uses; Rog could give a visitor the special treatment, rushing him right in to see me, leave him alone with me—and stop in Penny's office and write me a note, which would then be projected on the viewer—such quick tips as, "Kiss him to death and promise nothing," or, "All he really wants is for his wife to be presented at court. Promise him that and get rid of him," or even, "Easy on this one. It's a 'swing' district and he is smarter than he looks. Turn him over to me and I'll dicker."

I don't know who ran the government. The senior career men, probably. There would be a stack of papers on my desk each morning, I would sign Bonforte's sloppy signature to them, and Penny would take them away. I never had time to read them. The very size of the Imperial machinery dismayed me. Once when we had to attend a meeting outside the offices, Penny had led me on what she called a short cut through the Archives—miles on miles of endless files, each one chockablock with microfilm and all of them with moving belts scooting past them so that a clerk would not take all day to fetch one file.

But Penny told me that she had taken me through only one wing of it. The file of the files, she said, occupied a cavern the size of the Grand Assembly Hall. It made me glad that government was not a career with me, but merely a passing hobby, so to speak.

Seeing people was an unavoidable chore, largely useless since Rog, or Bonforte through Rog, made the decisions. My real job was to make campaign speeches. A discreet rumor had been spread that my doctor had been afraid that my heart had been strained by the "virus infection" and had advised me to stay in the low gravity of the Moon throughout the campaign. I did not dare risk taking the impersonation on a tour of Earth, much less make a trip to Venus; the Farleyfile system would break down if I attempted to mix with crowds, not to mention the unknown hazards of the Actionist goon squads—what I would babble with a minim dose of neodexocaine in the fore-brain none of us liked to think about, me least of all.

Quiroga was hitting all continents on Earth, making his stereo appearances as personal appearances on platforms in front of crowds. But it did not worry Rog Clifton. He shrugged and said, "Let him. There are no new votes to be picked up by personal appearances at political rallies. All it does is wear out the speaker. Those rallies are attended only by the faithful."

I hoped that he knew what he was talking about. The campaign was short, only six weeks from Quiroga's resignation to the day he had set for the election before resigning, and I was speaking almost every day, either on a grand network with time shared precisely with the Humanity Party, or speeches canned and sent by shuttle for later release to particular audiences. We had a set routine; a draft would come to me, perhaps from Bill although I never saw him, and then I would rework it. Rog would take the revised draft away; usually it would come back approved—and once in a while there would be corrections made in Bonforte's handwriting, now so sloppy as to be almost illegible.

I never ad-libbed at all on those parts he corrected, though I often did on the rest—when you get rolling there is often a better, more alive way to say a thing. I began to notice the nature of his corrections; they were almost always eliminations of qualifiers—make it blunter, let 'em like it or lump it!

After a while there were fewer corrections. I was getting with it.

I still never saw him. I felt that I could not "wear his head" if I looked at him on his sickbed. But I was not the only one of his intimate family who was not seeing him; Capek had chucked Penny out—for her own good. I did not know it at the time. I did know that Penny had become irritable, absent-minded, and moody after we reached New Batavia. She got circles under her eyes like a raccoon—all of which I could not miss, but I attributed it to the pressure of the campaign combined with worry about Bonforte's health. I was only partly right. Capek spotted it and took action, put her under light hypnosis and asked her questions—then he flatly forbade her to see Bonforte again until I was done and finished and shipped away.

The poor girl was going almost out of her mind from visiting the sickroom of the man she hopelessly loved—then going straight in to work closely with a man who looked and talked and sounded just like him, but in good health. She was probably beginning to hate me.

Good old Doc Capek got at the root of her trouble, gave her helpful and soothing post-hypnotic suggestions, and kept her out of the sickroom after that. Naturally I was not told about it at the time; it wasn't any of my business. But

Penny perked up and again was her lovable, incredibly efficient self.

It made a lot of difference to me. Let's admit it; at least twice I would have walked out on the whole incredible rat race if it had not been for Penny.

There was one sort of meeting I had to attend, that of the campaign executive committee. Since the Expansionist Party was a minority party, being merely the largest fraction of a coalition of several parties held together by the leadership and personality of John Joseph Bonforte, I had to stand in for him and peddle soothing syrup to those prima donnas. I was briefed for it with painstaking care, and Rog sat beside me and could hint the proper direction if I faltered. But it could not be delegated.

Less than two weeks before election day we were due for a meeting at which the safe districts would be parceled out. The organization always had thirty to forty districts which could be used to make someone eligible for cabinet office, or to provide for a political secretary (a person like Penny was much more valuable if he or she was fully qualified, able to move and speak on the floor of the Assembly, had the right to be present at closed caucuses, and so forth), or for other party reasons. Bonforte himself represented a "safe" district; it relieved him from the necessity of precinct campaigning. Clifton had another. Dak would have had one if he had needed it, but he actually commanded the support of his guild brethren. Rog even hinted to me once that if I wanted to come back in my proper person, I could say the word and my name would go on the next list.

Some of the spots were always saved for party wheel horses willing to resign at a moment's notice and thereby provide the Party with a place through a by-election if it proved necessary to qualify a man for cabinet office, or something.

But the whole thing had somewhat the flavor of patronage and, the coalition being what it was, it was necessary for Bonforte to straighten out conflicting claims and submit a list to the campaign executive committee. It was a last-minute job, to be done just before the ballots were prepared, to allow for late changes.

When Rog and Dak came in I was working on a speech and had told Penny to hold off anything but five-alarm fires. Quiroga had made a wild statement in Sydney, Australia, the night before, of such a nature that we could expose the lie and make him squirm. I was trying my hand at a speech in answer, without waiting for a draft to be handed me; I had high hopes of getting my own version approved.

When they came in I said, "Listen to this," and read them the key paragraph. "How do you like it?"

"That ought to nail his hide to the door," agreed Rog. "Here's the 'safe' list, Chief. Want to look it over? We're due there in twenty minutes."

"Oh, that damned meeting. I don't see why I should look at the list. Anything you want to tell me about it?" Nevertheless, I took the list and glanced down it. I knew them all from their Farleyfiles and a few of them from contact; I knew already why each one had to be taken care of.

Then I struck the name: *Corpsman, William J.*

I fought down what I felt was justifiable annoyance and said quietly, "I see Bill is on the list, Rog."

"Oh, yes. I wanted to tell you about that. You see, Chief, as we all know, there has been a certain amount of bad blood between you and Bill. Now I'm not blaming you; it's been Bill's fault. But there are always two sides. What you may not have realized is that Bill has been carrying around a tremendous inferiority feeling; it gives him a chip on the shoulder. This will fix it up."

"So?"

"Yes. It is what he has always wanted. You see, the rest of us all have official status, we're members of the G.A., I mean. I'm talking about those who work closely around, uh, *you*. Bill feels it. I've heard him say, after the third drink, that he was just a hired man. He's bitter about it. You don't mind, do you? The Party can afford it and it's an easy price to pay for elimination of friction at headquarters."

I had myself under full control by now. "It's none of my business. Why should I mind, if that is what Mr. Bonforte wants?"

I caught just a flicker of a glance from Dak to Clifton. I added, "That *is* what Mr. B. wants? Isn't it, Rog?"

Dak said harshly, "Tell him, Rog."

Rog said slowly, "Dak and I whipped this up ourselves. We think it is for the best."

"Then Mr. Bonforte did not approve it? You asked him, surely?"

"No, we didn't."

"Why not?"

"Chief, this is not the sort of thing to bother him with. He's a tired, old, sick man. I have not been worrying him with anything less than major policy decisions—which this isn't. It is a district we command no matter who stands for it."

"Then why ask my opinion about it at all?"

"Well, we felt you should know—and know why. We think you ought to approve it."

"Me? You're asking me for a decision as if I were Mr. Bonforte. I'm not." I tapped the desk in his nervous gesture. "Either this decision is at his level, and you should ask *him*—or it's not, and you should never have asked *me*."

Rog chewed his cigar, then said, "All right, I'm not asking you."

"*No!*"

"What do you mean?"

"I mean 'No!' You did ask me; therefore there is doubt in your mind. So if you expect me to present that name to the committee—*as if* I were Bonforte—then go in and ask him."

They both sat and said nothing. Finally Dak sighed and said, "Tell the rest, Rog. Or I will."

I waited. Clifton took his cigar out of his mouth and said, "Chief, Mr. Bonforte had a stroke four days ago. He's in no shape to be disturbed."

I held still, and recited to myself all of "the cloud-capp'd towers, the gorgeous palaces," and so forth. When I was back in shape I said, "How is his mind?"

"His mind seems clear enough, but he is terribly tired. That week as a prisoner was more of an ordeal than we realized. The stroke left him in a coma for twenty-four hours. He's out of it now, but the left side of his face is paralyzed and his entire left side is partly out of service."

"Uh, what does Dr. Capek say?"

"He thinks that as the clot clears up, you'll never be able to tell the difference. But he'll have to take it easier than he used to. But, Chief, right now he is *ill*. We'll just have to carry on through the balance of the campaign without him."

I felt a ghost of the lost feeling I had had when my father died. I had never seen Bonforte, I had had nothing from him but a few scrawled corrections on typescript. But I leaned on him all the way. The fact that he was in that room next door had made the whole thing possible.

I took a long breath, let it out, and said, "Okay, Rog. We'll have to."

"Yes, Chief." He stood up. "We've got to get over to that meeting. How about *that?*" He nodded toward the safe-districts list.

"Oh." I tried to think. Maybe it was possible that Bonforte would reward Bill with the privilege of calling himself "the Honorable," just to keep him happy. He wasn't small about such things; he did not bind the mouths of the kine who tread the grain. In one of his essays on politics he had said, "I am not an intellectual man. If I have any special talent, it lies in picking men of ability and letting them work."

"How long has Bill been with him?" I asked suddenly.

"Eh? About four years. A little over."

Bonforte evidently had liked his work. "That's past one general election, isn't it? Why didn't he make him an Assembly-man then?"

"Why, I don't know. The matter never came up."

"When was Penny put in?"

"About three years ago. A by-election."

"There's your answer, Rog."

"I don't follow you."

"Bonforte could have made Bill a Grand Assemblyman at any time. He didn't choose to. Change that nomination to a 'resigner.' Then if Mr. Bonforte wants Bill to have it, he can arrange a by-election for him later—when he's feeling himself."

Clifton showed no expression. He simply picked up the list and said, "Very well, Chief."

Later that same day Bill quit. I suppose Rog had to tell him that his arm-twisting had not worked. But when Rog told me about it I felt sick, realizing that my stiff-necked attitude had us all in acute danger. I told him so. He shook his head.

"But he knows it *all!* It was his scheme from the start. Look at the load of dirt he can haul over to the Humanity camp."

"Forget it, Chief. Bill may be a louse—I've no use for a man who will quit in the middle of a campaign; you just don't do that, ever. But he is not a rat. In his profession you don't spill a client's secrets, even if you fall out with him."

"I hope you are right."

"You'll see. Don't worry about it. Just get on with the job."

As the next few days passed I came to the conclusion that Rog knew Bill better than I did. We heard nothing from him or about him and the campaign went ahead as usual, getting rougher all the time, but with not a peep to show that our giant hoax was compromised. I began to feel better and buckled down to making the best Bonforte speeches I could manage— sometimes with Rog's help; sometimes just with his okay. Mr. Bonforte was steadily improving again, but Capek had him on absolute quiet.

Rog had to go to Earth during the last week; there are types of fence-mending that simply can't be done by remote control. After all, votes come from the precincts and the field managers count for more than the speechmakers. But speeches still had to be made and press conferences given; I carried on, with Dak and Penny at my elbow—of course I was much more closely with it now; most questions I could answer without stopping to think.

There was the usual twice-weekly press conference in the offices the day Rog was due back. I had been hoping that he would be back in time for it, but there was no reason I could not take it alone. Penny walked in ahead of me, carrying her gear; I heard her gasp.

I saw then that Bill was at the far end of the table.

But I looked around the room as usual and said, "Good morning, gentlemen."

"Good morning, Mr. Minister!" most of them answered.

I added, "Good morning, Bill. Didn't know you were here. Whom are you representing?"

They gave him dead silence to reply. Every one of them knew that Bill had quit us—or had been fired. He grinned at me, and answered, "Good morning, *Mister Bonforte.* I'm with the Krein Syndicate."

I knew it was coming then; I tried not to give him the satisfaction of letting it show. "A fine outfit. I hope they are paying you what you are worth. Now to business—— The written questions first. You have them, Penny?"

I went rapidly through the written questions, giving out answers I had already had time to think over, then sat back as usual and said, "We have time to bat it around a bit, gentlemen. Any other questions?"

There were several. I was forced to answer "No comment" only once—an answer Bonforte preferred to an ambiguous one. Finally I glanced at my watch and said, "That will be all this morning, gentlemen," and started to stand up.

"Smythe!" Bill shouted.

I kept right on getting to my feet, did not look toward him.

"I mean you, Mr. Phony Bonforte-Smythe!" he went on angrily, raising his voice still more.

This time I did look at him, with astonishment—just the amount appropriate, I think, to an important official subjected to rudeness under unlikely conditions. Bill was pointing at me and his face was red. "You impostor! You small-time actor! You *fraud!*"

The London *Times* man on my right said quietly, "Do you want me to call the guard, sir?"

I said, "No. He's harmless."

Bill laughed. "So I'm harmless, huh? You'll find out."

"I really think I should, sir," the *Times* man insisted.

"No." I then said sharply, "That's enough, Bill. You had better leave quietly."

"Don't you wish I would?" He started spewing forth the basic story, talking rapidly. He made no mention of the kidnaping and did not mention his own part in the hoax, but implied that he had left us rather than be mixed up in any such swindle. The impersonation was attributed, correctly as far as it went, to illness on the part of Bonforte—with a strong hint that we might have doped him.

I listened patiently. Most of the reporters simply listened at first, with that stunned expression of outsiders exposed unwillingly to a vicious family argument. Then some of them started scribbling or dictating into minicorders.

When he stopped I said, "Are you through, Bill?"

"That's enough, isn't it?"

"More than enough. I'm sorry, Bill. That's all, gentlemen. I must get back to work."

"Just a moment, Mr. Minister!" someone called out. "Do you want to issue a denial?" Someone else added, "Are you going to sue?"

I answered the latter question first. "No, I shan't sue. One doesn't sue a sick man."

"Sick, am I?" shouted Bill.

"Quiet down, Bill. As for issuing a denial, I hardly think it is called for. However, I see that some of you have been taking notes. While I doubt if any of your publishers would run this story, if they do, this anecdote may add something to it. Did you ever hear of the professor who spent forty years of his life proving that the *Odyssey* was not written by Homer—but by another Greek of the *same name?*"

It got a polite laugh. I smiled and started to turn away again. Bill came rushing around the table and grabbed at my arm. "You can't laugh it off!" The *Times* man—Mr. Ackroyd, it was —pulled him away from me.

I said, "Thank you, sir." Then to Corpsman I added, "What do you want me to do, Bill? I've tried to avoid having you arrested."

"Call the guards if you like, you phony! We'll see who stays in jail longest! *Wait until they take your fingerprints!*"

I sighed and made the understatement of my life. "This is ceasing to be a joke. Gentlemen, I think I had better put an end to this. Penny my dear, will you please have someone send in fingerprinting equipment?" I knew I was sunk—but, damn it, if you are caught by the Birkenhead Drill, the least you owe yourself is to stand at attention while the ship goes down. Even a villain should make a good exit.

Bill did not wait. He grabbed the water glass that had been sitting in front of me; I had handled it several times. "The hell with that! This will do."

"I've told you before, Bill, to mind your language in the presence of ladies. But you may keep the glass."

"You're bloody well right I'll keep it."

"Very well. Please leave. If not, I'll be forced to summon the guard."

He walked out. Nobody said anything. I said, "May I provide fingerprints for any of the rest of you?"

Ackroyd said hastily, "Oh, I'm sure we don't want them, Mr. Minister."

"Oh, by all means! If there is a story in this, you'll want to be covered." I insisted because it was in character—and in the second and third place, you can't be a little bit pregnant, or slightly unmasked—and I did not want my friends present to be scooped by Bill; it was the last thing I could do for them.

We did not have to send for formal equipment. Penny had carbon sheets and someone had one of those lifetime memo pads with plastic sheets; they took prints nicely. Then I said good morning and left.

We got as far as Penny's private office; once inside she fainted dead. I carried her into my office, laid her on the couch, then sat down at my desk and simply shook for several minutes.

Neither one of us was worth much the rest of the day. We carried on as usual except that Penny brushed off all callers, claiming excuses of some sort. I was due to make a speech that night and thought seriously of canceling it. But I left the news turned on all day and there was not a word about the incident of that morning. I realized that they were checking the prints before risking it—after all, I *was* supposed to be His Imperial Majesty's first minister; they would want confirmation. So I decided to make the speech since I had already written it and the time was scheduled. I couldn't even consult Dak; he was away in Tycho City.

It was the best one I made. I put into it the same stuff a comic uses to quiet a panic in a burning theater. After the pickup was dead I just sunk my face in my hands and wept, while Penny patted my shoulder. We had not discussed the horrible mess at all.

Rog grounded at twenty hundred Greenwich, about as I finished, and checked in with me as soon as he was back. In a dull monotone I told him the whole dirty story; he listened, chewing on a dead cigar, his face expressionless.

At the end I said almost pleadingly, "I *had* to give the fingerprints, Rog. You see that, don't you? To refuse would not have been in character."

Rog said, "Don't worry."

"Huh?"

"I said, 'Don't worry.' When the reports on those prints come back from the Identification Bureau at The Hague, you are in for a small but pleasant surprise—and our ex-friend Bill is in for a much bigger one, but not pleasant. If he has collected any of his blood money in advance, they will probably take it out of his hide. I hope they do."

I could not mistake what he meant. "Oh! But, Rog—they won't stop there. There are a dozen other places. Social Security . . . Uh, lots of places."

"You think perhaps we were not thorough? Chief, I knew this could happen, one way or another. From the moment Dak sent word to complete Plan Mardi Gras, the necessary cover-up started. Everywhere. But I didn't think it necessary to tell Bill." He sucked on his dead cigar, took it out of his mouth, and looked at it. "Poor Bill."

Penny sighed softly and fainted again.

X

SOMEHOW WE got to the final day. We did not hear from Bill again; the passenger lists showed that he went Earthside two days after his fiasco. If any news service ran anything I did not hear of it, nor did Quiroga's speeches hint at it.

Mr. Bonforte steadily improved until it was a safe bet that he could take up his duties after the election. His paralysis continued in part but we even had that covered: he would go on vacation right after election, a routine practice that almost every politician indulges in. The vacation would be in the *Tommie*, safe from everything. Sometime in the course of the trip I would be transferred and smuggled back—and the Chief would have a mild stroke, brought on by the strain of the campaign.

Rog would have to unsort some fingerprints, but he could safely wait a year or more for that.

Election day I was happy as a puppy in a shoe closet. The impersonation was over, although I was going to do one more short turn. I had already canned two five-minute speeches for grand network, one magnanimously accepting victory, the other gallantly conceding defeat; my job was finished. When the last one was in the can, I grabbed Penny and kissed her. She didn't even seem to mind.

The remaining short turn was a command performance; Mr. Bonforte wanted to see me—as *him*—before he let me drop it. I did not mind. Now that the strain was over, it did not worry me to see him; playing him for his entertainment would be like a comedy skit, except that I would do it straight. What am I saying? Playing straight is the essence of comedy.

The whole family would gather in the upper living room—there because Mr. Bonforte had not seen the sky in some weeks and wanted to—and there we would listen to the returns, and either drink to victory or drown our sorrows and swear to do better next time. Strike me out of the last part; I had had my first and last political campaign and I wanted no more politics. I was not even sure I wanted to act again. Acting every minute for over six weeks adds up to about five hundred ordinary performances. That's a long run.

*

They brought him up the lift in a wheel chair. I stayed out of sight and let them arrange him on a couch before I came in; a man is entitled not to have his weakness displayed before strangers. Besides, I wanted to make an entrance.

I was almost startled out of character. He looked like my father! Oh, it was just a "family" resemblance; he and I looked much more alike than either one of us looked like my father, but the likeness was there—and the age was right, for he looked *old*. I had not guessed how much he had aged. He was thin and his hair was white.

I made an immediate mental note that during the coming vacation in space I must help them prepare for the transition, the resubstitution. No doubt Capek could put weight back on him; if not, there were ways to make a man appear fleshier without obvious padding. I would dye his hair myself. The delayed announcement of the stroke he had suffered would cover the inevitable discrepancies. After all, he *had* changed this much in only a few weeks; the need was to keep the fact from calling attention to the impersonation.

But these practical details were going on by themselves in a corner of my mind; my own being was welling with emotion. Ill though he was, the man gave off a force both spiritual and virile. I felt that warm, almost holy, shock one feels when first coming into sight of that great statue of Abraham Lincoln. I was reminded of another statue, too, seeing him lying there with his legs and his helpless left side covered with a shawl: the wounded Lion of Lucerne. He had that massive strength and dignity, even when helpless: "The guard dies, but never surrenders."

He looked up as I came in and smiled the warm, tolerant, and friendly smile I had learned to portray, and motioned with his good hand for me to come to him. I smiled the same smile back and went to him. He shook hands with a grip surprisingly strong and said warmly, "I am happy to meet you at last." His speech was slightly blurred and I could now see the slackness on the side of his face away from me.

"I am honored and happy to meet you, sir." I had to think about it to keep from matching the blurring of paralysis.

He looked me up and down, and grinned. "It looks to me as if you had already met me."

I glanced down at myself. "I have tried, sir."

"'Tried'! You succeeded. It is an odd thing to see one's own self."

I realized with sudden painful empathy that he was not emotionally aware of his own appearance; my present appearance was "his"—and any change in himself was merely incidental to illness, temporary, not to be noticed. But he went on speaking. "Would you mind moving around a bit for me, sir? I want to see me—you—us. I want the audience's viewpoint for once."

So I straightened up, moved around the room, spoke to Penny (the poor child was looking from one to the other of us with a dazed expression), picked up a paper, scratched my collarbone and rubbed my chin, moved his wand from under my arm to my hand and fiddled with it.

He was watching with delight. So I added an encore. Taking the middle of the rug, I gave the peroration of one of his finest speeches, not trying to do it word for word, but interpreting it, letting it roll and thunder as he would have done—and ending with his own exact ending: "A slave cannot be freed, save he do it himself. Nor can you enslave a free man; the very most you can do is kill him!"

There was that wonderful hushed silence, then a ripple of clapping—and Bonforte himself was pounding the couch with his good hand and calling, "Bravo!"

It was the only applause I ever got in the role. It was enough.

He had me pull up a chair then and sit with him. I saw him glance at the wand, so I handed it to him. "The safety is on, sir."

"I know how to use it." He looked at it closely, then handed it back. I had thought perhaps he would keep it. Since he did not, I decided to turn it over to Dak to deliver to him. He asked me about myself and told me that he did not recall ever seeing me play, but that he had seen my father's *Cyrano*. He was making a great effort to control the errant muscles of his mouth and his speech was clear but labored.

Then he asked me what I intended to do now. I told him that I had no plans as yet. He nodded and said, "We'll see. There is a place for you. There is work to be done." He made no mention of pay, which made me proud.

The returns were beginning to come in and he turned his

attention to the stereo tank. Returns had been coming in, of course, for forty-eight hours, since the outer worlds and the districtless constituencies vote before Earth does, and even on Earth an election "day" is more than thirty hours long, as the globe turns. But now we began to get the important districts of the great land masses of Earth. We had forged far ahead the day before in the outer returns and Rog had had to tell me that it meant nothing; the Expansionists always carried the outer worlds. What the billions of people still on Earth who had never been out and never would thought about it was what mattered.

But we needed every outer vote we could get. The Agrarian Party on Ganymede had swept five out of six districts; they were part of our coalition, and the Expansionist Party as such did not put up even token candidates. The situation on Venus was more ticklish, with the Venerians split into dozens of splinter parties divided on fine points of theology impossible for a human being to understand. Nevertheless, we expected most of the native vote, either directly or through caucused coalition later, and we should get practically all of the human vote there. The Imperial restriction that the natives must select human beings to represent them at New Batavia was a thing Bonforte was pledged to remove; it gained us votes on Venus; we did not know yet how many votes it would lose us on Earth.

Since the nests sent only observers to the Assembly the only vote we worried about on Mars was the human vote. We had the popular sentiment; they had the patronage. But with an honest count we expected a shoo-in there.

Dak was bending over a slide rule at Rog's side; Rog had a big sheet of paper laid out in some complicated weighting formula of his own. A dozen or more of the giant metal brains through the Solar System were doing the same thing that night, but Rog preferred his own guesses. He told me once that he could walk through a district, "sniffing" it, and come within two per cent of its results. I think he could.

Doc Capek was sitting back, with his hands over his paunch, as relaxed as an angleworm. Penny was moving around, pushing straight things crooked and vice versa and fetching us drinks. She never seemed to look directly at either me or Mr. Bonforte.

I had never before experienced an election-night party; they are not like any other. There is a cozy, warm rapport of all passion spent. It really does not matter too much how the people decide; you have done your best, you are with your friends and comrades, and for a while there is no worry and no pressure despite the over-all excitement, like frosting on a cake, of the incoming returns.

I don't know when I've had so good a time.

Rog looked up, looked at me, then spoke to Mr. Bonforte. "The Continent is seesaw. The Americas are testing the water with a toe before coming in on our side; the only question is, how deep?"

"Can you make a projection, Rog?"

"Not yet. Oh, we have the popular vote but in the G.A. it could swing either way by half a dozen seats." He stood up. "I think I had better mosey out into town."

Properly speaking, I should have gone, as "Mr. Bonforte." The party leader should certainly appear at the main headquarters of the Party sometime during election night. But I had never been in headquarters, it being the sort of a buttonholing place where my impersonation might be easily breached. My "illness" had excused me from it during the campaign; tonight it was not worth the risk, so Rog would go instead, and shake hands and grin and let the keyed-up girls who had done the hard and endless paperwork throw their arms around him and weep. "Back in an hour."

Even our little party should have been down on the lower level, to include all the office staff, especially Jimmie Washington. But it would not work, not without shutting Mr. Bonforte himself out of it. They were having their own party of course. I stood up. "Rog, I'll go down with you and say hello to Jimmie's harem."

"Eh? You don't have to, you know."

"It's the proper thing to do, isn't it? And it really isn't any trouble or risk." I turned to Mr. Bonforte. "How about it, sir?"

"I would appreciate it very much."

We went down the lift and through the silent, empty private quarters and on through my office and Penny's. Beyond her door was bedlam. A stereo receiver, moved in for the purpose, was blasting at full gain, the floor was littered, and everybody was drinking, or smoking, or both. Even Jimmie Washington was holding a drink while he listened to the returns. He was not drinking it; he neither drank nor smoked. No doubt someone had handed it to him and he had kept it. Jimmie had a fine sense of fitness.

I made the rounds, with Rog at my side, thanked Jimmie warmly and very sincerely, and apologized that I was feeling tired. "I'm going up and spread the bones, Jimmie. Make my excuses to people, will you?"

"Yes, sir. You've got to take care of yourself, Mr. Minister."

I went back up while Rog went on out into the public tunnels.

Penny shushed me with a finger to her lips when I came into the upper living room. Bonforte seemed to have dropped off to sleep and the receiver was muted down. Dak still sat in front of it, filling in figures on the big sheet against Rog's return. Capek had not moved. He nodded and raised his glass to me.

I let Penny fix me a scotch and water, then stepped out into the bubble balcony. It was night both by clock and by fact and Earth was almost full, dazzling in a Tiffany spread of stars. I searched North America and tried to pick out the little dot I had left only weeks earlier, and tried to get my emotions straight.

After a while I came back in; night on Luna is rather overpowering. Rog returned a little later and sat back down at his work sheets without speaking. I noticed that Bonforte was awake again.

The critical returns were coming in now and everybody kept quiet, letting Rog with his pencil and Dak with his slide rule have peace to work. At long, long last Rog shoved his chair back. "That's it, Chief," he said without looking up. "We're in. Majority not less than seven seats, probably nineteen, possibly over thirty."

After a pause Bonforte said quietly, "You're sure?"

"Positive. Penny, try another channel and see what we get."

I went over and sat by Bonforte; I could not talk. He reached out and patted my hand in a fatherly way and we both watched the receiver. The first station Penny got said: "—doubt about it, folks; eight of the robot brains say yes, *Curiac* says maybe. The Expansionist Party has won a decisive——" She switched to another.

"—confirms his temporary post for another five years. Mr. Quiroga cannot be reached for a statement but his general manager in New Chicago admits that the present trend cannot be over——"

Rog got up and went to the phone; Penny muted the news down until nothing could be heard. The announcer continued mouthing; he was simply saying in different words what we already knew.

Rog came back; Penny turned up the gain. The announcer went on for a moment, then stopped, read something that was handed to him, and turned back with a broad grin. "Friends and fellow citizens, I now bring you for a statement the *Supreme Minister!*"

The picture changed to my victory speech.

I sat there luxuriating in it, with my feelings as mixed up as possible but all good, painfully good. I had done a job on the speech and I knew it; I looked tired, sweaty, and calmly triumphant. It sounded ad-lib.

I had just reached: "Let us go forward together, with freedom for all——" when I heard a noise behind me.

"Mr. Bonforte!" I said. "Doc! *Doc!* Come quickly!"

Mr. Bonforte was pawing at me with his right hand and trying very urgently to tell me something. But it was no use; his poor mouth failed him and his mighty indomitable will could not make the weak flesh obey.

I took him in my arms—then he went into Cheyne-Stokes breathing and quickly into termination.

They took his body back down in the lift, Dak and Capek together; I was no use to them. Rog came up and patted me on the shoulder, then he went away. Penny had followed the others down. Presently I went again out onto the balcony. I needed "fresh air" even though it was the same machine-pumped air as the living room. But it felt fresher.

They had killed him. His enemies had killed him as certainly as if they had put a knife in his ribs. Despite all that we had done, the risks we had taken, in the end they had murdered him. "Murder most foul"!

I felt dead inside me, numb with the shock. I had seen "myself" die, I had again seen my father die. I knew then why they so rarely manage to save one of a pair of Siamese twins. I was empty.

I don't know how long I stayed out there. Eventually I heard Rog's voice behind me. "Chief?"

I turned. "Rog," I said urgently, "don't call me that. Please!"

"Chief," he persisted, "you know what you have to do now? Don't you?"

I felt dizzy and his face blurred. I did not know what he was talking about—I did not *want* to know what he was talking about.

"What do you mean?"

"Chief—one man dies—but the show goes on. You can't quit now."

My head ached and my eyes would not focus. He seemed to pull toward me and away while his voice drove on. ". . . robbed him of his chance to finish his work. So you've got to do it for him. You've got to make him live again!"

I shook my head and made a great effort to pull myself together and reply. "Rog, you don't know what you are saying. It's preposterous—ridiculous! I'm no statesman. I'm just a bloody actor! I make faces and make people laugh. That's all I'm good for."

To my own horror I heard myself say it in Bonforte's voice.

Rog looked at me. "Seems to me you've done all right so far."

I tried to change my voice, tried to gain control of the situation. "Rog, you're upset. When you've calmed down you will see how ridiculous this is. You're right; the show goes on. But not that way. The proper thing to do—the *only* thing to do—is for you yourself to move on up. The election is won; you've got your majority—now you take office and carry out the program."

He looked at me and shook his head sadly. "I would if I could. I admit it. But I can't. Chief, you remember those confounded executive committee meetings? You kept them in line. The whole coalition has been kept glued together by the personal force and leadership of one man. If you don't follow through now, all that he lived for—and died for—will fall apart."

I had no answering argument; he might be right—I had seen the wheels within wheels of politics in the past month and a half. "Rog, even if what you say is true, the solution you offer is impossible. We've barely managed to keep up this pretense by letting me be seen only under carefully stage-managed conditions—and we've just missed being caught out as it is. But to make it work week after week, month after month, even year after year, if I understand you—no, it couldn't be done. It is impossible. I *can't* do it!"

"You *can!*" He leaned toward me and said forcefully, "We've all talked it over and we know the hazards as well as you do. But you'll have a chance to grow into it. Two weeks in space to start with—hell, a month if you want it! You'll study all the time—his journals, his boyhood diaries, his scrapbooks, you'll soak yourself in them. And we'll all help you."

I did not answer. He went on, "Look, Chief, you've learned that a political personality is not one man; it's a team—it's a team bound together by common purposes and common beliefs. We've lost our team captain and we've got to have another one. But the team is still there."

Capek was out on the balcony; I had not seen him come out. I turned to him. "Are you for this too?"

"Yes."

"It's your duty," Rog added.

Capek said slowly, "I won't go that far. I hope you will do it. But, damn it, I won't be your conscience. I believe in free will, frivolous as that may sound from a medical man." He turned to Clifton. "We had better leave him alone, Rog. He knows. Now it's up to him."

But, although they left, I was not to be alone just yet. Dak came out. To my relief and gratitude he did not call me "Chief."

"Hello, Dak."

"Howdy." He was silent for a moment, smoking and looking out at the stars. Then he turned to me. "Old son, we've been through some things together. I know you now, and I'll back you with a gun, or money, or fists any time, and never ask why. If you choose to drop out now, I won't have a word of blame and I won't think any the less of you. You've done a noble best."

"Uh, thanks, Dak."

"One more word and I'll smoke out. Just remember this: if you decide you can't do it, the foul scum who brainwashed him will win. In spite of everything they win." He went inside.

I felt torn apart in my mind—then I gave way to sheer self-pity. It wasn't fair! I had my *own* life to live. I was at the top of my powers, with my greatest professional triumphs still ahead of me. It wasn't right to expect me to bury myself, perhaps for years, in the anonymity of another man's role—while the public forgot me, producers and agents forgot me—would probably believe I was dead.

It wasn't fair. It was too much to ask.

Presently I pulled out of it and for a time did not think. Mother Earth was still serene and beautiful and changeless in the sky; I wondered what the election-night celebrations there sounded like. Mars and Jupiter and Venus were all in sight, strung like prizes along the zodiac. Ganymede I could not see, of course, nor the lonely colony out on far Pluto.

"Worlds of Hope," Bonforte had called them.

But he was dead. He was gone. They had taken away from him his birthright at its ripe fullness. He was dead.

And they had put it up to me to re-create him, make him live again.

Was I up to it? Could I possibly measure up to his noble standards? What would he want me to do? If he were in my place—what would Bonforte do? Again and again in the campaign I had asked myself: "What would Bonforte do?"

Someone moved behind me, I turned and saw Penny. I looked at her and said, "Did they send you out? Did you come to plead with me?"

"No."

She added nothing and did not seem to expect me to answer, nor did we look at each other. The silence went on. At last I said, "Penny? If I try to do it—will you help?"

She turned suddenly toward me. "Yes. Oh yes, Chief! I'll help!"

"Then I'll try," I said humbly.

I wrote all of the above twenty-five years ago to try to straighten out my own confusion. I tried to tell the truth and not spare myself because it was not meant to be read by anyone but myself and my therapist, Dr. Capek. It is strange, after a quarter of a century, to reread the foolish and emotional words of that young man. I remember him, yet I have trouble realizing that I was ever he. My wife Penelope claims that she remembers him better than I do—and that she never loved anyone else. So time changes us.

I find I can "remember" Bonforte's early life better than I remember my actual life as that rather pathetic person, Lawrence Smith, or—as he liked to style himself—"The Great Lorenzo." Does that make me insane? Schizophrenic, perhaps? If so, it is a necessary insanity for the role I have had to play, for in order to let Bonforte live again, that seedy actor had to be suppressed—completely.

Insane or not, I am aware that he once existed and that I was he. He was never a success as an actor, not really—though I think he was sometimes touched with the true madness. He made his final exit still perfectly in character; I have a yellowed newspaper clipping somewhere which states that he was "found dead" in a Jersey City hotel room from an overdose of sleeping pills—apparently taken in a fit of despondency, for his agent issued a statement that he had not had a part in several months. Personally, I feel that they need not have mentioned that about his being out of work; if not libelous, it was at least unkind. The date of the clipping proves, incidentally, that he could not have been in New Batavia, or anywhere else, during the campaign of '15.

I suppose I should burn it.

But there is no one left alive today who knows the truth other than Dak and Penelope—except the men who murdered Bonforte's body.

I have been in and out of office three times now and perhaps this term will be my last. I was knocked out the first time when we finally put the eetees—Venerians and Martians and Outer Jovians—into the Grand Assembly. But the nonhuman peoples are still there and I came back. The people will take a certain amount of reform, then they want a rest. But the reforms stay. People don't really want change, any change at all—and xenophobia is very deep-rooted. But we progress, as we must—if we are to go out to the stars.

Again and again I have asked myself: "What would Bonforte do?" I am not sure that my answers have always been right (although I am sure that I am the best-read student in his works in the System). But I have tried to stay in character in his role. A long time ago someone—Voltaire?—someone said, "If Satan should ever replace God he would find it necessary to assume the attributes of Divinity."

I have never regretted my lost profession. In a way, I have not lost it; Willem was right. There is other applause besides handclapping and there is always the warm glow of a good performance. I have tried, I suppose, to create the perfect work of art. Perhaps I have not fully succeeded—but I think my father would rate it as a "good performance."

No, I do not regret it, even though I was happier then—at least I slept better. But there is solemn satisfaction in doing the best you can for eight billion people.

Perhaps their lives have no cosmic significance, but they have feelings. They can hurt.

THE STARS MY DESTINATION

Alfred Bester

To

Truman M. Talley

Part 1

Tiger! Tiger! burning bright
In the forests of the night,
What immortal hand or eye
Could frame thy fearful symmetry?
                              Blake

Prologue

THIS was a Golden Age, a time of high adventure, rich living, and hard dying . . . but nobody thought so. This was a future of fortune and theft, pillage and rapine, culture and vice . . . but nobody admitted it. This was an age of extremes, a fascinating century of freaks . . . but nobody loved it.

All the habitable worlds of the solar system were occupied. Three planets and eight satellites and eleven million million people swarmed in one of the most exciting ages ever known, yet minds still yearned for other times, as always. The solar system seethed with activity . . . fighting, feeding, and breeding, learning the new technologies that spewed forth almost before the old had been mastered, girding itself for the first exploration of the far stars in deep space; but—

"Where are the new frontiers?" the Romantics cried, unaware that the frontier of the mind had opened in a laboratory on Callisto at the turn of the twenty-fourth century. A researcher named Jaunte set fire to his bench and himself (accidentally) and let out a yell for help with particular reference to a fire extinguisher. Who so surprised as Jaunte and his colleagues when he found himself standing alongside said extinguisher, seventy feet removed from his lab bench.

They put Jaunte out and went into the whys and wherefores of his instantaneous seventy-foot journey. Teleportation . . . the transportation of oneself through space by an effort of the mind alone . . . had long been a theoretic concept, and there were a few hundred badly documented proofs that it had happened in the past. This was the first time that it had ever taken place before professional observers.

They investigated the Jaunte Effect savagely. This was something too earth-shaking to handle with kid gloves, and Jaunte was anxious to make his name immortal. He made his will and said farewell to his friends. Jaunte knew he was going to die because his fellow researchers were determined to kill him, if necessary. There was no doubt about that.

Twelve psychologists, parapsychologists and neurometrists of varying specialization were called in as observers. The experimenters sealed Jaunte into an unbreakable crystal tank. They opened a water valve, feeding water into the tank, and let Jaunte watch them smash the valve handle. It was impossible to open the tank; it was impossible to stop the flow of water.

The theory was that if it had required the threat of death to goad Jaunte into teleporting himself in the first place, they'd damned well threaten him with death again. The tank filled quickly. The observers collected data with the tense precision of an eclipse camera crew. Jaunte began to drown. Then he was outside the tank, dripping and coughing explosively. He'd teleported again.

The experts examined and questioned him. They studied graphs and X-rays, neural patterns and body chemistry. They began to get an inkling of how Jaunte had teleported. On the technical grapevine (this had to be kept secret) they sent out a call for suicide volunteers. They were still in the primitive stage of teleportation; death was the only spur they knew.

They briefed the volunteers thoroughly. Jaunte lectured on what he had done and how he thought he had done it. Then they proceeded to murder the volunteers. They drowned them, hanged them, burned them; they invented new forms of slow and controlled death. There was never any doubt in any of the subjects that death was the object.

Eighty per cent of the volunteers died, and the agonies and remorse of their murderers would make a fascinating and horrible study, but that has no place in this history except to highlight the monstrosity of the times. Eighty per cent of the volunteers died, but 20 per cent jaunted. (The name became a word almost immediately.)

"Bring back the romantic age," the Romantics pleaded, "when men could risk their lives in high adventure."

The body of knowledge grew rapidly. By the first decade of the twenty-fourth century the principles of jaunting were established and the first school was opened by Charles Fort Jaunte himself, then fifty-seven, immortalized, and ashamed to admit that he had never dared jaunte again. But the primitive days were past; it was no longer necessary to threaten a man with death to make him teleport. They had learned how to teach man to recognize, discipline, and exploit yet another resource of his limitless mind.

How, exactly, did man teleport? One of the most unsatisfactory explanations was provided by Spencer Thompson, publicity representative of the Jaunte Schools, in a press interview.

THOMPSON: Jaunting is like seeing; it is a natural aptitude of almost every human organism, but it can only be developed by training and experience.

REPORTER: You mean we couldn't see without practice?

THOMPSON: Obviously you're either unmarried or have no children . . . preferably both.

(*Laughter*)

REPORTER: I don't understand.

THOMPSON: Anyone who's observed an infant learning to use its eyes, would.

REPORTER: But what *is* teleportation?

THOMPSON: The transportation of oneself from one locality to another by an effort of the mind alone.

REPORTER: You mean we can *think* ourselves from . . . say . . . New York to Chicago?

THOMPSON: Precisely; provided one thing is clearly understood. In jaunting from New York to Chicago it is necessary for the person teleporting himself to know exactly where he is when he starts and where he's going.

REPORTER: How's that?

THOMPSON: If you were in a dark room and unaware of where you were, it would be impossible to jaunte anywhere with safety. And if you knew where you were but intended to jaunte to a place you had never seen, you would never arrive alive. One cannot jaunte from an unknown departure point to an unknown destination. *Both* must be known, memorized and visualized.

REPORTER: But if we know where we are and where we're going . . . ?

THOMPSON: We can be pretty sure we'll jaunte and arrive.

REPORTER: Would we arrive naked?

THOMPSON: If you started naked.

(*Laughter*)

REPORTER: I mean, would our clothes teleport with us?

THOMPSON: When people teleport, they also teleport the clothes they wear and whatever they are strong enough to carry. I hate to disappoint you, but even ladies' clothes would arrive with them.

(*Laughter*)

REPORTER: But how do we do it?

THOMPSON: How do we think?

REPORTER: With our minds.

THOMPSON: And how does the mind think? What is the thinking process? Exactly how do we remember, imagine, deduce, create? Exactly how do the brain cells operate?

REPORTER: I don't know. Nobody knows.

THOMPSON: And nobody knows exactly how we teleport either, but we know we can do it—just as we know that we can think. Have you ever heard of Descartes? He said: *Cogito ergo sum*. I think, therefore I am. We say: *Cogito ergo jaunteo*. I think, therefore I jaunte.

If it is thought that Thompson's explanation is exasperating, inspect this report of Sir John Kelvin to the Royal Society on the mechanism of jaunting:

> We have established that the teleportative ability is associated with the Nissl bodies, or Tigroid Substance in nerve cells. The Tigroid Substance is easiest demonstrated by Nissl's method using 3.75 g. of methylen blue and 1.75 g. of Venetian soap dissolved in 1,000 cc. of water.
> Where the Tigroid Substance does not appear, jaunting is impossible. Teleportation is a Tigroid Function.
> (*Applause*)

Any man was capable of jaunting provided he developed two faculties, visualization and concentration. He had to visualize, completely and precisely, the spot to which he desired to teleport himself; and he had to concentrate the latent energy of his mind into a single thrust to get him there. Above all, he had to have faith . . . the faith that Charles Fort Jaunte never recovered. He had to believe he would jaunte. The slightest doubt would block the mind-thrust necessary for teleportation.

The limitations with which every man is born necessarily

limited the ability to jaunte. Some could visualize magnificently and set the co-ordinates of their destination with precision, but lacked the power to get there. Others had the power but could not, so to speak, see where they were jaunting. And space set a final limitation, for no man had ever jaunted further than a thousand miles. He could work his way in jaunting jumps over land and water from Nome to Mexico, but no jump could exceed a thousand miles.

By the 2420's, this form of employment application blank had become a commonplace:

This space
reserved for
retina pattern
identification

NAME (Capital Letters):......................................
                    Last   Middle   First

RESIDENCE (Legal):...
                    Continent   Country   County

JAUNTE CLASS (Official rating: Check one Only):

   M (1,000 miles): . . . . . .   L (50 miles): . . . .
   D (500 miles): . . . .   X (10 miles): . . . .
   C (100 miles): . . . .   V (5 miles): . . . .

The old Bureau of Motor Vehicles took over the new job and regularly tested and classed jaunte applicants, and the old American Automobile Association changed its initials to AJA.

Despite all efforts, no man had ever jaunted across the voids of space, although many experts and fools had tried. Helmut Grant, for one, who spent a month memorizing the co-ordinates of a jaunte stage on the moon and visualized every mile of the two hundred and forty thousand–mile trajectory from Times Square to Kepler City. Grant jaunted and disappeared. They never found him. They never found Enzio Dandridge, a Los Angeles revivalist looking for Heaven; Jacob Maria Freundlich, a paraphysicist who should have known better than to jaunte into deep space searching for metadimensions; Shipwreck Cogan, a professional seeker after notoriety; and hundreds of others, lunatic-fringers, neurotics, escapists and suicides. Space was closed to teleportation. Jaunting was restricted to the surfaces of the planets of the solar system.

But within three generations the entire solar system was on the jaunte. The transition was more spectacular than the changeover from horse and buggy to gasoline age four centuries before. On three planets and eight satellites, social, legal, and economic structures crashed while the new customs and laws demanded by universal jaunting mushroomed in their place.

There were land riots as the jaunting poor deserted slums to squat in plains and forests, raiding the livestock and wildlife. There was a revolution in home and office building: labyrinths and masking devices had to be introduced to prevent unlawful entry by jaunting. There were crashes and panics and strikes and famines as pre-jaunte industries failed.

Plagues and pandemics raged as jaunting vagrants carried disease and vermin into defenseless countries. Malaria, elephantiasis, and the breakbone fever came north to Greenland; rabies returned to England after an absence of three hundred years. The Japanese beetle, the citrus scale, the chestnut blight, and the elm borer spread to every corner of the world, and from one forgotten pesthole in Borneo, leprosy, long imagined extinct, reappeared.

Crime waves swept the planets and satellites as their underworlds took to jaunting with the night around the clock, and there were brutalities as the police fought them without quarter. There came a hideous return to the worst prudery of Victorianism as society fought the sexual and moral dangers of jaunting with protocol and taboo. A cruel and vicious war broke out between the Inner Planets—Venus, Terra and Mars —and the Outer Satellites . . . a war brought on by the economic and political pressures of teleportation.

Until the Jaunte Age dawned, the three Inner Planets (and the Moon) had lived in delicate economic balance with the seven inhabited Outer Satellites: Io, Europa, Ganymede, and

Callisto of Jupiter; Rhea and Titan of Saturn; and Lassell of Neptune. The United Outer Satellites supplied raw materials for the Inner Planets' manufactories, and a market for their finished goods. Within a decade this balance was destroyed by jaunting.

The Outer Satellites, raw young worlds in the making, had bought 70 per cent of the I.P. transportation production. Jaunting ended that. They had bought 90 per cent of the I.P. communications production. Jaunting ended that too. In consequence I.P. purchase of O.S. raw materials fell off.

With trade exchange destroyed it was inevitable that the economic war would degenerate into a shooting war. Inner Planets' cartels refused to ship manufacturing equipment to the Outer Satellites, attempting to protect themselves against competition. The O.S. confiscated the plants already in operation on their worlds, broke patent agreements, ignored royalty obligations . . . and the war was on.

It was an age of freaks, monsters, and grotesques. All the world was misshapen in marvelous and malevolent ways. The Classicists and Romantics who hated it were unaware of the potential greatness of the twenty-fifth century. They were blind to a cold fact of evolution . . . that progress stems from the clashing merger of antagonistic extremes, out of the marriage of pinnacle freaks. Classicists and Romantics alike were unaware that the Solar System was trembling on the verge of a human explosion that would transform man and make him the master of the universe.

It is against this seething background of the twenty-fifth century that the vengeful history of Gulliver Foyle begins.

One

HE was one hundred and seventy days dying and not yet dead. He fought for survival with the passion of a beast in a trap. He was delirious and rotting, but occasionally his primitive mind emerged from the burning nightmare of survival into something resembling sanity. Then he lifted his mute face to Eternity and muttered: "What's a matter, me? Help, you goddamn gods! Help, is all."

Blasphemy came easily to him: it was half his speech, all his life. He had been raised in the gutter school of the twenty-fifth century and spoke nothing but the gutter tongue. Of all brutes in the world he was among the least valuable alive and most likely to survive. So he struggled and prayed in blasphemy; but occasionally his raveling mind leaped backward thirty years to his childhood and remembered a nursery jingle:

> Gully Foyle is my name
> And Terra is my nation.
> Deep space is my dwelling place
> And death's my destination.

He was Gulliver Foyle, Mechanic's Mate 3rd Class, thirty years old, big boned and rough . . . and one hundred and seventy days adrift in space. He was Gully Foyle, the oiler, wiper, bunkerman; too easy for trouble, too slow for fun, too empty for friendship, too lazy for love. The lethargic outlines of his character showed in the official Merchant Marine records:

FOYLE, GULLIVER ------------- AS-128/127:006

EDUCATION:	NONE
SKILLS:	NONE
MERITS:	NONE
RECOMMENDATIONS:	NONE

(PERSONNEL COMMENTS)

A man of physical strength and intellectual
potential stunted by lack of ambition. Energizes

<u>at minimum. The stereotype Common Man. Some
unexpected shock might possibly awaken him, but
Psych cannot find the key. Not recommended for
promotion. Has reached a dead end.</u>

He had reached a dead end. He had been content to drift
from moment to moment of existence for thirty years like some
heavily armored creature, sluggish and indifferent—Gully
Foyle, the stereotype Common Man—but now he was adrift
in space for one hundred and seventy days, and the key to his
awakening was in the lock. Presently it would turn and open
the door to holocaust.

The spaceship "Nomad" drifted halfway between Mars and Jupiter. Whatever war catastrophe had wrecked it had taken a sleek
steel rocket, one hundred yards long and one hundred feet
broad, and mangled it into a skeleton on which was mounted
the remains of cabins, holds, decks and bulkheads. Great rents
in the hull were blazes of light on the sunside and frosty blotches
of stars on the darkside. The S.S. "Nomad" was a weightless
emptiness of blinding sun and jet shadow, frozen and silent.

The wreck was filled with a floating conglomerate of frozen
debris that hung within the destroyed vessel like an instantaneous photograph of an explosion. The minute gravitational
attraction of the bits of rubble for each other was slowly drawing
them into clusters which were periodically torn apart by the
passage through them of the one survivor still alive on the
wreck, Gulliver Foyle, AS:128/127:006.

He lived in the only airtight room left intact in the wreck, a
tool locker off the main-deck corridor. The locker was four
feet wide, four feet deep and nine feet high. It was the size of a
giant's coffin. Six hundred years before, it had been judged the
most exquisite Oriental torture to imprison a man in a cage
that size for a few weeks. Yet Foyle had existed in this lightless
coffin for five months, twenty days, and four hours.

"Who are you?"
    "Gully Foyle is my name."
    "Where are you from?"
    "Terra is my nation."

"Where are you now?"

"Deep space is my dwelling place."

"Where are you bound?"

"Death's my destination."

On the one hundred and seventy-first day of his fight for survival, Foyle answered these questions and awoke. His heart hammered and his throat burned. He groped in the dark for the air tank which shared his coffin with him and checked it. The tank was empty. Another would have to be moved in at once. So this day would commence with an extra skirmish with death which Foyle accepted with mute endurance.

He felt through the locker shelves and located a torn space-suit. It was the only one aboard "Nomad" and Foyle no longer remembered where or how he had found it. He had sealed the tear with emergency spray, but had no way of refilling or replacing the empty oxygen cartridges on the back. Foyle got into the suit. It would hold enough air from the locker to allow him five minutes in vacuum . . . no more.

Foyle opened the locker door and plunged out into the black frost of space. The air in the locker puffed out with him and its moisture congealed into a tiny snow cloud that drifted down the torn main-deck corridor. Foyle heaved at the exhausted air tank, floated it out of the locker and abandoned it. One minute was gone.

He turned and propelled himself through the floating debris toward the hatch to the ballast hold. He did not run: his gait was the unique locomotion of free-fall and weightlessness . . . thrusts with foot, elbow and hand against deck, wall and corner, a slow-motion darting through space like a bat flying under water. Foyle shot through the hatch into the darkside ballast hold. Two minutes were gone.

Like all spaceships, "Nomad" was ballasted and stiffened with the mass of her gas tanks laid down the length of her keel like a long lumber raft tapped at the sides by a labyrinth of pipe fittings. Foyle took a minute disconnecting an air tank. He had no way of knowing whether it was full or already exhausted; whether he would fight it back to his locker only to discover that it was empty and his life was ended. Once a week he endured this game of space roulette.

There was a roaring in his ears; the air in his spacesuit was rapidly going foul. He yanked the massy cylinder toward the ballast hatch, ducked to let it sail over his head, then thrust himself after it. He swung the tank through the hatch. Four minutes had elapsed and he was shaking and blacking out. He guided the tank down the main-deck corridor and bulled it into the tool locker.

He slammed the locker door, dogged it, found a hammer on a shelf and swung it thrice against the frozen tank to loosen the valve. Foyle twisted the handle grimly. With the last of his strength he unsealed the helmet of his spacesuit, lest he suffocate within the suit while the locker filled with air . . . if this tank contained air. He fainted, as he had fainted so often before, never knowing whether this was death.

"Who are you?"
  "Gully Foyle."
  "Where are you from?"
  "Terra."
  "Where are you now?"
  "Space."
  "Where are you bound?"
He awoke. He was alive. He wasted no time on prayer or thanks but continued the business of survival. In the darkness he explored the locker shelves where he kept his rations. There were only a few packets left. Since he was already wearing the patched spacesuit he might just as well run the gantlet of vacuum again and replenish his supplies.

He flooded his spacesuit with air from the tank, resealed his helmet and sailed out into the frost and light again. He squirmed down the main-deck corridor and ascended the remains of a stairway, to the control deck which was no more than a roofed corridor in space. Most of the walls were destroyed.

With the sun on his right and the stars on his left, Foyle shot aft toward the galley storeroom. Halfway down the corridor he passed a door frame still standing foursquare between deck and roof. The leaf still hung on its hinges, half-open, a door to nowhere. Behind it was all space and the steady stars.

As Foyle passed the door he had a quick view of himself reflected in the polished chrome of the leaf . . . Gully Foyle, a giant black creature, bearded, crusted with dried blood and filth, emaciated, with sick, patient eyes . . . and followed always by a stream of floating debris, the raffle disturbed by his motion and following him through space like the tail of a festering comet.

Foyle turned into the galley storeroom and began looting with the methodical speed of five months' habit. Most of the bottled goods were frozen solid and exploded. Much of the canned goods had lost their containers, for tin crumbles to dust in the absolute zero of space. Foyle gathered up ration packets, concentrates, and a chunk of ice from the burst water tank. He threw everything into a large copper cauldron, turned and darted out of the storeroom, carrying the cauldron.

At the door to nowhere Foyle glanced at himself again, reflected in the chrome leaf framed in the stars. Then he stopped his motion in bewilderment. He stared at the stars behind the door which had become familiar friends after five months. There was an intruder among them; a comet, it seemed, with an invisible head and a short, spurting tail. Then Foyle realized he was staring at a spaceship, stern rockets flaring as it accelerated on a sunward course that must pass him.

"No," he muttered. "No, man. No."

He was continually suffering from hallucinations. He turned to resume the journey back to his coffin. Then he looked again. It was still a spaceship, stern rockets flaring as it accelerated on a sunward course which must pass him. He discussed the illusion with Eternity.

"Six months already," he said in his gutter tongue. "Is it now? You listen a me, lousy gods. I talkin' a deal, is all. I look again, sweet prayer-men. If it's a ship, I'm yours. You own me. But if it's a gaff, man . . . if it's no ship . . . I unseal right now and blow my guts. We both ballast level, us. Now reach me the sign, yes or no, is all."

He looked for a third time. For the third time he saw a spaceship, stern rockets flaring as it accelerated on a sunward course which must pass him.

It was the sign. He believed. He was saved.

Foyle shoved off and went hurtling down control-deck corridor toward the bridge. But at the companionway stairs he restrained himself. He could not remain conscious for more than a few more moments without refilling his spacesuit. He gave the approaching spaceship one pleading look, then shot down to the tool locker and pumped his suit full.

He mounted to the control bridge. Through the starboard observation port he saw the spaceship, stern rockets still flaring, evidently making a major alteration in course, for it was bearing down on him very slowly.

On a panel marked FLARES, Foyle pressed the DISTRESS button. There was a three-second pause during which he suffered. Then white radiance blinded him as the distress signal went off in three triple bursts, nine prayers for help. Foyle pressed the button twice again, and twice more the flares flashed in space while the radioactives incorporated in their combustion set up a static howl that must register on any waveband of any receiver.

The stranger's jets cut off. He had been seen. He would be saved. He was reborn. He exulted.

Foyle darted back to his locker and replenished his spacesuit again. He began to weep. He started to gather his possessions—a faceless clock which he kept wound just to listen to the ticking, a lug wrench with a hand-shaped handle which he would hold in lonely moments, an egg slicer upon whose wires he would pluck primitive tunes. . . . He dropped them in his excitement, hunted for them in the dark, then began to laugh at himself.

He filled his spacesuit with air once more and capered back to the bridge. He punched a flare button labelled: RESCUE. From the hull of the "Nomad" shot a sunlet that burst and hung, flooding miles of space with harsh white light.

"Come on, baby you," Foyle crooned. "Hurry up, man. Come on, baby baby you."

Like a ghost torpedo, the stranger slid into the outermost rim of light, approaching slowly, looking him over. For a moment Foyle's heart constricted; the ship was behaving so cautiously that he feared she was an enemy vessel from the Outer Satellites. Then he saw the famous red and blue emblem on her side, the trademark of the mighty industrial clan of Presteign; Presteign of Terra, powerful, munificent, beneficent. And he knew this was a sister ship, for the "Nomad" was also Presteign-owned. He knew this was an angel from space hovering over him.

"Sweet sister," Foyle crooned. "Baby angel, fly away home with me."

The ship came abreast of Foyle, illuminated ports along its side glowing with friendly light, its name and registry number clearly visible in illuminated figures on the hull: Vorga-T:1339. The ship was alongside him in a moment, passing him in a second, disappearing in a third.

The sister had spurned him; the angel had abandoned him.

Foyle stopped dancing and crooning. He stared in dismay. He leaped to the flare panel and slapped buttons. Distress signals, landing, take-off, and quarantine flares burst from the hull of the "Nomad" in a madness of white, red and green light, pulsing, pleading . . . and "Vorga-T:1339" passed silently and implacably, stern jets flaring again as it accelerated on a sunward course.

So, in five seconds, he was born, he lived, and he died. After thirty years of existence and six months of torture, Gully Foyle, the stereotype Common Man, was no more. The key turned in the lock of his soul and the door was opened. What emerged expunged the Common Man forever.

"You pass me by," he said with slow mounting fury. "You leave me rot like a dog. You leave me die, 'Vorga' . . . 'Vorga-T:1339.' No. I get out of here, me. I follow you, 'Vorga.' I find you, 'Vorga.' I pay you back, me. I rot you. I kill you, 'Vorga.' I kill you filthy."

The acid of fury ran through him, eating away the brute patience and sluggishness that had made a cipher of Gully Foyle, precipitating a chain of reactions that would make an infernal machine of Gully Foyle. He was dedicated.

" 'Vorga,' I kill you filthy."

He did what the cipher could not do; he rescued himself.

For two days he combed the wreckage in five-minute forays, and devised a harness for his shoulders. He attached an air tank to the harness and connected the tank to his spacesuit helmet with an improvised hose. He wriggled through space like an ant dragging a log, but he had the freedom of the "Nomad" for all time.

He thought.

In the control bridge he taught himself to use the few navigation instruments that were still unbroken, studying the standard manuals that littered the wrecked navigation room.

In the ten years of his service in space he had never dreamed of attempting such a thing, despite the rewards of promotion and pay; but now he had "Vorga-T:1339" to reward him.

He took sights. The "Nomad" was drifting in space on the ecliptic, three hundred million miles from the sun. Before him were spread the constellations Perseus, Andromeda and Pisces. Hanging almost in the foreground was a dusty orange spot that was Jupiter, distinctly a planetary disc to the naked eye. With any luck he could make a course for Jupiter and rescue.

Jupiter was not, could never be habitable. Like all the outer planets beyond the asteroid orbits, it was a frozen mass of methane and ammonia; but its four largest satellites swarmed with cities and populations now at war with the Inner Planets. He would be a war prisoner, but he had to stay alive to settle accounts with "Vorga-T:1339."

Foyle inspected the engine room of the "Nomad." There was Hi-Thrust fuel remaining in the tanks and one of the four tail jets was still in operative condition. Foyle found the engine room manuals and studied them. He repaired the connection between fuel tanks and the one jet chamber. The tanks were on the sunside of the wreck and warmed above freezing point. The Hi-Thrust was still liquid, but it would not flow. In free-fall there was no gravity to draw the fuel down the pipes.

Foyle studied a space manual and learned something about theoretical gravity. If he could put the "Nomad" into a spin, centrifugal force would impart enough gravitation to the ship to draw fuel down into the combustion chamber of the jet. If he could fire the combustion chamber, the unequal thrust of the one jet would impart a spin to the "Nomad."

But he couldn't fire the jet without first having the spin; and he couldn't get the spin without first firing the jet.

He thought his way out of the deadlock; he was inspired by "Vorga."

Foyle opened the drainage petcock in the combustion chamber of the jet and tortuously filled the chamber with fuel by hand. He had primed the pump. Now, if he ignited the fuel, it would fire long enough to impart the spin and start gravity. Then the flow from the tanks would commence and the rocketing would continue.

He tried matches.

Matches will not burn in the vacuum of space.

He tried flint and steel.

Sparks will not glow in the absolute zero of space.

He thought of red-hot filaments.

He had no electric power of any description aboard the "Nomad" to make a filament red hot.

He found texts and read. Although he was blacking out frequently and close to complete collapse, he thought and planned. He was inspired to greatness by "Vorga."

Foyle brought ice from the frozen galley tanks, melted it with his own body heat, and added water to the jet combustion chamber. The fuel and the water were nonmiscible, they did not mix. The water floated in a thin layer over the fuel.

From the chemical stores Foyle brought a silvery bit of wire, pure sodium metal. He poked the wire through the open pet-cock. The sodium ignited when it touched the water and flared with high heat. The heat touched off the Hi-Thrust which burst in a needle flame from the petcock. Foyle closed the petcock with a wrench. The ignition held in the chamber and the lone aft jet slammed out flame with a soundless vibration that shook the ship.

The off-center thrust of the jet twisted the "Nomad" into a slow spin. The torque imparted a slight gravity. Weight returned. The floating debris that cluttered the hull fell to decks, walls and ceilings; and the gravity kept the fuel feeding from tanks to combustion chamber.

Foyle wasted no time on cheers. He left the engine room and struggled forward in desperate haste for a final, fatal observation from the control bridge. This would tell him whether the "Nomad" was committed to a wild plunge out into the no-return of deep space, or a course for Jupiter and rescue.

The slight gravity made his air tank almost impossible to drag. The sudden forward surge of acceleration shook loose masses of debris which flew backward through the "Nomad." As Foyle struggled up the companionway stairs to the control deck, the rubble from the bridge came hurtling back down the corridor and smashed into him. He was caught up in this tumbleweed in space, rolled back the length of the empty corridor, and brought up against the galley bulkhead with an impact that shattered his last hold on consciousness. He lay pinned in the center of half a ton of wreckage, helpless, barely alive, but still raging for vengeance.

"Who are you?"

"Where are you from?"

"Where are you now?"

"Where are you bound?"

Two

BETWEEN Mars and Jupiter is spread the broad belt of the asteroids. Of the thousands, known and unknown, most unique to the Freak Century was the Sargasso Asteroid, a tiny planet manufactured of natural rock and wreckage salvaged by its inhabitants in the course of two hundred years.

They were savages, the only savages of the twenty-fourth century; descendants of a research team of scientists that had been lost and marooned in the asteroid belt two centuries before when their ship had failed. By the time their descendants were rediscovered they had built up a world and a culture of their own, and preferred to remain in space, salvaging and spoiling, and practicing a barbaric travesty of the scientific method they remembered from their forebears. They called themselves The Scientific People. The world promptly forgot them.

S.S. "Nomad" looped through space, neither on a course for Jupiter nor the far stars, but drifting across the asteroid belt in the slow spiral of a dying animalcule. It passed within a mile of the Sargasso Asteroid, and it was immediately captured by The Scientific People to be incorporated into their little planet. They found Foyle.

He awoke once while he was being carried in triumph on a litter through the natural and artificial passages within the scavenger asteroid. They were constructed of meteor metal, stone, and hull plates. Some of the plates still bore names long forgotten in the history of space travel: INDUS QUEEN, TERRA; SYRTUS RAMBLER, MARS; THREE RING CIR-CUS, SATURN. The passages led to great halls, storerooms, apartments, and homes, all built of salvaged ships cemented into the asteroid.

In rapid succession Foyle was borne through an ancient Ganymede scow, a Lassell ice borer, a captain's barge, a Callisto heavy cruiser, a twenty-second-century fuel transport with glass tanks still filled with smoky rocket fuel. Two centuries of salvage were gathered in this hive: armories of weapons, libraries of books, museums of costumes, warehouses of machinery, tools, rations, drink, chemicals, synthetics, and surrogates.

A crowd around the litter was howling triumphantly. "Quant Suff!" they shouted. A woman's chorus began an excited bleating:

> Ammonium bromide . . . . gr. 1½
> Potassium bromide. . . . . gr. 3
> Sodium bromide . . . . gr. 2
> Citric acid . . . . quant. suff.

"Quant Suff!" The Scientific People roared. "Quant Suff!" Foyle fainted.

He awoke again. He had been taken out of his spacesuit. He was in the greenhouse of the asteroid where plants were grown for fresh oxygen. The hundred-yard hull of an old ore carrier formed the room, and one wall had been entirely fitted with salvaged windows . . . round ports, square ports, diamond, hexagonal . . . every shape and age of port had been introduced until the vast wall was a crazy quilt of glass and light.

The distant sun blazed through; the air was hot and moist. Foyle gazed around dimly. A devil face peered at him. Cheeks, chin, nose, and eyelids were hideously tattooed like an ancient Maori mask. Across the brow was tattooed JO'SEPH. The "O" in JO'SEPH had a tiny arrow thrust up from the right shoulder, turning it into the symbol of Mars, used by scientists to designate male sex.

"We are the Scientific Race," Jo'seph said. "I am Jo'seph; these are my people."

He gestured. Foyle gazed at the grinning crowd surrounding his litter. All faces were tattooed into devil masks; all brows had names blazoned across them.

"How long did you drift?" Jo'seph asked.

"Vorga," Foyle mumbled.

"You are the first to arrive alive in fifty years. You are a puissant man. Very. Arrival of the fittest is the doctrine of Holy Darwin. Most scientific."

"Quant Suff!" the crowd bellowed.

Jŏseph seized Foyle's elbow in the manner of a physician taking a pulse. His devil mouth counted solemnly up to ninety-eight.

"Your pulse. Ninety-eight-point-six," Jŏseph said, producing a thermometer and shaking it reverently. "Most scientific."

"Quant Suff!" came the chorus.

Jŏseph proffered an Erlenmeyer flask. It was labeled: *Lung, Cat, c.s., hematoxylin & eosin.* "Vitamin?" Jŏseph inquired.

When Foyle did not respond, Jŏseph removed a large pill from the flask, placed it in the bowl of a pipe, and lit it. He puffed once and then gestured. Three girls appeared before Foyle. Their faces were hideously tattooed. Across each brow was a name: JOAN and MOIRA and POLLY. The "O" of each name had a tiny cross at the base.

"Choose," Jŏseph said. "The Scientific People practice Natural Selection. Be scientific in your choice. Be genetic."

As Foyle fainted again, his arm slid off the litter and glanced against Moira.

"Quant Suff!"

He was in a circular hall with a domed roof. The hall was filled with rusting antique apparatus: a centrifuge, an operating table, a wrecked fluoroscope, autoclaves, cases of corroded surgical instruments.

They strapped Foyle down on the operating table while he raved and rambled. They fed him. They shaved and bathed him. Two men began turning the ancient centrifuge by hand. It emitted a rhythmic clanking like the pounding of a war drum. Those assembled began tramping and chanting.

They turned on the ancient autoclave. It boiled and geysered, filling the hall with howling steam. They turned on the old fluoroscope. It was short-circuited and spat sizzling bolts of lightning across the steaming hall.

A ten foot figure loomed up to the table. It was Jŏseph on stilts. He wore a surgical cap, a surgical mask, and a surgeon's gown that hung from his shoulders to the floor. The gown was

heavily embroidered with red and black thread illustrating anatomical sections of the body. Jŏseph was a lurid tapestry out of
a surgical text.

"I pronounce you Nomad!" Jŏseph intoned.

The uproar became deafening. Jŏseph tilted a rusty can over
Foyle's body. There was the reek of ether.

Foyle lost his tatters of consciousness and darkness enveloped him. Out of the darkness "Vorga-T:1339" surged again
and again, accelerating on a sunward course that burst through
Foyle's blood and brains until he could not stop screaming silently for vengeance.

He was dimly aware of washings and feedings and trampings
and chantings. At last he awoke to a lucid interval. There was
silence. He was in a bed. The girl, Moira, was in bed with him.

"Who you?" Foyle croaked.

"Your wife, Nomad."

"What?"

"Your wife. You chose me, Nomad. We are gametes."

"What?"

"Scientifically mated," Moira said proudly. She pulled up the
sleeve of her nightgown and showed him her arm. It was disfigured by four ugly slashes. "I have been inoculated with
something old, something new, something borrowed and something blue."

Foyle struggled out of the bed.

"Where we now?"

"In our home."

"What home?"

"Yours. You are one of us, Nomad. You must marry every
month and beget many children. That will be scientific. But I
am the first."

Foyle ignored her and explored. He was in the main cabin of
a small rocket launch of the early 2300's . . . once a private
yacht. The main cabin had been converted into a bedroom.

He lurched to the ports and looked out. The launch was
sealed into the mass of the asteroid, connected by passages to
the main body. He went aft. Two smaller cabins were filled
with growing plants for oxygen. The engine room had been
converted into a kitchen. There was Hi-Thrust in the fuel
tanks, but it fed the burners of a small stove atop the rocket

chambers. Foyle went forward. The control cabin was now a parlor, but the controls were still operative.

He thought.

He went aft to the kitchen and dismantled the stove. He reconnected the fuel tanks to the original jet combustion chambers. Moira followed him curiously.

"What are you doing, Nomad?"

"Got to get out of here, girl," Foyle mumbled. "Got business with a ship called 'Vorga.' You dig me, girl? Going to ram out in this boat, is all."

Moira backed away in alarm. Foyle saw the look in her eyes and leaped for her. He was so crippled that she avoided him easily. She opened her mouth and let out a piercing scream. At that moment a mighty clangor filled the launch; it was Jŏseph and his devil-faced Scientific People outside, banging on the metal hull, going through the ritual of a scientific charivari for the newlyweds.

Moira screamed and dodged while Foyle pursued her patiently. He trapped her in a corner, ripped her nightgown off and bound and gagged her with it. Moira made enough noise to split the asteroid open, but the scientific charivari was louder.

Foyle finished his rough patching of the engine room; he was almost an expert by now. He picked up the writhing girl and took her to the main hatch.

"Leaving," he shouted in Moira's ear. "Takeoff. Blast right out of asteroid. Hell of a smash, girl. Maybe all die, you. Everything busted wide open. Guesses for grabs what happens. No more air. No more asteroid. Go tell'm. Warn'm. Go, girl."

He opened the hatch, shoved Moira out, slammed the hatch and dogged it. The charivari stopped abruptly.

At the controls Foyle pressed ignition. The automatic take-off siren began a howl that had not sounded in decades. The jet chambers ignited with dull concussions. Foyle waited for the temperature to reach firing heat. While he waited he suffered. The launch was cemented into the asteroid. It was surrounded by stone and iron. Its rear jets were flush on the hull of another ship packed into the mass. He didn't know what would happen when his jets began their thrust, but he was driven to gamble by "Vorga."

He fired the jets. There was a hollow explosion as Hi-Thrust flamed out of the stern of the ship. The launch shuddered, yawed, heated. A squeal of metal began. Then the launch grated forward. Metal, stone and glass split asunder and the ship burst out of the asteroid into space.

The Inner Planets navy picked him up ninety thousand miles outside Mars's orbit. After seven months of shooting war, the I.P. patrols were alert but reckless. When the launch failed to answer and give recognition countersigns, it should have been shattered with a blast and questions could have been asked of the wreckage later. But the launch was small and the cruiser crew was hot for prize money. They closed and grappled.

They found Foyle inside, crawling like a headless worm through a junk heap of spaceship and home furnishings. He was bleeding again, ripe with stinking gangrene, and one side of his head was pulpy. They brought him into the sick bay aboard the cruiser and carefully curtained his tank. Foyle was no sight even for the tough stomachs of lower deck navy men.

They patched his carcass in the amniotic tank while they completed their tour of duty. On the jet back to Terra, Foyle recovered consciousness and bubbled words beginning with V. He knew he was saved. He knew that only time stood between him and vengeance. The sick bay orderly heard him exulting in his tank and parted the curtains. Foyle's filmed eyes looked up. The orderly could not restrain his curiosity.

"You hear me, man?" he whispered.

Foyle grunted. The orderly bent lower.

"What happened? Who in hell done that to you?"

"What?" Foyle croaked.

"Don't you know?"

"What? What's a matter, you?"

"Wait a minute, is all."

The orderly disappeared as he jaunted to a supply cabin, and reappeared alongside the tank five seconds later. Foyle struggled up out of the fluid. His eyes blazed.

"It's coming back, man. Some of it. Jaunte. I couldn't jaunte on the 'Nomad,' me."

"What?"

"I was off my head."

"Man, you didn't have no head left, you."

"I couldn't jaunte. I forgot how, is all. I forgot everything, me. Still don't remember much. I—"

He recoiled in terror as the orderly thrust the picture of a hideous tattooed face before him. It was a Maori mask. Cheeks, chin, nose, and eyelids were decorated with stripes and swirls. Across the brow was blazoned NOʹMAD. Foyle stared, then cried out in agony. The picture was a mirror. The face was his own.

Three

"BRAVO, Mr. Harris! Well done! L-E-S, gentlemen. Never forget. Location. Elevation. Situation. That's the only way to remember your jaunte co-ordinates. *Etre entre le marteau et l'enclume. French.* Don't jaunte yet, Mr. Peters. Wait your turn. Be patient, you'll all be C class by and by. Has anyone seen Mr. Foyle? He's missing. *Oh, look at that heavenly brown thrasher. Listen to him.* Oh dear, I'm thinking all over the place . . . or have I been speaking, gentlemen?"

"Half and half, m'am."

"It does seem unfair. One-way telepathy is a nuisance. I do apologize for shrapneling you with my thoughts."

"We like it, m'am. You think pretty."

"*How sweet of you, Mr. Gorgas.* All right, class; all back to school and we start again. Has Mr. Foyle jaunted already? I never can keep track of him."

Robin Wednesbury was conducting her re-education class in jaunting on its tour through New York City, and it was as exciting a business for the cerebral cases as it was for the children in her primer class. She treated the adults like children and they rather enjoyed it. For the past month they had been memorizing jaunte stages at street intersections, chanting: "L-E-S, m'am. Location. Elevation. Situation."

She was a tall, lovely Negro girl, brilliant and cultivated, but handicapped by the fact that she was a telesend, a one-way telepath. She could broadcast her thoughts to the world, but could receive nothing. This was a disadvantage that barred her from more glamorous careers, yet suited her for teaching. Despite her volatile temperament, Robin Wednesbury was a thorough and methodical jaunte instructor.

The men were brought down from General War Hospital to the jaunte school, which occupied an entire building in the Hudson Bridge at 42nd Street. They started from the school and marched in a sedate crocodile to the vast Times Square jaunte stage, which they earnestly memorized. Then they all jaunted to the school and back to Times Square. The crocodile reformed and they marched up to Columbus Circle and memorized its co-ordinates. Then all jaunted back to school via Times Square and returned by the same route to Columbus Circle. Once more the crocodile formed and off they went to Grand Army Plaza to repeat the memorizing and the jaunting.

Robin was re-educating the patients (all head injuries who had lost the power to jaunte) to the express stops, so to speak, of the public jaunte stages. Later they would memorize the local stops at street intersections. As their horizons expanded (and their powers returned) they would memorize jaunte stages in widening circles, limited as much by income as ability; for one thing was certain: you had to actually see a place to memorize it, which meant you first had to pay for the transportation to get you there. Even 3D photographs would not do the trick. The Grand Tour had taken on a new significance for the rich.

"Location. Elevation. Situation," Robin Wednesbury lectured, and the class jaunted by express stages from Washington Heights to the Hudson Bridge and back again in primer jumps of a quarter mile each; following their lovely Negro teacher earnestly.

The little technical sergeant with the platinum skull suddenly spoke in the gutter tongue: "But there ain't no elevation, m'am. We're on the ground, us."

"*Isn't, Sgt. Logan. 'Isn't any' would be better.* I beg your pardon. Teaching becomes a habit and I'm having trouble controlling my thinking today. The war news is so bad. We'll get to Elevation when we start memorizing the stages on top of skyscrapers, Sgt. Logan."

The man with the rebuilt skull digested that, then asked: "We hear you when you think, is a matter you?"

"Exactly."

"But you don't hear us?"

"Never. I'm a one-way telepath."

"We all hear you, or just I, is all?"

"That depends, Sgt. Logan. When I'm concentrating, just the one I'm thinking at; when I'm at loose ends, anybody and everybody . . . poor souls. Excuse me." Robin turned and called: "Don't hesitate before jaunting, Chief Harris. That starts doubting, and doubting ends jaunting. Just step up and bang off."

"I worry sometimes, m'am," a chief petty officer with a tightly bandaged head answered. He was obviously stalling at the edge of the jaunte stage.

"Worry? About what?"

"Maybe there's gonna be somebody standing where I arrive. Then there'll be a hell of a real bang, m'am. Excuse me."

"Now I've explained that a hundred times. Experts have gauged every jaunte stage in the world to accommodate peak traffic. That's why private jaunte stages are small, and the Times Square stage is two hundred yards wide. It's all been worked out mathematically and there isn't one chance in ten million of a simultaneous arrival. That's less than your chance of being killed in a jet accident."

The bandaged C.P.O. nodded dubiously and stepped up on the raised stage. It was of white concrete, round, and decorated on its face with vivid black and white patterns as an aid to memory. In the center was an illuminated plaque which gave its name and jaunte co-ordinates of latitude, longitude, and elevation.

At the moment when the bandaged man was gathering courage for his primer jaunte, the stage began to flicker with a sudden flurry of arrivals and departures. Figures appeared momentarily as they jaunted in, hesitated while they checked their surroundings and set new co-ordinates, and then disappeared as they jaunted off. At each disappearance there was a faint "Pop" as displaced air rushed into the space formerly occupied by a body.

"Wait, class," Robin called. "There's a rush on. Everybody off the stage, please."

Laborers in heavy work clothes, still spattered with snow, were on their way south to their homes after a shift in the north woods. Fifty white clad dairy clerks were headed west toward St. Louis. They followed the morning from the Eastern Time Zone to the Pacific Zone. And from eastern Greenland, where it was already noon, a horde of white-collar office workers was pouring into New York for their lunch hour.

The rush was over in a few moments. "All right, class," Robin called. "We'll continue. Oh dear, where *is* Mr. Foyle? He always seems to be missing."

"With a face like he's got, him, you can't blame him for hiding it, m'am. Up in the cerebral ward we call him Boogey."

"He does look dreadful, doesn't he, Sgt. Logan. Can't they get those marks off?"

"They're trying, Miss Robin, but they don't know how yet. It's called 'tattooing' and it's sort of forgotten, is all."

"Then how did Mr. Foyle acquire his face?"

"Nobody knows, Miss Robin. He's up in cerebral because he's lost his mind, him. Can't remember nothing. Me personal, if I had a face like that I wouldn't want to remember nothing too."

"It's a pity. He looks frightful. Sgt. Logan, d'you suppose I've let a thought about Mr. Foyle slip and hurt his feelings?"

The little man with the platinum skull considered. "No, m'am. You wouldn't hurt nobody's feelings, you. And Foyle ain't got none to hurt, him. He's just a big, dumb ox, is all."

"I have to be so careful, Sgt. Logan. You see, no one likes to know what another person really thinks about him. We imagine that we do, but we don't. *This telesending of mine makes me loathed. And lonesome. I—Please don't listen to me. I'm having trouble controlling my thinking.* Ah! There you are, Mr. Foyle. Where in the world have you been wandering?"

Foyle had jaunted in on the stage and stepped off quietly, his hideous face averted. "Been practicing, me," he mumbled.

Robin repressed the shudder of revulsion in her and went to him sympathetically. She took his arm. "You really should be with us more. We're all friends and having a lovely time. Join in."

Foyle refused to meet her glance. As he pulled his arm away from her sullenly, Robin suddenly realized that his sleeve was soaking wet. His entire hospital uniform was drenched.

"Wet? He's been in the rain somewhere. But I've seen the morning weather reports. No rain east of St. Louis. Then he must have

jaunted further than that. But he's not supposed to be able. He's supposed to have lost all memory and ability to jaunte. He's ma-lingering."

Foyle leapt at her. "Shut up, you!" The savagery of his face was terrifying.

"Then you are malingering."

"How much do you know?"

"That you're a fool. Stop making a scene."

"Did they hear you?"

"*I don't know. Let go of me.*" Robin turned away from Foyle. "All right, class. We're finished for the day. All back to school for the hospital bus. You jaunte first, Sgt. Logan. Remember: L-E-S. Location. Elevation. Situation . . ."

"What do you want?" Foyle growled. "A pay-off, you?"

"*Be quiet. Stop making a scene.* Now don't hesitate, Chief Harris. Step up and jaunte off."

"I want to talk to you."

"*Certainly not.* Wait your turn, Mr. Peters. Don't be in such a hurry."

"You going to report me in the hospital?"

"Naturally."

"I want to talk to you."

"No."

"They gone now, all. We got time. I'll meet you in your apartment."

"My apartment?" Robin was genuinely frightened.

"In Green Bay, Wisconsin."

"This is absurd. I've got nothing to discuss with this—"

"You got plenty, Miss Robin. You got a family to discuss."

Foyle grinned at the terror she radiated. "Meet you in your apartment," he repeated.

"You can't possibly know where it is," she faltered.

"Just told you, didn't I?"

"Y-You couldn't possibly jaunte that far. You—"

"No?" The mask grinned. "You just told me I was mal— that word. You told the truth, you. We got half an hour. Meet you there."

Robin Wednesbury's apartment was in a massive building set alone on the shore of Green Bay. The apartment house looked as though a magician had removed it from a city residential area and abandoned it amidst the Wisconsin pines. Buildings like this were a commonplace in the jaunting world. With self-contained heat and light plants, and jaunting to solve the transportation problem, single and multiple dwellings were built in desert, forest, and wilderness.

The apartment itself was a four-room flat, heavily insulated to protect neighbors from Robin's telesending. It was crammed with books, music, paintings, and prints . . . all evidence of the cultured and lonely life of this unfortunate wrong-way telepath.

Robin jaunted into the living room of the apartment a few seconds after Foyle who was waiting for her with ferocious impatience.

"So now you know for sure," he began without preamble. He seized her arm in a painful grip. "But you ain't gonna tell nobody in the hospital about me, Miss Robin. Nobody."

"Let go of me!" Robin lashed him across his face. *"Beast! Savage! Don't you dare touch me!"*

Foyle released her and stepped back. The impact of her revulsion made him turn away angrily to conceal his face.

"So you've been malingering. You knew how to jaunte. You've been jaunting all the while you've been pretending to learn in the primer class . . . taking big jumps around the country; around the world, for all I know."

"Yeah. I go from Times Square to Columbus Circle by way of . . . most anywhere, Miss Robin."

"And that's why you're always missing. But why? Why? What are you up to?"

An expression of possessed cunning appeared on the hideous face. "I'm holed up in General Hospital, me. It's my base of operations, see? I'm settling something, Miss Robin. I got a debt to pay off, me. I had to find out where a certain ship is. Now I got to pay her back. Now I rot you, 'Vorga.' I kill you, 'Vorga.' I kill you filthy!"

He stopped shouting and glared at her in wild triumph. Robin backed away in alarm.

"For God's sake, what are you talking about?"

" 'Vorga.' 'Vorga-T:1339.' Ever hear of her, Miss Robin? I found out where she is from Bo'ness & Uig's ship registry. Bo'ness & Uig are out in SanFran. I went there, me, the time when you was learning us the crosstown jaunte stages. Went out to SanFran, me. Found 'Vorga,' me. She's in Vancouver shipyards. She's owned by Presteign of Presteign. Heard of him, Miss Robin? Presteign's the biggest man on Terra, is all. But he won't stop me. I'll kill 'Vorga' filthy. And you won't stop me neither, Miss Robin."

Foyle thrust his face close to hers. "Because I cover myself, Miss Robin. I cover every weak spot down the line. I got something on everybody who could stop me before I kill 'Vorga' . . . including you, Miss Robin."

"No."

"Yeah. I found out where you live. They know up at the hospital. I come here and looked around. I read your diary, Miss Robin. You got a family on Callisto, mother and two sisters."

"For God's sake!"

"So that makes you alien-belligerent. When the war started you and all the rest was given one month to get out of the Inner Planets and go home. Any which didn't became spies by law." Foyle opened his hand. "I got you right here, girl." He clenched his hand.

"My mother and sisters have been trying to leave Callisto for a year and a half. We belong here. We—"

"Got you right here," Foyle repeated. "You know what they do to spies? They cut information out of them. They cut you apart, Miss Robin. They take you apart, piece by piece—"

The Negro girl screamed. Foyle nodded happily and took her shaking shoulders in his hands. "I got you, is all, girl. You can't even run from me because all I got to do is tip Intelligence and where are you? There ain't nothing nobody can do to stop me; not the hospital or even Mr. Holy Mighty Presteign of Presteign."

"Get out, you filthy, hideous . . . thing. Get out!"

"You don't like my face, Miss Robin? There ain't nothing you can do about that either."

Suddenly he picked her up and carried her to a deep couch. He threw her down on the couch.

"Nothing," he repeated.

Devoted to the principle of conspicuous waste, on which all society is based, Presteign of Presteign had fitted his Victorian mansion in Central Park with elevators, house phones, dumb-waiters and all the other labor-saving devices which jaunting had made obsolete. The servants in that giant gingerbread castle walked dutifully from room to room, opening and closing doors, and climbing stairs.

Presteign of Presteign arose, dressed with the aid of his valet and barber, descended to the morning room with the aid of an elevator, and breakfasted, assisted by a butler, footman, and waitresses. He left the morning room and entered his study. In an age when communication systems were virtually extinct—when it was far easier to jaunte directly to a man's office for a discussion than to telephone or telegraph—Presteign still maintained an antique telephone switchboard with an operator in his study.

"Get me Dagenham," he said.

The operator struggled and at last put a call through to Dagenham Couriers, Inc. This was a hundred million credit organization of bonded jaunters guaranteed to perform any public or confidential service for any principal. Their fee was ₵r 1 per mile. Dagenham guaranteed to get a courier around the world in eighty minutes.

Eighty seconds after Presteign's call was put through, a Dagenham courier appeared on the private jaunte stage outside Presteign's home, was identified and admitted through the jaunte-proof labyrinth behind the entrance. Like every member of the Dagenham staff, he was an M class jaunter, capable of teleporting a thousand miles a jump indefinitely, and familiar with thousands of jaunte co-ordinates. He was a senior specialist in chicanery and cajolery, trained to the incisive efficiency and boldness that characterized Dagenham Couriers and reflected the ruthlessness of its founder.

"Presteign?" he said, wasting no time on protocol.

"I want to hire Dagenham."

"Ready, Presteign."

"Not you. I want Saul Dagenham himself."

"Mr. Dagenham no longer gives personal service for less than ₵r 100,000."

"The amount will be five times that."

"Fee or percentage?"

"Both. Quarter of a million fee, and a quarter of a million guaranteed against 10 per cent of the total amount at risk."

"Agreed. The matter?"

"PyrE."

"Spell it, please."

"The name means nothing to you?"

"No."

"Good. It will to Dagenham. PyrE. Capital P-y-r Capital E. Pronounced "pyre" as in funeral pyre. Tell Dagenham we've located the PyrE. He's engaged to get it . . . at all costs . . . through a man named Foyle. Gulliver Foyle."

The courier produced a tiny silver pearl, a memo-bead, repeated Presteign's instructions into it, and left without another word. Presteign turned to his telephone operator. "Get me Regis Sheffield," he directed.

Ten minutes after the call went through to Regis Sheffield's law office, a young law clerk appeared on Presteign's private jaunte stage, was vetted and admitted through the maze. He was a bright young man with a scrubbed face and the expression of a delighted rabbit.

"Excuse the delay, Presteign," he said. "We got your call in Chicago and I'm still only a D class five hundred miler. Took me a while getting here."

"Is your chief trying a case in Chicago?"

"Chicago, New York *and* Washington. He's been on the jaunte from court to court all morning. We fill in for him when he's in another court."

"I want to retain him."

"Honored, Presteign, but Mr. Sheffield's pretty busy."

"Not too busy for PyrE."

"Sorry, sir; I don't quite—"

"No, you don't, but Sheffield will. Just tell him: PyrE as in funeral pyre, and the amount of his fee."

"Which is?"

"Quarter of a million retainer and a quarter of a million guaranteed against 10 per cent of the total amount at risk."

"And what performance is required of Mr. Sheffield?"

"To prepare every known legal device for kidnaping a man and holding him against the army, the navy and the police."

"Quite. And the man?"

"Gulliver Foyle."

The law clerk muttered quick notes into a memo-bead,

thrust the bead into his ear, listened, nodded and departed. Presteign left the study and ascended the plush stairs to his daughter's suite to pay his morning respects.

In the homes of the wealthy, the rooms of the female members were blind, without windows or doors, open only to the jaunting of intimate members of the family. Thus was morality maintained and chastity defended. But since Olivia Presteign was herself blind to normal sight, she could not jaunte. Consequently her suite was entered through doors closely guarded by ancient retainers in the Presteign clan livery.

Olivia Presteign was a glorious albino. Her hair was white silk, her skin was white satin, her nails, her lips, and her eyes were coral. She was beautiful and blind in a wonderful way, for she could see in the infrared only, from 7,500 angstroms to one millimeter wavelengths. She saw heat waves, magnetic fields, radio waves, radar, sonar, and electromagnetic fields.

She was holding her Grand Levee in the drawing room of the suite. She sat in a brocaded wing chair, sipping tea, guarded by her duenna, holding court, chatting with a dozen men and women standing about the room. She looked like an exquisite statue of marble and coral, her blind eyes flashing as she saw and yet did not see.

She saw the drawing room as a pulsating flow of heat emanations ranging from hot highlights to cool shadows. She saw the dazzling magnetic patterns of clocks, phones, lights, and locks. She saw and recognized people by the characteristic heat patterns radiated by their faces and bodies. She saw, around each head, an aura of the faint electromagnetic brain pattern, and sparkling through the heat radiation of each body, the everchanging tone of muscle and nerve.

Presteign did not care for the artists, musicians, and fops Olivia kept about her, but he was pleased to see a scattering of society notables this morning. There was a Sears-Roebuck, a Gillette, young Sidney Kodak who would one day be Kodak of Kodak, a Houbigant, Buick of Buick, and R. H. Macy XVI, head of the powerful Saks-Gimbel clan.

Presteign paid his respects to his daughter and left the house. He set off for his clan headquarters at 99 Wall Street in a coach and four driven by a coachman assisted by a groom, both wearing the Presteign trademark of red, black, and blue. That black "P" on a field of scarlet and cobalt was one of the most ancient and distinguished trademarks in the social register, rivaling the "57" of the Heinz clan and the "RR" of the Rolls-Royce dynasty in antiquity.

The head of the Presteign clan was a familiar sight to New York jaunters. Iron gray, handsome, powerful, impeccably dressed and mannered in the old-fashioned style, Presteign of Presteign was the epitome of the socially elect, for he was so exalted in station that he employed coachmen, grooms, hostlers, stableboys, and horses to perform a function for him which ordinary mortals performed by jaunting.

As men climbed the social ladder, they displayed their position by their refusal to jaunte. The newly adopted into a great commercial clan rode an expensive bicycle. A rising clansman drove a small sports car. The captain of a sept was transported in a chauffeur-driven antique from the old days, a vintage Bentley or Cadillac or a towering Lagonda. An heir presumptive in direct line of succession to the clan chieftainship staffed a yacht or a plane. Presteign of Presteign, head of the clan Presteign, owned carriages, cars, yachts, planes, and trains. His position in society was so lofty that he had not jaunted in forty years. Secretly he scorned the bustling new-rich like the Dagenhams and Sheffields who still jaunted and were unashamed.

Presteign entered the crenelated keep at 99 Wall Street that was Castle Presteign. It was staffed and guarded by his famous Jaunte-Watch, all in clan livery. Presteign walked with the stately gait of a chieftain as they piped him to his office. Indeed he was grander than a chieftain, as an importunate government official awaiting audience discovered to his dismay. That unfortunate man leaped forward from the waiting crowd of petitioners as Presteign passed.

"Mr. Presteign," he began. "I'm from the Internal Revenue Department, I must see you this morn—" Presteign cut him short with an icy stare.

"There are thousands of Presteigns," he pronounced. "All are addressed as Mister. But I am Presteign of Presteign, head of house and sept, first of the family, chieftain of the clan. I am addressed as Presteign. Not 'Mister' Presteign. Presteign."

He turned and entered his office where his staff greeted him with a muted chorus: "Good morning, Presteign."

Presteign nodded, smiled his basilisk smile and seated himself behind the enthroned desk while the Jaunte-Watch skirled their pipes and ruffled their drums. Presteign signaled for the audience to begin. The Household Equerry stepped forward with a scroll. Presteign disdained memo-beads and all mechanical business devices.

"Report on Clan Presteign enterprises," the Equerry began. "Common Stock: High—201½, Low—201¼. Average quotations New York, Paris, Ceylon, Tokyo—"

Presteign waved his hand irritably. The Equerry retired to be replaced by Black Rod.

"Another Mr. Presto to be invested, Presteign."

Presteign restrained his impatience and went through the tedious ceremony of swearing in the 497th Mr. Presto in the hierarchy of Presteign Prestos who managed the shops in the Presteign retail division. Until recently the man had had a face and body of his own. Now, after years of cautious testing and careful indoctrination, he had been elected to join the Prestos.

After six months of surgery and psycho-conditioning, he was identical with the other 496 Mr. Prestos and to the idealized portrait of Mr. Presto which hung behind Presteign's dais . . . a kindly, honest man resembling Abraham Lincoln, a man who instantly inspired affection and trust. Around the world purchasers entered an identical Presteign store and were greeted by an identical manager, Mr. Presto. He was rivaled, but not surpassed, by the Kodak clan's Mr. Kwik and Montgomery Ward's Uncle Monty.

When the ceremony was completed, Presteign arose abruptly to indicate that the public investiture was ended. The office was cleared of all but the high officials. Presteign paced, obviously repressing his seething impatience. He never swore, but his restraint was more terrifying than profanity.

"Foyle," he said in a suffocated voice. "A common sailor. Dirt. Dregs. Gutter scum. But that man stands between me and—"

"If you please, Presteign," Black Rod interrupted timidly. "It's eleven o'clock Eastern time; eight o'clock Pacific time."

"What?"

"If you please, Presteign, may I remind you that there is a launching ceremony at nine, Pacific time? You are to preside at the Vancouver shipyards."

"Launching?"

"Our new freighter, the Presteign 'Princess.' It will take some time to establish three dimensional broadcast contact with the shipyard so we had better—"

"I will attend in person."

"In person!" Black Rod faltered. "But we cannot possibly fly to Vancouver in an hour, Presteign. We—"

"I will jaunte," Presteign of Presteign snapped. Such was his agitation.

His appalled staff made hasty preparations. Messengers jaunted ahead to warn the Presteign offices across the country, and the private jaunte stages were cleared. Presteign was ushered to the stage within his New York office. It was a circular platform in a black-hung room without windows—a masking and concealment necessary to prevent unauthorized persons from discovering and memorizing co-ordinates. For the same reason, all homes and offices had one-way windows and confusion labyrinths behind their doors.

To jaunte it was necessary (among other things) for a man to know exactly where he was and where he was going, or there was little hope of arriving anywhere alive. It was as impossible to jaunte from an undetermined starting point as it was to arrive at an unknown destination. Like shooting a pistol, one had to know where to aim and which end of the gun to hold. But a glance through a window or door might be enough to enable a man to memorize the L-E-S co-ordinates of a place.

Presteign stepped on the stage, visualized the co-ordinates of his destination in the Philadelphia office, seeing the picture clearly and the position accurately. He relaxed and energized one concentrated thrust of will and belief toward the target. He jaunted. There was a dizzy moment in which his eyes blurred. The New York stage faded out of focus; the Philadelphia stage blurred into focus. There was a sensation of falling down, and then up. He arrived. Black Rod and others of his staff arrived a respectful moment later.

So, in jauntes of one and two hundred miles each, Presteign crossed the continent, and arrived outside the Vancouver shipping yards at exactly nine o'clock in the morning, Pacific time.

He had left New York at 11 A.M. He had gained two hours of daylight. This, too, was a commonplace in a jaunting world.

The square mile of unfenced concrete (what fence could bar a jaunter?) comprising the shipyard, looked like a white table covered with black pennies neatly arranged in concentric circles. But on closer approach, the pennies enlarged into the hundred-foot mouths of black pits dug deep into the bowels of the earth. Each circular mouth was rimmed with concrete buildings, offices, check rooms, canteens, changing rooms.

These were the take-off and landing pits, the drydock and construction pits of the shipyards. Spaceships, like sailing vessels, were never designed to support their own weight unaided against the drag of gravity. Normal terran gravity would crack the spine of a spaceship like an eggshell. The ships were built in deep pits, standing vertically in a network of catwalks and construction grids, braced and supported by anti-gravity screens. They took off from similar pits, riding the anti-grav beams upward like motes mounting the vertical shaft of a searchlight until at last they reached the Roche Limit and could thrust with their own jets. Landing spacecraft cut drive jets and rode the same beams downward into the pits.

As the Presteign entourage entered the Vancouver yards they could see which of the pits were in use. From some the noses and hulls of spaceships extruded, raised a quarterway or halfway above ground by the anti-grav screens as workmen in the pits below brought their aft sections to particular operational levels. Three Presteign V-class transports, "Vega," "Vestal," and "Vorga," stood partially raised near the center of the yards, undergoing flaking and replating, as the heat-lightning flicker of torches around "Vorga" indicated.

At the concrete building marked: ENTRY, the Presteign entourage stopped before a sign that read:

> YOU ARE ENDANGERING YOUR LIFE
> IF YOU ENTER THESE PREMISES UN-
> LAWFULLY. *YOU HAVE BEEN WARNED!*

Visitor badges were distributed to the party, and even Presteign of Presteign received a badge. He dutifully pinned it on for he well knew what the result of entry without such a protective badge would be. The entourage continued, winding its way through pits until it arrived at 0-3, where the pit mouth was decorated with bunting in the Presteign colors and a small grandstand had been erected.

Presteign was welcomed and, in turn, greeted his various officials. The Presteign band struck up the clan song, bright and brassy, but one of the instruments appeared to have gone insane. It struck a brazen note that blared louder and louder until it engulfed the entire band and the surprised exclamations. Only then did Presteign realize that it was not an instrument sounding, but the shipyard alarm.

An intruder was in the yard, someone not wearing an identification or visitor's badge. The radar field of the protection system was tripped and the alarm sounded. Through the raucous bellow of the alarm, Presteign could hear a multitude of "pops" as the yard guards jaunted from the grandstand and took positions around the square mile of concrete field. His own Jaunte-Watch closed in around him, looking wary and alert.

A voice began blaring on the P.A., co-ordinating defense. "UNKNOWN IN YARD. UNKNOWN IN YARD AT E FOR EDWARD NINE. E FOR EDWARD NINE MOVING WEST ON FOOT."

"Someone must have broken in," Black Rod shouted.

"I'm aware of that," Presteign answered calmly.

"He must be a stranger if he's not jaunting in here."

"I'm aware of that also."

"UNKNOWN APPROACHING D FOR DAVID FIVE. D FOR DAVID FIVE. STILL ON FOOT. D FOR DAVID FIVE ALERT."

"What in God's name is he up to?" Black Rod exclaimed.

"You are aware of my rule, sir," Presteign said coldly. "No associate of the Presteign clan may take the name of the Divinity in vain. You forget yourself."

"UNKNOWN NOW APPROACHING C FOR CHARLEY FIVE. NOW APPROACHING C FOR CHARLEY FIVE."

Black Rod touched Presteign's arm. "He's coming this way, Presteign. Will you take cover, please?"

"I will not."

"Presteign, there have been assassination attempts before. Three of them. If—"

"How do I get to the top of this stand?"

"Presteign!"

"Help me up."

Aided by Black Rod, still protesting hysterically, Presteign climbed to the top of the grandstand to watch the power of the Presteign clan in action against danger. Below he could see workmen in white jumpers swarming out of the pits to watch the excitement. Guards were appearing as they jaunted from distant sectors toward the focal point of the action.

"UNKNOWN MOVING SOUTH TOWARD B FOR BAKER THREE. B FOR BAKER THREE."

Presteign watched the B-3 pit. A figure appeared, dashing swiftly toward the pit, veering, dodging, bulling forward. It was a giant man in hospital blues with a wild thatch of black hair and a distorted face that appeared, in the distance, to be painted in livid colors. His clothes were flickering like heat lightning as the protective induction field of the defense system seared him.

"B FOR BAKER THREE ALERT. B FOR BAKER THREE CLOSE IN."

There were shouts and a distant rattle of shots, the pneumatic whine of scope guns. Half a dozen workmen in white leaped for the intruder. He scattered them like ninepins and drove on and on toward B-3 where the nose of "Vorga" showed. He was a lightning bolt driving through workmen and guards, pivoting, bludgeoning, boring forward implacably.

Suddenly he stopped, reached inside his flaming jacket and withdrew a black cannister. With the convulsive gesture of an animal writhing in death throes, he bit the end of the cannister and hurled it, straight and true on a high arc toward "Vorga." The next instant he was struck down.

"EXPLOSIVE. TAKE COVER. EXPLOSIVE. TAKE COVER. COVER."

"Presteign!" Black Rod squawked.

Presteign shook him off and watched the cannister curve up and then down toward the nose of "Vorga," spinning and glinting in the cold sunlight. At the edge of the pit it was caught by the anti-grav beam and flicked upwards as by a giant invisible thumbnail. Up and up and up it whirled, one hundred, five hundred, a thousand feet. Then there was a blinding flash, and an instant later a titanic clap of thunder that smote ears and jarred teeth and bone.

Presteign picked himself up and descended the grandstand to the launching podium. He placed his finger on the launching button of the Presteign "Princess."

"Bring me that man, if he's still alive," he said to Black Rod. He pressed the button. "I christen thee . . . the Presteign 'Power,'" he called in triumph.

Four

THE star chamber in Castle Presteign was an oval room with ivory panels picked out with gold, high mirrors, and stained glass windows. It contained a gold organ with robot organist by Tiffany, a gold-tooled library with android librarian on library ladder, a Louis Quinze desk with android secretary before a manual memo-bead recorder, an American bar with robot bartender. Presteign would have preferred human servants, but androids and robots kept secrets.

"Be seated, Captain Yeovil," he said courteously. "This is Mr. Regis Sheffield, representing me in this matter. That young man is Mr. Sheffield's assistant."

"Bunny's my portable law library," Sheffield grunted.

Presteign touched a control. The still life in the star chamber came alive. The organist played, the librarian sorted books, the secretary typed, the bartender shook drinks. It was spectacular; and the impact, carefully calculated by industrial psychometrists, established control for Presteign and put visitors at a disadvantage.

"You spoke of a man named Foyle, Captain Yeovil?" Presteign prompted.

Captain Peter Y'ang-Yeovil of Central Intelligence was a lineal descendant of the learned Mencius and belonged to the Intelligence Tong of the Inner Planets Armed Forces. For two hundred years the IPAF had entrusted its intelligence work to the Chinese who, with a five thousand–year history of cultivated subtlety behind them, had achieved wonders. Captain Y'ang-Yeovil was a member of the dreaded Society of Paper Men, an adept of the Tientsin Image Makers, a Master of Superstition, and fluent in the Secret Speech. He did not look Chinese.

Y'ang-Yeovil hesitated, fully aware of the psychological pressures operating against him. He examined Presteign's ascetic, basilisk face; Sheffield's blunt, aggressive expression; and the eager young man named Bunny whose rabbit features had an unmistakable Oriental cast. It was necessary for Yeovil to reestablish control or effect a compromise.

He opened with a flanking movement. "Are we related anywhere within fifteen degrees of consanguinity?" he asked Bunny in the Mandarin dialect. "I am of the house of the learned Meng-Tse whom the barbarians call Mencius."

"Then we are hereditary enemies," Bunny answered in faltering Mandarin. "For the formidable ancestor of my line was deposed as governor of Shan-tung in 342 B.C. by the earth pig Meng-Tse."

"With all courtesy I shave your ill-formed eyebrows," Y'ang-Yeovil said.

"Most respectfully I singe your snaggle teeth." Bunny laughed.

"Come, sirs," Presteign protested.

"We are reaffirming a three thousand–year blood feud," Y'ang-Yeovil explained to Presteign, who looked sufficiently unsettled by the conversation and the laughter which he did not understand. He tried a direct thrust. "When will you be finished with Foyle?" he asked.

"What Foyle?" Sheffield cut in.

"What Foyle have you got?"

"There are thirteen of that name associated with the clan Presteign."

"An interesting number. Did you know I was a Master of Superstition? Some day I must show you the Mirror-And-Listen Mystery. I refer to the Foyle involved in a reported attempt on Mr. Presteign's life this morning."

"Presteign," Presteign corrected. "I am not 'Mister.' I am Presteign of Presteign."

"Three attempts have been made on Presteign's life," Sheffield said. "You'll have to be more specific."

"Three this morning? Presteign must have been busy." Y'ang-Yeovil sighed. Sheffield was proving himself a resolute opponent. The Intelligence man tried another diversion. "I do wish our Mr. Presto had been more specific."

"*Your* Mr. Presto!" Presteign exclaimed.

"Oh yes. Didn't you know one of your five hundred Prestos was an agent of ours? That's odd. We took it for granted you'd find out and went ahead with a confusion operation."

Presteign looked appalled. Y'ang-Yeovil crossed his legs and continued to chat breezily. "That's the basic weakness in routine intelligence procedure; you start finessing before finesse is required."

"He's bluffing," Presteign burst out. "None of our Prestos could possibly have any knowledge of Gulliver Foyle."

"Thank you." Y'ang-Yeovil smiled. "That's the Foyle I want. When can you let us have him?"

Sheffield scowled at Presteign and then turned on Y'ang-Yeovil. "Who's 'us'?" he demanded.

"Central Intelligence."

"Why do you want him?"

"Do you make love to a woman before or after you take your clothes off?"

"That's a damned impertinent question to ask."

"And so was yours. When can you let us have Foyle?"

"When you show cause."

"To whom?"

"To me." Sheffield hammered a heavy forefinger against his palm. "This is a civilian matter concerning civilians. Unless war material, war personnel, or the strategy and tactics of a war-in-being are involved, civilian jurisdiction shall always prevail."

"303 Terran Appeals 191," murmured Bunny.

"The 'Nomad' was carrying war material."

"The 'Nomad' was transporting platinum bullion to Mars Bank," Presteign snapped. "If money is a—"

"*I* am leading this discussion," Sheffield interrupted. He swung around on Y'ang-Yeovil. "Name the war material."

This blunt challenge knocked Y'ang-Yeovil off balance. He knew that the crux of the "Nomad" situation was the presence on board the ship of 20 pounds of PyrE, the total world supply, which was probably irreplaceable now that its discoverer had disappeared. He knew that Sheffield knew that they both knew this. He had assumed that Sheffield would prefer to keep

PyrE unnamed. And yet, here was the challenge to name the unnamable.

He attempted to meet bluntness with bluntness. "All right, gentlemen, I'll name it now. The 'Nomad' was transporting twenty pounds of a substance called PyrE."

Presteign started; Sheffield silenced him. "What's PyrE?"

"According to our reports—"

"From Presteign's Mr. Presto?"

"Oh, that was bluff," Y'ang-Yeovil laughed, and momentarily regained control. "According to Intelligence, PyrE was developed for Presteign by a man who subsequently disappeared. PyrE is a Misch Metal, a pyrophore. That's all we know for a fact. But we've had vague reports about it . . . Unbelievable reports from reputable agents. If a fraction of our inferences are correct, PyrE could make the difference between a victory and a defeat."

"Nonsense. No war material has ever made that much difference."

"No? I cite the fission bomb of 1945. I cite the Null-G antigravity installations of 2022. Talley's All-Field Radar Trip Screen of 2194. Material can often make the difference, especially when there's the chance of the enemy getting it first."

"There's no such chance now."

"Thank you for admitting the importance of PyrE."

"I admit nothing; I deny everything."

"Central Intelligence is prepared to offer an exchange. A man for a man. The inventor of PyrE for Gully Foyle."

"You've got him?" Sheffield demanded. "Then why badger us for Foyle?"

"Because we've got a corpse!" Y'ang-Yeovil flared. "The Outer Satellites command had him on Lassell for six months trying to carve information out of him. We pulled him out with a raid at a cost of 79 per cent casualties. We rescued a corpse. We still don't know if the Outer Satellites were having a cynical laugh at our expense letting us recapture a body. We still don't know how much they ripped out of him."

Presteign sat bolt upright at this. His merciless fingers tapped slowly and sharply.

"Damn it," Y'ang-Yeovil stormed. "Can't you recognize a crisis, Sheffield? We're on a tightrope. What the devil are you

doing backing Presteign in this shabby deal? You're the leader
of the Liberal party . . . Terra's archpatriot. You're Presteign's
political archenemy. Sell him out, you fool, before he sells us
all out."

"Captain Yeovil," Presteign broke in with icy venom. "These
expressions cannot be countenanced."

"We want and need PyrE," Y'ang-Yeovil continued. "We'll
have to investigate that twenty pounds of PyrE, rediscover the
synthesis, learn to apply it to the war effort . . . and all this
before the O.S. beats us to the punch, if they haven't already.
But Presteign refuses to co-operate. Why? Because he's opposed
to the party in power. He wants no military victories for the
Liberals. He'd rather we lost the war for the sake of politics
because rich men like Presteign never lose. Come to your
senses, Sheffield. You've been retained by a traitor. What in
God's name are you trying to do?"

Before Sheffield could answer, there was a discreet tap on
the door of the Star Chamber and Saul Dagenham was ushered
in. Time was when Dagenham was one of the Inner Planets'
research wizards, a physicist with inspired intuition, total recall,
and a sixth-order computer for a brain. But there was an accident at Tycho Sands, and the fission blast that should have
killed him did not. Instead it turned him dangerously radioactive; it turned him "hot"; it transformed him into a twenty-
fifth century "Typhoid Mary."

He was paid ₵r 25,000 a year by the Inner Planets government to take precautions which they trusted him to carry out.
He avoided physical contact with any person for more than five
minutes per day. He could not occupy any room other than his
own for more than thirty minutes a day. Commanded and paid
by the IP to isolate himself, Dagenham had abandoned research
and built the colossus of Dagenham Couriers, Inc.

When Y'ang-Yeovil saw the short blond cadaver with leaden
skin and death's-head smile enter the Star Chamber, he knew
he was assured of defeat in this encounter. He was no match
for the three men together. He arose at once.

"I'm getting an Admiralty order for Foyle," he said. "As far
as Intelligence is concerned, all negotiations are ended. From
now on it's war."

"Captain Yeovil is leaving," Presteign called to the Jaunte-

Watch officer who had guided Dagenham in. "Please see him out through the maze."

Y'ang-Yeovil waited until the officer stepped alongside him and bowed. Then, as the man courteously motioned to the door, Y'ang-Yeovil looked directly at Presteign, smiled ironically, and disappeared with a faint Pop!

"Presteign!" Bunny exclaimed. "He jaunted. This room isn't blind to him. He—"

"Evidently," Presteign said icily. "Inform the Master of the Household," he instructed the amazed Watch officer. "The co-ordinates of the Star Chamber are no longer secret. They must be changed within twenty-four hours. And now, Mr. Dagenham . . ."

"One minute," Dagenham said. "There's that Admiralty order."

Without apology or explanation he disappeared too. Presteign raised his eyebrows. "Another party to the Star Chamber secret," he murmured. "But at least he had the tact to conceal his knowledge until the secret was out."

Dagenham reappeared. "No point wasting time going through the motions of the maze," he said. "I've given orders in Washington. They'll hold Yeovil up; two hours guaranteed, three hours probably, four hours possible."

"How will they hold him up?" Bunny asked.

Dagenham gave him his deadly smile. "Standard FFCC Operation of Dagenham Couriers. Fun, fantasy, confusion, catastrophe. . . . We'll need all four hours. Damn! I've disrupted your dolls, Presteign." The robots were suddenly capering in lunatic fashion as Dagenham's hard radiation penetrated their electronic systems. "No matter, I'll be on my way."

"Foyle?" Presteign asked.

"Nothing yet." Dagenham grinned his death's-head smile. "He's really unique. I've tried all the standard drugs and routines on him . . . Nothing. Outside, he's just an ordinary spaceman . . . if you forget the tattoo on his face . . . but inside he's got steel guts. Something's got hold of him and he won't give."

"What's got hold of him?" Sheffield asked.

"I hope to find out."

"How?"

"Don't ask; you'd be an accessory. Have you got a ship ready, Presteign?"

Presteign nodded.

"I'm not guaranteeing there'll be any 'Nomad' for us to find, but we'll have to get a jump on the navy if there is. Law ready, Sheffield?"

"Ready. I'm hoping we won't have to use it."

"I'm hoping too; but again, I'm not guaranteeing. All right. Stand by for instructions. I'm on my way to crack Foyle."

"Where have you got him?"

Dagenham shook his head. "This room isn't secure." He disappeared.

He jaunted Cincinnati–New Orleans–Monterey to Mexico City, where he appeared in the Psychiatry Wing of the giant hospital of the Combined Terran Universities. Wing was hardly an adequate name for this section which occupied an entire city in the metropolis which was the hospital. Dagenham jaunted up to the 43rd floor of the Therapy Division and looked into the isolated tank where Foyle floated, unconscious. He glanced at the distinguished bearded gentlemen in attendance.

"Hello, Fritz."

"Hello, Saul."

"Hell of a thing, the Head of Psychiatry minding a patient for me."

"I think we owe you favors, Saul."

"You still brooding about Tycho Sands, Fritz? I'm not. Am I lousing your wing with radiation?"

"I've had everything shielded."

"Ready for the dirty work?"

"I wish I knew what you were after."

"Information."

"And you have to turn my therapy department into an inquisition to get it?"

"That was the idea."

"Why not use ordinary drugs?"

"Tried them already. No good. He's not an ordinary man."

"You know this is illegal."

"I know. Changed your mind? Want to back out? I can duplicate your equipment for a quarter of a million."

"No, Saul. We'll always owe you favors."

"Then let's go. Nightmare Theater first."

They trundled the tank down a corridor and into a hundred feet square padded room. It was one of therapy's by-passed experiments. Nightmare Theater had been an early attempt to shock schizophrenics back into the objective world by rendering the phantasy world into which they were withdrawing uninhabitable. But the shattering and laceration of patients' emotions had proved to be too cruel and dubious a treatment.

For Dagenham's sake, the head of Psychiatry had dusted off the 3D visual projectors and reconnected all sensory projectors. They decanted Foyle from his tank, gave him a reviving shot and left him in the middle of the floor. They removed the tank, turned off the lights and entered the concealed control booth. There, they turned on the projectors.

Every child in the world imagines that its phantasy world is unique to itself. Psychiatry knows that the joys and terrors of private phantasies are a common heritage shared by all mankind. Fears, guilts, terrors, and shames could be interchanged, from one man to the next, and none would notice the difference. The therapy department at Combined Hospital had recorded thousands of emotional tapes and boiled them down to one all-inclusive all-terrifying performance in Nightmare Theater.

Foyle awoke, panting and sweating, and never knew that he had awakened. He was in the clutch of the serpent-haired bloody-eyed Eumenides. He was pursued, entrapped, precipitated from heights, burned, flayed, bowstringed, vermin-covered, devoured. He screamed. He ran. The radar Hobble-Field in the Theater clogged his steps and turned them into the ghastly slow motion of dream-running. And through the cacophony of grinding, shrieking, moaning, pursuing that assailed his ears, muttered the thread of a persistent voice.

"Where is 'Nomad' where is 'Nomad' where is 'Nomad' where is 'Nomad' where is 'Nomad'?"

" 'Vorga,' " Foyle croaked. " 'Vorga.' "

He had been inoculated by his own fixation. His own nightmare had rendered him immune.

"Where is 'Nomad'? where have you left 'Nomad'? what happened to 'Nomad'? where is 'Nomad'?"

"'Vorga,'" Foyle shouted. "'Vorga.' 'Vorga.' 'Vorga.'"

In the control booth, Dagenham swore. The head of psychiatry, monitoring the projectors, glanced at the clock. "One minute and forty-five seconds, Saul. He can't stand much more."

"He's got to break. Give him the final effect."

They buried Foyle alive, slowly, inexorably, hideously. He was carried down into black depths and enclosed in stinking slime that cut off light and air. He slowly suffocated while a distant voice boomed: "WHERE IS 'NOMAD'? WHERE HAVE YOU LEFT 'NOMAD'? YOU CAN ESCAPE IF YOU FIND 'NOMAD.' WHERE IS 'NOMAD'?"

But Foyle was back aboard "Nomad" in his lightless, airless coffin, floating comfortably between deck and roof. He curled into a tight foetal ball and prepared to sleep. He was content. He would escape. He would find "Vorga."

"Impervious bastard!" Dagenham swore. "Has anyone ever resisted Nightmare Theater before, Fritz?"

"Not many. You're right. That's an uncommon man, Saul."

"He's got to be ripped open. All right, to hell with any more of this. We'll try the Megal Mood next. Are the actors ready?"

"All ready."

"Then let's go."

There are six directions in which delusions of grandeur can run. The Megal (short for Megalomania) Mood was therapy's dramatic diagnosis technique for establishing and plotting the particular course of megalomania.

Foyle awoke in a luxurious four-poster bed. He was in a bedroom hung with brocade, papered in velvet. He glanced around curiously. Soft sunlight filtered through latticed windows. Across the room a valet was quietly laying out clothes.

"Hey . . ." Foyle grunted.

The valet turned. "Good morning, Mr. Fourmyle," he murmured.

"What?"

"It's a lovely morning, sir. I've laid out the brown twill and the cordovan pumps, sir."

"What's a matter, you?"

"I've—" The valet gazed at Foyle curiously. "Is anything wrong, Mr. Fourmyle?"

"What you call me, man?"

"By your name, sir."

"My name is . . . Fourmyle?" Foyle struggled up in the bed. "No, it's not. It's Foyle. Gully Foyle, that's my name, me."

The valet bit his lip. "One moment, sir . . ." He stepped outside and called. Then he murmured. A lovely girl in white came running into the bedroom and sat down on the edge of the bed. She took Foyle's hands and gazed into his eyes. Her face was distressed.

"Darling, darling, darling," she whispered. "You aren't going to start all that again, are you? The doctor swore you were over it."

"Start what again?"

"All that Gulliver Foyle nonsense about your being a common sailor and—"

"I am Gully Foyle. That's my name, Gully Foyle."

"Sweetheart, you're not. That's just a delusion you've had for weeks. You've been overworking and drinking too much."

"Been Gully Foyle all my life, me."

"Yes, I know darling. That's the way it's seemed to you. But you're not. You're Geoffrey Fourmyle. *The* Geoffrey Fourmyle. You're— Oh, what's the sense telling you? Get dressed, my love. You've got to come downstairs. Your office has been frantic."

Foyle permitted the valet to dress him and went downstairs in a daze. The lovely girl, who evidently adored him, conducted him through a giant studio littered with drawing tables, easels, and half-finished canvases. She took him into a vast hall filled with desks, filing cabinets, stock tickers, clerks, secretaries, office personnel. They entered a lofty laboratory cluttered with glass and chrome. Burners flickered and hissed; bright colored liquids bubbled and churned; there was a pleasant odor of interesting chemicals and odd experiments.

"What's all this?" Foyle asked.

The girl seated Foyle in a plush armchair alongside a giant desk littered with interesting papers scribbled with fascinating symbols. On some Foyle saw the name: Geoffrey Fourmyle, scrawled in an imposing, authoritative signature.

"There's some crazy kind of mistake, is all," Foyle began.

The girl silenced him. "Here's Doctor Regan. He'll explain."

An impressive gentleman with a crisp, comforting manner,

came to Foyle, touched his pulse, inspected his eyes, and nodded in satisfaction.

"Good," he said. "Excellent. You are close to complete recovery, Mr. Fourmyle. Now you will listen to me for a moment, eh?"

Foyle nodded.

"You remember nothing of the past. You have only a false memory. You were overworked. You are an important man and there were too many demands on you. You started to drink heavily a month ago— No, no, denial is useless. You drank. You lost yourself."

"I—"

"You became convinced you were not the famous Jeff Fourmyle. An infantile attempt to escape responsibility. You imagined you were a common spaceman named Foyle. Gulliver Foyle, yes? With an odd number . . ."

"Gully Foyle. AS:128/127:006. But that's me. That's—"

"It is not you. *This* is you." Dr. Regan waved at the interesting offices they could see through the transparent glass wall.

"You can only recapture the true memory if you discharge the old. All this glorious reality is yours, if we can help you discard the dream of the spaceman." Dr. Regan leaned forward, his polished spectacles glittering hypnotically. "Reconstruct this false memory of yours in detail, and I will tear it down. Where do you imagine you left the spaceship 'Nomad'? How did you escape? Where do you imagine the 'Nomad' is now?"

Foyle wavered before the romantic glamour of the scene which seemed to be just within his grasp.

"It seems to me I left 'Nomad' out in—" He stopped short.

A devil-face peered at him from the highlights reflected in Dr. Regan's spectacles . . . a hideous tiger mask with NOMAD blazoned across the distorted brow. Foyle stood up.

"Liars!" he growled. "It's real, me. This here is phoney. What happened to me is real. I'm real, me."

Saul Dagenham walked into the laboratory. "All right," he called. "Strike. It's a washout."

The bustling scene in laboratory, office, and studio ended. The actors quietly disappeared without another glance at Foyle. Dagenham gave Foyle his deadly smile. "Tough, aren't you?

You're really unique. My name is Saul Dagenham. We've got five minutes for a talk. Come into the garden."

The Sedative Garden atop the Therapy Building was a triumph of therapeutic planning. Every perspective, every color, every contour had been designed to placate hostility, soothe resistance, melt anger, evaporate hysteria, absorb melancholia and depression.

"Sit down," Dagenham said, pointing to a bench alongside a pool in which crystal waters tinkled. "Don't try to jaunte—you're drugged. I'll have to walk around a bit. Can't come too close to you. I'm 'hot.' D'you know what that means?"

Foyle shook his head sullenly. Dagenham cupped both hands around the flaming blossom of an orchid and held them there for a moment. "Watch that flower," he said. "You'll see."

He paced up a path and turned suddenly. "You're right, of course. Everything that happened to you is real. . . . Only what did happen?"

"Go to hell," Foyle growled.

"You know, Foyle, I admire you."

"Go to hell."

"In your own primitive way you've got ingenuity and guts. You're Cro-Magnon, Foyle. I've been checking on you. That bomb you threw in the Presteign shipyards was lovely, and you nearly wrecked General Hospital getting the money and material together." Dagenham counted fingers. "You looted lockers, stole from the blind ward, stole drugs from the pharmacy, stole apparatus from the lab stockrooms."

"Go to hell, you."

"But what have you got against Presteign? Why'd you try to blow up his shipyard? They tell me you broke in and went tearing through the pits like a wild man. What were you trying to do, Foyle?"

"Go to hell."

Dagenham smiled. "If we're going to chat," he said. "You'll have to hold up your end. Your conversation's getting monotonous. What happened to 'Nomad'?"

"I don't know about 'Nomad,' nothing."

"The ship was last reported over seven months ago. Are you the sole survivor? And what have you been doing all this time? Having your face decorated?"

"I don't know about 'Nomad,' nothing."

"No, no, Foyle, that won't do. You show up with 'Nomad' tattooed across your face. Fresh tattooed. Intelligence checks and finds you were aboard 'Nomad' when she sailed. Foyle, Gulliver: AS:128/127:006, Mechanic's Mate, 3rd Class. As if all this isn't enough to throw Intelligence into a tizzy, you come back in a private launch that's been missing fifty years. Man, you're cooking in the reactor. Intelligence wants the answers to all these questions. And you ought to know how Central Intelligence butchers its answers out of people."

Foyle started. Dagenham nodded as he saw his point sink home. "Which is why I think you'll listen to reason. We want information, Foyle. I tried to trick it out of you; admitted. I failed because you're too tough; admitted. Now I'm offering an honest deal. We'll protect you if you'll co-operate. If you don't, you'll spend five years in an Intelligence lab having information chopped out of you."

It was not the prospect of the butchery that frightened Foyle, but the thought of the loss of freedom. A man had to be free to avenge himself, to raise money and find "Vorga" again, to rip and tear and gut "VORGA."

"What kind of deal?" he asked.

"Tell us what happened to 'Nomad' and where you left her."

"Why, man?"

"Why? Because of the salvage, man."

"There ain't nothing to salvage. She's a wreck, is all."

"Even a wreck's salvageable."

"You mean you'd jet out a million miles to pick up pieces? Don't joker me, man."

"All right," Dagenham said in exasperation. "There's the cargo."

"She was split wide open. No cargo left."

"It was a cargo you don't know about," Dagenham said confidentially. " 'Nomad' was transporting platinum bullion to Mars Bank. Every so often, banks have to adjust accounts. Normally, enough trade goes on between planets so that accounts can be balanced on paper. The war's disrupted normal trade, and Mars Bank found that Presteign owed them twenty odd million credits without any way of getting the money short of actual delivery. Presteign was delivering the money in bar platinum aboard the 'Nomad.' It was locked in the purser's safe."

"Twenty million," Foyle whispered.

"Give or take a few thousand. The ship was insured, but that just means that the underwriters, Bo'ness and Uig, get the salvage rights and they're even tougher than Presteign. However, there'll be a reward for you. Say . . . twenty thousand credits."

"Twenty million," Foyle whispered again.

"We're assuming that an O.S. raider caught up with 'Nomad' somewhere on course and let her have it. They couldn't have boarded and looted or you wouldn't have been left alive. This means that the purser's safe is still— Are you listening, Foyle?"

But Foyle was not listening. He was seeing twenty million . . . not twenty thousand . . . twenty million in platinum bullion as a broad highway to "Vorga." No more petty thefts from lockers and labs; twenty million for the taking and the razing of "Vorga."

"Foyle!"

Foyle awoke. He looked at Dagenham. "I don't know about 'Nomad,' nothing," he said.

"What the hell's got into you now? Why're you dummying up again?"

"I don't know about 'Nomad,' nothing."

"I'm offering a fair reward. A spaceman can go on a hell of a tear with twenty thousand credits . . . a one-year tear. What more do you want?"

"I don't know about 'Nomad,' nothing."

"It's us or Intelligence, Foyle."

"You ain't so anxious for them to get me, or you wouldn't be flipping through all this. But it ain't no use, anyway. I don't know about 'Nomad,' nothing."

"You son of a ——" Dagenham tried to repress his anger. He had revealed just a little too much to this cunning, primitive creature. "You're right," he said. "We're not anxious for Intelligence to get you. But we've made our own preparations." His voice hardened. "You think you can dummy up and stand us off. You think you can leave us to whistle for 'Nomad.' You've even got an idea that you can beat us to the salvage."

"No," Foyle said.

"Now listen to this. We've got a lawyer waiting in New York. He's got a criminal prosecution for piracy pending against you; piracy in space, murder, and looting. We're going to throw the book at you. Presteign will get a conviction in twenty-four hours. If you've got a criminal record of any kind, that means a lobotomy. They'll open up the top of your skull and burn out half your brain to stop you from ever jaunting again."

Dagenham stopped and looked hard at Foyle. When Foyle shook his head, Dagenham continued.

"If you haven't got a record, they'll hand you ten years of what is laughingly known as medical treatment. We don't punish criminals in our enlightened age, we cure 'em; and the cure is worse than punishment. They'll stash you in a black hole in one of the cave hospitals. You'll be kept in permanent darkness and solitary confinement so you can't jaunte out. They'll go through the motions of giving you shots and therapy, but you'll be rotting in the dark. You'll stay there and rot until you decide to talk. We'll keep you there forever. So make up your mind."

"I don't know nothing about 'Nomad.' Nothing!" Foyle said.

"All right," Dagenham spat. Suddenly he pointed to the orchid blossom he had enclosed with his hands. It was blighted and rotting. "That's what's going to happen to you."

Five

SOUTH of Saint-Girons near the Spanish-French border is the deepest abyss in France, the Gouffre Martel. Its caverns twist for miles under the Pyrenees. It is the most formidable cavern hospital on Terra. No patient has ever jaunted out of its pitch darkness. No patient has ever succeeded in getting his bearings and learning the jaunte co-ordinates of the black hospital depths.

Short of prefrontal lobotomy, there are only three ways to stop a man from jaunting: a blow on the head producing concussion, sedation which prevents concentration, and concealment of jaunte co-ordinates. Of the three, the jaunting age considered concealment the most practical.

The cells that line the winding passages of Gouffre Martel are cut out of living rock. They are never illuminated. The passages are never illuminated. Infrared lamps flood the darkness. It is black light visible only to guards and attendants wearing snooper goggles with specially treated lenses. For the patients there is only the black silence of Gouffre Martel broken by the distant rush of underground waters.

For Foyle there was only the silence, the rushing, and the hospital routine. At eight o'clock (or it may have been any hour in this timeless abyss) he was awakened by a bell. He arose and received his morning meal, slotted into the cell by pneumatic tube. It had to be eaten at once, for the china surrogate of cups and plates was timed to dissolve in fifteen minutes. At eight-thirty the cell door opened and Foyle and hundreds of others shuffled blindly through the twisting corridors to Sanitation.

Here, still in darkness, they were processed like beef in a slaughter house: cleansed, shaved, irradiated, disinfected, dosed, and inoculated. Their paper uniforms were removed and sent back to the shops to be pulped. New uniforms were issued. Then they shuffled back to their cells which had been automatically scrubbed out while they were in Sanitation. In his cell, Foyle listened to interminable therapeutic talks, lectures, moral and ethical guidance for the rest of the morning. Then there was silence again, and nothing but the rush of distant water and the quiet steps of goggled guards in the corridors.

In the afternoon came occupational therapy. The TV screen in each cell illuminated and the patient thrust his hands into the shadow frame of the screen. He saw three-dimensionally and he felt the broadcast objects and tools. He cut hospital uniforms, sewed them, manufactured kitchen utensils, and prepared foods. Although actually he touched nothing, his motions were transmitted to the shops where the work was accomplished by remote control. After one short hour of this relief came the darkness and silence again.

But every so often . . . once or twice a week (or perhaps once or twice a year) came the muffled thud of a distant explosion. The concussions were startling enough to distract Foyle from the furnace of vengeance that he stoked all through the silences. He whispered questions to the invisible figures around him in Sanitation.

"What's them explosions?"

"Explosions?"

"Blow-ups. Hear 'em a long way off, me."

"Them's Blue Jauntes."

"What?"

"Blue Jauntes. Every sometime a guy gets fed up with old Jeffrey. Can't take it no more, him. Jauntes into the wild blue yonder."

"Jesus."

"Yep. Don't know where they are, them. Don't know where they're going. Blue Jaunte into the dark . . . and we hear 'em exploding in the mountains. Boom! Blue Jaunte."

He was appalled, but he could understand. The darkness, the silence, the monotony destroyed sense and brought on desperation. The loneliness was intolerable. The patients buried in Gouffre Martel prison hospital looked forward eagerly to the morning Sanitation period for a chance to whisper a word and hear a word. But these fragments were not enough, and desperation came. Then there would be another distant explosion.

Sometimes the suffering men would turn on each other and then a savage fight would break out in Sanitation. These were instantly broken up by the goggled guards, and the morning lecture would switch on the Moral Fiber record preaching the Virtue of Patience.

Foyle learned the records by heart, every word, every click and crack in the tapes. He learned to loathe the voices of the lecturers: the Understanding Baritone, the Cheerful Tenor, the Man-to-Man Bass. He learned to deafen himself to the therapeutic monotony and perform his occupational therapy mechanically, but he was without resources to withstand the endless solitary hours. Fury was not enough.

He lost count of the days, of meals, of sermons. He no longer whispered in Sanitation. His mind came adrift and he began to wander. He imagined he was back aboard "Nomad," reliving his fight for survival. Then he lost even this feeble grasp on illusion and began to sink deeper and deeper into the pit of catatonia: of womb silence, womb darkness, and womb sleep.

There were fleeting dreams. An angel hummed to him once. Another time she sang quietly. Thrice he heard her speak: "Oh

God . . ." and "God damn!" and "Oh . . ." in a heart-rending descending note.

He sank into his abyss, listening to her.

"There is a way out," his angel murmured in his ear, sweetly, comforting. Her voice was soft and warm, yet it burned with anger. It was the voice of a furious angel. "There is a way out."

It whispered in his ear from nowhere, and suddenly, with the logic of desperation, it came to him that there was a way out of Gouffre Martel. He had been a fool not to see it before.

"Yes," he croaked. "There's a way out."

There was a soft gasp, then a soft question: "Who's there?"

"Me, is all," Foyle said. "You know me."

"Where are you?"

"Here. Where I always been, me."

"But there's no one. I'm alone."

"Got to thank you for helping me."

"Hearing voices is bad," the furious angel murmured. "The first step off the deep end. I've got to stop."

"You showed me the way out. Blue Jaunte."

"Blue Jaunte! My God, this must be real. You're talking the gutter lingo. You must be real. Who are you?"

"Gully Foyle."

"But you're not in my cell. You're not even near. Men are in the north quadrant of Gouffre Martel. Women are in the south. I'm South-900. Where are you?"

"North-111."

"You're a quarter of a mile away. How can we— Of course! It's the Whisper Line. I always thought that was a legend, but it's true. It's working now."

"Here I go, me," Foyle whispered. "Blue Jaunte."

"Foyle, listen to me. Forget the Blue Jaunte. Don't throw this away. It's a miracle."

"What's a miracle?"

"There's an acoustical freak in Gouffre Martel . . . they happen in underground caves . . . a freak of echoes, passages and whispering galleries. Old-timers call it the Whisper Line. I never believed them. No one ever did, but it's true. We're talking to each other over the Whisper Line. No one can hear us but us. We can talk, Foyle. We can plan. Maybe we can escape."

*

Her name was Jisbella McQueen. She was hot-tempered, independent, intelligent, and she was serving five years of cure in Gouffre Martel for larceny. Jisbella gave Foyle a cheerfully furious account of her revolt against society.

"You don't know what jaunting's done to women, Gully. It's locked us up, sent us back to the seraglio."

"What's seraglio, girl?"

"A harem. A place where women are kept on ice. After a thousand years of civilization (it says here) we're still property. Jaunting's such a danger to our virtue, our value, our mint condition, that we're locked up like gold plate in a safe. There's nothing for us to do . . . nothing respectable. No jobs. No careers. There's no getting out, Gully, unless you bust out and smash all the rules."

"Did you have to, Jiz?"

"I had to be independent, Gully. I had to live my own life, and that's the only way society would let me. So I ran away from home and turned crook." And Jiz went on to describe the lurid details of her revolt: the Temper Racket, the Cataract Racket, the Honeymoon and Obituary Robs, the Badger Jaunte, and the Glim-Drop.

Foyle told her about "Nomad" and "Vorga," his hatred and his plans. He did not tell Jisbella about his face or the twenty millions in platinum bullion waiting out in the asteroids.

"What happened to 'Nomad'?" Jisbella asked. "Was it like that man, Dagenham, said? Was she blasted by an O.S. raider?"

"I don't know, me. Can't remember, girl."

"The blast probably wiped out your memory. Shock. And being marooned for six months didn't help. Did you notice anything worth salvaging from 'Nomad'?"

"No."

"Did Dagenham mention anything?"

"No," Foyle lied.

"Then he must have another reason for hounding you into Gouffre Martel. There must be something else he wants from 'Nomad.'"

"Yeah, Jiz."

"But you were a fool trying to blow up 'Vorga' like that. You're like a wild beast trying to punish the trap that injured it. Steel isn't alive. It doesn't think. You can't punish 'Vorga.'"

"Don't know what you mean, girl. 'Vorga' passed me by."

"You punish the brain, Gully. The brain that sets the trap. Find out who was aboard 'Vorga.' Find out who gave the order to pass you by. Punish him."

"Yeah. How?"

"Learn to think, Gully. The head that could figure out how to get 'Nomad' under way and how to put a bomb together ought to be able to figure that out. But no more bombs; brains instead. Locate a member of 'Vorga's' crew. He'll tell you who was aboard. Track them down. Find out who gave the order. Then punish him. But it'll take time, Gully . . . time and money; more than you've got."

"I got a whole life, me."

They murmured for hours across the Whisper Line, their voices sounding small yet close to the ear. There was only one particular spot in each cell where the other could be heard, which was why so much time had passed before they discovered the miracle. But now they made up for lost time. And Jisbella educated Foyle.

"If we ever break out of Gouffre Martel, Gully, it'll have to be together, and I'm not trusting myself to an illiterate partner."

"Who's illiterate?"

"You are," Jisbella answered firmly. "I have to talk gutter a you half the time, me."

"I can read and write."

"And that's about all . . . which means that outside of brute strength you'll be useless."

"Talk sense, you," he said angrily.

"I am talking sense, me. What's the use of the strongest chisel in the world if it doesn't have an edge? We've got to sharpen your wits, Gully. Got to educate you, man, is all."

He submitted. He realized she was right. He would need training not only for the bust-out but for the search for "Vorga" as well. Jisbella was the daughter of an architect and had received an education. This she drilled into Foyle, leavened with the cynical experience of five years in the underworld. Occasionally he rebelled against the hard work, and then there would be whispered quarrels, but in the end he would apologize and submit again. And sometimes Jisbella would tire of teaching, and then they would ramble on, sharing dreams in the dark.

"I think we're falling in love, Gully."

"I think so too, Jiz."

"I'm an old hag, Gully. A hundred and five years old. What are you like?"

"Awful."

"How awful?"

"My face."

"You make yourself sound romantic. Is it one of those exciting scars that make a man attractive?"

"No. You'll see when we meet, us. That's wrong, isn't it, Jiz? Just plain: 'When we meet.' Period."

"Good boy."

"We will meet some day, won't we, Jiz?"

"Soon, I hope, Gully." Jisbella's faraway voice became crisp and businesslike. "But we've got to stop hoping and get down to work. We've got to plan and prepare."

From the underworld, Jisbella had inherited a mass of information about Gouffre Martel. No one had ever jaunted out of the cavern hospitals, but for decades the underworld had been collecting and collating information about them. It was from this data that Jisbella had formed her quick recognition of the Whisper Line that joined them. It was on the basis of this information that she began to discuss escape.

"We can pull it off, Gully. Never doubt that for a minute. There must be dozens of loopholes in their security system."

"No one's ever found them before."

"No one's ever worked with a partner before. We'll pool our information and we'll make it."

He no longer shambled to Sanitation and back. He felt the corridor walls, noted doors, noted their texture, counted, listened, deduced, and reported. He made a note of every separate step in the Sanitation pens and reported them to Jiz. The questions he whispered to the men around him in the shower and scrub rooms had purpose. Together, Foyle and Jisbella built up a picture of the routine of Gouffre Martel and its security system.

One morning, on the return from Sanitation, he was stopped as he was about to step back into his cell.

"Stay in line, Foyle."

"This is North-111. I know where to get off by now."

"Keep moving."

"But—" He was terrified. "You're changing me?"

"Visitor to see you."

He was marched up to the end of the north corridor where it met the three other main corridors that formed the huge cross of the hospital. In the center of the cross were the administration offices, maintenance workshops, clinics, and plants. Foyle was thrust into a room, as dark as his cell. The door was shut behind him. He became aware of a faint shimmering outline in the blackness. It was no more than the ghost of an image with a blurred body and a death's head. Two black discs on the skull face were either eye sockets or infrared goggles.

"Good morning," said Saul Dagenham.

"You?" Foyle exclaimed.

"Me. I've got five minutes. Sit down. Chair behind you."

Foyle felt for the chair and sat down slowly.

"Enjoying yourself?" Dagenham inquired.

"What do you want, Dagenham?"

"There's been a change," Dagenham said dryly. "Last time we talked your dialogue consisted entirely of 'Go to hell.'"

"Go to hell, Dagenham, if it'll make you feel any better."

"Your repartee's improved; your speech, too. You've changed," Dagenham said. "Changed a damned sight too much and a damned sight too fast. I don't like it. What's happened to you?"

"I've been going to night school."

"You've had ten months in this night school."

"Ten months!" Foyle echoed in amazement. "That long?"

"Ten months without sight and without sound. Ten months in solitary. You ought to be broke."

"Oh, I'm broke, all right."

"You ought to be whining. I was right. You're unusual. At this rate it's going to take too long. We can't wait. I'd like to make a new offer."

"Make it."

"Ten per cent of 'Nomad's' bullion. Two million."

"Two million!" Foyle exclaimed. "Why didn't you offer that in the first place?"

"Because I didn't know your caliber. Is it a deal?"

"Almost. Not yet."

"What else?"

"I get out of Gouffre Martel."

"Naturally."

"And someone else, too."

"It can be arranged." Dagenham's voice sharpened. "Anything else?"

"I get access to Presteign's files."

"Out of the question. Are you insane? Be reasonable."

"His shipping files."

"What for?"

"A list of personnel aboard one of his ships."

"Oh." Dagenham's eagerness revived. "That, I can arrange. Anything else?"

"No."

"Then it's a deal." Dagenham was delighted. The ghostly blur of light arose from its chair. "We'll have you out in six hours. We'll start arrangements for your friend at once. It's a pity we wasted this time, but no one can figure you, Foyle."

"Why didn't you send in a telepath to work me over?"

"A telepath? Be reasonable, Foyle. There aren't ten full telepaths in all the Inner Planets. Their time is earmarked for the next ten years. We couldn't persuade one to interrupt his schedule for love or money."

"I apologize, Dagenham. I thought you didn't know your business."

"You very nearly hurt my feelings."

"Now I know you're just lying."

"You're flattering me."

"You could have hired a telepath. For a cut in twenty million you could have hired one easy."

"The government would never—"

"They don't all work for the government. No. You've got something too hot to let a telepath get near."

The blur of light leaped across the room and seized Foyle. "How much do you know, Foyle? What are you covering? Who are you working for?" Dagenham's hands shook. "Christ! What a fool I've been. Of course you're unusual. You're no common spaceman. I asked you: who are you working for?"

Foyle tore Dagenham's hands away from him. "No one," he said. "No one, except myself."

"No one, eh? Including your friend in Gouffre Martel you're

so eager to rescue? By God, you almost swindled me, Foyle. Tell Captain Y'ang-Yeovil I congratulate him. He's got a better staff than I thought."

"I never heard of any Y'ang-Yeovil."

"You and your colleague are going to rot here. It's no deal. You'll fester here. I'll have you moved to the worst cell in the hospital. I'll sink you to the bottom of Gouffre Martel. I'll— Guard, here! G—"

Foyle grasped Dagenham's throat, dragged him down to the floor and hammered his head on the flagstones. Dagenham squirmed once and then was still. Foyle ripped the goggles off his face and put them on. Sight returned in soft red and rose lights and shadows.

He was in a small reception room with a table and two chairs. Foyle stripped Dagenham's jacket off and put it on with two quick jerks that split the shoulders. Dagenham's cocked highwayman's hat lay on the table. Foyle clapped it over his head and pulled the brim down before his face.

On opposite walls were two doors. Foyle opened one a crack. It led out to the north corridor. He closed it, leaped across the room and tried the other. It opened onto a jaunte-proof maze. Foyle slipped through the door and entered the maze. Without a guide to lead him through the labyrinth, he was immediately lost. He began to run around the twists and turns and found himself back at the reception room. Dagenham was struggling to his knees.

Foyle turned back into the maze again. He ran. He came to a closed door and thrust it open. It revealed a large workshop illuminated by normal light. Two technicians working at a machine bench looked up in surprise.

Foyle snatched up a sledge hammer, leaped on them like a caveman, and felled them. Behind him he heard Dagenham shouting in the distance. He looked around wildly, dreading the discovery that he was trapped in a cul-de-sac. The workshop was L-shaped. Foyle tore around the corner, burst through the entrance of another jaunte-proof maze and was lost again. The Gouffre Martel alarm system began clattering. Foyle battered at the walls of the labyrinth with the sledge, shattered the thin plastic masking, and found himself in the infrared-lit south corridor of the women's quadrant.

Two women guards came up the corridor, running hard. Foyle swung the sledge and dropped them. He was near the head of the corridor. Before him stretched a long perspective of cell doors, each bearing a glowing red number. Overhead the corridor was lit by glowing red globes. Foyle stood on tiptoe and clubbed the globe above him. He hammered through the socket and smashed the current cable. The entire corridor went dark . . . even to goggles.

"Evens us up; all in the dark now," Foyle gasped and tore down the corridor feeling the wall as he ran and counting cell doors. Jisbella had given him an accurate word picture of the South Quadrant. He was counting his way toward South-900. He blundered into a figure, another guard. Foyle hacked at her once with his sledge. She shrieked and fell. The women patients began shrieking. Foyle lost count, ran on, stopped.

"Jiz!" he bellowed.

He heard her voice. He encountered another guard, disposed of her, ran, located Jisbella's cell.

"Gully, for God's sake . . ." Her voice was muffled.

"Get back, girl. Back." He hammered thrice against the door with his sledge and it burst inward. He staggered in and fell against a figure.

"Jiz?" he gasped. "Excuse me . . . Was passing by. Thought I'd drop in."

"Gully, in the name of—"

"Yeah. Hell of a way to meet, eh? Come on. Out, girl. Out!" He dragged her out of the cell. "We can't try a break through the offices. They don't like me back there. Which way to your Sanitation pens?"

"Gully, you're crazy."

"Whole quadrant's dark. I smashed the power cable. We've got half a chance. Go, girl. Go."

He gave her a powerful thrust and she led him down the passages to the automatic stalls of the women's Sanitation pens. While mechanical hands removed their uniforms, soaped, soaked, sprayed and disinfected them, Foyle felt for the glass pane of the medical observation window. He found it, swung the sledge and smashed it.

"Get in, Jiz."

He hurled her through the window and followed. They

were both stripped, greasy with soap, slashed and bleeding. Foyle slipped and crashed through the blackness searching for the door through which the medical officers entered.

"Can't find the door, Jiz. Door from the clinic. I—"

"Shh!"

"But—"

"Be quiet, Gully."

A soapy hand found his mouth and clamped over it. She gripped his shoulder so hard that her fingernails pierced his skin. Through the bedlam in the caverns sounded the clatter of steps close at hand. Guards were running blindly through the Sanitation stalls. The infrared lights had not yet been repaired.

"They may not notice the window," Jisbella hissed. "Be quiet."

They crouched on the floor. Steps trampled through the pens in bewildering succession. Then they were gone.

"All clear, now," Jisbella whispered. "But they'll have search-lights any minute. Come on, Gully. Out."

"But the door to the clinic, Jiz. I thought—"

"There is no door. They use spiral stairs and they pull them up. They've thought of this escape too. We'll have to try the laundry lift. God knows what good it'll do us. Oh Gully, you fool! You utter fool!"

They climbed through the observation window back into the pens. They searched through the darkness for the lifts by which soiled uniforms were removed and fresh uniforms issued. And in the darkness the automatic hands again soaped, sprayed and disinfected them. They could find nothing.

The caterwauling of a siren suddenly echoed through the caverns, silencing all other sound. There came a hush as suffocating as the darkness.

"They're using the G-phone to track us, Gully."

"The what?"

"Geophone. It can trace a whisper through half a mile of solid rock. That's why they've sirened for silence."

"The laundry lift?"

"Can't find it."

"Then come on."

"Where?"

"We're running."

"Where?"

"I don't know, but I'm not getting caught flat-footed. Come on. The exercise'll do you good."

Again he thrust Jisbella before him and they ran, gasping and stumbling, through the blackness, down into the deepest reaches of South Quadrant. Jisbella fell twice, blundering against turns in the passages. Foyle took the lead and ran, holding the twenty-pound sledge in his hand, the handle extended before him as an antenna. Then they crashed into a blank wall and realized they had reached the dead end of the corridor. They were boxed, trapped.

"What now?"

"Don't know. Looks like the dead end of my ideas, too. We can't go back for sure. I clobbered Dagenham in the offices. Hate that man. Looks like a poison label. You got a flash, girl?"

"Oh Gully . . . Gully . . ." Jisbella sobbed.

"Was counting on you for ideas. 'No more bombs,' you said. Wish I had one now. Could— Wait a minute." He touched the oozing wall against which they were leaning. He felt the checkerboard indentations of mortar seams. "Bulletin from G. Foyle. This isn't a natural cave wall. It's made. Brick and stone. Feel."

Jisbella felt the wall. "So?"

"Means this passage don't end here. Goes on. They blocked it off. Out of the way."

He shoved Jisbella up the passage, ground his hands into the floor to grit his soapy palms, and began swinging the sledge against the wall. He swung in steady rhythm, grunting and gasping. The steel sledge struck the wall with the blunt concussion of stones struck under water.

"They're coming," Jiz said. "I hear them."

The blunt blows took on a crumbling, crushing overtone. There was a whisper, then a steady pebble-fall of loose mortar. Foyle redoubled his efforts. Suddenly there was a crash and a gush of icy air blew in their faces.

"Through," Foyle muttered.

He attacked the edges of the hole pierced through the wall with ferocity. Bricks, stones, and old mortar flew. Foyle stopped and called Jisbella.

"Try it."

He dropped the sledge, seized her, and held her up to the chest-high opening. She cried out in pain as she tried to wriggle past the sharp edges. Foyle pressed her relentlessly until she got her shoulders and then her hips through. He let go of her legs and heard her fall on the other side.

Foyle pulled himself up and tore himself through the jagged breach in the wall. He felt Jisbella's hands trying to break his fall as he crashed down in a mass of loose brick and mortar. They were both through into the icy blackness of the unoccupied caverns of Gouffre Martel . . . miles of unexplored grottos and caves.

"By God, we'll make it yet," Foyle mumbled.

"I don't know if there's a way out, Gully." Jisbella was shaking with cold. "Maybe this is all cul-de-sac, walled off from the hospital."

"There has to be a way out."

"I don't know if we can find it."

"We've got to find it. Let's go, girl."

They blundered forward in the darkness. Foyle tore the useless set of goggles from his eyes. They crashed against ledges, corners, low ceilings; they fell down slopes and steep steps. They climbed over a razor-back ridge to a level plain and their feet shot from under them. Both fell heavily to a glassy floor. Foyle felt it and touched it with his tongue.

"Ice," he muttered. "Good sign. We're in an ice cavern, Jiz. Underground glacier."

They arose shakily, straddling their legs and worked their way across the ice that had been forming in the Gouffre Martel abyss for millennia. They climbed into a forest of stone saplings that were stalagmites and stalactites thrusting up from the jagged floor and down from the ceilings. The vibrations of every step loosened the huge stalactites; ponderous stone spears thundered down from overhead. At the edge of the forest, Foyle stopped, reached out and tugged. There was a clear metallic ring. He took Jisbella's hand and placed the long tapering cone of a stalagmite in it.

"Cane," he grunted. "Use it like a blind man."

He broke off another and they went tapping, feeling, stumbling through the darkness. There was no sound but the gallop of panic . . . their gasping breath and racing hearts, the taps of their stone canes, the multitudinous drip of water, the distant rushing of the underground river beneath Gouffre Martel.

"Not that way, girl." Foyle nudged her shoulder. "More to the left."

"Have you the faintest notion where we're headed, Gully?"

"Down, Jiz. Follow any slope that leads down."

"You've got an idea?"

"Yeah. Surprise, surprise! Brains instead of bombs."

"Brains instead of—" Jisbella shrieked with hysterical laughter. "You exploded into South Quadrant w-with a sledge hammer and th-that's your idea of b-brains instead of b-b-b—" She brayed and hooted beyond all control until Foyle grasped her and shook her.

"Shut up, Jiz. If they're tracking us by G-phone they could hear you from Mars."

"S-sorry, Gully. Sorry. I . . ." She took a breath. "Why down?"

"The river, the one we hear all the time. It must be near. It probably melts off the glacier back there."

"The river?"

"The only sure way out. It must break out of the mountain somewhere. We'll swim."

"Gully, you're insane!"

"What's a matter, you? You can't swim?"

"I can swim, but—"

"Then we've got to try. Got to, Jiz. Come on."

The rush of the river grew louder as their strength began to fail. Jisbella pulled to a halt at last, gasping.

"Gully, I've got to rest."

"Too cold. Keep moving."

"I can't."

"Keep moving." He felt for her arm.

"Get your hands off me," she cried furiously. In an instant she was all spitfire. He released her in amazement.

"What's the matter with you? Keep your head, Jiz. I'm depending on you."

"For what? I told you we had to plan . . . work out an escape . . . and now you've trapped us into this."

"I was trapped myself. Dagenham was going to change my

cell. No more Whisper Line for us. I had to, Jiz . . . and we're out, aren't we?"

"Out where? Lost in Gouffre Martel. Looking for a damned river to drown in. You're a fool, Gully, and I'm an idiot for letting you trap me into this. Damn you! Damn you! You pull everything down to your imbecile level and you've pulled me down too. Run. Fight. Punch. That's all you know. Beat. Break. Blast. Destroy— Gully!"

Jisbella screamed. There was a clatter of loose stone in the darkness, and her scream faded down and away to a heavy splash. Foyle heard the thrash of her body in water. He leaped forward, shouted: "Jiz!" and staggered over the edge of a precipice.

He fell and struck the water flat with a stunning impact. The icy river enclosed him, and he could not tell where the surface was. He struggled, suffocated, felt the swift current drag him against the chill slime of rocks, and then was borne bubbling to the surface. He coughed and shouted. He heard Jisbella answer, her voice faint and muffled by the roaring torrent. He swam with the current, trying to overtake her.

He shouted and heard her answering voice growing fainter and fainter. The roaring grew louder, and abruptly he was shot down the hissing sheet of a waterfall. He plunged to the bottom of a deep pool and struggled once more to the surface. The whirling current entangled him with a cold body bracing itself against a smooth rock wall.

"Jiz!"

"Gully! Thank God!"

They clung together for a moment while the water tore at them.

"Gully . . ." Jisbella coughed. "It goes through here."

"The river?"

"Yes."

He squirmed past her, bracing himself against the wall, and felt the mouth of an underwater tunnel. The current was sucking them into it.

"Hold on," Foyle gasped. He explored to the left and the right. The walls of the pool were smooth, without handhold.

"We can't climb out. Have to go through."

"There's no air, Gully. No surface."

"Couldn't be forever. We'll hold our breath."

"It could be longer than we can hold our breath."

"Have to gamble."

"I can't do it."

"You must. No other way. Pump your lungs. Hold on to me."

They supported each other in the water, gasping for breath, filling their lungs. Foyle nudged Jisbella toward the underwater tunnel. "You go first. I'll be right behind. . . . Help you if you get into trouble."

"Trouble!" Jisbella cried in a shaking voice. She submerged and permitted the current to suck her into the tunnel mouth. Foyle followed. The fierce waters drew them down, down, down, caroming from side to side of a tunnel that had been worn glass-smooth. Foyle swam close behind Jisbella, feeling her thrashing legs beat his head and shoulders.

They shot through the tunnel until their lungs burst and their blind eyes started. Then there was a roaring again and a surface, and they could breathe. The glassy tunnel sides were replaced by jagged rocks. Foyle caught Jisbella's leg and seized a stone projection at the side of the river.

"Got to climb out here," he shouted.

"What?"

"Got to climb out. You hear that roaring up ahead? Cataracts. Rapids. Be torn to pieces. Out, Jiz."

She was too weak to climb out of the water. He thrust her body up onto the rocks and followed. They lay on the dripping stones, too exhausted to speak. At last Foyle got wearily to his feet.

"Have to keep on," he said. "Follow the river. Ready?"

She could not answer; she could not protest. He pulled her up and they went stumbling through the darkness, trying to follow the bank of the torrent. The boulders they traversed were gigantic, standing like dolmens, heaped, jumbled, scattered into a labyrinth. They staggered and twisted through them and lost the river. They could hear it in the darkness; they could not get back to it. They could get nowhere.

"Lost . . ." Foyle grunted in disgust. "We're lost again. Really lost this time. What are we going to do?"

Jisbella began to cry. She made helpless yet furious sounds.

Foyle lurched to a stop and sat down, drawing her down with him.

"Maybe you're right, girl," he said wearily. "Maybe I am a damned fool. I got us trapped into this no-jaunte jam, and we're licked."

She didn't answer.

"So much for brainwork. Hell of an education you gave me." He hesitated. "You think we ought to try backtracking to the hospital?"

"We'll never make it."

"Guess not. Was just practicing m'brain. Should we start a racket? Make a noise so they can track us by G-phone?"

"They'd never hear us . . . Never find us in time."

"We could make enough noise. You could knock me around a little. Be a pleasure for both of us."

"Shut up."

"What a mess!" He sagged back, cushioning his head on a tuft of soft grass. "At least I had a chance aboard 'Nomad.' There was food and I could see where I was trying to go. I could—" He broke off and sat bolt upright. "Jiz!"

"Don't talk so much."

He felt the ground under him and clawed up sods of earth and tufts of grass. He thrust them into her face.

"Smell this," he laughed. "Taste it. It's grass, Jiz. Earth and grass. We must be out of Gouffre Martel."

"What?"

"It's night outside. Pitch-black. Overcast. We came out of the caves and never knew it. We're out, Jiz! We made it."

They leaped to their feet, peering, listening, sniffing. The night was impenetrable, but they heard the soft sigh of night winds, and the sweet scent of green growing things came to their nostrils. Far in the distance a dog barked.

"My God, Gully," Jisbella whispered incredulously. "You're right. We're out of Gouffre Martel. All we have to do is wait for dawn."

She laughed. She flung her arms about him and kissed him, and he returned the embrace. They babbled excitedly. They sank down on the soft grass again, weary, but unable to rest, eager, impatient, all life before them.

"Hello, Gully, darling Gully. Hello Gully, after all this time."

"Hello, Jiz."

"I told you we'd meet some day . . . some day soon. I told you, darling. And this is the day."

"The night."

"The night, so it is. But no more murmuring in the night along the Whisper Line. No more night for us, Gully, dear."

Suddenly they became aware that they were nude, lying close, no longer separated. Jisbella fell silent but did not move. He clasped her, almost angrily, and enveloped her with a desire that was no less than hers.

When dawn came, he saw that she was lovely: long and lean with smoky red hair and a generous mouth.

But when dawn came, she saw his face.

Six

HARLEY BAKER, M.D., had a small general practice in Montana-Oregon which was legitimate and barely paid for the diesel oil he consumed each weekend participating in the rallies for vintage tractors which were the vogue in Sahara. His real income was earned in his Freak Factory in Trenton to which Baker jaunted every Monday, Wednesday, and Friday night. There, for enormous fees and no questions asked, Baker created monstrosities for the entertainment business and refashioned skin, muscle, and bone for the underworld.

Looking like a male midwife, Baker sat on the cool veranda of his Spokane mansion listening to Jiz McQueen finish the story of her escape.

"Once we hit the open country outside Gouffre Martel it was easy. We found a shooting lodge, broke in, and got some clothes. There were guns there too . . . lovely old steel things for killing with explosives. We took them and sold them to some locals. Then we bought rides to the nearest jaunte stage we had memorized."

"Which?"

"Biarritz."

"Traveled by night, eh?"

"Naturally."

"Do anything about Foyle's face?"

"We tried makeup but that didn't work. The damned tattooing showed through. Then I bought a dark skin-surrogate and sprayed it on."

"Did that do it?"

"No," Jiz said angrily. "You have to keep your face quiet or else the surrogate cracks and peels. Foyle couldn't control himself. He never can. It was hell."

"Where is he now?"

"Sam Quatt's got him in tow."

"I thought Sam retired from the rackets."

"He did," Jisbella said grimly, "but he owes me a favor. He's minding Foyle. They're circulating on the jaunte to stay ahead of the cops."

"Interesting," Baker murmured. "Haven't seen a tattoo case in all my life. Thought it was a dead art. I'd like to add him to my collection. You know I collect curios, Jiz?"

"Everybody knows that zoo of yours in Trenton, Baker. It's ghastly."

"I picked up a genuine fraternal cyst last month," Baker began enthusiastically.

"I don't want to hear about it," Jiz snapped. "And I don't want Foyle in your zoo. Can you get the muck off his face? Clean it up? He says they were stymied at General Hospital."

"They haven't had my experience, dear. Hmm. I seem to remember reading something once . . . somewhere . . . Now where did I—? Wait a minute." Baker stood up and disappeared with a faint pop. Jisbella paced the veranda furiously until he reappeared twenty minutes later with a tattered book in his hands and a triumphant expression on his face.

"Got it," Baker said. "Saw it in the Caltech stacks three years ago. You may admire my memory."

"To hell with your memory. What about his face?"

"It can be done." Baker flipped the fragile pages and meditated. "Yes, it can be done. Indigotin disulphonic acid. I may have to synthesize the acid but . . ." Baker closed the text and nodded emphatically. "I can do it. Only it seems a pity to tamper with that face if it's as unique as you describe."

"Will you get off your hobby," Jisbella exclaimed in exasperation. "We're hot, understand? The first that ever broke out of Gouffre Martel. The cops won't rest until they've got us back. This is extra-special for them."

"But—"

"How long d'you think we can stay out of Gouffre Martel with Foyle running around with that tattooed face?"

"What are you so angry about?"

"I'm not angry. I'm explaining."

"He'd be happy in the zoo," Baker said persuasively. "And he'd be under cover there. I'd put him in the room next to the cyclops girl—"

"The zoo is out. That's definite."

"All right, dear. But why are you worried about Foyle being recaptured? It won't have anything to do with you."

"Why should you worry about me worrying? I'm asking you to do a job. I'm paying for the job."

"It'll be expensive, dear, and I'm fond of you. I'm trying to save you money."

"No you're not."

"Then I'm curious."

"Then let's say I'm grateful. He helped me; now I'm helping him."

Baker smiled cynically. "Then let's help him by giving him a brand new face."

"No."

"I thought so. You want his face cleaned up because you're interested in his face."

"Damn you, Baker, will you do the job or not?"

"It'll cost five thousand."

"Break that down."

"A thousand to synthesize the acid. Three thousand for the surgery. And one thousand for—"

"Your curiosity?"

"No, dear." Baker smiled again. "A thousand for the anesthetist."

"Why anesthesia?"

Baker reopened the ancient text. "It looks like a painful operation. You know how they tattoo? They take a needle, dip it in dye, and hammer it into the skin. To bleach that dye out I'll have to go over his face with a needle, pore by pore, and hammer in the indigotin disulphonic. It'll hurt."

Jisbella's eyes flashed. "Can you do it without the dope?"

"I can, dear, but Foyle—"

"To hell with Foyle. I'm paying four thousand. No dope, Baker. Let Foyle suffer."

"Jiz! You don't know what you're letting him in for."

"I know. Let him suffer." She laughed so furiously that she startled Baker. "Let his face make him suffer too."

Baker's Freak Factory occupied a round brick three-story building that had once been the roundhouse in a suburban railway yard before jaunting ended the need for suburban railroads. The ancient ivy-covered roundhouse was alongside the Trenton rocket pits, and the rear windows looked out on the mouths of the pits thrusting their anti-grav beams upward, and Baker's patients could amuse themselves watching the spaceships riding silently up and down the beams, their portholes blazing, recognition signals blinking, their hulls rippling with St. Elmo's fire as the atmosphere carried off the electrostatic charges built up in outer space.

The basement floor of the factory contained Baker's zoo of anatomical curiosities, natural freaks and monsters bought, and/or abducted. Baker, like the rest of his world, was passionately devoted to these creatures and spent long hours with them, drinking in the spectacle of their distortions the way other men saturated themselves with the beauty of art. The middle floor of the roundhouse contained bedrooms for post-operative patients, laboratories, staff rooms, and kitchens. The top floor contained the operating theaters.

In one of the latter, a small room usually used for retinal experiments, Baker was at work on Foyle's face. Under a harsh battery of lamps, he bent over the operating table working meticulously with a small steel hammer and a platinum needle. Baker was following the pattern of the old tattooing on Foyle's face, searching out each minute scar in the skin, and driving the needle into it. Foyle's head was gripped in a clamp, but his body was unstrapped. His muscles writhed at each tap of the hammer, but he never moved his body. He gripped the sides of the operating table.

"Control," he said through his teeth. "You wanted me to learn control, Jiz. I'm practicing." He winced.

"Don't move," Baker ordered.

"I'm playing it for laughs."

"You're doing all right, son," Sam Quatt said, looking sick. He glanced sidelong at Jisbella's furious face. "What do you say, Jiz?"

"He's learning."

Baker continued dipping and hammering the needle.

"Listen, Sam," Foyle mumbled, barely audible. "Jiz told me you own a private ship. Crime pays, huh?"

"Yeah. Crime pays. I got a little four-man job. Twin-jet. Kind they call a Saturn Weekender."

"Why Saturn Weekender?"

"Because a weekend on Saturn would last ninety days. She can carry food and fuel for three months."

"Just right for me," Foyle muttered. He writhed and controlled himself. "Sam, I want to rent your ship."

"What for?"

"Something hot."

"Legitimate?"

"No."

"Then it's not for me, son. I've lost my nerve. Jaunting the circuit with you, one step ahead of the cops, showed me that. I've retired for keeps. All I want is peace."

"I'll pay fifty thousand. Don't you want fifty thousand? You could spend Sundays counting it."

The needle hammered remorselessly. Foyle's body was twitching at each impact.

"I already got fifty thousand. I got ten times that in cash in a bank in Vienna." Quatt reached into his pocket and took out a ring of glittering radioactive keys. "Here's the key for the bank. This is the key to my place in Joburg. Twenty rooms; twenty acres. This here's the key to my Weekender in Montauk. You ain't temptin' me, son. I quit while I was ahead. I'm jaunting back to Joburg and live happy for the rest of my life."

"Let me have the Weekender. You can sit safe in Joburg and collect."

"Collect when?"

"When I get back."

"You want my ship on trust and a promise to pay?"

"A guarantee."

Quatt snorted. "What guarantee?"

"It's a salvage job in the asteroids. Ship named 'Nomad.' "

"What's on the 'Nomad'? What makes the salvage pay off?"

"I don't know."

"You're lying."

"I don't know," Foyle mumbled stubbornly. "But there has to be something valuable. Ask Jiz."

"Listen," Quatt said, "I'm going to teach you something. We do business legitimate, see? We don't slash and scalp. We don't hold out. I know what's on your mind. You got something juicy but you don't want to cut anybody else in on it. That's why you're begging for favors . . ."

Foyle writhed under the needle, but, still gripped in the vice of his possession, was forced to repeat: "I don't know, Sam. Ask Jiz."

"If you've got an honest deal, make an honest proposition," Quatt said angrily. "Don't come prowling around like a damned tattooed tiger figuring how to pounce. We're the only friends you got. Don't try to slash and scalp—"

Quatt was interrupted by a cry torn from Foyle's lips.

"Don't move," Baker said in an abstracted voice. "When you twitch your face I can't control the needle." He looked hard and long at Jisbella. Her lips trembled. Suddenly she opened her purse and took out two ₡r 500 banknotes. She dropped them alongside the beaker of acid.

"We'll wait outside," she said.

She fainted in the hall. Quatt dragged her to a chair, and found a nurse who revived her with aromatic ammonia. She began to cry so violently that Quatt was frightened. He dismissed the nurse and hovered until the sobbing subsided.

"What the hell has been going on?" he demanded. "What was that money supposed to mean?"

"It was blood money."

"For what?"

"I don't want to talk about it."

"Are you all right?"

"No."

"Anything I can do?"

"No."

There was a long pause. Then Jisbella asked in a weary voice: "Are you going to make that deal with Gully?"

"Me? No. It sounds like a thousand-to-one shot."

"There has to be something valuable on the 'Nomad.' Otherwise Dagenham wouldn't have hounded Gully."

"I'm still not interested. What about you?"

"Me? Not interested either. I don't want any part of Gully Foyle again."

After another pause, Quatt asked: "Can I go home now?"

"You've had a rough time, haven't you, Sam?"

"I think I died about a thousand times nurse-maidin' that tiger around the circuit."

"I'm sorry, Sam."

"I had it coming to me after what I did to you when you were copped in Memphis."

"Running out on me was only natural, Sam."

"We always do what's natural, only sometimes we shouldn't do it."

"I know, Sam. I know."

"And you spend the rest of your life trying to make up for it. I figure I'm lucky, Jiz. I was able to square it tonight. Can I go home now?"

"Back to Joburg and the happy life?"

"Uh-huh."

"Don't leave me alone, yet, Sam. I'm ashamed of myself."

"What for?"

"Cruelty to dumb animals."

"What's that supposed to mean?"

"Never mind. Hang around a little. Tell me about the happy life. What's so happy about it?"

"Well," Quatt said reflectively. "It's having everything you wanted when you were a kid. If you can have everything at fifty that you wanted when you were fifteen, you're happy. Now when I was fifteen . . ." And Quatt went on and on describing the symbols, ambitions, and frustrations of his boyhood which he was now satisfying until Baker came out of the operating theater.

"Finished?" Jisbella asked eagerly.

"Finished. After I put him under I was able to work faster. They're bandaging his face now. He'll be out in a few minutes."

"Weak?"

"Naturally."

"How long before the bandages come off?"

"Six or seven days."

"His face'll be clean?"

"I thought you weren't interested in his face, dear. It ought to be clean. I don't think I missed a spot of pigment. You may admire my skill, Jisbella . . . also my sagacity. I'm going to back Foyle's salvage trip."

"What?" Quatt laughed. "You taking a thousand-to-one gamble, Baker? I thought you were smart."

"I am. The pain was too much for him and he talked under the anesthesia. There's twenty million in platinum bullion aboard the 'Nomad.'"

"Twenty million!" Sam Quatt's face darkened and he turned on Jisbella. But she was furious too.

"Don't look at me, Sam. I didn't know. He held out on me too. Swore he never knew why Dagenham was hounding him."

"It was Dagenham who told him," Baker said. "He let that slip too."

"I'll kill him," Jisbella said. "I'll tear him apart with my own two hands and you won't find anything inside his carcass but black rot. He'll be a curio for your zoo, Baker; I wish to God I'd let you have him!"

The door of the operating theater opened and two orderlies wheeled out a trolley on which Foyle lay, twitching slightly. His entire head was one white globe of bandage.

"Is he conscious?" Quatt asked Baker.

"I'll handle this," Jisbella burst out. "I'll talk to the son of a— Foyle!"

Foyle answered faintly through the mask of bandage. As Jisbella drew a furious breath for her onslaught, one wall of the hospital disappeared and there was a clap of thunder that knocked them to their feet. The entire building rocked from repeated explosions, and through the gaps in the walls uniformed men began jaunting in from the streets outside, like rooks swooping into the gut of a battlefield.

"Raid!" Baker shouted. "Raid!"

"Christ Jesus!" Quatt shook.

The uniformed men were swarming all over the building, shouting: "Foyle! Foyle! Foyle! Foyle!" Baker disappeared with a pop. The attendants jaunted too, deserting the trolley on which Foyle waved his arms and legs feebly, making faint sounds.

"It's a goddamn raid!" Quatt shook Jisbella. "Go, girl! Go!"

"We can't leave Foyle!" Jisbella cried.

"Wake up, girl! Go!"

"We can't run out on him."

Jisbella seized the trolley and ran it down the corridor. Quatt pounded alongside her. The roaring in the hospital grew louder: "Foyle! Foyle! Foyle!"

"Leave him, for God's sake!" Quatt urged. "Let them have him."

"No."

"It's a lobo for us, girl, if they get us."

"We can't run out on him."

They skidded around a corner into a shrieking mob of post-operative patients, bird men with fluttering wings, mermaids dragging themselves along the floor like seals, hermaphrodites, giants, pygmies, two-headed twins, centaurs, and a mewling sphinx. They clawed at Jisbella and Quatt in terror.

"Get him off the trolley," Jisbella yelled.

Quatt yanked Foyle off the trolley. Foyle came to his feet and sagged. Jisbella took his arm, and between them Sam and Jiz hauled him through a door into a ward filled with Baker's temporal freaks . . . subjects with accelerated time sense, darting about the ward with the lightning rapidity of humming birds and emitting piercing batlike squeals.

"Jaunte him out, Sam."

"After the way he tried to cross and scalp us?"

"We can't run out on him, Sam. You ought to know that by now. Jaunte him out. Caister's place!"

Jisbella helped Quatt haul Foyle to his shoulder. The temporal freaks seemed to fill the ward with shrieking streaks. The ward doors burst open. A dozen bolts from pneumatic guns whined through the ward, dropping the temporal patients in their gyrations. Quatt was slammed back against a wall, dropping Foyle. A black and blue bruise appeared on his temple.

"Get to hell out of here," Quatt roared. "I'm done."

"Sam!"

"I'm done. Can't jaunte. Go, girl!"

Trying to shake off the concussion that prevented him from jaunting, Quatt straightened and charged forward, meeting the uniformed men who poured into the ward. Jisbella took Foyle's arm and dragged him out the back of the ward, through a pantry, a clinic, a laundry supply, and down flights of ancient stairs that buckled and threw up clouds of termite dust.

They came into a victual cellar. Baker's zoo had broken out of their cells in the chaos and were raiding the cellar like bees glutting themselves with honey in an attacked hive. A Cyclops girl was cramming her mouth with handfuls of butter scooped from a tub. Her single eye above the bridge of her nose leered at them.

Jisbella dragged Foyle through the victual cellar, found a bolted wooden door and kicked it open. They stumbled down a flight of crumbling steps and found themselves in what had once been a coal cellar. The concussions and roarings overhead sounded deeper and hollow. A chute slot on one side of the cellar was barred with an iron door held by iron clamps. Jisbella placed Foyle's hands on the clamps. Together they opened them and climbed out of the cellar through the coal chute.

They were outside the Freak Factory, huddled against the rear wall. Before them were the Trenton rocket pits, and as they gasped for breath, Jiz saw a freighter come sliding down an anti-grav beam into a waiting pit. Its portholes blazed and its recognition signals blinked like a lurid neon sign, illuminating the back wall of the hospital.

A figure leaped from the roof of the hospital. It was Sam Quatt, attempting a desperate flight. He sailed out into space, arms and legs flailing, trying to reach the up-thrusting anti-grav beam of the nearest pit which might catch him in mid-flight and cushion his fall. His aim was perfect. Seventy feet above ground he dropped squarely into the shaft of the beam. It was not in operation. He fell and was smashed on the edge of the pit.

Jisbella sobbed. Still automatically retaining her grip on Foyle's arm, she ran across the seamed concrete to Sam Quatt's body. There she let go of Foyle and touched Quatt's head tenderly. Her fingers were stained with blood. Foyle tore at the bandage before his eyes, working eye holes through the gauze. He muttered to himself, listening to Jisbella weep and hearing the shouts behind him from Baker's factory. His hands fumbled at Quatt's body, then he arose and tried to pull Jisbella up.

"Got to go," he croaked. "Got to get out. They've seen us."

Jisbella never moved. Foyle mustered all his strength and pulled her upright.

"Times Square," he muttered. "Jaunte, Jiz!"

Uniformed figures appeared around them. Foyle shook Jisbella's arm and jaunted to Times Square where masses of jaunters on the gigantic stage stared in amazement at the huge man with the white bandaged globe for a head. The stage was the size of two football fields. Foyle stared around dimly through the bandages. There was no sign of Jisbella but she might be anywhere. He lifted his voice to a shout.

"Montauk, Jiz! Montauk! The Folly Stage!"

Foyle jaunted with a last thrust of energy and a prayer. An icy nor'easter was blowing in from Block Island and sweeping brittle ice crystals across the stage on the site of a medieval ruin known as Fisher's Folly. There was another figure on the stage. Foyle tottered to it through the wind and the snow. It was Jisbella, looking frozen and lost.

"Thank God," Foyle muttered. "Thank God. Where does Sam keep his Weekender?" He shook Jisbella's elbow. "Where does Sam keep his Weekender?"

"Sam's dead."

"Where does he keep that Saturn Weekender?"

"He's retired, Sam is. He's not scared any more."

"Where's the ship, Jiz?"

"In the yards down at the lighthouse."

"Come on."

"Where?"

"To Sam's ship." Foyle thrust his big hand before Jisbella's eyes; a bunch of radiant keys lay in his palm. "I took his keys. Come on."

"He gave them to you?"

"I took them off his body."

"Ghoul!" She began to laugh. "Liar . . . Lecher . . . Tiger . . . Ghoul. The walking cancer . . . Gully Foyle."

Nevertheless she followed him through the snowstorm to Montauk Light.

*

To three acrobats wearing powdered wigs, four flamboyant women carrying pythons, a child with golden curls and a cynical mouth, a professional duellist in medieval armor, and a man wearing a hollow glass leg in which goldfish swam, Saul Dagenham said: "All right, the operation's finished. Call the rest off and tell them to report back to Courier headquarters."

The side show jaunted and disappeared. Regis Sheffield rubbed his eyes and asked: "What was that lunacy supposed to be, Dagenham?"

"Disturbs your legal mind, eh? That was part of the cast of our FFCC operation. Fun, fantasy, confusion, and catastrophe." Dagenham turned to Presteign and smiled his death's-head smile. "I'll return your fee if you like, Presteign."

"You're not quitting?"

"No, I'm enjoying myself. I'll work for nothing. I've never tangled with a man of Foyle's caliber before. He's unique."

"How?" Sheffield demanded.

"I arranged for him to escape from Gouffre Martel. He escaped, all right, but not my way. I tried to keep him out of police hands with confusion and catastrophe. He ducked the police, but not my way . . . his own way. I tried to keep him out of Central Intelligence's hands with fun and fantasy. He stayed clear . . . again his own way. I tried to detour him into a ship so he could make his try for 'Nomad.' He wouldn't detour, but he got his ship. He's on his way out now."

"You're following?"

"Naturally." Dagenham hesitated. "But what was he doing in Baker's factory?"

"Plastic surgery?" Sheffield suggested. "A new face?"

"Not possible. Baker's good, but he can't do a plastic that quick. It was minor surgery. Foyle was on his feet with his head bandaged."

"The tattoo," Presteign said.

Dagenham nodded and the smile left his lips. "That's what's worrying me. You realize, Presteign, that if Baker removed the tattooing we'll never recognize Foyle?"

"My dear Dagenham, his face won't be changed."

"We've never seen his face . . . only the mask."

"I haven't met the man at all," Sheffield said. "What's the mask like?"

"Like a tiger. I was with Foyle for two long sessions. I ought to know his face by heart, but I don't. All I know is the tattooing."

"Ridiculous," Sheffield said bluntly.

"No. Foyle has to be seen to be believed. However, it doesn't matter. He'll lead us out to 'Nomad.' He'll lead us to your bullion and PyrE, Presteign. I'm almost sorry it's all over. Or nearly. As I said, I've been enjoying myself. He really is unique."

Seven

THE Saturn Weekender was built like a pleasure yacht; it was ample for four, spacious for two, but not spacious enough for Foyle and Jiz McQueen. Foyle slept in the main cabin; Jiz kept to herself in the stateroom.

On the seventh day out, Jisbella spoke to Foyle for the second time: "Let's get those bandages off, Ghoul."

Foyle left the galley where he was sullenly heating coffee, and kicked back to the bathroom. He floated in after Jisbella and wedged himself into the alcove before the washbasin mirror. Jisbella braced herself on the basin, opened an ether capsule and began soaking and stripping the bandage off with hard, hating hands. The strips of gauze peeled slowly. Foyle was in agony of suspense.

"D'you think Baker did the job?" he asked.

No answer.

"Could he have missed anywhere?"

The stripping continued.

"It stopped hurting two days ago."

No answer.

"For God's sake, Jiz! Is it still war between us?"

Jisbella's hands stopped. She looked at Foyle's bandaged face with hatred. "What do you think?"

"I asked you."

"The answer is yes."

"Why?"

"You'll never understand."

"Make me understand."

"Shut up."

"If it's war, why'd you come with me?"

"To get what's coming to Sam and me."

"Money?"

"Shut up."

"You didn't have to. You could have trusted me."

"Trusted you? You?" Jisbella laughed without mirth and recommenced the peeling. Foyle struck her hands away.

"I'll do it myself."

She lashed him across his bandaged face. "You'll do what I tell you. Be still, Ghoul!"

She continued unwinding the bandage. A strip came away revealing Foyle's eyes. They stared at Jisbella, dark and brooding. The eyelids were clean; the bridge of the nose was clean. A strip came away from Foyle's chin. It was blue-black. Foyle, watching intently in the mirror, gasped.

"He missed the chin!" he exclaimed. "Baker goofed—"

"Shut up," Jiz answered shortly. "That's beard."

The innermost strips came away quickly, revealing cheeks, mouth, and brow. The brow was clean. The cheeks under the eyes were clean. The rest was covered with a blue-black seven day beard.

"Shave," Jiz commanded.

Foyle ran water, soaked his face, rubbed in shave ointment, and washed the beard off. Then he leaned close to the mirror and inspected himself, unaware that Jisbella's head was close to his as she too stared into the mirror. Not a mark of tattooing remained. Both sighed.

"It's clean," Foyle said. "Clean. He did the job." Suddenly he leaned further forward and inspected himself more closely. His face looked new to him, as new as it looked to Jisbella. "I'm changed. I don't remember looking like this. Did he do surgery on me too?"

"No," Jisbella said. "What's inside you changed it. That's the ghoul you're seeing, along with the liar and the cheat."

"For God's sake! Lay off. Let me alone!"

"Ghoul," Jisbella repeated, staring at Foyle's face with glowing eyes. "Liar. Cheat."

He took her shoulders and shoved her out into the

companionway. She went sailing down into the main lounge, caught a guide bar and spun herself around. "Ghoul!" she cried. "Liar! Cheat! Ghoul! Lecher! Beast!"

Foyle pursued her, seized her again and shook her violently. Her red hair burst out of the clip that gathered it at the nape of her neck and floated out like a mermaid's tresses. The burning expression on her face transformed Foyle's anger into passion. He enveloped her and buried his new face in her breast.

"Lecher," Jiz murmured. "Animal . . ."

"Oh, Jiz . . ."

"The light," Jisbella whispered. Foyle reached out blindly toward the wall switches and pressed buttons, and the Saturn Weekender drove on toward the asteroids with darkened portholes.

They floated together in the cabin, drowsing, murmuring, touching tenderly for hours.

"Poor Gully," Jisbella whispered. "Poor darling Gully . . ."

"Not poor," he said. "Rich . . . soon."

"Yes, rich and empty. You've got nothing inside you, Gully dear . . . Nothing but hatred and revenge."

"It's enough."

"Enough for now. But later?"

"Later? That depends."

"It depends on your inside, Gully; what you get hold of."

"No. My future depends on what I get rid of."

"Gully . . . why did you hold out on me in Gouffre Martel? Why didn't you tell me you knew there was a fortune aboard 'Nomad'?"

"I couldn't."

"Didn't you trust me?"

"It wasn't that. I couldn't help myself. That's what's inside me . . . what I have to get rid of."

"Control again, eh Gully? You're driven."

"Yes, I'm driven. I can't learn control, Jiz. I want to, but I can't."

"Do you try?"

"I do. God knows, I do. But then something happens, and—"

"And then you pounce like a tiger."

"If I could carry you in my pocket, Jiz . . . to warn me . . . stick a pin in me . . ."

"Nobody can do it for you, Gully. You have to learn yourself."

He digested that for a long moment. Then he spoke hesitantly: "Jiz . . . about the money . . . ?"

"To hell with the money."

"Can I hold you to that?"

"Oh, Gully."

"Not that I . . . that I'm trying to hold out on you. If it wasn't for 'Vorga,' I'd give you all you wanted. All! I'll give you every cent left over when I'm finished. But I'm scared, Jiz. 'Vorga' is tough . . . what with Presteign and Dagenham and that lawyer, Sheffield. I've got to hold on to every cent, Jiz. I'm afraid if I let you take one credit, that could make the difference between 'Vorga' and I."

"Me."

"Me." He waited. "Well?"

"You're all possessed," she said wearily. "Not just a part of you, but all of you."

"No."

"Yes, Gully. All of you. It's just your skin making love to me. The rest is feeding on 'Vorga.'"

At that moment the radar alarm in the forward control cabin burst upon them, unwelcome and warning.

"Destination zero," Foyle muttered, no longer relaxed, once more possessed. He shot forward into the control cabin.

So he returned to the freak planetoid in the asteroid belt between Mars and Jupiter, the Sargasso planet manufactured of rock and wreckage and the spoils of space disaster salvaged by the Scientific People. He returned to the home of Jŏseph and his People who had tattooed NOMAD across his face and scientifically mated him to the girl named Mǫira.

Foyle overran the asteroid with the sudden fury of a Vandal raid. He came blasting out of space, braked with a spume of flame from the forward jets, and kicked the Weekender into a tight spin around the junkheap. They whirled around, passing the blackened ports, the big hatch from which Jŏseph and his Scientific People emerged to collect the drifting debris of space, the new crater Foyle had torn out of the side of the asteroid in his first plunge back to Terra. They whipped past the giant patchwork windows of the asteroid greenhouse and saw hundreds of faces peering out at them, tiny white dots mottled with tattooing.

"So I didn't murder them," Foyle grunted. "They've pulled back into the asteroid . . . Probably living deep inside while they get the rest repaired."

"Will you help them, Gully?"

"Why?"

"You did the damage."

"To hell with them. I've got my own problems. But it's a relief. They won't be bothering us."

He circled the asteroid once more and brought the Weekender down in the mouth of the new crater.

"We'll work from here," he said. "Get into a suit, Jiz. Let's go! Let's go!"

He drove her, mad with impatience; he drove himself. They corked up in their spacesuits, left the Weekender, and went sprawling through the debris in the crater into the bleak bowels of the asteroid. It was like squirming through the crawling tunnels of giant worm-holes. Foyle switched on his micro-wave suit set and spoke to Jiz.

"Be easy to get lost in here. Stay with me. Stay close."

"Where are we going, Gully?"

"After 'Nomad.' I remember they were cementing her into the asteroid when I left. Don't remember where. Have to find her."

The passages were airless, and their progress was soundless, but the vibrations carried through metal and rock. They paused once for breath alongside the pitted hull of an ancient warship. As they leaned against it they felt the vibrations of signals from within, a rhythmic knocking.

Foyle smiled grimly. "That's Joseph and The Scientific People inside," he said. "Requesting a few words. I'll give 'em an evasive answer." He pounded twice on the hull. "And now a personal message for my wife." His face darkened. He smote the hull angrily and turned away. "Come on. Let's go."

But as they continued the search, the signals followed them. It became apparent that the outer periphery of the asteroid had been abandoned; the tribe had withdrawn to the center. Then, far down a shaft wrought of beaten aluminium, a hatch opened, light blazed forth, and Jo͡seph appeared in an ancient spacesuit fashioned of glass cloth. He stood in the clumsy sack, his devil face staring, his hands clutched in supplication, his devil mouth making motions.

Foyle stared at the old man, took a step toward him, and then stopped, fists clenched, throat working as fury arose within him. And Jisbella, looking at Foyle, cried out in horror. The old tattooing had returned to his face, blood red against the pallor of the skin, scarlet instead of black, truly a tiger mask in color as well as design.

"Gully!" she cried. "My God! Your face!"

Foyle ignored her and stood glaring at Jo͡seph while the old man made beseeching gestures, motioned to them to enter the interior of the asteroid, and then disappeared. Only then did Foyle turn to Jisbella and ask: "What? What did you say?"

Through the clear globe of the helmet she could see his face distinctly. And as the rage within Foyle died away, Jisbella saw the blood-red tattooing fade and disappear.

"Did you see that joker?" Foyle demanded. "That was Joseph. Did you see him begging and pleading after what he did to me . . . ? What did you say?"

"Your face, Gully. I know what's happened to your face."

"What are you talking about?"

"You wanted something that would control you, Gully. Well, you've got it. Your face. It—" Jisbella began to laugh hysterically. "You'll have to learn control now, Gully. You'll never be able to give way to emotion . . . any emotion . . . because—"

But he was staring past her and suddenly he shot up the aluminium shaft with a yell. He jerked to a stop before an open door and began to whoop in triumph. The door opened into a tool locker, four by four by nine. There were shelves in the locker and a jumble of old provisions and discarded containers. It was Foyle's coffin aboard the "Nomad."

Jo͡seph and his people had succeeded in sealing the wreck into their asteroid before the holocaust of Foyle's escape had rendered further work impossible. The interior of the ship was virtually untouched. Foyle took Jisbella's arm and dragged her on a quick tour of the ship and finally to the purser's locker where Foyle tore at the windrows of wreckage and debris until he disclosed a massive steel face, blank and impenetrable.

"We've got a choice," he panted. "Either we tear the safe out of the hull and carry it back to Terra where we can work on it, or we open it here. I vote for here. Maybe Dagenham was lying. All depends on what tools Sam has in the Weekender anyway. Come back to the ship, Jiz."

He never noticed her silence and preoccupation until they were back aboard the Weekender and he had finished his urgent search for tools.

"Nothing!" he exclaimed impatiently. "There isn't a hammer or a drill aboard. Nothing but gadgets for opening bottles and rations."

Jisbella didn't answer. She never took her eyes off his face.

"Why are you staring at me like that?" Foyle demanded.

"I'm fascinated," Jisbella answered slowly.

"By what?"

"I'm going to show you something, Gully."

"What?"

"How much I despise you."

Jisbella slapped him thrice. Stung by the blows, Foyle started up furiously. Jisbella picked up a hand mirror and held it before him.

"Look at yourself, Gully," she said quietly. "Look at your face."

He looked. He saw the old tattoo marks flaming blood-red under the skin, turning his face into a scarlet and white tiger mask. He was so chilled by the appalling spectacle that his rage died at once, and simultaneously the mask disappeared.

"My God . . ." he whispered. "Oh my God . . ."

"I had to make you lose your temper to show you," Jisbella said.

"What's it mean, Jiz? Did Baker goof the job?"

"I don't think so. I think you've got scars under the skin, Gully . . . from the original tattooing and then from the bleaching. Needle scars. They don't show normally, but they do show, blood red, when your emotions take over and your heart begins pumping blood . . . when you're furious or frightened or passionate or possessed . . . Do you understand?"

He shook his head, still staring at his face, touching it in bewilderment.

"You said you wished you could carry me in your pocket to stick pins in you when you lose control. You've got something better than that, Gully, or worse, poor darling. You've got your face."

"No!" he said. "No!"

"You can't ever lose control, Gully. You'll never be able to drink too much, eat too much, love too much, hate too much . . . You'll have to hold yourself with an iron grip."

"No!" he insisted desperately. "It can be fixed. Baker can do it, or somebody else. I can't walk around afraid to feel anything because it'll turn me into a freak!"

"I don't think this can be fixed, Gully."

"Skin-graft . . ."

"No. The scars are too deep for graft. You'll never get rid of this stigmata, Gully. You'll have to learn to live with it."

Foyle flung the mirror from him in sudden rage, and again the blood-red mask flared up under his skin. He lunged out of the main cabin to the main hatch where he pulled his spacesuit down and began to squirm into it.

"Gully! Where are you going? What are you going to do?"

"Get tools," he shouted. "Tools for the safe."

"Where?"

"In the asteroid. They've got dozens of warehouses stuffed with tools from wrecked ships. There have to be drills there, everything I need. Don't come with me. There may be trouble. How is my God damned face now? Showing it? By Christ, I hope there *is* trouble!"

He corked his suit and went into the asteroid. He found a hatch separating the habited core from the outer void. He banged on the door. He waited and banged again and continued the imperious summons until at last the hatch was opened. Arms reached out and yanked him in, and the hatch was closed behind him. It had no air lock.

He blinked in the light and scowled at Jŏseph and his innocent people gathering before him, their faces hideously decorated. And he knew that his own face must be flaming red and white for he saw Jŏseph start, and he saw the devil mouth shape the syllables: NOMAD.

Foyle strode through the crowd, scattering them brutally. He smashed Joseph with a backhand blow from his mailed fist. He searched through the inhabited corridors, recognizing them dimly, and he came at last to the chamber, half natural cave, half antique hull, where the tools were stored.

He rooted and ferreted, gathering up drills, diamond bits, acids, thermites, crystallants, dynamite jellies, fuses. In the gently revolving asteroid the gross weight of the equipment was reduced to less than a hundred pounds. He lumped it into a mass, roughly bound it together with cable, and started out of the store-cave.

Joseph and his Scientific People were waiting for him, like fleas waiting for a wolf. They darted at him and he battered through them, harried, delighted, savage. The armor of his spacesuit protected him from their attacks and he went down the passages searching for a hatch that would lead out into the void.

Jisbella's voice came to him, tinny on the earphones and agitated: "Gully, can you hear me? This is Jiz. Gully, listen to me."

"Go ahead."

"Another ship came up two minutes ago. It's drifting on the other side of the asteroid."

"What!"

"It's marked with yellow and black colors, like a hornet."

"Dagenham's colors!"

"Then we've been followed."

"What else? Dagenham's probably had a fix on me ever since we busted out of Gouffre Martel. I was a fool not to think of it. We've got to work fast, Jiz. Cork up in a suit and meet me aboard 'Nomad.' The purser's room. Go, girl."

"But Gully . . ."

"Sign off. They may be monitoring our waveband. Go!"

He drove through the asteroid, reached a barred hatch, broke through the guard before it, smashed it open and went into the void of the outer passages. The Scientific People were too desperate getting the hatch closed to stop him. But he knew they would follow him; they were raging.

He hauled the bulk of his equipment through twists and turns to the wreck of the "Nomad." Jisbella was waiting for him in the purser's room. She made a move to turn on her micro-wave set and Foyle stopped her. He placed his helmet against hers and shouted: "No shortwave. They'll be monitoring and they'll locate us by D/F. You can hear me like this, can't you?"

She nodded.

"All right. We've got maybe an hour before Dagenham locates us. We've got maybe an hour before Joseph and his mob come after us. We're in a hell of a jam. We've got to work fast."

She nodded again.

"No time to open the safe and transport the bullion."

"If it's there."

"Dagenham's here, isn't he? That's proof it's there. We'll have to cut the whole safe out of the 'Nomad' and get it into the Weekender. Then we blast."

"But—"

"Just listen to me and do what I say. Go back to the Weekender. Empty it out. Jettison everything we don't need . . . all supplies except emergency rations."

"Why?"

"Because I don't know how many tons this safe weighs, and the ship may not be able to handle it when we come back to gravity. We've got to make allowances in advance. It'll mean a tough trip back but it's worth it. Strip the ship. Fast! Go, girl. Go!"

He pushed her away and without another glance in her direction, attacked the safe. It was built into the structural steel of the hull, a massive steel ball some four feet in diameter. It was welded to the strakes and ribs of the "Nomad" at twelve different spots. Foyle attacked each weld in turn with acids, drills, thermite, and refrigerants. He was operating on the theory of structural strain . . . to heat, freeze, and etch the steel until its crystalline structure was distorted and its physical strength destroyed. He was fatiguing the metal.

Jisbella returned and he realized that forty-five minutes had passed. He was dripping and shaking but the globe of the safe hung free of the hull with a dozen rough knobs protruding from its surface. Foyle motioned urgently to Jisbella and she strained her weight against the safe with him. They could not budge its mass together. As they sank back in exhaustion and despair, a quick shadow eclipsed the sunlight pouring through the rents in the "Nomad" hull. They stared up. A spaceship was circling the asteroid less than a quarter of a mile off.

Foyle placed his helmet against Jisbella's. "Dagenham," he gasped. "Looking for us. Probably got a crew down here combing for us too. Soon as they talk to Joseph they'll be here."

"Oh Gully . . ."

"We've still got a chance. Maybe they won't spot Sam's Weekender until they've made a couple of revolutions. It's hidden in that crater. Maybe we can get the safe aboard in the meantime."

"How, Gully?"

"I don't know, damn it! I don't know." He pounded his fists together in frustration. "I'm finished."

"Couldn't we blast it out?"

"Blast . . . ? What, bombs instead of brains? Is this Mental McQueen speaking?"

"Listen. Blast it with something explosive. That would act like a rocket jet . . . give it a thrust."

"Yes, I've got that. But then what? How do we get it into the ship, girl? Can't keep on blasting. Haven't got time."

"No, we bring the ship to the safe."

"What?"

"Blast the safe straight out into space. Then bring the ship around and let the safe sail right into the main hatch. Like catching a ball in your hat. See?"

He saw. "By God, Jiz, we can do it." Foyle leaped to the pile of equipment and began sorting out sticks of dynamite gelatine, fuses and caps.

"We'll have to use the short-wave. One of us stays with the safe; one of us pilots the ship. Man with the safe talks the man with the ship into position. Right?"

"Right. You'd better pilot, Gully. I'll do the talking."

He nodded, fixing explosive to the face of the safe, attaching caps and fuses. Then he placed his helmet against hers. "Vacuum fuses, Jiz. Timed for two minutes. When I give the word by short-wave, just pull off the fuse heads and get the hell out of the way. Right?"

"Right."

"Stay with the safe. Once you've talked it into the ship, come right after it. Don't wait for anything. It's going to be close."

He thumped her shoulder and returned to the Weekender. He left the outer hatch open, and the inner door of the airlock as well. The ship's air emptied out immediately. Airless and stripped by Jisbella, it looked dismal and forlorn.

Foyle went directly to the controls, sat down and switched on his micro-wave set. "Stand by," he muttered. "I'm coming out now."

He ignited the jets, blew the laterals for three seconds and then the forwards. The Weekender lifted easily, shaking debris from her back and sides like a whale surfacing. As she slid up and back, Foyle called: "Dynamite, Jiz! Now!"

There was no blast; there was no flash. A new crater opened in the asteroid below him and a flower of rubble sprang upward, rapidly outdistancing a dull steel ball that followed leisurely, turning in a weary spin.

"Ease off." Jisbella's voice came cold and competent over the earphones. "You're backing too fast. And incidentally, trouble's arrived."

He braked with the rear jets, looking down in alarm. The surface of the asteroid was covered with a swarm of hornets. They were Dagenham's crew in yellow and black banded spacesuits. They were buzzing around a single figure in white that dodged and spun and eluded them. It was Jisbella.

"Steady as you go," Jiz said quietly, although he could hear how hard she was breathing. "Ease off a little more . . . Roll a quarter turn."

He obeyed her almost automatically, still watching the struggle below. The flank of the Weekender cut off any view of the trajectory of the safe as it approached him, but he could still see Jisbella and Dagenham's men. She ignited her suit rocket . . . he could see the tiny spurt of flame shoot out from her back . . . and came sailing up from the surface of the asteroid. A score of flames burst out from the backs of Dagenham's men as they followed. Half a dozen dropped the pursuit of Jisbella and came up after the Weekender.

"It's going to be close, Gully." Jisbella was gasping now, but her voice was still steady. "Dagenham's ship came down on the other side, but they've probably signaled him by now and he'll be on his way. Hold your position, Gully. About ten seconds now . . ."

The hornets closed in and engulfed the tiny white suit.

"Foyle! Can you hear me? Foyle!" Dagenham's voice came in fuzzily and finally cleared. "This is Dagenham calling on your band. Come in, Foyle!"

"Jiz! Jiz! Can you get clear of them?"

"Hold your position, Gully. . . . There she goes! It's a hole in one, son!"

A crushing shock racked the Weekender as the safe, moving slowly but massively, rammed into the main hatch. At the same moment the white suited figure broke out of the cluster of yellow wasps. It came rocketing up to the Weekender, hotly pursued.

"Come on, Jiz! Come on!" Foyle howled. "Come, girl! Come!"

As Jisbella disappeared from sight behind the flank of the Weekender, Foyle set controls and prepared for top acceleration.

"Foyle! Will you answer me? This is Dagenham speaking."

"To hell with you, Dagenham," Foyle shouted. "Give me the word when you're aboard, Jiz, and hold on."

"I can't make it, Gully."

"Come on, girl!"

"I can't get aboard. The safe's blocking the hatch. It's wedged in halfway . . ."

"Jiz!"

"There's no way in, I tell you," she cried in despair. "I'm blocked out."

He stared around wildly. Dagenham's men were boarding the hull of the Weekender with the menacing purpose of professional raiders. Dagenham's ship was lifting over the brief horizon of the asteroid on a dead course for him. His head began to spin.

"Foyle, you're finished. You and the girl. But I'll offer a deal . . ."

"Gully, help me. Do something, Gully. I'm lost!"

"Vorga," he said in a strangled voice. He closed his eyes and tripped the controls. The tail jets roared. The Weekender shook and shuddered forward. It broke free of Dagenham's boarders, of Jisbella, of warnings and pleas. It pressed Foyle back into the pilot's chair with the blackout of 10G acceleration, an acceleration that was less pressing, less painful, less treacherous than the passion that drove him.

And as he passed from sight there rose up on his face the blood-red stigmata of his possession.

Part 2

With a heart of furious fancies
  Whereof I am commander,
With a burning spear and a horse of air,
  To the wilderness I wander.
With a knight of ghosts and shadows
  I summoned am to tourney,
Ten leagues beyond the wide world's end—
  Methinks it is no journey.

                                 Tom-a-Bedlam

Eight

THE old year soured as pestilence poisoned the planets. The war gained momentum and grew from a distant affair of romantic raids and skirmishes in space to a holocaust in the making. It became evident that the last of the World Wars was done and the first of the Solar Wars had begun.

The belligerents slowly massed men and materiel for the havoc. The Outer Satellites introduced universal conscription, and the Inner Planets perforce followed suit. Industries, trades, sciences, skills, and professions were drafted; regulations and oppressions followed. The armies and navies requisitioned and commanded.

Commerce obeyed, for this war (like all wars) was the shooting phase of a commercial struggle. But populations rebelled, and draft-jaunting and labor-jaunting became critical problems. Spy scares and invasion scares spread. The hysterical became informers and lynchers. An ominous foreboding paralyzed every home from Baffin Island to the Falklands. The dying year was enlivened only by the advent of the Four Mile Circus.

This was the popular nickname for the grotesque entourage of Geoffrey Fourmyle of Ceres, a wealthy young buffoon from the largest of the asteroids. Fourmyle of Ceres was enormously rich; he was also enormously amusing. He was the classic *nouveau riche* of all time. His entourage was a cross between a country circus and the comic court of a Bulgarian kinglet, as witness this typical arrival in Green Bay, Wisconsin.

Early in the morning a lawyer, wearing the stovepipe hat of a legal clan, appeared with a list of camp sites in his hand and a small fortune in his pocket. He settled on a four-acre meadow facing Lake Michigan and rented it for an exorbitant fee. He was followed by a gang of surveyors from the Mason & Dixon clan. In twenty minutes the surveyors had laid out a camp site and the word had spread that the Four Mile Circus was arriving. Locals from Wisconsin, Michigan, and Minnesota came to watch the fun.

Twenty roustabouts jaunted in, each carrying a tent pack on his back. There was a mighty overture of bawled orders, shouts, curses, and the tortured scream of compressed air. Twenty giant tents ballooned upward, their lac and latex surfaces gleaming as they dried in the winter sun. The spectators cheered.

A six-motor helicopter drifted down and hovered over a giant trampoline. Its belly opened and a cascade of furnishings came down. Servants, valets, chefs, and waiters jaunted in. They furnished and decorated the tents. The kitchens began smoking and the odor of frying, broiling, and baking pervaded the camp. Fourmyle's private police were already on duty, patrolling the four acres, keeping the huge crowd of spectators back.

Then, by plane, by car, by bus, by truck, by bike and by jaunte came Fourmyle's entourage. Librarians and books, scientists and laboratories, philosophers, poets, athletes. Racks of swords and sabres were set up, and judo mats and a boxing ring. A fifty-foot pool was sunk in the ground and filled by pump from the lake. An interesting altercation arose between two beefy athletes as to whether the pool should be warmed for swimming or frozen for skating.

Musicians, actors, jugglers, and acrobats arrived. The uproar became deafening. A crew of mechanics melted a grease-pit and began revving up Fourmyle's collection of vintage diesel harvesters. Last of all came the camp followers: wives, daughters, mistresses, whores, beggars, chiselers, and grafters. By midmorning the roar of the circus could be heard for four miles, hence the nickname.

At noon, Fourmyle of Ceres arrived with a display of conspicuous transportation so outlandish that it had been known to make seven-year melancholics laugh. A giant amphibian thrummed up from the south and landed on the lake. An LST barge emerged from the plane and droned across the water to the shore. Its forward wall banged down into a drawbridge and out came a twentieth century staff car. Wonder piled on wonder for the delighted spectators, for the staff car drove a matter of twenty yards to the center of camp and then stopped.

"What can possibly come next? Bike?"

"No, roller skates."

"He'll come out on a pogo stick."

Fourmyle capped their wildest speculations. The muzzle of a circus cannon thrust up from the staff car. There was the bang of a black-powder explosion and Fourmyle of Ceres was shot out of the cannon in a graceful arc to the very door of his tent where he was caught in a net by four valets. The applause that greeted him could be heard for six miles. Fourmyle climbed onto his valets' shoulders and motioned for silence.

"Friends, Romans, Countrymen," Fourmyle began earnestly. "Lend me your ears, Shakespeare. 1564–1616. Damn!" Four white doves shook themselves out of Fourmyle's sleeves and fluttered away. He regarded them with astonishment, then continued. "Friends, greetings, salutations, *bonjour, bon ton, bon vivant, bon voyage, bon*— What the hell?" Fourmyle's pockets caught fire and rocketed forth Roman Candles. He tried to put himself out. Streamers and confetti burst from him. "Friends . . . Shut up! I'll get this speech straight. Quiet! Friends—!" Fourmyle looked down at himself in dismay. His clothes were melting away, revealing lurid scarlet underwear. "Kleinmann!" he bellowed furiously. "Kleinmann! What's happened to your goddamned hypno-training?"

A hairy head thrust out of a tent. "You stoodied for dis sbeech last night, Fourmyle?"

"Damn right. For two hours I stoodied. Never took my head out of the hypno-oven. Kleinmann on Prestidigitation."

"No, no, no!" the hairy man bawled. "How many times must I tell you? Prestidigitation is not sbeechmaking. Is magic. *Dumbkopf!* You haff the wrong hypnosis taken!"

The scarlet underwear began melting. Fourmyle toppled from the shoulders of his shaking valets and disappeared within his tent. There was a roar of laughter and cheering and the Four Mile Circus ripped into high gear. The kitchens sizzled and smoked. There was a perpetuity of eating and drinking. The music never stopped. The vaudeville never ceased.

Inside his tent, Fourmyle changed his clothes, changed his mind, changed again, undressed again, kicked his valets, and called for his tailor in a bastard tongue of French, Mayfair, and affectation. Halfway into a new suit, he recollected he had neglected to bathe. He slapped his tailor, ordered ten gallons of scent to be decanted into the pool, and was stricken with poetic inspiration. He summoned his resident poet.

"Take this down," Fourmyle commanded. "*Le roi est mort, les*— Wait. What rhymes to moon?"

"June," his poet suggested. "Croon, soon, dune, loon, noon, rune, tune, boon . . ."

"I forgot my experiment!" Fourmyle exclaimed. "Dr. Bohun! Dr. Bohun!"

Half-naked, he rushed pell-mell into the laboratory where he blew himself and Dr. Bohun, his resident chemist, halfway across the tent. As the chemist attempted to raise himself from the floor he found himself seized in a most painful and embarrassing strangle hold.

"Nogouchi!" Fourmyle shouted. "Hi! Nogouchi! I just invented a new judo hold."

Fourmyle stood up, lifted the suffocating chemist and jaunted to the judo mat where the little Japanese inspected the hold and shook his head.

"No, please." He hissed politely. "Hfffff. Pressure on windpipe are not perpetually lethal. Hfffff. I show you, please." He seized the dazed chemist, whirled him and deposited him on the mat in a position of perpetual self-strangulation. "You observe, please, Fourmyle?"

But Fourmyle was in the library bludgeoning his librarian over the head with Bloch's "*Das Sexual Leben*" (eight pounds, nine ounces) because that unhappy man could produce no text on the manufacture of perpetual motion machines. He rushed to his physics laboratory where he destroyed an expensive chronometer to experiment with cog wheels, jaunted to the bandstand where he seized a baton and led the orchestra into confusion, put on skates and fell into the scented swimming pool, was hauled out, swearing fulminously at the lack of ice, and was heard to express a desire for solitude.

"I wish to commute with myself," Fourmyle said, kicking his valets in all directions. He was snoring before the last of them limped to the door and closed it behind him.

The snoring stopped and Foyle arose. "That ought to hold them for today," he muttered, and went into his dressing room. He stood before a mirror, took a deep breath and held it, meanwhile watching his face. At the expiration of one minute it was still untainted. He continued to hold his breath, maintaining rigid control over pulse and muscle, mastering the strain with iron calm. At two minutes and twenty seconds the stigmata appeared, blood-red. Foyle let out his breath. The tiger mask faded.

"Better," he murmured. "Much better. The old fakir was right, Yoga is the answer. Control. Pulse, breath, bowels, brains."

He stripped and examined his body. He was in magnificent condition, but his skin still showed delicate silver seams in a network from neck to ankles. It looked as though someone had carved an outline of the nervous system into Foyle's flesh. The silver seams were the scars of an operation that had not yet faded.

That operation had cost Foyle a ₵r 200,000 bribe to the chief surgeon of the Mars Commando Brigade and had transformed him into an extraordinary fighting machine. Every nerve plexus had been rewired, microscopic transistors and transformers had been buried in muscle and bone, a minute platinum outlet showed at the base of his spine. To this Foyle affixed a power-pack the size of a pea and switched it on. His body began an internal electronic vibration that was almost mechanical.

"More machine than man," he thought. He dressed, rejected the extravagant apparel of Fourmyle of Ceres for the anonymous black coverall of action.

He jaunted to Robin Wednesbury's apartment in the lonely building amidst the Wisconsin pines. It was the real reason for the advent of the Four Mile Circus in Green Bay. He jaunted and arrived in darkness and empty space and immediately plummeted down. "Wrong co-ordinates!" he thought. "Misjaunted?" The broken end of a rafter dealt him a bruising blow and he landed heavily on a shattered floor upon the putrefying remains of a corpse.

Foyle leaped up in calm revulsion. He pressed hard with his tongue against his right upper first molar. The operation that had transformed half his body into an electronic machine, had located the control switchboard in his teeth. Foyle pressed a tooth with his tongue and the peripheral cells of his retina were excited into emitting a soft light. He looked down two pale beams at the corpse of a man.

The corpse lay in the apartment below Robin Wednesbury's flat. It was gutted. Foyle looked up. Above him was a ten-foot hole where the floor of Robin's living room had been. The entire building stank of fire, smoke, and rot.

"Jacked," Foyle said softly. "This place has been jacked. What happened?"

The jaunting age had crystallized the hoboes, tramps, and vagabonds of the world into a new class. They followed the night from east to west, always in darkness, always in search of loot, the leavings of disaster, carrion. If earthquake shattered a warehouse, they were jacking it the following night. If fire opened a house or explosion split the defenses of a shop, they jaunted in and scavenged. They called themselves Jack-jaunters. They were jackals.

Foyle climbed up through the wreckage to the corridor on the floor above. The Jack-jaunters had a camp there. A whole calf roasted before a fire which sparked up to the sky through a rent in the roof. There were a dozen men and three women around the fire, rough, dangerous, jabbering in the Cockney rhyming slang of the jackals. They were dressed in mismatched clothes and drinking potato beer from champagne glasses.

An ominous growl of anger and terror met Foyle's appearance as the big man in black came up through the rubble, his intent eyes emitting pale beams of light. Calmly, he strode through the rising mob to the entrance of Robin Wednesbury's flat. His iron control gave him an air of detachment.

"If she's dead," he thought, "I'm finished. I've got to use her. But if she's dead . . ."

Robin's apartment was gutted like the rest of the building. The living room was an oval of floor around the jagged hole in the center. Foyle searched for a body. Two men and a woman were in the bed in the bedroom. The men cursed. The woman shrieked at the apparition. The men hurled themselves at Foyle. He backed a step and pressed his tongue against his upper incisors. Neural circuits buzzed and every sense and response in his body was accelerated by a factor of five.

The effect was an instantaneous reduction of the external world to extreme slow motion. Sound became a deep garble. Color shifted down the spectrum to the red. The two assailants seemed to float toward him with dreamlike languor. To the rest of the world Foyle became a blur of action. He sidestepped the blow inching toward him, walked around the man, raised him and threw him toward the crater in the living room. He threw the second man after the first jackal. To Foyle's accelerated senses their bodies seemed to drift slowly, still in mid-stride, fists inching forward, open mouths emitting heavy clotted sounds.

Foyle whipped to the woman cowering in the bed.

"Wsthrabdy?" the blur asked.

The woman shrieked.

Foyle pressed his upper incisors again, cutting off the accel-eration. The external world shook itself out of slow motion back to normal. Sound and color leaped up the spectrum and the two jackals disappeared through the crater and crashed into the apartment below.

"Was there a body?" Foyle repeated gently. "A Negro girl?" The woman was unintelligible. He took her by the hair and shook her, then hurled her through the crater in the living room floor.

His search for a clue to Robin's fate was interrupted by the mob from the hall. They carried torches and makeshift weap-ons. The Jack-jaunters were not professional killers. They only worried defenseless prey to death. "Don't bother me," Foyle warned quietly, ferreting intently through closets and under overturned furniture.

They edged closer, goaded by a ruffian in a mink suit and a tricornered hat, and inspired by the curses percolating up from the floor below. The man in the tricorne threw a torch at Foyle. It burned him. Foyle accelerated again and the Jack-jaunters were transformed into living statues. Foyle picked up half a chair and calmly clubbed the slow-motion figures. They re-mained upright. He thrust the man in the tricorne down on the floor and knelt on him. Then he decelerated.

Again the external world came to life. The jackals dropped in their tracks, pole-axed. The man in the tricorne hat and mink suit roared.

"Was there a body in here?" Foyle asked. "Negro girl. Very tall. Very beautiful."

The man writhed and attempted to gouge Foyle's eyes.

"You keep track of bodies," Foyle said gently. "Some of you Jacks like dead girls better than live ones. Did you find her body in here?"

Receiving no satisfactory answer, he picked up a torch and set fire to the mink suit. He followed the Jack-jaunter into the living room and watched him with detached interest. The man howled, toppled over the edge of the crater and flamed down into the darkness below.

"Was there a body?" Foyle called down quietly. He shook his head at the answer. "Not very deft," he murmured. "I've got to learn how to extract information. Dagenham could teach me a thing or two."

He switched off his electronic system and jaunted.

He appeared in Green Bay, smelling so abominably of singed hair and scorched skin that he entered the local Presteign shop (jewels, perfumes, cosmetics, ionics & surrogates) to buy a deodorant. But the local Mr. Presto had evidently witnessed the arrival of the Four Mile Circus and recognized him. Foyle at once awoke from his detached intensity and became the outlandish Fourmyle of Ceres. He clowned and cavorted, bought a twelve-ounce flagon of *Euge No. 5* at ₢r 100 the ounce, dabbed himself delicately and tossed the bottle into the street to the edification and delight of Mr. Presto.

The record clerk at the County Record Office was unaware of Foyle's identity and was obdurate and uncompromising.

"No, Sir. County Records Are Not Viewed Without Proper Court Order For Sufficient Cause. That Must Be Final."

Foyle examined him keenly and without rancor. "Asthenic type," he decided. "Slender, long-boned, no strength. Epileptoid character. Self-centered, pedantic, single-minded, shallow. Not bribable; too repressed and straitlaced. But repression's the chink in his armor."

An hour later six followers from the Four Mile Circus waylaid the record clerk. They were of the female persuasion and richly endowed with vice. Two hours later, the record clerk, dazed by flesh and the devil, delivered up his information. The apartment building had been opened to Jack-jaunting by a gas explosion two weeks earlier. All tenants had been forced to move. Robin Wednesbury was in protective confinement in Mercy Hospital near the Iron Mountain Proving Grounds.

"Protective confinement?" Foyle wondered. "What for? What's she done?"

It took thirty minutes to organize a Christmas party in the Four Mile Circus. It was made up of musicians, singers, actors, and rabble who knew the Iron Mountain co-ordinates. Led by their chief buffoon, they jaunted up with music, fireworks, firewater, and gifts. They paraded through the town spreading largess and laughter. They blundered into the radar field of the Proving Ground protection system and were driven out with laughter. Fourmyle of Ceres, dressed as Santa Claus, scattering bank notes from a huge sack over his shoulder and, leaping in agony as the induction field of the protection system burned his bottom, made an entrancing spectacle. They burst into Mercy Hospital, following Santa Claus who roared and cavorted with the detached calm of a solemn elephant. He kissed the nurses, made drunk the attendants, pestered the patients with gifts, littered the corridors with money, and abruptly disappeared when the happy rioting reached such heights that the police had to be called. Much later it was discovered that a patient had disappeared too, despite the fact that she had been under sedation and was incapable of jaunting. As a matter of fact she departed from the hospital inside Santa's sack.

Foyle jaunted with her over his shoulder to the hospital grounds. There, in a quiet grove of pines under a frosty sky, he helped her out of the sack. She wore severe white hospital pajamas and was beautiful. He removed his own costume, watching the girl intently, waiting to see if she would recognize him and remember him.

She was alarmed and confused; her telesending was like heat lightning: *"My God! Who is he? What's happened? The music. The uproar. Why kidnapped in a sack? Drunks slurring on trombones. 'Yes, Virginia, there is a Santa Claus.' Adeste Fideles. What's he want from me? Who is he?"*

"I'm Fourmyle of Ceres," Foyle said.

"What? Who? Fourmyle of—? Yes, of course. *The buffoon. The bourgeois gentilhomme. Vulgarity. Imbecility. Obscenity. The Four Mile Circus.* My God! Am I telesending? Can you hear me?"

"I hear you, Miss Wednesbury," Foyle said quietly.

"What have you done? Why? What do you want with me? I—"

"I want you to look at me."

"*Bonjour, Madame. Into my sack, Madame. Ecco! Look at me.* I'm looking," Robin said, trying to control the jangle of her thoughts. She gazed up into his face without recognition. *"It's a face. I've seen so many like it. The faces of men, oh God! The features of masculinity. Everyman in rut. Will God never save us from brute desire?"*

"My rutting season's over, Miss Wednesbury."

"I'm sorry you heard that. I'm terrified, naturally. I— You know me?"

"I know you."

"We've met before?" She scrutinized him closely, but still without recognition. Deep down inside Foyle there was a surge of triumph. If this woman of all women failed to remember him he was safe, provided he kept blood and brains and face under control.

"We've never met," he said. "I've heard of you. I want something from you. That's why we're here; to talk about it. If you don't like my offer you can go back to the hospital."

"You want something? *But I've got nothing . . . nothing. Nothing's left but shame and—Oh God! Why did the suicide fail? Why couldn't I—"*

"So that's it?" Foyle interrupted softly. "You tried to commit suicide, eh? That accounts for the gas explosion that opened the building . . . And your protective confinement. Attempted suicide. Why weren't you hurt in the explosion?"

"So many were hurt. So many died. But I didn't. I'm unlucky, I suppose. I've been unlucky all my life."

"Why suicide?"

"I'm tired. I'm finished. I've lost everything . . . I'm on the army gray list . . . suspected, watched, reported. No job. No family. No— Why suicide? Dear God, what else but suicide?"

"You can work for me."

"I can . . . What did you say?"

"I want you to work for me, Miss Wednesbury."

She burst into hysterical laughter. "For you? *Another camp follower in the Circus?* Work for you, Fourmyle?"

"You've got sex on the brain," he said gently. "I'm not looking for tarts. They look for me, as a rule."

"I'm sorry. *I'm obsessed by the brute who destroyed me. I—* I'll try to make sense." Robin calmed herself. "Let me understand you. You've taken me out of the hospital to offer me a job. You've heard of me. That means you want something special. My specialty is telesending."

"And charm."

"What?"

"I want to buy your charm, Miss Wednesbury."

"I don't understand."

"Why," Foyle said mildly. "It ought to be simple for you. I'm the buffoon. I'm vulgarity, imbecility, obscenity. That's got to stop. I want you to be my social secretary."

"You expect me to believe that? You could hire a hundred social secretaries . . . a thousand, with your money. You expect me to believe that I'm the only one for you? That you had to kidnap me from protective confinement to get me?"

Foyle nodded. "That's right, there are thousands, but only one that can telesend."

"What's that got to do with it?"

"You're going to be the ventriloquist; I'm going to be your dummy. I don't know the upper classes; you do. They have their own talk, their own jokes, their own manners. If a man wants to be accepted by them he's got to talk their language. I can't, but you can. You'll talk for me, through my mouth . . ."

"But you could learn."

"No. It would take too long. And charm can't be learned. I want to buy your charm, Miss Wednesbury. Now, about salary. I'll pay you a thousand a month."

Her eyes widened. "You're very generous, Fourmyle."

"I'll clean up this suicide charge for you."

"You're very kind."

"And I'll guarantee to get you off the army gray list. You'll be back on the white list by the time you finish working for me. You can start with a clean slate and a bonus. You can start living again."

Robin's lips trembled and then she began to cry. She sobbed and shook and Foyle had to steady her. "Well," he asked. "Will you do it?"

She nodded. "You're so kind . . . It's . . . I'm not used to kindness any more."

The dull concussion of a distant explosion made Foyle stiffen. "Christ!" he exclaimed in sudden panic. "Another Blue Jaunte. I—"

"No," Robin said. "I don't know what blue jaunte is, but that's the Proving Ground. They—" She looked up at Foyle's face and screamed. The unexpected shock of the explosion and the vivid chain of associations had wrenched loose his iron control. The blood-red scars of tattooing showed under his skin. She stared at him in horror, still screaming.

He touched his face once, then leaped forward and gagged her. Once again he had hold of himself.

"It shows, eh?" he murmured with a ghastly smile. "Lost my grip for a minute. Thought I was back in Gouffre Martel listening to a Blue Jaunte. Yes, I'm Foyle. The brute who destroyed you. You had to know, sooner or later, but I'd hoped it would be later. I'm Foyle, back again. Will you be quiet and listen to me?"

She shook her head frantically, trying to struggle out of his grasp. With detached calm he punched her jaw. Robin sagged. Foyle picked her up, wrapped her in his coat and held her in his arms, waiting for consciousness to return. When he saw her eyelids flutter he spoke again.

"Don't move or you'll be sick. Maybe I didn't pull that punch enough."

"*Brute . . . Beast . . .*"

"I could do this the wrong way," he said. "I could blackmail you. I know your mother and sisters are on Callisto, that you're classed as an alien belligerent by association. That puts you on the black list, *ipso facto*. Is that right? *Ipso facto.* 'By the very fact.' Latin. You can't trust hypno-learning. I could point out that all I have to do is send anonymous information to Central Intelligence and you wouldn't be just suspect any more. They'd be ripping information out of you inside twelve hours . . ."

He felt her shudder. "But I'm not going to do it that way. I'm going to tell you the truth because I want to turn you into a partner. Your mother's in the Inner Planets. She's in the Inner Planets," he repeated. "She may be on Terra."

"Safe?" she whispered.

"I don't know."

"Put me down."

"You're cold."

"Put me down."

He set her on her feet.

"You destroyed me once," she said in choked tones. "Are you trying to destroy me again?"

"No. Will you listen?"

She nodded.

"I was lost in space. I was dead and rotting for six months. A ship came up that could have saved me. It passed me by. It let me die. A ship named 'Vorga.' 'Vorga-T:1339.' Does that mean anything to you?"

"No."

"Jiz McQueen—a friend of mine who's dead now—once told me to find out why I was left to rot. That would be the answer to who gave the order. So I started buying information about 'Vorga.' Any information."

"What's that to do with my mother?"

"Just listen. Information was tough to buy. The 'Vorga' records were removed from the Bo'ness & Uig files. I managed to locate three names . . . three out of a standard crew of four officers and twelve men. Nobody knew anything or nobody would talk. And I found this." Foyle took a silver locket from his pocket and handed it to Robin. "It was pawned by some spaceman off the 'Vorga.' That's all I could find out."

Robin uttered a cry and opened the locket with trembling fingers. Inside was her picture and the pictures of two other girls. As the locket was opened, the 3D photos smiled and whispered: "Love from Robin, Mama . . . Love from Holly, Mama . . . Love from Wendy, Mama . . ."

"It is my mother's," Robin wept. "It . . . She . . . For pity's sake, where is she? What happened?"

"I don't know," Foyle said steadily. "But I can guess. I think your mother got out of that concentration camp . . . one way or another."

"And my sisters too. She'd never leave them."

"Maybe your sisters too. I think 'Vorga' was running refugees out of Callisto. Your family paid with money and jewelry to get aboard and be taken to the Inner Planets. That's how a spaceman off the 'Vorga' came to pawn this locket."

"Then where are they?"

"I don't know. Maybe they were dumped on Mars or Venus. Most probably they were sold to a labor camp on the Moon, which is why they haven't been able to get in touch with you. I don't know where they are, but 'Vorga' can tell us."

"Are you lying? Tricking me?"

"Is that locket a lie? I'm telling the truth . . . all the truth I know. I want to find out why they left me to die, and who gave the order. The man who gave the order will know where your mother and sisters are. He'll tell you . . . before I kill him. He'll have plenty of time. He'll be a long time dying."

Robin looked at him in horror. The passion that gripped him was making his face once again show the scarlet stigmata. He looked like a tiger closing in for the kill.

"I've got a fortune to spend . . . never mind how I got it. I've got three months to finish the job. I've learned enough maths to compute the probabilities. Three months is the outside before they figure that Fourmyle of Ceres is Gully Foyle. Ninety days. From New Year's to All Fools. Will you join me?"

"You?" Robin cried with loathing. "Join you?"

"All this Four Mile Circus is camouflage. Nobody ever suspects a clown. But I've been studying, learning, preparing for the finish. All I need now is you."

"Why?"

"I don't know where the hunt is going to lead me . . . society or slums. I've got to be prepared for both. The slums I can handle alone. I haven't forgotten the gutter, but I need you for society. Will you come in with me?"

"You're hurting me." Robin wrenched her arm out of Foyle's grasp.

"Sorry. I lose control when I think about 'Vorga.' Will you help me find 'Vorga' and your family?"

"I hate you," Robin burst out. "I despise you. You're rotten. You destroy everything you touch. Someday I'll pay you back."

"But we work together from New Year's to All Fools?"

"We work together."

Nine

ON New Year's Eve, Geoffrey Fourmyle of Ceres made his onslaught on society. He appeared first in Canberra at the Government House ball, half an hour before midnight. This was a highly formal affair, bursting with color and pageantry, for it was the custom at formals for society to wear the evening dress that had been fashionable the year its clan was founded or its trademark patented.

Thus, the Morses (Telephone and Telegraph) wore nineteenth century frock coats and their women wore Victorian hoop skirts. The Skodas (Powder & Guns) harked back to the late eighteenth century, wearing Regency tights and crinolines. The daring Peenemundes (Rockets & Reactors), dating from the 1920's, wore tuxedos, and their women unashamedly revealed legs, arms, and necks in the décolleté of antique Worth and Mainbocher gowns.

Fourmyle of Ceres appeared in evening clothes, very modern and very black, relieved only by a white sunburst on his shoulder, the trademark of the Ceres clan. With him was Robin Wednesbury in a glittering white gown, her slender waist tight in whalebone, the bustle of the gown accentuating her long, straight back and graceful step.

The black and white contrast was so arresting that an orderly was sent to check the sunburst trademark in the Almanac of Peerages and Patents. He returned with the news that it was of the Ceres Mining Company, organized in 2250 for the exploitation of the mineral resources of Ceres, Pallas, and Vesta. The resources had never manifested themselves and the House of Ceres had gone into eclipse but had never become extinct. Apparently it was now being revived.

"Fourmyle? The Clown?"

"Yes. The Four Mile Circus. Everybody's talking about him."

"Is that the same man?"

"Couldn't be. He looks human."

Society clustered around Fourmyle, curious but wary.

"Here they come," Foyle muttered to Robin.

"Relax. They want the light touch. They'll accept anything if it's amusing. Stay tuned."

"Are you that dreadful man with the circus, Fourmyle?"

"Sure you are. Smile."

"I am, madam. You may touch me."

"Why, you actually seem proud. Are you proud of your bad taste?"

"The problem today is to have any taste at all."

"The problem today is to have any taste at all. I think I'm lucky."

"Lucky but dreadfully indecent."

"Indecent but not dull."

"And dreadful but delightful. Why aren't you cavorting now?"

"I'm 'under the influence,' Madam."

"Oh dear. Are you drunk? I'm Lady Shrapnel. When will you be sober again?"

"I'm under your influence, Lady Shrapnel."

"You wicked young man. Charles! Charles, come here and save Fourmyle. I'm ruining him."

"That's Victor of RCA Victor."

"Fourmyle, is it? Delighted. What's that entourage of yours cost?"

"Tell him the truth."

"Forty thousand, Victor."

"Good *Lord!* A week?"

"A day."

"A day! What on earth d'you want to spend all that money for?"

"The truth!"

"For notoriety, Victor."

"Ha! Are you serious?"

"I told you he was wicked, Charles."

"Damned refreshing. Klaus! Here a moment. This impudent young man is spending forty thousand a day . . . for notoriety, if you please."

"Skoda of Skoda."

"Good evening, Fourmyle. I am much interested in this revival of the name. You are, perhaps, a cadet descendant of the original founding board of Ceres, Inc.?"

"Give him the truth."

"No, Skoda. It's a title by purchase. I bought the company. I'm an upstart."

"Good. Toujours de l'audace!"

"My word, Fourmyle! You're frank."

"Told you he was impudent. Very refreshing. There's a parcel of damned upstarts about, young man, but they don't admit it. Elizabeth, come and meet Fourmyle of Ceres."

"Fourmyle! I've been dying to meet you."

"Lady Elizabeth Citroen."

"Is it true you travel with a portable college?"

"The light touch here."

"A portable high school, Lady Elizabeth."

"But why on earth, Fourmyle?"

"Oh, madam, it's so difficult to spend money these days. We have to find the silliest excuses. If only someone would invent a new extravagance."

"You ought to travel with a portable inventor, Fourmyle."

"I've got one. Haven't I, Robin? But he wastes his time on perpetual motion. What I need is a resident spendthrift. Would any of your clans care to lend me a younger son?"

"Would any of us care to!? There's many a clan would pay for the privilege of unloading."

"Isn't perpetual motion spendthrift enough for you, Fourmyle?"

"No. It's a shocking waste of money. The whole point of extravagance is to act like a fool and feel like a fool, but enjoy it. Where's the joy in perpetual motion? Is there any extravagance in entropy? Millions for nonsense but not one cent for entropy. My slogan."

They laughed and the crowd clustering around Fourmyle grew. They were delighted and amused. He was a new toy. Then it was midnight, and as the great clock tolled in the New Year, the gathering prepared to jaunte with midnight around the world.

"Come with us to Java, Fourmyle. Regis Sheffield's giving a marvelous legal party. We're going to play 'Sober The Judge.'"

"Hong Kong, Fourmyle."

"Tokyo, Fourmyle. It's raining in Hong Kong. Come to Tokyo and bring your circus."

"Thank you, no. Shanghai for me. The Soviet Duomo. I promise an extravagant reward to the first one who discovers the deception of my costume. Meet you all in two hours. Ready, Robin?"

"Don't jaunte. Bad manners. Walk out. Slowly. Languor is chic. Respects to the Governor . . . To the Commissioner . . . Their Ladies . . . Bien. Don't forget to tip the attendants. Not him, idiot! That's the Lieutenant Governor. All right. You made a hit. You're accepted. Now what?"

"Now what we came to Canberra for."

"I thought we came for the ball."

"The ball *and* a man named Forrest."

"Who's that?"

"Ben Forrest, spaceman off the 'Vorga.' I've got three leads to the man who gave the order to let me die. Three names. A cook in Rome named Poggi; a quack in Shanghai named Orel; and this man, Forrest. This is a combined operation . . . society and search. Understand?"

"I understand."

"We've got two hours to rip Forrest open. D'you know the co-ordinates of the Aussie Cannery? The company town?"

"I don't want any part of your 'Vorga' revenge. I'm searching for my family."

"This is a combined operation . . . every way," he said with such detached savagery that she winced and at once jaunted. When Foyle arrived in his tent in the Four Mile Circus on Jervis Beach, she was already changing into travel clothes. Foyle looked at her. Although he forced her to live in his tent for security reasons, he had never touched her again. Robin caught his glance, stopped changing and waited.

He shook his head. "That's all finished."

"How interesting. You've given up rape?"

"Get dressed," he said, controlling himself. "Tell them they've got two hours to get the camp up to Shanghai."

It was twelve-thirty when Foyle and Robin arrived at the front office of the Aussie Cannery company town. They applied for identification tags and were greeted by the mayor himself.

"Happy New Year," he caroled. "Happy! Happy! Happy! Visiting? A pleasure to drive you around. Permit me." He bundled them into a lush helicopter and took off. "Lots of visitors tonight. Ours is a friendly town. Friendliest company town in the world." The plane circled giant buildings. "That's our ice palace . . . Swimming baths on the left . . . Big dome is the ski jump. Snow all year 'round . . . Tropical gardens under that glass roof. Palms, parrots, orchids, fruit. There's our market . . . theater . . . got our own broadcasting company, too. 3D-5S. Take a look at the football stadium. Two of our boys made All-American this year. Turner at Right Rockne and Otis at Left Thorpe."

"Do tell," Foyle murmured.

"Yessir, we've got everything. Everything. You don't have to jaunte around the world looking for fun. Aussie Cannery brings the world to you. Our town's a little universe. Happiest little universe in the world."

"Having absentee problems, I see."

The mayor refused to falter in his sales pitch. "Look down at the streets. See those bikes? Motorcycles? Cars? We can afford more luxury transportation per capita than any other town on earth. Look at those homes. Mansions. Our people are rich and happy. We keep 'em rich and happy."

"But do you keep them?"

"What d'you mean? Of course we—"

"You can tell us the truth. We're not job prospects. Do you keep them?"

"We can't keep 'em more than six months," the mayor groaned. "It's a hell of a headache. We give 'em everything but we can't hold on to 'em. They get the wanderlust and jaunte. Absenteeism's cut our production by 12 per cent. We can't hold on to steady labor."

"Nobody can."

"There ought to be a law. Forrest, you said? Right here."

He landed them before a Swiss chalet set in an acre of gardens and took off, mumbling to himself. Foyle and Robin stepped before the door of the house, waiting for the monitor to pick them up and announce them. Instead, the door flashed red, and a white skull and crossbones appeared on it. A canned voice spoke: "WARNING. THIS RESIDENCE IS MAN-TRAPPED BY THE LETHAL DEFENSE CORPORATION OF SWEDEN. R:77-23. YOU HAVE BEEN LEGALLY NO-TIFIED."

"What the hell?" Foyle muttered. "On New Year's Eve? Friendly fella. Let's try the back."

They walked around the chalet, pursued by the skull and crossbones flashing at intervals, and the canned warning. At one side, they saw the top of a cellar window brightly illuminated and heard the muffled chant of voices: "The Lord is my shepherd, I shall not want . . ."

"Cellar Christians!" Foyle exclaimed. He and Robin peered through the window. Thirty worshippers of assorted faiths

were celebrating the New Year with a combined and highly illegal service. The twenty-fifth century had not yet abolished
God, but it had abolished organized religion.

"No wonder the house is man-trapped," Foyle said. "Filthy
practices like that. Look, they've got a priest and a rabbi, and
that thing behind them is a crucifix."

"Did you ever stop to think what swearing is?" Robin asked
quietly. "You say 'Jesus' and 'Jesus Christ.' Do you know what
that is?"

"Just swearing, that's all. Like 'ouch' or 'damn.'"

"No, it's religion. You don't know it, but there are two
thousand years of meaning behind words like that."

"This is no time for dirty talk," Foyle said impatiently. "Save
it for later. Come on."

The rear of the chalet was a solid wall of glass, the picture
window of a dimly lit, empty living room.

"Down on your face," Foyle ordered. "I'm going in."

Robin lay prone on the marble patio. Foyle triggered his
body, accelerated into a lightning blur, and smashed a hole in
the glass wall. Far down on the sound spectrum he heard dull
concussions. They were shots. Quick projectiles laced toward
him. Foyle dropped to the floor and tuned his ears, sweeping
from low bass to supersonic until at last he picked up the hum
of the Man-Trap control mechanism. He turned his head gently, pin-pointed the location by binaural D/F, wove in through
the stream of shots and demolished the mechanism. He decelerated.

"Come in, quick!"

Robin joined him in the living room, trembling. The Cellar
Christians were pouring up into the house somewhere, emitting the sounds of martyrs.

"Wait here," Foyle grunted. He accelerated, blurred through
the house, located the Cellar Christians in poses of frozen flight,
and sorted through them. He returned to Robin and decelerated.

"None of them is Forrest," he reported. "Maybe he's upstairs.
The back way, while they're going out the front. Come on!"

They raced up the back stairs. On the landing they paused
to take bearings.

"Have to work fast," Foyle muttered. "Between the shots and the religion riot, the world and his wife'll be jaunting around asking questions—" He broke off. A low mewling sound came from a door at the head of the stairs. Foyle sniffed.

"Analogue!" he exclaimed. "Must be Forrest. How about that? Religion in the cellar and dope upstairs."

"What are you talking about?"

"I'll explain later. In here. I only hope he isn't on a gorilla kick."

Foyle went through the door like a diesel tractor. They were in a large, bare room. A heavy rope was suspended from the ceiling. A naked man was entwined with the rope midway in the air. He squirmed and slithered up and down the rope, emitting a mewling sound and a musky odor.

"Python," Foyle said. "That's a break. Don't go near him. He'll mash your bones if he touches you."

Voices below began to call: "Forrest! What's all the shooting? Happy New Year, Forrest! Where in hell's the celebration?"

"Here they come," Foyle grunted. "Have to jaunte him out of here. Meet you back at the beach. Go!"

He whipped a knife out of his pocket, cut the rope, swung the squirming man to his back and jaunted. Robin was on the empty Jervis beach a moment before him. Foyle arrived with the squirming man oozing over his neck and shoulders like a python, crushing him in a terrifying embrace. The red stigmata suddenly burst out on Foyle's face.

"Sinbad," he said in a strangled voice. "Old Man of the Sea. Quick girl! Right pockets. Three over. Two down. Sting ampule. Let him have it anywh—" His voice was choked off.

Robin opened the pocket, found a packet of glass beads and took them out. Each bead had a bee-sting end. She thrust the sting of an ampule into the writhing man's neck. He collapsed. Foyle shook him off and arose from the sand.

"Christ!" he muttered, massaging his throat. He took a deep breath. "Blood and bowels. Control," he said, resuming his air of detached calm. The scarlet tattooing faded from his face.

"What was all that horror?" Robin asked.

"Analogue. Psychiatric dope for psychotics. Illegal. A twitch has to release himself somehow, revert back to the primitive.

He identifies with a particular kind of animal . . . gorilla, grizzly, brood bull, wolf . . . Takes the dope and turns into the animal he admires. Forrest was queer for snakes, seems as if."

"How do you know all this?"

"Told you I've been studying . . . preparing for 'Vorga.' This is one of the things I learned. Show you something else I've learned, if you're not chicken-livered. How to bring a twitch out of Analogue."

Foyle opened another pocket in his battle coveralls and got to work on Forrest. Robin watched for a moment, then uttered a horrified cry, turned and walked to the edge of the water. She stood, staring blindly at the surf and the stars, until the mewling and the twisting ceased and Foyle called to her.

"You can come back now."

Robin returned to find a shattered creature seated upright on the beach gazing at Foyle with dull, sober eyes.

"You're Forrest?"

"Who the hell are you?"

"You're Ben Forrest, leading spaceman. Formerly aboard the Presteign 'Vorga.'"

Forrest cried out in terror.

"You were aboard the 'Vorga' on September 16, 2436."

The man sobbed and shook his head.

"On September sixteen you passed a wreck. Out near the asteroid belt. Wreck of the 'Nomad,' your sister ship. She signalled for help. 'Vorga' passed her by. Left her to drift and die. Why did 'Vorga' pass her by?"

Forrest began to scream hysterically.

"Who gave the order to pass her by?"

"Jesus, no! No! No!"

"The records are all gone from the Bo'ness & Uig files. Someone got to them before me. Who was that? Who was aboard 'Vorga'? Who shipped with you? I want officers and crew. Who was in command?"

"No," Forrest screamed. "No!"

Foyle held a sheaf of bank notes before the hysterical man's face. "I'll pay for the information. Fifty thousand. Analogue for the rest of your life. Who gave the order to let me die, Forrest? Who?"

The man smote the bank notes from Foyle's hand, leaped up

and ran down the beach. Foyle tackled him at the edge of the surf. Forrest fell headlong, his face in the water. Foyle held him there.

"Who commanded 'Vorga,' Forrest? Who gave the order?"

"You're drowning him!" Robin cried.

"Let him suffer a little. Water's easier than vacuum. I suffered for six months. Who gave the order, Forrest?"

The man bubbled and choked. Foyle lifted his head out of the water. "What are you? Loyal? Crazy? Scared? Your kind would sell out for five thousand. I'm offering fifty. Fifty thousand for information, you son of a bitch, or you die slow and hard." The tattooing appeared on Foyle's face. He forced Forrest's head back into the water and held the struggling man. Robin tried to pull him off.

"You're murdering him!"

Foyle turned his terrifying face on Robin. "Get your hands off me, bitch! Who was aboard with you, Forrest? Who gave the order? Why?"

Forrest twisted his head out of the water. "Twelve of us on 'Vorga,'" he screamed. "Christ save me! There was me and Kemp—"

He jerked spasmodically and sagged. Foyle pulled his body out of the surf.

"Go on. You and who? Kemp? Who else? Talk."

There was no response. Foyle examined the body.

"Dead," he growled.

"Oh my God! My God!"

"One lead shot to hell. Just when he was opening up. What a damned break." He took a deep breath and drew calm about him like an iron cloak. The tattooing disappeared from his face. He adjusted his watch for 120 degrees east longitude. "Almost midnight in Shanghai. Let's go. Maybe we'll have better luck with Sergei Orel, pharmacist's mate off the 'Vorga.' Don't look so scared. This is only the beginning. Go, girl. Jaunte!"

Robin gasped. He saw that she was staring over his shoulder with an expression of incredulity. Foyle turned. A flaming figure loomed on the beach, a huge man with burning clothes and a hideously tattooed face. It was himself.

"Christ!" Foyle exclaimed. He took a step toward his burning image, and abruptly it was gone.

He turned to Robin, ashen and trembling. "Did you see that?"

"Yes."

"What was it?"

"You."

"For God's sake! Me? How's that possible? How—"

"It was you."

"But—" He faltered, the strength and furious possession drained out of him. "Was it illusion? Hallucination?"

"I don't know. I saw it too."

"Christ Almighty! To see yourself . . . face to face . . . The clothes were on fire. Did you see that? What in God's name was it?"

"It was Gully Foyle," Robin said, "burning in hell."

"All right," Foyle burst out angrily. "It was me in hell, but I'm still going through with it. If I burn in hell, Vorga'll burn with me." He pounded his palms together, stinging himself back to strength and purpose. "I'm still going through with it, by God! Shanghai next. Jaunte!"

Ten

AT the costume ball in Shanghai, Fourmyle of Ceres electrified society by appearing as Death in Dürer's "Death and the Maiden" with a dazzling blonde creature clad in transparent veils. A Victorian society which stifled its women in purdah, and which regarded the 1920 gowns of the Peenemunde clan as excessively daring, was shocked, despite the fact that Robin Wednesbury was chaperoning the pair. But when Fourmyle revealed that the female was a magnificent android, there was an instant reversal of opinion in his favor. Society was delighted with the deception. The naked body, shameful in humans, was merely a sexless curiosity in androids.

At midnight, Fourmyle auctioned off the android to the gentlemen of the ball.

"The money to go to charity, Fourmyle?"

"Certainly not. You know my slogan: Not one cent for entropy. Do I hear a hundred credits for this expensive and lovely creature? One hundred, gentlemen? She's all beauty and highly adaptable. Two? Thank you. Three and a half? Thank you. I'm bid— Five? Eight? Thank you. Any more bids for this remarkable product of the resident genius of the Four Mile Circus? She walks. She talks. She adapts. She has been conditioned to respond to the highest bidder. Nine? Do I hear any more bids? Are you all done? Are you all through? Sold, to Lord Yale for nine hundred credits."

Tumultuous applause and appalled ciphering: "An android like that must have cost ninety thousand! How can he afford it?"

"Will you turn the money over to the android, Lord Yale? She will respond suitably. Until we meet again in Rome, ladies and gentlemen . . . The Borghese Palace at midnight. Happy New Year."

Fourmyle had already departed when Lord Yale discovered, to the delight of himself and the other bachelors, that a double deception had been perpetrated. The android was, in fact, a living, human creature, all beauty and highly adaptable. She responded magnificently to nine hundred credits. The trick was the smoking room story of the year. The stags waited eagerly to congratulate Fourmyle.

But Foyle and Robin Wednesbury were passing under a sign that read: "DOUBLE YOUR JAUNTING OR DOUBLE YOUR MONEY BACK" in seven languages, and entering the emporium of "DR. SERGEI OREL, CELESTIAL ENLARGER OF CRANIAL CAPABILITIES."

The waiting room was decorated with lurid brain charts demonstrating how Dr. Orel poulticed, cupped, balsamed, and electrolyzed the brain into double its capacity or double your money back. He also doubled your memory with anti-febrile purgatives, magnified your morals with tonic roborants, and adjusted all anguished psyches with Orel's Epulotic Vulnerary.

The waiting room was empty. Foyle opened a door at a venture. He and Robin had a glimpse of a long hospital ward. Foyle grunted in disgust.

"A Snow Joint. Might have known he'd be running a dive for sick heads too."

This den catered to Disease Collectors, the most hopeless of neurotic-addicts. They lay in their hospital beds, suffering mildly from illegally induced para-measles, para-flu, para-malaria;

devotedly attended by nurses in starched white uniforms, and avidly enjoying their illegal illness and the attention it brought.

"Look at them," Foyle said contemptuously. "Disgusting. If there's anything filthier than a religion-junkey, it's a disease-bird."

"Good evening," a voice spoke behind them.

Foyle shut the door and turned. Dr. Sergei Orel bowed. The good doctor was crisp and sterile in the classic white cap, gown, and surgical mask of the medical clans, to which he belonged by fraudulent assertion only. He was short, swarthy, and olive-eyed, recognizably Russian by his name alone. More than a century of jaunting had so mingled the many populations of the world that racial types were disappearing.

"Didn't expect to find you open for business on New Year's Eve," Foyle said.

"Our Russian New Year comes two weeks later," Dr. Orel answered. "Step this way, please." He pointed to a door and disappeared with a "pop." The door revealed a long flight of stairs. As Foyle and Robin started up the stairs, Dr. Orel appeared above them. "This way, please. Oh . . . one moment." He disappeared and appeared again behind them. "You forgot to close the door." He shut the door and jaunted again. This time he reappeared high at the head of the stairs. "In here, please."

"Showing off," Foyle muttered. "Double your jaunting or double your money back. All the same, he's pretty fast. I'll have to be faster."

They entered the consultation room. It was a glass-roofed penthouse. The walls were lined with gaudy but antiquated medical apparatus: a sedative-bath machine, an electric chair for administering shock treatment to schizophrenics, an EKG analyzer for tracing psychotic patterns, old optical and electronic microscopes.

The quack waited for them behind his desk. He jaunted to the door, closed it, jaunted back to his desk, bowed, indicated chairs, jaunted behind Robin's and held it for her, jaunted to the window and adjusted the shade, jaunted to the light switch and adjusted the lights, then reappeared behind his desk.

"One year ago," he smiled, "I could not jaunte at all. Then I discovered the secret, the Salutiferous Abstersive which . . ."

Foyle touched his tongue to the switchboard wired into the nerve endings of his teeth. He accelerated. He arose without haste, stepped to the slow-motion figure "Bloo-hwoo-fwaa-mawwing" behind the desk, took out a heavy sap, and scientifically smote Orel across the brow, concussing the frontal lobes and stunning the jaunte center. He picked the quack up and strapped him into the electric chair. All this took approximately five seconds. To Robin Wednesbury it was a blur of motion.

Foyle decelerated. The quack opened his eyes, stirred, discovered where he was, and started in anger and perplexity.

"You're Sergei Orel, pharmacist's mate off the 'Vorga,'" Foyle said quietly. "You were aboard the 'Vorga' on September 16, 2436."

The anger and perplexity turned to terror.

"On September sixteen you passed a wreck. Out near the asteroid belt. It was the wreck of the 'Nomad.' She signalled for help and 'Vorga' passed her by. You left her to drift and die. Why?"

Orel rolled his eyes but did not answer.

"Who gave the order to pass me by? Who was willing to let me rot and die?"

Orel began to gibber.

"Who was aboard 'Vorga'? Who shipped with you? Who was in command? I'm going to get an answer. Don't think I'm not," Foyle said with calm ferocity. "I'll buy it or tear it out of you. Why was I left to die? Who told you to let me die?"

Orel screamed. "I can't talk abou— Wait I'll tell—"

He sagged.

Foyle examined the body.

"Dead," he muttered. "Just when he was ready to talk. Just like Forrest."

"Murdered."

"No. I never touched him. It was suicide." Foyle cackled without humor.

"You're insane."

"No, amused. I didn't kill them; I forced them to kill themselves."

"What nonsense is this?"

"They've been given Sympathetic Blocks. You know about SBs, girl? Intelligence uses them for espionage agents. Take a certain body of information you don't want told. Link it with the sympathetic nervous system that controls automatic respiration and heart beat. As soon as the subject tries to reveal that information, the block comes down, the heart and lungs stop, the man dies, your secret's kept. An agent doesn't have to worry about killing himself to avoid torture; it's been done for him."

"It was done to these men?"

"Obviously."

"But why?"

"How do I know? Refugee running isn't the answer. 'Vorga' must have been operating worse rackets than that to take this precaution. But we've got a problem. Our last lead is Poggi in Rome. Angelo Poggi, chef's assistant off the 'Vorga.' How are we going to get information out of him without—" He broke off.

His image stood before him, silent, ominous, face burning blood-red, clothes flaming.

Foyle was paralyzed. He took a breath and spoke in a shaking voice. "Who are you? What do you—"

The image disappeared.

Foyle turned to Robin, moistening his lips. "Did you see it?" Her expression answered him. "Was it real?"

She pointed to Sergei Orel's desk, alongside which the image had stood. Papers on the desk had caught fire and were burning briskly. Foyle backed away, still frightened and bewildered. He passed a hand across his face. It came away wet.

Robin rushed to the desk and tried to beat out the flames. She picked up wads of paper and letters and slammed helplessly. Foyle did not move.

"I can't stop it," she gasped at last. "We've got to get out of here."

Foyle nodded, then pulled himself together with power and resolution. "Rome," he croaked. "We jaunte to Rome. There's got to be some explanation for this. I'll find it, by God! And in the meantime I'm not quitting. Rome. Go, girl. Jaunte!"

Since the Middle Ages the Spanish Stairs have been the center of corruption in Rome. Rising from the Piazza di Spagna to the gardens of the Villa Borghese in a broad, long sweep, the

Spanish Stairs are, have been, and always will be swarming with vice. Pimps lounge on the stairs, whores, perverts, lesbians, catamites. Insolent and arrogant, they display themselves and jeer at the respectables who sometimes pass.

The Spanish Stairs were destroyed in the fission wars of the late twentieth century. They were rebuilt and destroyed again in the war of the World Restoration in the twenty-first century. Once more they were rebuilt and this time covered over with blast-proof crystal, turning the stairs into a stepped Galleria. The dome of the Galleria cut off the view from the death chamber in Keats's house. No longer would visitors peep through the narrow window and see the last sight that met the dying poet's eyes. Now they saw the smoky dome of the Spanish Stairs, and through it the distorted figures of corruption below.

The Galleria of the Stairs was illuminated at night, and this New Year's Eve was chaotic. For a thousand years Rome has welcomed the New Year with a bombardment . . . firecrackers, rockets, torpedoes, gunshots, bottles, shoes, old pots and pans. For months Romans save junk to be hurled out of top-floor windows when midnight strikes. The roar of fireworks inside the Stairs, and the clatter of debris clashing on the Galleria roof, were deafening as Foyle and Robin Wednesbury climbed down from the carnival in the Borghese Palace.

They were still in costume: Foyle in the livid crimson-and-black tights and doublet of Cesare Borgia, Robin wearing the silver-encrusted gown of Lucrezia Borgia. They wore grotesque velvet masks. The contrast between their Renaissance costumes and the modern clothes around them brought forth jeers and catcalls. Even the Lobos who frequented the Spanish Stairs, the unfortunate habitual criminals who had had a quarter of their brains burned out by prefrontal lobotomy, were aroused from their dreary apathy to stare. The mob seethed around the couple as they descended the Galleria.

"Poggi," Foyle called quietly. "Angelo Poggi?"

A bawd bellowed anatomical adjurations at him.

"Poggi? Angelo Poggi?" Foyle was impassive. "I'm told he can be found on the Stairs at night. Angelo Poggi?"

A whore maligned his mother.

"Angelo Poggi? Ten credits to anyone who brings me to him."

Foyle was ringed with extended hands, some filthy, some scented, all greedy. He shook his head. "Show me, first."

Roman rage crackled around him.

"Poggi? Angelo Poggi?"

After six weeks of loitering on the Spanish Stairs, Captain Peter Y'ang-Yeovil at last heard the words he had hoped to hear. Six weeks of tedious assumption of the identity of one Angelo Poggi, chef's assistant off the "Vorga," long dead, was finally paying off. It had been a gamble, first risked when Intelligence had brought the news to Captain Y'ang-Yeovil that someone was making cautious inquiries about the crew of the Presteign "Vorga," and paying heavily for information.

"It's a long shot," Y'ang-Yeovil had said, "but Gully Foyle, AS:128/127:006, *did* make that lunatic attempt to blow up 'Vorga.' And twenty pounds of PyrE is worth a long shot."

Now he waddled up the stairs toward the man in the Renaissance costume and mask. He had put on forty pounds with glandular shots. He had darkened his complexion with diet manipulation. His features, never of an Oriental cast but cut more along the hawklike lines of the ancient American Indian, easily fell into an unreliable pattern with a little muscular control.

The Intelligence man waddled up the Spanish Stairs, a gross cook with a larcenous countenance. He extended a package of soiled envelopes toward Foyle.

"Filthy pictures, signore? Cellar Christians, kneeling, praying, singing psalms, kissing cross? Very naughty. Very smutty, signore. Entertain your friends . . . Excite the ladies."

"No," Foyle brushed the pornography aside. "I'm looking for Angelo Poggi."

Y'ang-Yeovil signalled microscopically. His crew on the stairs began photographing and recording the interview without ceasing its pimping and whoring. The Secret Speech of the Intelligence Tong of the Inner Planets Armed Forces wig-wagged around Foyle and Robin in a hail of tiny tics, sniffs, gestures, attitudes, motions. It was the ancient Chinese sign language of eyelids, eyebrows, fingertips, and infinitesimal body motions.

"Signore?" Y'ang-Yeovil wheezed.

"Angelo Poggi?"

"Si, signore. I am Angelo Poggi."

"Chef's assistant off the 'Vorga'?" Expecting the same start of terror manifested by Forrest and Orel, which he at last understood, Foyle shot out a hand and grabbed Y'ang-Yeovil's elbow. "Yes?"

"Si, signore," Y'ang-Yeovil replied tranquilly. "How can I serve your worship?"

"Maybe this one can come through," Foyle murmured to Robin. "He's not scared. Maybe he knows a way around the Block. I want information from you, Poggi."

"Of what nature, signore, and at what price?"

"I want to buy all you've got. Anything you've got. Name your price."

"But signore! I am a man full of years and experience. I am not to be bought in wholesale lots. I must be paid item by item. Make your selection and I will name the price. What do you want?"

"You were aboard 'Vorga' on September 16, 2436?"

"The cost of that item is ₡r 10."

Foyle smiled mirthlessly and paid.

"I was, signore."

"I want to know about a ship you passed out near the asteroid belt. The wreck of the 'Nomad.' You passed her on September 16. 'Nomad' signalled for help and 'Vorga' passed her by. Who gave that order?"

"Ah, signore!"

"Who gave you that order, and why?"

"Why do you ask, signore?"

"Never mind why I ask. Name the price and talk."

"I must know why a question is asked before I answer, signore." Y'ang-Yeovil smiled greasily. "And I will pay for my caution by cutting the price. Why are you interested in 'Vorga' and 'Nomad' and this shocking abandonment in space? Were you, perhaps, the unfortunate who was so cruelly treated?"

"He's not Italian! His accent's perfect, but the speech pattern's all wrong. No Italian would frame sentences like that."

Foyle stiffened in alarm. Y'ang-Yeovil's eyes, sharpened to

detect and deduce from minutiae, caught the change in attitude. He realized at once that he had slipped somehow. He signalled to his crew urgently.

A white-hot brawl broke out on the Spanish Stairs. In an instant, Foyle and Robin were caught up in a screaming, struggling mob. The crews of the Intelligence Tong were past masters of this OP-I maneuver, designed to outwit a jaunting world. Their split-second timing could knock any man off balance and strip him for identification. Their success was based on the simple fact that between unexpected assault and defensive response there must always be a recognition lag. Within the space of that lag, the Intelligence Tong guaranteed to prevent any man from saving himself.

In three-fifths of a second Foyle was battered, kneed, hammered across the forehead, dropped to the steps and spread-eagled. The mask was plucked from his face, portions of his clothes torn away, and he was ripe and helpless for the rape of the identification cameras. Then, for the first time in the history of the tong, their schedule was interrupted.

A man appeared, straddling Foyle's body . . . a huge man with a hideously tattooed face and clothes that smoked and flamed. The apparition was so appalling that the crew stopped dead and stared. A howl went up from the crowd on the Stairs at the dreadful spectacle.

"The Burning Man! Look! The Burning Man!"

"But *that's* Foyle," Y'ang-Yeovil whispered.

For perhaps a quarter of a minute the apparition stood, silent, burning, staring with blind eyes. Then it disappeared. The man spread-eagled on the ground disappeared too. He turned into a lightning blur of action that whipped through the crew, locating and destroying cameras, recorders, all identification apparatus. Then the blur seized the girl in the Renaissance gown and vanished.

The Spanish Stairs came to life again, painfully, as though struggling out of a nightmare. The bewildered Intelligence crew clustered around Y'ang-Yeovil.

"What in God's name was that, Yeo?"

"I think it was our man. Gully Foyle. You saw that tattooed face."

"And the burning clothes!"

"Looked like a witch at the stake."

"But if that burning man was Foyle, who in hell were we wasting our time on?"

"I don't know. Does the Commando Brigade have an Intelligence service they haven't bothered to mention to us?"

"Why the Commandos, Yeo?"

"You saw the way he accelerated, didn't you? He destroyed every record we made."

"I still can't believe my eyes."

"Oh, you can believe what you didn't see, all right. That was top secret Commando technique. They take their men apart and rewire and regear them. I'll have to check with Mars HQ and find out whether Commando Brigade's running a parallel investigation."

"Does the army tell the navy?"

"They'll tell Intelligence," Y'ang-Yeovil said angrily. "This case is critical enough without jurisdictional hassels. And another thing: there was no need to manhandle that girl in the maneuver. It was undisciplined and unnecessary." Y'ang-Yeovil paused, for once unaware of the significant glances passing around him. "I must find out who she is," he added dreamily.

"If she's been regeared too, it'll be real interesting, Yeo," a bland voice, markedly devoid of implication, said. "Boy Meets Commando."

Y'ang-Yeovil flushed. "All right," he blurted. "I'm transparent."

"Just repetitious, Yeo. All your romances start the same way. 'There's no need to manhandle that girl . . .' And then— Dolly Quaker, Jean Webster, Gwynn Roget, Marion—"

"No names, please!" a shocked voice interrupted. "Does Romeo tell Juliet?"

"You're all going on latrine assignment tomorrow," Y'ang-Yeovil said. "I'm damned if I'll stand for this salacious insubordination. No, not tomorrow; but as soon as this case is closed." His hawk face darkened. "My God, what a mess! Will you ever forget Foyle standing there like a burning brand? But where is he? What's he up to? What's it all mean?"

Eleven

PRESTEIGN of Presteign's mansion in Central Park was ablaze for the New Year. Charming antique electric bulbs with zigzag filaments and pointed tips shed yellow light. The jaunte-proof maze had been removed and the great door was open for the special occasion. The interior of the house was protected from the gaze of the crowd outside by a jeweled screen just inside the door.

The sightseers buzzed and exclaimed as the famous and near-famous of clan and sept arrived by car, by coach, by litter, by every form of luxurious transportation. Presteign of Presteign himself stood before the door, iron gray, handsome, smiling his basilisk smile, and welcomed society to his open house. Hardly had a celebrity stepped through the door and disappeared behind the screen when another, even more famous, came clattering up in a vehicle even more fabulous.

The Colas arrived in a band wagon. The Esso family (six sons, three daughters) was magnificent in a glass-topped Greyhound bus. But Greyhound arrived (in an Edison electric runabout) hard on their heels and there was much laughter and chaffing at the door. But when Edison of Westinghouse dismounted from his Esso-fueled gasoline buggy, completing the circle, the laughter on the steps turned into a roar.

Just as the crowd of guests turned to enter Presteign's home, a distant commotion attracted their attention. It was a rumble, a fierce chatter of pneumatic punches, and an outrageous metallic bellowing. It approached rapidly. The outer fringe of sightseers opened a broad lane. A heavy truck rumbled down the lane. Six men were tumbling baulks of timber out the back of the truck. Following them came a crew of twenty arranging the baulks neatly in rows.

Presteign and his guests watched with amazement. A giant machine, bellowing and pounding, approached, crawling over the ties. Behind it were deposited parallel rails of welded steel. Crews with sledges and pneumatic punches spiked the rails to the timber ties. The track was laid to Presteign's door in a sweeping arc and then curved away. The bellowing engine and crews disappeared into the darkness.

"Good God!" Presteign was distinctly heard to say. Guests poured out of the house to watch.

A shrill whistle sounded in the distance. Down the track came a man on a white horse, carrying a large red flag. Behind him panted a steam locomotive drawing a single observation car. The train stopped before Presteign's door. A conductor swung down from the car followed by a Pullman porter. The porter arranged steps. A lady and gentleman in evening clothes descended.

"Shan't be long," the gentleman told the conductor. "Come back for me in an hour."

"Good God!" Presteign exclaimed again.

The train puffed off. The couple mounted the steps.

"Good evening, Presteign," the gentleman said. "Terribly sorry about that horse messing up your grounds, but the old New York franchise still insists on the red flag in front of trains."

"Fourmyle!" the guests shouted.

"Fourmyle of Ceres!" the sightseers cheered.

Presteign's party was now an assured success.

Inside the vast velvet and plush reception hall, Presteign examined Fourmyle curiously. Foyle endured the keen iron-gray gaze with equanimity, meanwhile nodding and smiling to the enthusiastic admirers he had acquired from Canberra to New York, with whom Robin Wednesbury was chatting.

"Control," he thought. *"Blood, bowels and brain. He grilled me in his office for one hour after that crazy attempt I made on 'Vorga.' Will he recognize me?* Your face is familiar, Presteign," Fourmyle said. "Have we met before?"

"I have not had the honor of meeting a Fourmyle until to-night," Presteign answered ambiguously. Foyle had trained himself to read men, but Presteign's hard, handsome face was inscrutable. Standing face to face, the one detached and compelled, the other reserved and indomitable, they looked like a pair of brazen statues at white heat on the verge of running molten.

"I'm told that you boast of being an upstart, Fourmyle."

"Yes. I've patterned myself after the first Presteign."

"Indeed?"

"You will remember that he boasted of starting the family fortune in the plasma blackmarket during the third World War."

"It was the second war, Fourmyle. But the hypocrites of our clan never acknowledge him. The name was Payne then."

"I hadn't known."

"And what was your unhappy name before you changed it to Fourmyle?"

"It was Presteign."

"Indeed?" The basilisk smile acknowledged the hit. "You claim a relationship with our clan?"

"I will claim it in time."

"Of what degree?"

"Let's say . . . a blood relationship."

"How interesting. I detect a certain fascination for blood in you, Fourmyle."

"No doubt a family weakness, Presteign."

"You're pleased to be cynical," Presteign said, not without cynicism, "but you speak the truth. We have always had a fatal weakness for blood and money. It is our vice. I admit it."

"And I share it."

"A passion for blood and money?"

"Indeed I do. Most passionately."

"Without mercy, without forgiveness, without hypocrisy?"

"Without mercy, without forgiveness, without hypocrisy."

"Fourmyle, you are a young man after my own heart. If you do not claim a relationship with our clan I shall be forced to adopt you."

"You're too late, Presteign. I've already adopted you."

Presteign took Foyle's arm. "You must be presented to my daughter, Lady Olivia. Will you allow me?"

They crossed the reception hall. Foyle hesitated, wondering whether he should call Robin to his side for impending emergencies, but he was too triumphant. *He doesn't know. He'll never know.* Then doubt came: *But I'll never know if he does know. He's crucible steel. He could teach me a thing or two about control.*

Acquaintances hailed Fourmyle.

"Wonderful deception you worked in Shanghai."

"Marvelous carnival in Rome, wasn't it? Did you hear about the burning man who appeared on the Spanish Stairs?"

"We looked for you in London."

"What a heavenly entrance that was," Harry Sherwin-

Williams called. "Outdid us all, Fourmyle. Made us look like a pack of damned pikers."

"You forget yourself, Harry," Presteign said coldly. "You know I permit no profanity in my home."

"Sorry, Presteign. Where's the circus now, Fourmyle?"

"I don't know," Foyle said. "Just a moment."

A crowd gathered, grinning in anticipation of the latest Fourmyle folly. He took out a platinum watch and snapped open the case. The face of a valet appeared on the dial.

"Ahhh . . . whatever your name is . . . Where are we staying just now?"

The answer was tiny and tinny. "You gave orders to make New York your permanent residence, Fourmyle."

"Oh? Did I? And?"

"We bought St. Patrick's Cathedral, Fourmyle."

"And where is that?"

"Old St. Patrick's, Fourmyle. On Fifth Avenue and what was formerly 50th Street. We've pitched the camp inside."

"Thank you." Fourmyle closed the platinum Hunter. "My address is Old St. Patrick's, New York. There's one thing to be said for the outlawed religions . . . At least they built churches big enough to house a circus."

Olivia Presteign was seated on a dais, surrounded by admirers paying court to this beautiful albino daughter of Presteign. She was strangely and wonderfully blind, for she could see in the infrared only, from 7,500 angstroms to one millimeter wavelengths, far below the normal visible spectrum. She saw heat waves, magnetic fields, radio waves; she saw her admirers in a strange light of organic emanations against a background of red radiation.

She was a Snow Maiden, an Ice Princess with coral eyes and coral lips, imperious, mysterious, unattainable. Foyle looked at her once and lowered his eyes in confusion before the blind gaze that could only see him as electromagnetic waves and infrared light. His pulse began to beat faster; a hundred lightning fantasies about himself and Olivia Presteign flashed in his heart.

"Don't be a fool!" he thought desperately. *"Control yourself. Stop dreaming. This can be dangerous . . ."*

He was introduced; was addressed in a husky, silvery voice; was given a cool, slim hand; but the hand seemed to explode within his with an electric shock. It was almost a start of mutual recognition . . . almost a joining of emotional impact.

"This is insane. *She's a symbol. The Dream Princess . . . The Unattainable . . . Control!*"

He was fighting so hard that he scarcely realized he had been dismissed, graciously and indifferently. He could not believe it. He stood, gaping like a lout.

"What? Are you still here, Fourmyle?"

"I couldn't believe I'd been dismissed, Lady Olivia."

"Hardly that, but I'm afraid you *are* in the way of my friends."

"I'm not used to being dismissed. (*No. No. All wrong!*) At least by someone I'd like to count as a friend."

"Don't be tedious, Fourmyle. Do step down."

"How have I offended you?"

"Offended me? Now you're being ridiculous."

"Lady Olivia . . . (*Can't I say anything right? Where's Robin?*) Can we start again, please?"

"If you're trying to be gauche, Fourmyle, you're succeeding admirably."

"Your hand again, please. Thank you. I'm Fourmyle of Ceres."

"All right." She laughed. "I'll concede you're a clown. Now do step down. I'm sure you can find someone to amuse."

"What's happened this time?"

"Really, sir, are you trying to make me angry?"

"No. (*Yes, I am. Trying to touch you somehow . . . cut through the ice.*) The first time our handclasp was . . . violent. Now it's nothing. What happened?"

"Fourmyle," Olivia said wearily, "I'll concede that you're amusing, original, witty, fascinating . . . anything, if you will only go away."

He stumbled off the dais. *"Bitch. Bitch. Bitch. No. She's the dream just as I dreamed her. The icy pinnacle to be stormed and taken. To lay siege . . . invade . . . ravish . . . force to her knees . . ."*

He came face to face with Saul Dagenham.

He stood paralyzed, coercing blood and bowels.

"Ah, Fourmyle," Presteign said. "This is Saul Dagenham.

He can only give us thirty minutes and he insists on spending one of them with you."

"*Does he know? Did he send for Dagenham to make sure? Attack. Toujours de l'audace.* What happened to your face, Dagenham?" Fourmyle asked with detached curiosity.

The death's head smiled. "And I thought I was famous. Radiation poisoning. I'm hot. Time was when they said 'Hotter than a pistol.' Now they say 'Hotter than Dagenham.'" The deadly eyes raked Foyle. "What's behind that circus of yours?"

"A passion for notoriety."

"I'm an old hand at camouflage myself. I recognize the signs. What's your larceny?"

"Did Dillinger tell Capone?" Foyle smiled back, beginning to relax, restraining his triumph. "*I've outfaced them both.* You look happier, Dagenham." Instantly he realized the slip.

Dagenham picked it up in a flash. "Happier than when? Where did we meet before?"

"Not happier than when; happier than me." Foyle turned to Presteign. "I've fallen desperately in love with Lady Olivia."

"Saul, your half hour's up."

Dagenham and Presteign, on either side of Foyle, turned. A tall woman approached, stately in an emerald evening gown, her red hair gleaming. It was Jisbella McQueen. Their glances met. Before the shock could seethe into his face, Foyle turned, ran six steps to the first door he saw, opened it and darted through.

The door slammed behind him. He was in a short blind corridor. There was a click, a pause, and then a canned voice spoke courteously: "You have invaded a private portion of this residence. Please retire."

Foyle gasped and struggled with himself.

"You have invaded a private portion of this residence. Please retire."

"*I never knew . . . Thought she was killed out there . . . She recognized me . . .*"

"You have invaded a private portion of this residence. Please retire."

"*I'm finished . . . She'll never forgive me . . . Must be telling Dagenham and Presteign now.*"

The door from the reception hall opened, and for a moment

Foyle thought he saw his flaming image. Then he realized he was looking at Jisbella's flaming hair. She made no move, just stood and smiled at him in furious triumph. He straightened.

"By God, I won't go down whining."

Without haste, Foyle sauntered out of the corridor, took Jisbella's arm and led her back to the reception hall. He never bothered to look around for Dagenham or Presteign. They would present themselves, with force and arms, in due time. He smiled at Jisbella; she smiled back, still in triumph.

"Thanks for running away, Gully. I never dreamed it could be so satisfying."

"Running away? My dear Jiz!"

"Well?"

"I can't tell you how lovely you're looking tonight. We've come a long way from Gouffre Martel, haven't we?" Foyle motioned to the ballroom. "Dance?"

Her eyes widened in surprise at his composure. She permitted him to escort her to the ballroom and take her in his arms.

"By the way, Jiz, how did you manage to keep out of Gouffre Martel?"

"Dagenham arranged it. So you dance now, Gully?"

"I dance, speak four languages miserably, study science and philosophy, write pitiful poetry, blow myself up with idiotic experiments, fence like a fool, box like a buffoon . . . In short, I'm the notorious Fourmyle of Ceres."

"No longer Gully Foyle."

"Only to you, dear, and whoever you've told."

"Just Dagenham. Are you sorry I blew your secret?"

"You couldn't help yourself any more than I could."

"No, I couldn't. Your name just popped out of me. What would you have paid me to keep my mouth shut?"

"Don't be a fool, Jiz. This accident's going to earn you about ₡r 17,980,000."

"What d'you mean?"

"I told you I'd give you whatever was left after I finished 'Vorga.'"

"You've finished 'Vorga'?" she said in surprise.

"No, dear, you've finished me. But I'll keep my promise."

She laughed. "Generous Gully Foyle. Be real generous, Gully. Make a run for it. Entertain me a little."

"Squealing like a rat? I don't know how, Jiz. I'm trained for hunting, nothing else."

"And I killed the tiger. Give me one satisfaction, Gully. Say you were close to 'Vorga.' I ruined you when you were half a step from the finish. Yes?"

"I wish I could, Jiz, but I can't. I'm nowhere. I was trying to pick up another lead here tonight."

"Poor Gully. Maybe I can help you out of this jam. I can say . . . oh . . . that I made a mistake . . . or a joke . . . that you really aren't Gully Foyle. I know how to confuse Saul. I can do it, Gully . . . if you still love me."

He looked down at her and shook his head. "It's never been love between us, Jiz. You know that. I'm too one-track to be anything but a hunter."

"Too one-track to be anything but a fool!"

"What did you mean, Jiz . . . Dagenham arranged to keep you out of Gouffre Martel . . . You know how to confuse Saul Dagenham? What have you got to do with him?"

"I work for him. I'm one of his couriers."

"You mean he's blackmailing you? Threatening to send you back if you don't . . ."

"No. We hit it off the minute we met. He started off capturing me; I ended up capturing him."

"How do you mean?"

"Can't you guess?"

He stared at her. Her eyes were veiled, but he understood. "Jiz! With *him?*"

"Yes."

"But how? He—"

"There are precautions. It's . . . I don't want to talk about it, Gully."

"Sorry. He's a long time returning."

"Returning?"

"Dagenham. With his army."

"Oh. Yes, of course." Jisbella laughed again, then spoke in a low, furious tone. "You don't know what a tightrope you've been walking, Gully. If you'd begged or bribed or tried to romance me . . . By God, I'd have ruined you. I'd have told the world who you were . . . Screamed it from the house-tops . . ."

"What are you talking about?"

"Saul isn't returning. He doesn't know. You can go to hell on your own."

"I don't believe you."

"D'you think it would take him *this* long to get you? Saul Dagenham?"

"But why didn't you tell him? After the way I ran out on you . . ."

"Because I don't want him going to hell with you. I'm not talking about 'Vorga.' I mean something else. PyrE. That's why they hunted you. That's what they're after. Twenty pounds of PyrE."

"What's that?"

"When you got the safe open was there a small box in it? Made of ILI . . . Inert Lead Isomer?"

"Yes."

"What was inside the ILI box?"

"Twenty slugs that looked like compressed iodine crystals."

"What did you do with the slugs?"

"Sent two out for analysis. No one could find out what they are. I'm trying to run an analysis on a third in my lab . . . when I'm not clowning for the public."

"Oh, you are, are you? Why?"

"I'm growing up, Jiz," Foyle said gently. "It didn't take much to figure out *that* was what Presteign and Dagenham were after."

"Where have you got the rest of the slugs?"

"In a safe place."

"They're not safe. They can't ever be safe. I don't know what PyrE is, but I know it's the road to hell, and I don't want Saul walking it."

"You love him that much?"

"I respect him that much. He's the first man that ever showed me an excuse for the double standard."

"Jiz, what *is* PyrE? You know."

"I've guessed. I've pieced together the hints I've heard. I've got an idea. And I could tell you, Gully, but I won't." The fury in her face was luminous. "I'm running out on *you*, this time. I'm leaving you to hang helpless in the dark. See what it feels like, boy! Enjoy!"

She broke away from him and swept across the ballroom floor. At that moment the first bombs fell.

They came in like meteor swarms; not so many, but far more deadly. They came in on the morning quadrant, that quarter of the globe in darkness from midnight to dawn. They collided head on with the forward side of the earth in its revolution around the sun. They had been traveling a distance of four hundred million miles.

Their excessive speed was matched by the rapidity of the Terran defense computors which traced and intercepted these New Year gifts from the Outer Satellites within the space of micro-seconds. A multitude of fierce new stars prickled in the sky and vanished; they were bombs detected and detonated five hundred miles above their target.

But so narrow was the margin between speed of defense and speed of attack that many got through. They shot through the aurora level, the meteor level, the twilight limit, the stratosphere, and down to earth. The invisible trajectories ended in titanic convulsions.

The first atomic explosion which destroyed Newark shook the Presteign mansion with an unbelievable quake. Floors and walls shuddered and the guests were thrown in heaps along with furniture and decorations. Quake followed quake as the random shower descended around New York. They were deafening, numbing, chilling. The sounds, the shocks, the flares of lurid light on the horizon were so enormous, that reason was stripped from humanity, leaving nothing but flayed animals to shriek, cower, and run. Within the space of five seconds Presteign's New Year party was transformed from elegance into anarchy.

Foyle arose from the floor. He looked at the struggling bodies on the ballroom parquet, saw Jisbella fighting to free herself, took a step toward her and then stopped. He revolved his head, dazedly, feeling it was no part of him. The thunder never ceased. He saw Robin Wednesbury in the reception hall, reeling and battered. He took a step toward her and then stopped again. He knew where he must go.

He accelerated. The thunder and lightning dropped down the spectrum to grinding and flickering. The shuddering quakes turned into greasy undulations. Foyle blurred through the giant house, searching, until at last he found her, standing in the garden, standing tiptoe on a marble bench looking like a marble statue to his accelerated senses . . . the statue of exaltation.

He decelerated. Sensation leaped up the spectrum again and once more he was buffeted by that bigger-than-death size bombardment.

"Lady Olivia," he called.

"Who is that?"

"The clown."

"Fourmyle?"

"Yes."

"And you came searching for me? I'm touched, really touched."

"You're insane to be standing out here like this. I beg you to let me—"

"No, no, no. It's beautiful . . . Magnificent!"

"Let me jaunte with you to some place that's safe."

"Ah, you see yourself as a knight in armor? Chivalry to the rescue. It doesn't suit you, my dear. You haven't the flair for it. You'd best go."

"I'll stay."

"As a beauty lover?"

"As a lover."

"You're still tedious, Fourmyle. Come, be inspired. This Armageddon . . . Flowering Monstrosity. Tell me what you see."

"There's nothing much," he answered, looking around and wincing. "There's light all over the horizon. Quick clouds of it. Above, there's a . . . a sort of sparkling effect. Like Christmas lights twinkling."

"Oh, you see so little with your eyes. See what I see! There's a dome in the sky, a rainbow dome. The colors run from deep tang to brilliant burn. That's what I've named the colors I see. What would that dome be?"

"The radar screen," Foyle muttered.

"And then there are vasty shafts of fire thrusting up and swaying, weaving, dancing, sweeping. What are they?"

"Interceptor beams. You're seeing the whole electronic defense system."

"And I can see the bombs coming down too . . . quick

streaks of what you call red. But not your red; mine. Why can I see them?"

"They're heated by air friction, but the inert lead casing doesn't show the color to us."

"See how much better you're doing as Galileo than Galahad. Oh! There's one coming down in the east. Watch for it! It's coming, coming, coming . . . Now!"

A flare of light on the eastern horizon proved it was not her imagination.

"There's another to the north. Very close. Very. Now!"

A shock tore down from the north.

"And the explosions, Fourmyle . . . They're not just clouds of light. They're fabrics, webs, tapestries of meshing colors. So beautiful. Like exquisite shrouds."

"Which they are, Lady Olivia."

"Are you afraid?"

"Yes."

"Then run away."

"No."

"Ah, you're defiant."

"I don't know what I am. I'm scared, but I won't run."

"Then you're brazening it out. Making a show of knightly courage." The husky voice sounded amused. "Just think, Fourmyle. How long does it take to jaunte? You could be safe in seconds . . . in Mexico, Canada, Alaska. So safe. There must be millions there now. We're probably the last left in the city."

"Not everybody can jaunte so far and so fast."

"Then we're the last left who count. Why don't you leave me? Be safe. I'll be killed soon. No one will ever know your pretense turned tail."

"Bitch!"

"Ah, you're angry. What shocking language. It's the first sign of weakness. Why don't you exercise your better judgment and carry me off? That would be the second sign."

"Damn you!"

He stepped close to her, clenching his fists in rage. She touched his cheek with a cool, quiet hand, but once again there was that electric shock.

"No, it's too late, my dear," she said quietly. "Here comes a whole cluster of red streaks . . . down, down, down . . . directly at us. There'll be no escaping this. Quick, now! Run! Jaunte! Take me with you. Quick! Quick!"

He swept her off the bench. "Bitch! Never!"

He held her, found the soft coral mouth and kissed her; bruised her lips with his, waiting for the final blackout.

The concussion never came.

"Tricked!" he exclaimed. She laughed. He kissed her again and at last forced himself to release her. She gasped for breath, then laughed again, her coral eyes blazing.

"It's over," she said.

"It hasn't begun yet."

"What d'you mean?"

"The war between us."

"Make it a human war," she said fiercely. "You're the first not to be deceived by my looks. Oh God! The boredom of the chivalrous knights and their milk-warm passion for the fairy tale princess. But I'm not like that . . . inside. I'm not. I'm not. Never. Make it a savage war between us. Don't win me . . . destroy me!"

Suddenly she was Lady Olivia again, the gracious snow maiden. "I'm afraid the bombardment has finished, my dear Fourmyle. The show is over. But what an exciting prelude to the New Year. Good night."

"Good night?" he echoed incredulously.

"Good night," she repeated. "Really, my dear Fourmyle, are you so gauche that you never know when you're dismissed? You may go now. Good night."

He hesitated, searched for words, and at last turned and lurched out of the house. He was trembling with elation and confusion. He walked in a daze, scarcely aware of the confusion and disaster around him. The horizon now was lit with the light of red flames. The shock waves of the assault had stirred the atmosphere so violently that winds still whistled in strange gusts. The tremor of the explosions had shaken the city so hard that brick, cornice, glass, and metal were tumbling and crashing. And this despite the fact that no direct hit had been made on New York.

The streets were empty; the city was deserted. The entire population of New York, of every city, had jaunted in a desperate search for safety . . . to the limit of their ability . . . five miles, fifty miles, five hundred miles. Some had jaunted into the center of a direct hit. Thousands died in jaunte-explosions, for the public jaunte stages had never been designed to accommodate the crowding of mass exodus.

Foyle became aware of white-armored Disaster Crews appearing on the streets. An imperious signal directed at him warned him that he was about to be summarily drafted for disaster work. The problem of jaunting was not to get populations out of cities, but to force them to return and restore order. Foyle had no intention of spending a week fighting fire and looters. He accelerated and evaded the Disaster Crew.

At Fifth Avenue he decelerated; the drain of acceleration on his energy was so enormous that he was reluctant to maintain it for more than a few moments. Long periods of acceleration demanded days of recuperation.

The looters and Jack-jaunters were already at work on the avenue, singly, in swarms, furtive yet savage; jackals rending the body of a living but helpless animal. They descended on Foyle. Anything was their prey tonight.

"I'm not in the mood," he told them. "Play with somebody else."

He emptied the money out of his pockets and tossed it to them. They snapped it up but were not satisfied. They desired entertainment and he was obviously a helpless gentleman. Half a dozen surrounded Foyle and closed in to torment him.

"Kind gentleman," they smiled. "We're going to have a party."

Foyle had once seen the mutilated body of one of their party guests. He sighed and detached his mind from visions of Olivia Presteign.

"All right, jackals," he said. "Let's have a party."

They prepared to send him into a screaming dance. Foyle tripped the switchboard in his mouth and became for twelve devastating seconds the most murderous machine ever devised . . . the Commando killer. It was done without conscious thought or volition; his body merely followed the directive taped into muscle and reflex. He left six bodies stretched on the street.

Old St. Pat's still stood, unblemished, eternal, the distant fires flickering on the green copper of its roof. Inside, it was deserted. The tents of the Four Mile Circus filled the nave, il-luminated and furnished, but the circus personnel was gone. Servants, chefs, valets, athletes, philosophers, camp followers and crooks had fled.

"But they'll be back to loot," Foyle murmured.

He entered his own tent. The first thing he saw was a figure in white, crouched on a rug, crooning sunnily to itself. It was Robin Wednesbury, her gown in tatters, her mind in tatters.

"Robin!"

She went on crooning wordlessly. He pulled her up, shook her, and slapped her. She beamed and crooned. He filled a syringe and gave her a tremendous shot of Niacin. The sobering wrench of the drug on her pathetic flight from reality was ghastly. Her satin skin turned ashen. The beautiful face twisted. She recognized Foyle, remembered what she had tried to forget, screamed and sank to her knees. She began to cry.

"That's better," he told her. "You're a great one for escape, aren't you? First suicide. Now this. What next?"

"Go away."

"Probably religion. I can see you joining a cellar sect with passwords like *Pax Vobiscum*. Bible smuggling and martyrdom for the faith. Can't you ever face up to anything?"

"Don't you ever run away?"

"Never. Escape is for cripples. Neurotics."

"Neurotics. The favorite word of the Johnny-Come-Lately educated. You're so educated, aren't you? So poised. So balanced. You've been running away all your life."

"Me? Never. I've been hunting all my life."

"You've been running. Haven't you ever heard of Attack-Escape? To run away from reality by attacking it . . . denying it . . . destroying it? That's what you've been doing."

"Attack-Escape?" Foyle was brought up with a jolt. "You mean I've been running away from something?"

"Obviously."

"From what?"

"From reality. You can't accept life as it is. You refuse. You attack it . . . try to force it into your own pattern. You attack and destroy everything that stands in the way of your own insane pattern." She lifted her tearstained face. "I can't stand it any more. I want you to let me go."

"Go? Where?"

"To live my own life."

"What about your family?"

"And find them my own way."

"Why? What now?"

"It's too much . . . you *and* the war . . . because you're as bad as the war. Worse. What happened to me tonight is what happens to me every moment I'm with you. I can stand one or the other; not both."

"No," he said. "I need you."

"I'm prepared to buy my way out."

"How?"

"You've lost all your leads to 'Vorga,' haven't you?"

"And?"

"I've found another."

"Where?"

"Never mind where. Will you agree to let me go if I turn it over to you?"

"I can take it from you."

"Go ahead. Take it." Her eyes flashed. "If you know what it is, you won't have any trouble."

"I can make you give it to me."

"Can you? After the bombing tonight? Try."

He was taken aback by her defiance. "How do I know you're not bluffing?"

"I'll give you one hint. Remember the man in Australia?"

"Forrest?"

"Yes. He tried to tell you the names of the crew. Do you remember the only name he got out?"

"Kemp."

"He died before he could finish it. The name is Kempsey."

"That's your lead?"

"Yes. Kempsey. Name and address. In return for your promise to let me go."

"It's a sale," he said. "You can go. Give it to me."

She went at once to the travel dress she had worn in Shanghai. From the pocket she took out a sheet of partially burned paper.

"I saw this on Sergei Orel's desk when I was trying to put the fire out . . . the fire the Burning Man started . . ."

She handed him the sheet of paper. It was a fragment of a begging letter. It read: . . . *do anything to get out of these bacteria fields. Why should a man just because he can't jaunte get treated like a dog? Please help me, Serg. Help an old shipmate off a ship we don't mention. You can spare Ç r 100. Remember all the favors I done you? Send Ç r 100 or even Ç r 50. Don't let me down.*

> Rodg Kempsey
> Barrack 3
> Bacteria, Inc.
> Mare Nubium
> Moon

"By God!" Foyle exclaimed. "This *is* the lead. We can't fail this time. We'll know what to do. He'll spill everything . . . everything." He grinned at Robin. "We leave for the moon tomorrow night. Book passage. No, there'll be trouble on account of the attack. Buy a ship. They'll be unloading them cheap anyway."

"We?" Robin said. "You mean you."

"I mean we," Foyle answered. "We're going to the moon. Both of us."

"I'm leaving."

"You're not leaving. You're staying with me."

"But you swore you'd—"

"Grow up, girl. I had to swear to anything to get this. I need you more than ever now. Not for 'Vorga.' I'll handle 'Vorga' myself. For something much more important."

He looked at her incredulous face and smiled ruefully. "It's too bad, girl. If you'd given me this letter two hours ago I'd have kept my word. But it's too late now. I need a Romance Secretary. I'm in love with Olivia Presteign."

She leaped to her feet in a blaze of fury. *"You're in love with her? Olivia Presteign? In love with that white corpse!"* The bitter fury of her telesending was a startling revelation to him. *"Ah, now you have lost me. Forever. Now I'll destroy you!"*

She disappeared.

Twelve

CAPTAIN Peter Y'ang-Yeovil was handling reports at Central Intelligence Hq. in London at the rate of six per minute. Information was phoned in, wired in, cabled in, jaunted in. The bombardment picture unfolded rapidly.

ATTACK SATURATED N & S AMERICA FROM 60° TO 120° WEST LONGITUDE . . . LABRADOR TO ALASKA IN N . . . RIO TO ECUADOR IN S . . . ESTIMATED TEN PER CENT (10%) MISSILES PENETRATED INTERCEPTION SCREEN . . . ESTIMATED POPULATION LOSS: TEN TO TWELVE MILLION . . .

"If it wasn't for jaunting," Y'ang-Yeovil said, "the losses would have been five times that. All the same, it's close to a knockout. One more punch like that and Terra's finished."

He addressed this to the assistants jaunting in and out of his office, appearing and disappearing, dropping reports on his desk and chalking results and equations on the glass blackboard that covered one entire wall. Informality was the rule, and Y'ang-Yeovil was surprised and suspicious when an assistant knocked on his door and entered with elaborate formality.

"What larceny now?" he asked.

"Lady to see you, Yeo."

"Is this the time for comedy?" Y'ang-Yeovil said in exasperated tones. He pointed to the Whitehead equations spelling disaster on the transparent blackboard. "Read that and weep on the way out."

"Very special lady, Yeo. Your Venus from the Spanish Stairs."

"Who? What Venus?"

"Your Congo Venus."

"Oh? That one?" Y'ang-Yeovil hesitated. "Send her in."

"You'll interview her in private, of course."

"Of course nothing. There's a war on. Keep those reports coming, but tip everybody to switch to Secret Speech if they have to talk to me."

Robin Wednesbury entered the office, still wearing the torn white evening gown. She had jaunted immediately from New York to London without bothering to change. Her face was strained, but lovely. Y'ang-Yeovil gave her a split-second inspection and realized that his first appreciation of her had not been mistaken. Robin returned the inspection and her eyes dilated. "But you're the cook from the Spanish Stairs! Angelo Poggi!"

As an Intelligence Officer, Y'ang-Yeovil was prepared to deal with this crisis. "Not a cook, madam. I haven't had time to change back to my usual fascinating self. Please sit here, Miss . . . ?"

"Wednesbury. Robin Wednesbury."

"Charmed. I'm Captain Y'ang-Yeovil. How nice of you to come and see me, Miss Wednesbury. You've saved me a long, hard search."

"B-But I don't understand. What were you doing on the Spanish Stairs? Why were you hunting—?"

Y'ang-Yeovil saw that her lips weren't moving. "Ah? You're a telepath, Miss Wednesbury? How is that possible? I thought I knew every telepath in the system."

"I'm not a full telepath. I'm a telesend. I can only send . . . not receive."

"Which, of course, makes you worthless to the world. I see." Y'ang-Yeovil cocked a sympathetic eye at her. "What a dirty trick, Miss Wednesbury . . . to be saddled with all the disadvantages of telepathy, and be deprived of all the advantages. I do sympathize. Believe me."

"Bless him! He's the first ever to realize that without being told."

"Careful, Miss Wednesbury, I'm receiving you. Now, about the Spanish Stairs?"

He paused, listening intently to her agitated telesending: *"Why was he hunting? Me? Alien Bellig—Oh God! Will they hurt me? Cut and— Information. I—"*

"My dear girl," Y'ang-Yeovil said gently. He took her hands and held them sympathetically. "Listen to me a moment. You're alarmed over nothing. Apparently you're an Alien Belligerent. Yes?"

She nodded.

"That's unfortunate, but we won't worry about it now. About Intelligence cutting and slicing information out of people . . . that's all propaganda."

"Propaganda?"

"We're not maladroits, Miss Wednesbury. We know how to

extract information without being medieval. But we spread the legend to soften people up in advance, so to speak."

"Is that true? He's lying. It's a trick."

"It's true, Miss Wednesbury. I do finesse, but there's no need now. Not when you've evidently come of your own free will to offer information."

"He's too adroit . . . too quick . . . He—"

"You sound as though you've been badly tricked recently, Miss Wednesbury . . . Badly burned."

"I have. I have. *By myself, mostly. I'm a fool. A hateful fool.*"

"Never a fool, Miss Wednesbury, and never hateful. I don't know what's happened to shatter your opinion of yourself, but I hope to restore it. So . . . you've been deceived, have you? By yourself, mostly? We all do that. But you've been helped by someone. Who?"

"I'm betraying him."

"Then don't tell me."

"But I've got to find my mother and sisters . . . I can't trust him any more . . . I've got to do it myself." Robin took a deep breath. "I want to tell you about a man named Gulliver Foyle."

Y'ang-Yeovil at once got down to business.

"Is it true he arrived by railroad?" Olivia Presteign asked. "In a locomotive and observation car? What wonderful audacity."

"Yes, he's a remarkable young man," Presteign answered. He stood, iron gray and iron hard, in the reception hall of his home, alone with his daughter. He was guarding honor and life while he waited for servants and staff to return from their panic-stricken jaunte to safety. He chatted imperturbably with Olivia, never once permitting her to realize their grave danger.

"Father, I'm exhausted."

"It's been a trying night, my dear. But please don't retire yet."

"Why not?"

Presteign refrained from telling her that she would be safer with him. "I'm lonely, Olivia. We'll talk for a few minutes."

"I did a daring thing, Father. I watched the attack from the garden."

"My dear! Alone?"

"No. With Fourmyle."

A heavy pounding began to shake the front door which Presteign had closed.

"What's that?"

"Looters," Presteign answered calmly. "Don't be alarmed, Olivia. They won't get in." He stepped to a table on which he had laid out an assortment of weapons as neatly as a game of patience. "There's no danger, my love." He tried to distract her. "You were telling me about Fourmyle. . . ."

"Oh, yes. We watched together . . . describing the bombing to each other."

"Unchaperoned? That wasn't discreet, Olivia."

"I know. I know. I behaved disgracefully. He seemed so big, so sure of himself, that I gave him the Lady Hauteur treatment. You remember Miss Post, my governess, who was so dignified and aloof that I called her Lady Hauteur? I acted like Miss Post. He was furious, father. That's why he came looking for me in the garden."

"And you permitted him to remain? I'm shocked, dear."

"I am too. I think I was half out of my mind with excitement. What's he like, father? Tell me. What's he look like to you?"

"He *is* big. Tall, very dark, rather enigmatic. Like a Borgia. He seems to alternate between assurance and savagery."

"Ah, he is savage, then? I could see it myself. He glows with danger. Most people just shimmer . . . he looks like a lightning bolt. It's terribly fascinating."

"My dear," Presteign remonstrated gently. "Unmarried females are too modest to talk like that. It would displease me, my love, if you were to form a romantic attachment for a parvenu like Fourmyle of Ceres."

The Presteign staff jaunted into the reception hall, cooks, waitresses, footmen, pages, coachmen, valets, maids. All were shaken and hang-dog after their flight from death.

"You have deserted your posts. It will be remembered," Presteign said coldly. "My safety and honor are again in your hands. Guard them. Lady Olivia and I will retire."

He took his daughter's arm and led her up the stairs, savagely protective of his ice-pure princess. "Blood and money," Presteign murmured.

"What, father?"

"I was thinking of a family vice, Olivia. I was thanking the Deity that you have not inherited it."

"What vice is that?"

"There's no need for you to know. It's one that Fourmyle shares."

"Ah, he's wicked? I knew it. Like a Borgia, you said. A wicked Borgia with black eyes and lines in his face. That must account for the pattern."

"Pattern, my dear?"

"Yes. I can see a strange pattern over his face . . . not the usual electricity of nerve and muscle. Something laid over that. It fascinated me from the beginning."

"What sort of pattern do you mean?"

"Fantastic . . . Wonderfully evil. I can't describe it. Give me something to write with. I'll show you."

They stopped before a six hundred year–old Chippendale cabinet. Presteign took out a silver-mounted slab of crystal and handed it to Olivia. She touched it with her fingertip; a black dot appeared. She moved her finger and the dot elongated into a line. With quick strokes she sketched the hideous swirls and blazons of a devil mask.

Saul Dagenham left the darkened bedroom. A moment later it was flooded with light as one wall illuminated. It seemed as though a giant mirror reflected Jisbella's bedroom, but with one odd quirk. Jisbella lay in the bed alone, but in the reflection Saul Dagenham sat on the edge of the bed alone. The mirror was, in fact, a sheet of lead glass separating identical rooms. Dagenham had just illuminated his.

"Love by the clock." Dagenham's voice came through a speaker. "Disgusting."

"No, Saul. Never."

"Frustrating."

"Not that, either."

"But unhappy."

"No. You're greedy. Be content with what you've got."

"It's more than I ever had. You're magnificent."

"You're extravagant. Now go to sleep, darling. We're skiing tomorrow."

"No, there's been a change of plan. I've got to work."

"Oh Saul . . . you promised me. No more working and fretting and running. Aren't you going to keep your promise?"

"I can't with a war on."

"To hell with the war. You sacrificed enough up at Tycho Sands. They can't ask any more of you."

"I've got one job to finish."

"I'll help you finish it."

"No. You'd best keep out of this, Jisbella."

"You don't trust me."

"I don't want you hurt."

"Nothing can hurt us."

"Foyle can."

"W-What?"

"Fourmyle is Foyle. You know that. I know you know."

"But I never—"

"No, you never told me. You're magnificent. Keep faith with me the same way, Jisbella."

"Then how did you find out?"

"Foyle slipped."

"How?"

"The name."

"Fourmyle of Ceres? He bought the Ceres company."

"But Geoffrey Fourmyle?"

"He invented it."

"He thinks he invented it. He remembered it. Geoffrey Fourmyle is the name they use in the megalomania test down in Combined Hospital in Mexico City. I used the Megal Mood on Foyle when I tried to open him up. The name must have stayed buried in his memory. He dredged it up and thought it was original. That tipped me."

"Poor Gully."

Dagenham smiled. "Yes, no matter how we defend ourselves against the outside we're always licked by something from the inside. There's no defense against betrayal, and we all betray ourselves."

"What are you going to do, Saul?"

"Do? Finish him, of course."

"For twenty pounds of PyrE?"

"No. To win a lost war."

"What?" Jisbella came to the glass wall separating the rooms. "You, Saul? Patriotic?"

He nodded, almost guiltily. "It's ridiculous. Grotesque. But I am. You've changed me completely. I'm a sane man again."

He pressed his face to the wall too, and they kissed through three inches of lead glass.

Mare Nubium was ideally suited to the growth of anaerobic bacteria, soil organisms, phage, rare moulds, and all those microscopic life forms, essential to medicine and industry, which required airless culture. Bacteria, Inc. was a huge mosaic of culture fields traversed by catwalks spread around a central clump of barracks, offices, and plant. Each field was a giant glass vat, one hundred feet in diameter, twelve inches high and no more than two molecules thick.

A day before the sunrise line, creeping across the face of the moon, reached Mare Nubium, the vats were filled with culture medium. At sunrise, abrupt and blinding on the airless moon, the vats were seeded, and for the next fourteen days of continuous sun they were tended, shielded, regulated, nurtured . . . the field workers trudging up and down the catwalks in spacesuits. As the sunset line crept toward Mare Nubium, the vats were harvested and then left to freeze and sterilize in the two week frost of the lunar night.

Jaunting was of no use in this tedious step-by-step cultivation. Hence Bacteria, Inc. hired unfortunates incapable of jaunting and paid them slave wages. This was the lowest form of labor, the dregs and scum of the Solar System; and the barracks of Bacteria, Inc. resembled an inferno during the two week lay-off period. Foyle discovered this when he entered Barrack 3.

He was met by an appalling spectacle. There were two hundred men in the giant room; there were whores and their hard-eyed pimps, professional gamblers and their portable tables, dope peddlers, money lenders. There was a haze of acrid smoke and the stench of alcohol and Analogue. Furniture, bedding, clothes, unconscious bodies, empty bottles, rotting food were scattered on the floor.

A roar challenged Foyle's appearance, but he was equipped to handle this situation. He spoke to the first hairy face thrust into his.

"Kempsey?" he asked quietly. He was answered outrageously. Nevertheless he grinned and handed the man a ₵r 100 note. "Kempsey?" he asked another. He was insulted. He paid again and continued his saunter down the barracks distributing ₵r 100 notes in calm thanks for insult and invective. In the center of the barracks he found his key man, the obvious barracks bully, a monster of a man, naked, hairless, fondling two bawds and being fed whiskey by sycophants.

"Kempsey?" Foyle asked in the old gutter tongue. "I'm diggin' Rodger Kempsey."

"I'm diggin' you for broke," the man answered, thrusting out a huge paw for Foyle's money. "Gimmie."

There was a delighted howl from the crowd. Foyle smiled and spat in his eye. There was an abject hush. The hairless man dumped the bawds and surged up to annihilate Foyle. Five seconds later he was groveling on the floor with Foyle's foot planted on his neck.

"Still diggin' Kempsey," Foyle said gently. "Diggin' hard, man. You better finger him, man, or you're gone, is all."

"Washroom!" the hairless man howled. "Holed up. Washroom."

"Now you broke me," Foyle said. He dumped the rest of his money on the floor before the hairless man and walked quickly to the washroom.

Kempsey was cowering in the corner of a shower, face pressed to the wall, moaning in a dull rhythm that showed he had been at it for hours.

"Kempsey?"

The moaning answered him.

"What's a matter, you?"

"Clothes," Kempsey wept. "Clothes. All over, clothes. Like filth, like sick, like dirt. Clothes. All over, clothes."

"Up, man. Get up."

"Clothes. All over, clothes. Like filth, like sick, like dirt . . ."

"Kempsey, mind me, man. Orel sent me."

Kempsey stopped weeping and turned his sodden countenance to Foyle. "Who? Who?"

"Sergei Orel sent me. I've bought your release. You're free. We'll blow."

"When?"

"Now."

"Oh God! God bless him. Bless him!" Kempsey began to caper in weary exultation. The bruised and bloated face split into a facsimile of laughter. He laughed and capered and Foyle led him out of the washroom. But in the barracks he screamed and wept again, and as Foyle led him down the long room, the naked bawds swept up armfuls of dirty clothes and shook them before his eyes. Kempsey foamed and gibbered.

"What's a matter, him?" Foyle inquired of the hairless man in the gutter patois.

The hairless man was now a respectful neutral if not a friend. "Guesses for grabs," he answered. "Always like that, him. Show old clothes and he twitch. Man!"

"For why, already?"

"For why? Crazy, is all."

At the main-office airlock, Foyle got Kempsey and himself corked in suits and then led him out to the rocket field where a score of anti-grav beams pointed their pale fingers upward from pits to the gibbous earth hanging in the night sky. They entered a pit, entered Foyle's yawl and uncorked. Foyle took a bottle and a sting ampule from a cabinet. He poured a drink and handed it to Kempsey. He hefted the ampule in his palm, smiling.

Kempsey drank the whiskey, still dazed, still exulting. "Free," he muttered. "God bless him! Free. You don't know what I've been through." He drank again. "I still can't believe it. It's like a dream. Why don't you take off, man? I—" Kempsey choked and dropped the glass, staring at Foyle in horror. "Your face!" he exclaimed. "My God, your face! What happened to it?"

"You happened to it, you son of a bitch!" Foyle cried. He leaped up, his tiger face burning, and flung the ampule like a knife. It pierced Kempsey's neck and hung quivering. Kempsey toppled.

Foyle accelerated, blurred to the body, picked it up in mid-fall and carried it aft to the starboard stateroom. There were two main staterooms in the yawl, and Foyle had prepared both of them in advance. The starboard room had been stripped and turned into a surgery. Foyle strapped the body on the operating table, opened a case of surgical instruments, and began the delicate operation he had learned by hypno-training that morning . . . an operation made possible only by his five-to-one acceleration.

He cut through skin and fascia, sawed through the rib cage, exposed the heart, dissected it out and connected veins and arteries to the intricate blood pump alongside the table. He started the pump. Twenty seconds, objective time, had elapsed. He placed an oxygen mask over Kempsey's face and switched on the alternating suction and ructation of the oxygen pump.

Foyle decelerated, checked Kempsey's temperature, shot an anti-shock series into his veins and waited. Blood gurgled through the pump and Kempsey's body. After five minutes, Foyle removed the oxygen mask. The respiration reflex continued. Kempsey was without a heart, yet alive. Foyle sat down alongside the operating table and waited. The stigmata still showed on his face.

Kempsey remained unconscious.

Foyle waited.

Kempsey awoke, screaming.

Foyle leaped up, tightened the straps and leaned over the heartless man.

"Hallo, Kempsey," he said.

Kempsey screamed.

"Look at yourself, Kempsey. You're dead."

Kempsey fainted. Foyle brought him to with the oxygen mask.

"Let me die, for God's sake!"

"What's the matter? Does it hurt? I died for six months, and I didn't whine."

"Let me die."

"In time, Kempsey. Your sympathetic block's been bypassed, but I'll let you die in time, if you behave. You were aboard 'Vorga' on September 16, 2436?"

"For Christ's sake, let me die."

"You were aboard 'Vorga'?"

"Yes."

"You passed a wreck out in space. Wreck of the 'Nomad.' She signalled for help and you passed her by. Yes?"

"Yes."

"Why?"

"Christ! Oh Christ help me!"

"Why?"

"Oh Jesus!"

"I was aboard 'Nomad,' Kempsey. Why did you leave me to rot?"

"Sweet Jesus help me! Christ, deliver me!"

"I'll deliver you, Kempsey, if you answer questions. Why did you leave me to rot?"

"Couldn't pick you up."

"Why not?"

"Reffs aboard."

"Oh? I guessed right, then. You were running refugees in from Callisto?"

"Yes."

"How many?"

"Six hundred."

"That's a lot, but you could have made room for one more. Why didn't you pick me up?"

"We were scuttling the reffs."

"What!" Foyle cried.

"Overboard . . . all of them . . . six hundred . . . Stripped 'em . . . took their clothes, money, jewels, baggage . . . Put 'em through the airlock in batches. Christ! The clothes all over the ship . . . The shrieking and the—Jesus! If I could only forget! The naked women . . . blue . . . busting wide open . . . spinning behind us . . . The clothes all over the ship . . . Six hundred . . . Scuttled!"

"You son of a bitch! It was a racket? You took their money and never intended bringing them to earth?"

"It was a racket."

"And that's why you didn't pick me up?"

"Would have had to scuttle you anyway."

"Who gave the order?"

"Captain."

"Name?"

"Joyce. Lindsey Joyce."

"Address?"

"Skoptsy Colony, Mars."

"What!" Foyle was thunderstruck. "He's a Skoptsy? You

mean after hunting him for a year, I can't touch him . . . hurt
him . . . make him feel what I felt?" He turned away from
the tortured man on the table, equally tortured himself by
frustration. "A Skoptsy! The one thing I never figured on . . .
After preparing that port stateroom for him . . . What am I
going to do? What, in God's name am I going to do?" he
roared in fury, the stigmata showing livid on his face.

He was recalled by a desperate moan from Kempsey. He returned to the table and bent over the dissected body. "Let's
get it straight for the last time. This Skoptsy, Lindsey Joyce,
gave the order to scuttle the reffs?"

"Yes."

"And to let me rot?"

"Yes. Yes. Yes. That's enough. Let me die."

"Live, you pig-man . . . filthy heartless bastard! Live without a heart. Live and suffer. I'll keep you alive forever, you—"

A lurid flash of light caught Foyle's eye. He looked up. His
burning image was peering through the large square porthole
of the stateroom. As he leaped to the porthole, the burning
man disappeared.

Foyle left the stateroom and darted forward to main controls
where the observation bubble gave him two hundred and
seventy degrees of vision. The Burning Man was nowhere in
sight.

"It's not real," he muttered. "It couldn't be real. It's a sign, a
good luck sign . . . a Guardian Angel. It saved me on the Spanish Stairs. It's telling me to go ahead and find Lindsey Joyce."

He strapped himself into the pilot chair, ignited the yawl's
jets, and slammed into full acceleration.

"Lindsey Joyce, Skoptsy Colony, Mars," he thought as he
was thrust back deep into the pneumatic chair. "A Skoptsy . . .
Without senses, without pleasure, without pain. The ultimate
in Stoic escape. How am I going to punish him? Torture him?
Put him in the port stateroom and make him feel what I felt
aboard 'Nomad'? Damnation! It's as though he's dead. He *is*
dead. And I've got to figure how to beat a dead body and
make it feel pain. To come so close to the end and have the
door slammed in your face . . . The damnable frustration of
revenge. Revenge is for dreams . . . never for reality."

An hour later he released himself from the acceleration and his fury, unbuckled himself from the chair, and remembered Kempsey. He went aft to the surgery. The extreme acceleration of the take-off had choked the blood pump enough to kill Kempsey. Suddenly Foyle was overcome with a novel passionate revulsion for himself. He fought it helplessly.

"What's a matter, you?" he whispered. "Think of the six hundred, scuttled . . . Think of yourself . . . Are you turning into a white-livered Cellar Christian turning the other cheek and whining forgiveness? Olivia, what are you doing to me? Give me strength, not cowardice . . ."

Nevertheless he averted his eyes as he scuttled the body.

Thirteen

ALL PERSONS KNOWN TO BE IN THE

EMPLOY OF FOURMYLE OF CERES OR ASSOCIATED

WITH HIM IN ANY CAPACITY TO BE HELD FOR

QUESTIONING. Y-Y: CENTRAL INTELLIGENCE.

ALL EMPLOYEES OF THIS COMPANY TO

MAINTAIN STRICT WATCH FOR ONE FOURMYLE OF

CERES, AND REPORT AT ONCE TO LOCAL MR.

PRESTO. PRESTEIGN.

ALL COURIERS WILL ABANDON PRESENT

ASSIGNMENTS AND REPORT FOR REASSIGNMENT

TO FOYLE CASE. DAGENHAM.

A BANK HOLIDAY WILL BE DECLARED
IMMEDIATELY IN THE NAME OF THE WAR CRISIS
TO CUT FOURMYLE OFF FROM ALL FUNDS. Y–Y:
CENTRAL INTELLIGENCE.

ANYONE MAKING INQUIRIES RE: S.S.
"VORGA" TO BE TAKEN TO CASTLE PRESTEIGN
FOR EXAMINATION. PRESTEIGN.

ALL PORTS AND FIELDS IN INNER PLANETS
TO BE ALERTED FOR ARRIVAL OF FOURMYLE.
QUARANTINE AND CUSTOMS TO CHECK ALL
LANDINGS. Y–Y: CENTRAL INTELLIGENCE.

OLD ST. PATRICK'S TO BE SEARCHED AND
WATCHED. DAGENHAM.

THE FILES OF BO'NESS & UIG TO BE
CHECKED FOR NAMES OF OFFICERS AND MEN OF
VORGA TO ANTICIPATE, IF POSSIBLE, FOYLE'S
NEXT MOVE. PRESTEIGN.

WAR CRIMES COMMISSION TO MAKE UP
LIST OF PUBLIC ENEMIES GIVING FOYLE NUMBER
ONE SPOT. Y–Y: CENTRAL INTELLIGENCE.

₵r 1,000,000 REWARD OFFERED FOR

INFORMATION LEADING TO APPREHENSION OF

FOURMYLE OF CERES, ALIAS GULLIVER FOYLE,

ALIAS GULLY FOYLE, NOW AT LARGE IN THE

INNER PLANETS. PRIORITY!

After two centuries of colonization, the air struggle on Mars was still so critical that the V-L Law, the Vegetative-Lynch Law, was still in effect. It was a killing offense to endanger or destroy any plant vital to the transformation of Mars' carbon dioxide atmosphere into an oxygen atmosphere. Even blades of grass were sacred. There was no need to erect KEEP OFF THE GRASS neons. The man who wandered off a path onto a lawn would be instantly shot. The woman who picked a flower would be killed without mercy. Two centuries of sudden death had inspired a reverence for green growing things that almost amounted to a religion.

Foyle remembered this as he raced up the center of the causeway leading to Mars St. Michel. He had jaunted direct from the Syrtis airport to the St. Michel stage at the foot of the causeway which stretched for a quarter of a mile through green fields to Mars St. Michel. The rest of the distance had to be traversed on foot.

Like the original Mont St. Michel on the French coast, Mars St. Michel was a majestic Gothic cathedral of spires and buttresses looming on a hill and yearning toward the sky. Ocean tides surrounded Mont St. Michel on earth. Green tides of grass surrounded Mars St. Michel. Both were fortresses. Mont St. Michel had been a fortress of faith before organized religion was abolished. Mars St. Michel was a fortress of telepathy. Within it lived Mars's sole full telepath, Sigurd Magsman.

"Now these are the defenses protecting Sigurd Magsman," Foyle chanted, halfway between hysteria and litany. "Firstly, the Solar System; secondly, martial law; thirdly, Dagenham-Presteign & Co.; fourthly, the fortress itself; fifthly, the uniformed guards, attendants, servants, and admirers of the bearded sage we all know so well, Sigurd Magsman, selling his awesome powers for awesome prices. . . ."

Foyle laughed immoderately: "But there's a Sixthly that I know: Sigurd Magsman's Achilles' Heel . . . For I've paid ₡r 1,000,000 to Sigurd III . . . or was he IV?"

He passed through the outer labyrinth of Mars St. Michel with his forged credentials and was tempted to bluff or proceed directly by commando action to an audience with the Great Man himself, but time was pressing and his enemies were closing in and he could not afford to satisfy his curiosity. Instead, he accelerated, blurred, and found a humble cottage set in a walled garden within the Mars St. Michel home farm. It had drab windows and a thatched roof and might have been mistaken for a stable. Foyle slipped inside.

The cottage was a nursery. Three pleasant nannies sat motionless in rocking chairs, knitting poised in their frozen hands. The blur that was Foyle came up behind them and quietly stung them with ampules. Then he decelerated. He looked at the ancient, ancient child; the wizened, shriveled boy who was seated on the floor playing with electronic trains.

"Hello, Sigurd," Foyle said.

The child began to cry.

"Crybaby! What are you afraid of? I'm not going to hurt you."

"You're a bad man with a bad face."

"I'm your friend, Sigurd."

"No, you're not. You want me to do b-bad things."

"I'm your friend. Look, I know all about those big hairy men who pretend to be you, but I won't tell. Read me and see."

"You're going to hurt him and y-you want me to tell him."

"Who?"

"The captain-man. The Skl— Skot—" The child fumbled with the word, wailing louder. *"Go away. You're bad. Badness in your head and burning mens and—"*

"Come here, Sigurd."

"No. NANNIE! NAN-N-I-E!"

"Shut up, you little bastard!"

Foyle grabbed the seventy-year-old child and shook it. "This is going to be a brand new experience for you, Sigurd. The first time you've ever been walloped into anything. Understand?"

The ancient child read him and howled.

"Shut up! We're going on a trip to the Skoptsy Colony. If you behave yourself and do what you're told, I'll bring you back safe and give you a lolly or whatever the hell they bribe you with. If you don't behave, I'll beat the living daylights out of you."

"No, you won't. . . . You won't. I'm Sigurd Magsman. I'm Sigurd the telepath. You wouldn't dare."

"Sonny, I'm Gully Foyle, Solar Enemy Number One. I'm just a step away from the finish of a year-long hunt . . . I'm risking my neck because I need you to settle accounts with a son of a bitch who— Sonny, I'm Gully Foyle. There isn't anything I wouldn't dare."

The telepath began broadcasting terror with such an uproar that alarms sounded all over Mars St. Michel. Foyle took a firm grip on the ancient child, accelerated and carried him out of the fortress. Then he jaunted.

URGENT. SIGURD MAGSMAN KIDNAPED BY

MAN TENTATIVELY IDENTIFIED AS GULLIVER

FOYLE, ALIAS FOURMYLE OF CERES, SOLAR

ENEMY NUMBER ONE. DESTINATION

TENTATIVELY FIXED. ALERT COMMANDO

BRIGADE. INFORM CENTRAL INTELLIGENCE.

URGENT!

The ancient Skoptsy sect of White Russia, believing that sex was the root of all evil, practiced an atrocious self-castration to extirpate the root. The modern Skoptsys, believing that sensation was the root of all evil, practiced an even more barbaric custom. Having entered the Skoptsy Colony and paid a fortune for the privilege, the initiates submitted joyously to an operation that severed the sensory nervous system, and lived out their days without sight, sound, speech, smell, taste, or touch.

When they first entered the monastery, the initiates were shown elegant ivory cells in which it was intimated they would spend the remainder of their lives in rapt contemplation, lovingly tended. In actuality, the senseless creatures were packed in catacombs where they sat on rough stone slabs and were fed and exercised once a day. For twenty-three out of twenty-four hours they sat alone in the dark, untended, unguarded, unloved.

"The living dead," Foyle muttered. He decelerated, put Sigurd Magsman down, and switched on the retinal light in his eyes, trying to pierce the wombgloom. It was midnight above ground. It was permanent midnight down in the catacombs. Sigurd Magsman was broadcasting terror and anguish with such a telepathic bray that Foyle was forced to shake the child again.

"Shut up!" he whispered. "You can't wake these dead. Now find me Lindsey Joyce."

"They're sick . . . all sick . . . like worms in their heads . . . worms and sickness and—"

"Christ, don't I know it. Come on, let's get it over with. There's worse to come."

They went down the twisting labyrinth of the catacombs. The stone slabs shelved the walls from floor to ceiling. The Skoptsys, white as slugs, mute as corpses, motionless as Buddhas, filled the caverns with the odor of living death. The telepathic child wept and shrieked. Foyle never relaxed his relentless grip on him; he never relaxed the hunt.

"Johnson, Wright, Keeley, Graff, Nastro, Underwood . . . God, there's thousands here." Foyle read off the bronze identification plates attached to the slabs. "Reach out, Sigurd. Find Lindsey Joyce for me. We can't go over them name by name. Regal, Cone, Brady, Vincent— What in the—?"

Foyle started back. One of the bone-white figures had cuffed his brow. It was swaying and writhing, its face twitching. All the white slugs on their shelves were squirming and writhing. Sigurd Magsman's constant telepathic broadcast of anguish and terror was reaching them and torturing them.

"Shut up!" Foyle snapped. "Stop it. Find Lindsey Joyce and we'll get out of here. Reach out and find him."

"Down there." Sigurd wept. *"Straight down there. Seven, eight, nine shelves down. I want to go home. I'm sick. I—"*

Foyle went pell-mell down the catacombs with Sigurd, reading off identification plates until at last he came to: "LINDSEY JOYCE. BOUGAINVILLE. VENUS."

This was his enemy, the instigator of his death and the deaths of the six hundred from Callisto. This was the enemy for whom he had planned vengeance and hunted for months. This was the enemy for whom he had prepared the agony of the port stateroom aboard his yawl. This was "Vorga." It was a woman.

Foyle was thunderstruck. In these days of the double standard, with women kept in purdah, there were many reported cases of women masquerading as men to enter the worlds closed to them, but he had never yet heard of a woman in the merchant marine . . . masquerading her way to top officer rank.

"This?" he exclaimed furiously. "This is Lindsey Joyce? Lindsey Joyce off the 'Vorga'? Ask her."

"I don't know what 'Vorga' is."

"Ask her!"

"But I don't— She was . . . She like gave orders."

"Captain?"

"I don't like what's inside her. It's all sick and dark. It hurts. I want to go home."

"Ask her. Was she captain of the 'Vorga'?"

"Yes. Please, please, please don't make me go inside her any more. It's twisty and hurts. I don't like her."

"Tell her I'm the man she wouldn't pick up on September 16, 2436. Tell her it's taken a long time but I've finally come to settle the account. Tell her I'm going to pay her back."

"I d-don't understand. Don't understand."

"Tell her I'm going to kill her, slow and hard. Tell her I've got a stateroom aboard my yawl, fitted up just like my locker aboard 'Nomad' where I rotted for six months . . . where she ordered 'Vorga' to leave me to die. Tell her she's going to rot and die just like me. Tell her!" Foyle shook the wizened child furiously. "Make her feel it. Don't let her get away by turning Skoptsy. Tell her I kill her filthy. Read me and tell her!"

"She . . . Sh-She didn't give that order."

"What!"

"I c-can't understand her."

"She didn't give the order to scuttle me?"

"I'm afraid to go in."

"Go in, you little son of a bitch, or I'll take you apart. What does she mean?"

The child wailed; the woman writhed; Foyle fumed. "Go in! Go in! Get it out of her. Jesus Christ, why does the only telepath on Mars have to be a child? Sigurd! Sigurd, listen to me. Ask her: Did she give the order to scuttle the reffs?"

"No. No!"

"No she didn't or no you won't?"

"She didn't."

"Did she give the order to pass 'Nomad' by?"

"She's twisty and sicky. Oh please! NAN-N-I-E! I want to go home. Want to go."

"Did she give the order to pass 'Nomad' by?"

"No."

"She didn't?"

"No. Take me home."

"Ask her who did."

"I want my Nannie."

"Ask her who could give her an order. She was captain aboard her own ship. Who could command her? Ask her!"

"I want my Nannie."

"Ask her!"

"No. No. No. I'm afraid. She's sick. She's dark and black. She's bad. I don't understand her. I want my Nannie. I want to go home."

The child was shrieking and shaking; Foyle was shouting. The echoes thundered. As Foyle reached for the child in a rage, his eyes were blinded by brilliant light. The entire catacomb was illuminated by the Burning Man. Foyle's image stood before him, face hideous, clothes on fire, the blazing eyes fixed on the convulsing Skoptsy that had been Lindsey Joyce.

The Burning Man opened his tiger mouth. A grating sound emerged. It was like flaming laughter.

"She hurts," he said.

"Who are you?" Foyle whispered.

The Burning Man winced. "Too bright," he said. "Less light."

Foyle took a step forward. The Burning Man clapped hands

over his ears in agony. "Too loud," he cried. "Don't move so loud."

"Are you my guardian angel?"

"You're blinding me. Shhh!" Suddenly he laughed again. "Listen to her. She's screaming. Begging. She doesn't want to die. She doesn't want to be hurt. Listen to her."

Foyle trembled.

"She's telling us who gave the order. Can't you hear? Listen with your eyes." The Burning Man pointed a talon finger at the writhing Skoptsy. "She says Olivia."

"What!"

"She says Olivia. Olivia Presteign. Olivia Presteign. Olivia Presteign."

The Burning Man vanished.

The catacombs were dark again.

Colored lights and cacophonies whirled around Foyle. He gasped and staggered. "Blue jaunte," he muttered. "Olivia. No. Not. Never. Olivia. I—"

He felt a hand reach for his. "Jiz?" he croaked.

He became aware that Sigurd Magsman was holding on to his hand and weeping. He picked the boy up.

"*I hurt*," Sigurd whimpered.

"I hurt too, son."

"Want to go home."

"I'll take you home."

Still holding the boy in his arms, he blundered through the catacombs.

"The living dead," he mumbled.

And then: "I've joined them."

He found the stone steps that led up from the depths to the monastery cloister above ground. He trudged up the steps, tasting death and desolation. There was bright light above him, and for a moment he imagined that dawn had come already. Then he realized that the cloister was brilliantly lit with artificial light. There was the tramp of shod feet and the low growl of commands. Halfway up the steps, Foyle stopped and mustered himself.

"Sigurd," he whispered. "Who's above us? Find out."

"*Sogers*," the child answered.

"Soldiers? What soldiers?"

"Commando sogers." Sigurd's crumpled face brightened. *"They come for me. To take me home to Nannie. HERE I AM! HERE I AM!"*

The telepathic clamor brought a shout from overhead. Foyle accelerated and blurred up the rest of the steps to the cloister. It was a square of Romanesque arches surrounding a green lawn. In the center of the lawn was a giant cedar of Lebanon. The flagged walks swarmed with Commando search parties, and Foyle came face to face with his match; for an instant after they saw his blur whip up from the catacombs they accelerated too, and all were on even terms.

But Foyle had the boy. Shooting was impossible. Cradling Sigurd in his arms, he wove through the cloister like a broken-field runner hurtling toward a goal. No one dared block him, for at plus-five acceleration a head-on collision between two bodies would be instantly fatal to both. Objectively, this break-neck skirmish looked like a five second zigzag of lightning.

Foyle broke out of the cloister, went through the main hall of the monastery, passed through the labyrinth, and reached the public jaunte stage outside the main gate. There he stopped, decelerated and jaunted to the monastery airfield, half a mile distant. The field, too, was ablaze with lights and swarming with Commandos. Every anti-grav pit was occupied by a Brigade ship. His own yawl was under guard.

A fifth of a second after Foyle arrived at the field, the pursuers from the monastery jaunted in. He looked around desperately. He was surrounded by half a regiment of Commandos, all under acceleration, all geared for lethal-action, all his equal or better. The odds were impossible.

And then the Outer Satellites altered the odds. Exactly one week after the saturation raid on Terra, they struck at Mars.

Again the missiles came down on the midnight to dawn quadrant. Again the heavens twinkled with interceptions and detonations, and the horizon exploded great puffs of light while the ground shook. But this time there was a ghastly variation, for a brilliant nova burst overhead, flooding the nightside of the planet with garish light. A swarm of fission heads had struck Mars's tiny satellite, Phobos, instantly vaporizing it into a sunlet.

The recognition lag of the Commandos to this appalling attack gave Foyle his opportunity. He accelerated again and burst through them to his yawl. He stopped before the main hatch and saw the stunned guard party hesitate between a continuance of the old action and a response to the new. Foyle hurled Sigurd Magsman up into the air like an ancient Scotsman tossing the caber. As the guard party rushed to catch the boy, Foyle dove through them into his yawl, slammed the hatch, and dogged it.

Still under acceleration, never pausing to see if anyone was inside the yawl, he shot forward to controls, tripped the release lever, and as the yawl started to float up the anti-grav beam, threw on full 10-G propulsion. He was not strapped into the pilot chair. The effect of the 10-G drive on his accelerated and unprotected body was monstrous.

A creeping force took hold of him and spilled him out of the chair. He inched back toward the rear wall of the control chamber like a sleepwalker. The wall appeared, to his accelerated senses, to approach him. He thrust out both arms, palms flat against the wall to brace himself. The sluggish power thrusting him back split his arms apart and forced him against the wall, gently at first, then harder and harder until face, jaw, chest, and body were crushed against the metal.

The mounting pressure became agonizing. He tried to trip the switchboard in his mouth with his tongue, but the propulsion crushing him against the wall made it impossible for him to move his distorted mouth. A burst of explosions, so far down the sound spectrum that they sounded like sodden rock slides, told him that the Commando Brigade was bombarding him with shots from below. As the yawl tore up into the blue-black of outer space, he began to scream in a bat screech before he mercifully lost consciousness.

Fourteen

FOYLE awoke in darkness. He was decelerated, but the exhaustion of his body told him he had been under acceleration while he had been unconscious. Either his power pack had run out or . . . He inched a hand to the small of his back. The pack was gone. It had been removed.

He explored with trembling fingers. He was in a bed. He listened to the murmur of ventilators and air-conditioners and the click and buzz of servo-mechanisms. He was aboard a ship. He was strapped to the bed. The ship was in free fall.

Foyle unfastened himself, pressed his elbows against the mattress and floated up. He drifted through the darkness searching for a light switch or a call button. His hands brushed against a water carafe with raised letters on the glass. He read them with his fingertips. SS, he felt. V, O, R, G, A. VORGA. He cried out.

The door of the stateroom opened. A figure drifted through the door, silhouetted against the light of a luxurious private lounge behind it.

"This time we picked you up," a voice said.

"Olivia?"

"Yes."

"Then it's true?"

"Yes, Gully."

Foyle began to cry.

"You're still weak," Olivia Presteign said gently. "Come and lie down."

She urged him into the lounge and strapped him into a chaise longue. It was still warm from her body. "You've been like this for six days. We never thought you'd live. Everything was drained out of you before the surgeon found that battery on your back."

"Where is it?" he croaked.

"You can have it whenever you want it. Don't fret, my dear."

He looked at her for a long moment, his Snow Maiden, his beloved Ice Princess . . . the white satin skin, the blind coral eyes and exquisite coral mouth. She touched his moist eyelids with a scented handkerchief.

"I love you," he said.

"Shhh. I know, Gully."

"You've known all about me. For how long?"

"I knew Gully Foyle the spaceman off the 'Nomad,' was my enemy from the beginning. I never knew you were Fourmyle until we met. Ah, if only I'd known before. How much would have been saved."

"You knew and you've been laughing at me."

"No."

"Standing by and shaking with laughter."

"Standing by and loving you. No, don't interrupt. I'm try-ing to be rational and it's not easy." A flush cascaded across the marble face. "I'm not playing with you now. I . . . I betrayed you to my father. I did. Self-defense, I thought. Now that I've met him at last I can see he's too dangerous. An hour later I knew it was a mistake because I realized I was in love with you. I'm paying for it now. You need never have known."

"You expect me to believe that?"

"Then why am I here?" She trembled slightly. "Why did I follow you? That bombing was ghastly. You'd have been dead in another minute when we picked you up. Your yawl was a wreck. . . ."

"Where are we now?"

"What difference does it make?"

"I'm stalling for time."

"Time for what?"

"Not for time . . . I'm stalling for courage."

"We're orbiting earth."

"How did you follow me?"

"I knew you'd be after Lindsey Joyce. I took over one of my father's ships. It happened to be 'Vorga' again."

"Does he know?"

"He never knows. I live my own private life."

He could not take his eyes off her, and yet it hurt him to look at her. He was yearning and hating . . . yearning for the real-ity to be undone, hating the truth for what it was. He discovered that he was stroking her handkerchief with tremulous fingers.

"I love you, Olivia."

"I love you, Gully, my enemy."

"For God's sake!" he burst out. "Why did you do it? You were aboard 'Vorga' running the reff racket. You gave the order to scuttle them. You gave the order to pass me by. Why! Why!"

"What?" she lashed back. "Are you demanding apologies?"

"I'm demanding an explanation."

"You'll get none from me!"

"Blood and money, your father said. He was right. Oh . . . Bitch! Bitch! Bitch!"

"Blood and money, yes; and unashamed."

"I'm drowning, Olivia. Throw me a lifeline."

"Then drown. Nobody ever saved me. No— No . . . This is wrong, all wrong. Wait, my dear. Wait." She composed herself and began speaking very tenderly. "I could lie, Gully dear, and make you believe it, but I'm going to be honest. There's a simple explanation. I live my own private life. We all do. You do."

"What's yours?"

"No different from yours . . . from the rest of the world. I cheat, I lie, I destroy . . . like all of us. I'm criminal . . . like all of us."

"Why? For money? You don't need money."

"No."

"For control . . . power?"

"Not for power."

"Then why?"

She took a deep breath, as though this truth was the first truth and was crucifying her. "For hatred . . . To pay you back, all of you."

"For what?"

"For being blind," she said in a smoldering voice. "For being cheated. For being helpless . . . They should have killed me when I was born. Do you know what it's like to be blind . . . to receive life secondhand? To be dependent, begging, crippled? 'Bring them down to your level,' I told my secret life. 'If you're blind make them blinder. If you're helpless, cripple them. Pay them back . . . all of them.'"

"Olivia, you're insane."

"And you?"

"I'm in love with a monster."

"We're a pair of monsters."

"No!"

"No? Not you?" she flared. "What have you been doing but paying the world back, like me? What's your revenge but settling your own private account with bad luck? Who wouldn't call you a crazy monster? I tell you, we're a pair, Gully. We couldn't help falling in love."

He was stunned by the truth of what she said. He tried on the shroud of her revelation and it fit, clung tighter than the tiger mask tattooed on his face.

"It's true," he said slowly. "I'm no better than you. Worse. But before God I never murdered six hundred."

"You're murdering six million."

"What?"

"Perhaps more. You've got something they need to end the war, and you're holding out."

"You mean PyrE?"

"Yes."

"What is it, this bringer of peace, this twenty pounds of miracle that they're fighting for?"

"I don't know, but I know they need it, and I don't care. Yes, I'm being honest now. I don't care. Let millions be murdered. It makes no difference to us. Not to us, Gully, because we stand apart. We stand apart and shape our own world. We're the strong."

"We're the damned."

"We're the blessed. We've found each other." Suddenly she laughed and held out her arms. "I'm arguing when there's no need for words. Come to me, my love. . . . Wherever you are, come to me. . . ."

He touched her and then put his arms around her. He found her mouth and devoured her. But he was forced to release her.

"What is it, Gully darling?"

"I'm not a child any more," he said wearily. "I've learned to understand that nothing is simple. There's never a simple answer. You can love someone and loathe them."

"Can you, Gully?"

"And you're making me loathe myself."

"No, my dear."

"I've been a tiger all my life. I trained myself . . . educated myself . . . pulled myself up by my stripes to make me a stronger tiger with a longer claw and a sharper tooth . . . quick and deadly. . . ."

"And you are. You are. The deadliest."

"No. I'm not. I went too far. I went beyond simplicity. I turned myself into a thinking creature. I look through your blind eyes, my love whom I loathe, and I see myself. The tiger's gone."

"There's no place for the tiger to go. You're trapped, Gully; by Dagenham, Intelligence, my father, the world."

"I know."

"But you're safe with me. We're safe together, the pair of us. They'll never dream of looking for you near me. We can plan together, fight together, destroy them together. . . ."

"No. Not together."

"What is it?" she flared again. "Are you still hunting me? Is that what's wrong? Do you still want revenge? Then take it. Here I am. Go ahead . . . destroy me."

"No. Destruction's finished for me."

"Ah, I know what it is." She became tender again in an instant. "It's your face, poor darling. You're ashamed of your tiger face, but I love it. You burn so brightly for me. You burn through the blindness. Believe me . . ."

"My God! What a pair of loathsome freaks we are."

"What's happened to you?" she demanded. She broke away from him, her coral eyes glittering. "Where's the man who watched the raid with me? Where's the unashamed savage who—"

"Gone, Olivia. You've lost him. We both have."

"Gully!"

"He's lost."

"But why? What have I done?"

"You don't understand, Olivia."

"Where are you?" she reached out, touched him and then clung to him. "Listen to me, darling. You're tired. You're exhausted. That's all. Nothing is lost." The words tumbled out of her. "You're right. Of course you're right. We've been bad, both of us. Loathsome. But all that's gone now. Nothing is lost. We were wicked because we were alone and unhappy. But we've found each other; we can save each other. Be my love, darling. Always. Forever. I've looked for you so long, waited and hoped and prayed . . ."

"No. You're lying, Olivia, and you know it."

"For God's sake, Gully!"

"Put 'Vorga' down, Olivia."

"Land?"

"Yes."

"On Terra?"

"Yes."

"What are you going to do? You're insane. They're hunting

you . . . waiting for you . . . watching. What are you going to do?"

"Do you think this is easy for me?" he said. "I'm doing what I have to do. I'm still driven. No man ever escapes from that. But there's a different compulsion in the saddle, and the spurs hurt, damn it. They hurt like hell."

He stifled his anger and controlled himself. He took her hands and kissed her palms.

"It's all finished, Olivia," he said gently. "But I love you. Always. Forever."

"I'll sum it up," Dagenham rapped. "We were bombed the night we found Foyle. We lost him on the Moon and found him a week later on Mars. We were bombed again. We lost him again. He's been lost for a week. Another bombing's due. Which one of the Inner Planets? Venus? The Moon? Terra again? Who knows. But we all know this: one more raid without retaliation and we're lost."

He glanced around the table. Against the ivory-and-gold background of the Star Chamber of Castle Presteign, his face, all three faces, looked strained. Y'ang-Yeovil slitted his eyes in a frown. Presteign compressed his thin lips.

"And we know this too," Dagenham continued. "We can't retaliate without PyrE and we can't locate the PyrE without Foyle."

"My instructions were," Presteign interposed, "that PyrE was not to be mentioned in public."

"In the first place, this is not public," Dagenham snapped. "It's a private information pool. In the second place, we've gone beyond property rights. We're discussing survival, and we've all got equal rights in that. Yes, Jiz?"

Jisbella McQueen had jaunted into the Star Chamber, looking intent and furious.

"Still no sign of Foyle."

"Old St. Pat's still being watched?"

"Yes."

"Commando Brigade's report in from Mars yet?"

"No."

"That's my business and Most Secret," Y'ang-Yeovil objected mildly.

"You've got as few secrets from me as I have from you."
Dagenham grinned mirthlessly. "See if you can beat Central
Intelligence back here with that report, Jiz. Go."

She disappeared.

"About property rights," Y'ang-Yeovil murmured. "May I
suggest to Presteign that Central Intelligence will guarantee
full payment to him for his right, title, and interest in PyrE?"

"Don't coddle him, Yeovil."

"This conference is being recorded," Presteign said, coldly.
"The Captain's offer is now on file." He turned his basilisk face
to Dagenham. "You are in my employ, Mr. Dagenham. Please
control your references to myself."

"And to your property?" Dagenham inquired with a deadly
smile. "You and your damned property. All of you and all of
your damned property have put us in this hole. The system's
on the edge of total annihilation for the sake of your property.
I'm not exaggerating. It will be a shooting war to end all wars
if we can't stop it."

"We can always surrender," Presteign answered.

"No," Y'ang-Yeovil said. "That's already been discussed and
discarded at HQ. We know the post-victory plans of the Outer
Satellites. They involve total exploitation of the Inner Planets.
We're to be gutted and worked until nothing's left. Surrender
would be as disastrous as defeat."

"But not for Presteign," Dagenham added.

"Shall we say . . . present company excluded?" Y'ang-
Yeovil replied gracefully.

"All right, Presteign." Dagenham swiveled in his chair. "Give."

"I beg your pardon, sir?"

"Let's hear all about PyrE. I've got an idea how we can bring
Foyle out into the open and locate the stuff, but I've got to
know all about it first. Make your contribution."

"No," Presteign answered.

"No, what?"

"I have decided to withdraw from this information pool. I
will reveal nothing about PyrE."

"For God's sake, Presteign! Are you insane? What's got into
you? Are you fighting Regis Sheffield's Liberal party again?"

"It's quite simple, Dagenham," Y'ang-Yeovil interposed. "My
information about the surrender-defeat situation has shown

Presteign a way to better his position. No doubt he intends negotiating a sale to the enemy in return for . . . property advantages."

"Can nothing move you?" Dagenham asked Presteign scornfully. "Can nothing touch you? Are you all property and nothing else? Go away, Jiz! The whole thing's fallen apart."

Jisbella had jaunted into the Star Chamber again. "Commando Brigade's reported," she said. "We know what happened to Foyle."

"What?"

"Presteign's got him."

"What!" Both Dagenham and Y'ang-Yeovil started to their feet.

"He left Mars in a private yawl, was shot up, and was observed being picked up by the Presteign S.S. 'Vorga.'"

"Damn you, Presteign," Dagenham snapped. "So that's why you've been—"

"Wait," Y'ang-Yeovil commanded. "It's news to him too, Dagenham. Look at him."

Presteign's handsome face had gone the color of ashes. He tried to rise and fell back stiffly in his chair. "Olivia . . ." he whispered. "With him . . . That scum . . ."

"Presteign?"

"My daughter, gentlemen, has . . . for some time been engaged in . . . certain activities. The family vice. Blood and— I . . . have managed to close my eyes to it . . . Had almost convinced myself that I was mistaken. I . . . But Foyle! Dirt! Filth! He must be destroyed!" Presteign's voice soared alarmingly. His head twisted back like a hanged man's and his body began to shudder.

"What in the—?"

"Epilepsy," Y'ang-Yeovil said. He pulled Presteign out of the chair onto the floor. "A spoon, Miss McQueen. Quick!" He levered Presteign's teeth open and placed a spoon between them to protect the tongue. As suddenly as it had begun, the seizure was over. The shuddering stopped. Presteign opened his eyes.

"*Petit mal*," Y'ang-Yeovil murmured, withdrawing the spoon. "But he'll be dazed for a while."

Suddenly Presteign began speaking in a low monotone. "PyrE is a pyrophoric alloy. A pyrophore is a metal which emits sparks when scraped or struck. PyrE emits energy, which is why E, the energy symbol, was added to the prefix Pyr. PyrE is a solid solution of transplutonian isotopes, releasing thermonuclear energy on the order of stellar Phoenix action. Its discoverer was of the opinion that he had produced the equivalent of the primordial protomatter which exploded into the Universe."

"My God!" Jisbella exclaimed.

Dagenham silenced her with a gesture and bent over Presteign. "How is it brought to critical mass, Presteign? How is the energy released?"

"As the original energy was generated in the beginning of time," Presteign droned. "Through Will and Idea."

"I'm convinced he's a Cellar Christian," Dagenham muttered to Y'ang-Yeovil. He raised his voice. "Will you explain, Presteign?"

"Through Will and Idea," Presteign repeated. "PyrE can only be exploded by psychokinesis. Its energy can only be released by thought. It must be willed to explode and the thought directed at it. That is the only way."

"There's no key? No formula?"

"No. Only Will and Idea are necessary." The glazed eyes closed.

"God in heaven!" Dagenham mopped his brow. "Will this give the Outer Satellites pause, Yeovil?"

"It'll give us all pause."

"It's the road to hell," Jisbella said.

"Then let's find it and get off the road. Here's my idea, Yeovil. Foyle was tinkering with that hell brew in his lab in Old St. Pat's, trying to analyze it."

"I told you that in strict confidence," Jisbella said furiously.

"I'm sorry, dear. We're past honor and the decencies. Now look, Yeovil, there must be some fragments of the stuff lying about . . . as dust, in solution, in precipitates . . . We've got to detonate those fragments and blow the hell out of Foyle's circus."

"Why?"

"To bring him running. He must have the bulk of the PyrE hidden there somewhere. He'll come to salvage it."

"What if it blows up too?"

"It can't, not inside an Inert Lead Isotope safe."

"Maybe it's not all inside."

"Jiz says it is . . . at least so Foyle reported."

"Leave me out of this," Jisbella said.

"Anyway, we'll have to gamble."

"Gamble!" Y'ang-Yeovil exclaimed. "On a Phoenix action? You'll gamble the solar system into a brand new nova."

"What else can we do? Pick any other road . . . and it's the road to destruction too. Have we got any choice?"

"We can wait," Jisbella said.

"For what? For Foyle to blow us up himself with his tinkering?"

"We can warn him."

"We don't know where he is."

"We can find him."

"How soon? Won't that be a gamble too? And what about that stuff lying around waiting for someone to think it into energy? Suppose a Jack-jaunter gets in and cracks the safe, looking for goodies? And then we don't just have dust waiting for an accidental thought, but twenty pounds."

Jisbella turned pale. Dagenham turned to the Intelligence man. "You make the decision, Yeovil. Do we try it my way or do we wait?"

Y'ang-Yeovil sighed. "I was afraid of this," he said. "Damn all scientists. I'll have to make my decision for a reason you don't know, Dagenham. The Outer Satellites are on to this too. We've got reason to believe that they've got agents looking for Foyle in the worst way. If we wait they may pick him up before us. In fact, they may have him now."

"So your decision is . . . ?"

"The blow-up. Let's bring Foyle running if we can."

"No!" Jisbella cried.

"How?" Dagenham asked, ignoring her.

"Oh, I've got just the one for the job. A one-way telepath named Robin Wednesbury."

"When?"

"At once. We'll clear the entire neighborhood. We'll get full news coverage and do a full broadcast. If Foyle's anywhere in the Inner Planets, he'll hear about it."

"Not *about* it," Jisbella said in despair. "He'll *hear* it. It'll be the last thing any of us hear."

"Will and Idea," Presteign whispered.

As always, when he returned from a stormy civil court session in Leningrad, Regis Sheffield was pleased and complacent, rather like a cocky prizefighter who's won a tough fight. He stopped off at Blekmann's in Berlin for a drink and some war talk, had a second and more war talk in a legal hangout on the Quai D'Orsay, and a third session in the Skin & Bones opposite Temple Bar. By the time he arrived in his New York office he was pleasantly illuminated.

As he strode through the clattering corridors and outer rooms, he was greeted by his secretary with a handful of memo-beads.

"Knocked Djargo-Dantchenko for a loop," Sheffield reported triumphantly. "Judgment and full damages. Old DD's sore as a boil. This makes the score eleven to five, my favor." He took the beads, juggled them, and then began tossing them into unlikely receptacles all over the office, including the open mouth of a gaping clerk.

"Really, Mr. Sheffield! Have you been drinking?"

"No more work today. The war news is too damned gloomy. Have to do something to stay cheerful. What say we brawl in the streets?"

"Mr. Sheffield!"

"Anything waiting for me that can't wait another day?"

"There's a gentleman in your office."

"He made you let him get that far?" Sheffield looked impressed. "Who is he? God, or somebody?"

"He won't give his name. He gave me this."

The secretary handed Sheffield a sealed envelope. On it was scrawled: "URGENT." Sheffield tore it open, his blunt features crinkling with curiosity. Then his eyes widened. Inside the envelope were two ₡r 50,000 notes. Sheffield turned without a word and burst into his private office. Foyle arose from his chair.

"These are genuine," Sheffield blurted.

"To the best of my knowledge."

"Exactly twenty of these notes were minted last year. All are on deposit in Terran treasuries. How did you get hold of these two?"

"Mr. Sheffield?"

"Who else? How did you get hold of these notes?"

"Bribery."

"Why?"

"I thought at the time that it might be convenient to have them available."

"For what? More bribery?"

"If legal fees are bribery."

"I set my own fees," Sheffield said. He tossed the notes back to Foyle. "You can produce them again *if* I decide to take your case and *if* I decide I've been worth that to you. What's your problem?"

"Criminal."

"Don't be too specific yet. And . . . ?"

"I want to give myself up."

"To the police?"

"Yes."

"For what crime?"

"Crimes."

"Name two."

"Robbery and rape."

"Name two more."

"Blackmail and murder."

"Any other items?"

"Treason and genocide."

"Does that exhaust your catalogue?"

"I think so. We may be able to unveil a few more when we get specific."

"Been busy, haven't you? Either you're the Prince of Villains or insane."

"I've been both, Mr. Sheffield."

"Why do you want to give yourself up?"

"I've come to my senses," Foyle answered bitterly.

"I don't mean that. A criminal never surrenders while he's ahead. You're obviously ahead. What's the reason?"

"The most damnable thing that ever happened to a man. I picked up a rare disease called conscience."

Sheffield snorted. "That can often turn fatal."

"It is fatal. I've realized that I've been behaving like an animal."

"And now you want to purge yourself?"

"No, it isn't that simple," Foyle said grimly. "That's why I've come to you . . . for major surgery. The man who upsets the morphology of society is a cancer. The man who gives his own decisions priority over society is a criminal. But there are chain reactions. Purging yourself with punishment isn't enough. Everything's got to be set right. I wish to God everything could be cured just by sending me back to Gouffre Martel or shooting me . . ."

"Back?" Sheffield cut in keenly.

"Shall I be specific?"

"Not yet. Go on. You sound as though you've got ethical growing pains."

"That's it exactly." Foyle paced in agitation, crumpling the banknotes with nervous fingers. "This is one hell of a mess, Sheffield. There's a girl that's got to pay for a vicious, rotten crime. The fact that I love her— No, never mind that. She has a cancer that's got to be cut out . . . like me. Which means I'll have to add informing to my catalogue. The fact that I'm giving myself up too doesn't make any difference."

"What *is* all this mish-mash?"

Foyle turned on Sheffield. "One of the New Year's bombs has just walked into your office, and it's saying: 'Put it all right. Put me together again and send me home. Put together the city I flattened and the people I shattered.' That's what I want to hire you for. I don't know how most criminals feel, but—"

"Sensible, matter-of-fact, like good businessmen who've had bad luck," Sheffield answered promptly. "That's the usual attitude of the professional criminal. It's obvious you're an amateur, if you're a criminal at all. My dear sir, do be sensible. You come here, extravagantly accusing yourself of robbery, rape, murder, genocide, treason, and God knows what else. D'you expect me to take you seriously?"

Bunny, Sheffield's assistant, jaunted into the private office. "Chief!" he shouted in excitement. "Something brand new's turned up. A lech-jaunte! Two society kids bribed a C-class tart to— Ooop. Sorry. Didn't realize you had—" Bunny broke off and stared. "Fourmyle!" he exclaimed.

"What? Who?" Sheffield demanded.

"Don't you know him, Chief?" Bunny stammered. "That's Fourmyle of Ceres. Gully Foyle."

More than a year ago, Regis Sheffield had been hypnotically fulminated and triggered for this moment. His body had been prepared to respond without thought, and the response was lightning. Sheffield struck Foyle in half a second; temple, throat and groin. It had been decided not to depend on weapons since none might be available.

Foyle fell. Sheffield turned on Bunny and battered him back across the office. Then he spat into his palm. It had been decided not to depend on drugs since drugs might not be available. Sheffield's salivary glands had been prepared to respond with an anaphylaxis secretion to the stimulus. He ripped open Foyle's sleeve, dug a nail deep into the hollow of Foyle's elbow and slashed. He pressed his spittle into the ragged cut and pinched the skin together.

A strange cry was torn from Foyle's lips; the tattooing showed livid on his face. Before the stunned law assistant could make a move, Sheffield swung Foyle up to his shoulder and jaunted.

He arrived in the middle of the Four Mile Circus in Old St. Pat's. It was a daring but calculated move. This was the last place he would be expected to go, and the first place where he might expect to locate the PyrE. He was prepared to deal with anyone he might meet in the cathedral, but the interior of the circus was empty.

The vacant tents ballooning up in the nave looked tattered; they had already been looted. Sheffield plunged into the first he saw. It was Fourmyle's traveling library, filled with hundreds of books and thousands of glittering novel-beads. The Jack-jaunters were not interested in literature. Sheffield threw Foyle down on the floor. Only then did he take a gun from his pocket.

Foyle's eyelids fluttered; his eyes opened.

"You're drugged," Sheffield said rapidly. "Don't try to jaunte. And don't move. I'm warning you, I'm prepared for anything."

Dazedly, Foyle tried to rise. Sheffield instantly fired and seared his shoulder. Foyle was slammed back against the stone flooring. He was numbed and bewildered. There was a roaring in his ears and a poison coursing through his blood.

"I'm warning you," Sheffield repeated. "I'm prepared for anything."

"What do you want?" Foyle whispered.

"Two things. Twenty pounds of PyrE, and you. You most of all."

"You lunatic! You damned maniac! I came into your office to give it up . . . hand it over . . ."

"To the O.S.?"

"To the . . . what?"

"The Outer Satellites? Shall I spell it for you?"

"No . . ." Foyle muttered. "I might have known. The patriot, Sheffield, an O.S. agent. I should have known. I'm a fool."

"You're the most valuable fool in the world, Foyle. We want you even more than the PyrE. That's an unknown to us, but we know what you are."

"What are you talking about?"

"My God! You don't know, do you? You still don't know. You haven't an inkling."

"Of what?"

"Listen to me," Sheffield said in a pounding voice. "I'm taking you back two years to 'Nomad.' Understand? Back to the death of the 'Nomad.' One of our raiders finished her off and they found you aboard the wreck. The last man alive."

"So an O.S. ship did blast 'Nomad'?"

"Yes. You don't remember?"

"I don't remember anything about that. I never could."

"I'm telling you why. The raider got a clever idea. They'd turn you into a decoy . . . a sitting duck, understand? You were half dead, but they took you aboard and patched you up. They put you into a spacesuit and cast you adrift with your microwave on. You were broadcasting distress signals and mumbling for help on every wave band. The idea was, they'd lurk nearby and pick off the IP ships that came to rescue you."

Foyle began to laugh. "I'm getting up," he said recklessly. "Shoot again, you son of a bitch, but I'm getting up." He struggled to his feet, clutching his shoulder. "So 'Vorga' shouldn't have picked me up anyway," Foyle laughed. "I was a decoy. Nobody should have come near me. I was a shill, a lure, death bait . . . Isn't that the final irony? 'Nomad' didn't have any right to be rescued in the first place. I didn't have any right to revenge."

"You still don't understand," Sheffield pounded. "They were nowhere near 'Nomad' when they set you adrift. They were six hundred thousand miles from 'Nomad.'"

"Six hundred thous—?"

"'Nomad' was too far out of the shipping lanes. They wanted you to drift where ships would pass. They took you six hundred thousand miles sunward and set you adrift. They put you through the air lock and backed off, watching you drift. Your suit lights were blinking and you were moaning for help on the micro-wave. Then you disappeared."

"Disappeared?"

"You were gone. No more lights, no more broadcast. They came back to check. You were gone without a trace. And the next thing we learned . . . you got back aboard 'Nomad.'"

"Impossible."

"Man, you space-jaunted!" Sheffield said savagely. "You were patched and delirious, but you space-jaunted. You space-jaunted six hundred thousand miles through the void back to the wreck of the 'Nomad.' You did something that's never been done before. God knows how. You don't even know yourself, but we're going to find out. I'm taking you out to the Satellites with me and we'll get that secret out of you if we have to tear it out."

He took Foyle's throat in his powerful hand and hefted the gun in the other. "But first I want the PyrE. You'll produce it, Foyle. Don't think you won't." He lashed Foyle across the forehead with the gun. "I'll do anything to get it. Don't think I won't." He smashed Foyle again, coldly, efficiently. "If you're looking for a purge, man, you've found it!"

Bunny leaped off the public jaunte stage at Five-Points and streaked into the main entrance of Central Intelligence's New York Office like a frightened rabbit. He shot past the outermost guard cordon, through the protective labyrinth, and into the inner offices. He acquired a train of excited pursuers and found himself face to face with the more seasoned guards who had calmly jaunted to positions ahead of him and were waiting.

Bunny began to shout: "Yeovil! Yeovil! Yeovil!"

Still running, he dodged around desks, kicked over chairs, and created an incredible uproar. He continued his yelling: "Yeovil! Yeovil! Yeovil!" Just before they were about to put him out of his misery, Y'ang-Yeovil appeared.

"What's all this?" he snapped. "I gave orders that Miss Wednesbury was to have absolute quiet."

"Yeovil!" Bunny shouted.

"Who's that?"

"Sheffield's assistant."

"What . . . Bunny?"

"Foyle!" Bunny howled. "Gully Foyle."

Y'ang-Yeovil covered the fifty feet between them in exactly one-point-six-six seconds. "What about Foyle?"

"Sheffield's got him," Bunny gasped.

"Sheffield? When?"

"Half an hour ago."

"Why didn't he bring him here?"

"He abducted him. I think Sheffield's an O.S. agent . . ."

"Why didn't you come at once?"

"Sheffield jaunted with Foyle. . . . Knocked him stiff and disappeared. I went looking. All over. Took a chance. Must have made fifty jauntes in twenty minutes. . . ."

"Amateur!" Y'ang-Yeovil exclaimed in exasperation. "Why didn't you leave that to the pros?"

"Found 'em."

"You found them? Where?"

"Old St. Pat's. Sheffield's after the—"

But Y'ang-Yeovil had turned on his heel and was tearing back up the corridor, shouting: "Robin! Robin! Stop! Stop!"

And then their ears were bruised by the bellow of thunder.

Fifteen

LIKE widening rings in a pond, the Will and the Idea spread, searching out, touching and tripping the delicate subatomic trigger of PyrE. The thought found particles, dust, smoke, vapor, motes, molecules. The Will and the Idea transformed them all.

In Sicily, where Dott. Franco Torre had worked for an exhausting month attempting to unlock the secret of one slug of PyrE, the residues and the precipitates had been dumped down a drain which led to the sea. For many months the Mediterranean currents had drifted these residues across the sea bottom. In an instant a hump-backed mound of water towering fifty feet high traced the courses, northeast to Sardinia and southwest to Tripoli. In a micro-second the surface of the Mediterranean was raised into the twisted casting of a giant earthworm that wound around the islands of Pantelleria, Lampedusa, Linosa, and Malta.

Some of the residues had been burned off; had gone up the chimney with smoke and vapor to drift for hundreds of miles before settling. These minute particles showed where they had finally settled in Morocco, Algeria, Libya, and Greece with blinding pin-point explosions of incredible minuteness and intensity. And some motes, still drifting in the stratosphere, revealed their presence with brilliant gleams like daylight stars.

In Texas, where Prof. John Mantley had had the same baffling experience with PyrE, most of the residues had gone down the shaft of an exhausted oil well which was also used to accommodate radioactive wastes. A deep water table had absorbed much of the matter and spread it slowly over an area of some ten square miles. Ten square miles of Texas flats shook themselves into corduroy. A vast untapped deposit of natural gas at last found a vent and came shrieking up to the surface where sparks from flying stones ignited it into a roaring torch, two hundred feet high.

A milligram of PyrE deposited on a disk of filter paper long since discarded, forgotten, rounded up in a waste paper drive and at last pulped into a mold for type metal, destroyed the entire late night edition of the *Glasgow Observer*. A fragment of PyrE spattered on a lab smock long since converted into rag paper, destroyed a Thank You note written by Lady Shrapnel, and destroyed an additional ton of first class mail in the process.

A shirt cuff, inadvertently dipped into an acid solution of PyrE, long abandoned along with the shirt, and now worn under his mink suit by a Jack-jaunter, blasted off the wrist and hand of the Jack-jaunter in one fiery amputation. A decimilligram of PyrE, still adhering to a former evaporation crystal now in use as an ash tray, kindled a fire that scorched the office of one Baker, dealer in freaks and purveyor of monsters.

Across the length and breadth of the planet were isolated explosions, chains of explosions, traceries of fire, pin points of fire, meteor flares in the sky, great craters and narrow channels plowed in the earth, exploded in the earth, vomited forth from the earth.

In Old St. Pat's nearly a tenth of a gram of PyrE was exposed in Fourmyle's laboratory. The rest was sealed in its Inert Lead Isotope safe, protected from accidental and intentional psycho-kinetic ignition. The blinding blast of energy generated from that tenth of a gram blew out the walls and split the floors as though an internal earthquake had convulsed the building. The buttresses held the pillars for a split second and then crumbled. Down came towers, spires, pillars, buttresses, and roof in a thundering avalanche to hesitate above the yawning crater of the floor in a tangled, precarious equilibrium. A breath of wind, a distant vibration, and the collapse would continue until the crater was filled solid with pulverized rubble.

The star-like heat of the explosion ignited a hundred fires and melted the ancient thick copper of the collapsed roof. If a milligram more of PyrE had been exposed to detonation, the heat would have been intense enough to vaporize the metal immediately. Instead, it glowed white and began to flow. It streamed off the wreckage of the crumbled roof and began searching its way downward through the jumbled stone, iron, wood, and glass, like some monstrous molten mold creeping through a tangled web.

Dagenham and Y'ang-Yeovil arrived almost simultaneously. A moment later Robin Wednesbury appeared and then Jisbella McQueen. A dozen Intelligence operatives and six Dagenham couriers arrived along with Presteign's Jaunte-Watch and the police. They formed a cordon around the blazing block, but there were very few spectators. After the shock of the New Year's Eve raid, that single explosion had frightened half New York into another wild jaunte for safety.

The uproar of the fire was frightful, and the massive grind of tons of wreckage in uneasy balance was ominous. Everyone was forced to shout and yet was fearful of the vibrations. Y'ang-

Yeovil bawled the news about Foyle and Sheffield into Dagenham's ear. Dagenham nodded and displayed his deadly smile.

"We'll have to go in," he shouted.

"Fire suits," Y'ang-Yeovil shouted.

He disappeared and reappeared with a pair of white Disaster Crew fire suits. At the sight of these, Robin and Jisbella began shouting hysterical objections. The two men ignored them, wriggled into the Inert Isomer armor and inched into the inferno.

Within Old St. Pat's it was as though a monstrous hand had churned a log jam of wood, stone, and metal. Through every interstice crawled tongues of molten copper, slowly working downward, igniting wood, crumbling stone, shattering glass. Where the copper flowed it merely glowed, but where it poured it spattered dazzling droplets of white hot metal.

Beneath the log jam yawned a black crater where formerly the floor of the cathedral had been. The explosion had split the flagstone asunder, revealing the cellars, subcellars, and vaults deep below the building. These too were filled with a snarl of stones, beams, pipes, wire, the remnants of the Four Mile circus tents; all fitfully lit small fires. Then the first of the copper dripped down into the crater and illuminated it with a brilliant molten splash.

Dagenham pounded Y'ang-Yeovil's shoulder to attract his attention and pointed. Halfway down the crater, in the midst of the tangle, lay the body of Regis Sheffield, drawn and quartered by the explosion. Y'ang-Yeovil pounded Dagenham's shoulder and pointed. Almost at the bottom of the crater lay Gully Foyle, and as the blazing spatter of molten copper illuminated him, they saw him move. The two men at once turned and crawled out of the cathedral for a conference.

"He's alive."

"How's it possible?"

"I can guess. Did you see the shreds of tent wadded near him? It must have been a freak explosion up at the other end of the cathedral and the tents in between cushioned Foyle. Then he dropped through the floor before anything else could hit him."

"I'll buy that. We've got to get him out. He's the only man who knows where the PyrE is."

"Could it still be here . . . unexploded?"

"If it's in the ILI safe, yes. That stuff is inert to anything. Never mind that now. How are we going to get him out?"

"Well we can't work down from above."

"Why not?"

"Isn't it obvious? One false step and the whole mess will collapse."

"Did you see that copper flowing down?"

"God, yes!"

"Well if we don't get him out in ten minutes, he'll be at the bottom of a pool of molten copper."

"What can we do?"

"I've got a long shot."

"What?"

"The cellars of the old RCA buildings across the street are as deep as St. Pat's."

"And?"

"We'll go down and try to hole through. Maybe we can pull Foyle out from the bottom."

A squad broke into the ancient RCA buildings, abandoned and sealed up for two generations. They went down into the cellar arcades, crumbling museums of the retail stores of centuries past. They located the ancient elevator shafts and dropped through them into the subcellars filled with electric installations, heat plants and refrigeration systems. They went down into the sump cellars, waist deep in water from the streams of prehistoric Manhattan Island, streams that still flowed beneath the streets that covered them.

As they waded through the sump cellars, bearing east-northeast to bring up opposite the St. Pat's vaults, they suddenly discovered that the pitch dark was illuminated by a fiery flickering up ahead. Dagenham shouted and flung himself forward. The explosion that had opened the subcellars of St. Pat's had split the septum between its vaults and those of the RCA buildings. Through a jagged rent in stone and earth they could peer into the bottom of the inferno.

Fifty feet inside was Foyle, trapped in a labyrinth of twisted beams, stones, pipe, metal, and wire. He was illuminated by a roaring glow from above him and fitful flames around him. His clothes were on fire and the tattooing was livid on his face. He moved feebly, like a bewildered animal in a maze.

"My God!" Y'ang-Yeovil exclaimed. "The Burning Man!"

"What?"

"The Burning Man I saw on the Spanish Stairs. Never mind that now. What can we do?"

"Go in, of course."

A brilliant white gob of copper suddenly oozed down close to Foyle and splashed ten feet below him. It was followed by a second, a third, a slow steady stream. A pool began to form. Dagenham and Y'ang-Yeovil sealed the face plates of their armor and crawled through the break in the septum. After three minutes of agonized struggling they realized that they could not get through the labyrinth to Foyle. It was locked to the outside but not from the inside. Dagenham and Y'ang-Yeovil backed up to confer.

"We can't get to him," Dagenham shouted, "but he can get out."

"How? He can't jaunte, obviously, or he wouldn't be there."

"No, he can climb. Look. He goes left, then up, reverses, makes a turn along that beam, slides under it and pushes through that tangle of wire. The wire can't be pushed in, which is why we can't get to him, but it *can* push out, which is how he can get out. It's a one-way door."

The pool of molten copper crept up toward Foyle.

"If he doesn't get out soon he'll be roasted alive."

"We'll have to talk him out . . . Tell him what to do."

The men began shouting: "Foyle! Foyle! Foyle!"

The Burning Man in the maze continued to move feebly. The downpour of sizzling copper increased.

"Foyle! Turn left. Can you hear me? Foyle! Turn left and climb up. You can get out if you'll listen to me. Turn left and climb up. Then— Foyle!"

"He's not listening. Foyle! Gully Foyle! Can you hear us?"

"Send for Jiz. Maybe he'll listen to her."

"No, Robin. She'll telesend. He'll have to listen."

"But will she do it? Save *him* of all people?"

"She'll have to. This is bigger than hatred. It's the biggest damned thing the world's ever encountered. I'll get her." Y'ang-Yeovil started to crawl out. Dagenham stopped him.

"Wait, Yeo. Look at him. He's flickering."

"Flickering?"

"Look! He's . . . blinking like a glow-worm. Watch! Now you see him and now you don't."

The figure of Foyle was appearing, disappearing, and reappearing in rapid succession, like a firefly caught in a flaming trap.

"What's he doing now? What's he trying to do? What's happening?"

He was trying to escape. Like a trapped firefly or some seabird caught in the blazing brazier of a naked beacon fire, he was beating about in a frenzy . . . a blackened, burning creature, dashing himself against the unknown.

Sound came as sight to him, as light in strange patterns. He saw the sound of his shouted name in vivid rhythms:

```
F  O Y L  E      F  O Y L  E      F  O Y L  E
F  O Y L  E      F  O Y L  E      F  O Y L  E
F  O Y L  E      F  O Y L  E      F  O Y L  E
F  O Y L  E      F  O Y L  E      F  O Y L  E
F  O Y L  E      F  O Y L  E      F  O Y L  E
```

Motion came as sound to him. He heard the writhing of the flames, he heard the swirls of smoke, he heard the flickering, jeering shadows . . . all speaking deafeningly in strange tongues:

"BURUU GYARR?" the steam asked.

"Asha. Asha, rit-kit-dit-zit m'gid," the quick shadows answered.

"Ohhh. Ahhh. Heee. Teee," the heat ripples clamored.

Even the flames smoldering on his own clothes roared gibberish in his ears. "MANTERGEISTMANN!" they bellowed.

Color was pain to him . . . heat, cold, pressure; sensations of intolerable heights and plunging depths, of tremendous accelerations and crushing compressions:

RED RECEDED FROM HIM

GREEN LIGHT ATTACKED

GLIDING UNDULATED WITH SICKENING SPEED LIKE A SHUDDERING SNAKE

Touch was taste to him . . . the feel of wood was acrid and chalky in his mouth, metal was salt, stone tasted sour-sweet to the touch of his fingers, and the feel of glass cloyed his palate like over-rich pastry.

Smell was touch . . . Hot stone smelled like velvet caressing his cheek. Smoke and ash were harsh tweeds rasping his skin, almost the feel of wet canvas. Molten metal smelled like blow hammering his heart, and the ionization of the PyrE explosion filled the air with ozone that smelled like water trickling through his fingers.

He was not blind, not deaf, not senseless. Sensation came to him, but filtered through a nervous system twisted and short-circuited by the shock of the PyrE concussion. He was suffering from Synaesthesia, that rare condition in which perception receives messages from the objective world and relays these messages to the brain, but there in the brain the sensory perceptions are confused with one another. So, in Foyle, sound registered as sight, motion registered as sound, colors became pain sensations, touch became taste, and smell became touch. He was not only trapped within the labyrinth of the inferno under Old St. Pat's; he was trapped in the kaleidoscope of his own cross-senses.

Again desperate, on the ghastly verge of extinction, he abandoned all disciplines and habits of living; or, perhaps, they were stripped from him. He reverted from a conditioned product of environment and experience to an inchoate creature craving escape and survival and exercising every power it possessed. And again the miracle of two years ago took place. The undivided energy of an entire human organism, of every cell, fiber, nerve, and muscle empowered that craving, and again Foyle space-jaunted.

He went hurtling along the geodesical space lines of the curving universe at the speed of thought, far exceeding that of light. His spatial velocity was so frightful that his time axis was twisted from the vertical line drawn from the Past through Now to the Future. He went flickering along the new near-horizontal axis, this new space-time geodesic, driven by the miracle of a human mind no longer inhibited by concepts of the impossible.

Again he achieved what Helmut Grant and Enzio Dandridge and scores of other experimenters had failed to do, because his blind panic forced him to abandon the spatio-temporal inhibitions that had defeated previous attempts. He did not jaunte to Elsewhere, but to Elsewhen. But most important, the fourth dimensional awareness, the complete picture of the Arrow of Time and his position on it which is born in every man but deeply submerged by the trivia of living, was in Foyle close to the surface. He jaunted along the space-time geodesics to Elsewheres and Elsewhens, translating "i," the square root of minus one, from an imaginary number into reality by a magnificent act of imagination.

He jaunted.

He jaunted back through time to his past. He became the Burning Man who had inspired himself with terror and perplexity on the beach in Australia, in a quack's office in Shanghai, on the Spanish Stairs in Rome, on the Moon, in the Skoptsy Colony on Mars. He jaunted back through time, revisiting the savage battles that he himself had fought in Gully Foyle's tiger hunt for vengeance. His flaming appearances were sometimes noted; other times not.

He jaunted.

He was aboard "Nomad," drifting in the empty frost of space.

He stood in the door to nowhere.

The cold was the taste of lemons and the vacuum was a rake of talons on his skin. The sun and the stars were a shaking ague that racked his bones.

"GLOMMHA FREDNIS!" motion roared in his ears.

It was a figure with its back to him vanishing down the corridor; a figure with a copper cauldron of provisions over its shoulder; a figure darting, floating, squirming through free fall. It was Gully Foyle.

"MEEHAT JESSROT," the sight of his motion bellowed.

"Aha! Oh-ho! M'git not to kak," the flicker of light and shade answered.

"Oooooooh? Soooooo?" the whirling raffle of debris in his wake murmured.

The lemon taste in his mouth became unbearable. The rake of talons on his skin was torture.

He jaunted.

He reappeared in the furnace beneath Old St. Pat's less than a second after he had disappeared from there. He was drawn, as the seabird is drawn, again and again to the flames from which it is struggling to escape. He endured the roaring torture for only another moment.

He jaunted.

He was in the depths of Gouffre Martel.

The velvet black darkness was bliss, paradise, euphoria.

"Ah!" he cried in relief.

"AH!" came the echo of his voice, and the sound was translated into a blinding pattern of light.

```
  A HA HA HA HA HA HA HA HA H
   HA HA HA HA HA HA HA HA HA
    A HA HA HA HA HA HA HA HA H
     HA HA HA HA HA HA HA HA HA
      A HA HA HA HA HA HA HA HA H
       HA HA HA HA HA HA HA HA HA
```

The Burning Man winced. "Stop!" he called, blinded by the noise. Again came the dazzling pattern of the echo:

```
        StOpStOpStOp
       OpStOpStOpStOp
      StOpStOpStOpStOp
     OpStOpStOpStOpStOp
      OpStOpStOpStOpSt
       OpStOpStOpStOp
        OpStOpStOpSt
```

A distant clatter of steps came to his eyes in soft patterns of vertical borealis streamers:

```
  c       c       c       c       c       c
   l       l       l       l       l       l
    a       a       a       a       a       a
   t       t       t       t       t       t
   t       t       t       t       t       t
   e       e       e       e       e       e
    r       r       r       r       r       r
```

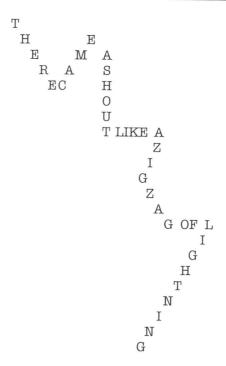

THE
RECTANGULAR SMASHOUT LIKE A ZIGZAG OF LIGHTNING

A BEAM OF LIGHT ATTACKED

It was the search party from the Gouffre Martel hospital, tracking Foyle and Jisbella McQueen by geophone. The Burning Man disappeared, but not before he had unwittingly decoyed the searchers from the trail of the vanished fugitives.

He was back under Old St. Pat's, reappearing only an instant after his last disappearance. His wild beatings into the unknown sent him stumbling up geodesic space-time lines that inevitably brought him back to the Now he was trying to escape, for in the inverted saddle curve of space-time, his Now was the deepest depression in the curve.

He could drive himself up, up, up the geodesic lines into the past or future, but inevitably he must fall back into his own Now, like a thrown ball hurled up the sloping walls of an infinite pit, to land, hang poised for a moment, and then roll back into the depths.

But still he beat into the unknown in his desperation.

Again he jaunted.

He was on Jervis beach on the Australian coast.

The motion of the surf was bawling: "LOGGERMIST CROTEHAVEN!"

The churning of the surf blinded him with the lights of batteries of footlights:

Gully Foyle and Robin Wednesbury stood before him. The body of a man lay on the sand which felt like vinegar in the Burning Man's mouth. The wind brushing his face tasted like brown paper.

Foyle opened his mouth and exclaimed. The sound came out in burning star-bubbles.

Foyle took a step. "GRASH?" the motion blared.

The Burning Man jaunted.

He was in the office of Dr. Sergei Orel in Shanghai.

Foyle was again before him, speaking in light patterns:

```
W    A   Y        W   A   Y   W   A   Y
  H   R   O     H   R   O      H   R   O
    O   E   U   O   E   U        O   E   U
```

He flickered back to the agony of Old St. Pat's and jaunted again.

HE WAS ON THE BRAWLING SPANISH
STAIRS. HE WAS ON THE BRAWLING
SPANISH STAIRS. HE WAS ON THE
BRAWLING SPANISH STAIRS. HE WAS
ON THE BRAWLING SPANISH STAIRS.
HE WAS ON THE BRAWLING SPANISH
STAIRS. HE WAS ON THE BRAWLING
SPANISH STAIRS. HE WAS ON THE
BRAWLING SPANISH STAIRS. HE WAS
ON THE BRAWLING SPANISH STAIRS.

The Burning Man jaunted.

It was cold again, with the taste of lemons, and vacuum raked his skin with unspeakable talons. He was peering through the porthole of a silvery yawl. The jagged mountains of the Moon towered in the background. Through the porthole he could see the jangling racket of blood pumps and oxygen pumps and hear the uproar of the motion Gully Foyle made toward him. The clawing of the vacuum caught his throat in an agonizing grip.

The geodesic lines of space-time rolled him back to Now under Old St. Pat's, where less than two seconds had elapsed since he first began his frenzied struggle. Once more, like a burning spear, he hurled himself into the unknown.

He was in the Skoptsy Catacomb on Mars. The white slug that was Lindsey Joyce was writhing before him.

"NO! NO! NO!" her motion screamed. "DON'T HURT ME. DON'T KILL ME. NO PLEASE . . . PLEASE . . . PLEASE . . ."

The Burning Man opened his tiger mouth and laughed. "She hurts," he said. The sound of his voice burned his eyes.

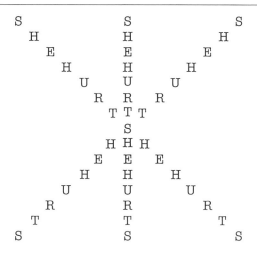

"Who are you?" Foyle whispered.

```
WWWWWWWWWWWWWWWWWWW
HHHHHHHHHHHHHHHHHHH
OOOOOOOOOOOOOOOOOOO
AREAREAREAREAREAREARE
AREAREAREAREAREAREARE
AREAREAREAREAREAREARE
YYYYYYYYYYYYYYYYYYY
OOOOOOOOOOOOOOOOOOO
UUUUUUUUUUUUUUUUUUU
```

The Burning Man winced. "Too bright," he said. "Less light."

Foyle took a step forward. "BLAA-GAA-DAA-MAWW!" the motion roared.

The Burning Man clapped his hands over his ears in agony. "Too loud," he cried. "Don't move so loud."

The writhing Skoptsy's motion was still screaming, beseeching: "DON'T HURT ME. DON'T HURT ME."

The Burning Man laughed again. She was mute to normal men, but to his freak-crossed senses her meaning was clear.

"Listen to her. She's screaming. Begging. She doesn't want to die. She doesn't want to be hurt. Listen to her."

"IT WAS OLIVIA PRESTEIGN GAVE THE ORDER. OLIVIA PRESTEIGN. NOT ME. DON'T HURT ME. OLIVIA PRESTEIGN."

"She's telling who gave the order. Can't you hear? Listen with your eyes. She says Olivia."

```
WHAT?        WHAT?        WHAT?
      WHAT?        WHAT?        WHAT?
WHAT?        WHAT?        WHAT?
      WHAT?        WHAT?        WHAT?
WHAT?        WHAT?        WHAT?
```

The checkerboard glitter of Foyle's question was too much for him. The Burning Man interpreted the Skoptsy's agony again.

"She says Olivia. Olivia Presteign. Olivia Presteign. Olivia Presteign."

He jaunted.

He fell back into the pit under Old St. Pat's, and suddenly his confusion and despair told him he was dead. This was the finish of Gully Foyle. This was eternity, and hell was real. What he had seen was the past passing before his crumbling senses in the final moment of death. What he was enduring he must endure through all time. He was dead. He knew he was dead.

He refused to submit to eternity.

He beat again into the unknown.

The Burning Man jaunted.

He was in a scintillating mist a snowflake cluster of stars

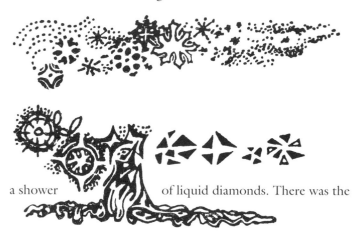

a shower of liquid diamonds. There was the

touch of butterfly wings on his skin. There was the

taste of a strand of cool pearls in his mouth. His crossed kalei-

doscopic senses could not tell him where he was, but he knew
he wanted to remain in this Nowhere forever.

"Hello, Gully."

"Who's that?"

"This is Robin."

"Robin?"

"Robin Wednesbury that was."

"That was?"

"Robin Yeovil that is."

"I don't understand. Am I dead?"

"No, Gully."

"Where am I?"

"A long, long way from Old St. Pat's."

"But where?"

"I can't take the time to explain, Gully. You've only got a few moments here."

"Why?"

"Because you haven't learned how to jaunte through space-time yet. You've got to go back and learn."

"But I do know. I must know. Sheffield said I space-jaunted to 'Nomad' . . . six hundred thousand miles."

"That was an accident then, Gully, and you'll do it again . . . after you teach yourself . . . But you're not doing it now. You don't know how to hold on yet . . . how to turn any Now into reality. You'll tumble back into Old St. Pat's in a moment."

"Robin, I've just remembered. I have bad news for you."

"I know, Gully."

"Your mother and sisters are dead."

"I've known for a long time, Gully."

"How long?"

"For thirty years."

"That's impossible."

"No it isn't. This is a long, long way from Old St. Pat's. I've been waiting to tell you how to save yourself from the fire, Gully. Will you listen?"

"I'm not dead?"

"No."

"I'll listen."

"Your senses are all confused. It'll pass soon, but I won't give the directions in left and right or up and down. I'll tell you what you can understand now."

"Why are you helping me . . . after what I've done to you?"

"That's all forgiven and forgotten, Gully. Now listen to me. When you get back to Old St. Pat's, turn around until you're facing the loudest shadows. Got that?"

"Yes."

"Go toward the noise until you feel a deep prickling on your skin. Then stop."

"Then stop."

"Make a half turn into compression and a feeling of falling. Follow that."

"Follow that."

"You'll pass through a solid sheet of light and come to the taste of quinine. That's really a mass of wire. Push straight through the quinine until you see something that sounds like trip hammers. You'll be safe."

"How do you know all this, Robin?"

"I've been briefed by an expert, Gully." There was the sensation of laughter. *"You'll be falling back into the past any moment now. Peter and Saul are here. They say au revoir and good luck. And Jiz Dagenham too. Good luck, Gully dear . . ."*

"The past? This is the future?"

"Yes, Gully."

"Am I here? Is . . . Olivia—?"

And then he was tumbling down, down, down the space-time lines back into the dreadful pit of Now.

Sixteen

HIS senses uncrossed in the ivory-and-gold star chamber of Castle Presteign. Sight became sight and he saw the high mirrors and stained glass windows, the gold tooled library with android librarian on library ladder. Sound became sound and he heard the android secretary tapping the manual bead-recorder at the Louis Quinze desk. Taste became taste as he sipped the cognac that the robot bartender handed him.

He knew he was at bay, faced with the decision of his life. He ignored his enemies and examined the perpetual beam carved in the robot face of the bartender, the classic Irish grin.

"Thank you," Foyle said.

"My pleasure, sir," the robot replied and awaited its next cue.

"Nice day," Foyle remarked.

"Always a lovely day somewhere, sir," the robot beamed.

"Awful day," Foyle said.

"Always a lovely day somewhere, sir," the robot responded.

"Day," Foyle said.

"Always a lovely day somewhere, sir," the robot said.

Foyle turned to the others. "That's me," he said, motioning to the robot. "That's all of us. We prattle about free will, but we're nothing but response . . . mechanical reaction in pre-scribed grooves. So . . . here I am, here I am, waiting to re-spond. Press the buttons and I'll jump." He aped the canned voice of the robot. "My pleasure to serve, sir." Suddenly his tone lashed them. "What do you want?"

They stirred with uneasy purpose. Foyle was burned, beaten, chastened . . . and yet he was taking control of all of them.

"We'll stipulate the threats," Foyle said. "I'm to be hung, drawn, and quartered, tortured in hell if I don't . . . What? What do you want?"

"I want my property," Presteign said, smiling coldly.

"Eighteen and some odd pounds of PyrE. Yes. What do you offer?"

"I make no offer, sir. I demand what is mine."

Y'ang-Yeovil and Dagenham began to speak. Foyle silenced them. "One button at a time, gentlemen. Presteign is trying to make me jump at present." He turned to Presteign. "Press harder, blood and money, or find another button. Who are you to make demands at this moment?"

Presteign tightened his lips. "The law . . ." he began.

"What? Threats?" Foyle laughed. "Am I to be frightened into anything? Don't be imbecile. Speak to me the way you did New Year's Eve, Presteign . . . without mercy, without for-giveness, without hypocrisy."

Presteign bowed, took a breath, and ceased to smile. "I offer you power," he said. "Adoption as my heir, partnership in Presteign Enterprises, the chieftainship of clan and sept. To-gether we can own the world."

"With PyrE?"

"Yes."

"Your proposal is noted and declined. Will you offer your daughter?"

"Olivia?" Presteign choked and clenched his fists.

"Yes, Olivia. Where is she?"

"You scum!" Presteign cried. "Filth . . . Common thief . . . You dare to . . ."

"Will you offer your daughter for the PyrE?"

"Yes," Presteign answered, barely audible.

Foyle turned to Dagenham. "Press your button, death's-head," he said.

"If the discussion's to be conducted on this level . . ." Dagenham snapped.

"It is. Without mercy, without forgiveness, without hypocrisy. What do you offer?"

"Glory."

"Ah?"

"We can't offer money or power. We can offer honor. Gully Foyle, the man who saved the Inner Planets from annihilation. We can offer security. We'll wipe out your criminal record, give you an honored name, guarantee a niche in the hall of fame."

"No," Jisbella McQueen cut in sharply. "Don't accept. If you want to be a savior, destroy the secret. Don't give PyrE to anyone."

"What is PyrE?"

"Quiet!" Dagenham snapped.

"It's a thermonuclear explosive that's detonated by thought alone . . . by psychokinesis," Jisbella said.

"What thought?"

"The desire of anyone to detonate it, directed at it. That brings it to critical mass if it's not insulated by Inert Lead Isotope."

"I told you to be quiet," Dagenham growled.

"If we're all to have a chance at him, I want mine."

"This is bigger than idealism."

"Nothing's bigger than idealism."

"Foyle's secret is," Y'ang-Yeovil murmured. "I know how relatively unimportant PyrE is just now." He smiled at Foyle. "Sheffield's law assistant overheard part of your little discussion in Old St. Pat's. We know about the space-jaunting."

There was a sudden hush.

"Space-jaunting," Dagenham exclaimed. "Impossible. You don't mean it."

"I do mean it. Foyle's demonstrated that space-jaunting is not impossible. He jaunted six hundred thousand miles from an O.S. raider to the wreck of the 'Nomad.' As I said, this is far bigger than PyrE. I should like to discuss that matter first."

"Everyone's been telling what they want," Robin Wednesbury said slowly. "What do you want, Gully Foyle?"

"Thank you," Foyle answered. "I want to be punished."

"What?"

"I want to be purged," he said in a suffocated voice. The stigmata began to appear on his bandaged face. "I want to pay for what I've done and settle the account. I want to get rid of this damnable cross I'm carrying . . . this ache that's cracking my spine. I want to go back to Gouffre Martel. I want a lobo, if I deserve it . . . and I know I do. I want—"

"You want escape," Dagenham interrupted. "There's no escape."

"I want release!"

"Out of the question," Y'ang-Yeovil said. "There's too much of value locked up in your head to be lost by lobotomy."

"We're beyond easy childish things like crime and punishment," Dagenham added.

"No," Robin objected. "There must always be sin and forgiveness. We're never beyond that."

"Profit and loss, sin and forgiveness, idealism and realism," Foyle smiled. "You're all so sure, so simple, so single-minded. I'm the only one in doubt. Let's see how sure you really are. You'll give up Olivia, Presteign? To me, yes? Will you give her up to the law? She's a killer."

Presteign tried to rise, and then fell back in his chair.

"There must be forgiveness, Robin? Will you forgive Olivia Presteign? She murdered your mother and sisters."

Robin turned ashen. Y'ang-Yeovil tried to protest.

"The Outer Satellites don't have PyrE, Yeovil. Sheffield revealed that. Would you use it on them anyway? Will you turn my name into common anathema . . . like Lynch and Boycott?"

Foyle turned to Jisbella. "Will your idealism take you back to Gouffre Martel to serve out your sentence? And you, Dagenham, will you give her up? Let her go?"

He listened to the outcries and watched the confusion for a moment, bitter and constrained.

"Life is so simple," he said. "This decision is so simple, isn't it? Am I to respect Presteign's property rights? The welfare of the planets? Jisbella's ideals? Dagenham's realism? Robin's conscience? Press the button and watch the robot jump. But I'm not a robot. I'm a freak of the universe . . . a thinking animal . . . and I'm trying to see my way clear through this morass. Am I to turn PyrE over to the world and let it destroy itself? Am

I to teach the world how to space-jaunte and let us spread our freak show from galaxy to galaxy through all the universe? What's the answer?"

The bartender robot hurled its mixing glass across the room with a resounding crash. In the amazed silence that followed, Dagenham grunted: "Damn! My radiation's disrupted your dolls again, Presteign."

"The answer is yes," the robot said, quite distinctly.

"What?" Foyle asked, taken aback.

"The answer to your question is yes."

"Thank you," Foyle said.

"My pleasure, sir," the robot responded. "A man is a member of society first, and an individual second. You must go along with society, whether it chooses destruction or not."

"Completely haywire," Dagenham said impatiently. "Switch it off, Presteign."

"Wait," Foyle commanded. He looked at the beaming grin engraved in the steel robot face. "But society can be so stupid. So confused. You've witnessed this conference."

"Yes, sir, but you must teach, not dictate. You must teach society."

"To space-jaunte? Why? Why reach out to the stars and galaxies? What for?"

"Because you're alive, sir. You might as well ask: Why is life? Don't ask about it. Live it."

"Quite mad," Dagenham muttered.

"But fascinating," Y'ang-Yeovil murmured.

"There's got to be more to life than just living," Foyle said to the robot.

"Then find it for yourself, sir. Don't ask the world to stop moving because you have doubts."

"Why can't we all move forward together?"

"Because you're all different. You're not lemmings. Some must lead, and hope that the rest will follow."

"Who leads?"

"The men who must . . . driven men, compelled men."

"Freak men."

"You're all freaks, sir. But you always have been freaks. Life is a freak. That's its hope and glory."

"Thank you very much."

"My pleasure, sir."

"You've saved the day."

"Always a lovely day somewhere, sir," the robot beamed. Then it fizzed, jangled, and collapsed.

Foyle turned on the others. "That thing's right," he said, "and you're wrong. Who are we, any of us, to make a decision for the world? Let the world make its own decisions. Who are we to keep secrets from the world? Let the world know and decide for itself. Come to Old St. Pat's."

He jaunted; they followed. The square block was still cordoned and by now an enormous crowd had gathered. So many of the rash and curious were jaunting into the smoking ruins that the police had set up a protective induction field to keep them out. Even so, urchins, curio seekers and irresponsibles attempted to jaunte into the wreckage, only to be burned by the induction field and depart, squawking.

At a signal from Y'ang-Yeovil, the field was turned off. Foyle went through the hot rubble to the east wall of the cathedral which stood to a height of fifteen feet. He felt the smoking stones, pressed, and levered. There came a grinding grumble and a three-by-five-foot section jarred open and then stuck. Foyle gripped it and pulled. The section trembled; then the roasted hinges collapsed and the stone panel crumbled.

Two centuries before, when organized religion had been abolished and orthodox worshippers of all faiths had been driven underground, some devout souls had constructed this secret niche in Old St. Pat's and turned it into an altar. The gold of the crucifix still shone with the brilliance of eternal faith. At the foot of the cross rested a small black box of Inert Lead Isotope.

"Is this a sign?" Foyle panted. "Is this the answer I want?"

He snatched the heavy safe before any could seize it. He jaunted a hundred yards to the remnants of the cathedral steps facing Fifth Avenue. There he opened the safe in full view of the gaping crowds. A shout of consternation went up from the Intelligence crews who knew the truth of its contents.

"Foyle!" Dagenham cried.

"For God's sake, Foyle!" Y'ang-Yeovil shouted.

Foyle withdrew a slug of PyrE, the color of iodine crystals, the size of a cigarette . . . one pound of transplutonian isotopes in solid solution.

"PyrE!" he roared to the mob. "Take it! Keep it! It's your future. PyrE!" He hurled the slug into the crowd and roared over his shoulder: "SanFran. Russian Hill stage."

He jaunted St. Louis–Denver to San Francisco, arriving at the Russian Hill stage where it was four in the afternoon and the streets were bustling with late-shopper jaunters.

"PyrE!" Foyle bellowed. His devil face glowed blood red. He was an appalling sight. "PyrE. It's danger! It's death! It's yours. Make them tell you what it is. Nome!" he called to his pursuit as it arrived, and jaunted.

It was lunch hour in Nome, and the lumberjacks jaunting down from the sawmills for their beefsteak and beer were startled by the tiger-faced man who hurled a one pound slug of iodine colored alloy into their midst and shouted in the gutter tongue: "PyrE! You hear me, man? You listen a me, you. PyrE is filthy death for us. Alla us! Grab no guesses, you. Make 'em tell you about PyrE, is all!"

To Dagenham, Y'ang-Yeovil and others jaunting in after him, as always, seconds too late, he shouted: "Tokyo. Imperial stage!" He disappeared a split second before their shots reached him.

It was nine o'clock of a crisp, winey morning in Tokyo, and the morning rush hour crowd milling around the Imperial stage alongside the carp ponds was paralyzed by a tiger-faced Samurai who appeared and hurled a slug of curious metal and unforgettable warnings and admonitions at them.

Foyle continued to Bangkok where it was pouring rain, and Delhi where a monsoon raged . . . always pursued in his mad-dog course. In Baghdad it was three in the morning and the night-club crowd and pub crawlers who stayed a perpetual half hour ahead of closing time around the world, cheered him alcoholically. In Paris and again in London it was midnight and the mobs on the Champs Élysées and in Piccadilly Circus were galvanized by Foyle's appearance and passionate exhortation.

Having led his pursuers three-quarters of the way around the world in fifty minutes, Foyle permitted them to overtake him in London. He permitted them to knock him down, take the ILI safe from his arms, count the remaining slugs of PyrE, and slam the safe shut.

"There's enough left for a war. Plenty left for destruction . . . annihilation . . . if you dare." He was laughing and sobbing in hysterical triumph. "Millions for defense, but not one cent for survival."

"D'you realize what you've done, you damned killer?" Dagenham shouted.

"I know what I've done."

"Nine pounds of PyrE scattered around the world! One thought and we'll— How can we get it back without telling them the truth? For God's sake, Yeo, keep that crowd back. Don't let them hear this."

"Impossible."

"Then let's jaunte."

"No," Foyle roared. "Let them hear this. Let them hear everything."

"You're insane, man. You've handed a loaded gun to children."

"Stop treating them like children and they'll stop behaving like children. Who the hell are you to play monitor?"

"What are you talking about?"

"Stop treating them like children. Explain the loaded gun to them. Bring it all out into the open." Foyle laughed savagely. "I've ended the last star-chamber conference in the world. I've blown the last secret wide open. No more secrets from now on. . . . No more telling the children what's best for them to know. . . . Let 'em all grow up. It's about time."

"Christ, he *is* insane."

"Am I? I've handed life and death back to the people who do the living and dying. The common man's been whipped and led long enough by driven men like us. . . . Compulsive men . . . Tiger men who can't help lashing the world before them. We're all tigers, the three of us, but who the hell are we to make decisions for the world just because we're compulsive? Let the world make its own choice between life and death. Why should we be saddled with the responsibility?"

"We're not saddled," Y'ang-Yeovil said quietly. "We're driven. We're forced to seize the responsibility that the average man shirks."

"Then let him stop shirking it. Let him stop tossing his duty and guilt onto the shoulders of the first freak who comes along grabbing at it. Are we to be scapegoats for the world forever?"

"Damn you!" Dagenham raged. "Don't you realize that you can't trust people? They don't know enough for their own good."

"Then let them learn or die. We're all in this together. Let's live together or die together."

"D'you want to die in their ignorance? You've got to figure out how we can get those slugs back without blowing everything wide open."

"No. I believe in them. I was one of them before I turned tiger. They can all turn uncommon if they're kicked awake like I was."

Foyle shook himself and abruptly jaunted to the bronze head of Eros, fifty feet above the counter of Piccadilly Circus. He perched precariously and bawled: "Listen a me, all you! Listen, man! Gonna sermonize, me. Dig this, you!"

He was answered with a roar.

"You pigs, you. You goof like pigs, is all. You got the most in you, and you use the least. You hear me, you? Got a million in you and spend pennies. Got a genius in you and think crazies. Got a heart in you and feel empties. All a you. Every you . . ."

He was jeered. He continued with the hysterical passion of the possessed.

"Take a war to make you spend. Take a jam to make you think. Take a challenge to make you great. Rest of the time you sit around lazy, you. Pigs, you! All right, God damn you! I challenge you, me. Die or live and be great. Blow yourselves to Christ gone or come and find me, Gully Foyle, and I make you men. I make you great. I give you the stars."

He disappeared.

He jaunted up the geodesic lines of space-time to an Elsewhere and an Elsewhen. He arrived in chaos. He hung in a precarious para-Now for a moment and then tumbled back into chaos.

"*It can be done,*" he thought. "*It must be done.*"

He jaunted again, a burning spear flung from unknown into unknown, and again he tumbled back into a chaos of para-space and para-time. He was lost in Nowhere.

"*I believe*," he thought. "*I have faith.*"

He jaunted again and failed again.

"*Faith in what?*" he asked himself, adrift in limbo.

"*Faith in faith*," he answered himself. *"It isn't necessary to have something to believe in. It's only necessary to believe that somewhere there's something worthy of belief."*

He jaunted for the last time and the power of his willingness to believe transformed the para-Now of his random destination into a real . . .

NOW: Rigel in Orion, burning blue-white, five hundred and forty light years from earth, ten thousand times more luminous than the sun, a cauldron of energy circled by thirty-seven massive planets . . . Foyle hung, freezing and suffocating in space, face to face with the incredible destiny in which he believed, but which was still inconceivable. He hung in space for a blinding moment, as helpless, as amazed, and yet as inevitable as the first gilled creature to come out of the sea and hang gulping on a primeval beach in the dawn-history of life on earth.

He space-jaunted, turning para-Now into . . .

NOW: Vega in Lyra, an AO star twenty-six light years from earth, burning bluer than Rigel, planetless, but encircled by swarms of blazing comets whose gaseous tails scintillated across the blue-black firmament . . .

And again he turned now into NOW: Canopus, yellow as the sun, gigantic, thunderous in the silent wastes of space at last invaded by a creature that once was gilled. The creature hung, gulping on the beach of the universe, nearer death than life, nearer the future than the past, ten leagues beyond the wide world's end. It wondered at the masses of dust, meteors, and motes that girdled Canopus in a broad, flat ring like the rings of Saturn and of the breadth of Saturn's orbit . . .

NOW: Aldebaran in Taurus, a monstrous red star of a pair of stars whose sixteen planets wove high velocity ellipses around their gyrating parents. He was hurling himself through space-time with growing assurance . . .

NOW: Antares, an MI red giant, paired like Aldebaran, two hundred and fifty light years from earth, encircled by two hundred and fifty planetoids of the size of Mercury, of the climate of Eden . . .

And lastly . . . NOW.

He was drawn to the womb of his birth. He returned to the "Nomad," now welded into the mass of the Sargasso asteroid, home of the lost Scientific People who scavenged the spaceways between Mars and Jupiter . . . home of Jŏseph who had tattooed Foyle's tiger face and mated him to the girl, Mǫira.

He was back aboard "Nomad."

> *Gully Foyle is my name*
> *And Terra is my nation.*
> *Deep space is my dwelling place,*
> *The stars my destination.*

The girl, Mǫira, found him in his tool locker aboard "Nomad," curled in a tight foetal ball, his face hollow, his eyes burning with divine revelation. Although the asteroid had long since been repaired and made airtight, Foyle still went through the motions of the perilous existence that had given birth to him years before.

But now he slept and meditated, digesting and encompassing the magnificence he had learned. He awoke from reverie to trance and drifted out of the locker, passing Mǫira with blind eyes, brushing past the awed girl who stepped aside and sank to her knees. He wandered through the empty passages and returned to the womb of the locker. He curled up again and was lost.

She touched him once; he made no move. She spoke the name that had been emblazoned on his face. He made no answer. She turned and fled to the interior of the asteroid, to the holy of holies in which Jŏseph reigned.

"My husband has returned to us," Mǫira said.

"Your husband?"

"The god-man who almost destroyed us."

Jŏseph's face darkened with anger.

"Where is he? Show me!"

"You will not hurt him?"

"All debts must be paid. Show me."

Jo͡seph followed her to the locker aboard "Nomad" and gazed intently at Foyle. The anger in his face was replaced by wonder. He touched Foyle and spoke to him; there was still no response.

"You cannot punish him," Mǫira said. "He is dying."

"No," Jo͡seph answered quietly. "He is dreaming. I, a priest, know these dreams. Presently he will awaken and read to us, his people, his thoughts."

"And then you will punish him."

"He has found it already in himself," Jo͡seph said.

He settled down outside the locker. The girl, Mǫira, ran up the twisted corridors and returned a few moments later with a silver basin of warm water and a silver tray of food. She bathed Foyle gently and then set the tray before him as an offering. Then she settled down alongside Jo͡seph . . . alongside the world . . . prepared to await the awakening.

A CASE OF CONSCIENCE

James Blish

I schal declare the disposcioun of rome fro hys first makyng . . . and the seconde part schal declar ye holynesse of ye same place fro his first crystendom; I schal not write but that I fynde in auctores or ellis that I sey with eye.

    —John Capgrave: The Solace of Pilgrims

to LARRY SHAW

Pronunciation Key

For any reader who cares, the Lithian words and names he will encounter here and there in this story are to be pronounced as follows:

Xoredeshch—"X" as English "K" or Greek chi, hard; "shch" contains two separate sounds, as in Russian, or in English "fish-*ch*urch."

Sfath: As in English, with a broad "a."

Gton: Guttural "G," against the hard palate, like hawking.

Chtexa: Like German "Stuka," but with the flat "e."

gchteht: Guttural "g" followed by the soft "sh" sound, a flat "e," and the "h" serving as equivalent of the Old Russian mute sign; thus, a four-syllable word, with a palatal tick at the end, but sounded as one syllable.

Gleshchtehk—As indicated, with the guttural "G," the "fish-*ch*urch" middle consonants, and the mute "h" throwing the "k" back against the soft palate.

THE RULE is that "ch" is always English "sh" in the initial position, always English "ch" as in "chip" elsewhere in the word; and "h" in isolation is an accented rest which always *precedes*, never follows, a consonant. As Agronski somewhere remarks, anybody who can spit can speak Lithian.

BOOK ONE

I

THE stone door slammed. It was Cleaver's trade-mark: there had never been a door too heavy, complex, or cleverly tracked to prevent him from closing it with a sound like a clap of doom. And no planet in the universe could possess an air sufficiently thick and curtained with damp to muffle that sound—not even Lithia.

Father Ramon Ruiz-Sanchez, late of Peru, and always Clerk Regular of the Society of Jesus, professed father of the four vows, continued to read. It would take Paul Cleaver's impatient fingers quite a while to free him from his jungle suit, and in the meantime the problem remained. It was a century-old problem, first propounded in 1939, but the Church had never cracked it. And it was diabolically complex (that adverb was official, precisely chosen, and intended to be taken literally.) Even the novel which had proposed the case was on the Index Expurgatorius, and Father Ruiz-Sanchez had spiritual access to it only by virtue of his Order.

He turned the page, scarcely hearing the stamping and muttering in the hall. On and on the text ran, becoming more tangled, more evil, more insoluble with every word:

> . . . Magravius threatens to have Anita molested by Sulla, an orthodox savage (and leader of a band of twelve mercenaries, the Sullivani,) who desires to procure Felicia for Gregorius, Leo Vitellius and Macdugalius, four excavators, if she will not yield to him and also deceive Honuphrius by rendering conjugal duty when demanded. Anita who claims to have discovered incestuous temptations from Jeremias and Eugenius—

There now, he was lost again. Jeremias and Eugenius were—? Oh, yes, the "philadelphians" or brotherly lovers (another crime hidden there, no doubt) at the beginning of the case, consanguineous to the lowest degree with both Felicia and Honuphrius—the latter the apparent prime villain and husband of Anita. It was Magravius, who seemed to admire Honuphrius, who had been urged by the slave Mauritius to solicit Anita,

377

seemingly under the aegis of Honuphrius himself. This, however, had come to Anita through her tirewoman Fortissa, who
was or at one time had been the common-law wife of Mauritius
and had borne him children—so that the whole story had to
be weighed with the utmost caution. And that entire initial
confession of Honuphrius had come out under torture—
voluntarily consented to, to be sure, but still torture. The
Fortissa-Mauritius relationship was even more dubious, really
only a supposition of the commentator Father Ware—

"Ramon, give me a hand, will you?" Cleaver shouted suddenly. "I'm stuck, and—and I don't feel well."

The Jesuit biologist arose in alarm, putting the novel aside.
Such an admission from Cleaver was unprecedented.

The physicist was sitting on a pouf of woven rushes, stuffed
with a sphagnumlike moss, which was bulging at the equator
under his weight. He was half-way out of his glass-fiber jungle
suit, and his face was white and beaded with sweat, although
his helmet was already off. His uncertain, stubby fingers tore at
a jammed zipper.

"Paul! Why didn't you say you were ill in the first place? Here,
let go of that; you're only making things worse. What happened?"

"Don't know exactly," Cleaver said, breathing heavily but
relinquishing the zipper. Ruiz-Sanchez knelt beside him and
began to work it carefully back onto its tracks. "Went a ways
into the jungle to see if I could spot more pegmatite lies. It's
been in the back of my mind that a pilot-plant for turning out
tritium might locate here eventually—ought to be able to produce on a prodigious scale."

"God forbid," Ruiz-Sanchez said under his breath.

"Hm? Anyhow, I didn't see anything. A few lizards, hoppers,
the usual thing. Then I ran up against a plant that looked a little
like a pineapple, and one of the spines jabbed right through
my suit and nicked me. Didn't seem serious, but—"

"But we don't have the suits for nothing. Let's look at it.
Here, put up your feet and we'll haul those boots off. Where
did you get the—oh. Well, it's angry-looking, I'll give it that.
Any other symptoms?"

"My mouth feels raw," Cleaver complained.

"Open up," the Jesuit commanded. When Cleaver complied,

it became evident that his complaint had been the understatement of the year. The mucosa inside his mouth was nearly covered with ugly and undoubtedly painful ulcers, their edges as sharply defined as though they had been cut with a cookie punch.

Ruiz-Sanchez made no comment, however, and deliberately changed his expression to one of carefully calculated dismissal. If the physicist needed to minimize his ailments, that was all right with Ruiz-Sanchez. An alien planet is not a good place to strip a man of his inner defenses.

"Come into the lab," he said. "You've got some inflammation in there."

Cleaver arose, a little unsteadily, and followed the Jesuit into the laboratory. There Ruiz-Sanchez took smears from several of the ulcers onto microscope slides, and Gram-stained them. He filled the time consumed by the staining process with the ritual of aiming the microscope's substage mirror out the window at a brilliant white cloud. When the timer's alarm went off, he rinsed and flame-dried the slide and slipped it under the clips.

As he had half-feared, he saw few of the mixed bacilli and spirochetes which would have indicated a case of ordinary, Earthly, Vincent's angina—"trench mouth," which the clinical picture certainly suggested, and which he could have cured overnight with a spectrosigmin pastille. Cleaver's oral flora were normal, though on the increase because of all the exposed tissue.

"I'm going to give you a shot," Ruiz-Sanchez said gently. "And then I think you'd better go to bed."

"The hell with that," Cleaver said. "I've got nine times as much work to do as I can hope to clean up now, without any additional handicaps."

"Illness is never convenient," Ruiz-Sanchez agreed. "But why worry about losing a day or so, since you're in over your head anyhow?"

"What have I got?" Cleaver asked suspiciously.

"You haven't *got* anything," Ruiz-Sanchez said, almost regretfully. "That is, you aren't infected. But your 'pineapple' did you a bad turn. Most plants of that family on Lithia bear thorns or leaves coated with polysaccharides that are poisonous to us.

The particular glucoside you ran up against today was evidently squill, or something closely related to it. It produces symptoms like those of trench mouth, but a lot harder to clear up."

"How long will that take?" Cleaver said. He was still balking, but he was on the defensive now.

"Several days at least—until you've built up an immunity. The shot I'm going to give you is a gamma globulin specific against squill, and it ought to moderate the symptoms until you've developed a high antibody titer of your own. But in the process you're going to run quite a fever, Paul; and I'll have to keep you well stuffed with antipyretics, because even a little fever is dangerous in this climate."

"I know it," Cleaver said, mollified. "The more I learn about this place, the less disposed I am to vote 'aye' when the time comes. Well, bring on your shot—and your aspirin. I suppose I ought to be glad it isn't a bacterial infection, or the Snakes would be jabbing me full of antibiotics."

"Small chance of that," Ruiz-Sanchez said. "I don't doubt that the Lithians have at least a hundred different drugs we'll be able to use eventually, but—there, that's all there is to it; you can relax now—but we'll have to study their pharmacology from the ground up, first. All right, Paul, hit the hammock. In about ten minutes you're going to be wishing you'd been born dead, that I promise you."

Cleaver grinned. His sweaty face under its thatch of dirty blond hair was craggy and powerful even in illness. He stood up and deliberately rolled down his sleeve.

"Not much doubt about how you'll vote, either," he said. "You like this planet, don't you, Ramon? It's a biologist's paradise, as far as I can see."

"I do like it," the priest said, smiling back. He followed Cleaver into the small room which served them both as sleeping quarters. Except for the window, it strongly resembled the inside of a jug. The walls were curving and continuous, and were made of some ceramic material which never beaded or felt wet, but never seemed to be quite dry, either. The hammocks were slung from hooks which projected smoothly from the walls, as though they had been baked from clay along with the rest of the house. "I wish my colleague Dr. Meid were able to see it. She would be even more delighted with it than I am."

"I don't hold with women in the sciences," Cleaver said, with abstract, irrelevant irritation. "Get their emotions all mixed up with their hypotheses. Meid—what kind of name is that, anyhow?"

"Japanese," Ruiz-Sanchez said. "Her first name is Liu—the family follows the Western custom of putting the family name last."

"Oh," Cleaver said, losing interest. "We were talking about Lithia."

"Well, don't forget that Lithia is my first extrasolar planet," Ruiz-Sanchez said. "I think I'd find *any* new, habitable world fascinating. The infinite mutability of life forms, and the cunning inherent in each of them. . . . It's all amazing, and quite delightful."

"Why shouldn't that be sufficient?" Cleaver said. "Why do you have to have the God bit too? It doesn't make sense."

"On the contrary, it's what gives everything else meaning," Ruiz-Sanchez said. "Belief and science aren't mutually exclusive—quite the contrary. But if you place scientific standards first, and exclude belief, admit nothing that's not proven, then what you have is a series of empty gestures. For me, biology *is* an act of religion, because I know that all creatures are God's—each new planet, with all its manifestations, is an affirmation of God's power."

"A dedicated man," Cleaver said. "All right. So am I. To the greater glory of man, that's what *I* say."

He sprawled heavily in his hammock. After a decent interval, Ruiz-Sanchez took the liberty of heaving up after him the foot he seemed to have forgotten. Cleaver didn't notice. The reaction was setting in.

"Exactly so," Ruiz-Sanchez said. "But that's only half the story. The other half reads, '. . . and to the greater glory of God.'"

"Read me no tracts, Father," Cleaver said. Then: "I didn't mean that. I'm sorry. . . . But for a physicist, this place is hell. . . . You'd better get me that aspirin. I'm cold."

"Surely, Paul."

Ruiz-Sanchez went quickly back into the lab, made up a salicylate-barbiturate paste in one of the Lithians' superb mortars, and pressed it into a set of pills. (Storing such pills was impossible in Lithia's humid atmosphere; they were too hygroscopic.) He wished he could stamp each pill "Bayer" before it set—if Cleaver's personal cure-all was aspirin, it would have been just as well to let him think he was taking aspirin— but of course he had no dies for the purpose. He took two of the pills back to Cleaver, with a mug and a carafe of Berkefeld- filtered water.

The big man was already asleep; Ruiz-Sanchez woke him, more or less. Cleaver would sleep longer, and awaken farther along the road to recovery, for having been done that small un- kindness now. As it was, he hardly noticed when the pills were put down him, and soon resumed his heavy, troubled breath- ing.

That done, Ruiz-Sanchez returned to the front room of the house, sat down, and began to inspect the jungle suit. The tear which the plant spine had made was not difficult to find, and would be easy to repair. It would be much harder to repair Cleaver's notion that the defenses of Earthmen on Lithia were invulnerable, and that plant-spines could be blundered against with impunity. Ruiz-Sanchez wondered whether either of the other two members of the Lithian Review Commission still shared that notion.

Cleaver had called the thing which had brought him low a "pineapple." Any biologist could have told Cleaver that even on Earth the pineapple is a prolific and dangerous weed, edible only by a happy and irrelevant accident. In Hawaii, as Ruiz- Sanchez remembered, the tropical forest was quite impassable to anyone not wearing heavy boots and tough trousers. Even inside the Dole plantations, the close-packed irrepressible pineapples could tear unprotected legs to ribbons.

The Jesuit turned the suit over. The zipper that Cleaver had jammed was made of a plastic into the molecule of which had been incorporated radicals from various terrestrial anti-fungal substances, chiefly the protoplasmic poison thiolutin. The fungi of Lithia respected these, all right, but the elaborate molecule of the plastic itself had a tendency, under Lithian humidities and heats, to undergo polymerization more or less spontaneously. That was what had happened here. One of the teeth of the zipper had changed into something resembling a kernel of popped corn.

The air grew dark as Ruiz-Sanchez worked. There was a

muted puff of sound, and the room was illuminated with small, soft yellow flames from recesses in every wall. The burning substance was natural gas, of which Lithia had an inexhaustible and constantly renewed supply. The flames were lit by adsorption against a catalyst, as soon as the gas came on from the system. A lime mantle, which worked on a rack and pinion of heatproof glass, could be moved into the flame to provide a brighter light; but the priest liked the yellow light the Lithians themselves preferred, and used the limelight only in the laboratory.

For some purposes, of course, the Earthmen had to have electricity, for which they had been forced to supply their own generators. The Lithians had a far more advanced science of electrostatics than Earth had, but of electrodynamics they knew comparatively little. They had discovered magnetism only a few years before the Commission had arrived, since natural magnets were unknown on the planet. They had first observed the phenomenon, not in iron, of which they had next to none, but in liquid oxygen—a difficult substance from which to make generator cores!

The results in terms of Lithian civilization were peculiar, to an Earthman. The twelve-foot-tall, reptilian people had built several huge electrostatic generators and scores of little ones, but had nothing even vaguely resembling telephones. They knew a great deal on the practical level about electrolysis, but carrying a current over a long distance—say a mile—was regarded by them as a technical triumph. They had no electric motors as an Earthman would understand the term, but made fast intercontinental flights in jet aircraft powered by *static* electricity. Cleaver said he understood this feat, but Ruiz-Sanchez certainly did not (and after Cleaver's description of electron-ion plasmas heated by radio-frequency induction, he felt more in the dark than ever.)

They had a completely marvelous radio network, which among other things provided a "live" navigational grid for the whole planet, zeroed on (and here perhaps was the epitome of the Lithian genius for paradox) a tree. Yet they had never produced a standardized vacuum tube, and their atomic theory was not much more sophisticated than Democritus' had been!

These paradoxes, of course, could be explained in part by

the things that Lithia lacked. Like any large rotating mass, Lithia had a magnetic field of its own, but a planet which almost entirely lacks iron provides its people with no easy way to discover magnetism. Radioactivity had been entirely unknown on the surface of Lithia, at least until the Earthmen had arrived, which explained the hazy atomic theory. Like the Greeks, the Lithians had discovered that friction between silk and glass produces one kind of energy or charge, and between silk and amber another; they had gone on from there to van de Graaff generators, electrochemistry, and the static jet—but without suitable metals they were unable to make heavy-duty batteries, or to do more than begin to study electricity in motion.

In the fields where they had been given fair clues, they had made enormous progress. Despite the constant cloudiness and endemic drizzle, their descriptive astronomy was excellent, thanks to the fortunate presence of a small moon which had drawn their attention outward early. This in turn made for basic advances in optics, and thence for a downright staggering versatility in the working of glass. Their chemistry took full advantage of both the seas and the jungles. From the one they took such vital and diversified products as agar, iodine, salt, trace metals, and foods of many kinds. The other provided nearly everything else that they needed: resins, rubbers, woods of all degrees of hardness, edible and essential oils, vegetable "butters," rope and other fibers, fruits and nuts, tannins, dyes, drugs, cork, paper. Indeed, the sole forest product which they did *not* take was game, and the reason for this neglect was hard to find. It seemed to the Jesuit to be religious—yet the Lithians had no religion, and they certainly ate many of the creatures of the sea without qualms of conscience.

He dropped the jungle suit into his lap with a sigh, though the popcorned tooth still was not completely trimmed back into shape. Outside, in the humid darkness, Lithia was in full concert. It was a vital, somehow fresh, new-sounding drone, covering most of the sound spectrum audible to an Earthman. It came from the myriad insects of Lithia. Many of these had wiry, trilling songs, almost like birds, in addition to the scrapes and chirrups and wing-case buzzes of the insects of Earth. In a way this was lucky, for there were no birds on Lithia.

Had Eden sounded like that, before evil had come into the world? Ruiz-Sanchez wondered. Certainly his native Peru sang no such song . . .

Qualms of conscience—these were, in the long run, his essential business, rather than the taxonomical mazes of biology, which had already become tangled into near-hopelessness on Earth before space flight had come along to add whole new layers of labyrinths for each planet, new dimensions of labyrinths for each star. It was only interesting that the Lithians were bipedal, evolved from reptiles, with marsupial-like pouches and pteropsid circulatory systems. But it was vital that they had qualms of conscience—if they did.

The calendar caught his eye. It was an "art" calendar Cleaver had produced from his luggage back in the beginning; the girl on it was now unintentionally modest beneath large patches of brilliant orange mold. The date was April 19, 2049. Almost Easter—the most pointed of reminders that to the inner life, the body was only a garment. To Ruiz-Sanchez personally, however, the year date was almost equally significant, for 2050 was to be a Holy Year.

The Church had returned to the ancient custom, first recognized officially in 1300 by Boniface VIII, of proclaiming the great pardon only once every half-century. If Ruiz-Sanchez was not in Rome next year when the Holy Door was opened, it would never be opened again in his lifetime.

Hurry, hurry! some personal demon whispered inside his brain. Or was it the voice of his own conscience? Were his sins already so burdensome—unknown to himself—as to put him in mortal need of the pilgrimage? Or was that, in turn, only a minor temptation, to the sin of pride?

In any event, the work could not be hurried. He and the other three men were on Lithia to decide whether or not the planet would be suitable as a port of call for Earth, without risk of damage either to Earthmen or to Lithians. The other three men on the commission were primarily scientists, as was Ruiz-Sanchez; but he knew that his own recommendation would in the long run depend upon conscience, not upon taxonomy.

And conscience, like creation, cannot be hurried. It cannot even be scheduled.

He looked down at the still-imperfect jungle suit with a troubled face until he heard Cleaver moan. Then he arose and left the room to the softly hissing flames.

II

FROM the oval front window of the house to which Cleaver and Ruiz-Sanchez had been assigned, the land slanted away with insidious gentleness toward the ill-defined south edge of Lower Bay, a part of the Gulf of Sfath. Most of the area was salt marsh, as was the seaside nearly everywhere on Lithia. When the tide was in, the flats were covered to a depth of a yard or so almost half the way to the house. When it was out, as it was tonight, the jungle symphony was augmented by the agonized barking of a species of lungfish, sometimes as many as a score of them at once. Occasionally, when the small moon was unoccluded and the light from the city was unusually bright, one could see the leaping shadow of some amphibian, or the sinuously advancing sigmoid track of the Lithian crocodile, in pursuit of some prey faster than itself but which it would nonetheless capture in its own geological good time.

Still farther—and usually invisible even in daytime because of the pervasive mists—was the opposite shore of Lower Bay, beginning with tidal flats again, and then more jungle, which ran unbroken thereafter for hundreds of miles north to the equatorial sea.

Behind the house, visible from the sleeping room, was the rest of the city, Xoredeshch Sfath, capital of the great southern continent. As was the case in all the cities the Lithians built, its most striking characteristic to an Earthman was that it hardly seemed to be there at all. The Lithian houses were low, and made of the earth which had been dug from their foundations, so that they tended to fade into the soil even to a trained observer.

Most of the older buildings were rectangular, put together without mortar of rammed-earth blocks. Over the course of decades the blocks continued to pack and settle themselves until it became easier to abandon an unwanted building than to tear it down. One of the first setbacks the Earthmen had suffered on Lithia had come about through Agronski's ill-advised offer to raze one such structure with TDX; this was a gravity-polarized explosive, unknown to the Lithians, which had the property of exploding in a flat plane which could cut through steel girders as if they were cheese. The warehouse in question, however, was large, thick-walled, and three Lithian centuries old—312 years by Earth time. The explosion created an uproar which greatly distressed the Lithians, but when it was over, the storehouse still stood, unshaken.

Newer structures were more conspicuous when the sun was out, for just during the past half-century the Lithians had begun to apply their enormous knowledge of ceramics to house con-struction. The new houses assumed thousands of fantastic, quasi-biological shapes, not quite amorphous but not quite re-sembling any form in experience, either; they looked a little like the dream constructions once made by an Earth painter named Dalí out of such materials as boiled beans. Each one was unique and to the choice of its owner, yet all markedly shared the character of the community and the earth from which they sprang. These houses, too, would have blended well with the background of soil and jungle, except that most of them were glazed and so shone blindingly for brief moments on sunny days, when the light and the angle of observation were just right. These shifting coruscations, seen from the air, had been the Earthmen's first clue as to where the intelligent life was hiding in the ubiquitous Lithian jungle. (There had never been any doubt that there was intelligent life there; the tremendous radio pulses emanating from the planet had made that much plain from afar.)

Ruiz-Sanchez looked out through the sleeping-room win-dow at the city, for at least the ten thousandth time, on his way to Cleaver's hammock. Xoredeshch Sfath was alive to him; it never looked the same twice. He found it singularly beautiful. And singularly strange: though the cities of Earth were very various, none was like this.

He checked Cleaver's pulse and respiration. Both were fast, even for Lithia, where a high partial pressure of carbon dioxide raised the pH of the blood of Earthmen and stimulated the breathing reflex. The priest judged, however, that Cleaver was in little danger as long as his actual oxygen utilization was not increased. At the moment he was certainly sleeping deeply—if not very restfully—and it would do no harm to leave him alone for a little while.

Of course, if a wild allosaur blundered into the city. . . . But that was just about as likely as the blundering of an untended elephant into the heart of New Delhi. It could happen, but it almost never did. And no other dangerous Lithian animal could break into the house if it was closed. Even the rats—or the abundant monotreme creatures which were Lithia's equivalent—found it impossible to infest a pottery house.

Ruiz-Sanchez changed the carafe of fresh water in the niche beside the hammock, went into the hall, and donned boots, mackintosh and waterproof hat. The night sounds of Lithia burst in upon him as he opened the stone door, along with a gust of sea air bearing the characteristic halogen odor always called "salty." There was a thin drizzle falling, making halos around the lights of Xoredeshch Sfath. Far out, on the water, another light moved. That was probably the coastal side-wheeler to Yllith, the enormous island which stood athwart the Upper Bay, barring the Gulf of Sfath as a whole from the equatorial sea.

Outside, Ruiz-Sanchez turned the wheel which extended bolts on every margin of the door. Drawing from his mackintosh a piece of soft chalk, he marked on the sheltered tablet designed for such uses the Lithian symbols which meant "Illness is here." That would be sufficient. Anybody who chose to could open the door simply by turning the wheel—the Lithians had never heard of locks—but the Lithians, too, were overridingly social beings, who respected their own conventions as they respected natural law.

That done, Ruiz-Sanchez set out for the center of the city and the Message Tree. The asphalt streets shone in the yellow lights cast from windows, and in the white light of the mantled, wide-spaced street lanterns. Occasionally he passed the twelve-foot, kangaroo-like shape of a Lithian, and the two exchanged glances of frank curiosity, but there were not many Lithians abroad now. They kept to their houses at night, doing Ruiz-Sanchez knew not what. He could see them frequently, alone or by twos or threes, moving behind the oval windows of the houses he passed. Sometimes they seemed to be talking.

What about?

It was a nice question. The Lithians had no crime, no newspapers, no house-to-house communications systems, no arts that could be differentiated clearly from their crafts, no political parties, no public amusements, no nations, no games, no religions, no sports, no cults, no celebrations. Surely they didn't spend every waking minute of their lives exchanging knowledge, making things go, discussing philosophy or history, or planning for tomorrow! Or did they? Perhaps, Ruiz-Sanchez thought suddenly, they simply went inert once they were inside their jugs, like so many pickles! But even as the thought came, the priest passed another house, and saw their silhouettes moving to and fro. . . .

A puff of wind scattered cool droplets in his face. Automatically, he quickened his step. If the night were to turn out to be especially windy, there would doubtless be many voices coming and going in the Message Tree. It loomed ahead of him now, a sequoialike giant, standing at the mouth of the valley of the River Sfath—the valley which led in great serpentine folds into the heart of the continent, where Gleshchtehk Sfath, or Blood Lake in English, poured out its massive torrents.

As the winds came and went along the valley, the tree nodded and swayed—only a little, but that little was enough. With every movement, the tree's root system, which underlay the entire city, tugged and distorted the buried crystalline cliff upon which the city had been founded, as long ago in Lithian prehistory as was the founding of Rome on Earth. At every such pressure, the buried cliff responded with a vast heart-pulse of radio waves—a pulse detectable not only all over Lithia, but far out in space as well. The four Commission members had heard those pulses first on shipboard, when Alpha Arietis, Lithia's sun, was still only a point of light ahead of them, and had looked into each other's faces with eyes gleaming with conjecture.

The bursts, however, were sheer noise. How the Lithians modulated them to carry information—not only messages, but the amazing navigational grid, the planet-wide time-signal system, and much more—was something as remote from Ruiz-Sanchez' understanding as affine theory, although Cleaver said it was all perfectly simple once you understood it. It had something to do with semi-conduction and solid-state physics, which (again according to Cleaver) the Lithians understood better than any Earthman.

A free-association jump which startled him momentarily reminded him of the current *doyen* of Earthly affine theory, a man who signed his papers "H. O. Petard," though his real (if scarcely more likely) name was Lucien le Comte des Bois-d'Averoigne. Nor was the association as free as it appeared on the surface, Ruiz-Sanchez realized, for the count was a striking example of the now almost total alienation of modern physics from the common physical experiences of mankind. His title was not a patent of nobility, but merely a part of his name which had been maintained in his family long after the political system which had granted the patent had vanished away, a victim of the dividing up of Earth under the Shelter economy. There was more honor appertaining to the name itself than to the title, for the count had pretensions to hereditary grandeur which reached all the way back into thirteenth-century England, to the author of *Lucien Wycham His Boke of Magick*.

A high ecclesiastic heritage to be sure, but the latter-day Lucien, a lapsed Catholic, was a political figure, insofar as the Shelter economy sheltered any such thing: he carried the additional title of Procurator of Canarsie—a title which a moment's examination would also show to be nonsense, but which paid a small honorarium in exemptions from weekly labor. The subdivided and deeply buried world of Earth was full of such labels, all of them pasted on top of large sums of money which had no place to go now that speculation was dead and shareholding had become the only way by which an ordinary citizen could exercise any control over the keeps in which he lived. The remaining fortune-holders had no outlet left but that of conspicuous consumption, on a scale which would have made Veblen doubt that there had ever been such a thing in the world before. Had they attempted to assert any control over the economy they would have been toppled, if not by the shareholders, then by the grim defenders of the by now indefensible Shelter cities.

Not that the count was a drone. At last reports, he had been involved in some highly esoteric tampering with the Haertel equations—that description of the space-time continuum which, by swallowing up the Lorentz-Fitzgerald contraction exactly as Einstein had swallowed Newton (that is, alive) had made interstellar flight possible. Ruiz-Sanchez did not understand a word of it, but, he reflected with amusement, it was doubtless perfectly simple once you understood it.

Almost all knowledge, after all, fell into that category. It was either perfectly simple once you understood it, or else it fell apart into fiction. As a Jesuit—even here, fifty light-years from Rome—Ruiz-Sanchez knew something about knowledge that Lucien le Comte des Bois-d'Averoigne had forgotten, and that Cleaver would never learn: that all knowledge goes through *both* stages, the annunciation out of noise into fact, and the disintegration back into noise again. The process involved was the making of increasingly finer distinctions. The outcome was an endless series of theoretical catastrophes.

The residuum was faith.

The high, sharply vaulted chamber, like an egg stood on its large end, which had been burned out in the base of the Message Tree, was droning with life as Ruiz-Sanchez entered it. It would have been difficult to imagine anything less like an Earthly telegraph office or other message center, however.

Around the circumference of the lower end of the egg there was a continual whirling of tall figures, Lithians, entering and leaving through the many doorless entrances, and changing places in the swirl of movement like so many electrons passing from orbit to orbit. Despite their numbers, their voices were pitched so low that Ruiz-Sanchez could hear, blended in with their murmuring, the soughing of the wind through the enormous branches far above.

The inner side of this band of moving figures was bounded by a high railing of black, polished wood, evidently cut from the phloem of the Tree itself. On the other side of this token division, which reminded Ruiz-Sanchez irresistibly of the Encke division in the Saturnian rings, a thin circlet of Lithians took and passed out messages steadily and without a moment's break, handling the total load faultlessly—if one were to judge by the way the outer band was kept in motion—and without apparent effort, by memory alone. Occasionally one of these specialists would leave the circlet and go to one of the desks which were scattered over most of the rest of the sloping floor,

increasingly thinly, like a Crape ring, to confer there with the
desk's occupant. Then he went back to the black rail, or sometimes he took the desk, and its previous occupant went to the
rail.

The bowl deepened, the desks thinned, and at the very center stood a single, aged Lithian, his hands clapped to the ear
whorls behind his heavy jaws, his eyes covered by their nictitat-
ing membranes, only his nasal fossae and heat-receptive post-
nasal pits uncovered. He spoke to no one, and no one consulted
him—but the absolute stasis in which he stood was obviously
the reason, the sole reason, for the torrents and counter-torrents
of people which poured along the outermost ring.

Ruiz-Sanchez stopped, astonished. He had never been to
the Message Tree himself before—communicating with Michelis and Agronski, the other two Earthmen on Lithia, had
until now been one of Cleaver's tasks—and the priest found
that he had no idea what to do. The scene before him was
more suggestive of a bourse than of a message center in any
ordinary sense. It seemed unlikely that so many Lithians could
have urgent personal messages to send each time the winds
were active; yet it seemed equally uncharacteristic that the
Lithians, with their stable, abundance-based economy, should
have any equivalent for stock or commodity brokerage.

There seemed to be no choice, however, but to plunge in,
try to reach the polished black rail, and ask one of the Lithians
who stood on the other side to try to raise Agronski or Michelis
again. At worst, he supposed, he could only be refused, or fail
to get a hearing at all. He took a deep breath.

Simultaneously his left arm was caught in a firm four-fingered
grip which ran all the way from his elbow to his shoulder. Letting the stored breath out again in a snort of surprise, the priest
looked around and up at the solicitously bent head of a Lithian. Under the long, trap-like mouth, the being's wattles were
a delicate, curious aquamarine, in contrast to its vestigial comb,
which was a permanent and silvery sapphire, shot through with
veins of fuchsia.

"You are Ruiz-Sanchez," the Lithian said in his own language. The priest's name, unlike those of the other Earthmen,
fell easily in that tongue. "I know you by your robe."

That was pure accident. Any Earthman out in the rain in a

mackintosh would have been identified as Ruiz-Sanchez, because the priest was the only Earthman who seemed to the Lithians to wear the same garment indoors and out.

"I am," Ruiz-Sanchez said, a little apprehensively.

"I am Chtexa, the metallurgist, who consulted with you earlier on problems of chemistry and medicine and your mission here, and some other smaller matters."

"Oh. Yes, of course; I should have remembered your comb."

"You do me honor. We have not seen you here before. Do you wish to talk with the Tree?"

"I do," Ruiz-Sanchez said gratefully. "It is true that I am new here. Can you explain to me what to do?"

"Yes, but not to any profit," Chtexa said, tilting his head so that his completely inky pupils shone down into Ruiz-Sanchez' eyes. "One must have observed the ritual, which is very complex, until it is habit. We have grown up with it, but I think you lack the coordination to follow it on the first attempt. If I may bear your message instead—"

"I would be most indebted. It is for our colleagues Agronski and Michelis; they are at Xoredeshch Gton on the northeast continent, at about thirty-two degrees east, thirty-two degrees north—"

"Yes, the second bench mark at the outlet of the Lesser Lakes; that is the city of the potters, I know it well. And you would say?"

"That they are to join us now, here, at Xoredeshch Sfath. And that our time on Lithia is almost up."

"That me regards," Chtexa said. "But I will bear it."

The Lithian leapt into the whirling cloud, and Ruiz-Sanchez was left behind, considering again his thankfulness that he had been moved to study the painfully difficult Lithian language. Two of the four commission members had shown a regrettable lack of interest in that world-wide tongue: "Let 'em learn English" had been Cleaver's unknowingly classic formulation. Ruiz-Sanchez had been all the less likely to view this notion sympathetically for the facts that his own native language was Spanish, and that, of the five foreign languages in which he was really fluent, the one he liked best was West High German.

Agronski had taken a slightly more sophisticated stand. It

was not, he said, that Lithian was too difficult to pronounce—
certainly it wasn't any harder on the soft palate than Arabic or
Russian—but, after all, "it's hopeless to attempt to grasp the
concepts that lie *behind* a really alien language, isn't it? At least
in the time we have to spend here?"

To both views, Michelis had said nothing; he had simply set
out to learn to read the language first, and if he found his way
from there into speaking it, he would not be surprised and
neither would his confreres. That was Michelis' way of doing
things, thorough and untheoretical at the same time. As for
the other two approaches, Ruiz-Sanchez thought privately that
it was close to criminal to allow any contact man for a new
planet ever to leave Earth with such parochial notions. In understanding a new culture, language is of the essence; if one
doesn't start there, where under God does one start?

Of Cleaver's penchant for referring to the Lithians themselves as "the Snakes," Ruiz-Sanchez' opinion was of a color
admissible only to his remote confessor.

And in view of what lay before him now in this egg-shaped
hollow, what was Ruiz-Sanchez to think of Cleaver's conduct
as communications officer for the commission? Surely he could
never have transmitted or received a single message through
the Tree, as he had claimed to have done. Probably he had
never been closer to the Tree than Ruiz-Sanchez was now.

Of course, it went without saying that he had been in contact with Agronski and Michelis by *some* method, but that
method had evidently been something private—a transmitter
concealed in his luggage, or. . . . No, that wouldn't do.
Physicist though he most definitely was not, Ruiz-Sanchez rejected that solution on the spot; he had some idea of the
practical difficulties of operating a ham radio on a world like
Lithia, swamped as that world was on all wave-lengths by the
tremendous pulses which the Tree wrung from the buried
crystalline cliff. The problem was beginning to make him feel
decidedly uncomfortable.

Then Chtexa was back, recognizable not so much by any
physical detail—for his wattles were now the same ambiguous
royal purple as those of most of the other Lithians in the crowd
—as by the fact that he was bearing down upon the Earthman.

"I have sent your message," he said at once. "It is recorded at Xoredeshch Gton. But the other Earthmen are not there. They have not been in the city for some days."

That was impossible. Cleaver had said he had spoken to Michelis only a day ago. "Are you sure?" Ruiz-Sanchez said cautiously.

"It admits of no uncertainty. The house which we gave them stands empty. The many things which they brought with them to the house are gone." The tall shape raised its four-fingered hands in a gesture which might have been solicitous. "I think this is an ill word. I dislike to bring it you. The words you brought me when first we met were full of good."

"Thank you. Don't worry," Ruiz-Sanchez said distractedly. "No man could hold the bearer responsible for the word, surely."

"The bearer also has responsibilities; at least, that is our custom," Chtexa said. "No act is wholly free. And as we see it, you have lost by our exchange. Your words on iron have been shown to contain great good. I would take pleasure in showing you how we have used them, especially since I have brought you in return an ill message. If you could share my house to-night, without prejudice to your work, I could expose this matter. Is that possible?"

Sternly Ruiz-Sanchez stifled his sudden excitement. Here was the first chance, at long last, to see something of the private life of Lithia, and through that, perhaps, to gain some inkling of the moral life, the role in which God had cast the Lithians in the ancient drama of good and evil, in the past and in the times to come. Until that was known, the Lithians in their Eden might be only spuriously good: all reason, all organic thinking machines, ULTIMACs with tails—and without souls.

But there remained the hard fact that he had left behind in his house a sick man. There was not much chance that Cleaver would awaken before morning. He had been given nearly fifteen milligrams of sedative per kilogram of body weight. But sick men are like children, whose schedules persistently defy all rules. If Cleaver's burly frame should somehow throw that dose off, driven perhaps by some anaphylactic crisis impossible to rule out this early in his illness, he would need prompt attention. At the very least, he would want badly for the sound of a human voice on this planet which he hated, and which had struck him down almost without noticing that he existed.

Still, the danger to Cleaver was not great. He most certainly did not require a minute-by-minute vigil; he was, after all, not a child, but an almost ostentatiously strong man.

And there was such a thing as an excess of devotion, a form of pride among the pious which the Church had long found peculiarly difficult to make clear to them. At its worst, it produced the hospital saints, whose attraction to noisomeness so peculiarly resembled the vermin-worship of the Hindi sects—or a St. Simon Stylites, who though undoubtedly acceptable to God had been for centuries very bad public relations for the Church. And had Cleaver really earned the kind of devotion Ruiz-Sanchez had been proposing, up to now, to tender him as a creature of God—or, to come closer to the mark, a godly creature?

And with a whole planet at stake, a whole people—no, more than that, a whole problem in theology, an imminent solution to the vast, tragic riddle of original sin. . . . What a gift to bring to the Holy Father in a jubilee year—a grander and more solemn thing than the proclamation of the conquest of Everest had been at the coronation of Elizabeth II of England!

Always providing, of course, that this would be the ultimate outcome of the study of Lithia. The planet was not lacking in hints that something quite different, and fearful beyond all else, might emerge under Ruiz-Sanchez' prolonged attention. Not even prayer had yet resolved that doubt. But should he sacrifice even the possibility of this, for Cleaver?

A lifetime of meditation over just such cases of conscience had made Ruiz-Sanchez, like most other gifted members of his order, quick to find his way to a decision through all but the most complicated of ethical labyrinths. All Catholics must be devout; but a Jesuit must be, in addition, agile.

"Thank you," he said to Chtexa, a little shakily. "I will share your house very gladly."

III

(*A voice*): "Cleaver? Cleaver! Wake up, you big slob. Cleaver! Where the hell have you been?"

Cleaver groaned and tried to turn over. At his first motion, the world began to rock, gently, sickeningly. He was awash in fever. His mouth seemed to be filled with burning pitch.

"Cleaver, turn out. It's me—Agronski. Where's the Father? What's wrong? Why didn't we ever hear from you? *Look out*, you'll—"

The warning came too late, and Cleaver could not have understood it anyhow. He had been profoundly asleep, and had no notion of his situation in space or time. At his convulsive twist away from the nagging voice, the hammock rotated on its hooks and dumped him.

He struck the floor stunningly, taking the main blow across his right shoulder, though he hardly felt it yet. His feet, not yet part of him at all, still remained far aloft, twisted in the hammock webbing.

"What the hell—"

There was a brief chain of footsteps, like chestnuts dropping on a roof, and then a hollow noise of something hitting the floor near his head.

"Cleaver, are you sick? Here, lie still a minute and let me get your feet free. Mike—Mike, can't you turn the gas up in this jug? Something's wrong back here."

After a moment, yellow light began to pour from the glistening walls, and then the white glare of the mantles. Cleaver dragged an arm across his eyes, but it did him no good; it tired too quickly. Agronski's mild face, plump and anxious, floated directly above him like a captive balloon. He could not see Michelis anywhere, and at the moment he was just as glad he couldn't. Agronski's presence was hard enough to understand.

"How . . . the hell . . ." he said. At the words, his lips split painfully at both corners. He realized for the first time that they had become gummed together, somehow, while he was asleep. He had no idea how long he had been out of the picture.

Agronski seemed to understand the aborted question. "We came in from the Lakes in the 'copter," he said. "We didn't like the silence down here, and we figured we'd better come in under our own power, instead of registering in on the regular jet liner and tipping the Lithians off—just in case there'd been any dirty work afloat—"

"Stop jawing him," Michelis said, appearing suddenly, magically in the doorway. "He's got a bug, that's obvious. I don't like to feel pleased about misery, but I'm glad it's that instead of the Lithians."

The rangy, long-jawed chemist helped Agronski lift Cleaver to his feet. Tentatively, despite the pain, Cleaver got his mouth open again. Nothing came out but a hoarse croak.

"Shut up," Michelis said, not unkindly. "Let's get him back into the hammock. Where's the Father, I wonder? He's the only one capable of dealing with sickness here."

"I'll bet he's dead," Agronski burst out suddenly, his face glistening with alarm. "He'd be here if he could. It must be catching, Mike."

"I didn't bring my mitt," Michelis said drily. "Cleaver, lie still or I'll have to clobber you. Agronski, you seem to have dumped his water bottle; better go get him some more, he needs it. And see if the Father left anything in the lab that looks like medicine."

Agronski went out, and, maddeningly, so did Michelis—at least out of Cleaver's field of vision. Setting his every muscle against the pain, Cleaver pulled his lips apart once more.

"Mike."

Instantly, Michelis was there. He had a pad of cotton between thumb and forefinger, wet with some solution, with which he gently cleaned Cleaver's lips and chin.

"Easy. Agronski's getting you a drink. We'll let you talk in a little while, Paul. Don't rush it."

Cleaver relaxed a little. He could trust Michelis. Nevertheless, the vivid and absurd insult of having to be swabbed like a baby was more than he could bear; he felt tears of helpless rage swelling on either side of his nose. With two deft, noncommittal swipes, Michelis removed them.

Agronski came back, holding out one hand tentatively, palm up.

"I found these," he said. "There's more in the lab, and the Father's pill press is still out. So are his mortar and pestle, though they've been cleaned."

"All right, let's have 'em," Michelis said. "Anything else?"

"No. Well, there's a syringe cooking in the sterilizer, if that means anything."

Michelis swore briefly and to the point.

"It means that there's a pertinent antitoxin in the shop some-place," he added. "But unless Ramon left notes, we'll not have a prayer of figuring out which one it is."

As he spoke, he lifted Cleaver's head and tipped the pills into his mouth, onto his tongue. The water which followed was cold at the first contact, but a split second later it was liquid fire. Cleaver choked, and at that precise instant Michelis pinched his nostrils shut. The pills went down with a gulp.

"There's no sign of the Father?" Michelis said.

"Not a one, Mike. Everything's in good order, and his gear's still here. Both jungle suits are in the locker."

"Maybe he went visiting," Michelis said thoughtfully. "He must have gotten to know quite a few of the Lithians by now. He liked them."

"With a sick man on his hands? That's not like him, Mike. Not unless there was some kind of emergency. Or maybe he went on a routine errand, expected to be back in just a few minutes, and—"

"And was set upon by trolls, for forgetting to stamp his foot three times before crossing a bridge."

"All right, laugh."

"I'm not laughing, believe me. That's just the kind of damn fool thing that can kill a man in a strange culture. But some-how I can't see it happening to Ramon."

"*Mike. . . .*"

Michelis took a step and looked down at Cleaver. His face was drifting as if detached through a haze of tears. He said:

"All right, Paul. Tell us what it is. We're listening."

But it was too late. The doubled sedative dose had gotten to Cleaver first. He could only shake his head, and with the mo-tion Michelis seemed to go reeling away into a whirlpool of fuzzy rainbows.

Curiously, he did not quite go to sleep. He had had nearly a normal night's sleep, and he had started out his enormously long day a powerful and healthy man. The conversation of the two commissioners, and an obsessive consciousness of his need to speak to them before Ruiz-Sanchez returned, helped to keep him, if not totally awake, at least not far below a state of light trance. In addition, the presence in his system of thirty grains of acetylsalicylic acid had seriously raised his oxygen consumption, bringing with it not only dizziness but also a precarious, emotionally untethered alertness. That the fuel which was being burned to maintain it was in part the protein substrate of his own cells he did not know, and it could not have alarmed him had he known it.

The voices continued to reach him, and to convey a little meaning. With them were mixed fleeting, fragmentary dreams, so slightly removed from the surface of his waking life as to seem peculiarly real, yet at the same time peculiarly pointless and depressing. In the semiconscious intervals there came plans, a whole succession of them, all simple and grandiose at once, for taking command of the expedition, for communicating with the authorities on Earth, for bringing forward secret papers proving that Lithia was uninhabitable, for digging a tunnel under Mexico to Peru, for detonating Lithia in one single mighty fusion of all its lightweight atoms into one single atom of cleaverium, the element of which the monobloc had been made, whose cardinal number was Aleph-Null. . . .

AGRONSKI: Mike, come here and look at this; you read Lithian. There's a mark on the front door, on the message tablet.

(*Footsteps.*)

MICHELIS: It says "Sickness inside." The strokes aren't casual or deft enough to be the work of the natives. Ideograms are hard to write rapidly without long practice. Ramon must have written it there.

AGRONSKI: I wish we knew where he went afterwards. Funny we didn't see it when we came in.

MICHELIS: I don't think so. It was dark, and we weren't looking for it.

(*Footsteps. Door shutting, not loudly. Footsteps. Hassock creaking.*)

AGRONSKI: Well, we'd better start thinking about getting up a report. Unless this damn twenty-hour day has me thrown completely off, our time's just about up. Are you still set on opening up the planet?

MICHELIS: Yes. I've seen nothing to convince me that there's anything on Lithia that's dangerous to us. Except maybe Cleaver in there, and I'm not prepared to say that the Father would have left him if he were in any serious danger. And I don't see how Earthmen could harm this society; it's too stable emotionally, economically, in every other way.

(Danger, danger, *said somebody in Cleaver's dream.* It will explode. It's all a popish plot. *Then he was marginally awake again, and conscious of how much his mouth hurt.*)

AGRONSKI: Why do you suppose those two jokers never called us after we went north?

MICHELIS: I don't have any answer. I won't even guess until I talk to Ramon. Or until Paul's able to sit up and take notice.

AGRONSKI: I don't like it, Mike. It smells bad to me. This town's right at the heart of the communications system of the planet—that's why we picked it, for Crisake! And yet— no messages, Cleaver sick, the Father not here. . . . There's a hell of a lot we don't know about Lithia, that's for damn sure.

MICHELIS: There's a hell of a lot we don't know about central Brazil—let alone Mars, or the Moon.

AGRONSKI: Nothing essential, Mike. What we know about the periphery of Brazil gives us all the clues we need about the interior—even to those fish that eat people, the what-are-they, the piranhas. That's not true on Lithia. We don't know whether our peripheral clues about Lithia are germane or just incidental. Something enormous could be hidden under the surface without our being able to detect it.

MICHELIS: Agronski, stop sounding like a Sunday supplement. You underestimate your own intelligence. What kind of enormous secret could that be? That the Lithians eat people? That they're cattle for unknown gods that live in the jungle? That they're actually mind-wrenching, soul-twisting, heart-stopping, blood-freezing, bowel-moving superbeings in disguise? The moment you state any such proposition, you'll deflate it yourself; it's only in the abstract that it's able to scare you. I wouldn't even take the trouble of examining it, or discussing how we might meet it if it were true.

AGRONSKI: All right, all right. I'll reserve judgment for the time being, anyhow. If everything turns out to be all right here, with the Father and Cleaver I mean, I'll probably go along with you. I don't have any reason I could defend for voting against the planet, I admit that.

MICHELIS: Good for you. I'm sure Ramon is for opening it up, so that should make it unanimous. I can't see why Cleaver would object.

(Cleaver was testifying before a packed court convened in the UN General Assembly chambers in New York, with one finger pointed dramatically, but less in triumph than in sorrow, at Ramon Ruiz-Sanchez, S. J. At the sound of his name the dream collapsed, and he realized that the room had grown a little lighter. Dawn—or the dripping, wool-gray travesty of it which prevailed on Lithia—was on its way.

He wondered what he had just said to the court. It had been conclusive, damning, good enough to be used when he awoke; but he could not remember a word of it. All that remained of it was a sensation, almost the taste of the words, but nothing of their substance.)

AGRONSKI: It's getting light. I suppose we'd better knock off.

MICHELIS: Did you stake down the 'copter? The winds down here are higher than they are up north, I seem to remember.

AGRONSKI: Yes. And covered it with the tarp. Nothing left to do now but sling our hammocks—

(A sound)

MICHELIS: Shhh. What's that?

AGRONSKI: Eh?

MICHELIS: Listen.

(Footsteps. Faint ones, but Cleaver knew them. He forced his eyes to open a little, but there was nothing to see but the ceiling. Its even color, and its smooth, ever-changing slope into a dome of nowhereness, drew him almost immediately upward into the mists of trance once more.)

AGRONSKI: Somebody's coming.

(Footsteps.)

AGRONSKI: It's the Father, Mike—look out here and you can

see him. He seems to be all right. Dragging his feet a bit, but who wouldn't after being out helling all night?

MICHELIS: Maybe you'd better meet him at the door. It'd probably be better than our springing out at him after he gets inside. After all he doesn't expect us. I'll get to unpacking the hammocks.

AGRONSKI: Sure thing, Mike.

(*Footsteps, going away from Cleaver. A grating sound of stone on stone: the door wheel being turned.*)

AGRONSKI: Welcome home, Father! We just got in a little while ago and—My God, what's wrong? Are you ill too? Is there something that—Mike! *Mike!*

(*Somebody was running. Cleaver willed his neck muscles to lift his head, but they refused to obey. Instead, the back of his head seemed to force itself deeper into the stiff pillow of the hammock. After a momentary and endless agony, he cried out*):

CLEAVER: Mike!

AGRONSKI: Mike!

(*With a gasp, Cleaver lost the long battle at last. He was asleep.*)

IV

As the door of Chtexa's house closed behind him, Ruiz-Sanchez looked about the gently glowing foyer with a feeling of almost unbearable anticipation, although he could hardly have said what it was that he hoped to see. Actually, it looked exactly like his own quarters, which was all he could in justice have expected—all the furniture at "home" was Lithian, except of course for the lab equipment and a few other terrestrial trappings.

"We have cut up several of the metal meteors from our museums, and hammered them as you suggested," Chtexa was saying behind him, while he struggled out of his raincoat and boots. "They show very definite, very strong magnetism, as you predicted. We now have the whole of our world alerted to pick up these nickel-iron meteorites and send them to our electrical laboratory here, regardless of where they are found.

The staff of the observatory is attempting to predict possible falls. Unhappily, meteors are rare here. Our astronomers say that we have never had a 'shower' such as you describe as frequent on your native planet."

"No; I should have thought of that," Ruiz-Sanchez said, following the Lithian into the front room. This, too, was quite ordinary by Lithian standards, and empty except for the two of them.

"Ah, that is interesting. Why?"

"Because in our system we have a sort of giant grinding-wheel—a whole ring of little planets, many thousands of them, distributed around an orbit where we had expected to find only one normal-sized world."

"Expected? By the harmonic rule?" Chtexa said, sitting down and pointing out another hassock to his guest. "We have often wondered whether that relationship was real."

"So have we. It broke down in this instance. Collisions between all those small bodies are incessant, and our plague of meteors is the result."

"It is hard to understand how so unstable an arrangement could have come about," Chtexa said. "Have you any explanation?"

"Not a good one," Ruiz-Sanchez said. "Some of us think that there really was a respectable planet in that orbit ages ago, which exploded somehow. A similar accident happened to a satellite in our system, creating a great flat ring of debris around its primary. Others think that at the formation of our solar system the raw materials of what might have been a planet just never succeeded in coalescing. Both ideas have many flaws, but each satisfies certain objections to the other, so perhaps there is some truth in both."

Chtexa's eyes filmed with the mildly disquieting "inner blink" characteristic of Lithians at their most thoughtful.

"There would seem to be no way to test either answer," he said at length. "By our logic, the lack of such tests makes the original question meaningless."

"That rule of logic has many adherents on Earth. My colleague Dr. Cleaver would certainly agree with it."

Ruiz-Sanchez smiled suddenly. He had labored long and hard to master the Lithian language, and to have recognized and understood so completely abstract a point as the one just made by Chtexa was a bigger victory than any quantitative gains in vocabulary alone could have been.

"But I can see that you are going to have difficulties in collecting these meteorites," he said. "Have you offered incentives?"

"Oh, certainly. Everyone understands the importance of the program. We are all eager to advance it."

This was not quite what the priest had meant by his question. He searched his memory for some Lithian equivalent for "reward," but found nothing but the word he had already used, "incentive." He realized that he knew no Lithian word for "greed," either. Evidently offering Lithians a hundred dollars for every meteorite they found would simply baffle them. He had to abandon that tack.

"Since the potential meteor fall is so small," he said instead, "you're not likely to get anything like the supply of metal that you need for a real study—no matter how thoroughly you co-operate on the search. A high percentage of the finds will be stony rather than metallic, too. What you need is another, supplementary iron-finding program."

"We know that," Chtexa said ruefully. "But we have been able to think of none."

"If only you had some way of concentrating the traces of the metal you actually have on the planet now. . . . Our smelting methods would be useless to you, since you have no ore beds. Hmm. . . . Chtexa, what about the iron-fixing bacteria?"

"Are there such?" Chtexa said, cocking his head dubiously.

"I don't know. Ask your bacteriologists. If you have any bacteria here that belong to the genus we call *Leptothrix*, one of them should be an iron-fixing species. In all the millions of years that this planet has had life on it, that mutation must have occurred, and probably very early."

"But why have we never seen it before? We have done perhaps more research in bacteriology than we have in any other field."

"Because," Ruiz-Sanchez said earnestly, "you don't know what to look for, and because such a species would be as rare on Lithia as iron itself. On Earth, because we have iron in abundance, our *Leptothrix ochracea* has found plenty of opportunity to grow. We find their fossil sheaths by uncountable billions in our great ore beds. It used to be thought, as a matter of fact, that the bacteria *produced* the ore beds, but I've always doubted that. They get their energy by oxidizing ferrous iron into ferric—but that's a change that can happen spontaneously if the oxidation-reduction potential and the pH of the solution are right, and both of those conditions can be affected by ordinary decay bacteria. On our planet the bacteria grew in the ore beds because the iron was there, not the other way around—but on Lithia the process will have to be worked in reverse."

"We will start a soil-sampling program at once," Chtexa said, his wattles flaring a subdued orchid. "Our antibiotics research centers screen soil samples by the thousands each month, in search of new microflora of therapeutic importance. If these iron-fixing bacteria exist, we are certain to find them eventually."

"They must exist. Do you have a bacterium that is a sulphur-concentrating obligate anaerobe?"

"Yes—yes, certainly!"

"There you are," the Jesuit said, leaning back contentedly and clasping his hands across one knee. "You have plenty of sulphur, and so you have the bacterium. Please let me know when you find the iron-fixing species. I'd like to make a subculture and take it home with me when I leave. There are two Earth scientists whose noses I'd like to rub in it."

The Lithian stiffened and thrust his head forward a little, as if puzzled.

"Pardon me," Ruiz-Sanchez said hastily. "I was translating literally an aggressive idiom of my own tongue. It was not meant to describe an actual plan of action."

"I think I understand," Chtexa said. Ruiz-Sanchez wondered if he did. In the rich storehouse of the Lithian language he had yet to discover any metaphors, either living or dead. Neither did the Lithians have any poetry or other creative arts. "You are of course welcome to any of the results of this program, which you would honor us by accepting. One problem in the social sciences which has long puzzled us is just how one may adequately honor the innovator. When we consider how new ideas change our lives, we despair of giving in kind, and it is helpful when the innovator himself has wishes which society can gratify."

Ruiz-Sanchez was at first not quite sure that he had understood the formulation. After he had gone over it once more in his mind, he was not sure that he could bring himself to like it, although it was admirable enough. From an Earthman it would have sounded intolerably pompous, but it was evident that Chtexa meant it.

It was probably just as well that the commission's report on Lithia was about to fall due. Ruiz-Sanchez had begun to think that he could absorb only a little more of this kind of calm sanity. And all of it—a disquieting thought from somewhere near his heart reminded him—all of it derived from reason, none from precept, none from faith. The Lithians did not know God. They did things rightly, and thought righteously, because it was reasonable and efficient and natural to do and to think that way. They seemed to need nothing else.

Did they never have night thoughts? Was it possible that there could exist in the universe a reasoning being of a high order, which was never for an instant paralyzed by the sudden question, the terror of seeing through to the meaninglessness of action, the blindness of knowledge, the barrenness of having been born at all? "Only upon this firm foundation of unyielding despair," a famous atheist once had written, "may the soul's habitation henceforth be safely built."

Or could it be that the Lithians thought and acted as they did because, not being born of man, and never in effect having left the Garden in which they lived, they did not share the terrible burden of original sin? The fact that Lithia had never once had a glacial epoch, that its climate had been left unchanged for seven hundred million years, was a geological fact that an alert theologian could scarcely afford to ignore. Could it be that, free from the burden, they were also free from the curse of Adam?

And if they were—could men bear to live among them?

"I have some questions to ask you, Chtexa," the priest said after a moment. "You owe me no debt whatsoever—it is our custom to regard all knowledge as community property—but we four Earthmen have a hard decision to make shortly. You know what it is. And I don't believe that we know enough yet about your planet to make that decision properly."

"Then of course you must ask questions," Chtexa said immediately. "I will answer, wherever I can."

"Well then—do your people die? I see you have the word, but perhaps it isn't the same in meaning as our word."

"It means to stop changing and to go back to existing," Chtexa said. "A machine exists, but only a living thing, like a tree, progresses along a line of changing equilibriums. When that progress stops, the entity is dead."

"And that happens to you?"

"It always happens. Even the great trees, like the Message Tree, die sooner or later. Is that not true on Earth?"

"Yes," Ruiz-Sanchez said, "yes, it is. For reasons which it would take me a long time to explain, it occurred to me that you might have escaped this evil."

"It is not evil as we look at it," Chtexa said. "Lithia lives because of death. The death of plants supplies our oil and gas. The death of some creatures is always necessary to feed the lives of others. Bacteria must die, and viruses be prevented from living, if illness is to be cured. We ourselves must die simply to make room for others, at least until we can slow the rate at which our people arrive in the world—a thing impossible to us at present."

"But desirable, in your eyes?"

"Surely desirable," Chtexa said. "Our world is rich, but not inexhaustible. And other planets, you have taught us, have peoples of their own. Thus we cannot hope to spread to other planets when we have overpopulated this one."

"No real thing is ever exhaustible," Ruiz-Sanchez said abruptly, frowning at the iridescent floor. "That we have found to be true over many thousands of years of our history."

"But exhaustible in what way?" Chtexa said. "I grant you that any small object, any stone, any drop of water, any bit of soil can be explored without end. The amount of information which can be gotten from it is quite literally infinite. But a given soil can be exhausted of nitrates. It is difficult, but with bad cultivation it can be done. Or take iron, about which we have been talking. To allow our economy to develop a demand for iron which exceeds the total known supply of Lithia—and

exceeds it beyond any possibility of supplementation by meteorites or by import—would be folly. This is not a question of
information. It is a question of whether or not the information
can be used. If it cannot, then limitless information is of no
help."

"You could certainly get along without more iron if you had
to," Ruiz-Sanchez admitted. "Your wooden machinery is precise enough to satisfy any engineer. Most of them, I think,
don't remember that we used to have something similar: I've a
sample in my own home. It's a kind of timer called a cuckoo
clock, nearly two of our centuries old, made entirely of wood
except for the weights, and still nearly a hundred per cent accurate. For that matter, long after we began to build seagoing
vessels of metal, we continued to use lignum vitae for ships'
bearings."

"Wood is an excellent material for most uses," Chtexa agreed.
"Its only deficiency, compared to ceramic materials or perhaps
metal, is that it is variable. One must know it quite well to be
able to assess its qualities from one tree to the next. And of
course complicated parts can always be grown inside suitable
ceramic molds; the growth pressure inside the mold rises so
high that the resulting part is very dense. Larger parts can be
ground direct from the plank with soft sandstone and polished
with slate. It is a gratifying material to work, we find."

Ruiz-Sanchez felt, for some reason, a little ashamed. It was a
magnified version of the same shame he had always felt back
home toward that old Black Forest cuckoo clock. The electric
clocks elsewhere in his hacienda outside Lima all should have
been capable of performing silently, accurately, and in less
space—but the considerations which had gone into the making of them had been commercial as well as purely technical.
As a result, most of them operated with a thin, asthmatic whir,
or groaned softly but dismally at irregular hours. All of them
were "streamlined," oversize and ugly. None of them kept
good time, and several of them, since they were powered by
constant-speed motors driving very simple gearboxes, could
not be adjusted, but had been sent out from the factory with
built-in, ineluctable inaccuracies.

The wooden cuckoo clock, meanwhile, ticked evenly away.
A quail emerged from one of two wooden doors every quarter

of an hour and let you know about it, and on the hour first the quail came out, then the cuckoo, and there was a soft bell that rang just ahead of each cuckoo call. Midnight and noon were not just times of the day for that clock; they were productions. It was accurate to a minute a month, all for the price of running up the three weights which drove it, each night before bedtime.

The clock's maker had been dead before Ruiz-Sanchez was born. In contrast, the priest would probably buy and jettison at least a dozen cheap electric clocks in the course of one lifetime, as their makers had intended he should; they were linearly descended from "planned obsolescence," the craze for waste which had hit the Americas during the last half of the previous century.

"I'm sure it is," he said humbly. "I have one more question, if I may. It is really part of the same question. I have asked you if you die; now I should like to ask how you are born. I see many adults on your streets and sometimes in your houses—though I gather you yourself are alone—but never any children. Can you explain this to me? Or if the subject is not allowed to be discussed—"

"But why should it not be? There can never be any closed subjects," Chtexa said. "Our women, as I'm sure you know, have abdominal pouches where the eggs are carried. It was a lucky mutation for us, for there are a number of nest-robbing species on this planet."

"Yes, we have a few animals with a somewhat similar arrangement on Earth, although they are viviparous."

"Our eggs are laid in these pouches once a year," Chtexa said. "It is then that the women leave their own houses and seek out the man of their choice to fertilize the eggs. I am alone because, thus far, I am no woman's first choice this season; I will be elected in the Second Marriage, which is tomorrow."

"I see," Ruiz-Sanchez said carefully. "And how is the choice determined? Is it by emotion, or by reason alone?"

"The two are in the long run the same," Chtexa said. "Our ancestors did not leave our genetic needs to chance. Emotion with us no longer runs counter to our eugenic knowledge. It cannot, since it was itself modified to follow that knowledge by selective breeding for such behavior.

"At the end of the season, then, comes Migration Day. At that time all the eggs are fertilized, and ready to hatch. On that day—you will not be here to see it, I am afraid, for your scheduled date of departure precedes it by a short time—our whole people goes to the seashores. There, with the men to protect them from predators, the women wade out to swimming depth, and the children are born."

"In the sea?" Ruiz-Sanchez said faintly.

"Yes, in the sea. Then we all return, and resume our other affairs until the next mating season."

"But—but what happens to the children?"

"Why, they take care of themselves, if they can. Of course many perish, particularly to our voracious brother the great fish-lizard, whom for that reason we kill when we can. But a majority return home when the time comes."

"Return? Chtexa, I don't understand. Why don't they drown when they are born? And if they return, why have we never seen one?"

"But you have," Chtexa said. "And you have heard them often. Can it be that you yourselves do not—ah, of course, you are mammals; that is doubtless the difficulty. You keep your children in the nest with you; you know who they are, and they know their parents."

"Yes," Ruiz-Sanchez said. "We know who they are, and they know us."

"That is not possible with us," Chtexa said. "Here, come with me; I will show you."

He arose and led the way out into the foyer. Ruiz-Sanchez followed, his head whirling with surmises.

Chtexa opened the door. The night, the priest saw with a subdued shock, was on the wane; there was the faintest of pearly glimmers in the cloudy sky to the east. The multifarious humming and singing of the jungle continued unabated. There was a high, hissing whistle, and the shadow of a pterodon drifted over the city toward the sea. Out on the water, an indistinct blob that could only be one of Lithia's sailplaning squid broke the surface and glided low over the oily swell for nearly sixty yards before it hit the waves again. From the mud flats came a hoarse barking.

"There," Chtexa said softly. "Did you hear it?"

The stranded creature, or another of its kind—it was impossible to tell which—croaked protestingly again.

"It is hard for them at first," Chtexa said. "But actually the worst of their dangers are over. They have come ashore."

"Chtexa," Ruiz-Sanchez said. "Your children—*the lungfish?*"

"Yes," Chtexa said. "Those are our children."

V

IN the last analysis it was the incessant barking of the lungfish which caused Ruiz-Sanchez to stumble when Agronski opened the door for him. The late hour, and the dual strains of Cleaver's illness and the subsequent discovery of Cleaver's direct lying, contributed. So did the increasing sense of guilt toward Cleaver which the priest had felt while walking home under the gradually brightening, weeping sky; and so, of course, did the shock of discovering that Agronski and Michelis had arrived some time during the night while he had been neglecting his charge to satisfy his curiosity.

But primarily it was the diminishing, gasping clamor of the children of Lithia, battering at his every mental citadel, all the way from Chtexa's house to his own.

The sudden fugue lasted only a few moments. He fought his way back to self-control to find that Agronski and Michelis had propped him up on a stool in the lab and were trying to remove his mackintosh without unbalancing him or awakening him—as difficult a problem in topology as removing a man's vest without taking off his jacket. Wearily, the priest pulled his own arm out of a mackintosh sleeve and looked up at Michelis.

"Good morning, Mike. Please excuse my bad manners."

"Don't be an idiot," Michelis said evenly. "You don't have to talk now, anyhow. I've already spent much of tonight trying to keep Cleaver quiet until he's better. Don't put me through it again, please, Ramon."

"I won't. I'm not ill; I'm just tired and a little overwrought."

"What's the matter with Cleaver?" Agronski demanded. Michelis made as if to shoo him off.

"No, no, Mike, it's a fair question. I'm all right, I assure you. As for Paul, he got a dose of glucoside poisoning when a plant spine stabbed him this afternoon. No, it's yesterday afternoon now. How has he been since you arrived?"

"He's sick," Michelis said. "Since you weren't here, we didn't know what to do for him. We settled for two of the pills you'd left out."

"You did?" Ruiz-Sanchez slid his feet heavily to the floor and tried to stand up. "As you say, you couldn't have known what else to do—but you did overdose him. I think I'd better look in on him—"

"Sit down, please, Ramon." Michelis spoke gently, but his tone showed that he meant the request to be honored. Obscurely glad to be forced to yield to the big man's well-meant implacability, the priest let himself be propped back on the stool. His boots fell off his feet to the floor.

"Mike, who's the Father here?" he asked tiredly. "Still, I'm sure you've done a good job. He's in no apparent danger?"

"Well, he seems pretty sick. But he had energy enough to keep himself awake most of the night. He only passed out a short while ago."

"Good. Let him stay out. Tomorrow we'll probably have to begin intravenous feeding, though. In this atmosphere one doesn't give a salicylate overdose without penalties." He sighed. "Since I'll be sleeping in the same room, I'll be on hand if there's a crisis. So. Can we put off further questions?"

"If there's nothing else wrong here, of course we can."

"Oh," Ruiz-Sanchez said, "there's a great deal wrong, I'm afraid."

"I knew it!" Agronski said. "I knew damn well there was. I told you so, Mike, didn't I?"

"Is it urgent?"

"No, Mike—there's no danger to us, of that I'm positive. It's nothing that won't keep until we've all had a rest. You two look as though you need one as badly as I."

"We're tired," Michelis agreed.

"But why didn't you ever call us?" Agronski burst in

aggrievedly. "You had us scared half to death, Father. If there's really something wrong here, you should have—"

"There's no immediate danger," Ruiz-Sanchez repeated patiently. "As for why we didn't call you, I don't understand that any more than you do. Up to last night, I thought we were in regular contact with you both. That was Paul's job and he seemed to be carrying it out. I didn't discover that he hadn't been doing it until after he became ill."

"Then obviously we'll have to wait for him," Michelis said. "Let's hit the hammock, in God's name. Flying that whirlybird through twenty-five hundred miles of fog banks wasn't exactly restful, either; I'll be glad to turn in. . . . But, Ramon—"

"Yes, Mike?"

"I have to say that I don't like this any better than Agronski does. Tomorrow we've got to clear it up, and get our commission business done. We've only a day or so to make our decision before the ship comes and takes us off Lithia for good, and by that time we *must* know everything there is to know, and just what we're going to tell the Earth about it."

"Yes," Ruiz-Sanchez said. "Just as you say, Mike—in God's name."

The Peruvian priest-biologist awoke before the others; actually, he had undergone far less purely physical strain than had the other three. It was just beginning to be cloudy dusk when he rolled out of his hammock and padded over to look at Cleaver.

The physicist was in coma. His face was a dirty gray, and looked oddly shrunken. It was high time that the neglect and inadvertent abuse to which he had been subjected was rectified. Happily, his pulse and respiration were close to normal now.

Ruiz-Sanchez went quietly into the lab and made up a fructose intravenous feeding. At the same time he reconstituted a can of powdered eggs into a sort of soufflé, setting it in a covered crucible to bake at the back of the little oven; that was for the rest of them.

In the sleeping chamber, the priest set up his I-V stand. Cleaver did not stir when the needle entered the big vein just above the inside of his elbow. Ruiz-Sanchez taped the tubing in place, checked the drip from the inverted bottle, and went back into the lab.

There he sat, on the stool before the microscope, in a sort of suspension of feeling while the new night drew on. He was still poisoned-tired, but at least now he could stay awake without constantly fighting himself. The slowly rising soufflé in the oven went *plup-plup*, *plup-plup*, and after a while a thin tendril of aroma suggested that it was beginning to brown on top, or at least thinking about it.

Outside, it abruptly rained buckets. Just as abruptly, it stopped. Lithia's short, hot summer was drawing to a close; its winter would be long and mild, the temperature never dropping below 20° centigrade in this latitude. Even at the poles the winter temperature stayed throughout well above freezing, usually averaging about 15° C.

"Is that breakfast I smell, Ramon?"

"Yes, Mike, in the oven. In a few minutes now."

"Right."

Michelis went away again. On the back of the workbench, Ruiz-Sanchez saw the dark blue book with the gold stamping which he had brought with him all the way from Earth. Almost automatically he pulled it to him, and almost automatically it fell open at page 573. It would at least give him something to think about with which he was not personally involved.

He had last quitted the text with Anita, who "would yield to the lewdness of Honuphrius to appease the savagery of Sulla and the mercenariness of the twelve Sullivani, and (as Gilbert at first suggested) to save the virginity of Felicia for Magravius"—now hold on a moment, how could Felicia still be considered a virgin at this point? Ah ". . . when converted by Michael after the death of Gillia"; that covered it, since Felicia had been guilty only of simple infidelities in the first place. ". . . but she fears that, by allowing his marital rights, she may cause reprehensible conduct between Eugenius and Jeremias. Michael, who has formerly debauched Anita, dispenses her from yielding to Honuphrius"—yes, that made sense, since Michael also had had designs on Eugenius. "Anita is disturbed, but Michael comminates that he will reserve her case tomorrow for the ordinary

Guglielmus even if she should practice a pious fraud during affrication, which, from experience, she knows (according to Wadding) to be leading to nullity."

Well. This was all very well. The novel even seemed to be shaping up into sense, for the first time; evidently the author had known exactly what he was doing, every step of the way. Still, Ruiz-Sanchez reflected, he would not like to have known the imaginary family hidden behind the conventional Latin aliases, or to have been the confessor to any member of it.

Yes, it added up, when one tried to view it without outrage either at the persons involved—they were, after all, fictitious, only characters in a novel—or at the author, who for all his mighty intellect, easily the greatest ever devoted to fiction in English and perhaps in any language, had still to be pitied as much as the meanest victim of the Evil One. To view it, as it were, in a sort of gray twilight of emotion, wherein everything, even the barnacle-like commentaries the text had accumulated since it had been begun in the 1920's, could be seen in the same light.

"Is it done, Father?"

"Smells like it, Agronski. Take it out and help yourself, why don't you?"

"Thanks. Can I bring Cleaver—"

"No, he's getting an I-V."

"Check."

Unless his impression that he understood the problem at last was once more going to turn out to be an illusion, he was now ready for the basic question, the stumper that had deeply disturbed both the Order and the Church for so many decades now. He reread it carefully. It asked:

"Has he hegemony and shall she submit?"

To his astonishment, he saw as if for the first time that it was two questions, despite the omission of a comma between the two. And so it demanded two answers. Did Honuphrius have hegemony? Yes, he did, because Michael, the only member of the whole complex who had been gifted from the beginning with the power of grace, had been egregiously compromised. Therefore, Honuphrius, regardless of whether all his sins were to be laid at his door or were real only in rumor, could not be divested of his privileges by anyone.

But should Anita submit? No, she should not. Michael had forfeited his right to dispense or to reserve her in any way, and so she could not be guided by the curate or by anyone else in the long run but her own conscience—which in view of the grave accusations against Honuphrius could lead her to no recourse but to deny him. As for Sulla's repentance, and Felicia's conversion, they meant nothing, since the defection of Michael had deprived both of them—and everyone else—of spiritual guidance.

The answer, then, had been obvious all the time. It was:

Yes, and No.

And it had hung throughout upon putting a comma in the right place. A writer's joke. A demonstration that it could take one of the greatest novelists of all time seventeen years to write a book the central problem of which is exactly where to put one comma; thus does the Adversary cloak his emptiness, and empty his votaries.

Ruiz-Sanchez closed the book with a shudder and looked up across the bench, feeling neither more nor less dazed than he had before, but with a small stirring of elation deep inside him which he could not suppress. In the eternal wrestling, the Adversary had taken another fall.

As he looked dazedly out of the window into the dripping darkness, a familiar, sculpturesque head and shoulders moved into the truncated tetrahedron of yellow light being cast out through the fine glass into the rain. Ruiz-Sanchez awoke with a start. The head was Chtexa's, moving away from the house.

Suddenly Ruiz-Sanchez realized that nobody had bothered to rub away the sickness ideograms on the door tablet. If Chtexa had come here on some errand, he had been turned back unnecessarily. The priest leaned forward, snatched up an empty slide box, and rapped with a corner of it against the inside of the glass.

Chtexa turned and looked in through the streaming curtains of rain, his eyes completely filmed against the downpour. Ruiz-Sanchez beckoned to him, and got stiffly off the stool to open the door.

In the oven the priest's share of breakfast dried slowly and began to burn.

The rapping on the window had summoned forth Agronski

and Michelis as well. Chtexa looked down at the three of them
with easy gravity, while drops of water ran like oil down the
minute, prismatic scales of his supple skin.

"I did not know that there was sickness here," the Lithian
said. "I called because your brother Ruiz-Sanchez left my
house this morning without the gift I had hoped to give him.
I will leave if I am invading your privacy in any way."

"You are not," Ruiz-Sanchez assured him. "And the sickness
is only a poisoning, not communicable and we think not likely
to end badly for our colleague. These are my friends from the
north, Agronski and Michelis."

"I am happy to see them. The message was not in vain, then?"

"What message is this?" Michelis said, in his pure but hesi-
tant Lithian.

"I sent a message, as your colleague Ruiz-Sanchez asked me
to do, last night. I was told by Xoredeshch Gton you had already departed."

"As we had," Michelis said. "Ramon, what's this? I thought
you told us that sending messages was Paul's job. And you
certainly implied that you didn't know how to do it yourself,
after Paul took sick."

"I didn't. I don't. I asked Chtexa to send it for me; he just
finished telling you that, Mike."

Michelis looked up at the Lithian.

"What did the message say?" he asked.

"That you were to join them now, here, at Xoredeshch Sfath.
And that your time on our world was almost up."

"What does that mean?" Agronski said. He had been trying
to follow the conversation, but he was not much of a linguist,
and evidently the few words he had been able to pick up had
served only to inflame his ready fears. "Mike, translate, please."

Michelis did so, briefly. Then he said:

"Ramon, was that really all you had to say to us, especially
after what you had found out? We knew that departure time
was coming, too, after all. We can keep a calendar as well as the
next man, I hope."

"I know that, Mike. But I had no idea what previous messages you'd received, if indeed you'd received any. For all I
knew, Cleaver might have been in touch with you some other
way, privately. I thought first of a transmitter in his personal

luggage, but later it occurred to me that he might have been sending dispatches over the regular jet liners; that would have been easier. He might have told you that we were going to stay on beyond the official departure time. Or he might have told you that I had been killed and that he was looking for the murderer. He might have told you anything. I had to make sure, as well as I could, that you'd arrive here *regardless* of what he had or had not said.

"And when I got to the local message center, I had to do all this message-revision on the spot, because I found that I couldn't communicate with you directly, or send anything that was at all detailed, anything that might have been garbled through being translated and passed through alien minds. Everything that goes out from Xoredeshch Sfath by radio goes out through the Tree, and until you've seen it you haven't any idea what an Earthman is up against there in sending even the simplest message."

"Is this true?" Michelis asked Chtexa.

"True?" Chtexa repeated. His wattles were stippled with confusion; though Ruiz-Sanchez and Michelis had both reverted to Lithian, there were a number of words they had used, such as "murderer," which simply did not exist in the Lithian language, and so had been thrown out hastily in English. "True? I do not know. Do you mean, is it valid? You must be the judge of that."

"But is it accurate, sir?"

"It is accurate," Chtexa said, "insofar as I understand it."

"Well, then," Ruiz-Sanchez, a little nettled despite himself, went on, "you can see why, when Chtexa appeared providentially in the Tree, recognized me, and offered to act as an intermediary, I had to give him only the gist of what I had to say. I couldn't hope to explain all the details to him, and I couldn't hope that any of those details would get to you undistorted after they'd passed through at least two Lithian intermediaries. All I could do was shout at the top of my voice for you two to get down here on the proper date—and hope that you'd hear me."

"This is a time of trouble, which is like a sickness in the house," Chtexa said. "I must not remain. I will wish to be left alone when I am troubled, and I cannot ask that, if I now force my presence on others who are troubled. I will bring my gift at a better time."

He ducked out through the door, without any formal gesture of farewell, but nevertheless leaving behind an overwhelming impression of graciousness. Ruiz-Sanchez watched him go helplessly, and a little forlornly. The Lithians always seemed to understand the essences of situations; they were never, unlike even the most cocksure of Earthmen, beset by the least apparent doubt. They had no night thoughts.

And why should they have? They were backed—if Ruiz-Sanchez was right—by the second-best Authority in the universe, and backed directly, without intermediary churches or conflicts of interpretations. The very fact that they were never tormented by indecision identified them as creatures of that Authority. Only the children of God had been given free will, and hence were often doubtful.

Nevertheless, Ruiz-Sanchez would have delayed Chtexa's departure had he been able. In a short-term argument it is helpful to have pure reason on your side—even though such an ally could be depended upon to stab you to the heart if you depended upon him too long.

"Let's go inside and thrash this thing out," Michelis said, shutting the door and turning back toward the front room. He spoke in Lithian still, and acknowledged it with a wry grimace over his shoulder after the departed Chtexa before switching to English. "It's a good thing we got some sleep, but we have so little time left now that it's going to be touch-and-go to have a formal decision ready when the ship comes."

"We can't go ahead yet," Agronski objected, although along with Ruiz-Sanchez, he followed Michelis obediently enough. "How can we do anything sensible without having heard what Cleaver has to say? Every man's voice counts on a job of this sort."

"That's very true," Michelis said. "And I don't like the present situation any better than you do—I've already said that. But I don't see that we have any choice. What do you think, Ramon?"

"I'd like to hold out for waiting," Ruiz-Sanchez said frankly. "Anything I may say now is, to put it realistically, somewhat compromised with you two. And don't tell me that you have every confidence in my integrity, because we had every confidence in Cleaver's, too. Right now, trying to maintain both confidences just cancels out both."

"You have a nasty way, Ramon, of saying aloud what everybody else is thinking," Michelis said, grinning bleakly. "What alternatives do you see, then?"

"None," Ruiz-Sanchez admitted. "Time is against us, as you said. We'll just have to go ahead without Cleaver."

"No you won't."

The voice, from the doorway to the sleeping chamber, was at once both uncertain and much harshened by weakness.

The others sprang up. Cleaver, clad only in his shorts, stood in the doorway, clinging to both sides of it. On one of his forearms Ruiz-Sanchez could see the marks where the adhesive tape which had held the I-V needle had been ripped away. Where the needle itself had been inserted, an ugly haematoma swelled bluely under the gray skin of Cleaver's upper arm.

VI

(*A silence.*)

"Paul, you must be crazy," Michelis said suddenly, almost angrily. "Get back into your hammock before you make things twice as bad for yourself. You're a sick man, can't you realize that?"

"Not as sick as I look," Cleaver said, with a ghastly grin. "Actually I feel pretty fair. My mouth is almost all cleared up, and I don't think I've got any fever. And I'll be damned if this commission is going to proceed one single damned inch without me. It isn't empowered to do it, and I'll appeal any decision —*any* decision, I hope you guys are listening—that it makes without me."

The commission was listening; the recorder had already been started, and the unalterable tapes were running into their sealed cans. The other two men turned dubiously to Ruiz-Sanchez.

"How about it, Ramon?" Michelis said, frowning. He shut off the recorder with his key. "Is it safe for him to be up like this?"

Ruiz-Sanchez was already at the physicist's side, peering into his mouth. The ulcers were indeed almost gone, with granulation tissue forming nicely over the few that still remained. Cleaver's eyes were still slightly suffused, indicating that the toxemia was not completely defeated, but except for these two signs the effect of the accidental squill inoculation was no longer visible. It was true that Cleaver looked awful, but that was inevitable in a man quite recently sick, and in one who had been burning his own body proteins for fuel to boot. As for the haematoma, a cold compress would fix that.

"If he wants to endanger himself, I guess he's got a right to do so, at least by indirection," Ruiz-Sanchez said. "Paul, the first thing you'll have to do is get off your feet, and get into a robe, and put a blanket around your legs. Then you'll have to eat something; I'll fix it for you. You've staged a wonderful recovery, but you're a sitting duck for a real infection if you abuse your time during convalescence."

"I'll compromise," Cleaver said immediately. "I don't want to be a hero, I just want to be heard. Give me a hand over to that hassock. I still don't walk very straight."

It took the better part of half an hour to get Cleaver settled to Ruiz-Sanchez' satisfaction. The physicist seemed in a wry way to be enjoying every minute of it. At last he had in his hand a mug of *gchteht*, a local herb tea so delicious that it would probably become a major article of export before long, and he said:

"All right, Mike, turn on the recorder and let's go."

"Are you sure?" Michelis said.

"One hundred per cent. Turn the goddam key."

Michelis turned the key, took it out and put it in his pocket. From now on, they were on the record.

"All right, Paul," Michelis said. "You've gone out of your way to put yourself on the spot. Evidently that's where you want to be. So let's have the answer: Why didn't you communicate with us?"

"I didn't want to."

"Now wait a minute," Agronski said. "Paul, you're going on record; don't break your neck to say the first damn thing that comes into your head. Your judgment may not be well yet, even if your talking apparatus is. Wasn't your silence just a matter of your being unable to work the local message system—the Tree or whatever it is?"

"No, it wasn't," Cleaver insisted. "Thanks, Agronski, but I don't need to be shepherded down the safe and easy road, or have any alibis set up for me. I know exactly what I did that was ticklish, and I know that it's going to be impossible for me to set up consistent alibis for it now. My chances for keeping anything under my hat depended upon my staying in complete control of everything I did. Naturally those chances went out the window when I got stuck by that damned pineapple. I realized that last night, when I fought like a demon to get through to you before the Father could get back, and found that I couldn't make it."

"You seem to take it calmly enough now," Michelis observed.

"Well, I'm feeling a little washed out. But I'm a realist. And I also know, Mike, that I had damned good reasons for what I did. I'm counting on the chance that you'll agree with me wholeheartedly, when I tell you why I did it."

"All right," Michelis said, "begin."

Cleaver sat back, folding his hands quietly in the lap of his robe. He looked almost ecclesiastical. He was obviously still enjoying the situation. He said:

"First of all, I didn't call you because I didn't want to, as I said. I could have mastered the problem of the Tree easily enough by doing what the Father did—that is, by getting a Snake to ferry my messages. Of course I don't speak Snake, but the Father does, so all I had to do was to take him into my confidence. Barring that, I could have mastered the Tree itself. I already know all the technical problems involved. Mike, wait till you see that Tree. Essentially it's a single-junction transistor, with the semi-conductor supplied by a huge lump of crystal buried under it; the crystal is piezoelectric and emits in the RF spectrum every time the Tree's roots stress it. It's fantastic—nothing like it anywhere else in this galaxy, I'd lay money on that.

"But I wanted a gap to spring up between our party and yours. I wanted both of you to be completely in the dark about what was going on, down here on this continent. I wanted you to imagine the worst, and blame it on the Snakes, too, if that could be managed. After you got here—if you did—I was going to be able to show you that I hadn't sent any messages because the Snakes wouldn't let me. I've got more plants to that effect squirreled away around here than I'll bother to list now; besides, there'd be no point in it, since it's all come to nothing. But I'm sure that it would have looked conclusive, regardless of anything the Father would have been able to offer to the contrary."

"Are you sure you don't want me to turn off the machine?" Michelis said quietly.

"Oh, throw away your damned key, will you, and listen. From my point of view it was just a bloody shame that I had to run up against a pineapple at the last minute. It gave the Father a chance to find out something about what was up. I'll swear that if that hadn't happened, he wouldn't have smelt anything until you actually got here—and by then it would have been too late."

"I probably wouldn't have, that's true," Ruiz-Sanchez said, watching Cleaver steadily. "But your running up against that 'pineapple' was no accident. If you'd been observing Lithia as you were sent here to do, instead of spending all your time building up a fictitious Lithia for purposes of your own, you'd have known enough about the planet to have been more careful about 'pineapples.' You'd also have spoken at least as much Lithian as Agronski, by this time."

"That," Cleaver said, "is probably true, and again it doesn't make any difference to me. I observed the one fact about Lithia that overrides all other facts, and that is going to turn out to be sufficient. Unlike you, Father, I have no respect for petty niceties in extreme situations, and I'm not the kind of man who thinks anyone learns anything from analysis after the fact."

"Let's not get to bickering this early," Michelis said. "You've told us your story without any visible decoration, and it's evident that you have a reason for confessing. You expect us to excuse you, or at least not to blame you too heavily, when you tell us what that reason is. Let's hear it."

"It's this," Cleaver said, and for the first time he seemed to become a little more animated. He leaned forward, the glowing gaslight bringing the bones of his face into sharp contrast with the sagging hollows of his cheeks, and pointed a not-quite-steady finger at Michelis.

"Do you know, Mike, what it is that we're sitting on here? Just to begin with, do you know how much rutile there is here?"

"Of course I know," Michelis said. "Agronski told me, and since then I've been working on practicable methods of refining the ore. If we decide to vote for opening the planet up, our titanium problem will be solved for a century, maybe even longer. I'm saying as much in my personal report. But what of it? We anticipated that that would be true even before we first landed here, as soon as we got accurate figures on the mass of the planet."

"And what about the pegmatite?" Cleaver demanded softly.

"Well, what about it?" Michelis said, looking more puzzled than before. "I suppose it's abundant—I really didn't bother to check. Titanium's important to us, but I don't quite see why lithium should be. The days when the metal was used as a rocket fuel are fifty years behind us."

"And a good thing, too," Agronski said. "Those old Li-Fluor engines used to go off like war heads. One little leak in the feed lines, and bloo-*ey!*"

"And yet the metal's still worth about twenty thousand dollars an English ton back home, Mike, and that's exactly the same price it was drawing in the nineteen-sixties, allowing for currency changes since then. Doesn't that mean anything to you?"

"I'm more interested in knowing what it means to you," Michelis said. "None of us can make a personal penny out of this trip, even if we find the planet solid platinum inside—which is hardly likely. And if price is the only consideration, surely the fact that lithium ore is common here will break the market for it. What's it good for, after all, on a large scale?"

"Bombs," Cleaver said. "Real bombs. Fusion bombs. It's no good for controlled fusion, for power, but the deuterium salt makes the prettiest multimegaton explosion you ever saw."

Ruiz-Sanchez suddenly felt sick and tired all over again. It was exactly what he had feared had been on Cleaver's mind; given a planet named Lithia only because it appeared to be mostly rock, and a certain kind of mind will abandon every other concern to find a metal called lithium on it. But he had not wanted to find himself right.

"Paul," he said, "I've changed my mind. I would have caught you out, even if you had never blundered against your 'pineapple.' That same day you mentioned to me that you were looking for pegmatite when you had your accident, and that you thought Lithia might be a good place for tritium production on a large scale. Evidently you thought that I wouldn't know what you were talking about. If you hadn't hit the 'pineapple,' you would have given yourself away to me before now by talk like that. Your estimate of me was based on as little observation as is your estimate of Lithia."

"It's easy," Cleaver observed indulgently, "to say 'I knew it all the time'—especially on a tape."

"Of course it's easy, when the other man is helping you," Ruiz-Sanchez said. "But I think that your view of Lithia as a potential cornucopia of hydrogen bombs is only the beginning of what you have in mind. I don't believe that it's even your real objective. What you would like most is to see Lithia removed from the universe as far as you're concerned. You hate the place. It's injured you. You'd like to think that it doesn't really exist. Hence the emphasis on Lithia as a source of munitions, to the exclusion of every other fact about the planet; for if that emphasis wins out, Lithia will be placed under security seal. Isn't that right?"

"Of course it's right, except for the phony mind reading," Cleaver said contemptuously. "When even a priest can see it, it's got to be obvious—and it's got to be written off by impugning the motives of the man who saw it first. To hell with that. Mike, listen to me. This is the most tremendous opportunity that any commission has ever had. This planet is made to order to be converted, root and branch, into a thermonuclear laboratory and production center. It has indefinitely large supplies of the most important raw materials. What's even more important, it has no nuclear knowledge of its own for us to worry about. All the clue materials, the radioactive elements and so on, which you need to work out real knowledge of the atom, we'll have to import; the Snakes don't know a thing about them. Furthermore, the instruments involved, the counters and particle-accelerators and so on, all depend on materials like iron that the Snakes don't have, and on principles that they don't know, ranging all the way from magnetism to quantum mechanics. We'll be able to stock our plants here with an immense reservoir of cheap labor which doesn't know, and—if we take proper precautions—never will have a prayer of learning enough to snitch classified techniques.

"All we need to do is to turn in a triple-E Unfavorable on the planet, to shut off any use of Lithia as a way station or any other kind of general base for a whole century. At the same time, we can report separately to the UN Review Committee exactly what we do have in Lithia: a triple-A arsenal for the whole of Earth, for the whole commonwealth of planets we control! Only the decision becomes general administrative property back home; the tape is protected; it's an opportunity it'd be a crime to flub!"

"Against whom?" Ruiz-Sanchez said.

"Eh? You've lost me."

"Against whom are you stocking this arsenal? Why do we need a whole planet devoted to nothing but making fusion bombs?"

"The UN can use weapons," Cleaver said drily. "The time isn't very far gone since there were still a few restive nations on Earth, and it could come around again. Don't forget also that thermonuclear weapons last only a few years—they can't be stock-piled indefinitely, like fission bombs. The half-life of tritium is very short, and lithium-6 isn't very long-lived either. I suppose you wouldn't know anything about that. But take my word for it, the UN police would be glad to know that they could have access to a virtually inexhaustible stock of fusion bombs, and to hell with the shelf-life problem!

"Besides, if you've thought about it at all, you know as well as I do that this endless consolidation of peaceful planets can't go on forever. Sooner or later—well, what happens if the next planet we touch down on is a place like Earth? If it is, its inhabitants may fight, and fight like a planetful of madmen, to stay *out* of our frame of influence. Or what happens if the next planet we hit is an outpost for a whole federation, maybe bigger than ours? When that day comes—and it will, it's in the cards—we'll be damned glad if we're able to plaster the enemy from pole to pole with fusion bombs, and clean up the matter with as little loss of life as possible."

"On our side," Ruiz-Sanchez added.

"Is there any other side?"

"By golly, that makes sense to me," Agronski said. "Mike, what do you think?"

"I'm not sure yet," Michelis said. "Paul, I still don't understand why you thought it necessary to go through all the cloak-and-dagger maneuvers. You tell your story fairly enough now, and it has its merits, but you also admit you were going to trick the three of us into going along with you, if you could. Why? Couldn't you trust the force of your argument alone?"

"No," Cleaver said bluntly. "I've never been on a commission like this before, where there was no single, definite chairman, where there was deliberately an even number of members so that a split opinion couldn't be settled if it occurred—and where the voice of a man whose head is filled with Pecksniffian, irrelevant moral distinctions and three-thousand-year old metaphysics carries the same weight as the voice of a scientist."

"That's mighty loaded language, Paul," Michelis said.

"I know it. If it comes to that, I'll say here or anywhere that I think the Father is a hell of a fine biologist. I've seen him in operation, and they don't come any better—and for that matter he may have just finished saving my life, for all any of the rest of us can tell. That makes him a scientist like the rest of us—insofar as biology's a science."

"Thank you," Ruiz-Sanchez said. "With a little history in your education, Paul, you would also have known that the Jesuits were among the first explorers to enter China, and Paraguay, and the North American wilderness. Then it would have been no surprise to you to find me here."

"That may well be. However, it has nothing to do with the paradox as I see it. I remember once visiting the labs at Notre Dame, where they have a complete little world of germ-free animals and plants and have pulled I don't know how many physiological miracles out of the hat. I wondered then how a man goes about being as good a scientist as that, and a good Catholic at the same time—or any other kind of churchman. I wondered in which compartment in their brains they filed their religion, and in which their science. I'm still wondering."

"They're not compartmented," Ruiz-Sanchez said. "They are a single whole."

"So you said, when I brought this up before. That answers nothing; in fact, it convinced me that what I was planning to do was absolutely necessary. I didn't propose to take any chances on the compartments getting interconnected on Lithia. I had every intention of cutting the Father down to a point where his voice would be nearly ignored by the rest of you. That's why I undertook the cloak-and-dagger stuff. Maybe it was stupidly done—I suppose that it takes training to be a successful agent-provocateur and that I should have realized that."

Ruiz-Sanchez wondered what Cleaver's reaction would be when he found, as he would very shortly now, that his purpose would have been accomplished without his having to lift a finger. Of course the dedicated man of science, working for the greater glory of man, could anticipate nothing but failure; that was the fallibility of man. But would Cleaver be able to understand, through his ordeal, what had happened to Ruiz-Sanchez when he had discovered the fallibility of God? It seemed unlikely.

"But I'm not sorry I tried," Cleaver was saying. *"I'm only sorry I failed."*

VII

THERE was a short, painful hiatus.

"Is that it, then?" Michelis said.

"That's it, Mike. Oh—one more thing. My vote, if anybody is still in any doubt about it, is to keep the planet closed. Take it from there."

"Ramon," Michelis said, "do you want to speak next? You're certainly entitled to it, on a point of personal privilege. The air's a mite murky at the moment, I'm afraid."

"No, Mike. Let's hear from you."

"I'm not ready to speak yet either, unless the majority wants me to. Agronski, how about you?"

"Sure," Agronski said. "Speaking as a geologist, and also as an ordinary slob that doesn't follow rarefied reasoning very well, I'm on Cleaver's side. I don't see anything either for or against the planet on any other grounds but Cleaver's. It's a fair planet as planets go, very quiet, not very rich in anything else we need—sure, that *gchteht* is marvelous stuff, but it's strictly for the luxury trade—and not subject to any kind of trouble that I've been able to detect. It'd make a good way station, but so would lots of other worlds hereabouts.

"It'd also make a good arsenal, the way Cleaver defines the term. In every other category it's as dull as ditch water, and it's got plenty of that. The only other thing it can have to offer is titanium, which isn't quite as scarce back home these days as Mike seems to think; and gem stones, particularly the semiprecious ones, which we can make at home without traveling fifty light-years to get them. I'd say, either set up a way station here and forget about the planet otherwise, or else handle the place as Cleaver suggested."

"But which?" Ruiz-Sanchez asked.

"Well, which is more important, Father? Aren't way stations a dime a dozen? Planets that can be used as thermonuclear labs, on the other hand, are rare—Lithia is the *first* one that can be used that way, at least in my experience. Why use a planet for a routine purpose if it's unique? Why not apply Occam's Razor—the law of parsimony? It works on every other scientific problem anybody's ever tackled. It's my bet that it's the best tool to use on this one."

"Occam's Razor isn't a natural law," Ruiz-Sanchez said. "It's only a heuristic convenience—in short, a learning gimmick. And besides, Agronski, it calls for the simplest solution of the problem that will fit all the facts. You don't have all the facts, not by a long shot."

"All right, show me," Agronski said piously. "I've got an open mind."

"You vote to close the planet, then," Michelis said.

"Sure. That's what I was saying, wasn't it, Mike?"

"I wanted to have it Yes or No for the tape," Michelis said. "Ramon, I guess it's up to us. Shall I speak first? I think I'm ready."

"Of course, Mike."

"Then," Michelis said evenly, and without changing in the slightest his accustomed tone of grave impartiality, "I'll say that I think both of these gentlemen are fools, and calamitous fools at that because they're supposed to be scientists. Paul, your maneuvers to set up a phony situation are perfectly beneath contempt, and I shan't mention them again. I shan't even appeal to have them cut from the tape, so you needn't feel that you have to mend any fences with me. I'm looking solely at the purpose those maneuvers were supposed to serve, just as you asked me to do."

Cleaver's obvious self-satisfaction began to dim a little around the edges. He said, "Go ahead," and wound the blanket a little bit tighter around his legs.

"Lithia is not even the beginning of an arsenal," Michelis said. "Every piece of evidence you offered to prove that it might be is either a half-truth or the purest trash. Take cheap labor, for instance. With what will you pay the Lithians? They have no money, and they can't be rewarded with goods. They have almost everything that they need, and they like the way they're living right now—God knows they're not even slightly jealous of the achievements we think make Earth great. They'd like to have space flight but, given a little time, they'll get it by themselves; they have the Coupling ion-jet right now, and they won't be needing the Haertel overdrive for another century."

He looked around the gently rounded room, which was shining softly in the gaslight.

"And I don't seem to see any place in here," he said, "where a vacuum cleaner with forty-five patented attachments would find any work to do. How will you pay the Lithians to work in your thermonuclear plants?"

"With knowledge," Cleaver said gruffly. "There's a lot they'd like to know."

"But what knowledge, Paul? The things they'd like to know are specifically the things you can't tell them, if they're to be valuable to you as a labor force. Are you going to teach them quantum mechanics? You can't; that would be dangerous. Are you going to teach them nucleonics, or Hilbert space, or the Haertel scholium? Again, any one of those would enable them to learn other things you think dangerous. Are you going to teach them how to extract titanium from rutile, or how to accumulate enough iron to develop a science of electrodynamics, or how to pass from this Stone Age they're living in now—this Pottery Age, I should say—into an Age of Plastics? Of course you aren't. As a matter of fact, we don't have a thing to offer them in that sense. It'd all be classified under the arrangement you propose—and they just wouldn't work for us under those terms."

"Offer them other terms," Cleaver said shortly. "If necessary, tell them what they're going to do, like it or lump it. It'd be easy enough to introduce a money system on this planet. You give a Snake a piece of paper that says it's worth a dollar, and if he asks you just what makes it worth a dollar—well, the answer is, an honest day's work."

"And we put a machine pistol to his belly to emphasize the point," Ruiz-Sanchez interjected.

"Do we make machine pistols for nothing? I never figured out what else they were good for. Either you point them at someone or you throw them away."

"Item: slavery," Michelis said. "That disposes, I think, of the argument of cheap labor. I won't vote for slavery. Ramon won't. Agronski?"

"No," Agronski said uneasily. "But isn't it a minor point?"

"The hell it is! It's the reason why we're here. We're supposed to think of the welfare of the Lithians as well as of ourselves—otherwise this commission procedure would be a waste of time, of thought, of energy. If we want cheap labor, we can enslave any planet."

"How do we do that?" Agronski said. "There aren't any other planets. I mean, none with intelligent life on them that we've hit so far. You can't enslave a Martian sand crab."

"Which brings up the point of our own welfare," Ruiz-Sanchez said. "We're supposed to be considering that, too. Do you know what it does to a people to be slave-owners? It kills them."

"Lots of people have worked for money without calling it slavery," Agronski said. "I don't mind getting a pay check for what I do."

"There is no money on Lithia," Michelis said stonily. "If we introduce it here, we do so only by force. Forced labor is slavery. Q. E. D."

Agronski was silent.

"Speak up," Michelis said. "Is that true, or isn't it?"

Agronski said, "I guess it is. Take it easy, Mike. There's nothing to get mad about."

"Cleaver?"

"Slavery's just a swearword," Cleaver said sullenly. "You're deliberately clouding the issue."

"Say that again."

"Oh, hell. All right, Mike, I know you wouldn't. But we could work out a fair pay scale somehow."

"I'll admit that the instant that you can demonstrate it to me," Michelis said. He got up abruptly from his hassock, walked over to the sloping window sill, and sat down again, looking out into the rain-stippled darkness. He seemed to be more deeply troubled than Ruiz-Sanchez had ever before thought possible for him. The priest was astonished, as much at himself as at Michelis; the argument from money had never occurred to him, and Michelis had unknowingly put his finger on a doctrinal sore spot which Ruiz-Sanchez had never been able to reconcile with his own beliefs. He remembered the lines of poetry that had summed it up for him—lines written way back in the 1950's:

The groggy old Church has gone toothless,
No longer holds against neshek; *the fat has covered their*
   croziers. . . .

Neshek was the lending of money at interest, once a sin called usury, for which Dante had put men into Hell. And now here was Mike, not a Christian at all, arguing that money itself was a form of slavery. It was, Ruiz-Sanchez discovered upon fingering it mentally once more, a *very* sore spot.

"In the meantime," Michelis had resumed, "I'll prosecute my own demonstration. What's to be said, now, about this theory of automatic security that you've propounded, Paul? You think that the Lithians can't learn the techniques they would need to be able to understand secret information and pass it on, and so they won't have to be screened. There again, you're wrong, as you'd have known if you'd bothered to study the Lithians even perfunctorily. The Lithians are highly intelligent, and they already have many of the clues they need. I've given them a hand toward pinning down magnetism, and they absorbed the material like magic and put it to work with enormous ingenuity."

"So did I," Ruiz-Sanchez said. "And I've suggested to them a technique for accumulating iron that should prove to be pretty powerful. I had only to suggest it, and they were already halfway down to the bottom of it and traveling fast. They can make the most of the smallest of clues."

"If I were the UN I'd regard both actions as the plainest kind of treason," Cleaver said harshly. "You'd better think again about using that key, Mike, on your own behalf—if it isn't already too late. Isn't it possible that the Snakes found out both items by themselves, and were only being polite to you?"

"Set me no traps," Michelis said. "The tape is on and it stays on, by your own request. If you have any second thoughts, file them in your individual report, but don't try to stampede me into hiding anything under the rug now, Paul. It won't work."

"That," Cleaver said, "is what I get for trying to help."

"If that's what you were trying to do, thanks. I'm not through, however. So far as the practical objective that you want to achieve is concerned, Paul, I think it's just as useless as it is impossible. The fact that we have here a planet that's especially rich in lithium doesn't mean that we're sitting on a bonanza, no matter what price per ton the metal commands back home.

"The fact of the matter is that you can't ship lithium home. Its density is so low that you couldn't send away more than a ton of it per shipload; by the time you got it to Earth, the shipping charges on it would more than outweigh the price you'd get for it on arrival. I should have thought that you'd know there's lots of lithium on Earth's own moon, too—and it isn't economical to fly it back to Earth even over that short a distance, less than a quarter of a million miles. Lithia is three hundred and fourteen trillion miles from Earth; that's what fifty light-years comes to. Not even radium is worth carrying over a gap that great!

"No more would it be economical to ship from Earth to Lithia all the heavy equipment that would be needed to make use of lithium here. There's no iron here for massive magnets. By the time you got your particle-accelerators and mass chromatographs and the rest of your needs to Lithia, you'd have cost the UN so much that no amount of locally available pegmatite could compensate for it. Isn't that so, Agronski?"

"I'm no physicist," Agronski said, frowning slightly. "But just getting the metal out of the ore and storing it would cost a fair sum, that's a cinch. Raw lithium would burn like phosphorus in this atmosphere; you'd have to store it and work it under oil. That's costly no matter how you look at it."

Michelis looked from Cleaver to Agronski and back again.

"Exactly so," he said. "And that's only the beginning. In fact, the whole scheme is just a chimera."

"Have you got a better one, Mike?" Cleaver said, very quietly.

"I hope so. It seems to me that we have a lot to learn from the Lithians, as well as they from us. Their social system works like the most perfect of our physical mechanisms, and it does so without any apparent repression of the individual. It's a thoroughly liberal society in terms of guarantees, yet all the same it never even begins to tip over toward the side of total disorganization, toward the kind of Gandhiism that keeps a people tied to the momma-and-poppa farm and the roving-brigand distribution system. It's in balance, and not in precarious balance either—it's in perfect chemical equilibrium.

"The notion of using Lithia as a fusion-bomb plant is easily the strangest anachronism I've ever encountered—it's as crude as proposing to equip an interstellar ship with galley slaves, oars and all. Right here on Lithia is the *real* secret, the secret that's going to make bombs of all kinds, and all the rest of the antisocial armament, as useless, unnecessary, obsolete as the iron boot!

"And on top of all of that—no, please, I'm not quite finished, Paul—on top of all that, the Lithians are decades ahead of us in some purely technical matters, just as we're ahead of them in others. You should see what they can do with mixed disciplines —scholia like histochemistry, immunodynamics, biophysics, terataxonomy, osmotic genetics, electrolimnology, and half a hundred more. If you'd been looking, you *would* have seen.

"We have much more to do, it seems to me, than just to vote to open the planet. That's only a passive move. We have to realize that being able to use Lithia is only the beginning. The fact of the matter is that we actively *need* Lithia. We should say so in our recommendation."

Michelis unfolded himself from the window sill and stood up, looking down on all of them, but most especially at Ruiz-Sanchez. The priest smiled at him, but as much in anguish as in admiration, and then had to look back down at his shoes.

"Well, Agronski?" Cleaver said, spitting the words out like bullets on which he had been clenching his teeth, like a Civil War casualty during an operation without anesthetics. "What d'you say now? Do you like the pretty picture?"

"Sure, I like it," Agronski said, slowly but forthrightly. It was a virtue in him, as well as a frequent source of exasperation, that he always said exactly what he was thinking, the moment he was asked to do so. "Mike makes sense. I wouldn't expect him not to, if you see what I mean. Also he's got another advantage: he told us what he thought, *without* trying to trick us first into his way of thinking."

"Oh, don't be a thumphead," Cleaver exclaimed. "Are we scientists or Boy Rangers? Any rational man up against a majority of do-gooders would have taken the same precautions I did."

"Maybe," Agronski said. "I'm none too sure. Why is it silly to be a do-gooder? Is it wrong to do good? Do you want to be a do-badder—whatever the hell that is? Your precautions still smell to me like a confession of weakness somewhere in the argument. As for me, I don't like to be finessed. And I don't much like being called a thumphead, either."

"Oh, for Christ's sake—"

"Now-you-listen-to-me," Agronski said, all in one breath. "Before you call me any more names, I'm going to say that I think you're more right than Mike is. I don't like your methods, but your aim seems sensible to me. Mike's shot some of your major arguments full of holes, that I'll admit. But as far as I'm concerned, you're still leading—by a nose."

He paused, breathing heavily and glaring at the physicist. Then he said:

"By a nose, Paul. That's all. Just bear that in mind."

Michelis remained standing for a moment longer. Then he shrugged, walked back to his hassock, and sat down, locking his hands awkwardly between his knees.

"I did my best, Ramon," he said. "But so far it looks like a draw. See what you can do."

Ruiz-Sanchez took a deep breath. What he was about to do

would hurt him, without doubt, for the rest of his life, regardless of the way time had of turning any blade. The decision had already cost him many hours of concentrated, agonized doubt. But he believed that it had to be done.

"I disagree with all of you," he said, "except Cleaver. I believe, as he does, that Lithia should be reported triple-E Unfavorable. But I think also that it should be given a special classification: X-One."

Michelis' eyes were glazed with shock. Even Cleaver seemed unable to credit what he had heard.

"X-One—but that's a quarantine label," Michelis said huskily. "As a matter of fact—"

"Yes, Mike, that's right," Ruiz-Sanchez said. "I vote to seal Lithia off from *all* contact with the human race. Not only now, or for the next century—but forever."

VIII

FOREVER.

The word did not produce the consternation that he had been dreading—or, perhaps, hoping for, somewhere in the back of his mind. Evidently they were all too tired for that. They took his announcement with a kind of stunned emptiness, as though it were so far out of the expected order of events as to be quite meaningless.

It was hard to say whether Cleaver or Michelis was the more overwhelmed. All that could be seen for certain was that Agronski recovered first, and was now ostentatiously reaming out his ears, as if in signal that he would be ready to listen again when Ruiz-Sanchez changed his mind.

"Well," Cleaver began. And then again, shaking his head amazedly, like an old man: "Well. . . ."

"Tell us why, Ramon," Michelis said, clenching and unclenching his fists. His voice was quite flat, but Ruiz-Sanchez thought he could feel the pain under it.

"Of course. But I warn you, I'm going to be very roundabout. What I have to say seems to me to be of the utmost importance. I don't want to see it rejected out of hand as just the product of my peculiar training and prejudices—interesting perhaps as a study in aberration, but not germane to the problem. The evidence for my view of Lithia is overwhelming. It overwhelmed me quite *against* my natural hopes and inclinations. I want you to hear that evidence."

The preamble, with its dry scholiast's tone and its buried suggestion, did its work well.

"He also wants us to understand," Cleaver said, recovering a little of his natural impatience, "that his reasons are religious and won't hold water if he states them right out."

"Hush," Michelis said intently. "Listen."

"Thank you, Mike. All right, here we go. This planet is what I think is called in English 'a set-up.' Let me describe it for you briefly as I see it, or rather as I've come to see it.

"Lithia is a paradise. It has resemblances to a number of other planets, but the closest correspondence is to the Earth in its pre-Adamic period, before the coming of the first glaciers. The resemblance ends there, because on Lithia the glaciers never came, and life continued to be spent in the paradise, as it was not allowed to do on Earth."

"Myths," Cleaver said sourly.

"I use the terms with which I'm most familiar; strip off those terms and what I am saying is still a fact that all of you know to be true. We find here a completely mixed forest, with plants that fall from one end of the creative spectrum to the other living side by side in perfect amity, cycad with cycladella, giant horsetail with flowering trees. To a great extent that's also true of the animals. The lion doesn't lie down with the lamb here because Lithia has neither animal, but as an allegory the phrase is apt. Parasitism occurs rather less often on Lithia than it does on Earth, and there are very few carnivores of any sort except in the sea. Almost all of the surviving land animals eat plants only, and by a neat arrangement which is typically Lithian, the plants are admirably set up to attack animals rather than each other.

"It's an unusual ecology, and one of the strangest things about it is its rationality, its extreme, almost single-minded insistence upon one-for-one relationships. In one respect it looks almost as though somebody had arranged the whole planet as a ballet about Mengenlehre—the theory of aggregates.

"Now, in this paradise we have a dominant creature, the Lithian, the man of Lithia. This creature is rational. It conforms, as if naturally and without constraint or guidance, to the highest ethical code we have evolved on Earth. It needs no laws to enforce this code. Somehow, everyone obeys it as a matter of course, although it has never even been written down. There are no criminals, no deviates, no aberrations of any kind. The people are not standardized—our own very bad and partial answer to the ethical dilemma—but instead are highly individual. They choose their own life courses without constraint—yet somehow no antisocial act of any kind is ever committed. There isn't even any word for such an act in the Lithian language."

The recorder made a soft, piercing pip of sound, announcing that it was threading a new tape. The enforced pause would last about eight seconds, and on a sudden inspiration, Ruiz-Sanchez put it to use. On the next pip, he said:

"Mike, let me stop here and ask you a question. What does this suggest to you, thus far?"

"Why, just what I've said before that it suggested," Michelis said slowly. "An enormously superior social science, evidently founded in a precise system of psychogenetics. I should think that would be more than enough."

"Very well, I'll go on. I felt as you did, at first. Then I came to ask myself some correlative questions. For instance: How does it happen that the Lithians not only have no deviates— think of that, *no* deviates!—but that the code by which they live so perfectly is, point for point, the code *we* strive to obey? If that just happened, it was by the uttermost of all coincidences. Consider, please, the imponderables involved. Even on Earth we have never known a society which evolved independently *exactly* the same precepts as the Christian precepts—by which I mean to include the Mosaic. Oh, there were some duplications of doctrine, enough to encourage the twentieth century's partiality toward synthetic religions like theosophism and Hollywood Vedanta, but no ethical system on Earth that grew up independently of Christianity agreed with it point for point. Not Mithraism, not Islam, not the Essenes—not even these, which influenced or were influenced by Christianity, were in good agreement with it in the matter of ethics.

"And yet here on Lithia, fifty light-years away from Earth

and among a race as unlike man as man is unlike the kangaroos, what do we find? A Christian people, lacking nothing but the specific proper names and the symbolic appurtenances of Christianity. I don't know how you three react to this, but I found it extraordinary and indeed completely impossible—mathematically impossible—under any assumption but one. I'll get to that assumption in a moment."

"You can't get there any too soon for me," Cleaver said morosely. "How a man can stand fifty light-years from home in deep space and talk such parochial nonsense is beyond my comprehension."

"Parochial?" Ruiz-Sanchez said, more angrily than he had intended. "Do you mean that what we think true on Earth is automatically made suspect just by the fact of its removal into deep space? I beg to remind you, Paul, that quantum mechanics seem to hold good on Lithia, and that you see nothing parochial about behaving as if it does. If I believe in Peru that God created and still rules the universe, I see nothing parochial in my continuing to believe it on Lithia. You brought your parish with you; so did I. This has been willed where what is willed must be."

As always, the great phrase shook him to the heart. But it was obvious that it meant nothing to anyone else in the room; were such men hopeless? No, no. That Gate could never slam behind them while they lived, no matter how the hornets buzzed for them behind the deviceless banner. Hope was with them yet.

"A while back I thought I had been provided an escape hatch, incidentally," he said. "Chtexa told me that the Lithians would like to modify the growth of their population, and he implied that they would welcome some form of birth control. But, as it turns out, birth control in the sense that the Church interdicts it is impossible to Lithia, and what Chtexa had in mind was obviously some form of fertility control, a proposition to which the Church gave its qualified assent many decades ago. So there I was, even on this small point forced again to realize that we had found on Lithia the most colossal rebuke to our aspirations that we had ever encountered: a people that seems to live with ease the kind of life which we associate with saints alone.

"Bear in mind that a Muslim who visited Lithia would find no such thing; though he would find a form of polygamy here, its purposes and methods would revolt him. Neither would a Taoist. Neither would a Zoroastrian, presuming that there were still such, or a classical Greek. But for the four of us—and I include you, Paul, for despite your tricks and your agnosticism you still subscribe to the Christian ethical doctrines enough to be put on the defensive when you flout them—what we four have here on Lithia is a coincidence which beggars description. It is more than an astronomical coincidence—that tired old metaphor for numbers that don't seem very large any more—it is a transfinite coincidence. It would take the shade of Cantor himself to do justice to the odds against it."

"Wait a minute," Agronski said. "Holy smoke. I don't know any anthropology, Mike, I'm lost here. I was with the Father up to the part about the mixed forest, but I don't have any standards to judge the rest. Is it so, what he says?"

"Yes, I think it's so," Michelis said slowly. "But there could be differences of opinion as to what it means, if anything. Ramon, go on."

"I will. There's still a good deal more to say. I'm still describing the planet, and more particularly the Lithians. The Lithians take a lot of explaining. What I've said about them thus far states only the most obvious fact. I could go on to point out many more, equally obvious facts. They have no nations and no regional rivalries, yet if you look at the map of Lithia—all those small continents and archipelagoes separated by thousands of miles of seas—you'll see every reason why they *should* have developed such rivalries. They have emotions and passions, but are never moved by them to irrational acts. They have only one language, and have never had more than this same one—which again should have been made impossible by the geography of Lithia. They exist in complete harmony with everything, large and small, that they find in their world. In short, they're a people that couldn't exist—and yet does.

"Mike, I'll go beyond your view to say that the Lithians are the most perfect example of how human beings *ought* to behave that we're ever likely to find, for the very simple reason that they behave now the way human beings once behaved before we fell in our own Garden. I'd go even farther: as an example, the Lithians are useless to us, because until the coming of the Kingdom of God no substantial number of human beings will ever be able to imitate Lithian conduct. Human beings seem to have built-in imperfections that the Lithians lack—original sin, if you like—so that after thousands of years of trying, we are farther away than ever from our original emblems of conduct, while the Lithians have never departed from theirs.

"And don't allow yourselves to forget for an instant that these emblems of conduct are the same on both planets. That couldn't ever have happened, either—but it did.

"I'm now going to adduce another interesting fact about Lithian civilization. It is a fact, whatever you may think of its merits as evidence. It is this: that your Lithian is a creature of logic. Unlike Earthmen of all stripes, he has no gods, no myths, no legends. He has no belief in the supernatural—or, as we're calling it in our barbarous jargon these days, the 'paranormal.' He has no traditions. He has no tabus. He has no faiths, except for an impersonal belief that he and his lot are indefinitely improvable. He is as rational as a machine. Indeed, the only way in which we can distinguish the Lithian from an organic computer is his possession and use of a moral code.

"And that, I beg you to observe, *is completely irrational*. It is based upon a set of axioms, a set of propositions which were 'given' from the beginning—though your Lithian sees no need to postulate any Giver. The Lithian, for instance Chtexa, believes in the sanctity of the individual. Why? Not by reason, surely, for there is no way to reason to that proposition. It is an axiom. Or: Chtexa believes in the right of juridical defense, in the equality of all before the code. Why? It's possible to behave rationally *from* the proposition, but it's impossible to reason one's way *to* it. It's given. If you assume that the responsibility to the code varies with the individual's age, or with what family he happens to belong to, logical behavior can follow from one of these assumptions, but there again one can't arrive *at* the principle by reason alone.

"One begins with belief: 'I think that all people ought to be equal before the law.' That is a statement of faith, nothing more. Yet Lithian civilization is so set up as to suggest that one can arrive at such basic axioms of Christianity, and of Western civilization on Earth as a whole, by reason alone—in the plain face of the fact that one cannot. One rationalist's axiom is another one's madness."

"Those *are* axioms," Cleaver growled. "You don't arrive at them by faith, either. You don't arrive at them at all. They're self-evident—that's the definition of an axiom."

"It was until the physicists kicked that definition to pieces," Ruiz-Sanchez said, with a certain grim relish. "There's the axiom that only one parallel can be drawn to a given line. It may be self-evident, but it's also untrue, isn't it? And it's self-evident that matter is solid. Go on, Paul, you're a physicist yourself. Kick a stone for me, and say, 'Thus I refute Bishop Berkeley.'"

"It's peculiar," Michelis said in a low voice, "that Lithian culture should be so axiom-ridden, without the Lithians being aware of it. I hadn't formulated it in quite these terms before, Paul, but I've been disturbed myself at the bottomless *assumptions* that lie behind Lithian reasoning—all utterly unprobed, although in other respects the Lithians are very subtle. Look at what they've done in solid-state chemistry, for instance. It's a structure of the purest kind of reason, and yet when you get down to its fundamental assumptions you discover the axiom: 'Matter is real.' How can they know that? How did logic lead them to it? It's a very shaky notion, in my opinion. If I say that the atom is just a-hole-inside-a-hole-through-a-hole, how can they controvert me?"

"But their system works," Cleaver said.

"So does our solid-state theory—but we work from opposite axioms," Michelis said. "Whether it works or not isn't the issue. The question is, what is it that's working? I don't myself see how this immense structure of reason which the Lithians have evolved can stand for an instant. It doesn't seem to rest on anything. 'Matter is real' is a crazy proposition, when you come right down to it; all the evidence points in exactly the opposite direction."

"I'm going to tell you," Ruiz-Sanchez said. "You won't believe me, but I'm going to tell you anyhow, because I have to. *It stands because it's being propped up.* That's the simple answer and the whole answer. But first I want to add one more fact about the Lithians:

"They have complete physical recapitulation outside the body."

"What does that mean?" Agronski said.

"You know how a human child grows inside its mother's body. It is a one-celled animal to begin with, and then a simple metazoan resembling the fresh-water hydra or a simple jelly-fish. Then, very rapidly, it goes through many other animal forms, including the fish, the amphibian, the reptile, the lower mammal, and finally becomes enough like a man to be born. I don't know how this was taught to you as a geologist, but biologists call the process *recapitulation*.

"The term assumes that the embryo is passing through the various stages of evolution which brought life from the single-celled organism to man, but on a contracted time scale. There is a point, for instance, in the development of the fetus when it has gills, though it never uses them. It has a tail almost to the very end of its time in the womb, and rarely it still has it when it is born; and the tail-wagging muscle, the pubococcygeus, persists in the adult—in women it becomes transformed into the contractile ring around the vestibule. The circulatory system of the fetus in the last month is still reptilian, and if it fails to be completely transformed before birth, the infant emerges as a 'blue baby' with patent ductus arteriosus, the tetralogy of Fallot, or a similar heart defect which allows venous blood to mix with arterial—which is the rule with terrestrial reptiles. And so on."

"I see," Agronski said. "It's a familiar idea; I just didn't recognize the term. I had no idea that the correspondence was that close either, come to think of it."

"Well, the Lithians, too, go through this series of metamorphoses as they grow up, but they go through it *outside* the bodies of their mothers. This whole planet is one huge womb. The Lithian female lays her eggs in her abdominal pouch, the eggs are fertilized, and then she goes to the sea to give birth to her children. What she bears is not a miniature of the marvelously evolved reptile which is the adult Lithian; far from it: instead, she hatches a fish, rather like a lamprey. The fish lives in the sea a while, and then develops rudimentary lungs and comes to live along the shore lines. Once it's stranded on the flats by the tides, the lungfish's pectoral fins become simple legs, and it squirms away through the mud, changing into an amphibian and learning to endure the rigors of living away from the sea. Gradually their limbs become stronger, and better set on their bodies, and they become the big froglike things we sometimes see down the hill, leaping in the moonlight, trying to get away from the crocodiles.

"Many of them do get away. They carry their habit of leaping with them into the jungle, and there they change once again, into the small, kangaroo-like reptiles we've all seen, fleeing from us among the trees—the things we called the 'hoppers.' The last change is circulatory—from the sauropsid blood system which still permits some mixing of venous and arterial blood, to the pteropsid system we see in Earthly birds, which supplies nothing to the brain but oxygenated arterial blood. At about the same time, they become homeostatic and homeothermic, as mammals are. Eventually, they emerge, fully grown, from the jungles, and take their places among the folk of the cities as young Lithians, ready for education.

"But they have *already* learned every trick of every environment that their world has to offer. Nothing is left them to learn but their own civilization; their instincts are fully matured, fully under control; their rapport with nature on Lithia is absolute; their adolescence is passed and can't distract their intellects—they are ready to become social beings in every possible sense."

Michelis locked his hands together again in an agony of quiet excitement, and looked up at Ruiz-Sanchez.

"But that—that's a discovery beyond price!" he whispered. "Ramon, that alone is worth our trip to Lithia. What a stunning, elegant—what a *beautiful* sequence—and what a brilliant piece of analysis!"

"It is very elegant," Ruiz-Sanchez said dispiritedly. "He who would damn us often gives us gracefulness. It is not the same thing as Grace."

"But is it as serious as all that?" Michelis said, his voice charged with urgency. "Ramon, surely your Church can't object to it in any way. Your theorists accepted recapitulation in the human embryo, and also the geological record that showed the same process in action over longer spans of time. Why not this?"

"The Church accepts facts, as it always accepts facts," Ruiz-Sanchez said. "But—as you yourself suggested hardly ten minutes ago—facts have a way of pointing in several different directions at once. The Church is as hostile to the doctrine of evolution—particularly to that part of it which deals with the descent of man—as it ever was, and with good reason."

"Or with obdurate stupidity," Cleaver said.

"I confess that I haven't followed the ins and outs of all this," Michelis said. "What is the present position?"

"There are really two positions. You may assume that man evolved as the evidence attempts to suggest that he did, and that somewhere along the line God intervened and infused a soul; this the Church regards as a tenable position, but does not endorse it, because historically it has led to cruelty to animals, who are also creations of God. Or, you may assume that the soul evolved along with the body; this view the Church entirely condemns. But these positions are not important, at least not in this company, compared with the fact that the Church thinks *the evidence itself* to be highly dubious."

"Why?" Michelis said.

"Well, the Diet of Basra is hard to summarize in a few words, Mike; I hope you'll look it up when you get home. It's not exactly recent—it met in 1995, as I recall. In the meantime, look at the question very simply, with the original premises of the Scriptures in mind. If we assume that God created man, just for the sake of argument, did He create him perfect? I see no reason to suppose that He would have bothered with any lesser work. Is a man perfect without a navel? I don't know, but I'd be inclined to say that he isn't. Yet the first man—Adam, again for the sake of argument—wasn't born of woman, and so didn't really *need* to have a navel. Did he have one? All the great painters of the Creation show him with one: I'd say that their theology was surely as sound as their aesthetics."

"What does that prove?" Cleaver said.

"That the geological record, and recapitulation too, do not necessarily prove the doctrine of the descent of man. Given *my* initial axiom, which is that God created everything from scratch, it's perfectly logical that he should have given Adam a navel, Earth a geological record, and the embryo the process of recapitulation. None of these need indicate a real past; all might be there because the creations involved would have been imperfect otherwise."

"Wow," Cleaver said. "And I used to think that Haertel relativity was abstruse."

"Oh, that's not a new argument by any means, Paul; it dates back nearly two centuries—a man named Gosse invented it, not the Diet of Basra. Anyhow, any system of thought becomes abstruse if it's examined long enough. I don't see why my belief in a God you can't accept is any more rarefied than Mike's vision of the atom as a-hole-inside-a-hole-through-a-hole. I expect that in the long run, when we get right down to the fundamental stuff of the universe, we'll find that there's nothing there at all—just no-things moving no-place through no-time. On the day that that happens, I'll have God and you will not—otherwise there'll be no difference between us.

"But in the meantime, what we have here on Lithia is very clear indeed. We have—and now I'm prepared to be blunt—a planet and a people propped up by the Ultimate Enemy. It is a gigantic trap prepared for all of us—for every man on Earth and off it. We can do nothing with it but reject it, nothing but say to it, *Retro me, Sathanas.* If we compromise with it in any way, we are damned."

"Why, Father?" Michelis said quietly.

"Look at the premises, Mike. *One:* Reason is always a sufficient guide. *Two:* The self-evident is always the real. *Three:* Good works are an end in themselves. *Four:* Faith is irrelevant to right action. *Five:* Right action can exist without love. *Six:* Peace need not pass understanding. *Seven:* Ethics can exist without evil alternatives. *Eight:* Morals can exist without conscience. *Nine:* Goodness can exist without God. *Ten*—but do I really need to go on? We have heard all these propositions before, and we know What proposes them."

"A question," Michelis said, and his voice was painfully gentle. "To set such a trap, you must allow your Adversary to be creative. Isn't that—a heresy, Ramon? Aren't you now subscribing to a heretical belief? Or did the Diet of Basra—"

For a moment, Ruiz-Sanchez could not answer. The question cut to the heart. Michelis had found the priest out in the full agony of his defection, his belief betrayed, and he in full betrayal of his Church. He had hoped that it would not happen so soon.

"It is a heresy," he said at last, his voice like iron. "It is called Manichaeanism, and the Diet did not readmit it." He swallowed. "But since you ask, Mike, I do not see how we can avoid it now. I do not do this gladly, Mike, but we have seen these demonstrations before. The demonstration, for instance, in the rocks —the one that was supposed to show how the horse evolved from Eohippus, but which somehow never managed to convince the whole of mankind. If the Adversary *is* creative, there is at least some divine limitation that rules that Its creations be maimed. Then came the discovery of intra-uterine recapitulation, which was to have clinched the case for the descent of man. That one failed because the Adversary put it into the mouth of a man named Haeckel, who was so rabid an atheist that he took to faking the evidence to make the case still more convincing. Nevertheless, despite their flaws, these were both very subtle arguments, but the Church is not easily swayed; it is founded on a rock.

"But now we have, on Lithia, a new demonstration, both the subtlest and at the same time the crudest of all. It will sway many people who could have been swayed in no other way, and who lack the intelligence or the background to understand that it is a rigged demonstration. It seems to show us evolution in action on an inarguable scale. It is supposed to settle the question once and for all, to rule God out of the picture, to snap the chains that have held Peter's rock together all these many centuries. Henceforth there is to be no more question; henceforth there is to be no more God, but only phenomenology—and, of course, behind the scenes, within the hole that's inside the hole that's through a hole, the Great Nothing itself, the Thing that has never learned any word but *No* since it was cast flaming from heaven. It has many other names, but we know the name that counts. That will be all that's left us.

"Paul, Mike, Agronski, I have nothing more to say than this: We are all of us standing on the brink of Hell. By the grace of God, we may still turn back. We must turn back—for I at least think that this is our last chance."

IX

THE vote was cast, and that was that. The commission was tied, and the question would be thrown open again in higher echelons on Earth, which would mean tying Lithia up for years to come. *Proscripted area pending further study.* The planet was now, in effect, on the Index Expurgatorius.

The ship arrived the next day. The crew was not much surprised to find that the two opposing factions of the commission were hardly speaking to each other. It often happened that way.

The four commission members cleaned up in almost complete silence the house in Xoredeshch Sfath that the Lithians had given them. Ruiz-Sanchez packed the dark blue book with the gold stamping without being able to look at it except out of the corner of his eye, but even obliquely he could not help seeing its long-familiar title:

FINNEGANS WAKE
James Joyce

So much for his pride in his solution of the case of conscience the novel proposed. He felt as though he himself had been collated, bound and stamped, a tortured human text for future generations of Jesuits to explicate and argue.

He had rendered the verdict he had found it necessary for him to render. But he knew that it was not a final verdict, even for himself, and certainly not for the UN, let alone the Church. Instead, the verdict itself would be a knotty question for members of his Order yet unborn:

Did Father Ruiz-Sanchez correctly interpret the Divine case, and did this ruling, if so, follow from it?

Except, of course, that they would not use his name—but what good would it do them to use an alias? Surely there would never be any way to disguise the original of *this* problem. Or was that pride again—or misery? It had been Mephistopheles himself who had said, *Solamen miseris socios habuisse doloris. . . .*

"Let's go, Father. It'll be take-off time shortly."

"All ready, Mike."

It was only a short journey to the clearing, where the mighty spindle of the ship stood ready to weave its way back through the geodesics of deep space to the sun that shone on Peru. There was even some sunlight here, piercing now and then through low, scudding clouds; but it had been raining all morning, and would begin again soon enough.

The baggage went on board smoothly and without any fuss. So did the specimens, the films, the tapes, the special reports, the recordings, the sample cases, the slide boxes, the vivariums, the type cultures, the pressed plants, the animal cages, the tubes of soil, the chunks of ore, the Lithian manuscripts in their atmospheres of helium—everything was lifted decorously by the cranes and swung inside.

Agronski went up the cleats to the air lock first, with Michelis following him, a barracks bag slung over one shoulder. On the ground Cleaver was stowing some last-minute bit of gear, something that seemed to require delicate, almost reverent bedding down before the cranes could be allowed to take it in their indifferent grip; Cleaver was fanatically motherly about his electronic apparatus. Ruiz-Sanchez took advantage of the delay to look around once more at the near margins of the forest.

At once, he saw Chtexa. The Lithian was standing at the entrance to the path the Earthmen themselves had taken from the city to reach the ship. He was carrying something.

Cleaver swore under his breath and undid something he had just done to do it in another way. Ruiz-Sanchez raised his hand. Immediately Chtexa walked toward the ship, in great loping strides which nevertheless seemed almost leisurely.

"I wish you a good journey," the Lithian said, "wherever you may go. I wish also that your road may lead back to this world at some future time. I have brought you the gift that I sought before to give you, if the moment is now appropriate."

Cleaver had straightened and was now glaring up suspiciously at the Lithian. Since he did not understand the language, he was unable to find anything to which he could object. He simply stood there and radiated unwelcomeness.

"Thank you," Ruiz-Sanchez said. This creature of Satan made him miserable all over again, made him feel intolerably in the wrong. Yet how could Chtexa know—?

The Lithian was holding out to him a small vase, sealed at the top and provided with two gently looping handles. The gleaming porcelain of which it had been made still carried inside it, under the glaze, the fire which had formed it; it was iridescent, alive with long quivering festoons and plumes of rainbows, and the form as a whole would have made any potter of Greece abandon his trade in shame. It was so beautiful that one could imagine no use for it at all. Certainly one could not make a lamp of it, or fill it with leftover beets and put it in the refrigerator. Besides, it would take up too much space.

"This is the gift," Chtexa said. "It is the finest container yet to come out of Xoredeshch Gton. The material of which it is made includes traces of every element to be found on Lithia, even including iron, and thus, as you see, it shows the colors of every shade of emotion and of thought. On Earth, it will tell Earthmen much of Lithia."

"We will be unable to analyze it," Ruiz-Sanchez said. "It is too perfect to destroy, too perfect even to open."

"Ah, but we wish you to open it," Chtexa said. "For it contains our other gift."

"Another gift?"

"Yes, and a more important one. It is a fertilized, living egg of our species. Take it with you. By the time you reach Earth, it will have hatched, and will be ready to grow up with you in your strange and marvelous world. The container is the gift of all of us; but the child inside is my gift, for it is my child."

Appalled, Ruiz-Sanchez took the vase in trembling hands, as though he expected it to explode—as indeed he did. It shook with subdued flame in his grip.

"Good-bye," Chtexa said. He turned and walked away, back toward the entrance to the path. Cleaver watched him go, shading his eyes.

"Now what was that all about?" the physicist said. "The Snake couldn't have made a bigger thing of it if he'd been handing you his own head on a platter. And all the time it was only a jug!"

Ruiz-Sanchez did not answer. He could not have spoken even to himself. He turned away and began to ascend the cleats, cradling the vase carefully in one elbow. It was not the gift he had hoped to bring to the holy city for the grand indulgence of all mankind, no; but it was all he had.

While he was still climbing, a shadow passed rapidly over the hull: Cleaver's last crate, being borne aloft into the hold by a crane.

Then he was in the air lock, with the rising whine of the ship's Nernst generators around him. A long shaft of sunlight was cast ahead of him, picking out his shadow on the deck.

After a moment, a second shadow overlaid and blurred his own: Cleaver's. Then the light dimmed and went out.

The air lock door slammed.

BOOK TWO

X

AT first Egtverchi knew nothing, in the peculiarly regular and chilly womb where he floated, except his name. That was inherited, and marked in a twist of desoxyribonucleic acid upon one of his genes; farther up on the same chromosome, the x-chromosome, another gene carried his father's name: Chtexa. And that was all. At the moment he had begun his independent life, as a zygote or fertilized egg, that had been written down in letters of chromatin: his name was Egtverchi, his race Lithian, his sex male, his inheritance continuous back through Lithian centuries to the moment when the world of Lithia began. He did not need to understand this; it was implicit.

But it was dark, chilly, and too regular in the pouch. Tiny as a speck of pollen, Egtverchi drifted in the fluid which sustained him, from wall to smoothly curved and unnaturally glazed wall, not conscious yet, but constantly, chemically reminded that he was not in his mother's pouch. No gene that he carried bore his mother's name, but he knew—not in his brain, for he had none yet, but by feel, with purely chemical revulsion—whose child he was, of what race he was, and where he should be: *not here.*

And so he grew—and drifted, seeking to attach himself at every circuit to the chilly glass-lined pouch which rejected him always. By the time of gastrulation, the attachment reflex had run its course and he forgot it. Now he merely floated, knowing once more only what he had known at the beginning: his race Lithian, his sex male, his name Egtverchi, his father Chtexa, his life due to begin; and his birth world as bitter and black as the inside of a jug.

Then his notochord formed, and his nerve cells congregated in a tiny knot at one end of it. Now he had a front end and a hind end, as well as an address. He also had a brain—and now he was a fish—a spawn, not even a fingerling yet, circling and circling in the cold enclave of sea.

That sea was tideless and lightless, but there was some motion in it, the slow roll of convection currents. Sometimes, too, something went through it which was not a current, forcing him far down toward the bottom, or against the walls. He did not know the name of this force—as a fish he knew nothing, only circled with the endlessness of his hunger—but he fought it, as he would have fought cold or heat. There was a sense in his head, aft of his gills, which told him which way was up. It told him, too, that a fish in its natural medium has mass and inertia, but no weight. The sporadic waves of gravity—or acceleration—which whelmed through the lightless water were no part of his instinctual world, and when they were over he was often swimming desperately on his back.

There came a time when there was no more food in the little sea; but time and the calculations of his father were kind to him. Precisely at that time the weight force returned more powerfully than had even been suggested as possible before, and he was driven to sluggish immobility for a long period, fanning the water at the bottom of the jug past his gills with slow exhausted motions.

It was over at last, and then the little sea was moving jerkily from side to side, up and down, and forward. Egtverchi was now about the size of a larval fresh-water eel. Beneath his pectoral bones twin sacs were forming, which connected with no other system of his body, but were becoming more and more richly supplied with capillaries. There was nothing inside the sacs but a little gaseous nitrogen—just enough to equalize the pressure. In due course, they would be rudimentary lungs.

Then there was light.

To begin with, the top of the world was taken off. Egtverchi's eyes would not have focussed at this stage in any case and, like any evolved creature, he was subject to the neo-Lamarckian laws which provide that even a completely inherited ability will develop badly if it is formed in the absence of any opportunity to function. As a Lithian, with a Lithian's special sensitivity to the modifying pressures of environment, the long darkness had done him less potential damage than it surely would have done another creature—say, an Earth creature; nevertheless, he would pay for it in due course. Now, he could sense no more than that in the *up* direction (now quite stable and un-changing) there was light.

He rose toward it, his pectoral fins strumming the warm harps of the water.

Father Ramon Ruiz-Sanchez, late of Peru, late of Lithia, and always Fellow in the Society of Jesus, watched the surfacing, darting little creature with surfacing strange emotions. He could not help feeling for the sinuous eft the pity that he felt for every living thing, and an aesthetic delight in the flashing unpredictable certainty of its motions. But this little animal was Lithian.

He had had more time than he had wanted to explore the black ruin that underlay his position. Ruiz-Sanchez had never underestimated the powers which evil could still exercise, pow-ers retained—even by general agreement within the Church—after its fall from beside the throne of the Most High. As a Jesuit he had examined and debated far too many cases of con-science to believe that evil is unsubtle or impotent. But that among these powers the Adversary numbered the puissance to create—no, that had never entered his head, not until Lithia. That power, at least, had to be of God, and of God only. To think that there could be more than one demiurge was out-right heresy, and a very ancient heresy at that.

So be it, it was so, heretical or not. The whole of Lithia, and in particular the whole of the dominant, rational, infinitely admirable race of Lithians, had been created by Evil, out of Its need to confront men with a new, a specifically intellectual se-duction, springing like Minerva from the brow of Jove. Out of that unnatural birth, as out of the fabled one, there was to come a symbolic clapping of palms to foreheads for everyone who could admit for an instant that any power but God could create; a ringing, splitting ache in the skull of theology; a moral migraine; even a cosmological shell shock, for Minerva was the mistress of Mars, on Earth as—undoubtedly, Ruiz-Sanchez remembered with anguish—as it is in heaven.

After all, he had been there, and he knew.

But all that could wait a little while, at least. For the moment it was sufficient that the little creature, so harmlessly like a three-inch eel, was still alive and apparently healthy. Ruiz-Sanchez picked up a beaker of water, cloudy with thousands of cultured *Cladocera* and Cyclops, and poured nearly half of it into the subtly glowing amphora. The infant Lithian flashed instantly away into the darkness, in chase after the nearly microscopic crustaceans. Appetite, the priest reflected, is a universal barometer of health.

"Look at him go," a soft voice said beside his shoulder. He looked up, smiling. The speaker was Liu Meid, the UN laboratory chief whose principal charge the Lithian child would be for many months. A small, black-haired girl with an expression of almost childlike calm, she peered into the vase expectantly, waiting for the imago to reappear.

"They won't make him sick, do you think?" she said.

"I hope not," Ruiz-Sanchez said. "They're Earthly, it's true, but Lithian metabolism is remarkably like ours. Even the blood pigment is an analogue of hemoglobin, though the metal base isn't iron, of course. Their plankton includes forms very like Cyclops and the water flea. No; if he's survived the trip, I dare say our subsequent care won't kill him, not even with kindness."

"The trip?" Liu said slowly. "How could that have hurt him?"

"Well, I really can't say exactly. It was simply the chance that we took. Chtexa—that was his father—presented him to us inside this vase, already sealed in. We had no way of knowing what provisions Chtexa had made for his child against the various strains of space flight. And we didn't dare look inside to see; if there was one thing of which I was certain, it was that Chtexa wouldn't have sealed the vase without a reason; after all, he does know the physiology of his own race better than any of us, even Dr. Michelis or myself."

"That's what I was getting at," Liu said.

"I know; but you see, Liu, Chtexa *doesn't* know space flight. Oh, ordinary flight stresses are no secret to him—the Lithians fly jets; it was the Haertel overdrive that *I* was worried about. You'll remember the fantastic time effects that Garrard went through on that first successful Centaurus flight. I couldn't explain the Haertel equations to Chtexa even if I'd had the time. They're classified against him; besides, he couldn't have understood them, because Lithian math doesn't include transfinites. And time is of the utmost importance in Lithian gestation."

"Why?" Liu said. She peered down into the amphora again, with an instinctive smile.

The question touched a nerve which had lain exposed in Ruiz-Sanchez for a long time. He said carefully: "Because they have physical recapitulation outside the body, Liu. That's why that creature in there is a fish; as an adult, it will be a reptile, though with a pteropsid circulatory system and a number of other unreptilian features. The Lithian females lay their eggs in the sea—"

"But it's fresh water in the jug."

"No, it's sea water; the Lithian seas are not so salt as ours. The egg hatches into a fishlike creature, such as you see in there; then the fish develops lungs and is beached by the tides. I used to hear them barking in Xoredeshch Sfath—they barked all night long, blowing the water out of their lungs and developing their diaphragm masculature."

Unexpectedly, he shuddered. The recollection of the sound was far more disturbing than the sound itself had been. Then, he had not known what it was—or, no, he had known that, but he had not known what it meant.

"Eventually the lungfish develop legs and lose their tails, like a tadpole, and go off into the Lithian forests as true amphibians. After a while, their respiratory system loses its dependence upon the skin as an auxiliary source, so they no longer need to stay near water. Eventually, they become true adults, a very advanced type of reptile, marsupial, bipedal, homeostatic—and highly intelligent. The new adults come out of the jungle and are ready for education in the cities."

Liu took a deep breath. "How marvelous," she whispered.

"It is just that," he said somberly. "Our own children go through nearly the same changes in the womb, but they're protected throughout; the Lithian children have to run the gauntlet of every ecology their planet possesses. That's why I was afraid of the Haertel overdrive. We insulated the vase against the drive fields as best we could, but in a maturation process so keyed to the appearances of evolution, a time slow-down could have been crucial. In Garrard's case, he was slowed down to an hour a second, then whipped up to a second an hour, then back again, and so on along a sine wave. If there'd been the slightest break in the insulation, something like that

might have happened to Chtexa's child, with unknowable results. Evidently, there was no leak, but I was worried."

The girl thought about it. In order to keep himself from
thinking about it, for he had already pondered himself in
dwindling spirals to a complete, central impasse, Ruiz-Sanchez
watched her think. She was always restful to watch, and Ruiz-
Sanchez needed rest. It now seemed to him that he had had
no rest at all since the moment when he had fainted on the
threshold of the house in Xoredeshch Sfath, directly into the
astonished Agronski's arms.

Liu had been born and raised in the state of Greater New
York. It was Ruiz-Sanchez' most heartfelt compliment that nobody would have guessed it; as a Peruvian he hated the nineteen-
million-man megalopolis with an intensity he would have been
the first to characterize as unchristian. There was nothing in the
least hectic or harried about Liu. She was calm, slow, serene,
gentle, her reserve unshakable without being in the least cold or
compulsive, her responses to everything that impinged upon
her as direct and uncomplicated as a kitten's; her attitude toward
her fellow men virtually unsuspicious, not out of naïveté, but
out of her confidence that the essential Liu was so inviolable as
to prevent anyone even from wanting to violate it.

These were the abstract terms which first came to Ruiz-
Sanchez' mind, but immediately he came to grief over a transi-
tional thought. As nobody would take Liu for a New Yorker
—even her speech betrayed not a one of the eight dialects, all
becoming more and more mutually unintelligible, which were
spoken in the city, and in particular one would never have
guessed that her parents spoke nothing but Bronix—so nobody could have taken her for a female laboratory technician.

This was not a line of thought that Ruiz-Sanchez felt comfortable in following, but it was too obvious to ignore. Liu was
as small-boned and intensely nubile as a geisha. She dressed
with exquisite modesty, but it was not the modesty of concealment, but of quietness, of the desire to put around a firmly
feminine body clothes that would be ashamed of nothing, but
would also advertise nothing. Inside her soft colors, she was a
Venus Callipygous with a slow, sleepy smile, inexplicably unaware that she—let alone anybody else—was expected by na-

ture and legend to worship continually the firm dimpled slopes of her own back.

There now, that was quite enough; more than enough. The little eel chasing fresh-water crustaceae in the ceramic womb presented problems enough, some of which were about to become Liu's. It would hardly be suitable to complicate Liu's task by so much as an unworthy speculation, though it be communicated by no more than a curious glance. Ruiz-Sanchez was confident enough of his own ability to keep himself in the path ordained for him, but it would not do to burden this grave sweet girl with a suspicion her training had never equipped her to meet.

He turned away hastily and walked to the vast glass west wall of the laboratory, which looked out over the city thirty-four storeys from the street—not a great height, but more than sufficient for Ruiz-Sanchez. The thundering, heat-hazed, nineteen-million-man megalopolis repelled him, as usual—or perhaps even more than usual, after his long stay in the quiet streets of Xoredeshch Sfath. But at least he had the consolation of knowing that he did not have to live here the rest of his life.

In a way, the state of Manhattan was only a relict anyhow, not only politically, but physically. What could be seen of it from here was an enormous multi-headed ghost. The crumbling pinnacles were ninety per cent empty, and remained so right around the clock. At any given moment most of the population of the state (and of any other of the thousand-odd city-states around the globe) was underground.

The underground area was self-sufficient. It had its own thermonuclear power sources; its own tank farms, and its thousands of miles of illuminated plastic pipe through which algae suspensions flowed richly, grew unceasingly; decades' worth of food and medical supplies in cold storage; water-processing equipment which was a completely closed circuit, so that it could recover moisture even from the air and from the city's own sewage; and air intakes equipped to remove gas, virus, fall-out particles or all three at once. The city-states were equally independent of any central government; each was under the hegemony of a Target Area Authority modeled on the old, self-policing port authorities of the previous century—out of which, indeed, they had evolved inevitably.

This fragmentation of the Earth had come about as the end product of the international Shelter race of 1960–85. The fission-bomb race, which had begun in 1945, was effectively over five years later; the fusion-bomb race and the race for the intercontinental ballistic missile had each taken five years more. The Shelter race had taken longer, not because any new physical knowledge or techniques had been needed to bring it to fruition—quite the contrary—but because of the vastness of the building program it involved.

Defensive though the Shelter race seemed on the surface, it had taken on all the characteristics of a classical arms race—for the nation that lagged behind invited instant attack. Nevertheless, there had been a difference. The Shelter race had been undertaken under the dawning realization that the threat of nuclear war was not only imminent but transcendent; it could happen at any instant, but its failure to break out at any given time meant that it had to be lived with for at least a century, and perhaps five centuries. Thus the race was not only hectic, but long-range—

And, like all arms races, it defeated itself in the end, this time because those who planned it had planned for too long a span of time. The Shelter economy was world-wide now, but the race had hardly ended when signs began to appear that people simply would not live willingly under such an economy for long; certainly not for five hundred years, and probably not for a century. The Corridor Riots of 1993 were the first major sign; since then, there had been many more.

The riots had provided the United Nations with the excuse it needed to set up, at long last, a real supranational government—a world state with teeth in it. The riots had provided the excuse—and the Shelter economy, with its neo-Hellenic fragmentation of political power, had given the UN the means.

Theoretically, that should have solved everything. Nuclear war was no longer likely between the member states; the threat was gone . . . but how do you *un*build a Shelter economy? An economy which cost twenty-five billion dollars a year, every year for twenty-five years, to build? An economy now embedded in the face of the Earth in uncountable billions of tons of concrete and steel, to a depth of more than a mile? It could not be undone; the planet would be a mausoleum for the living from now until the Earth itself perished: gravestones, gravestones, gravestones . . .

The word tolled in Ruiz-Sanchez' ears, distantly. The infra-bass of the buried city's thunder shook the glass in front of him. Mingled with it there was an ominous grinding sound of unrest, more marked than he had ever heard it before—like the noise of a cannon ball rolling furiously around and around in a rickety, splintering wooden track. . . .

"Dreadful, isn't it?" Michelis' voice said at his shoulder. Ruiz-Sanchez shot a surprised glance at the big chemist—not surprised that he had not heard Michelis enter, but that Mike was speaking to him again.

"It is," he said. "I'm glad you noticed it too. I thought it just might be hypersensitivity on my part—from having been away so long."

"It might well be that," Michelis agreed gravely. "I was away myself."

Ruiz-Sanchez shook his head.

"No, I think it's real," he said. "These are intolerable conditions to ask people to live under. And it's more than a matter of making them live ninety days out of every hundred at the bottom of a hole. After all, they think of living every day of their lives on the verge of destruction. We trained their parents to think that way, otherwise there'd never have been enough taxes to pay for the shelters. And of course the children have been brought up to think that too. It's inhuman."

"Is it?" Michelis said. "People lived all their lives on the verge for centuries—all the way up until Pasteur. How long ago was that?"

"Only about 1860," Ruiz-Sanchez said. "But no, it's quite different now. The pestilence was capricious; one's children might survive it; but fusion bombs are catholic." He winced involuntarily. "And there it is. A moment ago, I caught myself thinking that the shadow of destruction we labor under now is not only imminent but transcendent; I was burlesquing a tragedy; death in premedical days was always both imminent and immanent, impending and indwelling—but it was never transcendent. In those days, only God was impending, indwelling *and* transcendent all at once, and that was their hope. Today, we've given them Death instead."

"Sorry," Michelis said, his bony face suddenly turning flinty. "You know I can't argue with you on those grounds, Ramon. I've already been burned once. Once is enough."

The chemist turned away. Liu, who had been making a serial dilution at the long bench, was holding the ranked test tubes up to the daylight, and peeping up at Michelis from under her half-shut eyelids. She looked promptly away again as Ruiz-Sanchez' gaze fell on her face. He did not know whether she knew that he had caught her; but the tubes rattled a little in the rack as she put them down again.

"Excuse me," he said. "Liu, this is Dr. Michelis, one of my confreres on the commission to Lithia. Mike, this is Dr. Liu Meid, who'll be taking care of Chtexa's child for an indefinite period, more or less under my supervision. She's one of the world's best xenozoologists."

"How do you do," Mike said gravely. "Then you and the Father stand *in loco parentis* to our Lithian guest. It's a heavy responsibility for a young woman, I should think."

The Jesuit felt a thoroughly unchristian impulse to kick the tall chemist in the shins; but there seemed to be no conscious malice in Michelis' voice.

The girl merely looked down at the ground and sucked in her breath between slightly parted lips. "*Ah*-so-*deska*," she said, almost inaudibly.

Michelis' eyebrows went up, but in a moment it became obvious that Liu was not going to say anything more, to him, right now. With a slight huff of embarrassment, Michelis addressed himself to the priest, catching him erasing the traces of a smile.

"So I'm all feet," Michelis said, grinning ruefully. "But I won't have time to practice my manners for a while yet. There are lots of loose ends to tie up. Ramon, how soon do you think you can leave Chtexa's child in Dr. Meid's hands? We've been asked to do a non-classified version of the Lithia report—"

"We?"

"Yes. Well, you and I."

"What about Cleaver and Agronski?"

"Cleaver's not available," Michelis said. "I don't offhand

know where he is. And for some reason they don't want Agronski; maybe he doesn't have enough letters after his name. It's *The Journal of Interstellar Research*, and you know how stuffy they are—they're *nouveau-riche* in terms of prestige, and that makes them more academic than the academicians. But I think it would be worth doing, just to get some of our data out into the open. Can you find the time?"

"I think so," Ruiz-Sanchez said thoughtfully. "Providing it can be sandwiched in between getting Chtexa's child born, and my pilgrimage."

Michelis raised his eyebrows again. "That's right, this is a Holy Year, isn't it?"

"Yes," Ruiz-Sanchez said.

"Well, I think we can work it in," Michelis said. "But—excuse me for prying, Ramon, but you don't strike me as a man in urgent need of the great pardon. Does this mean that you've changed your mind about Lithia?"

"No, I haven't changed my mind," Ruiz-Sanchez said quietly. "We are all in need of the great pardon, Mike. But I'm not going to Rome for that."

"Then—"

"I expect to be tried there for heresy."

XI

THERE was light on the mud flat where Egtverchi lay, somewhere eastward of Eden, but day and night had not been created yet, nor was there yet wind or tide to whelm him as he barked the water from his itchy lungs and whooped in the fiery air. Hopefully he squirmed with his new forelimbs, and there was motion; but there was no place to go, and no one and nothing from which to escape. The unvarying, glareless light was comfortingly like that of a perpetually overcast sky, but Somebody had failed to provide for that regular period of darkness and negation during which an animal consolidates its failures and seeks in the depths of its undreaming self for sufficient joy to greet still another morning.

"Animals have no souls," said Descartes, throwing a cat out

the window to prove, if not his point, at least his faith in it. The timid genius of mechanism, who threw cats well but Popes badly, had never met a true automaton, and so never saw that what the animal lacks is not a soul, but a mind. A computer which can fill the parameters of the Haertel equations for all possible values and deliver them in two and a half seconds is an intellectual genius but, compared even to a cat, it is an emotional moron.

As an animal which does not think, but instead responds to each minute experience with the fullness of immediately apprehended—and immediately forgotten—emotions which involve its whole body, needs the temporary death of nightfall to protract its life, so the newly emerged animal body requires the battles appointed to the day in order to become, at long last, the somnolent self-confident adult which has been written aforetime in its genes; and here, too, Somebody had failed Egtverchi. There was soap in his mud, a calculated percentage which allowed him to thrash on the floor of his cage without permitting him to make enough progress to bump his head against its walls. This was conservative of his head, but it wasted the muscles of his limbs. When his croaking days were over, and he was transformed into a totally air-breathing, leaping thing, he did not leap well.

This too had been arranged, in a sense. There was nothing in this childhood of his from which he needed to leap away in terror, nor was there any place in it to which a small leap could have carried him. Even the smallest jump ended with an invisible bang and a slithering fall for the end of which, harmless though it invariably proved to be, no instinct prepared him, and for which no learning-reflex helped him to cultivate a graceful recovery. Besides, an animal with a perpetually sprained tail cannot be graceful regardless of its instincts.

Finally, he forgot how to leap entirely, and simply sat huddled until the next transformation overcame him, looking back dully at the many bobbing heads that were beginning to ring him round during his every waking hour. By the time he realized that all these watchers were alive like himself, and much larger than he was, his instincts were so far submerged as to produce in him nothing more than a vague alarm which resulted in no action.

The new transformation turned him into a weak and spindly walker with no head for distance, oversized though it was. It was here that Somebody saw to it that he was transferred to the terrarium.

Here at last the hormones of his true adolescence awakened and began to flow in his blood. The proper responses for a world something like this tiny jungle had been written imperatively upon every chromosome in his body; here, all at once, he was almost at home. He roved through the verdure of the terrarium on his shaky shanks with a counterfeit of gladness, looking for something to flee, something to fight, something to eat, something to learn. Yet in the long run he hardly found even a place to sleep, for in the terrarium night was as unknown as ever.

Here he also became aware for the first time that there were differences among the creatures who looked in at him and sometimes molested him. There were two who were almost always to be seen, either alone or together. They were always the molesters, as well—except—except that it was not always exactly molestation, for sometimes these beings with their sharp stings and their rough hands would give him something to eat which he had never tasted before, or do something else to him which pleased as much as it annoyed. He did not understand this relationship at all, and he did not like it.

After a while, he hid from all the watchers except these two —and even from them most of the time, for he was always sleepy. When he wanted them, he would call: "Szan-tchez!" (For he could not say "Liu" at all; his mesentery-tied tongue and almost cleft palate would never master so demanding a combination of liquid sounds—that had to wait for his adulthood.)

But eventually he stopped calling, and took to squatting apathetically beside the pond in the center of the miniature jungle. When on the last night of his lizard existence he laid his bulging brain case again in that hollow of mosses where there was the most dimness, he knew in his blood that on the morrow, when he awoke into his doom as a thinking creature, he would be old with that age which curses those who have never even for an instant been young. Tomorrow he would be a thinking creature, but the weariness was on him tonight. . . .

And so he awoke; and so the world was changed. The multiple doors from sense to soul had closed; suddenly, the world was an abstract; he had made that crossing from animal to automaton which had caused all the trouble eastward of Eden in 4004 B.C.

He was not a man, but he would pay the toll on that bridge all the same. From this point on, nobody would ever be able to guess what he felt in his animal soul, least of all Egtverchi himself.

"But what is he thinking about?" Liu said wonderingly, staring up at the huge, grave Lithian head which bent down upon them from the other side of the transparent pyroceram door. Egtverchi—he had told them his name very early—could hear her, of course, despite the division of the laboratory into two; but he said nothing. Thus far, he was anything but talkative, though he was a voracious reader.

Ruiz did not respond for a while, though the nine-foot young Lithian awed and puzzled him quite as much as he did Liu—and for better reasons. He looked sidewise at Michelis.

The chemist was ignoring them both. Ruiz could understand that well enough, as far as he himself was concerned; the attempt to write a joint but impartial report on the Lithia expedition for the *J. I. R.* had proven disastrous for the already tense relationship between the two scientists. But that same tension, he could see, was distressing Liu without her being quite aware of it, and that he could not let pass; she was innocent. He mustered a last-ditch attempt to draw Mike out.

"This is their learning period," he said. "Necessarily, they spend most of it listening. They're like the old legend of the wolf boy, who is raised by animals and comes into human cities without even knowing human speech—except that the Lithians don't learn speech in infancy and so have no block against learning it in young adulthood. To do that, they must listen very hard—most wolf boys never learn to talk at all—and that's what he's doing."

"But why won't he at least answer questions?" Liu said troubledly, without quite looking at Michelis. "How is he going to learn if he won't practice?"

"He hasn't anything to tell us yet, by his lights," Ruiz said.

"And for him, we lack the authority to put questions. Any adult Lithian could question him, but obviously we don't qualify—and what Mike calls the foster-parent relationship couldn't mean anything to a creature adapted to a solitary childhood."

Michelis did not respond.

"He used to call us," Liu said sadly. "At least, he used to call you."

"That's different. That's the pleasure response; it has nothing to do with authority, or affection either. If you were to put an electrode into the septal or caudate nucleus areas in the brain of a cat, or a rat, so that they could stimulate themselves electrically by pushing a pedal, you could train them to do almost anything that's within their powers, for no other reward but that jolt in the head. In the same way, a cat or a rat or a dog will learn to respond to its name, or to initiate some action, in order to gain pleasure. But you don't expect the animal to talk to you or answer questions just because it can do that."

"I never heard of the brain experiments," Liu said. "I think that's horrible."

"I think so too," Ruiz said. "It's an old line of research that got sidetracked somehow. I've never understood why some of our megalomaniacs didn't follow it up in human beings. A dictatorship founded on that device might really last a thousand years. But it has nothing to do with what you're asking of Egtverchi. When he's ready to talk, he'll talk. In the meantime, we don't have the stature to compel him to answer questions. For that, we would have to be twelve-foot Lithian adults."

Egtverchi's eyes filmed, and he brought his hands together suddenly.

"You are already too tall," his harsh voice said over the annunciator system.

Liu clapped her hands together in delighted imitation.

"See, see, Ramon, you're wrong! Egtverchi, what do you mean? Tell us!"

Egtverchi said experimentally: "Liu. Liu. Liu."

"Yes, yes. That's right, Egtverchi. Go on, go on—what did you mean—tell us!"

"Liu." Egtverchi seemed satisfied. The colors in his wattles died down. He was again almost a statue.

After a moment, there was an explosive snort from Michelis. Liu turned to him with a start, and, without really meaning to, so did Ruiz.

But it was too late. The big New Englander had already turned his back on them, as though disgusted at himself for having broken his own silence. Slowly, Liu too turned her back, if only to hide her face from everyone, even Egtverchi. Ruiz was left standing alone at the vertex of the tetrahedron of disaffection.

"This is going to be a fine performance for a prospective citizen of the United Nations to turn in," Michelis said suddenly, bitterly, from somewhere behind his shoulder. "I suppose you expected nothing else when you asked me here. What moved you to tell me what vast progress he was making? As I got the story, he ought to have been propounding theorems by this time."

"Time," Egtverchi said, "is a function of change, and change is the expression of the relative validity of two propositions, one of which contains a time t and the other a time t-prime, which differ from each other in no respect except that one contains the coordinate t and the other the coordinate t-prime."

"That's all very well," Michelis said coldly, turning to look up at the great head. "But I know where you got it from. If you're only a parrot, you're not going to be a citizen of *this* culture; you can take that from me."

"Who are you?" Egtverchi said.

"I'm your sponsor, God help me," Michelis said. "I know my own name, and I know what kind of record goes with it. If you expect to be a citizen, Egtverchi, you'll have to do better than pass yourself off as Bertrand Russell, or Shakespeare for that matter."

"I don't think he has any such notion," Ruiz said. "We explained the citizenship proposal to him, but he didn't give us any sign that he understood it. He just finished reading the *Principia* last week, so there's nothing unlikely about his feeding it back. He does that now and then."

"In first-order feedback," Egtverchi said somnolently, "if the connections are reversed, any small disturbance will be self-aggravating. In second-order feedback, going outside normal limits will force random changes in the network which will stop only when the system is stable again."

"God damn it!" Mike said savagely. "Now where did he get *that?* Stop it, you! You don't fool me for a minute!"

Egtverchi closed his eyes and fell silent.

Suddenly Michelis shouted: "Speak up, damn it!"

Without opening his eyes, Egtverchi said: "Hence the system can develop vicarious function if some of its parts are destroyed." Then he was silent again; he was asleep. He was often asleep, even these days.

"Fugue," Ruiz said softly. "He thought you were threatening him."

"Mike," Liu said, turning to him with a kind of desperate earnestness, "what do you think you're doing? He won't answer you, he can't answer you, especially when you speak to him like that! He's only a child, whatever you think when you have to look up at him! Obviously he learns many of these things by rote. Sometimes he says them when they seem to be apposite, but when we question him, he never carries it any farther. Why don't you give him a chance? *He* didn't ask you to bring any citizenship committee here!"

"Why don't you give *me* a chance?" Michelis said raggedly. Then he turned white-on-white. After a moment, so did Liu.

Ruiz looked up again at the slumbering Lithian and, as assured as he could be that Egtverchi was truly asleep, pressed the button which brought the rumbling metal curtain down in front of the transparent door. To the last, Egtverchi did not seem to move. Now they were isolated and away from him; Ruiz did not know whether this would make any difference, but he had his doubts about the innocence of Egtverchi's responses. To be sure, he had not overtly done anything but make an enigmatic statement, ask a simple question, quote from his reading—yet somehow everything he said had helped matters to go more badly than before.

"Why did you do that?" Liu said.

"I wanted to clear the air," Ruiz said quietly. "He's asleep, anyhow. Besides, we don't have any argument with Egtverchi yet. He may not be equipped to argue with us. But we've got to talk to each other—you too, Mike."

"Haven't you had enough of that already, Ramon?" Michelis said, in a voice a little more like his own.

"Preaching is my vocation," Ruiz said. "If I make a vice of it, I expect to atone for that somewhere else than here. But in the meantime—Liu, part of our trouble is the quarrel that I mentioned to you. Mike and I sharply disagreed on what Lithia means to the human race, indeed we disagreed on whether Lithia poses us any philosophical question at all. I think the planet is a time bomb; Mike thinks that's nonsense. And he thought that a general article for a scientific audience was no place to raise such questions, especially since this particular question has been posed officially and hasn't been adjudicated yet. And that's one reason why we're all snarling at each other right now, without any surface reason for it."

"What a cold thing to be heated about!" Liu said. "Men are so exasperating. How could a problem like that matter now?"

"I can't tell you," Ruiz said helplessly. "I can't be specific—the whole issue is under security seal. Mike thinks even the general issues I wanted to raise are graveyarded for the time being."

"But what we're waiting for is to find out what's going to happen to Egtverchi," Liu said. "The UN examining group must be already on its way. What business do you have to be hatching philosophical mandrake's-eggs when the life of a—of a human being, there's no other way to put it—is hanging on the next half hour?"

"Liu," Ruiz said gently, "forgive me, but are you so convinced that Egtverchi is what you mean by a human being—a *hnau*, a rational soul? Does he talk like one? You were complaining yourself that he won't answer questions, and that very often when he speaks he doesn't make much sense. I've talked to adult Lithians, I knew Egtverchi's father well, and Egtverchi isn't much like them, let alone much like a human being. Hasn't anything that's happened in the past hour changed your mind?"

"Oh, no," Liu said warmly, reaching out her hands for the Jesuit's. "Ramon, you've heard him talk yourself, as much as I have—you've tended him with me—you know he's not just an animal! He can be brilliant when he wants to be!"

"You're right, the mandrake's eggs have nothing to do with the case," Michelis said, turning and looking at Liu with dark, astonishingly pain-haunted eyes. "But I can't make Ramon listen to me. He's becoming more and more bound in some rarefied theological torture of his own. I'm sorry Egtverchi isn't as far along as I'd thought, but I foresaw almost from the beginning, I think, that he was going to be a serious embarrassment to us all, the closer he approaches his full intelligence.

"And I didn't get all my information from Ramon. I've seen the protocol on the progressive intelligence tests. Either they're reports on something phenomenal, or else we have no really trustworthy way of measuring Egtverchi's intelligence at all—and that may add up to the same thing in the end. If the tests are right, what's going to happen when Egtverchi finally does grow up? He's the son of a highly intelligent inhuman culture, and he's turning out to be a genius to boot—and his present status is that of an animal in a zoo! Or far worse than that, he's an experimental animal; that's how most of the public tends to think of him. The Lithians aren't going to like that, and furthermore the public won't like it when it learns the facts.

"That's why I brought up this whole citizenship question in the beginning. I see no other way out; we've got to turn him loose."

He was silent a moment, and then added, with almost his wonted gentleness:

"Maybe I'm naïve. I'm not a biologist, let alone a psychometrist. But I'd thought he'd be ready by now, and he isn't, so I guess Ramon wins by default. The interviewers will take him as he is, and the results obviously can't be good."

This was precisely Ruiz-Sanchez' opinion, though he would hardly have put it that way.

"I'll be sorry to see him go, if he leaves," Liu said abstractedly. It was evident, however, that she was hardly thinking about Egtverchi at all any more. "But Mike, I *know* you're right, there's no other solution in the long run—he has to go free. He *is* brilliant, there's no doubt about that. Now that I come to think of it, even this silence isn't the natural reaction of an animal with no inner resources. Father, is there nothing we can do to help?"

Ruiz shrugged; there was nothing that he could say. Michelis' reaction to the apparent parroting and unresponsiveness of Egtverchi had of course been far too extreme for the actual situation, springing mostly from Michelis' own disappointment at the equivocal outcome of the Lithia expedition; he liked issues to be clear-cut, and evidently he had thought he had found in the citizenship maneuver a very sharp-edged tool indeed. But there was much more to it than that: some of it, of course, tied into the yet unadmitted bond which was forming between the chemist and the girl; in that single word "Father" she had shucked the priest off as a foster parent of Egtverchi, and put him in a position to give her away instead.

And what remained left over to be said would have no audience here. Michelis had already dismissed it as "some rarefied theological torture" which was personal to Ruiz and of no importance outside the priest's own skin. What Michelis dismissed would shortly fail to exist at all for Liu, if indeed it had not already been obliterated.

No, there was nothing further that could be done about Egtverchi; the Adversary was protecting his begotten son with all the old, divisive, puissant weapons; it was already too late. Michelis did not know how skilled UN naturalization commissions were at detecting intelligence and desirability in a candidate, even through the thickest smoke screen of language and cultural alienation, and at almost any age after the disease called "talking" had set in. And he did not realize how primed the commission would be to settle the Lithia question by a *fait accompli*. The visitors would see through Egtverchi within an hour at most, and then—

And then, Ruiz would be left with no allies at all. It seemed now to be the will of God that he be stripped of everything, and brought before the Holy Door with no baggage—not even such comforters as Job had, no, not even burdened by belief.

For Egtverchi would surely pass. He was as good as free—and closer to being a citizen in good standing than Ruiz himself.

XII

EGTVERCHI'S coming-out party was held at the underground mansion of Lucien le Comte des Bois-d'Averoigne, a fact which greatly complicated the already hysterical life of Aristide, the countess' caterer. Ordinarily, such a party would have presented Aristide with no problems reaching far beyond the technical ones with which he was already familiar, and used to drive the staff to that frantic peak which he regarded as the utmost in efficiency; but planning for the additional presence of a ten-foot monster was an affront to his conscience as well as to his artistry.

Aristide—born Michel di Giovanni in the timeless brutal peasantry of un-Sheltered Sicily—was a dramatist who knew well the intricate stage upon which he had to work. The count's New York mansion was many levels deep. The part of it in which the party was being held protruded one storey above the surface of Manhattan, as though the buried part of the city were coming out of hibernation—or not quite finished digging in for it. The structure had been a carbarn, Aristide had discovered, a dismal block-square red brick building which had been put up in 1887 when cable street cars had been the newest and most hopeful addition to the city's circulatory system. The trolley tracks, with their middle division for the cable grips, were still there in the asphalt floor, with only a superficial coating of rust—steel does not rust appreciably in less than two centuries. In the center of the top storey was a huge old steam elevator with a basketwork shaft, which had once been used to lower the trolley cars below ground for storage. There were more tracks in the basement and sub-basement, whose elaborate switches led toward the segments of rail in the huge elevator cab. Aristide had been stunned when he first encountered this underlying blueprint, but he had promptly put it to good use.

The countess' parties, thanks to his genius, were now confined in their most formal phase to the uppermost of these three levels, but Aristide had installed a serpentine of fourteen two-chair cars which wound its way sedately along the trolley tracks, picking up as passengers those who were already bored with nothing but chatter and drinking, and rumbled onto the elevator to be taken down—with a great hissing and a cloud of rising steam, for the countess was a stickler for surface authenticity in antiques—to the next level, where presumably more interesting things were happening.

As a dramatist, Aristide also knew his audience: it was his job to provide that whatever was seen on the next levels *was* more interesting than what had been going on above. And he knew his *dramatis personae*, too: he knew more about the countess' regular guests than they knew about themselves, and much of his knowledge would have been decidedly destructive had he been the talkative type. Aristide, however, was an artist; he did not bribe; the notion was as unthinkable to him as plagiarism (except, of course, self-plagiarism; that was how you kept going during slumps). Finally, as an artist, Aristide knew his patroness: he knew her to the point where he could judge just how many parties had to pass by before he could chance repeating an Effect, a Scene or a Sensation.

But what could you do with a ten-foot reptilian kangaroo?

From where he stood in a discrete pillared alcove on the above-ground entrance floor, Aristide watched the early guests filtering in from the reception room to the formal cocktail party, one of his favorite anachronisms, and one which the countess seemed prepared to allow him to repeat year after year. It required very little apparatus, but the most absurd and sub-lethal concoctions, and even more absurd costumes on the part of both staff and guests. The nice rigidity of the costumes provided a pleasant contrast to the unlimbering of the psyche which the drinks quickly induced.

Thus far, there were only the early comers: here, Senator Sharon, waggling her oversize eyebrows in wholesome cheeriness at the remaining guests, ostentatiously refusing drinks, secure in the knowledge that her good friend Aristide had provided for her below five strong young men no one of whom she had ever seen before; there, Prince William of East Orange, a young man whose curse was that he had no vices, and who came again and again to ride the serpentine in hopes of discovering one that he liked; and, nearby, Dr. Samuel P. Shovel, M. D., a jovial, red-cheeked, white-haired man who was the high priest of psichonetology, "the New Science of the Id," and a favorite of Aristide's, since he was easy to provide for—he was fundamentally nothing more complicated than a bottom-pincher.

Faulkner, the head butler, was approaching Aristide stiffly from the left. Ordinarily, Faulkner ran the countess' household like an oriental despot, but he was no longer in control while Aristide was on the premises.

"Shall I order in the embryos in wine?" Faulkner said.

"Don't be such a blind, stupid fool," Aristide said. He had learned his first English from sentimental 3-C 'casts, which gave his ordinary conversation decidedly odd overtones; he was well aware of it, and these days it was one of his principal weapons for driving his underlings, who could not tell when he said these things dispassionately from when he was really angry. "Go below, Faulkner. I'll call you when I need you—if I do."

Faulkner bowed slightly and vanished. Fuming mildly at the interruption, Aristide resumed his survey of the early comers.

In addition to the regulars, there was, of course, the countess, who had posed him no special problems yet. Her gilded make-up was still unmussed, and the mobiles in the little caves Stefano had contrived in her hair spun placidly or blinked their diamond eyes. Then there were the sponsors of the Lithian monster into Shelter society, Dr. Michelis and Dr. Meid; these two might present special problems, for he had been unable to find out enough about them to decide what personal tastes they might need to have catered to down below, despite the fact that they were key guests, second only to the impossible creature itself. There was an explosive potential here, Aristide knew with the certainty of fate, for that impossible creature was already more than an hour late, and the countess had let it be known to all the guests and to Aristide that the creature was to be the guest of honor; fully half of the party would be coming to see him.

There was no one else in the room at the moment but a UN man wearing a funny hat—a sort of crash helmet liberally provided with communications apparatus and other, unnamable devices, including bubble goggles which occasionally filmed over to become a miniature 3-V screen—and a Dr. Martin Agronski, whom Aristide could not place at all, and whom he regarded with the consequent intense suspicion he reserved for people whose weaknesses he could not even guess at. Agronski's face was as petulant as that of the Prince of East Orange, but he was a much older man, and it seemed unlikely that he was there for the same reasons. He had something to do with the guest of honor, which made Aristide all the more uneasy. Dr. Agronski seemed to know Dr. Michelis, but for an unaccountable reason shied away from him at every opportunity; he was spending most of his time at one of the most potent of Aristide's punches, with the glum determination of a non-drinker who believes that he can perfect his poise by poisoning his timidity. Perhaps a woman . . . ?

Aristide crooked a finger. His assistant scuttled around the back of the hanging floral decorations with a practiced stoop, covering even the sound of his movements by a brief delay which allowed the serpentine to come into its station, and cocked his ear to Aristide's mouth under the squeal of the train's brakes.

"Watch that one," Aristide said through motionless lips, pointing with the apex of one pelvic bone. "He will be drunk within the next half hour. Take him out before he falls down, but don't take him off the premises. She may ask for him later. Better put him in the recovery room and taper him off as soon as he begins to wobble."

The assistant nodded and pedaled away, bent double. Aristide was still talking to him in blunt, businesslike English; that was a good sign, as far as it went.

Aristide returned to watching the guests; their number was growing a little, but he was still most interested in assessing the countess' reaction to the absence of the guest of honor. For the moment Aristide himself was in no danger, though he could see that the countess' hints had begun to acquire a certain hardness. Thus far, however, she was directing them at the monster's sponsors, Dr. Michelis and Dr. Meid, and it was plain that they had no answer for these gambits.

Dr. Michelis could only say over and over again, with a politeness which was becoming more and more formal as his patience visibly evaporated:

"Madame, I don't know when he's coming. I don't even know where he lives now. He promised to come. I'm not surprised that he's late, but I think he'll show up eventually."

The countess turned away petulantly, swinging her hips. Here was the first danger point for Aristide. There was no other pressure that the countess could bring to bear upon the monster's sponsors, regardless of how ignorant they were of the actual situation in the countess' household. By some trick of heredity, Lucien le Comte des Bois-d'Averoigne, Procurator of Canarsie, had been shrewd enough to spend his money wisely: he gave ninety-eight per cent of it to his wife, and used the other two per cent to disappear with for most of the year. There were even rumors that he did scientific research, though nobody could say in what field; certainly it could not be psichonetology or ufonics, or the countess would have known about it, since both were currently fashionable. And without the count, the countess was socially a nullity supported only by money; if the Lithian creature failed to show up at all, there was nothing that the countess could do to his sponsors but fail to invite them to the next party—which she would probably fail to do anyhow. On the other hand, there was a great deal that she might do to Aristide. She could not fire him, of course—he had kept careful dossiers against that possibility—but she could make his professional life with her very difficult indeed.

He signaled his second-in-command.

"Give Senator Sharon the canapé with the jolt in it as soon as there are ten more people on the floor," he directed crisply. "I don't like the way this is going. As soon as we have a minimum crowd, we'll have to get them rolling on the trains—Sharon's not the best Judas goat for the purpose, but she'll have to do. Take my advice, Cyril, or you will rue the day."

"Very good, Maestro," the assistant, whose name was not Cyril at all, said respectfully.

Michelis had hardly noticed the serpentine at the beginning, except as a novelty, but somehow or other it became noisier as the party grew older. It seemed to wind along the floor about every five minutes, but he soon realized that there were actually three such trains: the first one collected passengers up here; the second returned parties from the second level, to discharge wildly exhilarated recruiters among the cautiously formal newcomers on the first level; and the third train, usually almost empty this early in the party's course, brought glassy-eyed party-poopers from the sub-basement, who were removed efficiently by the countess' livery in a covered station-stop well apart from the main entrance and well out of sight of new boarders for the nether levels. Then the whole cycle repeated itself.

Michelis had had every intention of staying off the serpentine entirely. He did not like the diplomatic service, especially

now that it had nothing left to be diplomatic about, and anyhow he was far too dedicated to loneliness to be comfortable
even at small parties, let alone anything like *this*. After a while,
however, he became bored with repeating that same apology
for Egtverchi, and aware that the top level of the party was
now so empty that his and Liu's presence there was keeping
their hostess against her will.

When Liu finally noticed that the serpentine not only toured
this level but went below, he lost his last excuse to stay off it;
and the elevator took all the rest of the newcomers down, leaving behind only the servants and a few bewildered scientific
attachés who probably were at the wrong party to begin with.
He looked about for Agronski, whose presence had astonished
him early, but the hollow-eyed geologist had disappeared.

Everyone on the train shouted with glee and mock terror as
the steam elevator took it down to the second level in utter
blackness and rusty-smelling humidity. Then the great doors
rolled up sharply in their eyes, and the train surged out, making an abrupt turn along its banked rails. Its plowlike nose
butted immediately through a set of swinging double doors,
plunged its passengers into even deeper darkness, and stopped
completely with a grinding shudder.

From out of the darkness came a barrage of shrieking, hysterical feminine laughter and the shouting of men's voices.

"Oh, I can't stand!"

"Henry, is that you?"

"Leggo of me, you bitch."

"I'm so dizzy!"

"Look out, the damn thing's speeding up again!"

"Get off my foot, you bastard."

"Hey, *you're* not my husband."

"Ugh. Lady, I couldn't care less."

"Woman's gone too far this—"

Then they were drowned out by a siren so prolonged and
deafening that Michelis' ears rang frighteningly even after the
sound had risen past the upper limits of audibility. Then there
was the groan of machinery, a dim violet glow—

The serpentine was turning over and over in midspace, supported by nothing. Many-colored stars, none of them very
bright, whirled past, rising on one side and sweeping over and

then under the train with a period of only ten seconds from one "horizon" to the other. The shouts and the laughter were heard again, accompanied by a frantic scrabbling sound—and there came the siren again, first as a pressure, then as a thin singing which seemed to be inside the skull, and then as a prolonged sickening slide toward the infrabass.

Liu clutched frantically at Michelis' arm, but he could do nothing but cling to his seat. Every cell in his brain was flaring with alarm, but he was paralyzed and sick with giddiness—

Lights.

The world stabilized instantly. The serpentine sat smugly on its tracks, which were supported by cantilever braces; it had never moved. At the bottom of a gigantic barrel, disheveled guests looked up at the nearly blinded passengers of the train and howled with savage mockery. The "stars" had been spots of fluorescent paint, brought to life by hidden ultraviolet lamps. The illusion of spinning in midspace had been made more real by the siren, which had disturbed their vestibular apparatus, the inner ear which maintains the sense of balance.

"All out!" a rough male voice shouted. Michelis looked down cautiously; he was still a little dizzy. The shouter was a man in rumpled black evening clothes and fire-red hair; his huge shoulders had burst one seam of his jacket. "You get the next train. That's the rules."

Michelis thought of refusing, and changed his mind. Being tumbled in the barrel was probably less likely to produce serious wounds than would fighting with two people who had already "earned" their passage out in his and Liu's seats. There were rules of conduct for everything. A gang ladder protruded up at them; when their turn came, he helped Liu down it.

"Try not to fight it," he told her in a low voice. "When it starts to revolve, slide if you can, roll if you can't. Got a pyrostyle? All right, here's mine—jab if anybody stays too close, but don't worry about the drum—it looks thoroughly waxed."

It was; but Liu was frightened and Michelis in a murderously ugly mood by the time the next train came through and took them out; he was glad that he had not decided to argue with his predecessors in the barrel. Anybody who had tried the same thing with him might well have been killed.

The fact that he was drenched with perfume as the serpentine passed through the next cell did not exactly improve his temper, but at least the cell did not require anyone's participation. It was a sizable and beautiful garden made of blown glass in every possible color, in which live Javanese models were posed in dioramas of discovered lust; the situations depicted were melodramatic in the extreme but, except for their almost imperceptible breathing, the models did not move a muscle; they were almost as motionless as the glass foliage. To Michelis' surprise—for outside the sciences he had almost no aesthetic sense—Liu regarded these lascivious, immobile scenes with a kind of withdrawn, grave approval.

"It's an art, to suggest a dance without moving," she murmured suddenly, as though she had sensed his uneasiness. "Difficult with the brush, far more difficult with the body. I think I know the man who designed this; there couldn't be but one."

He stared at her as though he had never seen her before, and by the pure current of jealousy that shot through him he knew for the first time that he loved her. "Who?" he said hoarsely.

"Oh, Tsien Hi, of course. The last classicist. I thought he was dead, but this isn't a copy—"

The serpentine slowed before the exit doors long enough for two models, looking obscenely alive in very modest movement, to hand them each a fan covered with brushed drawings in ink. A single glance was enough to make Michelis thrust his fan in his pocket, unwilling to acknowledge ownership of it by so definite a gesture as throwing it away; but Liu pointed mutely to an ideogram and folded hers with reverence. "Yes," she said. "It is he; these are the original sketches. I never thought I'd own one—"

The train lurched forward suddenly. The garden vanished, and they were plunged into a vague, colored chaos of meaningless emotions. There was nothing to see or hear or feel, yet Michelis was shaken to his soul, and then shaken again, and again. He cried out, and dimly heard others crying. He fought for control of himself, but it eluded him, and . . . no, he had it now, or almost had it. . . . If he could only *think* for an instant—

For an instant, he managed it, and saw what was happening. The new cell was a long corridor, divided by invisible currents of moving air into fifteen sub-cells. Inside each sub-cell was a colored smoke, and in each smoke was some gas which went instantly home to the hypothalamus. Michelis recognized some of them: they were crude hallucinogenic compounds which had been developed during the heyday of tranquilizer research in the mid-twentieth century. Under the waves of fright, religious exaltation, berserker bravery, lust for power, and less namable emotions which each induced, he felt a mounting intellectual anger at such irresponsible wholesale tampering with the pharmacology of the mind for the sake of a momentary "experience"; but he knew that this kind of jolt-breathing was anything but uncommon in the Shelter state. The smokes had the reputation of being non-addicting, which for the most part they were—but they were certainly habit-forming, which is quite a different thing, and not necessarily less dangerous.

A hazy, formless curtain of pink at the far end of the corridor proved to be a pure free-serotonin antagonist in high concentration, a true ataraxic which washed his mind free of every emotion but contentment with everything in all the wide universe. What must be, must be . . . it is all for the best . . . there is peace in everything—

In this state of uncritical yea-saying, the passengers on the serpentine were run through an assembly line of elaborate and bestial practical jokes. It ended with a 3-V tape re-creation of Belsen, in which the scenarist had cunningly made it appear that the people on the serpentine would be next into the ovens. As the furnace door closed behind them there was a blast of mind-cleansing oxygen; staggering with horror at what they had been about to accept with joy, the passengers were helped off the train to join a guffawing audience of previous victims.

Michelis' only impulse was to escape—above all he did not want to stay to laugh at the next load of passengers in shock—but he was too exhausted to get beyond the nearest bench in the amphitheater, and Liu could hardly walk even that far. They were forced to sit there in the press until they had made a better recovery.

It was fortunate that they did. While they were nursing their drinks—Michelis had been deeply suspicious of the warm amber cups, but their contents had proved to be nothing but

honest and welcome brandy—the next train was greeted with
a roar of delight and a unanimous surge of the crowd to its
feet.

Egtverchi had arrived.

There was a real mob now in the cocktail lounge above ground,
but Aristide was far from happy; he had already cut off quite a
few heads down below on the catering staff. He had somewhere inside him a very delicate sense which told him when a
party was going sour, and that sense had put up the red alarms
long before this. The arrival of the guest of honor in particular
had been an enormous fiasco. The countess had not been on
hand, the creature's sponsors had not been there, none of the
really important guests who had been invited specifically to see
the guest of honor had been there, and the guest himself had
betrayed Aristide into showing, before all the staff, that he was
frightened out of his wits.

He was bitterly ashamed of his fright, but the fact was now
beyond undoing. He had been told to anticipate a monster,
but not such a monster as this—a creature well *more* than ten
feet high, a reptile which walked more like a man than like a
kangaroo, with vast grinning jaws, wattles which changed color
every few moments, small clawlike hands which looked as
though they could pluck one like a chicken, a balancing tail
which kept sweeping trays off tables, and above all a braying
laugh and an enormous tenor voice which spoke English with
a perfection so cold and carefully calculated as to make Aristide
feel like a thumb-fingered leather-skinned Sicilian who had just
landed. And at the monster's entrance, nobody but Aristide
had been there to welcome him. . . .

A train rumbled into the atrium of the recovery room, but
before it stopped, Senator Sharon tumbled out with a vast
display of piano legs and black eyebrows. "Look at *him!*" she
squealed, full of the five-fold revival Aristide had conscien-
tiously arranged for her. "Isn't he *male!*"

Another failure for Aristide: it was one of the countess'
standing orders that the Senator had to be put through her cell
and fired out into the Shelter night long before the party
proper could be said to have begun; otherwise the Senator

would spend the rest of the evening, after her five-fold awak-ening, climbing from one pair of shoulders to another to a political, literary, scientific or any other eminence she could manage to attain at the expense of everyone else who could be bought with half an hour on a table top—and never mind that she would spend the rest of the next week falling down from that eminence into the swamps of nymphomania again. If Senator Sharon were not properly ejected this early, and with due assurances, in the warm glow of her aftermath, she was given to lawsuits.

The empty train pulled out invitingly into the lounge. The Lithian monster saw it and his grin got wider.

"I always wanted to be an engine driver," he said in a brassy English which nevertheless was more precise than anything to which Aristide would be able to pretend to the end of his life. "And there's the major-domo. Good sir, I've brought two, three, several guests of my own. Where is our hostess?"

Aristide pointed helplessly, and the tall reptile boarded the train at the front car, with a satisfied crow. He was scarcely settled in before the rest of his party was pouring across the lounge floor and piling in behind him. The train started with a jerk, and rumbled to the elevator. It sank down amid tall wisps of steam.

And that was that. Aristide had muffed the grand entrance. Had he had any doubts about it, they would have been laid to rest most directly: less than ten minutes later, he was snooted egregiously by Faulkner.

So much for being a dedicated artist with a loyal patroness, he thought dismally. Tomorrow, he would be a short-order cook in some Shelter commissariat, dossiers or no dossiers. And why? Because he had been unable to anticipate the time of arrival, let alone the desires or the friends, of some creature which had never been born on Earth at all.

He marched deliberately and morosely away from his post toward the recovery room, kicking assistants who were green enough to stay within range. He could think of nothing further to do but to supervise personally the tapering-off of Dr. Martin Agronski, the unknown guest who had something to do with the Lithian.

But he had no illusions. Tomorrow, Aristide, caterer to the Countess des Bois-d'Averoigne, would be lucky to be Michel di Giovanni, late of the malarial plains of Sicily.

Michelis was sorry he had allowed himself and Liu aboard the serpentine the moment he understood the construction of the second level, for he saw at once that they would have virtually no chance of seeing Egtverchi's arrival. Fundamentally, the second level was divided by soundproof walls into a number of smaller parties, some of them only slightly drunker and more unorthodox than the cocktail party had been, but the rest running a broad spectrum of frenetic exoticism. He and Liu were carried completely around the course before he was able to figure out how to get the girl and himself safely off the serpentine; and each time he was moved to attempt it, the train began to go faster in unpredictable spurts, producing a sensation rather like that of riding a roller coaster in the middle of the night.

Nevertheless, they saw the only entrance that counted. Egtverchi emerged from the last gas bath standing in the head car of the serpentine, and stepped out of the car under his own power. In the next five cars behind him, also standing, were ten nearly identical young men in uniforms of black and lizard-green with silver piping, their arms folded, their expressions stern, their eyes straight ahead.

"Greetings," Egtverchi said, with a deep bow which his disproportionately small dinosaurian arms and hands made both comical and mocking. "Madame the Countess, I am delighted. You are protected by many bad smells, but I have braved them all."

The crowd applauded. The countess' reply was lost in the noise, but evidently she had chided him with being naturally immune to smokes which would affect Earthmen, for he said promptly, with a trace of hurt in his voice:

"I thought you might say that, but I'm grieved to be caught in the right. To the pure all things are pure, however—did you ever see such upstanding, unshaken young men?" He gestured at the ten. "But of course I cheated. I stopped their nostrils with filters, as Ulysses stopped his men's ears with wax to pass the sirens. My entourage will stand for anything; they think I am a genius."

With the air of a conjurer, the Lithian produced a silver whistle which seemed small in his hand, and blew into the thick air a white, warbling note which was utterly inadequate to the gesture which had preceded it. The ten soldierly young men promptly melted. The forefront of the crowd gleefully toed the limp bodies, which took the abuse with lax indifference.

"Drunk," Egtverchi said with fatherly disapproval. "Of course. Actually I didn't stop their noses at all. I prevented their reticular formations from reporting the countess' smokes to their brains until I gave the cue. Now they have gotten all the messages at once; isn't it disgraceful? Madame, please have them removed, such dissoluteness embarrasses me. I shall have to institute discipline."

The countess clapped her hands. "Aristide! Aristide?" She touched the transceiver concealed in her hair, but there was no response that Michelis could detect. Her expression changed abruptly from childish delight to infant fury. "Where is that lousy rustic—"

Michelis, boiling, shouldered his way into Egtverchi's line of sight with difficulty.

"Just what the hell do you think you're doing?" he said in a hoarse voice.

"Good evening, Mike. I am attending a party, just as you are. Good evening, dear Liu. Countess, do you know my foster parents? But I am sure you do."

"Of course," the countess said, turning her bare shoulders and back unmistakably on Michelis and Liu, and looking up at Egtverchi's perpetually grinning head from under gilded eyelids. "Let's go next door—there's more room, and it will be quieter. We've all seen enough of these train riders. After you, their arrivals will seem all alike."

"I cultivate the unique," Egtverchi said. "But I must have Mike and Liu by my side, Countess. I am the only reptile in the universe with mammalian parents, and I cherish them. I have a notion that it may be a sin; isn't that interesting?"

The gilded eyelids lowered. It had been years since the countess' caterers had come up with a new sin interesting enough to be withheld from the next evening's guests for private testing; that was common knowledge. She looked as if she scented one now, Michelis thought; and since she was, in fact, a woman of small imagination, Michelis was not in much doubt as to what it was. For all his saurian shape and texture, there was something about Egtverchi that was intensely, overwhelmingly masculine.

And intensely childlike, too. That the combination was perfectly capable of overriding any repugnance people might feel toward his additionally overwhelming reptilian-ness had already been demonstrated, in the response to his first interview on 3-V. His wry and awry comments on Earthly events and customs had been startling enough, and perhaps it could have been predicted even then that the intelligentsia of the world would pick him up as a new fad before the week was out. But nobody had anticipated the flood of letters from children, from parents, from lonely women.

Egtverchi was a sponsored news commentator now, the first such ever to have an audience composed half-and-half of disaffected intellectuals and delighted children. There was no precedent for it in the present century, at least; learned men in communications compared him simultaneously with two historical figures named Adlai E. Stevenson and Oliver J. Dragon.

Egtverchi also had a lunatic following, though its composition had not yet been analyzed publicly by his 3-V network. Ten of these followers were being lugged limply out by the countess' livery right now, and Michelis' eyes followed them speculatively while he trailed with the crowd after Egtverchi and the countess, out of the amphitheater and into the huge lounge next door. The uniforms were suggestive—but of what? They might have been no more than costumes, designed for the party alone; had the ten young men who fell to the bleat of Egtverchi's silver whistle been physically different from each other, the effect would have been smaller, as Egtverchi would have known. And yet the whole notion of uniforms was foreign to Lithian psychology, while it was profoundly meaningful in Earth terms—and Egtverchi knew more about Earth than most Earthmen did, already.

Lunatics in uniforms, who thought Egtverchi to be a genius who could do no wrong; what could that mean?

Were Egtverchi a man, one would know instantly what it meant. But he was not a man, but a musician playing upon man as on an organ. The structure of the composition would not be evident for a long time to come—if it had a structure; Egtverchi might only be improvising, at least this early. That was a frightening thought in itself.

And all this had happened within a month of the awarding of citizenship to Egtverchi. That had been a pleasant surprise. Michelis was none too sure how he felt about the surprises that had followed; about those certain to come he was decidedly wary.

"I have been exploring this notion of parenthood," Egtverchi was saying. "I know who my father is, of course—it is a knowledge we are born with—but the concept that goes with the word is quite unlike anything you have here on Earth. *Your* concept is a tremendous network of inconsistencies."

"In what way?" the countess said, not very much interested.

"Why, it seems to be based on a reverence for the young, and an extremely patient and protective attitude toward their physical and mental welfare. Yet you make them live in these huge caves, utterly out of contact with the natural world, and you teach them to be afraid of death—which of course makes them a little insane, because there is nothing anybody can do about death. It is like teaching them to be afraid of the second law of thermodynamics, just because living matter sets that law aside for a very brief period. How they hate you!"

"I doubt that they know I exist," the countess said drily. She had no children.

"Oh, they hate their own parents first of all," Egtverchi said, "but there is enough hatred left over for every other adult on your planet. They write me about it. They have never had anybody to say this to before, but they see in me someone who has had no hand in their torment, who is critical of it, and who obviously is a comical, harmless fellow who won't betray them."

"You're exaggerating," Michelis said uneasily.

"Oh no, Mike. I have prevented several murders already. There was one five-year-old who had a most ingenious plan, something involving garbage disposal. He was ready to include his mother, his father, and his fourteen-year-old brother, and the whole affair would have been blamed on a computational error in his city's sanitation department. Amazing that a child that age could have planned anything so elaborate, but I believe it would have worked—these Shelter cities of yours are so complex, they become lethal engines if even the most minute errors creep into them. Do you doubt me, Mike? I shall show you the letter."

"No," Michelis said slowly. "I don't think I do."

Egtverchi's eyes filmed briefly. "Some day I will let one of these affairs proceed to completion," he said. "As a demonstration, perhaps. Something of the sort seems to be in order."

Somehow Michelis did not doubt that he would, nor that the results would be as predicted. People did not remember their childhoods clearly enough to take seriously the rages and frustrations that shook children—and the smaller the child, the less superego it had to keep the emotions tamed. It seemed more than likely that a figure like Egtverchi would be able to tap this vast, seething underworld of impotent fury more effectively and easily than any human analyst, no matter how skilled and subtle, had ever been able to do.

And there was where you had to tap it, if you were hoping to do any good. Tapping it by hindsight, through analysis of adults, was successful with neurotics, but it had never proved effective against the psychoses; those had to be attacked pharmacologically, by regulating serotonin metabolism with ataraxics—the carefully tailored chemical grandchildren of the countess' crude smokes. That worked, but it was not a cure, but a maintenance operation—like giving insulin or sulfonylureas to a diabetic. The organic damage had already been done. In the great raveled knot of the brain, the basic reverberating circuits, once set in motion, could be interrupted but never discontinued—except by destructive surgery, a barbarity now a century out of use.

And it all fitted some of the disturbing things he had been discovering about the Shelter economy since his return from his long sojourn on Lithia. Having been born into it, Michelis had always taken that economy pretty much for granted; or at least his adult memory of his childhood told him that. Maybe it had really been different, and perhaps a little less grim, back in those days, or maybe that was just an illusion cherished by the silent censor in his brain. But it seemed to him that in those days people had let themselves become reconciled to these endless caverns and corridors for the sake of their children, in the hope that the next generation would be out from under the fear and could know something a little better—a glimpse of sunlight, a little rain, the fall of a leaf.

Since then, the restrictions on surface living had been relaxed greatly—nobody now believed in the possibility of nuclear war, since the Shelter race had produced an obvious impasse—but somehow the psychic atmosphere was far worse instead of better. The number of juvenile gangs roaming the corridors had increased four hundred per cent while Michelis was out of the solar system; the UN was now spending about a hundred million dollars a year on elaborate recreation and rehabilitation programs for adolescents, but the rec centers stayed largely deserted, and the gangs continued to multiply. The latest measure taken against them was frankly punitive: a tremendous increase in the cost of compulsory insurance on power scooters, seemingly harmless, slow-moving vehicles which the gangs had adapted first to simple crimes like purse-snatching, and then to such more complicated and destructive games as mass raids on food warehouses, industrial distilleries, even utilities—it had been drag-racing in the air ducts that had finally triggered the confiscatory insurance rates.

In the light of what Egtverchi had said, the gangs made perfect and horrible sense. Nobody now believed in the possibility of nuclear war, but nobody could believe in the possibility of a full return to surface life, either. The billions of tons of concrete and steel were far too plainly there to stay. The adults no longer had hopes even for their children, let alone for themselves. While Michelis had been away in the Eden of Lithia, on Earth the number of individual crimes without motive—crimes committed just to distract the committer from the grinding monotony of corridor life—had passed the total of all other crimes put together. Only last week some fool on the UN's Public Polity Commission had proposed putting tranquilizers in the water supplies; the World Health Organization had had him ousted within twenty-four hours—actually putting the suggestion into effect would have doubled crimes of this kind, by cutting the population further free of its already feeble grip on responsibility—but it was too late to counteract the effect on morale of the suggestion alone.

The WHO had had good reason to be both swift and arbitrary about it. Its last demographic survey showed, under the grim heading of "Actual Insanity," a total of thirty-five million un-hospitalized early paranoid schizophrenics who had been clearly diagnosed, every one of whom should have been committed for treatment at once—except that, were the WHO to commit them, the Shelter economy would suffer a manpower loss more devastating than any a war had inflicted on mankind in all of its history. Every one of those thirty-five million persons was a major hazard to his neighbors and to his job, but the Shelter economy was too complicated to do without them—

—let alone do without the unrecognized, subclinical cases, which probably totaled twice as many. The Shelter economy obviously could not continue operating much longer without a major collapse; it was on the verge of a psychotic break at this instant.

With Egtverchi for a therapist?

Preposterous. But who else . . ?

"You're very gloomy tonight," the countess was complaining. "Won't you amuse anyone but children?"

"No one," Egtverchi said promptly. "Except, of course, myself. And of course I am also a child. There now: not only do I have mammals for parents, but I am myself my own uncle —these 3-V amusers of children are always everyone's uncle. You do not appreciate me properly, Countess; I become more interesting every minute, but you do not notice. In the next instant I may turn into your mother, and you will do nothing but yawn."

"You've already turned into my mother," the countess said, with a challenging, slumbrous look. "You even have her jowls, and all those impossibly even teeth. And the talk. My God. Turn into something else—and *don't* make it Lucien."

"I would turn into the count if I could," Egtverchi said, with what Michelis was almost sure was genuine regret. "But I have no affinity for affines; I don't even understand Haertel yet. Tomorrow, perhaps?"

"My God," the countess said again. "Why in the world did I think I should invite you? You're too dull to be borne. I don't know why I count on anything any more. I should know better by now."

Astonishingly, Egtverchi began to sing, in a high, pure, *castrato* tenor: "*Swef, swef, Susa. . . .*" For a moment Michelis thought the voice was coming from someone else, but the countess swung on Egtverchi instantly, her face twisted into a Greek mask of pure rage.

"Stop that," she said, her voice as raw as a wound. Her expression, under the gilded gaiety of her party paint, was savagely incongruous.

"Certainly," Egtverchi said soothingly. "You see I am not your mother after all. It pays to be careful with these accusations."

"You lousy snake-scaled demon!"

"Please, Countess; I have scales, you have breasts; this is proper and fitting. You ask me to amuse you; I thought you might enjoy my jongleur's lullaby."

"Where did you hear that song?"

"Nowhere," Egtverchi said. "I reconstructed it. I could see from the cast of your eyes that you were a born Norman."

"How did you do it?" Michelis said, interested in spite of himself. It was the first sign he had encountered that Egtverchi had any musical ability.

"Why, by the genes, Mike," Egtverchi said; his literal Lithian mind had gone to the substance of Michelis' question rather than to its sense. "This is the way I know my name, and the name of my father. E-G-T-V-E-R-C-H-I is the pattern of genes on one of my chromosomes; the G, V and I alleles are of course from my mother; my cerebral cortex has direct sensual access to my genetic composition. We see ancestry everywhere we look, just as you see colors—it is one of the spectra of the real world. Our ancestors bred that sense into us; you could do worse than imitate them. It is helpful to know what a man is before he even opens his mouth."

Michelis felt a faint but decided chill. He wondered if Chtexa had ever mentioned this to Ruiz. Probably not; a discovery so fascinating to a biologist would have driven the Jesuit to talking about it. In any event, it was too late to ask him, for he was on the way to Rome; Cleaver was even farther away by now; and Agronski wouldn't know.

"Dull, dull, dull," the countess said. She had got back most of her self-possession.

"To be sure, to the dull," Egtverchi said, with his eternal grin, which somehow managed to disarm almost anything that he said. "But I offered to amuse you; you did not enjoy my entertainment. It is your doom to amuse me, too, you know; I am the guest here. What do you have in the sub-basement, for instance? Let us go see. Where are my summer soldiers? Somebody wake them; we have a trip to take."

The packed guests had been listening intently, obviously enjoying the countess' floundering upon Egtverchi's long and multiple-barbed gaff. When she bowed her high-piled, gilded head and led the way back toward the trolley tracks, a blurred and almost animal cheer shook the lounge. Liu shrank back against Michelis; he put his arm tightly around her waist.

"Mike, let's not go," she whispered. "Let's go home. I've had enough."

XIII

ENTRY IN EGTVERCHI'S JOURNAL:

June 13th, 13th week of citizenship: This week I stayed home. Elevators on Earth never stop at this floor. Must check why. They have reasons for everything they do.

It was during the week Egtverchi's program was off the air that Agronski stumbled across the discovery that he no longer knew who he was. Though he had not recognized it for what it was at the time, the first forebodings of this vastation had come creeping over him as far back as that four-cornered debate in Xoredeshch Sfath, when he had begun to realize that he did not know what Mike, the Father and Cleaver were talking about. After a while, it had begun to seem to him that they didn't know, either; the long looping festoons of logic and emotion with which they so determinedly bedecked the humid Lithian air seemed to hang from nothing, and touch no ground on which he or any other human being he knew had ever stood.

Then, after he had come home, he had hardly even been angered—only vaguely irritated—when the *J. I. R.* had failed to include him in its invitation to prepare the preliminary article on Lithia. The Lithian experience had already begun to seem remote and dreamlike to him, and he already knew that he and the senior authors could have nothing more to say to each other on that subject which would make mutual sense.

So far, so good; but so far there was no explanation for the sensation of bottomless despair, loneliness and disgust which had swept over him here at the discovery, seemingly of no consequence in itself, that his favorite 3-V program would not be on tonight. Superficially, everything else was as it should be. He had been invited to a year of residency at Fordham's seismological laboratories on the basis of his previous publications on gravity waves—tidal and seismic tremors—and his arrival had been greeted with just the proper mixture of respect and enthusiasm by the Jesuits who ran the great university's science department. His apartment in the bachelor scientists' quarters was not at all monastic, indeed it was almost luxurious for a single man; he had as much apparatus as any geologist in his field could have dreamed of having under such an arrangement, he was virtually free of lecture duties, he had made several new friends among the graduate students assigned to him—and yet, tonight, looking blankly at the replacement program which had appeared instead of Egtverchi on his 3-V screen—

In retrospect, each of the steps toward this abyss seemed irrevocable, and yet they had all been so small! He had been looking forward to his return to Earth with an unfocussed but intense excitement, not directed toward any one aspect of Earthly life, but simply eager for the pat wink of all things familiar. But when he had returned, he found no reassurance in the familiar; indeed, it all seemed rather flat. He put it down to having been a relatively free-wheeling, nearly unique individual on a virtually unpopulated world; there was bound to be a certain jolt in readapting oneself to the life of one mole among billions.

And yet a jolt was precisely what it had not been. Instead, it had been a most peculiar kind of lack of all sensation, as though the familiar were powerless to move him or even to touch him. As the days wore by, this intellectual, emotional, sensual numbness became more and more pronounced, until it became a kind of sensation in itself, a sort of giddiness—as though he were about to fall, and yet could not see anything to grab hold of to steady himself, or indeed what kind of ground he was standing on at the moment.

Somewhere along in there he had taken up listening to Egtverchi's news broadcasts, out of simple curiosity insofar as he could remember any feeling so far removed in time. There had been something there that was useful to him, though he could not know what it was. At the very least, Egtverchi occasionally amused him. Sometimes the creature reminded him obscurely that on Lithia, no matter how divorced he had been from the thinking and the purposes of the other members of the commission, he had been almost unique; that was comforting, though it was a watery comfort. And sometimes, during Egtverchi's most savage sallies against Agronski's familiar Earth, he felt a slight surge of genuine pleasure, as though Egtverchi were his agent in acting out a long and complicated revenge against enemies hidden and unknown. More usually, however, Egtverchi failed to penetrate the slightly nauseating numbness which had closed around him; the broadcasts simply became a habit.

In the meantime, increasingly it came over him that he did not understand what his fellow men were doing or, in the minority of instances where he did understand it, it seemed to him to be something utterly trivial; why did people bind themselves to these regimes? Where were they going that was so important? The air of determined dull preoccupation with which the average troglodyte went to his job, got through it, and came away again to his cubby in his target area would have seemed tragic to him if the actors had not all been such utter ciphers; the eagerness, dedication, chicanery, short-cutting, brilliance, hard labor and total immersion of people who thought themselves or their jobs important would have seemed absurd had he been able to think of anything in the world more worth all this attention, but the savor was leaking rapidly out of everything now. Even the steaks he had dreamed of on Lithia were now only something else to be got through, an exercise in cutting, forking, swallowing, and disturbed cat naps.

In brief flashes of a few minutes at a time, he was able to envy the Jesuit scientists. They still believed geology to be important, an illusion which now seemed far in the past—a matter of weeks—to Agronski. Their religion, too, seemed to be a constant source of great intellectual excitement, especially during this Holy Year; Agronski had gathered from conversations with Ramon two years ago that the Jesuit order is the cerebral cortex of the Church, concerned with its knottiest moral, theological and organizational problems. In particular, Agronski remembered, the Jesuits were charged with weighing questions of polity and making recommendations to Rome, and it was here that the area of greatest excitement at Fordham was centered. Although he never did arouse himself sufficiently to find out the core of the issue, Agronski knew that this year was to mark the settlement by papal proclamation of one of the great dogmatic questions of Catholicism, comparable to the dogma of the Assumption of the Blessed Virgin which had been proclaimed a century ago; from the hot discussions he overheard in the refectory, and elsewhere after working hours, he gathered that the Society of Jesus had already made its recommendation, and all that remained to be debated was the most probable decision which Pope Hadrian would arrive at. That there should still be any question about the matter surprised him a little, until a scrap of conversation overheard in the commissariat told him that there was nothing in the least binding about the Order's decisions. The doctrine of the Assumption had been heavily recommended against by the Jesuits of the time, despite the fact that it had been an obvious personal preference of the then incumbent Pope, but it had been adopted all the same—the decision of St. Peter's was beyond all appeal.

Nothing in the world, Agronski was learning with this feeling of general giddiness and nausea, was that certain. In the end his colleagues here at Fordham came to seem as remote to him as Ruiz-Sanchez had on Lithia. The Catholic Church in 2050 was still fourth in rank in terms of number of adherents, with Islam, the Buddhists and the Hindi sects commanding the greater number of worshipers, in that order; after Catholicism, there was the confusing number of Protestant groups, which might well outnumber the Catholics if one included all those in the world who had no faith worth mentioning—and it was probable that the agnostics, atheists and don't-cares taken as a separate group were at least as numerous as the Jews, perhaps more so. As for Agronski, he knew grayly that he belonged no more with one of these groups than with any other; he had been cut adrift; he was slowly beginning to doubt the existence of the phenomenal universe itself, and he could not bring himself to care enough about the probably unreal to feel that it mattered what intellectual organization you imposed on it, whether it was High Episcopalian or Logical Positivist. If one no longer likes steak, what does it matter how well it has been aged, butchered, cooked or served?

The invitation to Egtverchi's coming-out party had almost succeeded in piercing the iron fog which had descended between Agronski and the rest of creation. He had had the notion that the sight of a live Lithian might do something for him, though what he could hardly have said; and besides, he had wanted to see Mike and the Father again, moved by memories of having been fond of them once. But the Father was not there, Mike had been removed light-years away from him by having taken up in the meantime with a woman—and of all the meaningless obsessions of mankind, Agronski was most determined now to avoid the tyranny of sex—and in person Egtverchi had turned out to be a grotesque and alarming Earthly caricature of the Lithians that Agronski remembered. Disgusted with himself, he kept sedulously away from all of them, and in the process, quite inadvertently, got drunk. He remembered no more of the party except scraps of a fight that he had had with some swarthy flunkey in a huge dark room bounded by metal webwork, like being inside the shaft of the Eiffel Tower at midnight—a memory which seemed to include inexplicable rising clouds of steam and a jerky intensification of his catholic, nauseating vertigo, as though he and his anonymous adversary were being lowered into hell on the end of a thousand-mile-long hydraulic piston.

He had awakened after noon the next day in his rooms with a thousand-fold increase in the giddiness, an awful sense of mission before a holocaust, and the worst hangover he had had since the drunk he had staged on cooking sherry in the first week of his freshman year in college. It took him two days to get rid of the hangover, but the rest remained, shutting him off utterly even from the things that he could see and touch in his own apartment. He could not taste his food; words on paper had no meaning; he could not make his way from his chair to the toilet without wondering if at the next step the room would turn upside down or vanish entirely. Nothing had any volume, texture, or mass, let alone any color; the secondary properties of things, which had been leaking steadily out of his world ever since Lithia, were gone entirely now, and the primary qualities were beginning to follow.

The end was clear and predictable. There was to be nothing left but the little plexus of habit patterns at the center of which lived the dwindling unknowable thing that was his *I*. By the time one of those habits brought him before the 3-V set and snapped open the switch, it was already too late to save anything else. There was nobody left in the universe but himself—nobody and nothing—

Except that, when the screen lighted and Egtverchi failed to appear, he discovered that even the *I* no longer had a name. Inside the thin shell of unwilling self-consciousness, it was as empty as an upended jug.

XIV

RUIZ-SANCHEZ put the much-folded, sleazy airletter down into his lap and looked blindly out the compartment window of the *rapido*. The train was already an hour out from Naples, slightly less than halfway to Rome, and as yet he had seen almost nothing of the country he had been hoping to reach all of his adult life; and now he had a headache. Michelis' sprawling cursive handwriting was under the best of circumstances about as legible as Beethoven's, and obviously he had written this letter under the worst circumstances imaginable.

And after emotion had done its considerable worst to Michelis' scrawl, the facsimile reducer had squeezed it all down onto a single piece of tissue for missile mail, so that only a man who knew the handwriting as well as Assyriologists know cuneiform could have deciphered the remaining ant tracks at all.

After a moment, he picked up where he had left off; the letter went on:

Which is why I missed the subsequent debacle. There is still some doubt in my mind as to whether or not Egtverchi was entirely responsible—it occurs to me that maybe the countess' smokes did affect him in some way after all, since his metabolism can't be *totally* different from ours—but you'd know much more about that than I would. It's perfectly possible that I'm just whistling past the graveyard.

In any event, I don't know any more about the sub-basement shambles than the papers have reported. In case you haven't seen them, what happened was that Egtverchi and his bravoes somehow became impatient with the progress the serpentine was making, or with the caliber of the entertainment they could see from it, and went on an expedition of their own, breaking down the barriers between cells when they couldn't find any other way in. Egtverchi is still pretty weak for a Lithian, but he's big, and the dividing walls apparently didn't pose him any problems.

What happened thereafter is confused—it depends on which reporter you believe. Insofar as I've been able to piece all these conflicting accounts together, Egtverchi himself didn't hurt anybody, and if his *condottieri* did, they got as good as they gave; one of them died. The major damage is to the countess, who is ruined. Some of the cells he broke into weren't on the serpentine's route at all, and contained public figures in private hells especially designed by the countess' caterers. The people who haven't themselves already succumbed to the sensation-mongers—though in some instances the publicity is no more vicious than they had coming—are out to revenge themselves on the whole house of Averoigne.

Of course the count can't be touched directly, since he wasn't even aware of what was going on. (Did you see that last paper from "H. O. Petard," by the way? Beautiful stuff: he has a fundamental twist on the Haertel equations which make it look possible to *see* around normal space-time, as well as travel around it. Theoretically you might photograph a star and get a contemporary image, not one light-years old. Another blow to the chops for poor old Einstein.) But he is already no longer Procurator of Canarsie and, unless he takes his money promptly out of the countess' hands, he will wind up as just another moderately comfortable troglodyte. And at the moment nobody knows where he is, so unless he has been reading the papers it is already too late for him to make a drastic enough move. In any event, whether he does or he doesn't, the countess will be *persona non grata* in her own circles to the day she dies.

And even now I haven't any idea whether Egtverchi intended exactly this, or whether it was all an accident springing out of a wild impulse. He says he will reply to the newspaper criticism of him on his 3-V program next week—this week nobody can reach him, for reasons he refuses to explain—but I don't see what he could possibly say that would salvage more than a fraction of the good will he'd accumulated before the party. He's already half-convinced that Earth's laws are only organized whims at best—and his present audience is more than half children!

I wish you were the kind of man who might say "I told you so"; at least I could get a melancholy pleasure out of nodding. But it's too late for that now. If you can spare any time for further advice, please send it post haste. We are in well over our heads.

—Mike

P.S.: Liu and I were married yesterday. It was earlier than we had planned, but we both feel a sense of urgency that we can't explain—almost a desperation. It's as though something crucial were about to happen. I believe something is; but what? Please write.—*M.*

Ruiz groaned involuntarily, drawing incurious glances from his compartment-mates: a Pole in a sheepskin coat who had spent the entire journey wordlessly cutting his way through a monstrous and smelly cheese he had boarded the train with, and a Hollywood Vedantist in sandals, burlap and beard whose smell was not that of cheese and whose business in Rome in a Holy Year was problematical.

He closed his eyes against them. Mike had had no business even thinking about such matters on his wedding morning. No wonder the letter was hard to read.

Cautiously, he opened his eyes again. The sunlight was almost intolerably bright, but for a moment he saw an olive grove sweeping by against burnt-umber hills lined beneath a sky of incredibly clear blue. Then the hills abruptly came piling down upon him and the express shot screaming into a tunnel.

Ruiz lifted the letter once more, but the ant tracks promptly puddled into a dirty blur; a sudden stab of pain lanced vertically through his left eye. Dear God, was he going blind? No, nonsense, that was hypochondria—there was nothing wrong with him but simple eyestrain. The stab through the eyeball was pressure in his left sphenoid sinus, which had been inflamed

ever since he left Lima for the wet North, and had begun to
become acute in the dripping atmosphere of Lithia.

His trouble was Michelis' letter, that was plain. Never mind
the temptation to blame eyes or sinuses, which were only surrogates for hands empty even of the amphora in which Egtverchi had been brought into the world. Nothing was left of his
gift but the letter.

And what answer could he give?

Why, only what Michelis obviously was already coming to
realize: that the reason for both Egtverchi's popularity and his
behavior lay in the fact that he was both mentally and emotionally a seriously displaced person. He had been deprived of
the normal Lithian upbringing which would have taught him
how fundamental it is to know how to survive in a predomi-
nantly predatory society. As for Earth's codes and beliefs, he
had only half-absorbed them when Michelis forcibly expelled
him from the classroom straight into citizenship. Now he had
already had ample opportunity to see the hypocrisy with which
some of those codes were served and, to the straight-line logic
of the Lithian mind, this could mean only that the codes must
therefore be only some kind of game at best. (He had encountered the concept of a game here, too; it was unknown on
Lithia.) But he had no Lithian code of conduct to substitute or
to fall back on, since he was as ignorant of Lithian civilization
as he was innocent of experience of Lithia's seas, savannas and
jungles.

In short, a wolf child.

The *rapido* hurled itself from the mouth of the tunnel as
impetuously as it had entered, and the renewed blast of sunlight forced Ruiz to close his eyes once more. When he opened
them he was rewarded by the sight of an extensive terraced
vineyard. This was obviously wine country and, judging by the
mountains, which were especially steep here, they must be
nearing Terracina. Soon, if he was lucky, he might see Mt.
Circeo; but he was far more interested in the vineyards.

From what he had been able to observe thus far, the Italian
states were far less deeply buried than was most of the rest of
the world, and the people were on the surface for much greater
proportions of their lifetimes. To some extent this was a product of poverty—Italy as a whole had not had the wealth to get

into the Shelter race early, or on anything like the scale which had been possible for the United States or even the other continental countries. Nevertheless, there was a huge Shelter installation at Naples, and the one under Rome was the world's fourth biggest; that one had got itself dug with funds from all over the Western world, and with a great deal of outright voluntary help, when the first deep excavations had begun to turn up an incredible wealth of unsuspected archaeological finds.

In part, however, sheer stubbornness was responsible. A high proportion of Italy's huge population, which had never known any living but in and by the sun, simply could not be driven underground on any permanent basis. Of all the Shelter nations—a class which excluded only countries still almost wholly undeveloped, or unrecoverably desert—Italy appeared to be the least thoroughly entombed.

If that turned out to hold true for Rome in particular, the Eternal City would also be by far the sanest major capital on the planet. And that, Ruiz realized suddenly, would be an outcome nobody would have dared predict for an enterprise founded in 753 B.C. by a wolf child.

Of course, about the Vatican he had never been in any doubt, but Vatican City is not Rome. The thought reminded him that he had been commanded to an *udienza speciale* with the Holy Father tomorrow, before the ring-kissing, which meant before 1000 at the latest—probably as early as 0700, for the Holy Father was an early riser, and in this year of all years would be holding audiences of all kinds nearly around the clock. Ruiz had had nearly a month to prepare, for the command had reached him very shortly after the order of the College to appear for inquisition, but he felt unreadier than ever. He wondered how long it had been since any Pope had personally examined a Jesuit convert to an admitted heresy, and what the man had found to say; doubtless the transcript was there in the Vatican library, as recorded by some papal master of ceremonies—assiduous as always in his duty toward history, as masters of ceremonies had been ever since the invaluable Burchard—but Ruiz would not have time to read it.

From here on out, there would be a thousand petty distractions to keep him from settling his mind and heart any further. Just getting his bearings was going to be a chore, and after that there was the matter of accommodations. None of the *case religiose* would take him in—word had apparently got around—and he had not the purse for a hotel, though if worse came to worst he had a confirmed-reservation slip from one of the most expensive which just might let him into some linen closet there. Finding a *pensione*, the only other tolerable alternative, was going to be particularly difficult, for the one which had been contracted for him by the tourist agency had become impossible the moment he received the papal summons; it was too far from St. Peter's. The agency had been able to do nothing else for him except suggest that he sleep in the Shelter, which he was resolved not to do. After all, the agent had told him belligerently, it's a Holy Year—almost as though he were saying, "Don't you know there's a war on?"

And of course his tone had been right. There was a war on. The Enemy was presently fifty light-years away, but He was at the gates all the same.

Something prompted him to check the date of Michelis' letter. It was, he discovered with astonishment and disquiet, nearly two weeks old. Yet the postmark read today; the letter had been mailed, in fact, only about six hours ago, just in time to catch the dawn missile to Naples. Michelis had been sitting on it—or perhaps adding to it, but the facsimile process and the ensmallment, together with Ruiz' gathering eyestrain, all conspired to make it impossible to detect differences in the handwriting or the ink.

After a moment, Ruiz realized what importance the discrepancy had for him. It meant that Egtverchi's 3-V answer to his newspaper critics had been broadcast a week ago—and that he was due on the air again tonight!

Egtverchi's program was broadcast at 0300 Rome time; Ruiz was going to be up earlier than the pontiff himself. In fact, he thought grimly, he was going to get no sleep at all.

The express pulled into the *Stazione Termini* in Rome five minutes ahead of schedule with a feminine shriek. Ruiz found a porter with no difficulty, tipped him the standard 100 lire for his two pieces of luggage, and gave directions. The priest's Italian was adequate, but hardly standard; it made the *facchino* grin with delight every time Ruiz opened his mouth. He had learned it by reading, partly in Dante, mostly in opera libretti, and consequently what he lacked in accent he made up for in flowery phrases: he was unable to ask the way to the nearest fruit stall without sounding as though he would throw himself into the Tiber unless he got an answer.

"*Be' 'a!*" the porter kept saying after every third sentence from Ruiz. "*Che be' 'a!*"

Still, that was easier to get along with than the French attitude had been, on Ruiz' one visit to Paris fifteen years ago. He remembered a taxi driver who had refused to understand his request to be taken to the Continental Hotel until he had written the name down, after which the hackie had said, miming sudden comprehension: "*Ah, ah! Lee Con-ti-nen-TAL!*" This he had found to be an almost universal pretense; the French wanted one to know that without a perfect accent one is not intelligible at all.

The Italians, apparently, were willing to meet one halfway. The porter grinned at Ruiz' purple prose, but he guided the priest deftly to a newsstand where he was able to buy a news magazine containing a high enough proportion of text over pictures to insure an adequate account of what Egtverchi had said last week; and then took him down the left incline from the station across the Piazza Cinquecento to the corner of the Via Viminale and the Via Diocletian, precisely as requested. Ruiz promptly doubled his tip without even a qualm; guidance like that would be invaluable now that time was so short, and he might see the man again.

He had been left in the Casa del Passegero, which had the reputation of being the finest travelers' way station in Italy— which, Ruiz quickly discovered, means the finest in the world, for there are no other institutions precisely like the *alberghi diurni* anywhere else. Here he was able to check his luggage, read his magazine over a pastry in the *caffè*, have his hair cut and his shoes shined, have a bath while his clothes were being pressed, and then begin the protracted series of telephone calls which, he hoped, would eventually allow him to spend the coming night in a bed—preferably near by, but at least anywhere in Rome but in a Shelter dormitory.

In the coffee shop, in the barber's chair, and even in the tub, he pored again and again over the account of Egtverchi's broadcast. The Italian reporter did not give a text, for obvious reasons—a thirteen-minute broadcast would have filled an entire page of the journal in which he was limited to a single column of type—but he digested it skillfully, and he had an inside story to go with it. Ruiz was impressed.

Evidently Egtverchi had composed his rebuttal by weaving together the news items of the evening, just as they had come in to him off the wires beyond any possibility of his selecting them, into a brilliant extempore attack upon Earthly moral assumptions and pretensions. The thread which wove them all together was summed up by the magazine's reporter in a phrase from the Inferno: *Perche mi scerpi?/non hai tu spirto di pietate alcuno?*—the cry of the Suicides, who can speak only when the Harpies rend them and the blood flows: "Wherefore pluckest *thou* me?" It had been a scathing indictment, at no point defending Egtverchi's own conduct, but by implication making ridiculous the notion that any man could be stainless enough to be casting stones. Egtverchi had obviously absorbed Schopenhauer's vicious *Rules for Debate* down to the last comma.

"And in fact," the Italian reporter added, "it is widely known in Manhattan that QBC officials were on the verge of cutting off the outworlder in mid-broadcast as he began to cover the Stockholm brothel war. They were dissuaded by the barrage of telephone calls, telegrams and radiograms which began to pour down upon QBC's main office at precisely that moment. The response of the public has hardly diminished since, and it continues to be overwhelmingly approving. The network, encouraged by Signor Egtverchi's major sponsor, Bridget Bifalco World Kitchens, now is issuing almost hourly releases containing statistics 'proving' the broadcast a spectacular success. Signor Egtverchi is now a hot property, and if past experience is any guide (and it is) this means that henceforth the Lithian will be encouraged to display those aspects of his public character for which formerly he was being widely condemned, for which the network was considering taking him off the air in the middle of a word. Suddenly, in short, he is worth a lot of money."

The report was both literate and overheated—a peculiarly Roman combination—but as long as Ruiz lacked the text of the broadcast itself, he could not take exception to a word of it. Both the reporter's editorializing and the precise passion of his language seemed no more than justified. Indeed, a case could be made for a claim that the man had indulged in understatement.

To Ruiz, at least, Egtverchi's voice came through. The accent was familiar and perfect. And this for an audience full of children! Had any independent person called Egtverchi ever really existed? If so, he was possessed—but Ruiz did not believe that for an instant. There had never been any real Egtverchi to possess. He was throughout a creature of the Adversary's imagination, as even Chtexa had been, as the whole of Lithia had been. In the figure of Egtverchi He had already abandoned subtlety; already He dared to show Himself more than half-naked, commanding money, fathering lies, poisoning discourse, compounding grief, corrupting children, killing love, building armies—

—and all in a Holy Year.

Ruiz-Sanchez froze, one arm halfway into his summer jacket, looking up at the ceiling of the dressing room. He had yet to make more than two telephone calls, neither of them to the general of his Order, but he had already changed his mind.

Had he really failed, all this time, to read such obvious signs —or was he as crazed as heretics are supposed to be, smelling the *Dies irae*, the day of the wrath of God, in the steam of nothing but a public bath? Armageddon—in 3-V? The pit opened to let loose a comedian for the amusement of children?

He did not know. He could only be sure that he needed to hunt for no bed tonight, after all; what he needed was stones. He got out of the Casa del Passegero as quickly as he could, leaving everything he owned behind, and found his way alone back to the Via del Termini; the guidebook showed a church just off there, on the Piazza della Republica, by the Baths of Diocletian.

The book was right. The church was there: Santa Maria d'Angeli. He did not stop in the porch to cool off, though the early evening sunlight was almost as hot as noon. Tomorrow might be much hotter—unredeemably hotter. He went through the portals at once.

Inside, in the chill darkness, he knelt; and in cold terror, he prayed.

It did not seem to do him much good.

XV

ALL about Michelis the jungle stood frozen in a riot of motionlessness. Filtered through it, the sourceless blue-gray daylight was tinged with deep green, and where the light fell on one or another clear reflection it seemed to penetrate rather than glance off, carrying the jungle on in an inversion of images to the eight corners of the universe. The illusion was made doubly real by the stillness of everything; at any moment it seemed as though a breeze would spring up and ruffle the reflections, but there was no breeze, and nothing but time would ever disturb those images.

Egtverchi moved, of course; though his figure was ensmalled as if by distance, he was about the right size for the rest of the jungle, and almost more convincingly colored and in the round. His circumscribed gestures seemed to be beckoning, as though he were attempting to lead Michelis out of this motionless wilderness.

Only his voice was jarring: it was at normal conversational volume, which meant that it was far too loud to be in scale with himself or his (and Michelis') surroundings. It seemed so loud to Michelis, indeed, that in his reverie he almost missed the content of Egtverchi's final speech. Only when Egtverchi had bowed ironically and faded away and his voice died, leaving behind only the omni-present muted insect buzz, did the meaning penetrate.

Michelis sat where he was, stunned. A full thirty seconds of commercial for Mammale Bifalco's Delicious Instant Knish Mix went by before he remembered to put his finger over the 3-V's cut-off stud. Then this year's Bridget Bifalco in turn faded in mid-mix, smothered before she reached her famous brogue tag-line ("Give it t' me a minute, dharlin', till I give it a lhashin'"). The scurrying electrons in the phosphor complex migrated back to the atoms from which they had been driven by the miniature de Broglie scanner imbedded in the picture frame. The atoms resumed their chemical identity, the molecules cooled, and the screen became a static reproduction of Paul Klee's "Caprice in February." The principle, Michelis recalled with gray irrelevancy, had emerged out of d'Averoigne's first "Petard" paper, the count's only venture into applied math, published when he was seventeen.

"What does he mean?" Liu said faintly. "I don't understand him at all any more. He calls it a demonstration—but what can he possibly demonstrate by that? It's childish!"

"Yes," Michelis said. For the moment he could think of nothing else to say. He needed to get his temper back; he was losing it more and more easily these days. That had been one of the reasons for his urgency in marrying Liu: he needed her calmness, for his own was vanishing with frightening rapidity.

No calmness seemed to be passing from her to him now. Even the apartment, originally such a source of satisfaction and repose for them both, felt like a trap. It was far above ground, in one of the mostly unused project buildings on the upper East Side of Manhattan. Originally Liu had had a far smaller set of rooms in the same building, and Michelis, after he had got used to the idea, had had them both installed in the present apartment with only a minimum of wire-pulling. It was not customary, it was certainly not fashionable, and they were officially warned that it was considered dangerous—the gangs raided surface structures now and then; but apparently it was no longer outright illegal, if one had the money to live that high up in the slums.

Given the additional space, the artist buried inside Liu's demure technician's exterior had run quietly wild. In the green glow of concealed light which washed the apartment, Michelis was surrounded by what seemed to be a miniature jungle. On small tables stood Japanese gardens with real Ming trees or dwarf cedars in them. An oriental lamp was fashioned out of a piece of fantastically sculptured driftwood. Long, deep, woven flower boxes ran completely around the room at eye level; they were thickly planted with ivy, wandering Jew, rubber plants, philodendron, and other nonflowering species, and behind each box a mirror ran up to the ceiling, unbroken anywhere except by the placidly witty Klee reproduction which was the

3-V set; the painting, made almost wholly of detached angles and glyphs like the symbols of mathematics, was a welcome oasis of dryness for which Liu had paid a premium—QBC's stock "covers" were mostly Sargents and van Goghs. Since the light tubes were hidden behind the planting boxes, the room gave an effect of extraterrestrial exuberance kept under control only with the greatest difficulty.

"I know what he means," Michelis said at last. "I just don't know quite how to put it. Let me think a minute—why don't you get dinner while I do it? We'd better eat early. We're going to have visitors, that's a cinch."

"Visitors? But— All right, Mike."

Michelis walked to the glass wall and looked out onto the sun porch. All of Liu's flowering plants were out there, a real garden, which had to be kept sealed off from the rest of the apartment; for in addition to being an ardent amateur gardener, Liu bred bees. There was a colony of them there, making singular and exotic honeys from the congeries of blossoms Liu had laid out so carefully. The honey was fabulous and ever-changing, sometimes too bitter to eat except in tiny fork-touches like Chinese mustard, sometimes containing a heady touch of opium from the sticky hybrid poppies that nodded in a soldierly squad along the sun porch railing, sometimes sickly-sweet and insipid until, with a surprisingly small amount of glassware, Liu converted it into a liqueur that mounted to the head like a breeze from the Garden of Allah. The bees that made it were tetraploid monsters the size of hummingbirds, with tempers as bad as Michelis' own was getting to be; only a few of them could kill even a big man. Luckily, they flew badly in the gusts common at this altitude, and would starve anywhere but in Liu's garden, otherwise Liu would never have been licensed to keep them on an open sun porch in the middle of the city. Michelis had been more than a little wary of them at first, but lately they had begun to fascinate him: their apparent intelligence was almost as phenomenal as their size and viciousness.

"Damn!" Liu said behind him.

"What's the matter?"

"Omelettes again. That's the second wrong number I've dialed this week."

Both the oath—mild though it was—and the error were uncharacteristic. Mike felt a twinge, a mixture of compassion and guilt. Liu was changing; she had never been so distractible before. Was he responsible?

"It's all right. I don't mind. Let's eat."

"All right."

They ate silently, but Michelis was conscious of the pressure of inquiry behind Liu's still expression. The chemist thought furiously, angry with himself, and yet unable to phrase what he wanted to say. He should never have got her into this at all. No, that couldn't have been prevented; she had been the logical scientist to handle Egtverchi in his infancy—probably nobody else could have brought him through it even this well. But surely it should have been possible to keep her from becoming emotionally involved—

No, that had not been possible either; that was the woman of it. And the man of it, now that he was forced to think about his own role. It was no use; he simply did not know what he should think; Egtverchi's broadcast had rattled him beyond the point of logical thought. He was going to wind up with his usual bad compromise with Liu, which was to say nothing at all. But that would not do either.

And yet it had been a simple enough piece of foolery that the Lithian had perpetrated—childish, as Liu had said. Egtverchi had been urged to be off beat, rebellious, irresponsible, and he had come through in spades. Not only had he voiced his disrespect for all established institutions and customs, but he had also challenged his audience to show the same disrespect. In the closing moments of his broadcast, he had even told them how: they were to mail anonymous, insulting messages to Egtverchi's own sponsors.

"A postcard will do," he had said, gently enough, through his grinning chops. "Just make the message pungent. If you hate that powdered concrete they call a knish mix, write and tell them so. If you can eat the knishes but our commercials make you sick, write them about that, and don't pull any punches. If you loathe *me*, tell the Bifalcos that, too, and make sure you're spitting mad about it. I'll read the five messages I think in the worst possible taste on my broadcast next week. And remember, don't sign your name; if you have to sign, use my name. Goodnight."

The omelette tasted like flannel.

"I'll tell you what I think," Michelis said suddenly, in a low voice. "I think he's whipping up a mob. Remember those kids in the uniforms? He's abandoned that now, or else he's keeping it under cover; in any event, he thinks he has something better. He has an audience of about sixty-five million, and maybe half of them are adults. Of those, another half is unsane to some degree, and that's what he's counting on now. He's going to turn that group into a lynch gang."

"But why, Mike?" Liu said. "What good will that do him?"

"I don't know. That's what stops me. He's not after power— he's got too many brains to think he can be a mccarthy. Maybe he just wants to destroy things. An elaborate act of revenge."

"Revenge!"

"I'm only guessing. I don't understand him any better than you do. Maybe worse."

"Revenge on whom?" Liu said steadily. "And for what?"

"Well—on us. For making such a bad job of him."

"I see," Liu said. "I see." She looked down into her untouched plate and began to weep, silently. At that moment, Michelis would gladly have killed either Egtverchi or himself, had he known where to begin.

The Klee chimed decorously. Michelis looked up at it with bitter resignation.

"The visitors," he said. He touched the phone stud.

The Klee faded, and the chairman of the citizenship committee which had examined Egtverchi looked out from the wall at them from under his elaborate helmet.

"Come on up," Michelis said to the silently inquiring image. "We've been expecting you."

It took a while for the UN committee chairman to stop touring the apartment and exclaiming over Liu's decor, but this evidently was a ceremony. As soon as he had uttered the last amenity, he dropped his social manner so abruptly that Michelis could almost see it break on the carpetite. Even the bees had sensed something hostile about him; he had no sooner peered through the glass at them than they began butting their eye-bulging heads at him. Michelis could hear them thumping doggedly away at the transparent barrier all through the subsequent conversation, with a rising and falling snarl of angry wings.

"We've gotten more than ten thousand facsimiles and telegrams in the half hour between when Egtverchi went off the air and the first analysis of the response," the UN man said grimly. "That was enough to tell us what we're up against, and that's why I came to see you. We've had a good many decades of experience at assessing public response. In the next week, we are going to get about two million of these things—"

"Who's 'we'?" Michelis said, and Liu added: "That doesn't seem like a large figure to me."

" 'We' is the network. And the figure's large for us, since we're nearly anonymous in the public mind. The Bifalcos are going to get a little over seven and a half million such missives."

"Are they really so bad?" Liu said, frowning.

"They are as bad as they could be and still get through the cables and the mail tubes," the UN man said flatly. "I've never seen anything like them, and I've been in QBC community relations for eleven years—this UN committee job is my other hat, you know how that goes. More than half of them are expressions of virulent, unrestrained hatred—pathological hatred. I have a few samples here, but I didn't bring the worst of them along. It's my policy not to show laymen anything that scares *me*."

"Let me see one," Michelis said promptly.

The UN man passed a facsimile over silently. Michelis read it. Then he gave it back.

"You're a little more calloused than you realize," he said in a gravelly voice. "I wouldn't have shown even that one to anyone but the director of research of an insane asylum."

The UN man smiled for the first time, looking at them both with quick, intelligent eyes. Somehow he seemed to be assessing them, not individually, but as a couple; Michelis had an overwhelming intuition that his privacy was somehow being violated, though there was nothing concrete in the man's behavior to which he could have taken exception.

"Not even to Dr. Meid?" the UN man said.

"To nobody," Michelis said angrily.

"Quite so. And yet I repeat that I didn't select it deliberately for shock value, Dr. Michelis. It's a bagatelle—very mild, compared to some of the stuff we've been getting. This Snake obviously has an audience of borderline madmen, and he means to use it. That's why I came to see you. We think you might have some idea as to what he intends to use it *for*."

"For nothing, if you people have any control over what you yourselves do," Michelis said. "Why don't you cut him off the air? If he's poisoning it, then you don't have any other choice."

"One man's poison is another man's knish mix," the UN man said smoothly. "The Bifalcos don't see this the way we do. They have their own analysts, and they know as well as we do that they're going to get more than seven and a half million dirty postcards in the next week. But they *like* the idea. In fact, they're positively wriggling with delight. They think it will sell products. They will probably give the Snake a whole half hour, solely sponsored by them, if the response comes through as predicted—and it will."

"Why can't you cut Egtverchi off anyhow?" Liu said.

"The charter prevents us from interfering with the right of free speech. As long as the Bifalcos put up the money, we are obligated to keep the program on the air. It's a good principle at bottom; we've had experiences with it before that threatened to turn out nastily, but in every case we sweated them out and the public got bored with them eventually. But that was a different public—the broad public, which used to be mostly sane. The Snake obviously has a selected audience, and that's not sane at all. This time—for the first time—we are thinking of interfering. That's why we came to you."

"I can't help you," Michelis said.

"You can, and you will, Dr. Michelis. I'm talking from under both my hats now. QBC wants him off the air, and the UN is beginning to smell something which might prove to be much worse than the 1993 Corridor Riots. You sponsored this Snake, and your wife raised him from an egg, or damn near an egg. You know him better than anyone else on Earth. You will have to give us the weapon that we need against him. That's what I came to tell you. Think about it. You are responsible under the naturalization law. It's not often that we have to invoke that clause, but we're invoking it now. You'll have to think fast, because we have to have him closed out before his next broadcast."

"And suppose we have nothing to offer?" Michelis said stonily.

"Then we will probably declare the Snake a minor, and you his guardians," the UN man said. "Which will hardly be a solution from our point of view, but you would probably find it painful—you'd be well advised to come up with something better. I'm sorry to bring such bad news, but the news *is* bad tonight; that sometimes happens. Good-night, and thank you."

He went out. He did not have to resume any of his three hats; he had never taken any of them off, visible or metaphorical.

Michelis and Liu stared at each other, appalled.

"We—we couldn't possibly have him as a ward *now*," Liu whispered.

"Well," Michelis said harshly, "we were talking about wanting a son—"

"Mike, don't!"

"I'm sorry," he said inadequately. "That officious son of a bitch. He was the man that passed on the application—and now he's throwing it right back in our laps. They must be really desperate. What are we going to do? I haven't an idea in my head."

Liu said, after a moment's hesitation: "Mike—we don't know enough to come up with anything useful in a week. At least I don't, and I don't think you do either. We've got to get through to the Father somehow."

"If we can," Michelis said slowly. "But even so, what good will that do? The UN won't listen to him—they've bypassed him."

"How? What do you mean?"

"They've made a *de facto* decision in favor of Cleaver," Michelis said. "It won't be announced until after Ramon's church has finished disavowing him, but it's already in effect. I knew about it before he left for Rome, but I didn't have the heart to tell him. Lithia has been closed; the UN is going to use it as a laboratory for the study of fusion power storage—not exactly what Cleaver had in mind originally, but close enough."

Liu was silent for a long time. She arose and went to the window, against which the huge bees were still butting like live battering-rams.

"Does Cleaver know?" she said, her back still turned.

"Oh yes, he knows," Michelis said. "He's in charge. He was

scheduled to land back at Xoredeshch Sfath yesterday. I tried to tip Ramon off indirectly as soon as I heard about it—that's why I promoted that collaboration for the *J. I. R.*—but Ramon just didn't seem to hear any of my hints. And I just couldn't tell him outright that his cause was already lost, before he'd even had a hearing."

"It's ugly," Liu said slowly. "Why won't they announce it until after Ramon is officially excommunicated? Why does that make any difference?"

"Because the decision is tainted, that's all," Michelis said fiercely. "Whether you agree with Ramon's theological arguments or not, to decide for Cleaver is a dirty act—impossible to defend except in terms of raw power. They know that well enough, damn them, and sooner or later they're going to have to let the public see what the arguments were on the other side. When that day comes, they want Ramon's arguments discredited in advance by his own church."

"What precisely is Cleaver doing?"

"I can't say, precisely. But they're building a big Nernst generator plant inland on the south continent, near Gleshchtehk Sfath, to turn out the power, so that much of his dream is already realized. Later they'll try to trap the power raw, as it comes off, instead of stepping it down and throwing away ninety-five per cent of it as heat. I don't know how Cleaver proposes to do that, but I should guess he'd begin with a modification of the Nernst effect itself—the 'magnetic bottle' dodge. He'd better be damned careful." He paused. "I suppose I'd have told Ramon if he'd asked me. But he didn't, so I didn't say anything. Now I feel like a coward."

Liu turned swiftly at that, and came back to sit on the arm of his chair. "That was right to do, Mike," she said. "It's not cowardice to refuse to rob a man of hope, I think."

"Maybe not," Michelis said, taking her hand gratefully. "But what it all comes out to is that Ramon can't help us now. Thanks to me, he doesn't even know yet that Cleaver is back on Lithia."

XVI

SHORTLY past dawn, Ruiz-Sanchez walked stiffly into the vast circle of the Piazza San Pietro toward the towering dome of St. Peter's itself. The piazza was swarming with pilgrims even this early, and the dome, more than twice as high as the Statue of Liberty, seemed frowning and ominous in the early light, rising from the forest of pillars like the forehead of God.

He passed under the right arch of the colonnade, past the Swiss Guards in their gorgeous, *outré* uniforms, and through the bronze door. Here he paused to murmur, with unexpected intensity, the prayers for the Pope's intentions obligatory for this year. The Apostolic Palace soared in front of him; he was astonished that any edifice so crowded with stone could at the same time contrive to be so spacious, but he had no time for further devotions now.

Near the first door on the right a man sat at a table. Ruiz-Sanchez told him: "I am commanded to a special audience with the Holy Father."

"God has blessed you. The major-domo's office is on the first floor, to the left. No, one moment—a *special* audience? May I see your letter, please?"

Ruiz-Sanchez showed it.

"Very good. But you will need to see the major-domo anyhow. The special audiences are in the throne room; he will show you where to go."

The throne room! Ruiz-Sanchez was more unsettled than ever. That was where the Holy Father received heads of state, and members of the college of cardinals. Certainly it was no place to receive a heretical Jesuit of very low rank—

"The throne room," the major-domo said. "That's the first room in the reception suite. I trust your business goes well, Father. Pray for me."

Hadrian VIII was a big man, a Norwegian by birth, whose curling beard had been only slightly peppered with gray at his election. It was white now, of course, but otherwise age seemed to have marked him little; indeed, he looked somewhat younger than his photographs and 3-V 'casts suggested, for they had a tendency to accentuate the crags and furrows of his huge, heavy face.

Ruiz-Sanchez found his person so overwhelming that he barely noticed the magnificence of his robes of state. Needless to say, there was nothing in the least Latin in the Holy Father's mien or temperament. In his rise to the gestatorial chair he had made a reputation as a Catholic with an almost Lutheran passion for the grimmer reaches of moral theology; there was something of Kierkegaard in him, and something of the Grand Inquisitor as well. After his election, he had surprised everyone by developing an interest—one might almost call it a business-man's interest—in temporal politics, though the characteristic coldness of Northern theological speculation continued to color everything he said and did. His choice of the name of a Roman emperor was perfectly appropriate, Ruiz-Sanchez realized: here was a face that might well have been stamped on imperial coin, for all the beneficence which tempered its harshness.

The Pope remained standing throughout the interview, staring down at Ruiz-Sanchez with what seemed at first to be nine-tenths frank curiosity.

"Of all the thousands of pilgrims here, you may stand in the greatest need of our indulgence," he observed in English. Near by, a tape recorder raced silently; Hadrian was an ardent archi-vist, and a stickler for the letter of the text. "Yet we have small hope of your winning it. It is incredible to us that a Jesuit, of all our shepherds, could have fallen into Manichaeanism. The errors of that heresy are taught most particularly in that col-lege."

"Holiness, the evidence—"

Hadrian raised his hand. "Let us not waste time. We have already informed ourself of your views and your reasoning. You are subtle, Father, but you have committed a grievous oversight all the same—but we wish to defer that subject for the moment. Tell us first of this creature Egtverchi—not as a sending of the Devil, but as you would see him were he a man."

Ruiz-Sanchez frowned. There was something about the word "sending" that touched some weakness inside him, like an obligation forgotten until too late to fulfill it. The feeling was like that which had informed a ridiculous recurrent nightmare of his student days, in which he was not to graduate because he had forgotten to attend all his Latin classes. Yet he could not put his finger on what it was.

"There are many ways to describe him, Holiness," he said. "He is the kind of personality that the twentieth-century critic Colin Wilson called an Outsider, and that is the kind of Earth man he appeals to—he is a preacher without a creed, an intellect without a culture, a seeker without a goal. I think he has a conscience as we would define the term; he's very different from the rest of his race in that and many other respects. He seems to take a deep interest in moral problems, but he's utterly contemptuous of all traditional moral frames of reference —including the kind of rationalized moral automation that prevails on Lithia."

"And this strikes some chord in his audience?"

"There can be no doubt of that, surely, Holiness. It remains to be seen how wide his appeal is. He ran off a very shrewdly designed experiment last night, obviously intended to test that very question; we should soon know just how great the response will be. But it already seems clear that he appeals to all those people who feel cut off, emotionally and intellectually, from our society and its dominant cultural traditions."

"Well put," Hadrian said, surprisingly. "We stand at the brink of unguessable events, that is certain; we have had forebodings that this might be the year. We have commanded the Inquisition to put away its bell, book and candle for the time being; we think such a move would be most unwise."

Ruiz-Sanchez was stunned. No trial—and no excommunication? The drumming of events around his head had begun to remind him of the numbing, incessant rains of Xoredeshch Sfath.

"Why, Holiness?" he said faintly.

"We believe you may be the man appointed by our Lord to bear St. Michael's arms," the Pope said, weighing every word.

"I, Holiness? A heretic?"

"Noah was not perfect, you will recall," Hadrian said, with what might have been a half-smile. "He was merely a man who was given another chance. Goethe, himself more than a little heretical, reshaped the legend of Faustus to the same lesson: redemption is always the crux of the great drama, and there must be a peripataea first. Besides, Father, consider for a moment the unique nature of this case of heresy. Is not the appearance of a solitary Manichaean in the twenty-first century either a wildly meaningless anachronism—or a grave sign?"

He paused and fingered his beads.

"Of course," he added, "it will be necessary for you to purge yourself, if you can. That is why we have called you. We believe as you do that the Adversary is the moving spirit behind this whole Lithian crisis; but we do not believe that any repudiation of dogma is required. It all hinges upon this question of creativity. Tell us, Father: when you first became convinced that the whole of Lithia was a sending, what did you do about it?"

"Do about it?" Ruiz-Sanchez said numbly. "Why, Holiness, I did only what was recorded. I could think of nothing else to do."

"Then did it never occur to you that sendings can be banished—and that God has given that power into your hands?"

Ruiz-Sanchez had no emotions left.

"Banished. . . . Holiness, perhaps I have been stupid. I feel stupid. But as far as I know, exorcism was abandoned by the Church more than two centuries ago. My college taught me that meteorology replaced the 'spirits and powers of the air,' and neurophysiology replaced 'possession.' It would never have occurred to me."

"Exorcism was not abandoned, merely discouraged," Hadrian said. "It had become limited, as you have just pointed out, and the Church wished to prevent its abuse by ignorant country priests—they were bringing the Church into disrepute trying to drive demons out of sick cows and perfectly healthy goats and cats. But I am not talking about animal health, the weather or mental illness now, Father."

"Then . . . is Your Holiness truly proposing that . . . that I should have attempted to . . . *to exorcise a whole planet?*"

"Why not?" Hadrian said. "Of course, the fact that you were standing on the planet at the time might have helped to prevent you, unconsciously, from thinking of it. We are convinced that God would have provided for you—in Heaven certainly, and possibly you might have received temporal help as well. But it was the only solution to your dilemma. Had the exorcism failed, *then* there might have been some excuse for falling into heresy. But surely it should be easier to believe in a planet-wide hallucination—which in principle we know the Adversary has the power to do—than in the heresy of satanic creativity!"

The Jesuit bowed his head. He felt overwhelmed by his own ignorance. He had spent almost all his leisure hours on Lithia minutely studying a book which to all intents and purposes might have been dictated by the Adversary himself, and he had seen nothing that mattered, not in all those 628 pages of compulsive demoniac chatter.

"It is not too late to try," Hadrian said, almost gently. "That is the only road left for you to travel." Suddenly his face became stern, flinty. "As we have pointed out to the Inquisition, your excommunication is automatic. It began the instant that you admitted this abomination into your soul. It does not need to be formalized to be a fact—and there are political reasons, as well as spiritual ones, for not formalizing it now. In the meantime, you must leave Rome. We withhold our blessing and our indulgence from you, Dr. Ruiz-Sanchez. This Holy Year is for you a year of battle, with the world as prize. When you have won that battle you may return to us—not before. Farewell."

Dr. Ramon Ruiz-Sanchez, a layman, damned, left Rome for New York that night by air. The deluge of happenstance was rising more rapidly around him; the time for the building of arks was almost at hand. And yet, as the waters rose, and the words, *Into your hand are they delivered*, passed incessantly across the tired surfaces of his brain, it was not of the swarming billions of the Shelter state that he was thinking. It was of Chtexa; and the notion that an exorcism might succeed in dissolving utterly that grave being and all his race and civilization, return them to the impotent mind of the Great Nothing as though they had never been, was an agony to him.

Into your hand. . . . Into your hand. . . .

XVII

THE figures were in. The people who had taken Egtverchi as both symbol and spokesman for their passionate discontents were now tallied, although they could not be known. Their nature was no surprise—the crime and mental disease statistics had long provided a clear picture of that—but their number was stunning. Apparently nearly a third of twenty-first-century society loathed that society from the bottom of its collective heart.

Ruiz-Sanchez wondered suddenly whether, had a similar tally been possible in every age, the proportion would have turned out to be stable.

"Do you think it would do any good to talk to Egtverchi?" he asked Michelis. Over his protests, he was staying in the Michelis' apartment for the time being.

"Well, it hasn't done any good for *me* to talk with him," Michelis said. "With you it might be a different story—though frankly, Ramon, I'm inclined to doubt even that. He's doubly hard to reason with because he himself seems to be getting no satisfaction out of the whole affair."

"He knows his audience better than we do," Liu added. "And the more the numbers pile up, the more embittered he seems to become. I think they remind him continually that he can never be fully accepted on Earth, fully at home on it. He thinks he's of interest only to people who themselves don't feel at home on their own planet. That's not true, of course, but that's how he feels."

"There's enough truth in it so that he'd be unlikely to be dissuaded of it," Ruiz-Sanchez agreed gloomily.

He shifted his chair so as not to be able to see Liu's bees, which were hard at work in the shafts of sunlight on the porch. At another time he could not have torn himself away from them, but he could not afford to be distracted now.

"And of course he's also well aware that he'll never know what it means to be a Lithian—regardless of his shape and in-heritance," he added. "Chtexa might get a shadow of that through to him, if only they could meet—but no, they don't even speak the same language."

"Egtverchi's been studying Lithian," Michelis said. "But it's true that he can't speak it, not even as well as I can. He has nothing to read but your grammar—the documents are still all classified against him—and nobody to talk to. He sounds as rusty as an iron hinge. But, Ramon, you could interpret."

"Yes, I could. But Mike, it's physically impossible. There just isn't time to get Chtexa here, even if we had the resources and the authority to do it."

"I wasn't thinking of that. I was thinking of CirCon—d'Averoigne's new circum-continuum radio. I don't know what shape it's in, but the Message Tree puts out a poweful signal—possibly d'Averoigne could pick it up. If so, you might be able to talk to Chtexa. I'll see what I can find out, anyhow."

"I'm willing to try," Ruiz-Sanchez said. "But it doesn't sound very promising."

He stopped to think, not of more answers—he had already hit his head against that wall more than often enough—but of what questions he still needed to ask. Michelis' appearance gave him the cue. It had shocked him at first, and he could still not quite get used to it. The big chemist had aged markedly: his face was drawn, and he had deeply cut, liverish circles under his eyes. Liu looked no better; while she had not seemed to age any, she looked miserable. There was a tension in the air between them, too, as though they had failed to find in each other sufficient release from the tensions of the world around them.

"It's possible that Agronski might know something that would be helpful," he said, only half-aloud.

"Maybe," Michelis said. "I've seen him only once—at a party, the one where Egtverchi caused such a stink. He was behaving very oddly. I'm sure he recognized us, but he wouldn't meet our eyes, let alone come and talk to us. As a matter of fact, I can't remember seeing him talking to anybody. He just sat in a corner and drank. It wasn't at all like him."

"Why did he come, do you suppose?"

"Oh, that's not hard to guess. He's a fan of Egtverchi's."

"*Martin?* How do you know?"

"Egtverchi bragged about it. He said he hoped to have the whole Lithia commission on his side eventually." Michelis grimaced. "The way Agronski was acting, he'll be of no use to Egtverchi or anybody else."

"And so we have still another soul on the way to damnation," Ruiz-Sanchez said grimly. "I should have suspected it. There's so little meaning in Agronski's life as it is, it won't take Egtverchi long to cut him off from any contact with reality at all. That is what evil does—it empties you."

"I'm none too sure Egtverchi's to blame," Michelis said, his voice steeped in gloom. "Except as a symptom. The Earth is riddled with schizophrenics already. If Agronski had any tendency that way, and obviously he did, then all he needed was to be planted here again for the tendency to flower."

"That wasn't my impression of him," Liu said. "From what little I saw of him, and from what you've told me, he seemed dreadfully normal—even simple-minded. I don't see how he could get deep enough into any question to be driven insane—or how he could be tempted to fall into your theological vacuum, Ramon."

"In this universe of discourse, Liu, we are all very much alike," Ruiz-Sanchez said dispiritedly. "And from what Mike tells me, I think we may be already too late to do much for Martin. And he's only—only a sample of what's happening everywhere within the sound of Egtverchi's voice."

"It's a mistake to think of schizophrenia as a disease of the wits, anyhow," Michelis said. "Back in the days when it was first being described, the English used to call it 'lorry-driver's disease.' When intellectuals get it, the results are spectacular only because they can articulate what they feel: Nijinski, van Gogh, T. E. Lawrence, Nietzsche, Wilson . . . it's a long list, but it's nothing compared to the ordinary people who've had it. And they get it fifty-to-one over intellectuals. Agronski is just the usual kind of victim, no more, no less."

"What has happened to that threat you mentioned?" Ruiz-Sanchez said. "Egtverchi got on the air again last night without his being made a ward of yours. Was your friend in the complicated hat just flailing the air?"

"I think that's partly the answer," Michelis said hopefully. "They haven't said another word to us, so I'm just guessing, but it may be that your arrival disconcerted them. They expected you to be publicly unfrocked—and the fact that you weren't has thrown their schedule for announcing the Lithia decision seriously out of joint. They're probably waiting to see what you will do now."

"So," Ruiz-Sanchez said grimly, "am I. I might just do nothing, which would probably be the most confusing thing I could do. I think their hands are tied, Mike. He's never mentioned the Bifalcos' products but that once, but obviously he must be selling them by the warehouse-load, so his sponsors won't cut him off. Nor can I see on what grounds the UN Communications Commission can do it." He laughed shortly. "They've been trying for decades to encourage more independent comment on 3-V anyhow—and Egtverchi is certainly a giant step in that direction."

"I should think he'd be open to charges of inciting to riot," Michelis said.

"He hasn't incited any riots that I've heard about," Ruiz-Sanchez said. "The Frisco affair happened spontaneously as far as anyone could see—and I noticed that the pictures didn't show a single one of those uniformed followers of his in the crowds."

"But he praised the rioters' spirit, and made fun of the police," Liu pointed out. "He as good as endorsed it."

"That's not incitement," Michelis said. "I see what Ramon means. He's smart enough to do nothing for which he could be brought to trial—and a false arrest would be suicide, the UN would be inciting a riot itself."

"Besides, what would they do with him if they got a conviction?" Ruiz asked. "He's a citizen, but his needs aren't like ours; they'd be chancing killing him with a thirty-day sentence. I suppose they could deport him, but they can't declare him an undesirable alien without declaring Lithia a foreign country—and until that report is released, Lithia is a protectorate, with a right to admission to the UN as a member state!"

"Small chance of that," Michelis said. "That would mean ditching Cleaver's project."

Ruiz-Sanchez felt the same sinking of the heart that had overcome him when Michelis first gave him that news. "How far advanced is it now?" he asked.

"I'm not sure. All I know is that they've been shipping equipment to him in huge amounts. There's another load scheduled to leave in two weeks. The scuttlebutt says that Cleaver has some kind of crucial experiment ready to go as soon as that shipment gets there. That puts it pretty close—the new ships make the trip in less than a month."

"Betrayed again," Ruiz-Sanchez said bitterly.

"Then is there *nothing* you can do, Ramon?" Liu asked.

"I'll interpret for Egtverchi and Chtexa, if anything comes of that project."

"Yes, but. . . ."

"I know what you mean," he said. "Yes, there is something decisive that I can do. And possibly it would work. In fact, it is something that I *must* do."

He stared blindly at them. The buzzing of the bees, so reminiscent of the singing of the jungles of Lithia, probed insistently at him.

"But," he said, "I don't think that I'm going to do it."

Michelis moved mountains. He was formidable enough under normal conditions, but when he was desperate and saw a possible way out, no bulldozer could have been more implacable in crushing through an opening.

Lucien le Comte des Bois-d'Averoigne, late Procurator of Canarsie, and always fellow in the brotherhood of science, received them all cordially in his Canadian retreat. Not even the sardonically silent figure of Egtverchi made him blink; he shook hands with the displaced Lithian as though they were old friends meeting again after a lapse of a few weeks. The count himself was a large, rotund man in his early sixties, with a protuberant belly, and he was brown all over: his remaining hair was brown, his suit was brown, he was deeply tanned, and he was smoking a long brown cigar.

The room in which he received them—Ruiz-Sanchez, Michelis, Liu, and Egtverchi—was a curious mixture of lodge and laboratory. It had an open fireplace, rough furniture, mounted guns, an elk's head, and an amazing mess of wires and apparatus.

"I am by no means sure that this is going to work," he told them promptly. "Everything I have is still in the breadboard stage, as you can see. It's been years since I last handled a soldering iron and a voltmeter, too, so we may well have a simple electronic failure somewhere in this mass of wiring—but it wasn't a task I could leave to a technician."

He waved them to seats while he made final adjustments. Egtverchi remained standing in the rear of the room in the shadows, motionless except for the gentle rise and fall of his great chest as he breathed, and an occasional sudden movement of his eyes.

"There will be no image, of course," the count said abstractedly. "This giant J-J coupling you describe obviously doesn't broadcast in that band. But if we are very lucky, we may get some sound. . . . Ah."

A loudspeaker almost hidden in the maze crackled and then began to emit distant, patterned bursts of hissing. Except for the pattern, it seemed to Ruiz-Sanchez to be nothing but noise, but the count said at once:

"I'm getting something in that region. I didn't expect to pick it up so soon. I don't make much sense of it, however."

Neither did Ruiz, and for a few moments he had all he could do to get over his amazement. "Those are—signals the Message Tree is broadcasting now?" he said, with a touch of incredulity.

"I hope so," the count said drily. "I have been busy all day installing chokes against any other possible signal."

The Jesuit's respect for the mathematician came close to awe. To think that this disorderly tangle of wiring, little black acorns, small red and brown objects like firecrackers, the shining interlocking blades of variable condensers, massively heavy coils, and flickering meters was even now reaching directly through the subether, around fifty light-years of space-time, to eavesdrop on the pulses of the crystalline cliff buried beneath Xoredeshch Sfath. . . .

"Can you tune it?" he said at last. "I think those must be the stutter pattern—what the Lithians use as a navigational grid for their ships and planes. There ought to be an audio band—"

Except, he recalled suddenly, that that band couldn't possibly be an "audio" band. Nobody ever spoke directly to the Message Tree—only to the single Lithian who stood in the center of the Tree's chamber. How *he* got the substance of the message transformed into radio waves had never been explained to any of the Earthmen.

And yet suddenly there was a voice.

"—a powerful tap on the Tree," the voice said in clear, even, cold Lithian. "Who is receiving? Do you hear me? I do not understand the direction your carrier is coming from. It seems inside the Tree, which is impossible. Does anyone understand me?"

Silently, the count thrust a microphone into Ruiz' hand. He discovered that he was trembling.

"We understand you," he said in Lithian in a shaky voice. "We are on Earth. Can you hear me?"

"I hear you," the voice said at once. "We understood that what you say is impossible. But what you say is not always accurate, we have found. What do you want?"

"I would like to speak to Chtexa, the metallist," Ruiz said. "This is Ruiz-Sanchez, who was in Xoredeshch Sfath last year."

"He can be summoned," said the cold, distant voice. There was a brief hashing sound from the speaker; then it went away again. "If he wishes to speak to you."

"Tell him," Ruiz-Sanchez said, "that his son Egtverchi also wishes to speak to him."

"Ah," said the voice after a pause. "Then no doubt he will come. But you cannot speak long on this channel. The direction from which your signal comes is damaging my sanity. Can you receive a sound-modulated signal if we can arrange to send one?"

Michelis murmured to the count, who nodded energetically and pointed to the loudspeaker.

"That is how we are receiving you now," Ruiz said. "How are you transmitting?"

"That I cannot explain to you," said the cold voice. "I cannot speak to you any longer or I will be damaged. Chtexa has been called."

The voice stopped and there was a long silence. Ruiz-Sanchez wiped the sweat off his forehead with the back of his hand.

"Telepathy?" Michelis muttered behind him. "No, it fits into the electro-magnetic spectrum somewhere. But where? Boy, there sure is a lot we don't know about that Tree."

The count nodded ruefully. He was watching his meters like a hawk but, judging from his expression, they were not telling him anything he did not already know.

"Ruiz-Sanchez," the loudspeaker said. Ruiz started.

It was Chtexa's voice, clear and strong.

Ruiz beckoned at the shadows, and Egtverchi came forward. He was in no hurry. There was something almost insolent in his very walk.

"This is Ruiz-Sanchez, Chtexa," Ruiz said. "I'm talking to you from Earth—a new experimental communications system one of our scientists has evolved. I need your help."

"I will be glad to do whatever I can," Chtexa said. "I was sorry that you did not return with the other Earthman. He was less welcome. He and his friends have razed one of our finest forests near Gleshchtehk Sfath, and built ugly buildings here in the city."

"I'm sorry, too," Ruiz-Sanchez said. The words seemed inadequate, but it would be impossible to explain to Chtexa exactly what the situation was—impossible, and illegal. "I still hope to come some day. But I am calling about your son."

There was a brief pause, during which the speaker emitted a series of muted, anomalous sounds, almost yet not quite recognizable. Evidently the Lithians' audio hookup was catching some background noise from inside the Tree, or even outside it. The clarity of the reception was astonishing; it was impossible to believe that the Tree was fifty light-years away.

"Egtverchi is an adult now," Chtexa's voice said. "He has seen many wonders on your world. Is he with you?"

"Yes," Ruiz-Sanchez said, beginning to sweat again. "But he does not know your language, Chtexa. I will interpret as best I can."

"That is strange," Chtexa said. "But I will hear his voice. Ask him when he is coming home; he has much to tell us."

Ruiz put the question.

"I have no home," Egtverchi said indifferently.

"I can't just tell him that, Egtverchi. Say something intelligible, in heaven's name. You owe your existence to Chtexa, you know that."

"I may visit Lithia some day," Egtverchi said, his eyes filming. "But I am in no hurry. There is still a great deal to be done on Earth."

"I hear him," Chtexa said. "His voice is high; he is not as tall as his inheritance provided, unless he is ill. What does he answer?"

There simply was not time to provide an interpretive translation; Ruiz-Sanchez told him the answer literally, word by word from English into Lithian.

"Ah," Chtexa said. "Then he has matters of import to his hand. That is good, and is generous of the Earth. He is right not to hurry. Ask him what he is doing."

"Breeding dissension," Egtverchi said, with a slight widening of his grin. Ruiz-Sanchez could not translate that literally; the concept was not in the Lithian language. It took him the better part of three long sentences to transmit even a dubious shadow of the idea to Chtexa.

"Then he *is* ill," Chtexa said. "You should have told me, Ruiz-Sanchez. You had best send him to us. You cannot treat him adequately there."

"He is not ill, and he will not go," Ruiz-Sanchez said carefully. "He is a citizen of Earth and cannot be compelled. This is why I called you. He is a trouble to us, Chtexa. He is doing us hurts. I had hoped you might reason with him; we can do nothing."

The anomalous sound, a sort of burring metallic whine, rose in the background and fell away again.

"That is not normal or natural," Chtexa said. "You do not recognize his illness. No more do I, but I am not a physician. You must send him here. I see I was in error in giving him to you. Tell him he is commanded home by the Law of the Whole."

"I never heard of the Law of the Whole," Egtverchi said when this was translated for him. "I doubt that there is any such thing. I make up my own laws as I go along. Tell him he is making Lithia sound like a bore, and that if he keeps it up I'll make a point of never going there at all."

"Blast it, Egtverchi—" Michelis burst in.

"Hush, Mike, one pilot is enough. Egtverchi, you were willing to co-operate with us up to now; at least, you came here with us. Did you do it just for the pleasure of defying and insulting your father? Chtexa is far wiser than you are; why don't you stop acting like a child and listen to him?"

"Because I don't choose to," Egtverchi said. "And you make me no more willing by wheedling, dear foster father. I didn't choose to be born a Lithian, and I didn't choose to be brought to Earth—but now that I'm a free agent I mean to make my own choices, and explain them to nobody if that's what pleases me."

"Then why did you come here?"

"There's no reason why I should explain that, but I will. I came to hear my father's voice. Now I've heard it. I don't understand what he says, and he makes no better sense in your translation, and that's all there is to it as far as I am concerned. Bid him farewell for me—I shan't speak to him again."

"What does he say?" Chtexa's voice said.

"That he does not acknowledge the Law of the Whole, and will not come home," Ruiz-Sanchez told the microphone. The little instrument was slippery with sweat in his palm. "And he says to bid you farewell."

"Farewell, then," Chtexa said. "And farewell to you, too, Ruiz-Sanchez. I am at fault, and this fills me with sorrow; but it is too late. I may not talk to you again, even by means of your marvelous instrument."

Behind the voice, the strange, half-familiar whine rose to a savage, snarling scream which lasted almost a minute. Ruiz-Sanchez waited until he thought he could be heard over it again.

"Why not, Chtexa?" he said huskily. "The fault is ours as much as it is yours. I am still your friend, and wish you well."

"And I am your friend, and wish you well," Chtexa's voice said. "But we may not talk again. Can you not hear the power saws?"

So that was what that sound was!

"Yes. Yes, I hear them."

"That is the reason," Chtexa said. "Your friend Xlevher is cutting down the Message Tree."

The gloom was thick in the Michelis apartment. As the time drew closer for Egtverchi's next broadcast, it became increasingly apparent that their analysis of the UN's essential helplessness had been correct. Egtverchi was not openly triumphant, though he was exposed to that temptation in several newspaper interviews; but he floated some disquieting hints of vast plans which might well be started in motion when he was next on the air.

Ruiz-Sanchez had not the least desire to listen to the broadcast, but he had to face the fact that he would be unable to stay away from it. He could not afford to be without any new data that the program might yield. Nothing he had learned had done him any good thus far, but there was always the slim chance that something would turn up.

In the meantime, there was the problem of Cleaver, and his associates. However you looked at it, they were human souls. If Ruiz-Sanchez were to be driven, somehow, to the step that Hadrian VIII had commanded, and it did not fail, more than a set of attractive hallucinations would be lost. It would plunge several hundred human souls into instant death and more than probable damnation; Ruiz-Sanchez did not believe that the hand of God would reach forth to pluck to salvation men who were involved in such a project as Cleaver's, but he was equally convinced that his should not be the hand to condemn any man to death, let alone to an unshriven death. Ruiz was condemned already—but not yet of murder.

It had been Tannhäuser who had been told that his salvation was as unlikely as the blossoming of the pilgrim's staff in his hand. And Ruiz-Sanchez' was as unlikely as sanctified murder.

Yet the Holy Father had commanded it; had said it was the only road back for Ruiz-Sanchez, and for the world. The Pope's clear implication had been that he shared with Ruiz-Sanchez the view that the world stood on the brink of Armageddon—and he had said flatly that only Ruiz-Sanchez could avert it. Their only difference was doctrinal, and in these matters the Pope could not err. . . .

But if it was possible that the dogma of the infertility of Satan was wrong, then it was possible that the dogma of Papal infallibility was wrong. After all, it was a recent invention; quite a few Popes in history had got along without it.

Heresies, Ruiz-Sanchez thought—not for the first time—come in snarls. It is impossible to pull free one thread; tug at one, and the whole mass begins to roll down upon you.

I believe, O Lord; help me in mine unbelief. But it was useless. It was as though he were praying to God's back.

There was a knock on his door. "Coming, Ramon?" Michelis' tired voice said. "He's due to go on in two minutes."

"All right, Mike."

They settled before the Klee, warily, already defeated, awaiting

—what? It could only be a proclamation of total war. They were ignorant only of the form it would take.

"Good evening," Egtverchi said warmly from the frame. "There will be no news tonight. Instead of reporting news, we will make some. The time has come, it is now plain, for the people to whom news happens—those hapless people whose grief-stricken, stunned faces look out at you from the newspapers and the 3-V 'casts such as mine—to throw off their helplessness. Tonight I call upon all of you to show your contempt for the hypocrites who are your bosses, and your total power to be free of them.

"You have a message for them. Tell them this: tell them, 'Your beasts, sirs, are a great people.'

"I will be the first. As of tonight, I renounce my citizenship in the United Nations, and my allegiance to the Shelter state. From now on I will be a citizen—"

Michelis was on his feet, shouting incoherently.

"—a citizen of no country but that bounded by the limits of my own mind. I do not know what those limits are, and I may never find out, but I shall devote my life to searching for them, in whatever manner seems good to me, and in no other manner whatsoever.

"You must do the same. Tear up your registration cards. If you are asked your serial number, tell them you never had one. Never fill in another form. Stay above ground when the siren sounds. Stake out plots; grow crops; abandon the corridors. Do not commit any violence; simply refuse to obey. Nobody has the right to compel you, as non-citizens. Passivity is the key. Renounce, resist, deny!

"Begin now. In half an hour they will overwhelm you. When—"

An urgent buzzer sounded over Egtverchi's voice, and for an instant a checkerboard pattern in red and black blotted out his figure: the UN's crash-priority signal, overriding the by-pass recording circuit. Then the face of the UN man looked out at them from under its funny hat, with Egtverchi underlying it dimly, his exhortations only a whisper in the background.

"Dr. Michelis," the UN man said exultantly. "He's done it. He's overreached himself. As a non-citizen, he's right in our hands. Get down here—we need you right away, before he gets off the air. Dr. Meid too."

"What for?"

"To sign pleas of *nolo contendere*. Both of you are under arrest for keeping a wild animal—a technicality only; don't be alarmed. But we have to have you. We mean to put Mr. Egtverchi in a cage for the rest of his life—a *soundproof* cage."

"You are making a mistake," Ruiz-Sanchez said quietly.

The UN man's face, a mask of triumph with blazing eyes, swung toward him briefly.

"I didn't ask what you thought, Mister," he said. "I have no orders concerning you, but as far as I'm concerned, you've been closed out of this case entirely. If you try to force your way back in, you'll get burned. Dr. Michelis, Dr. Meid? Do we have to come and get you?"

"We'll come," Michelis said stonily. "Sign off." He did not wait for the UN man, however, but killed the set himself.

"Do you think we should do it, Ramon?" he said. "If not, we'll stay right here, and the hell with him. Or we'll take you along if you want."

"No, no," Ruiz-Sanchez said. "Go ahead. No balking on your part will accomplish a thing but getting you both in deep trouble. Do me one favor, though."

"Gladly. What is it?"

"Stay off the streets. When you get to the UN offices, make them keep you there. As arrested citizens, you have the right to be jailed."

Michelis and Liu both stared at him. Then comprehension began to break over Michelis' face.

"You think it will be that bad?" he said.

"Yes, I do. Do I have your promise?"

Michelis looked at Liu and nodded grimly. They went out.

The collapse of the Shelter state had already begun.

XVIII

THE beast Chaos roared on unslaked for three days. Ruiz-Sanchez was able to follow much of its progress from the beginning, via the Michelises' 3-V set. There were times when he would also have liked to look out over the sun porch rail, but the roar of the mob, the shots, explosions, police whistles, sirens, and unnamable noises had driven the bees frantic; under such conditions he would not have trusted Liu's protective garments for an instant, even had they been large enough for him.

The UN squads had made a well-organized attempt to bear Egtverchi off directly from the broadcasting station, but Egtverchi was not there—in fact, he had never been there at all. The audio, video and tri-di signals had all been piped into the station via co-axial cable from some unspecified place. The necessary connections had been made at the last minute, when it became obvious that Egtverchi was not going to show up, by a technician who had volunteered word of the actual situation; a sacrifice piece in Egtverchi's gambit. The network had sent an alert to the proper UN officers at once, but another sacrifice piece saw to it that the alert was shunted through channels.

It took nearly all night to sweat out of the QBC technician the location of Egtverchi's studio (the stooge at the UN obviously did not know) and by that time, of course, he was no longer there either. Also by that time, the news of the attempted arrest and the misfire was being blared and headlined in every Shelter in the world.

Even this much did not get to Ruiz-Sanchez until somewhat later, for the noise in the street began immediately after the first announcement had been made. At first it was disconnected and random, as though the streets were gradually filling with people who were angry or upset but were divided over what, if anything, they ought to do about it. Then there was a sudden change in the quality of the sound, and instantly Ruiz-Sanchez knew that the transformation from a gathering to a mob had been made. The shouting could not very well have become any louder, but abruptly it was a frightening uniform growl, like the enormous voice of a single animal.

He had no way of knowing what had triggered the change, and perhaps the crowd itself never knew either. But now the shots began—not many, but one shot is a fusillade if there have been no shots before. A part of the overall roar detached itself and took on an odd and even more frightening hollow sound;

only when the floor shook slightly under him did he realize what that meant.

A pseudopod of the beast had thrust itself into the building. Ruiz-Sanchez realized that he should have expected nothing else. The fad of living above ground was still essentially a privilege, reserved to those UN employees and officials who knew how to get the necessary and elaborate permissions, and who furthermore had enough income to support such an inconvenient arrangement; it was the twenty-first century's version of commuting from Maine—*here* was where *they* lived—

Ruiz-Sanchez checked the door hastily. It had elaborate locks—left over from the last period of the Shelter race, when the great untended buildings had been natural targets for looters—but they had gone unused for years. Ruiz-Sanchez used them all now.

He was just in time. There was an obscene shouting in the corridor just outside as part of the mob burst into it from the fire stairs. They had avoided the elevator by instinct—it was too slow to sustain their thoughtless ferocity, too confined for lawlessness, too mechanical for men who were letting their muscles do their thinking.

Somebody rattled the door knob and then shook it.

"Locked," a muffled voice said.

"Break the damned thing down. Here, get out of the way—"

The door shuddered, but held easily. There was another, harder thump, as though several men had lunged against it at the same time; Ruiz-Sanchez could hear them grunt with the impact. Then there were five hammerlike blows.

"Open up in there! Open up, you lousy government fink, or we'll burn you out!"

The spontaneous threat seemed to surprise them all, even the utterer. There was a confused whispering. Then someone said hoarsely: "All right, but find some paper or something."

Ruiz-Sanchez thought confusedly of finding and filling a bucket, though he could not see how any fire could be introduced around the door—there was no transom, and the sill was snug—but at the same time a blurred shout from farther down the hall seemed to draw everyone outside stampeding away. The subsequent noises made it clear that they had found either an open, empty apartment, or an inadequately secured, occupied one where nobody was at home. Yes, it was occupied; Ruiz-Sanchez could hear them breaking furniture as well as windows.

Then, with a shock of terror, their voices began to come at him from behind his back. He whirled, but there seemed to be nobody in the apartment; the shouting was coming from the glassed-in sun porch, but of course there was nobody out there either—

"Jesus! Look, the guy's got his porch glassed in. It's a goddam garden."

"They don't let you have no goddam gardens in the Shelters."

"And you know who paid for it. Us, that's who."

He realized that they were on the neighboring balcony. He felt a surge of relief which he knew to be irrational. The next words confirmed its irrationality.

"Get some of that kindling out here. No, heavier stuff. Something to *throw*, you meathead."

"Can we get over there from here?"

"If we could throw a ladder across there—"

"It's a long way down—"

The leg of a chair burst through the glass on the sun porch. A heavy vase followed.

The bees came pouring out. Ruiz-Sanchez had not realized how many of them there were. The porch was black with them. For a moment they hovered uncertainly. They would have found the gaps in the glass almost at once in any event, but the men on the next porch, who could not have understood what it was they were seeing, gave the great insects the perfect cue. Something small and massive, possibly a torn-off piece of plumbing, shattered another pane and whirled through the midst of the cloud. Snarling like an old-fashioned aircraft engine, the bees swarmed.

There was an instant of dead silence across the way, and then a scream of agony and horror that made Ruiz-Sanchez' gut contort violently. Then they were all screaming. Briefly, he saw one of them, leaping straight out into space, his arms flailing, his head and chest swathed in golden-and-black furry bodies. Feet drummed past the door, and someone fell. The heavy buzzing threaded its way along the corridor after them.

From below, there were more screams. The great insects

could not fly in the open air, but they were free in the building now. Some of them might even make it all the way down to the street, by descending the stairwell.

After a while, there were no human sounds left in the building, only the pervasive insect snarl. Outside the door, somebody moaned and was silent.

Ruiz-Sanchez knew what he had to do. He went into the kitchen and vomited, and then he crammed himself into Liu's beekeeper's togs.

He was no longer a priest; indeed, he was no longer even a Catholic. Grace had been withdrawn from him. But it is the duty of any person to administer extreme unction if he knows how, as it is the duty of any person to administer baptism if he knows how. What happened to the soul so ministered to when it departed would be disposed by the Lord God, Who disposes all things; but He had commanded that no soul come before Him unshriven.

The man before the door was already dead. Ruiz-Sanchez crossed himself out of habit and stepped over the body, his eyes averted. A man who has died of massive histamine shock is not an edifying sight.

The open apartment had been thoroughly smashed up. There were three bodies there, all beyond help. The door to the kitchen, however, was closed; if one of them had had the sense to barricade himself in there before the swarm got to him, he might have been able to kill the few bees who had come in with him—

As if in confirmation, there was a groan behind the door. Ruiz-Sanchez pushed at it, but it was partly locked. He got it open about six inches and wormed through.

The contorted man on the floor, his incredibly puffed, taut skin slowly turning black, his eyes glassy with agony, was Agronski.

The geologist did not recognize him; he was already beyond that. There was no mind behind the eyes. Ruiz-Sanchez fell to his knees, clumsily in the tight protective clothing. He heard himself begin to mutter the rites, but he was no more hearing the Latin words than Agronski was.

This could be no coincidence. He had come here to give

grace, if such a one as he could still give grace; and before him was the most blameless of the Lithian commission, struck down where Ruiz-Sanchez would be sure to find him. It was the God of Job who was abroad in the world now, not the God of the Psalmist or the Christ. The face that was bent upon Ruiz-Sanchez was the face of the avenging, the jealous God— the God Who made hell before He made man, because He knew that He would have need of it. That terrible truth Dante had written down; and in the black face with the protruding tongue which rolled beside Ruiz-Sanchez' knee, he saw that Dante had been right, as every Catholic who reads the Divine Comedy knows in his heart of hearts.

There is a demonolater abroad in the world. He shall be deprived of grace, and then called upon to administer extreme unction to a friend. By this sign, let him know himself for what he is.

After a while, Agronski was dead, choked to death by his own tongue.

But still it was not over. It was necessary now to make Mike's apartment secure, kill any bees that might have got in, see to it that the escaped swarm died. It was easy enough. Ruiz-Sanchez simply papered over the broken panes on the sun porch. The bees could not feed anywhere but in Liu's garden; they would come back there within a few hours; denied entrance, they would die of starvation an hour or so later. A bee is not a well-designed flying-machine; it keeps itself in the air by expending energy—in short, by pure brute force. A trapped bumblebee can starve to death in half a day, and Liu's tetraploid monsters would die far sooner of their freedom.

The 3-V muttered away throughout the dreary business. The terror was not local, that was clear. The Corridor Riots of 1993 had been nothing but a premonitory flicker, compared to this.

Four target areas were blacked out completely. Egtverchi's uniformed thugs, suddenly reappearing from nowhere in force, had seized their control centers. At the moment, they were holding roughly twenty-five million people as hostages for Egt-verchi's safe-conduct, with the active collusion of perhaps five million of them. The violence elsewhere was not as systematic —though some of the outbursts of wrecking must have been carefully planned to allow for the placing of the explosives alone, there seemed to be no special pattern to it—but in no case could it be described as "passive" or "non-violent."

Sick, wretched and damned, Ruiz-Sanchez waited in the Michelises' jungle apartment, as though part of Lithia had followed him home and enfolded him there.

After the first three days, the fury had exhausted itself sufficiently to permit Michelis and Liu to risk the trip back to their apartment in a UN armored car. They were wan and ghastly-looking, as Ruiz-Sanchez supposed he was himself; they had had even less sleep than he had. He decided at once to say nothing about Agronski; that horror they could be spared. There was no way, however, that he could avoid explaining what had happened to the bees.

Liu's sad little shrug was somehow even harder to bear than Agronski.

"Did they find him yet?" Ruiz-Sanchez said huskily.

"We were going to ask you the same thing," Michelis said. The tall New Englander was able to get a glimpse of himself in a mirror above a planting box and winced. "Ugh, what a beard! At the UN everybody's too busy to tell you anything, except in fragments. We thought you might have heard an announcement."

"No, nothing. The Detroit vigilantes have surrendered, according to QBC."

"Yes, so have those goons in Smolensk; they ought to be putting that on the air in an hour or so. I never did think they'd succeed in pulling that operation off. They can't possibly know the corridors as well as the target area authorities themselves do. In Smolensk they got them with the fire door system—drained all the oxygen out of the area they were holding without their realizing what was going on. Two of them never came to."

Ruiz-Sanchez crossed himself automatically. Up on the wall, the Klee muttered in a low voice; it had not been off since Egtverchi's broadcast.

"I don't know whether I want to listen to that damn thing or not," Michelis said sourly. Nevertheless, he turned up the volume.

There was still essentially no news. The rioting was dying

back, though it was as bad as ever in some shelters. The Smolensk announcement was duly made, bare of detail. Egtverchi had not yet been located, but UN officials expected a break in the case "shortly."

"'Shortly,' hell," Michelis said. "They've run out of leads entirely. They thought they had him cold the next morning, when they found a trail to the hideaway where he'd arranged to tide himself over and direct things. But he wasn't there—apparently he'd gotten out in a hurry, some time before. And nobody in his organization knows where he would go next—he was *supposed* to be there, and they're thoroughly demoralized to be told that he's not."

"Which means that he's on the run," Ruiz-Sanchez suggested.

"Yes, I suppose that's some consolation," Michelis said. "But where could he run to, where he wouldn't be recognized? And *how* would he run? He couldn't just gallop naked through the streets, or take a public conveyance. It takes organization to ship something as *outré* as that secretly—and Egtverchi's organization is as baffled about it as the UN is." He turned the 3-V off with a savage gesture.

Liu turned to Ruiz-Sanchez, her expression appalled beneath its weariness.

"Then it's really not over after all?" she said hopelessly.

"Far from it," Ruiz-Sanchez said. "But maybe the violent phase of it is over. If Egtverchi stays vanished for a few days more, I'll conclude that he is dead. He couldn't stay unsighted that long if he were still moving about. Of course his death won't solve most of the major problems, but at least it would remove one sword from over our heads."

Even that, he recognized silently, was wishful thinking. Besides, can you kill a hallucination?

"Well, I hope the UN has learned something," Michelis said. "There's one thing you have to say for Egtverchi: he got the public to bring up all the unrest that's been smoldering down under the concrete for all these years. And underneath all the apparent conformity, too. We're going to have to do something about that now—maybe take sledgehammers in our hands and pound this damned Shelter system down into rubble and start over. It wouldn't cost any more than rebuilding what's already been destroyed. One thing's certain: the UN won't be able to smother a revolt of this size in slogans. They'll have to *do* something."

The Klee chimed.

"I won't answer it," Michelis said through gritted teeth. "I won't answer it. I've had enough."

"I think we'd better, Mike," Liu said. "It might be—news."

"News!" Michelis said, like a swearword. But he allowed himself to be persuaded. Underneath all the weariness, Ruiz-Sanchez thought he could detect something like a return of warmth between the two, as though, during the three days, some depth had been sounded which they had never touched before. The slight sign of something good astonished him. Was he beginning, like all demonolaters, to take pleasure in the prevalence of evil, or at least in the expectation of it?

The caller was the UN man. His face was very strange underneath his funny hat, and his head was cocked as if to catch the first word. Suddenly, blindingly, Ruiz-Sanchez saw the hat in the light of the attitude, and realized what it was: an elaborately disguised hearing aid. The UN man was deaf and, like most deaf people, ashamed of it. The rest of the apparatus was a decoy.

"Dr. Michelis, Dr. Meid, Dr. Ruiz," he said. "I don't know how to begin. Yes, I do. My deepest apologies for past rudeness. And past damn foolishness. We were wrong—my God, but we were wrong! It's your turn now. We need you badly, if you feel like doing us a favor. I won't blame you if you don't."

"No threats?" Michelis said, with unforgiving contempt.

"No, no threats. My apologies, please. No, this is purely a favor, requested by the Security Council." His face twisted suddenly, and then was composed once more. "I—volunteered to present the petition. We need you all, right away, on the Moon."

"On the Moon! Why?"

"We've found Egtverchi."

"Impossible," Ruiz-Sanchez said, more sharply than he had intended. "He could never have gotten passage. Is he dead?"

"No, he's not dead. And he's not on the Moon—I didn't mean to imply that."

"Then where *is* he, in God's name?"

"He's on his way back to Lithia."

*

The trip to the Moon, by ferry-rocket, was rough, hectic and long. As the sole space voyage now being made in which the Haertel overdrive could not be used—across so short a distance, a Haertel ship would have overshot the target—very little improvement in techniques had been made in the trip since the old von Braun days. It was only after they had been bundled off the rocket into the moonboat, for the slow, paddle-wheel-driven trip across the seas of dust to the Comte d'Averoigne's observatory, that Ruiz-Sanchez managed to piece the whole story together.

Egtverchi had been found aboard the vessel that was shipping the final installment of equipment to Cleaver, when the ship was two days out. He was half-dead. In a final, desperate improvisation, he had had himself crated, addressed to Cleaver, marked "FRAGILE — RADIOACTIVE — THIS END UP," and shipped via ordinary express into the spaceport. Even a normally raised Lithian would have been shaken up by this kind of treatment, and Egtverchi, in addition to being a spindling specimen of his race, had been on the run for many hours before being shipped.

The vessel, by no very great coincidence, was also carrying the pilot model of the Petard CirCon; the captain got the news back to the count on the first test, and the count passed it along to the UN by ordinary radio. Egtverchi was in irons now, but he was well and cheerful. Since it was impossible for the ship to turn back, the UN was now, in effect, doing his running for him, at a good many times the speed of light.

Ruiz-Sanchez found a trace of pity in his heart for the born exile, harried now like a wild animal, penned behind bars, on his way back to a fatherland for which no experience in his life had fitted him, whose very language he could not speak. But when the UN man began to question them all—what was needed was some knowledgeable estimate of what Egtverchi might do next—his pity did not survive his speculations. It was right and proper to pity children, but Ruiz-Sanchez was beginning to believe that adults generally deserve any misfortune that they get.

The impact of a creature like Egtverchi on the stable society of Lithia would be explosive. On Earth, at least, he had been a freak; on Lithia, he would soon be taken for another Lithian, however odd. And Earth had had centuries of experience with deranged and displaced messiahs like Egtverchi; such a thing had never happened before on Lithia. Egtverchi would infect that garden down to the roots, and remake it in his own image —transforming the planet into that hypothetical dangerous enemy against whose advent Cleaver had wanted to make it an arsenal!

Yet something like that had happened when Earth was a stable garden, too. Perhaps—*O felix culpa!*—it always happened that way, on every world. Perhaps the Tree of the Knowledge of Good and Evil was like the Yggdrasil of the legends of Pope Hadrian's birthland, with its roots in the floor of the universe, its branches bearing the planets—and whosoever would eat of its fruit might eat thereof. . . .

No, that must not be. Lithia as a rigged Garden had been dangerous enough; but Lithia transformed into a planet-wide fortress of Dis was a threat to Heaven itself.

The Count d'Averoigne's main observatory had been built by the UN, to his specifications, approximately in the center of the crater Stadius, a once towering cup which early in its history had been swamped and partially melted in the outpouring sea of lava which made the Mare Imbrium. What remained of its walls served the count's staff as a meteor-rampart during showers, yet they were low enough to be well below the horizon from the center of the crater, giving the count what was effectively a level plain in all directions.

He looked no different than he had when they had first met, except that he was wearing brown coveralls instead of a brown suit, but he seemed glad to see them. Ruiz-Sanchez suspected that he was sometimes lonely, or perhaps lonely all the time— not only because of his current isolation on the Moon, but in his continuing remoteness from his family and indeed the whole of ordinary humanity.

"I have a surprise for you," he told them. "We've just completed the new telescope—six hundred feet in diameter, all of sodium foil, perched on top of Mount Piton a few hundred miles north of here. The relay cables were brought through to

Stadius yesterday, and I was up all night testing my circuits. They have been made a little neater since you last saw them."

This was an understatement. The breadboard rigs had vanished entirely; the object the count was indicating now was nothing but a black enamel box about the size of a tape recorder, and with only about that many knobs.

"Of course to do this is simpler than picking up a broadcast from a transmitter that doesn't have CirCon, like the Tree," the count admitted. "But the results are just as gratifying. Regard."

He snapped a switch dramatically. On a large screen on the opposite wall of the dark observatory chamber, a cloud-wrapped planet swam placidly.

"My God!" Michelis said in a choked voice. "That's—*is* that Lithia, Count d'Averoigne? I'd swear it is."

"Please," the count said. "Here I'm Dr. Petard. But yes, that's Lithia; its sun is visible from the Moon a little over twelve days of the month. It's fifty light-years away, but here we see it at an apparent distance of a quarter of a million miles, give or take ten thousand—about the distance of the Moon from the Earth. It's remarkable how much light you can gather with a six-hundred-foot paraboloid of sodium when there's no atmosphere in the way. Of course with an atmosphere we couldn't maintain the foil, either—the gravity here is almost too much for it."

"It's stunning," Liu murmured.

"That's only the beginning, Dr. Meid. We have spanned not only the space, but also the time—both together, as is only appropriate. What we are seeing is Lithia *today*—right now, in fact—not Lithia fifty years ago."

"Congratulations," Michelis said, his voice hushed. "Of course the scholium was the real achievement—but you threw up an installation in record time, too, it seems to me."

"It seems that way to me, too," the count said, taking his cigar out of his mouth and regarding it complacently.

"Are we going to be able to catch the ship's landing?" the UN man said intensely.

"No, I'm afraid not, unless I have my dates wrong. According to the schedule you gave me, the landing was supposed to have taken place yesterday, and I can't back my device up and down the time spectrum. The equations nail it to simultaneity, and simultaneity is what I get—neither more, nor less."

His voice changed color suddenly. The change transformed him from a fat man delighted with a new toy into the philosopher-mathematician Henri Petard as no disclaimer of his hereditary title could ever have done.

"I invited you to hold your conference here," he said, "because I thought you should all be witnesses to an event which I hope profoundly is not going to happen. I will explain:

"Recently I was asked to check the reasoning on which Dr. Cleaver based the experiment he has programmed for today. Briefly, the experiment is an attempt to store the total output of a Nernst generator for a period of about ninety seconds, through a special adaptation of what is called the pinch effect.

"I found the reasoning faulty—not obviously, Dr. Cleaver is too careful a craftsman for that, but seriously, all the same. Since lithium 6 is ubiquitous on that planet, any failure would be totally disastrous. I sent Dr. Cleaver an urgent message on the CirCon, to be tape-recorded on the ship that landed yesterday; I would have used the Tree, but of course that has been cut down, and I doubt that he would have accepted any such message from a Lithian had it not been. The captain of the ship promised me that the tape would be delivered to Dr. Cleaver before any of the remaining apparatus was unloaded. But I know Dr. Cleaver. He is bullheaded. Is that not so?"

"Yes," Michelis said. "God knows that's so."

"Well, we are ready," Dr. Petard said. "As ready as we can be. I have instruments to record the event. Let us pray that I won't need them."

The count was a lapsed Catholic; his injunction was a habit. But Ruiz-Sanchez could no more pray for any such thing than the count could—and no more could he leave the outcome to chance. St. Michael's sword had been put into his hand now so unmistakably that even a fool could not fail to recognize it.

The Holy Father had known it would be so, and had planned for it with the skill of a Disraeli. Ruiz-Sanchez shuddered to think what a less politically minded Pope would have made of such an opportunity, but of course it had been God's will that this should happen in the time of Hadrian and not during any other pontificate. By specifically ruling out any formal excommunication, Hadrian had reserved to Ruiz-Sanchez' use the one gift of grace which was pertinent to the occasion at hand.

And perhaps he had seen, too, that the time Ruiz-Sanchez had devoted to the elaborate, capriciously hypercomplex case of conscience in the Joyce novel had been time wasted; there was a much simpler case, one of the classical situations, which applied if Ruiz-Sanchez could only see it. It was the case of the sick child, for whose recovery prayers were offered.

These days, most sick children recovered in a day or so, after a shot of spectrosigmin or some similar drug, even from the brink of the terminal coma. *Question*: Has prayer failed, and temporal science wrought the recovery?

Answer: No, for prayer is always answered, and no man may choose for God the means He uses to answer it. Surely a miracle like a life-saving antibiotic is not unworthy of the bounty of God.

And this, too, was the answer to the riddle of the Great Nothing. The Adversary is not creative, except in the sense that He always seeks evil, and always does good. He cannot claim any of the credit for temporal science, nor imply truthfully that a success for temporal science is a failure for prayer. In this as in all other matters, He is compelled to lie.

And there on Lithia was Cleaver, agent of the Great Nothing, foredoomed to failure, the very task to which he was putting his hand in the Adversary's service tottering on the edge of undoing all His work. The staff of Tannhauser had blossomed: *These fruits are shaken from the wrath-bearing tree.*

Yet even as Ruiz-Sanchez rose, the searing words of Pope Gregory VIII trembling on his lips, he hesitated still again. What if he were wrong after all? Suppose, just suppose, that Lithia were Eden, and that the Earth-bred Lithian who had just returned there were the Serpent foreordained for it? *Suppose it always happened that way, world without end?*

The voice of the Great Nothing, pouring forth lies to the last. Ruiz-Sanchez raised his hand. His shaken voice resounded and echoed in the cave of the observatory.

"I, A PRIEST OF CHRIST, DO COMMAND YE, MOST FOUL SPIRITS WHO DO STIR UP THESE CLOUDS—"

"What? For heaven's sake, be quiet," the UN man said

irritably. Everyone else was staring in wonder, and in Liu's glance there appeared to be a little fear. Only the count's glance was knowing and solemn.

"—THAT YE DEPART FROM THEM, AND DISPERSE YOURSELVES INTO WILD AND UNTILLED PLACES, THAT YE MAY BE NO LONGER ABLE TO HARM MEN OR ANIMALS OR FRUITS OR HERBS, OR WHATSOEVER IS DESIGNED FOR HUMAN USE:

"AND THOU GREAT NOTHING, THOU LUSTFUL AND STUPID ONE, *SCROFA STERCORATE*, THOU SOOTY SPIRIT FROM TARTARUS, I CAST THEE DOWN, *O PORCARIE PEDICOSE*, INTO THE INFERNAL KITCHEN:

"BY THE APOCALYPSE OF JESUS CHRIST, WHICH GOD HATH GIVEN TO MAKE KNOWN UNTO HIS SERVANTS THOSE THINGS WHICH ARE SHORTLY TO BE; AND HATH SIGNIFIED, SENDING BY HIS ANGEL; I EXORCISE THEE, ANGEL OF PERVERSITY:

"BY THE SEVEN GOLD CANDLESTICKS, AND BY ONE LIKE UNTO THE SON OF MAN, STANDING IN THE MIDST OF THE CANDLESTICKS; BY HIS VOICE, AS THE VOICE OF MANY WATERS; BY HIS WORDS, 'I AM LIVING, WHO WAS DEAD; AND BEHOLD, I LIVE FOREVER AND EVER; AND I HAVE THE KEYS OF DEATH AND OF HELL'; I SAY UNTO YOU, ANGEL OF PERDITION: DEPART, DEPART, DEPART!"

The echoes rang and dwindled. The lunar silence flowed back, underlined by the breathing of the people in the observatory and the sound of pumps laboring somewhere beneath.

And slowly, and without a sound, the cloudy planet on the screen turned white all over. The clouds and the dim oceans and continents blended into a blue-white glare which shone out from the screen like a searchlight. It seemed to penetrate their bloodless faces down to the bone.

Slowly, slowly, it all melted away: the chirruping forests, Chtexa's porcelain house, the barking lungfish, the stump of the Message Tree, the wild allosaurs, the single silver moon, the great beating heart of Blood Lake, the city of the potters, the flying squid, the Lithian crocodile and his winding track, the tall noble reasoning creatures and the mystery and the beauty around them. Suddenly the whole of Lithia began to swell, like a balloon—

The count tried to turn the screen off, but he was too late. Before he could touch the black box, the whole circuit went out with a puffing of fuses. The intolerable light vanished instantly; the screen went black, and the universe with it.

They sat blinded and stunned.

"An error in Equation Sixteen," the count's voice said harshly in the swimming darkness.

No, Ruiz-Sanchez thought; no. An instance of fulfilled desire. He had wanted to use Lithia to defend the faith, and he had been given that. Cleaver had wanted to turn it into a fusion-bomb plant, and he had got that in full measure, all at once. Michelis had seen in it a prophecy of infallible human love, and had been stretched on that rack ever since. And Agronski—Agronski had wanted nothing to change, and now was unchangeably nothing.

In the darkness, there was a long, ragged sigh. For a moment, Ruiz-Sanchez could not place the voice; he thought it was Liu. But no. It was Mike.

"When we have our eyesight back," the count's voice said, "I propose that we suit up and go outside. We have a nova to watch for."

That was only a maneuver, an act of misdirection on the count's part—an act of kindness. He knew well enough that that nova would not be visible to the naked eye until the next Holy Year, fifty years to come; and he knew that they knew.

Nevertheless, when Father Ramon Ruiz-Sanchez, sometime Clerk Regular in the Society of Jesus, could see again, they had left him alone with his God and his grief.

APPENDIX

The Planet Lithia (from Michelis, D., and Ruiz-Sanchez, R.: Lithia—a preliminary report. *J. I. R.* 4:225, 2050; abstract.)

Lithia is the second planet of the solar type star Alpha Arietis, which is located in the constellation Aries and is approximately 50 light-years from Sol.[1]

It revolves around its primary at a mean distance of 108,600,000 miles, with a year of approximately 380 terrestrial days. The orbit is definitely elliptical, with an eccentricity of 0.51, so that the long axis of the ellipse is approximately 15 per cent longer than the short axis.

The axis of the planet is essentially perpendicular to the orbit, and the planet rotates on its axis with a day of about 20 terrestrial hours. Hence, the Lithian year consists of 456 Lithian days. The eccentricity of the orbit produces mild seasons, with long, relatively cold winters, and short, hot summers.

The planet has one moon with a diameter of 1,256 miles, which revolves about its primary at a distance of 326,000 miles, twelve times in the Lithian year.

The outer planets of the system have not yet been explored.

Lithia is 8,267 miles in diameter, and has a surface gravity of 0.82 that of Earth. The light gravity of the planet is accounted for by the relatively low density, which in turn is the result of its composition. When the planet was formed there was a much lower percentage of the heavy elements with atomic numbers above 20 included in its make-up than was the case with the Earth. Furthermore, the odd-numbered elements are even rarer than they are on Earth; the only odd-numbered elements that appear in any quantity are hydrogen, nitrogen, sodium and chlorine. Potassium is quite rare, and the heavy odd-numbered elements (gold, silver, copper) appear only in microscopic quantities and never in the elemental form. In fact,

---

[1]An earlier figure of 40 light-years, often quoted in the literature, arose from application of the so-called Cosmological Constant. Einstein's reluctance to allow this "constant" into his scholium has now been fully justified. v. Haertel, *J. I. R.* 1:21, 2047.

the only uncombined metal that has ever appeared on the planet has been the nickel-iron of an occasional meteorite.

The metallic core of the planet is considerably smaller than that of the Earth, and the basaltic inner coating correspondingly thicker. The continents are built, as on Earth, basically of granite, overlaid with sedimentary deposits.

The scarcity of potassium has led to an extremely static geology. The natural radioactivity of K^{40} is the major source of the internal heat of the Earth, and Lithia has less than a tenth of the K^{40} content of the Earth. As a result, the interior of the planet is much cooler, vulcanism is extremely rare, and geological revolutions even rarer. The planet seems to have settled down early in life, and nothing very startling has happened since. The major part of its uneventful geological history is at best conjectural, because the scarcity of radioactive elements has led to great difficulties in dating the strata.

The atmosphere is somewhat similar to that of the Earth.[2] The atmospheric pressure is 815.3 mm at sea level, and the composition of dry air is as follows:

Nitrogen	66.26 per cent by volume
Oxygen	31.27
Argon, &c.	2.16
CO_2	0.31

The relatively high CO_2 concentration (partial pressure about 11 times that of the gas in the Earth's atmosphere) leads to a hothouse type of climate, with relatively slight temperature differences from pole to equator. The average summer temperature at the pole is about 30° C., at the equator near 38° C., while the winter temperatures are about 15° colder. The humidity is generally high and there is a lot of haze; gentle, drizzling rain is chronic.

There has been little change in the climate of the planet for about 700 million years. Since there is little vulcanism, the CO_2 content of the air does not rise appreciably from that cause, and the amount consumed in photosynthesis by the lush vegetation is compensated for by the rapid oxidation of dead vegetable matter induced by the high temperature, high humidity, and high oxygen content of the air. In fact, the climate

[2]Clark, J.: The climate of Lithia. *J. I. R.*, in press.

of the planet has been in equilibrium for more than half a billion years.

As has the geography of the planet. There are three continents, of which the largest is the southern continent, extending roughly from latitude 15° south to 60° south, and two-thirds of the way around the planet. The two northern continents are squarish in shape, and of sizes similar to each other. They extend from about 10° south to about 70° north, and each one about 80° east and west. One is located north of the eastern end of the southern continent, the other north of the western end. On the other side of the world there is an archipelago of large islands, the size of England and Ireland, running from 20° north to 10° south of the equator. There are thus five seas or oceans: the two polar seas; the equatorial sea separating the southern from the northern continents; the central sea between the two latter, and connecting the equatorial sea with the north polar sea; and the great sea, stretching from pole to pole, broken only by the archipelago, extending a third of the way around the planet.

The southern continent has one low mountain range (highest peak 2263 meters) paralleling its southern shore, and moderating the never very momentous effect of the south winds. The northwestern continent has two ranges, one paralleling the eastern and one the western sea, so that the polar winds have a free run, and give this continent a more variable climate than that of the southern one. The northeastern continent has a slight range along its southern shore. The islands of the archipelago have few hills, and possess an oceanic type of climate. The trade winds are much like those of Earth, but of lesser velocity, due to the lesser temperature differentials between the different parts of the planet. The equatorial sea is nearly windless.

Except for the few mountain ranges, the terrain of the continents is rather flat, particularly near the coasts, and the lower reaches of all the rivers are of the meandering type, bordered with marshes, and with low plains that are flooded, miles wide, every spring.

There are tides, milder than on Earth, producing an appreciable tidal current in the equatorial sea. As the coastal terrain is generally quite flat, except where the mountain ranges come to the sea, wide tidal flats separate the shore from the open sea.

The water is similar to that of Earth, but considerably less salty.[3] Life began in the sea, and evolved much as it did on Earth. There is a rich assortment of microscopic sea life, types resembling such forms as seaweed and sponges, and many crustacea and mollusklike forms. The latter are very highly developed and diversified, particularly the mobile types. Quite familiar fishlike forms have emerged and dominate the seas as they do on Earth.

Present-day Lithian land plant life would be unfamiliar, but not surprising, to a terrestrial observer. There are no plants exactly like those of Earth, but most of them have a noticeable similarity to those with which the visitor would be familiar. The most surprising aspect is that the forests are of a remarkably mixed type. Flowering and non-flowering trees, palms and pines, tree ferns, shrubs and grasses all grow together in remarkable amity. Since Lithia never had a glacial period, these mixed forests, rather than the uniform type prevailing on Earth, are the rule.

In general the vegetation is lush and the forests can be considered as typical rain-forests. There are several varieties of poisonous plants, including most of the edible-looking tubers. Their roots resemble potatoes and they produce extremely toxic alkaloids, whose structure has not yet been worked out, in large quantities. There are several types of bushes which grow thorns impregnated with glucosides which are extremely irritating to the skins of most vertebrates.

The grasses are more prevalent on the plains, shading into rushes and similar swamp-adapted plants in the marshes. There are few desert areas—even the mountains are rounded and smooth, and covered with grasses and shrubs. Seen from space, the land areas of the planet are almost entirely green. Bare rock is found only in the river valleys, where the streams have cut their way down to the lime and sandstone, and in ligneous outcroppings, where flint, quartz and quartzite are frequently found. Obsidian is rare, of course, because of the lack of volcanic activity. There is clay to be found in some of the river

[3]Ley, W.: The ecologies of Lithia. *J. I. R.*, in press.

valleys, with an appreciable alumina content, and rutile (titanium dioxide) is not uncommon. There are no concentrated deposits of iron ore, and hematite is almost unknown.

The land-living animal forms include orders similar to those found on Earth. There is a large variety of arthropods, including eight-legged insectlike forms of all sizes, up to a pseudo dragonfly with two pairs of wings and a wingspread which has been recorded at 86.5 cm. maximum. This variety lives exclusively on other insects, but there are several types dangerous to higher forms of animals. Several have dangerous bites (the poison is generally an alkaloid) and one insect can eject a stream of poisonous gas (reputed to be largely HCN) in quantity sufficient to immobilize a small animal. These insects are social in nature, like ants, living in colonies which are usually left severely alone by otherwise insectivorous organisms.

There are also many amphibians, small lizardlike forms with three fingers on each limb instead of the five that are common to terrestrial land vertebrates. They form an extremely important class, and there are some species that are as large as a St. Bernard dog at maturity. Except for some small and unimportant forms, however, the amphibians are confined to the marshy lowlands near the sea, and the rest of the land is dominated by a class resembling Earthly reptiles. Among these is the dominant species, a large, highly intelligent animal with a bipedal gait which balances itself with a rather stiff, heavy tail.

Two groups of the reptiles went back to the sea and engaged in successful competition with the fish. One adopted a completely streamlined form and is, outwardly, just another 30-foot fish. But its tail fin is in the horizontal plane and its internal structure shows its ancestry. It is the fastest thing in the waters of Lithia, doing nearly 80 knots when pressed (as it usually is by its insatiable appetite). The other group of returned reptiles resembles crocodiles, and is competent either in the open sea or on the mud flats, although it is not very fast in either situation.

Several genera of the reptiles have taken to the air, as did the terrestrial pteranodons. The largest of these has a wingspread of nearly three meters, but is very lightly built. It roosts mainly on the sea cliffs of the southern coast of the northeastern continent, and lives mainly on fish, and such of the gliding cephalopods as it can manage to catch above water. This flying reptile has a large assortment of sharp, backward-curving teeth in its long beak. One other species of flying reptile is of special interest, because it has developed something resembling feathers, in a many-colored crest down its long neck. They appear only on the mature reptile; the young are completely naked.

Some 100,000,000 years ago the land-living reptiles were almost completely wiped out by one of the smallest of their own family, which adopted the easiest method of making a living: eating the eggs of its larger relatives. The larger forms almost completely disappeared, and those that survived (such as the Lithian allosaur) are now almost as rare as the terrestrial elephant (as compared for instance, with the many elephant species of the Pleistocene). The smaller forms survived better, but are not nearly so abundant now as they once were.

The dominant species is an exception. The female of this species has an abdominal pouch in which the eggs are carried until they hatch. This animal is about twelve feet tall at the crown, with a head shaped for bifocal vision. One of the three fingers on the free forelimb is an opposable thumb.

WHO?

Algis Budrys

Chapter One

IT WAS near the middle of the night. The wind came up from the river, moaning under the filigreed iron bridges, and the weathercocks on the dark old buildings pointed their heads north.

The Military Police sergeant in charge had lined up his receiving squad on either side of the cobbled street. Blocking the street was a weathered concrete gateway with a black-and-white-striped wooden rail. The headlights of the M.P. super-jeeps and of the waiting Allied Nations Government sedan glinted from the raised shatterproof riot visors on the squad's varnished helmets. Over their heads was a sign, fluorescing in the lights:

YOU ARE <u>LEAVING</u> THE ALLIED SPHERE

YOU ARE <u>ENTERING</u> THE SOVIET SOCIALIST SPHERE

In the parked sedan, Shawn Rogers sat waiting with a man from the A.N.G. Foreign Ministry beside him. Rogers was Security Chief for this sector of the A.N.G.-administered Central European Frontier District. He waited patiently, his light green eyes brooding in the dark.

The Foreign Ministry representative looked at his thin gold wristwatch. "They'll be here with him in a minute." He drummed his fingertips on his briefcase. "If they keep to their schedule."

"They'll be on time," Rogers said. "That's the way they are. They held him four months, but now they'll be on time to prove their good faith all along." He looked out through the windscreen, past the silent driver's shoulders, at the gateway. The Soviet border guards on the other side—Slavs and stumpy Asiatics in shapeless quilted jackets—were ignoring the Allied squad. They were clustered around a fire in an oil drum in front of their checkpoint shack, holding their hands out to the warmth. Their shroud-barreled submachine guns were slung over their shoulders, hanging clumsily and unhandily. They were talking and joking, and none of them were bothering to watch the frontier.

"Look at them," the Foreign Ministry man said peevishly.

"They don't care what we do. They're not concerned if we drive up with an armed squad."

The Foreign Ministry man was from Geneva, five hundred kilometers away. Rogers had been here, in this sector, for seven years. He shrugged. "We're all old acquaintances by now. This frontier's been here forty years. They know we're not going to start shooting, any more than they are. This isn't where the war is."

He looked at the clustered Soviets again, remembering a song he'd heard years ago: "Give the Comrade With the Machine Gun the Right to Speak." He wondered if they knew of that song, over on their side of the line. There were many things on the other side of the line that he wanted to know. But there was little hope for it.

The war was in all the world's filing cabinets. The weapon was information: things you knew, things you'd found out about them, things they knew about you. You sent people over the line, or you had them planted from years ago, and you probed. Not many of your people got through. Some of them might. So you put together the little scraps of what you'd found out, hoping it wasn't too garbled, and in the end, if you were clever, you knew what the Soviets were going to do next.

And they probed back. Not many of their people got through—at least, you could be reasonably sure they didn't—but, in the end, they found out what you were going to do next. So neither side did anything. You probed, back and forth, and the deeper you tried to go, the harder it was. For a little distance on either side of the line, there was some light. Further on, there was only a dark fog. And some day, you had to hope, the balance would break in your favor.

The Foreign Ministry man was taking out his impatience in talk. "Why the devil did we give Martino a laboratory so near the border in the first place?"

Rogers shook his head. "I don't know. I don't handle strategy."

"Well, why couldn't we get a rescue team of our own in there after the explosion?"

"We did. Theirs just got in first. They moved fast and took him away." And he wondered if that had been a simple piece of luck.

"Why couldn't we take him back from them?"

"I don't handle tactics on that level. I imagine we might have had trouble, though, kidnaping a seriously hurt man out of a hospital." And the man was an American national. Suppose he'd died? The Soviet propaganda teams would have gone to work on the Americans, and when the next A.N.G. bill came up in their Congress, they might not be so quick with their share of next year's budget. Rogers grunted to himself. It was that kind of war.

"I think it's a ridiculous situation. An important man like Martino in their hands, and we're helpless. It's absurd."

"That's the kind of thing that gives you your work to do, isn't it?"

The Foreign Ministry representative changed his tack. "I wonder how he's taking it? He was rather badly knocked about in the explosion, I understand."

"Well, he's convalescent now."

"I'm told he lost an arm. But I imagine they'll have taken care of that. They're quite good at prosthetics, you know. Why, as far back as the nineteen forties, they were keeping dogs' heads alive with mechanical hearts and so forth."

"Mm." A man disappears over the line, Rogers was thinking, and you send out people to find him. Little by little, the reports come trickling in. He's dead, they say. He's lost an arm, but he's alive. He's dying. We don't know where he is. He's been shipped to Novoya Moskva. He's right here, in this city, in a hospital. At least, they've got *somebody* in a hospital here. What hospital?

Nobody knows. You're not going to find out any more. You give what you have to the Foreign Ministry, and the negotiations start. Your side closes down a highway across the line. Their side almost shoots down a plane. Your side impounds some fishing boats. And finally, not so much because of anything your side had done but for some reason of their own, their side gives in.

And all this time, a man from your side has been lying in one of their hospitals, broken and hurt, waiting for you to do something.

"There's a rumor he was quite close to completing something called a K-Eighty-eight," the Foreign Ministry man went on. "We had orders not to press too hard, for fear they'd realize how important he was. That is, in the event they didn't already know. But, of course, we were to get him back, so we couldn't go too soft. Delicate business."

"I can imagine."

"Do you think they got the K-Eighty-eight out of him?"

"They have a man on their side called Azarin. He's very good." How can I possibly know until I've talked to Martino? But Azarin's damned good. And I wonder if we shouldn't run this gossip through another security check?

Out beyond the gateway, two headlights bloomed up, turned sideward, and stopped. The rear door of a Tatra limousine snapped open, and at the same time one of the Soviet guards went over to the gate and flipped the rail up. The Allied M.P. sergeant called his men to attention.

Rogers and the Foreign Ministry representative got out of their car.

A man stepped out of the Tatra and came to the gateway. He hesitated at the border and then walked forward quickly between the two rows of M.P.'s.

"Good God!" the Foreign Ministry man whispered.

The lights glittered in a spray of bluish reflection from the man in the gateway. He was mostly metal.

2.

He was wearing one of their shapeless, drab civilian suits, with lumpy shoes and a striped brown shirt. His sleeves were too short, and his hands hung far out. One was flesh and one was not. His skull was a polished metal ovoid, completely featureless except for a grille where his mouth ought to be and a half-moon recess, curving upward at the ends, where his eyes lurked. He stood, looking ill at ease, at the end of two rows of soldiers. Rogers came up to him, holding out his hand. "Lucas Martino?"

The man nodded. "Yes." It was his right hand that was still good. He reached up and took Rogers' hand. His grip was strong and anxious. "I'm very glad to be here."

"My name's Rogers. This is Mr. Haller, of the Foreign Ministry."

Haller shook Martino's hand automatically, staring.

"How do you do?" Martino said.

"Very well, thank you," the Foreign Ministry man mumbled. "And you?"

"The car's over here, Mr. Martino," Rogers cut in. "I'm with the sector Security office. I'd appreciate it if you came with me. The sooner I interview you, the sooner this'll be completely over." Rogers touched Martino's shoulder and urged him lightly toward the sedan.

"Yes, of course. There's no need delaying." The man matched Rogers' quick pace and slipped in ahead of him at his gesture. Haller climbed in on the other side of Martino, and then the driver wheeled the car around and started them rolling for Rogers' office. Behind them, the M.P.'s got into their jeeps and followed. Rogers looked back through the car's rear window. The Soviet border guards were staring after them.

Martino sat stiffly against the upholstery, his hands in his lap. "It feels wonderful to be back," he said in a strained voice.

"I should think so," Haller said. "After what they—"

"I think Mr. Martino's only saying what he feels is expected of people in these situations, Mr. Haller. I doubt very much if he feels wonderful about anything."

Haller looked at Rogers with a certain shock. "You're quite blunt, Mr. Rogers."

"I feel blunt."

Martino looked from one to the other. "Please don't let me unsettle you," he said. "I'm sorry to be a source of upset. Perhaps it would help if I said I knew what I look like, and that I, for one, am used to it?"

"Sorry," Rogers said. "I didn't mean to start a squabble around you."

"Please accept my apologies, as well," Haller added. "I realize that, in my own way, I was being just as rude as Mr. Rogers."

Martino said, "And so now we've all apologized to each other."

So we have, Rogers thought. Everybody's sorry.

They pulled into the ramp which served the side door of Rogers' office building, and the driver stopped the car. "All right, Mr. Martino, this is where we get out," Rogers told the man. "Haller, you'll be checking into your office right away?"

"Immediately, Mr. Rogers."

"O.K. I guess your boss and my boss can start getting together on policy toward this."

"I'm quite sure my Ministry's role in this case was concluded with Mr. Martino's safe return," Haller said delicately. "I intend to go to bed after I make my report. Good night, Rogers. Pleasure working with you."

"Of course." They shook hands briefly, and Rogers followed Martino out of the car and through the side door.

"He washed his hands of me rather quickly, didn't he?" Martino commented as Rogers directed him down a flight of steps into the basement.

Rogers grunted. "Through this door, please, Mr. Martino."

They came out into a narrow, door-lined corridor with painted concrete walls and a gray linoleum tile floor. Rogers stopped and looked at the doors for a moment. "That one'll do, I guess. Please come in here with me, Mr. Martino." He took a bunch of keys out of his pocket and unlocked the door.

The room inside was small. It had a cot pushed against one wall, neatly made up with a white pillow and a tightly stretched army blanket. There was a small table, and one chair. An overhead bulb lit the room, and in a side wall there were two doors, one leading to a small closet and the other opening on a compact bathroom.

Martino looked around. "Is this where you always conduct your interviews with returnees?" he asked mildly.

Rogers shook his head. "I'm afraid not. I'll have to ask you to stay here for the time being." He stepped out of the room without giving Martino an opportunity to react. He closed and locked the door.

He relaxed a little. He leaned against the door's solid metal and lit a cigarette with only a faint tremor in his fingertips. Then he walked quickly down the corridor to the automatic elevator and up to the floor where his office was. As he snapped on the lights, his mouth twisted at the thought of what his staff would say when he started calling them out of their beds.

He picked up the telephone on his desk. But first, he had to talk to Deptford, the District Chief. He dialed the number.

Deptford answered almost immediately. "Hello?" Rogers had expected him to be awake.

"Rogers, Mr. Deptford."

"Hello, Shawn. I've been waiting for your call. Everything go all right with Martino?"

"No, sir. I need an emergency team down here as fast as possible. I want a whatdyoucallit—a man who knows about miniature mechanical devices—with as many assistants authorized as he needs. I want a surveillance device expert. And a psychologist. With the same additional staff authorizations for the last two. I want the three key men tonight or tomorrow morning. How much of a staff they'll need'll be up to them, but I want the authorizations in so there won't be any red tape to hold them up. I wish to hell nobody had ever thought of pumping key personnel full of truth-drug allergens."

"Rogers, what is this? What went wrong? Your offices aren't equipped for any such project as that."

"I'm sorry, sir. I don't dare move him. There're too many sensitive places in this city. I got him over here and into a cell, and I made damned sure he didn't even get near my office. God knows what he might be after, or can do."

"Rogers—did Martino come over the line tonight or didn't he?"

Rogers hesitated. "I don't know," he said.

3.

Rogers ignored the room full of waiting men and sat looking down at the two dossiers, not so much thinking as gathering his energy.

Both dossiers were open to the first page. One was thick, full of security check breakdowns, reports, career progress résumés, and all the other data that accumulate around a government employee through the years. It was labeled *Martino, Lucas Anthony*. The first page was made up of the usual identification statistics: height, weight, color of eyes, color of hair, date of birth, fingerprints, dental chart, distinguishing marks and scars. There was a set of standard nude photographs; front, back, and both profiles of a heavy-set, muscular man with controlled, pleasantly intelligent features and a slightly thickened nose.

The second dossier was much thinner. As yet, there was nothing in the folder but the photographs, and it was unlabeled beyond a note: See *Martino, L.A.* (?) The photographs showed a heavy-set, muscular man with broad scars running diagonally up from his left side, across his chest and around his back and both shoulders, like a ropey shawl. His left arm was mechanical up to the top of the shoulder, and seemed to have been grafted directly into his pectoral and dorsal musculature. He had thick scars around the base of his throat, and that metal head.

Rogers stood up behind his desk and looked at the waiting special team. "Well?"

Barrister, the English servomechanisms engineer, took the bit of his pipe out of his teeth. "I don't know. It's quite hard to tell on the basis of a few hours' tests." He took a deep breath. "As a matter of exact fact, I'm running tests but I've no idea what they'll show, if anything, or how soon." He gestured helplessly. "There's no getting *at* someone in his condition. There's no penetrating his surface, as it were. Half our instruments're worthless. There're so many electrical components in his mechanical parts that any readings we take are hopelessly blurred. We can't even do so simple a thing as determine the amperage they used. It hurts him to have us try." He dropped his voice apologetically. "It makes him scream."

Rogers grimaced. "But he *is* Martino?"

Barrister shrugged.

Rogers suddenly slammed his fist against the top of his desk. "What the hell are we going to do?"

"Get a can opener," Barrister suggested.

In the silence, Finchley, who was on loan to Rogers from the American Federal Bureau of Investigation, said, "Look at this."

He touched a switch and the film projector he'd brought began to hum while he went over and dimmed the office lights. He pointed the projector toward a blank wall and started the film running. "Overhead pickup," he explained. "Infra-red lighting. We believe he can't see it. We think he was asleep."

Martino—Rogers had to think of him by that name against his better judgment—was lying on his cot. The upturned crescent in his face was shuttered from the inside, with only the edges of a flexible gasket to mark its outline. Below it, the grille, centered just above the blunt curve of his jaw, was ajar. The impression created was vaguely that of a hairless man with his eyes shut, breathing through his mouth. Rogers had to remind himself that this man did not breathe.

"This was taken about two A.M. today," Finchley said. "He'd been lying there for a little over an hour and a half."

Rogers frowned at the tinge of bafflement in Finchley's voice. Yes, it was uncanny not being able to tell whether a man was asleep or not. But it was no use doing anything if they were all going to let their nerves go ragged. He almost said something about it until he realized his chest was aching. He relaxed his shoulders, shaking his head at himself.

A cue spot flickered on the film. "All right," Finchley said, "now listen." The tiny speaker in the projector began to crackle.

Martino had begun to thrash on his cot, his metal arm striking sparks from the wall.

Rogers winced.

Abruptly, the man started to babble in his sleep. The words poured out, each syllable distinct. But the speech was wildly faster than normal, and the voice was desperate:

"Name! Name! Name!

"Name Lucas Martino born Bridgetown New Jersey May tenth nineteen forty-eight, about . . . *face!* Detail . . . forward . . . *march!*

"Name! Name! Detail . . . Halt!

"Name Lucas Martino born Bridgetown New Jersey May tenth nineteen forty-eight!"

Rogers felt Finchley touch his arm. "Think they were walking him?"

Rogers shrugged. "If that's a genuine nightmare, and if that's Martino, then, yes—it sounds very much like they were walking him back and forth in a small room and firing questions at him. You know their technique: keep a man on his feet, keep him moving, keep asking questions. Change interrogation teams every few hours, so they'll be fresh. Don't let the subject sleep or get off his feet. Walk him delirious. Yes, that's what it might be."

"Do you think he's faking?"

"I don't know. He may have been. Then again, maybe he was asleep. Maybe he's one of their people, and he was dreaming we were trying to shake his story."

After a time, the man on the cot fell back. He lay still, his forearms raised stiffly from the elbows, his hands curled into rigid claws. He seemed to be looking straight up at the camera with his streamlined face, and no one could tell whether he was awake or asleep, thinking or not, afraid or in pain, or who or what he was.

Finchley shut off the projector.

4.

Rogers had been awake for thirty-six hours. It was a whole day, now, since the man had come back over the line. Rogers pawed angrily at his burning eyes as he let himself into his apartment. He left his clothes in a rumpled trail across the threadbare old carpet as he crossed the floor toward the bathroom. Fumbling in the medicine cabinet for an Alka-Seltzer, he envied the little wiry men like Finchley who could stay awake for days without their stomachs backing up on them.

The clanking pipes slowly filled the tub with hot brown water while he pulled at his beard with a razor. He clawed his fingers through the crisp, cropped red hair on his scalp, and scowled at the dandruff that came flaking out.

God, he thought wearily, I'm thirty-seven and I'm coming apart.

And as he slid into the tub, feeling the hot water working into the bad hip where he'd been hit by a cobblestone in a riot, looking down under his navel at the bulge that no exercise could quite flatten out any more, the thought drove home.

A few more years, and I'll really have a pot. When the damp weather comes, that hip's going to give me all kinds of hell. I used to be able to stay up two and three days at a clip—I'm never going to be able to do that again. Some day I'm going to try some stunt I could do the week before, and I won't make it.

Some day, too, I'm going to make a decision of some kind—some complex, either-or thing that's got to be right. I'll know I've got it right—and it'll be wrong. I'll start screwing up, and every time after that I'll get the inside sweats remembering how I was wrong. I'll start pressing, and worrying, and living on dexedrine, and if they spot it in time, upstairs, they'll give me a nice harmless job in a corner somewhere. And if they don't spot it, one of these days Azarin's going to put a really good one over on me, and everybody's kids'll talk Chinese.

He shivered. The phone rang in the living room.

He climbed out of the tub, holding carefully onto the edge, and wrapped himself in one of the huge towels that was the size of a blanket, and which he was going to take back to the States with him if he was ever assigned there. He padded out to the phone stand and picked up the head-piece. "Yeah?"

"Mr. Rogers?" He recognized one of the War Ministry operators.

"That's right."

"Mr. Deptford is on the line. Hold on, please."

"Thank you." He waited, wishing the cigarette box wasn't across the room beside his bed.

"Shawn? Your office said you'd be home."

"Yes, sir. My shirt was trying to walk off me."

"I'm here, at the Ministry. I've just been talking to the Undersecretary for Security. How are you doing on this Martino business? Have you reached any definite conclusions as yet?"

Rogers thought over the terms of his answer. "No, sir, I'm sorry. We've only had one day, so far."

"Yes, I know. Do you have any notion of how much more time you'll need?"

Rogers frowned. He had to calculate how much time they could possibly spare. "I'd say it'll take a week." He hoped.

"That long?"

"I'm afraid so. The team's set up and working smoothly now, but we're having a very rough time. He's like a big egg."

"I see." Deptford took a long breath that came clearly over the phone. "Shawn—Karl Schwenn asked me if you knew how important Martino is to us."

Rogers said quietly: "You can tell Mr. Undersecretary I know my job."

"All right, Shawn. He wasn't trying to rag you. He just wanted to be certain."

"What you mean is, he's riding you."

Deptford hesitated. "Someone's riding him, too, you know."

"I could still stand to do with a little less Teutonic discipline in this department."

"Have you been to sleep lately, Shawn?"

"No, sir. I'll be filing daily reports, and when we crack this, I'll phone."

"Very well, Shawn. I'll tell him. Good night."

"Good night, sir."

He hung up and the red scrambler bulb on the phone went out. He went back into the bathtub and lay there with his eyes closed, letting Martino's dossier drift up into the forepart of his brain.

There was still very little in it. The man was still five feet eleven inches tall. His weight was up to two hundred sixty-eight pounds. His arches had collapsed, but the thickness of his skull plating apparently made up the height differential.

Nothing else in the I.D. chart was applicable. There were no entries for eyes, hair, or complexion. There was no entry for Date of Birth, though a physiologist had given him an age, within the usual limits of error, that corresponded with 1948. Fingerprints? Distinguishing marks and scars?

Rogers' bitter smile was pale at the corners. He dried himself, kicked his old clothes into a corner, and dressed. He went back into the bathroom, dropped his toothbrush into his pocket, thought for a moment and added the tube of Alka-Seltzer, and went back to his office.

5.

It was early in the morning of the second day. Rogers looked across his desk at Willis, the psychologist.

"If they were going to let Martino go anyway," Rogers asked, "why would they go to so much trouble with him? He wouldn't have needed all that hardware just to keep him alive. Why did they carefully make an exhibition piece out of him?"

Willis rubbed a hand over the stubble on his face. "Assuming he's Martino, they may never have intended to let him go. I agree with you—if they were going to give him back to us originally, they'd probably just have patched him up any old way. Instead, they went to a great deal of trouble to rebuild him as close to a functioning human being as possible.

"I think what happened was that they knew he'd be useful to them. They expected a great deal of him, and they wanted him to be as physically capable of delivering it as they could make him. It's quite probable they never even considered how he'd look to us. Oh, they may have gone beyond the absolute necessary minimum in dressing him up—but perhaps it was him they wanted to impress. In any case, they probably thought he'd be grateful to them, and that might give them a wedge. And let's not discount this idea of arousing his purely professional admiration. Particularly since he's a physicist. That could be quite a bridge between him and their culture. If that was one of the considerations, I'd say it was excellent psychological technique."

Rogers lit a new cigarette, grimacing at the taste. "We've been over this before. We can play with almost any notion we want to and make it fit some of the few facts we know. What does it prove?"

"Well, as I said, they may never have intended to let us see him again. If we work with that as an assumption, then why did they finally let him go? Aside from the pressure we exerted on them, let's say he held out. Let's say they finally saw he wasn't going to be the gold mine they'd expected. Let's say they've got something else planned—next month, say, or next week. Looking at it that way, it's reasonable for them to have let him go, figuring also that if they give Martino back, maybe they can get away with their next stunt."

"That's too many assumptions. What's he got to say on the subject?"

Willis shrugged. "He says they made him some offers. He decided they were just bait and turned them down. He says they interrogated him and he didn't crack."

"Think it's possible?"

"Anything's possible. He hasn't gone insane yet. That's something in itself. He was always a pretty firmly balanced individual."

Rogers snorted. "Look—they cracked everybody they ever wanted to crack. Why not him?"

"I'm not saying they didn't. But there's a possibility he's telling the truth. Maybe they didn't have enough time. Maybe he had an advantage over their usual subjects. Not having mobile features and a convulsed respiratory cycle to show when they had him close to the ragged edge—that might be a big help."

"Yes," Rogers said. "I'm becoming aware of that possibility."

"His heartbeat's no indicator, either, with a good part of the load taken over by his powerplant. I'm told his entire metabolic cycle's non-kosher."

"I can't figure it," Rogers said. "I can't figure it at all. Either he's Martino or he isn't. They went to all this trouble. Now we've got him back. If he's Martino, I still don't see what they hope to gain. I can't accept the notion they don't hope to gain anything—that's not like them."

"Not like us, either."

"All right. Look—we're two sides, each convinced we're right and the other fellow's wrong. This century's thrashing out the world's way of life for the next thousand years. When you're playing for stakes like that, you don't miss a step. If he isn't Martino, they might have known we wouldn't just take him back without checking him. If this's their idea of a smart trick for slipping us a ringer, they're dumber than their past performance chart reads. But if he *is* Martino, why did they let him go? Did he go over to them? God knows, whole countries went Soviet that we never thought would."

He rubbed the top of his head. "They've got us chasing our tails over this guy."

Willis nodded sourly. "I know. Listen—how much do you know about the Russians?"

"Russians? About as much as I do about the other Soviets. Why?"

Willis said reluctantly, "Well, it's a trap to generalize about these things. But there's something we had to learn to take into account, down at PsychoWar. It's a Slav's idea of a joke. Particularly the Russians'. I keep thinking . . . whether it started out that way or not, every one of them that knows about this fellow is laughing at us now. They go in for deadpan practical jokes, and especially the kind where somebody bleeds a little. I've got a vision of the boys in Novoya Moskva clustered around the vodka at night and laughing and laughing and laughing."

"That's nice," Rogers said. "That's very fine." He wiped his palm over his jaw. "That helps."

"I thought you'd enjoy it."

"God damn it, Willis, I've got to crack that shell of his! We can't have him running around loose and unsolved. Martino was one of the very best in his business. He was right up there, right in the thick of every new wrinkle we're going to pleat for the next ten years. He was working on this K-Eighty-eight thing. And the Soviets had him four months. What'd they get out of him, what'd they do to him—do they still have him?"

"I know . . ." Willis said slowly. "I can see he might have given away almost anything, or even become an active agent of theirs. But on this business of his not being Martino at all—I frankly can't believe that. What about the fingerprints on his one good hand?"

Rogers cursed. "His right shoulder's a mass of scar tissue. If they can substitute mechanical parts for eyes and ears and lungs—if they can motorize an arm and graft it right into him—where does that leave us?"

Willis turned pale. "You mean—they could fake anything. It's definitely Martino's right arm, but it isn't necessarily Martino."

"That's right."

6.

The telephone rang. Rogers rolled over on his cot and lifted the receiver off the unit on the floor beside him. "Rogers," he mumbled. "Yes, Mr. Deptford." The radiant numerals on his watch were swimming before his eyes, and he blinked sharply to steady them. Eleven-thirty P.M. He'd been asleep a little under two hours.

"Hello, Shawn. I've got your third daily report in front of me here. I'm sorry to have awakened you, but you don't really seem to be making much progress, do you?"

"That's all right. About waking me up, I mean. No—no, I'm not getting far on this thing."

The office was dark except for the seep of light under the door from the hall. Across the hall, in a larger office Rogers had commandeered, a specialist clerical staff was collating and evaluating the reports Finchley, Barrister, Willis, and the rest of them had made. Rogers could faintly hear the restless clacking of typewriters and I.B.M. machines.

"Would it be of any value for me to come down?"

"And take over the investigation? Come ahead. Any time."

Deptford said nothing for a moment. Then he asked, "Would I get any farther than you have?"

"No."

"That's what I told Karl Schwenn."

"Still giving you the business, is he?"

"Shawn, he has to. The entire K-Eighty-eight program has been held up for months. No other project in the world would have been permitted to hang fire this long. At the first doubt of its security, it would have been washed out as a matter of routine. You know that, and that ought to tell you how important the K-Eighty-eight is. I think you're aware of what's going on in Africa at this moment. We've got to have something to show. We've got to quiet the Soviets down—at least until they've developed something to match it. The Ministry's putting pressure on the Department to reach a quick decision on this man."

"I'm sorry, sir. We're almost literally taking this man apart like a bomb. But we don't have anything to show whose bomb he is."

"There must be something."

"Mr. Deptford, when we send a man over the line, we provide him with their I.D. papers. We go further. We fill his pockets with their coins, their door keys, their cigarettes, their combs. We give him one of their billfolds, with their sales receipts and laundry tickets. We give him photographs of relatives and girls, printed on their kind of paper with their processes and chemicals —and yet every one of those items came out of our manufacturing shops and never saw the other side of the line before."

Deptford sighed. "I know. How's he taking it?"

"I can't tell. When one of our people goes over the line, he has a cover story. He's an auto mechanic, or a baker, or a tramway conductor. And if he's one of our good people—and for important jobs we only send the best—then, no matter what happens, no matter what they do to him—he *stays* a baker or a tramway conductor. He answers questions like a tramway conductor. He's as bewildered at it all as a tramway conductor would be. If necessary, he bleeds and screams and dies like a tramway conductor."

"Yes." Deptford's voice was quiet. "Yes, he does. Do you

suppose Azarin ever wonders if perhaps this man he's working on really *is* a tramway conductor?"

"Maybe he does, sir. But he can't ever act as if he did, or he wouldn't be doing his job."

"All right, Shawn. But we've got to have our answer soon."

"I know."

After a time, Deptford said: "It's been pretty rough on you, hasn't it, Shawn?"

"Some."

"You've always done the job for me." Deptford's voice was quiet, and then Rogers heard the peculiar click a man's drying lips make as he opens his mouth to wet them. "All right. I'll explain the situation upstairs, and you do what you can."

"Yes, sir. Thank you."

"Good night, Shawn. Go back to sleep, if you can."

"Good night, sir." Rogers hung up. He sat looking down at the darkness around his feet. It's funny, he thought. I wanted an education, and my family lived a half block away from the docks in Brooklyn. I wanted to be able to understand what a categorical imperative was, and recognize a quote from Byron when I heard one. I wanted to wear a tweed jacket and smoke a pipe under a campus oak somewhere. And during the summers while I was going to high school, I worked for this insurance company, file clerking in the claims investigation division. So when I got the chance to try for that A.N.G. scholarship, I took it. And when they found out I knew something about investigation work, they put me in with their Security trainees. And here I am, and I never thought about it one way or another. I've got a pretty good record. Pretty damned good. But I wonder, now, if I wouldn't have done just as well at something else?

Then he slowly put his shoes on, went to his desk, and clicked on the light.

7.

The week was almost over. They were beginning to learn things, but none of them were the slightest help.

Barrister laid the first engineering drawing down on Rogers' desk. "This is how his head works—we believe. It's a difficult thing, not being able to get clear X-rays."

Rogers looked down at the drawing and grunted. Barrister began pointing out specific details, using his pipestem to tap the drawing.

"There's his eye assembly. He has binocular vision, with servo-motored focusing and tracking. The motors are powered by this miniature pile, in his chest cavity, here. So are the remainder of his artificial components. It's interesting to note he's a complete selection of filters for his eye lenses. They did him up brown. By the by, he *can* see by infra-red if he wants to."

Rogers spat a shred of tobacco off his lower lip. "That's interesting."

Barrister said, "Now—right here, on each side of the eyes, are two acoustical pickups. Those are his ears. They must have felt it was better design to house both functions in that one central skull opening. It's directional, but not as effective as God intended. Here's something else; the shutter that closes that opening is quite tough—armored to protect all those delicate components. The result is he's deaf when his eyes're closed. He probably sleeps more restfully for it."

"When he isn't faking nightmares, yeah."

"Or having them." Barrister shrugged. "Not my department."

"I wish it wasn't mine. All right, now what about that other hole?"

"His mouth? Well, there's a false, immovable jaw over the working one—again, apparently, to protect the mechanism. His true jaws, his saliva ducts and teeth are artificial. His tongue isn't. The inside of the mouth is plastic-lined. Teflon, probably, or one of its kin. My people're having a little trouble breaking it down for analysis. But he's cooperative about letting us gouge out samples."

Rogers licked his lips. "Okay—fine," he said brusquely. "But how's all this hooked into his brain? How does he operate it?"

Barrister shook his head. "I don't know. He uses it all as if he were born with it, so there's some sort of connection into his voluntary and autonomic nervous centers. But we don't yet know exactly how it was done. He's cooperative, as I said, but I'm not the man to start disassembling any of this—we might not be able to put him back together again. All I know is that somewhere, behind all that machinery, there's a functioning human brain inside that skull. How the Soviets did it is something else again. You have to remember they've been fiddling with this sort of thing a long time." He laid another sheet atop the first one, paying no attention to the pallor of Rogers' face.

"Here's his powerplant. It's only roughed out in the drawing, but we think it's just a fairly ordinary pocket pile. It's located where his lungs were, next to the blower that operates his vocal cords and the most ingenious oxygen circulator I've ever heard of. The delivered power's electrical, of course, and it works his arm, his jaws, his audiovisual equipment, and everything else."

"How well's the pile shielded?"

Barrister let a measured amount of professional admiration show in his voice. "Well enough so we can get muddy X-rays right around it. There's *some* leakage, of course. He'll die in about fifteen years."

"Mm."

"Well, now, man, if they cared whether he lived or died, they'd have supplied us with blueprints."

"They cared at one time. And fifteen years might be plenty long enough for them, if he isn't Martino."

"And if he is Martino?"

"Then, if he is Martino, and they got to him with some of their persuasions, fifteen years might be plenty long enough for them."

"And if he's Martino and they didn't get to him? If he's the same man he always was, behind his new armor? If he isn't the Man from Mars? If he's simply plain Lucas Martino, physicist?"

Rogers shook his head slowly. "I don't know. I'm running out of ideas for quick answers. But we have to find out. Before we're through, we may have to find out everything he ever did or felt—everyone he talked to, everything he thought."

Chapter Two

LUCAS MARTINO was born in the hospital of the large town nearest to his father's farm. His mother was injured by the birth, and so he was both the eldest son and only child of Matteo and Serafina Martino, truck farmers, of Milano, near

Bridgetown, New Jersey. He was named after the uncle who had paid his parents' passage to the United States in 1947 and lent them the money for the farm.

Milano, New Jersey, was a community of tomato fields, peach orchards, and chicken farms, centering on a general store which sold household staples, stock feed, gasoline for the tractors, and was also the post office. One mile to the north, the four broad lanes of a concrete highway carried booming traffic between Camden-Philadelphia and Atlantic City. To the west, railroad tracks curved down from Camden to Cape May. To the south, forming the base of a triangle of communications, another highway ran from the Jersey shore to the Chester ferry across the mouth of the Delaware, and so connected to all the sprawling highways of the Eastern Seaboard. Bridgetown lay at the meeting of railroad and highway, but Milano was inside the triangle, never more than five minutes away from the world as most people know it, and yet far enough.

Half a century earlier, the clayey earth had been planted, acre-on-acre of vineyard, and the Malaga Processing Corporation had imported workers by the hundreds from old Italy. Communities had grown up, farms had been cleared, and the language of the area was Italian.

When the grape blight came, the tight cultural pattern was torn. Some, like Lucas Maggiore, left the farms their fathers had built and moved to the Italian communities in other cities. To a certain extent their places were taken by people from different parts of the world. And the newcomers, too, were all farmers by birth and blood. In a few years the small communities were once again reasonably prosperous, set in a new pattern of habits and customs that was much like the old. But the outside world had touched the little towns like Milano, and in turn Milano had sent out some of its own people to the world as most of us know it.

The country was warm in the summer, with mild winters. The outlying farms were set among patches of pine and underbrush, and there were wide-eyed deer that came into the kitchen gardens during the winter. Most of the roads were graded gravel, and the utility poles carried only one or two strands of cable. There were more pickup trucks than cars on the roads, though the cars were as likely to be new Dodges and

Mercurys as not. There was a tomato-packing plant a few miles up the road, and Matteo Martino's farm was devoted mostly to tomato vines. Except for occasional trips to Bridgetown for dress material and parts for the truck, the packing plant and general store were as far from home as Matteo ever found it necessary to go.

Young Lucas had heavy bones and an already powerful frame from Matteo's North Italian ancestry. His eyes were brown, but his hair at that age was almost light enough to be blond. His father had a habit of occasionally rumpling his hair and calling him Tedeschino—which means "the little German"—to his mother's faint annoyance. They lived together in a four-room farmhouse, a closely knit unit, and Lucas grew naturally into a share of the work. They were three people with three different but interdependent responsibilities, as they had to be if the work was to go properly. Serafina kept house and helped with the picking. Matteo did the heavy work, and Lucas, more and more as he grew older and stronger, did the necessary maintenance work that had to be kept up day by day. He weeded, he had charge of racking and storing the hand tools, and Matteo, who had worked in the Fiat plant before he came to America, was gradually teaching him how to repair and maintain the tractor. Lucas had a bent for mechanics.

Having no brothers or sisters, and being too busy to talk much with his parents during the day, he grew into early adolescence alone, but not lonely. For one thing, he had more than the ordinary share of work to keep him occupied. For another, he thought in terms of shaped parts that fitted into other parts to produce a whole, functioning mechanism. Having no one near his own age whose growth and development he could observe, he learned to observe himself—to stand a little to one side of the young boy and catalogue the things he did, putting each new discovery into its proper place in an already well-disciplined and instinctively systematic brain. From the outside, no doubt, he seemed to be an overly-serious, preoccupied youngster.

Through grammar school, which he attended near his home, he formed no important outside associations. He returned home for lunch and immediately after school, because there was always work to do and because he wanted to. He got high marks in all subjects but English, which he spoke fluently but not often enough or long enough to become interested in its grammatic structure. However, he did well enough at it, and when he was thirteen he was enrolled in the high school at Bridgetown, twelve road miles away by bus.

Twenty-four miles by bus, every day, in the company of twenty other people your own age—people named Morgan, Crosby, Muller, Kovacs, and Jones in addition to those named Del Bello and Scarpa—can do things. In particular, they can do things to a quiet, self-sufficient young boy with constantly inquiring eyes. His trouble with grammar disappeared overnight. Morgan taught him to smoke. Kovacs talked about the structure of music, and with Del Bello he went out for football. Most important, in his sophomore year he met Edmund Starke, a short, thickset, reticent man with rimless glasses who taught the physics class. It would take a little time, a little study, and a little growth. But Lucas Martino was on his way out into the world.

Chapter Three

I T WAS a week after the man had come across the line. Deptford's voice was tired and empty over the phone. Rogers, whose ears had been buzzing faintly but constantly during the past two days, had to jam the headpiece hard against his ear in order to make out what he was saying.

"I showed Karl Schwenn all your reports, Shawn, and I added a summary of my own. He agrees that nothing more could have been done."

"Yes, sir."

"He was a sector chief himself once, you know. He's aware of these things."

"Yes, sir."

"In a sense, this sort of thing happens to us every day. If anything, it happens to the Soviets even more often. I like to think we take longer to reach these decisions than they do."

"I suppose so."

Deptford's voice was oddly inconclusive in tone, now, as

though he were searching his mind for something to say that would round things off. But it was a conversation born to trail away rather than end, and Deptford gave up after only a short pause.

"That's it, then. Tomorrow you can disperse the team, and you're to stand by until you're notified what policy we're going to pursue with regard to Mar—to the man."

"All right, sir."

"Good bye, Shawn."

"Good night, Mr. Deptford." He put the receiver down and rubbed his ear.

2.

Rogers and Finchley sat on the edge of the cot and looked across the tiny room at the faceless man, who was sitting in the one chair beside the small table on which he ate his meals. He had been kept in this room through most of the week, and had gone out of it only to the laboratory rigged in the next room. He had been given new clothes. He had used the bathroom shower several times without rusting.

"Now, Mr. Martino," the F.B.I. man was saying politely, "I know we've asked before, but have you remembered anything new since our last talk?"

One last try, Rogers thought. You always give it one whack for luck before you give up.

He hadn't yet told anyone on the team that they were all through. He'd asked Finchley to come down here with him because it was always better to have more than one man in on an interrogation. If the subject started to weaken, you could ask questions alternately, bouncing him back and forth between you like a tennis ball, and his head would swing from one man to the other as though he were watching himself in flight.

No—no, Rogers thought, to hell with that. I just didn't want to come down here alone.

The overhead light winked on polished metal. It was only after a second or two that Rogers realized the man had shaken his head in answer to Finchley's question.

"No, I don't remember a thing. I can remember being caught in the blast—it looked like it was coming straight at my face."

He barked a savage, throaty laugh. "I guess it was. I woke up in their hospital and put my one hand up to my head." His right arm went up to his hard cheek as though to help him remember. It jerked back down abruptly, almost in shock, as if that were exactly what had happened the first time.

"Uh-huh," Finchley said quickly. "Then what?"

"That night they shot a needle full of some anesthetic into my spine. When I woke up again, I had this arm."

The motorized limb flashed up and his knuckles rang faintly against his skull. Either from the conducted sound or the memory of that first astonished moment, Martino winced visibly.

His face fascinated Rogers. The two lenses of his eyes, collecting light from all over the room, glinted darkly in their recess. The grilled shutter set flush in his mouth opening looked like a row of teeth bared in a desperate grimace.

Of course, behind that facade a man who wasn't Martino might be smiling in thin laughter at the team's efforts to crack past it.

"Lucas," Rogers said as softly as he could, not looking in the man's direction, fogging the verbal pitch low and inside.

Martino's head turned toward him without a second's hesitation. "Yes, Mr. Rogers?"

Ball One. If he'd been trained, he'd been well trained.

"Did they interrogate you extensively?"

The man nodded. "I don't know what you'd consider extensive in a case like this of course. But I was up and around after two months; they were able to talk to me for several weeks before that. In all, I'd say they spent about ten weeks trying to get me to tell them something they didn't already know."

"Something about the K-Eighty-eight, you mean?"

"I didn't mention the K-Eighty-eight. I don't think they know about it. They just asked general questions: what lines of investigation we were pursuing—things like that."

Ball Two.

"Well, look, Mr. Martino," Finchley said, and Martino's skull moved uncannily on his neck, like a tank's turret swiveling. "They went to a lot of trouble with you. Frankly, if we'd gotten to you first there's a chance you might be alive today, yes, but you wouldn't like yourself very much."

The metal arm twitched sharply against the side of the desk.

There was an over-long silence. Rogers half expected some bitter answer from the man.

"Yes, I see what you mean." Rogers was surprised at the complete detachment in the slightly muffled voice. "They wouldn't have done it if they hadn't expected some pretty positive return on their investment."

Finchley looked helplessly at Rogers. Then he shrugged. "I guess you've said it about as specifically as possible," he told Martino.

"They didn't get it, Mr. Finchley. Maybe because they out-did themselves. It's pretty tough to crack a man who doesn't show his nerves."

A home run, over the centerfield bleachers and still rising when last seen.

Rogers' calves pushed the cot back with a scrape against the cement floor when he stood up. "All right, Mr. Martino. Thank you. And I'm sorry we haven't been able to reach any conclusion."

The man nodded. "So am I."

Rogers watched him closely. "There's one more thing. You know one of the reasons we pushed you so hard was because the government was anxious about the future of the K-Eighty-eight program."

"Yes?"

Rogers bit his lip. "I'm afraid that's all over now. They couldn't wait any longer."

Martino looked quickly from Rogers to Finchley's face, and back again. Rogers could have sworn his eyes glowed with a light of their own. There was a splintering crack and Rogers stared at the edge of the desk where the man's hand had closed on it convulsively.

"I'm not ever going back to work, am I?" the man demanded.

He pushed himself away from the desk and stood as though his remaining muscles, too, had been replaced by steel cables under tension.

Rogers shook his head. "I couldn't say, officially. But I don't see how they'd dare let a man of your ability get near any critical work. Of course, there's still a policy decision due on your case. So I can't say definitely until it reaches me."

Martino paced three steps toward the end of the room, spun, and paced back.

Rogers found himself apologizing to the man. "They couldn't take the risk. They're probably trying some alternate approach to the problem K-Eighty-eight was supposed to handle."

Martino slapped his thigh.

"Probably that monstrosity of Besser's." He sat down abruptly, facing away from them. His hand fumbled at his shirt pocket and he pushed the end of a cigarette through his mouth grille. A motor whined, and the split soft rubber inner gasket closed around it. He lit the cigarette with jerky motions of his good arm.

"Damn it," he muttered savagely. "Damn it, K-Eighty-eight was *the* answer! They'll go broke trying to make that abortion of Besser's work." He took an angry drag on the cigarette.

Suddenly he spun his head around and looked squarely at Rogers. "What in hell are *you* staring at? I've got a throat and a tongue. Why shouldn't I smoke?"

"We know that, Mr. Martino," Finchley said gently.

Martino's red gaze shifted. "You just think you do." He turned back to face the wall. "Weren't you two about to leave?"

Rogers nodded silently before he spoke. "Yes. Yes, we were, Mr. Martino. We'll be going. Sorry."

"All right." He sat without speaking until they were almost out the door. Then he said, "Can you get me some lens tissue?"

"I'll send some in right away." Rogers closed the door gently. "His eyes must get dirty, at that," he commented to Finchley.

The F.B.I. man nodded absently, walking along the hall beside him.

Rogers said uncomfortably, "That was quite a show he put on. If he is Martino, I don't blame him."

Finchley grimaced. "And if he isn't, I don't blame him either."

"You know," Rogers said, "if we'd been able to crack him today, they would have kept the K-Eighty-eight program going. It won't actually be scrubbed until midnight. It was more or less up to me."

"Oh?"

Rogers nodded. "I told him it was washed out because I wanted to see what he'd do. I suppose I thought he might make some kind of break."

Rogers felt a peculiar kind of defeat. He had run down. He was empty of energy, and everything from now on would only be a falling downhill, back the way he had come.

"Well," Finchley said, "you can't say he didn't react."

"Yes, he did. He reacted." Rogers found himself disliking the sound of what he would say. "But he didn't react in any way that would help. All he did was act like a normal human being."

Chapter Four

THE PHYSICS laboratory at Bridgetown Memorial High School was a longish room with one wall formed by the windows of the building front. It was furnished with long, varnished, masonite-topped tables running toward the end of the room where Edmund Starke's desk was set on a raised platform. Blackboards ran along two of the remaining walls, and equipment cupboards took up the other. By and large, the room was adequate for its purpose, neither substandard nor good enough to satisfy Starke, neither originally designed to be a laboratory nor rendered hopelessly unsuited by its conversion from two ordinary classrooms. It was intended to serve as the space enclosing the usual high school physics class, and that was what it was.

Lucas Martino saw it as something else again, though he didn't realize it and for quite some time couldn't have said why. But never once did he remind himself that a highly similar class might have been held in any high school in the world. This was *his* physics class, taught by *his* instructor, in *his* laboratory. This was *the* place, in its place, as everything in his universe was in its place or beginning to near it. So when he came in each day he first looked around it searchingly before he took his chair at one of the tables, with an unmistakably contented and oddly proprietary expression. Consequently, Starke marked him out for an eager student.

Lucas Martino couldn't ignore a fact. He judged no fact; he only filed it away, like a machine part found on a workshop bench, confident that someday he would find the part to which it fitted, knowing that some day all these parts would, by inevitable process, join together in a complete mechanism which he would put to use. Furthermore, everything he saw represented a fact to him. He made no judgments, so nothing was trivial. Everything he had ever seen or heard was put somewhere in his brain. His memory was not photographic—he wasn't interested in a static picture of his past—but it was all-inclusive. People said his mind was a jumble of odd knowledge. And he was always trying to fit these things together, and see to what mechanism they led.

In classes, he was quiet and answered only when asked to. He had the habit of depending on himself to fit his own facts together, and the notion of consulting someone else—even Starke—by asking an impromptu question was foreign to him. He was accustomed to a natural order of things in which few answers were supplied. Asking Starke to help him with his grasp of facts would have seemed unfair to him.

Consequently, his marks showed unpredictable ups and downs. Like all high school science classes, the only thing Starke's physics class was supposed to teach was the principal part of the broad theoretical base. His students were given and expected to learn by rote the various simpler laws and formulae, like so many bricks ripped whole out of a misty and possibly useful structure. They were not yet—if ever—expected to construct anything of their own out of them. Lucas Martino failed to realize this. He would have been uncomfortable with the thought. It was his notion that Starke was throwing out hints, and he was presumed capable of filling in the rest for himself.

So there were times when he saw the inevitable direction of a lecture before its first sentences were cold, and when he leaped to the conclusion of an experiment before Starke had the apparatus fairly set up. One thing after another would fall into place for him, garnering its structure out of his storehouse of half-ideas, hints, and unrelated data. When this happened, he'd experienced what someone else would have called a flash of genius.

But there were other times when things only seemed to fit, when actually they did not, and then he shot down a blind alley in pursuit of a hare-brained mistake, making some ridiculous error no one else would have made or could have.

When this happened, he painfully worked his way back along

the false chain of facts, taking each in turn and examining it to see why he'd been fooled, eventually returning to the right track. But, having once built a structure, he found it impossible to discard it entirely. So another part of his mind was a storehouse of interesting ideas that hadn't worked, but were interesting— theories that were wild, but had seemed to hold together. To a certain extent, these phantom heresies stayed behind to color his thinking. He would never quite be an orthodox theory-spieler.

Meanwhile, he went on gathering facts.

Starke was a veteran of the high school teaching circuit. He'd seen his share of morning glories and of impassive average-mechanics working for the Valedictorian's chair on graduation night. He'd gotten past the point of resenting them, and long before that he'd gotten past the point of wasting his conversation on them. He'd found out early in the game that their interests were not in common with his own.

So Lucas Martino attracted him and he felt obligated to establish some kind of link with the boy. He took several weeks to find the opportunity, and even then he had to force it. He was clumsy, because sociability wasn't his forte. He was an economical man, saw no reason to establish social relations with anyone he didn't respect, and respected few people.

Lucas was finishing up a report at the end of a class when Starke levered himself out of his chair, waited for the rest of the class to start filing out, and walked over to the boy.

"Martino—"

Lucas looked up, surprised but not startled. "Yes, Mr. Starke?"

"Uh—you're not a member of the Physics Club, are you?"

"No, sir." The Physics Club existed as yet another excuse for a group picture in the yearbook.

"Well—I've been thinking of having the club perform some special experiments. Outside of class. Might even work up some demonstrations and stage them at an assembly. I thought the rest of the student body might be interested." All of this was sheer fabrication, arrived at on the spur of the moment, and Starke was astonished at himself. "Wondered if you'd care to join in."

Lucas shook his head. "Sorry, Mr. Starke. I don't have much extra time, with football practice and work at night."

Ordinarily, Starke wouldn't have pressed further. Now he said, "Come on, Martino. Frank Del Bello's on the team, too, and he's a member of the club."

For some reason, Lucas felt as though Starke were probing an exposed nerve. After all, as far as Lucas Martino knew up to this moment, he had no rational basis for considering the physics class any more important than his other courses. But he reacted sharply and quickly. "I'm afraid I'm not interested in popular science, Mr. Starke." He immediately passed over the fact that belonging to the club as it was and following Starke's new program were two different things. He wasn't interested in fine argumentative points. He clearly understood that Starke was after something else entirely, and that Starke, with his momentum gathered, would keep pushing. "I don't think that demonstrating nuclear fission by dropping a cork into a bunch of mousetraps has anything to do with physics. I'm sorry."

It was suddenly a ticklish moment for both of them. Starke was unused to being stopped once he'd started something. Lucas Martino lived by facts, and the facts of the circumstances left him only one position to take, as he saw it. In a very real sense, each felt the other's mass resisting him, and each knew that something violent could result unless they found some neutral way to disengage.

"What *is* your idea of physics, Martino?"

Lucas took the opening and turned into it gratefully. He found it led farther than he'd thought. "I think it's the most important thing in the world, sir," he said, and felt like a man stumbling out over a threshold.

"You do, eh? Why?" Starke slammed the door behind him.

Lucas fumbled for words. "The universe is a perfect structure. Everything in it is in balance. It's complete. Nothing can be added to it or taken away."

"And what does that mean?"

Bit by bit, facts were falling together in Lucas Martino's mind. Ideas, half-thoughts, bits of formulation that he failed to recognize as fragments of a philosophy—all these things suddenly arranged themselves in a systematic and natural order as he listened to what he'd just said on impulse. For the first time since the day he'd come to this class with a fresh, blank laboratory notebook, he understood exactly what he was doing here. He understood more than that; he understood himself. His picture of himself was complete, finished for all time.

That left him free to turn to something else.

"Well, Martino?"

Lucas took one deep breath, and stopped fumbling. "The universe is constructed of perfectly fitted parts. Every time you rearrange the position of one, you affect all the others. If you add something in one place, you had to take it away from somewhere else. Everything we do—everything that has ever been done—was accomplished by rearranging pieces of the universe. If we knew exactly where everything fitted, and what moving it would do to all the other pieces, we'd be able to do things more effectively. That's what physics is doing—investigating the structure of the universe and giving us a system to handle it with. That's the most basic thing there is. Everything else depends on it."

"That's an article of faith with you, is it?"

"That's the way it *is*." Faith has nothing to do with it." The answer came quickly. He didn't quite understand what Starke meant. He was too full of the realization that he had just learned what he was for.

Starke had run across carefully rehearsed speeches before. He got at least one a year from some bright boy who'd seen a movie about Young Tom Edison. He knew Martino wasn't likely to be giving him that, but he'd been fooled before. So he took his long look at the boy before he said anything.

He saw Lucas Martino looking back at him as though sixteen-year-old boys took their irrevocable vows every day.

It upset Starke. It made him uncomfortable, and it made him draw back for the first time in his life.

"Well. So that's your idea of physics. Planning to go on to Massachusetts Tech, are you?"

"If I can get the money together. And my grades aren't too high, are they?"

"The grades can be taken care of, if you'll work at it. The semester's not that far gone. And money's no problem. There're all kinds of science scholarships. If you miss on that, you can probably get one of the big outfits like G. E. to underwrite you."

Martino shook his head. "It's a three-factor problem. My

graduating average won't be that high, no matter what I do the next two years here. And I don't want to be tied to anybody's company, and third, scholarships don't cover everything. You've got to have decent clothes at college, and you've got to have some money in your pocket to relax on once in a while. I've heard about M.I.T. Nobody human can take their curriculum and earn money part-time. If you're there, you're there twenty-four hours a day. And I'm going for my doctorate. That's seven years, minimum. No, I'm going to New York after I graduate here and work in my Uncle Luke's place until I get some money put away. I'll be a New York resident and put in a cheap year at C.C.N.Y. I'll pile up an average there, and get my tuition scholarship to Massachusetts that way."

The plan unfolded easily and spontaneously. Starke couldn't have guessed it was being created on the spot. Martino had put all the facts together, seen how they fit, and what action they indicated. It was as easy as that.

"Talked it over with your parents, have you?"

"Not yet." For the first time, he showed hesitation. "It'll be rough on them. It'll be a long time before I can send them any money." Also, but never to be put in words for a stranger, the life of the family would be changed forever, never to be put back in the same way again.

2.

"I don't understand," his mother said. "Why should you suddenly want to go to this school in Boston? Boston is far away from here. Farther than New York."

He had no easy answer. He sat awkwardly at the dinner table, looking down at his plate.

"I don't understand it either," his father said to his mother. "But if he wants to go, that's his choice. He's not leaving right away, in any case. By the time he goes, he'll be a man. A man has a right to decide these things."

He looked from his mother to his father, and he could see it wasn't something he could explain. For a moment, he almost said he'd changed his mind.

Instead he said, "Thank you for your permission." Move one piece of the universe, and all the others are affected. Add something to one piece, and another must lose. What real choice did he have, when everything meshed together, one block of fact against another, and there was only one best way to act?

Chapter Five

O N THE eighth day after the man had come over the line, the annunciator buzzed on Rogers' desk.

"Yes?"

"Mr. Deptford is here to see you, sir."

Rogers grunted. He said, "Send him in, please," and sat waiting.

Deptford came into the office. He was a thin, gray-faced man in a dark suit, and he was carrying a briefcase. "How are you, Shawn?" he said quietly.

Rogers stood up. "Fine, thanks," he answered slowly. "How are you?"

Deptford shrugged. He sat down in the chair beside the end of Rogers' desk and laid the briefcase in his lap. "I thought I'd bring the decision on the Martino matter down with me." He opened the briefcase and handed Rogers a manila envelope. "In there's the usual file copy of the official policy directive, and a letter to you from Karl Schwenn's office."

Rogers picked up the envelope. "Did Schwenn give you a very bad time, sir?"

Deptford smiled thinly. "They didn't quite know what to do. It didn't seem to be anybody's fault. But they'd needed an answer very badly. Now, at the sacrifice of the K-Eighty-eight program, they don't need it so badly any more. But they still need it, of course."

Rogers nodded slowly.

"I'm replacing you here as sector chief. They've put a new man in my old job. And the letter from Schwenn reassigns you to follow up on Martino. Actually, I think Schwenn arrived at the best answer to a complicated situation."

Rogers felt his lips stretch in an uncomfortable grimace of surprise and embarrassment. "Well." There was nothing else to say.

2.

"Direct investigation won't do it," Rogers said to the man. "We tried, but it can't be done. We can't prove who you are."

The glinting eyes looked at him impassively. There was no telling what the man might be thinking. They were alone in the small room, and Rogers suddenly understood that this had turned into a personal thing between them. It had happened gradually, he could see now, built up in small increments over the past days, but this was the first time it had struck him, and so it had also happened suddenly. Rogers found himself feeling personally responsible for the man's being here, and for everything that had happened to him. It was an unprofessional way to feel, but the fact was that he and this man were here face to face, alone, and when it came down to the actual turn of the screw it was Rogers whose hand was on the wrench.

"I see what you mean," the man said. "I've been doing a lot of thinking about it." He was sitting stiffly in his chair, his metal hand across his lap and there was no telling whether he had been thinking of it coldly and dispassionately, or whether hopes and desperate ideas had gone echoing through his brain like men in prison hammering on the bars. "I thought I might be able to come up with something. What about skin pore patterns? Those couldn't have been changed."

Rogers shook his head. "I'm sorry, Mr. Martino. Believe me, we had experts in physical identification thrashing this thing back and forth for days. Pore patterns were mentioned, as a matter of fact. But unfortunately, that won't do us any good. We don't have verified records from before the explosion. Nobody ever thought we'd have to go into details as minute as that." He raised his hand, rubbed it wearily across the side of his head, and dropped it in resignation. "That's true of everything in that line, I'm afraid. We have your fingerprints and retinal photographs on file. Both are useless now."

And here we are, he thought, fencing around the entire question of whether you're really Martino but went over to them. There're limits to what civilized people can bring out into the open, no matter how savagely they can speculate. So it doesn't matter. There's no easy escape for either of us, no mat-

ter what we say or do now. We've had our try at the easy answers, and there aren't any. It's the long haul for both of us
now.

"Isn't there anything to work on at all?"

"I'm afraid not. No distinguishing marks or scars that
couldn't be faked, no tattoos, no anything. We've tried, Mr.
Martino. We've thought of every possibility. We accumulated
quite a team of specialists. The consensus is there's no fast
answer."

"That's hard to believe," the man said.

"Mr. Martino, you're more deeply involved in the problem
than any of us. You've been unable to offer anything useful.
And you're a pretty smart man."

"If I'm Lucas Martino," the man said drily.

"Even if you're not." Rogers brought his palms down on his
knees. "Let's look at it logically. Anything we can think of,
they could have thought of first. In trying to establish anything
about you, normal approaches are useless. We're the specialists
in charge of taking you apart, and a great many of us have
been in this kind of work a long time. I was head of A.N.G.
Security in this sector for seven years. I'm the fellow responsible
for the agents we drop into their organizations. But when I try
to crack you, I've got to face the possibility that just as many
experts on the other side worked at putting you together—and
you yourself can most likely match my own experience in
spades. What's opposed here are the total efforts of two efficient organizations, each with the resources of half the world.
That's the situation, and we're all stuck with it."

"What're you going to do?"

"That's what I'm here to tell you. We couldn't keep you
here indefinitely. We don't do things that way. So you're free
to go."

The man raised his head sharply. "There's a catch to it."

Rogers nodded. "Yes, there is. We can't let you go back to
sensitive work. That's the catch, and you already knew it. Now
it's official. You're free to go and do anything you like, as long
as it isn't physics."

"Yes." The man's voice was quiet. "You want to see me run.
How long does that injunction apply? How long're you going
to keep watching me?"

"Until we find out who you are."

The man began to laugh, quietly and bitterly.

3.

"So he's leaving here today?" Finchley asked.

"Tomorrow morning. He wants to go to New York. We're paying his flight transportation, we've assigned him a one-hundred-per cent disability pension, and given him four months' back pay at Martino's scale."

"Are you going to put a surveillance team on him in New York?"

"Yes. And I'll be on the plane with him."

"You will? You're dropping your job here?"

"Yes. Orders. He's my personal baby. I'll head up the New York A.N.G. surveillance unit."

Finchley looked at him curiously. Rogers kept his eyes level. After a moment, the F.B.I. man made an odd sucking noise between his two upper front teeth and let it go at that. But Rogers saw his mouth stretch into the peculiar grimace a man shows when a fellow professional falls from grace.

"What's your procedure going to be?" Finchley asked carefully. "Just keep him under constant watch until he makes a wrong move?"

Rogers shook his head. "No. We've got to screw it down tighter than that. There's only one possible means of identification left. We've got to build up a psychological profile on Lucas Martino. Then we'll match it against this fellow's pattern of actions and responses, in situations where we'd be able to tell exactly how the real Martino'd react. We're going to dig —deeper than any security clearance, deeper than the Recording Angel, if we have to. We're going to reduce Lucas Martino to so many points on a graph, and then we're going to chart this fellow against him. Once he does something Lucas Martino would never have done, we'll know. Once he expresses an attitude the old, loyal Lucas Martino didn't have, we'll come down on him like a ton of bricks."

"Yes—but . . ." Finchley looked umcomfortable. His specific assignment to Rogers' team was over. From now on he'd be only a liaison man between Rogers' A.N.G. surveillance unit and the F.B.I. As a member of a different organization, he'd be expected to give help when needed, but no unasked-for suggestions. And particularly now, with Rogers bound to be sensitive about rank, he was wary of overstepping.

"Well?" Rogers asked.

"Well, what you're going to do is wait for this man to make his mistake. He's a clever man, so he won't make it soon, and it won't be a big one. It'll be some little thing, and it may be years before he makes it. It may be fifteen years. He may die without making it. And all that time he'll be on the spot. All that time he may be Lucas Martino—and if he is, this system's never going to prove it."

Rogers' voice was soft. "Can you think of anything better? Anything at all?" It wasn't Finchley's fault they were in this mess. It wasn't the A.N.G.'s fault he'd had to be demoted. It wasn't Martino's fault this whole thing had started. It wasn't Roger's fault—still, wasn't it?, he thought—that Mr. Deptford had been demoted. They were caught up in a structure of cir-cumstances that were each fitted to one another in an inevitable pattern, each so shaped and so placed that they fell naturally into a trackless maze, and there was nothing for anyone to do but follow along.

"No," Finchley admitted, "I can't see any way out of it."

4.

There was a ground fog at the airfield and Rogers stood out-side alone, waiting for it to lift. He kept his back turned to the car parked ten feet away, beside the administration building, where the other man was sitting with Finchley. Rogers' topcoat collar was turned up, and his hands were in his pockets. He was staring out at the dirty metal skin of the airplane waiting on the apron. He was thinking of how aircraft in flight flashed molten in the sky, dazzling as angels, and how on the ground their purity was marred by countless grease-rimmed rivet heads, by oil stains, by scuff marks where mechanics' feet had slipped, and by droplets of water that dried away to each leave a speck of dirt behind.

He slipped two fingers inside his shirt, like a pickpocket, and pulled out a cigarette. Closing his thin lips around it, he stood bareheaded in the fog, his hair a corona of beaded moisture, and listened to the public address system announce that the fog was dissipating and passengers were requested to board their planes. He looked through the glass wall of the administration building into the passenger lounge and saw the people there getting to their feet, closing their coats, getting their tickets ready.

The man had to go out into the world sometime. This was an ordinary commercial civilian flight, and sixty-five people, not counting Rogers and Finchley, would be exposed to him at one blow.

Rogers hunched his shoulders, lit his cigarette, and wondered what would happen. The fog seemed to have worked its way into his nasal passages and settled at the back of his throat. He felt cold and depressed. The gate checker came out and took up his position, and people began filing out of the passenger lounge.

Rogers listened for the sound of the car door. When it didn't come at once, he wondered if the man was going to wait until everyone was aboard, in hopes of being able to take the last seat and so, for a little time, avoid being noticed.

The man waited until the passengers were collected in the inevitable knot around the ticket checker. Then he got out of the car, waited for Finchley to slide out, and slammed the door like a gunshot.

Rogers jerked his head in that direction, realizing everyone else was, too.

For a moment, the man stood there holding his overnight bag in one gloved hand, his hat pulled down low over his obscene skull, his topcoat buttoned to the neck, his collar up. Then he set the bag down and pulled off his gloves, raising his face to look directly at the other passengers. Then he lifted his metal hand and yanked his hat off.

In the silence he walked forward quickly, hat and bag in his good hand, taking his ticket out of his breast pocket with the other. He stopped, bent, and picked up a woman's handbag.

"I believe you dropped this?" he murmured.

The woman took her purse numbly. The man turned to Rogers and, in a deliberately cheerful voice, said, "Well, time to be getting aboard, isn't it?"

Chapter Six

Y OUNG LUCAS came to the city at a peculiar time.
The summer of 1966 was uncomfortable for New York.
It was usually cooler than expected, and it often rained. The
people who ordinarily spent their summer evenings in the
parks, walking back and forth and then sitting down to watch
other people walk past, felt disappointed in the year. The
grumbling old men who sold ice cream sticks from three-
wheeled carts rang their bells more vigorously than they would
have liked. Fewer people came to the band concerts on the
Mall in Central Park, and the music, instead of diffusing gently
through heat-softened air, had a tinny ring to the practiced
ear.

There were hot days here and there. There were weeks at a
time when it seemed that the weather had settled down at last,
and the city, like a machine late in shifting gears but shifting at
last, would try to fall into its true summer rhythm. But then it
would rain again. The rain glazed the sidewalks instead of
soaking into them, and the leaves on the trees curled rather
than opened. It would have been a perfectly good enough
summer for Boston, but New York had to force itself a little.
Everyone was just a fraction on edge, knowing how New York
summers ought to be, knowing how you ought to feel in the
summer, and knowing that this year just wasn't making it.

Young Lucas Martino knew only that the city seemed to be
a nervous, discontented place. His uncle, Lucas Maggiore,
who was his mother's older brother and who had been in the
States since 1936, was glad enough to see and hire him, but he
was growing old and he was moody. *Espresso Maggiore*, where
young Lucas was to work from noon to three A.M. each day
but Monday, grinding coffee, charging the noisy espresso machine, carrying armfuls of cups to the tables, had until recently
been a simple neighborhood trattoria for the neighborhood
Italians who didn't care to patronize the rival Greek kaffe-
neikons.

But the tourist area of Greenwich Village had spread down
to include the block where Lucas Maggiore had started his
coffee house when he stopped wrestling sacks of roasted beans

in a restaurant supply warehouse. So now there were murals on the walls, antique tables, music by Muzak, and a new I.B.M. electric cash register. Lucas Maggiore, a big, heavy, indrawn bachelor who had always managed to have enough money, now had more. He was able to pay his only nephew more than he deserved, and still had enough left to make him wonder if perhaps he shouldn't live more freely than he had in the past. But he had an ingrained caution against flying too far in the face of temptation, and so he was moody. He felt a vague resentment against the coffee house, hired a manager, and stayed away most of the time. He began stopping more and more often by the Park Department tables in Washington Square, where old men in black overcoats sat and played checkers with the concentration of chessmasters, and sometimes he was on the verge of asking to play.

When young Lucas came to New York, his uncle had embraced him at Pennsylvania Station, patted him between the shoulder blades, and held him off by both arms to look at him:

"Ah! Lucas! *Bello nipotino! E la Mama, il Papa—come lei portano?*"

"They're fine, Uncle Lucas. They send their love. I'm glad to see you."

"So. All right—I like you, you like me—we'll get along. Let's go." He took Lucas' suitcase in one big hand and led the way to the subway station. "Mrs. Dormiglione—my landlady—she has a room for you. Cheap. It's a good room. Nice place. Old lady Dormiglione, she's not much for cleaning up. You'll have to do that yourself. But that way, she won't bother you much. You're young, Lucas—you don't want old people bothering you all the time. You want to be with young people. You're eighteen—you want a little life." Lucas Maggiore inclined his head in the direction of a passing girl.

Young Lucas didn't quite know what to say. He followed his uncle into a downtown express car and stood holding on to the overhead bar as the train jerked to a start. Finally, having nothing conclusive to say, he said nothing. When the train reached Fourth Street, he and his uncle got off, and went to the furnished rooming house just off West Broadway where Lucas Maggiore lived on the top floor and Lucas Martino was to live in the basement—with an entrance separate from the main front door. After young Lucas had been introduced to Mrs. Dormiglione, shown his room, and given a few minutes to put his suitcase away and wash his face, his uncle took him to the coffee house.

On the way there, Lucas Maggiore turned to young Lucas.

"Lucas and Lucas—that's too many Lucases in one store. Does Matteo have another name for you?"

Lucas thought back. "Well, sometimes Papa calls me Tedeschino."

"Good! In the store, that's your name. All right?"

"Fine."

So that was the name by which Lucas was introduced to the employees of *Espresso Maggiore*. His uncle told him to be at work at noon the next day, advanced him a week's pay, and left him. They saw each other occasionally after that, and sometimes when his uncle wanted company, he asked young Lucas whether he would like to eat with him, or listen to music on the phonograph in Mrs. Dormiglione's parlor. But Lucas Maggiore had so arranged things that young Lucas had a life of his own, freedom to live it, and was still close enough so that the boy couldn't get into serious trouble. He felt that he'd done his best for the youngster, and he was right.

So Lucas spent his first day in New York with a firm base under his feet, but on his own. He thought that the city could have been pleasanter, but that he was being given a fair chance. He felt a little isolated, but that was something he felt was up to him to handle.

In another year, with a soft summer, he might have found it easier to slip quickly into the pattern of the city's life. But this year most people had not been lulled into relaxation—this year they took no vacations from the closed-up, preoccupied attitudes of winter, and so Lucas discovered that New Yorkers putting a meal in front of you in a diner, selling you a movie ticket, or rubbing against you on a crowded bus, could each of them be behind an impenetrable wall.

With another uncle, he might have been taken up into a family much like the one he had left behind. In another house, he might have had a room somewhere where people next door soon struck up an acquaintance. But, as everything was, things so combined that what kind of life he lived for the next year and a half was entirely up to him. He recognized the situation, and in his methodical, logical way, began to consider what kind of life he needed.

2.

Espresso Maggiore was essentially one large room, with a counter at one end where the espresso machine was and where the clean cups were kept. There were heavy, elaborately carved tables from Venice and Florence, some with marble tops and some not, and besides the murals executed in an Italianate modern style by one of the neighborhood artists, there were thickly varnished old oil paintings in flaking gilt frames on the walls. There was a sugar bowl on each table, with a small menu card listing the various kinds of coffee served and the small selection of ices and other sweets available. The walls were painted a warm cream-yellow, and the lights were dim. The music played in the background, from speakers concealed in two genuine Cinquecento cupboards, and from time to time one of the steady patrons would find a vaguely Roman bust or statuette—French neoclassic was close enough—which he would donate to the management for the satisfaction of seeing it displayed on a wooden pedestal somewhere in a corner.

The espresso machine dominated the room. When Lucas Maggiore first opened his trattoria, he had bought a second-hand but nearly new modern electric machine, shining in chrome, looking a good deal like the manifold of a liquid-cooled aircraft engine, with *ATALANTO* proclaiming the maker's name in raised block letters across the topmost tube. When the store was redecorated, the new machine was sold to a kaffeneikon and another machine—one of the old gas-fired models—was put up in its place. This was a great vertical cylinder with a bell top, nickel-plated, with the heads of cherubim bolted to its sides and an eagle rampant atop its bell. Rich with its ornamentation, its sides covered by engraved scrollwork, with spigots protruding from its base, the machine sat on the counter and screamed hisses as it forced steam through the charges of coffee. From noon to three A.M. each day except Monday, gathering thickest around midnight, Villagers and tourists crowded *Espresso Maggiore*, sitting in the wire-back chairs, most of them drinking capuccino in preference to true espresso, which is bitter, and interrupting their conversations whenever the machine hissed.

Besides Lucas, there were four other employees of *Espresso Maggiore*.

Carlo, the manager, was a heavy-set, almost unspeaking man of about thirty-five, cut from the same cloth as Lucas Maggiore and hired for that reason. He handled the machine, usually took cash, and supervised the work and cleaning up. He showed Lucas how to grind the coffee, told him to keep the tables wiped and the sugarbowls full, taught him how to wash cups and saucers with the greatest efficiency, and left him alone after that, since the youngster did his work well.

There were three waitresses. Two of them were more or less typical Village girls, one from the Midwest and the other from Schenectady, who were studying drama and came in to work from eight to one. The third waitress was a neighborhood girl, Barbara Costa, who was about seventeen or eighteen and worked the full shift every day. She was a pretty, thinnish girl who did her work expertly and wasted no time talking to the Village young men, who came in during the afternoons and sat for hours over their one cup of coffee because nobody minded as long as the store wasn't crowded. Because she was there all day, Lucas got to know her better than the other two girls. They got along well, and during the first few days she took the trouble to teach him the tricks of balancing four and five cups at a time, remembering complicated orders, and keeping a running tab in his head. Lucas liked her for her friendliness, respected her skill because it was organized in a way he understood, and was grateful for having one person he could talk to in the rare moments when he felt a desire to do so.

In a month, Lucas had acclimated himself to the city. He memorized the complicated network of straggling, unnumbered streets below Washington Square, knew the principal subway routes, found a good, inexpensive laundry and a delicatessen where he bought what few groceries he felt he needed. He had investigated the registration system and entrance requirements at City College, sent a letter of inquiry to Massachusetts, and registered with the local Selective Service Board, where his grade in the Technical Aptitude Examination gave him his conditional deferment. He'd have to be a registered physical sciences student within a year, but that was what he was in New York for. So, by and large, he had succeeded in arranging his circumstances to fit his needs.

But what his uncle had hinted at on his first day in the city was beginning to turn itself over in Lucas' mind. He sat down and thought it out systematically.

He was eighteen, and at or near his physical peak. His body was an excellently designed mechanism, with definite needs and functions. This particular year was the last even partly-free time he could expect for the next eight years.

Yes, he decided, if he was ever going to get himself a girl, there was no better time for it than now. He had the time, the means, and even the desire. Logic pointed the way, and so he began to look around.

Chapter Seven

THE PLANE went into its final downward glide over Long Island, slipping into the New York International landing pattern, and the lounge hostess asked Rogers and the man to take their seats.

The man lifted his highball gracefully, set the edge against the lip of his mouth, and finished his drink. He put the glass down, and the grille moved back into place. He dabbed at his chin with a paper cocktail napkin. "Alcohol is very bad for high-carbon steel, you know," he remarked to the hostess.

He had spent most of the trip in the lounge, occasionally ordering a drink, smoking at intervals, holding glass or cigarette in his metal hand. The passengers and crew had been forced to grow accustomed to him.

"Yes, sir," the hostess said politely.

Rogers shook his head to himself. As he followed the man down the aisle to their seats, he said, "Not if it's stainless steel, Mr. Martino. I've seen the metallurgical analyses on you."

"Yes," the man said, buckling his seatbelt and resting his

hands lightly on his kneecaps. "You have. But that hostess hasn't." He put a cigarette in his mouth and let it dangle there, unlit, while the plane banked and steadied on its new heading. He looked out the window beside him. "Odd," he said. "You wouldn't expect it to still be too early for daylight."

The moment the plane touched the runway, slowed, and began to taxi toward the offloading ramp, the man unfastened his seatbelt and lit his cigarette. "We seem to be here," he said conversationally, and stood up. "It's been a pleasant trip."

"Pretty good," Rogers said, unfastening his own belt. He looked toward Finchley, across the aisle, and shook his head helplessly as the F.B.I. man raised his eyebrows. There was no doubt about it—whoever this man was, Martino or not, they were going to have a bad time with him.

"Well," the man said, "I don't suppose we'll be meeting socially again, Mr. Rogers. I hardly know whether it's proper to say good-bye or not."

Rogers held out his hand wordlessly.

The man's right hand was warm and firm. "It'll be good to see New York again. I haven't been here in nearly twenty years. And you, Mr. Rogers?"

"Twelve, about. I was born here."

"Oh, were you?" They moved slowly along the aisle toward the rear door, with the man walking ahead of Rogers. "Then you'll be glad to get back."

Rogers shrugged uncomfortably.

The man's chuckle was rueful. "Pardon me—do you know, for a moment I actually forgot this was hardly a pleasure trip for either of us."

Rogers had no answer. He followed the man down the aisle to where the stewardesses gave them their coats. They stepped out on the escalator, with Rogers' eyes on a level with the top of the man's bare head.

The man half-turned, as though for another casual remark.

The first flashbulb exploded down at the foot of the escalator, and the man recoiled. He stumbled back against Rogers, and for a moment he was pressed against him. Rogers suddenly caught the stale, acrid smell of the perspiration that had been soaking the man's shirt for hours.

There was a cluster of photographers down on the apron,

pointing their cameras at the man and firing their flashguns in a ripple of sharp light.

The man tried to turn on the escalator. His hard hand closed on Rogers' shoulder as he tried to get him out of the way. The gaskets behind his mouth grille were up out of sight. Rogers heard his two food-grinding blades clash together.

Then Finchley somehow got past both of them, clattering down the escalator. He was reaching for his wallet as he went, and then the F.B.I. shield glittered briefly in the puffballs of light. The photographers stopped.

Rogers took a deep breath and pried the man's hand off his shoulder. "All right," he said gently, lowering the hand carefully as though it were no longer attached to anything. "It's all right, man, it's under control. The damned pilot must have radioed ahead or something. Finchley'll have a talk with the newspaper editors and the wire service chiefs. You won't get spread all over the world."

The man got his footing back, and stepped unsteadily off the escalator as they reached the ground. He mumbled something that had to be either thanks or a stumbling apology. Rogers was just as glad not to have heard it.

"We'll take care of the news media. The only thing you'll have left to worry about is the people you meet, but from what I've seen you can do a damn fine job of handling those."

The man's glittering eyes swung on Rogers savagely. "Just don't watch me too closely," he growled.

2.

Rogers stood in the local A.N.G. Security office that afternoon, massaging his shoulder from time to time while he talked. Twenty-two men sat in orderly rows of classroom chairs facing him, taking notes on standard pads rested on the broad right arms of the chairs.

"All right," Rogers said in a tired voice. "You've all got offset copies of the dossier on Martino. It's pretty complete, but that's only where we start. You'll get your individual assignments as you file out, but I want you all to know what the team's supposed to be doing as a whole. Any one of you may come up with something that'll seem unimportant unless we have the whole picture.

"Now—what we want is a diagram of a man, down to the last capillary and—" His lips twitched. "Rivet. Out of your in-dividual reports, we're going to put together a master descrip-tion of him that'll tell us everything from the day he was born to the day the lab went up. We want to know what foods he liked, what cigarettes he smoked, what vices he had, what kind of women he favored—and why. We want a list of the books he's read—and what he agreed with in them. Almost all of you are going to do nothing but intensive research on him. When we're through, we want to have read a man's mind." Rogers let his hand fall to his side. "Because his mind is all we have left to recognize him by.

"Some of you are going to be assigned to direct surveillance. It'll be your reports we'll check against the research. They'll have to be just as detailed, just as precise. Remember that he knows you're watching. That means his gross actions may very well be intended to mislead you. It'll be the small things that might trip him up. Watch who he talks to—but pay just as much attention to the way he lights his cigarettes.

"But remember you're dealing with a genius. He's either Lucas Martino or a Soviet ringer, but, whichever it is, he's sharper than any one of us. You'll have to face that, keep it in mind, and just remember there're more of us and we've got the system. Of course"—Rogers heard the frustrated undertone in his voice—"he may be part of a system, too. But it'd be much smarter of them to let him go it alone.

"As to what he's here for if he is a ringer: it might be any-thing. They might seriously have expected him to get back into the technological development program. If so, he's in a hole right now, with no place to go. He may make a break to get out of the Allied Sphere. Watch out for that. Again, he may be here for something else, figuring the Soviets expected us to handle him just the way we have. If so, there're all kinds of rabbits he could start pulling out of his hat. We're positive he isn't a human bomb or a walking arsenal full of hidden death-rays and other stuff out of the funnies. We're positive, but, Lord knows, we could be wrong. Watch out for him if he starts trying to buy electronic parts, or *anything* he could build something out of.

"Those of you who're going to dig into his history—if he ever fiddled with things in his cellar, or tossed an idea for some kind of nasty gimmick into a discussion, I want to hear about it quick. I don't know what this K-Eighty-eight thing he worked up was—I do know it must have had an awful punch. I think we'd all appreciate it if he didn't put one together in a back room somewhere."

Rogers sighed. "All right. Questions."

A man raised his hand. "Mr. Rogers?"

"Yes."

"How about the other end of this problem? I presume there're teams in Europe trying to penetrate the Soviet organization that worked on him?"

"There are. But they're only doing it because we're supposed to cover all loose ends for the record. They're not getting anywhere. The Soviets have a fellow named Azarin who's their equivalent to a sector security chief. He's good at his work. He's a stone wall. If we get anything out past him, it'll be pure luck. If I know him, everybody connected in any way with whatever happened is in Uzbekistan by now, and the records have been destroyed—if they were ever kept. I know one thing—we had some people I thought I'd planted over there. They're gone. Other questions?"

"Yes, sir. How long do you think it'll be before we can say for sure about this fellow?"

Rogers simply looked at the man.

3.

Rogers was sitting alone in his office when Finchley came in. It was growing dark again outside, and the room was gloomy in spite of the lamp on Rogers' desk. Finchley took a chair and waited while Rogers folded his reading glasses and put them back in his breast pocket.

"How'd you make out?" Rogers asked.

"I covered them all. Press, newsreel, and TV. He's not going to get publicity."

Rogers nodded. "Good. If we'd let him become a seven

days' wonder, we'd have lost our last chance. It'll be tough enough as it is. Thanks for doing all the work, Finchley. We'd never have gotten any accurate observations on him."

"I don't think he'd have enjoyed it, either," Finchley said.

Rogers looked at him for a moment, and then let it pass. "So as far as anyone connected with the news media is concerned, this isn't any higher up than F.B.I. level?"

"That's right. I kept the A.N.G. out of it."

"Fine. Thanks."

"That's one of the things I'm here for. What did Martino do after what happened at the airport?"

"He took a cab downtown and got off at the corner of Twelfth Street and Seventh Avenue. There's a luncheonette there. He had a hamburger and a glass of milk. Then he walked down to Greenwich Avenue, and down Greenwich to Sixth Avenue. He went down Sixth to Fourth Street. As of a few hours ago, he was walking back and forth on those streets down there."

"He went right out in public again. Just to prove he hadn't lost his nerve."

"It looks that way. He stirred up a mild fuss—people turning around to look at him, and a few people pointing. That was all there was to that. It wasn't anything he couldn't ignore. Of course, he hasn't looked for a place to stay yet, either. I'd say he was feeling a little lost right now. The next report's due within the next half hour—sooner if something drastic happens. We'll see. We're checking out the luncheonette."

Finchley looked up from his chair. "You know this whole business stinks, don't you?"

"Yes." Rogers frowned. "What's that got to do with it?"

"You saw him on the plane. He was dying by inches, and it never showed. He put himself up in front of sixty-odd people and rubbed their faces in what he was, just to prove to himself and to us, and to them, too, that he wasn't going to crawl into a hole. He fooled them, and he fooled us. He looks like nothing that ever walked this earth, and he proved he was as good a man as any of us."

"We knew that all along."

"And then, just when he'd done it, the world came up and hit him too hard. He saw himself being spread all over the whole Allied world in full-page color, and he saw himself being branded a freak for good and all. Well, who hasn't been hit too hard to stand? It's happened to me in my life, and I guess it's happened to you."

"I imagine it has."

"But he got up from it. He put himself on the sidewalk for everybody in New York to look at, and he got away with it. He knew what being hit felt like, and he went back for more. That's a man, Rogers—God damn it, that's a man!"

"What man?"

"Damn it, Rogers, give them a little time and the right chance, and there isn't an ID the Soviets couldn't fake! We don't have a man they couldn't replace with a ringer if they really wanted to. Nobody—nobody in this whole world—can prove who he is, but we're expecting this one man to do it."

"We have to. You can't do anything about it. This one man has to prove who he is."

"He could have just been put somewhere where he'd be harmless."

Rogers stood up and walked over to the window. His fingers played with the blind cord. "No man is harmless anywhere in this world. He may sit and do nothing, but he's there, and every other man has to solve the problem of who he is and what he's thinking, because until that problem's solved, that man is dangerous.

"The A.N.G. could have decided to put this man on a desert island, yes. And he might never have done anything. But the Soviets may have the K-Eighty-eight. And the real Martino might still be on their side of the line. By that much, this man on his desert island might be the most dangerous man in the world. And until we get evidence, that's exactly what he is, and equally so no matter where he is. If we're ever going to get evidence, it's going to be here. If we don't get it, then we'll stay close enough to stop him if he turns out not to be our Martino. That's the job, Finchley, and neither you nor I can get out of it. Neither of us'll be old enough for retirement before he dies."

"Look, damn it, Rogers, I know all that! I'm not trying to crawl out of the job. But we've been watching this man ever since he came back over the line. We've watched him, we've seen what he's going through—damn it, it's not going to make any difference in my work, but as far as I'm concerned—"

"You think he's Martino?"

Finchley stopped. "I don't have any evidence for it."

"But you can't help thinking he's Martino. Because he bleeds? Because he'd cry if he had tears? Because he's afraid, and desperate, and knows he has no place to go?" Rogers' hands jerked at the blind cord. "Don't we all? Aren't we all human beings?"

Chapter Eight

Young Lucas Martino turned away from the freshly-cleaned table, holding four dirty cups and saucers in his left hand, each cup in its saucer the way Barbara had taught him, with two saucers held overlapping between his fingers and the other two sets stacked on top. He carried his wiping sponge in his right hand, ready to clean up any dirty spots on tables he passed on the way to the counter. He liked working this way—it was efficient, it wasted no time, and it made no real difference that there was plenty of time, now that the late afternoon rush was over.

He wondered what created these freak rushes, as he set the cups and saucers down in the basket under the counter, first flipping the spoons into a smaller tray. There was no overt reason why, on indeterminate days, *Espresso Maggiore* should suddenly become crowded at four o'clock. Logically, people ought to have been working, or looking forward to supper, or walking in the park on a beautiful day like this. But, instead, they came here—all of them at almost the same time—and for half an hour, the store was crowded. Now, at a quarter of five, it was empty again, and the chairs were once more set in order against the clean tables. But it had been a busy time—so busy, with only Barbara and himself on shift, that Carlo had waited on some tables himself.

He looked at the stacks of dirty cups in the basket. There was a strong possibility, it seemed to him, that most of the customers had ordered the same thing, as well. Not capuccino, for a change, but plain espresso, and that was curious, too, as though a majority of people in the neighborhood had felt a need for a stimulant, rather than something sweet to drink.

But they all did different things—some were tavern-keepers, some were their employees, some were artists, some were idlers, some were tourists. Were there days when everyone simply grew tired, no matter what they did? Lucas frowned to himself. He tried to recall if he'd ever felt anything of the sort in himself. But one case provided no conclusive evidence. He'd have to file it away and think about it—check back when it happened again.

He let the thought drift to the back of his mind as Barbara cleaned up the last of her tables and came to the counter. She smiled ruefully, shook her head, and wiped her forehead with the back of her wrist. "Whew! Be glad when this day's over, Tedeschino?"

Lucas grinned. "Wait'll the night rush." He watched her bend to add her cups to the basket, and he blushed faintly as her uniform skirt tightened over her slight hips. He caught himself, and hastily pulled out the silverware tray to take into the small back room where the sink was.

"Night rush me no night rushes, Ted. Alice and Gloria'll be here—it won't be half as bad." Barbara winked at him. "I bet you'll be glad to see that Alice."

"Alice? Why?" Alice was an intense, sharp-faced girl who barely paid attention to her work and none at all to either the customers or the people she worked with.

Barbara put the tip of her tongue in her cheek and looked down at the floor. "Oh, I don't know," she said, pursing her lips. "But she was telling me just yesterday how much she liked you."

Lucas frowned over that. "I didn't know you and Alice talked to each other that much." It didn't sound like Alice at all. But he'd have to think about it. If it was true, it meant trouble. Getting involved with a girl where you worked never made sense—or so he'd heard, and he could plainly see the logic of it. Besides, he knew exactly what kind of girl he wanted for his present purposes. It couldn't be anybody he'd fall in love with—Alice fit that part of it well enough—but she also had to be fairly easy, because his time was limited, and she had to live far enough away so he'd never see her during the ordinary course of the day, when he'd be working or studying.

"You don't like Alice, huh?"

"What makes you say that?" He kept his eyes off Barbara's face.

"You got a look. Your eyes looked like you were thinking of something complicated, and your mouth got an expression that showed you didn't like it."

"You watch me pretty close, don't you?"

"Maybe. All right, if Alice doesn't suit, how about Gloria? Gloria's pretty."

"And not very bright." His girl would at least have to be somebody he could talk to sometimes.

"Well. You don't like Alice, you don't like Gloria—who do you like? Got a girl tucked away somewhere? Going to take her out tomorrow? Tomorrow's the big day to howl, you know. Monday."

Lucas shrugged. He knew. For the past three Mondays, he'd been cruising the city. "No. I hadn't even thought about the store being closed tomorrow, to tell you the truth."

"We got paid today, didn't we? Don't think *I* didn't know it. Mmm, boy—big date tomorrow, and everything."

Lucas felt his mouth twitch. "Steady boy?"

"Not yet. But he may be—he just may. Tell you what it is— he's the nicest fellow I ever had take me out. Smooth, good dancer, polite, and grown up. A girl doesn't meet very many fellows like that. When one comes along, she kind of gets taken up with him. But you wonder, sometimes, if you waited a little longer, maybe somebody nicer would come along—if you gave him a chance." She looked squarely at Lucas. "I guess you can imagine how it is."

"Yes—well, I guess I can." He gnawed his upper lip, looking down, and then blurted out, "I have to wash these now." He turned, carrying the silverware tray, and walked quickly into the back room. He spilled the silverware into the sink, slammed the hot water handle over, and stood staring down, his hands curled over the edge of the sink. But after a little while he felt better, even though he could not bring himself to ignore the thought of Barbara's having a steady.

By all logic, Barbara was the wrong girl.

2.

On that particular Monday, the weather held good. The sun shone down just warmly enough to make the streets comfortable, and the narrow Village sidewalks were crowded by the chairs that the old people sat on beside their front stoops, talking to each other and their old friends passing by. The younger men who did not have to go to work leaned against parked cars and sat on their fenders, and the Village girls walked by self-consciously. People brought their dogs out on the grass of Washington Square Park, and on the back streets there was laundry drying on the lines strung between fire escapes. The handball and tennis courts in the Parks Department enclosure were busy.

Lucas Martino came up to the street from his apartment a little past two-thirty, wearing a light shirt and trousers, and stepped into the midst of this life. He walked head-down to the subway station, not looking to either side, feeling restless and troubled. He hoped he'd find the right girl today, and at the same time he was nervous about how he'd approach her. He'd observed the manner in which the high school operators had handled the problem, and he was fairly confident of his ability to do as well. Furthermore, he had once or twice taken a girl to the movies, so he was not a complete novice at the particular social code that applied to girls and young men. But it was not a social partner he was looking for.

There was the matter of Barbara, as well, and it seemed that only self-discipline would be of any use there. He could not afford to become involved with any sort of long-term thing. He could not afford to leave a girl waiting while he went through all the years of training that were ahead of him. And after that, with this business in Asia last year, it looked very much as though, more than ever, any physical sciences specialist would go into government work. It meant a long time of living on a project base somewhere, with limited housing facilities and very little time for anything but work. He knew himself—once started working, he would plunge into it to the exclusion of everything else.

No, he thought, remembering his mother's look when he told her he was going to New York. No, a man with people depending on him had no choice, often, but to hurt either them or himself—and many times, both. Barbara couldn't be asked to place herself in a situation like that.

Besides, he reminded himself, that wasn't what he was looking for now. That wasn't what he needed.

He reached the subway station and took an uptown train to Columbus Circle, and not until he reached there did he raise his head and begin looking at girls.

He walked slowly into Central Park, moving in the general direction of Fifth Avenue. He walked a little self-consciously, sure that at least some of the people sitting on the benches must wonder what he was doing.

There were quite a few girls out in the park, mostly in pairs, and they paid him no attention. Most of them were walking toward the roller-skating rink, where he imagined they would have prearranged dates, or else were hoping to meet a pair of young men. He toyed with the notion of going down to the rink himself, but there was something so desperately purposeless in skating around and around in a circle to sticky organ music that he dropped the idea almost immediately. Instead, he cut up another path and skirted the bird sanctuary, without knowing what it was or what the high fence was for. When he suddenly saw a peacock step out into a glade, spreading its plumes like an unfolding dream, he stopped, entranced. He stood motionless for ten minutes before the bird walked away. Then he unhooked his fingers from the steel mesh and resumed his slow walk, still moving east.

The park was full of people in the clear sunshine. Every row of benches he passed was crowded, baby carriages jutting out into the path and small children trotting after the pigeons. Nursemaids sat talking together in white huddles, and old men read newspapers. Old women in black sat with their purses in their laps, looking out across the lake and working their empty fingers as though they were sewing.

There were a few girls out walking alone. He looked at them cautiously, out of the corners of his eyes, but there wasn't one who looked right for him. He always turned his head to the side of the path and walked by them quickly, or else he stopped and looked carefully at his wristwatch while they passed him in the other direction.

He felt that the right kind of girl for him ought to have a look about her—a way of dressing, or walking, or looking around, that would be different from most girls'. It seemed logical to him that a girl who would let strange young men speak to her in the park would have a special kind of attitude, a mark of identification that he couldn't describe but would certainly recognize. And, once or twice in his wanderings around the city, he had thought he'd found a girl like that. But when he walked closer to one of these girls, she was always chewing gum, or had thick orange lipstick, or in some other way gave him a peculiar feeling in the pit of the stomach that made him walk by her as quickly as he could without attracting attention.

Finally, he reached the zoo. He walked back and forth in front of the lion cages for a time. Then he went into the cafeteria and had a glass of milk, taking it outside and sitting at one of the tables on the terrace while he looked down at the seals in their pool. He was feeling increasingly awkward, as he usually did on one of these expeditions, and he took a long time over his milk. He looked at his watch again, and this time it was three-thirty. He had to look at his watch twice, because it seemed to him that he'd been in the park much longer than that. He lit a cigarette, smoked it down to the end, and found that this had taken only five minutes.

He stirred restlessly on the metal chair. He ought to get up and start moving around again, but he was haunted by the certainty that if he did that, his feet would carry him right out of the park and back to the downtown subway.

He ran his fingers over his forehead. He was sweating. There was a woman sitting at the next table, drinking iced tea. She was about thirty-five, he would have judged, dressed in expensive-looking clothes. She looked at him peculiarly, and he dropped his glance. He stood up, pushing his chair back with a harsh rattle of its legs on the terrace stones, and walked quickly down into the plaza where the seal tank was.

He watched the seals for a few minutes, his hands closed

over the fence rail. The thought that he was on the verge of giving the whole thing up bothered him tremendously.

He had thought this business out, after all, and come to a logical decision. He had always abided by his decisions before, and they had invariably worked out well.

It was this Barbara business, he decided. There was nothing wrong with being in love with her—there was plenty of room for illogic in his logic—but it was bound to complicate his immediate plan. Yet, it was obvious that there was nothing he could do but go ahead in spite of it. Barbara, or a girl like Barbara, would come later, when he had settled his life down. That all belonged in a different compartment of his mind, and ought not to be crossing over into this one.

It was the first time in his life that he found himself unable to do what he ought to do, and it bothered him deeply. It made him angry. He turned abruptly away from the seal tank and marched up the steps back toward the exit beyond the lion cages.

While he'd been drinking his milk, apparently, a girl had set up a camp stool in front of the cages and was sitting on it, sketching. He noticed her out of the corner of his eye, walked up to her, and without even having bothered to particularly look at her, said challengingly, "Haven't I seen you someplace before?"

3.

The girl was about his own age, with very pale blonde hair that was straight, cut close to her skull, and tapered at the back of the neck. She had high cheekbones with hollows under them, a thin nose, and a broad, full mouth which she did not lipstick to the corners. Her eyebrows were very thick and black, painted in with some gummy black cosmetic that looked like stage makeup more than eyebrow pencil. She was wearing flat ballet-ish slippers, a full printed skirt, and a peasant blouse. Her eyes were brown and a little startled.

Lucas realized that it was almost impossible to know what she really looked like, that she was probably quite plain, and, furthermore, that she was far from a girl he could even like. He saw that the sketch she was working on was completely lifeless. It was a fair enough rendering of a lioness, but it felt like a picture of something stuffed and carefully arranged in a window.

He felt angry at her for her looks, for her lack of talent, and for being there. "No, I suppose not," he said, and turned to walk away.

"You may have," the girl said. "My name's Edith Chester. What's yours?"

He stopped. Her voice was surprisingly gentle, and the very fact that she had reacted in any calm way at all was enough to make him feel like an idiot. "Luke," he said, and, for some reason, shrugged.

"Are you at the Art Students' League?" she asked.

He shook his head. "No. I'm not." He stopped, and then, just as she was opening her mouth to say something else, he blurted, "As a matter of fact, I don't know you at all. I was just—" He stopped again, feeling more foolish than ever, and getting angry again.

Surprisingly, now, she had a nervous laugh. "Well, that's all right, I guess. You're not going to bite my head off, are you?"

The association of ideas was fairly obvious. He looked down at her sketch pad and said, "That's not much of a lioness."

She looked at the drawing too, and said, "Well, no, I suppose it isn't."

He had wanted to draw a hostile reaction out of her—to start an argument he could walk away on. Now he was in deeper than ever, and he had no idea of what to do. "Look—I was going to the movies. You want to come along?"

"All right," she said, and once again he was trapped.

"I was going to see *Queen of Egypt*," he declared, picking a picture as far as possible from the taste of anyone with pretensions to intelligence.

"I haven't seen that," she said. "I wouldn't mind." She dropped her pencils into her purse, put the sketch pad under her arm, and folded the camp stool. "We can leave all this stuff at the League," she said. "Would you mind carrying the stool for me? It's only a couple of blocks from here."

He took it without a word, and the two of them walked out of the park together. As they crossed the plaza, going toward the Fifth Avenue exit, he looked over toward the terrace in front of the cafeteria, but the stylishly dressed woman who'd sat at the next table was gone.

4.

He stood in front of the League building, smoking, and waiting for the girl to come out. He didn't know what to do.

The thought of walking around the corner and taking a downtown bus had occurred to him. His hand in his pocket had already found the quarter for the farebox. But it was obvious by now that he'd picked on a girl not very many boys could be interested in, and that if he walked out on her now, he'd be hurting her badly. This whole thing wasn't her fault—he wished it was—and the only thing to do was to go through with it. So he waited for her, flipping the quarter angrily in his pocket, and in due course she came out.

By now he was feeling ashamed of himself. She came out quickly, and when she saw him, she smiled for the first time since he'd met her—a smile that transformed her face for a moment before she remembered not to show relief at his still being there. Then she dropped her eyes in quick decorum. "I'm ready."

"All right." Now he was annoyed again. She was so easy to read that he resented the lack of effort. He wanted someone with depth—someone he could come to know over a long period of time, someone whose total self could be unfolded gradually, would be always interesting and never quite completely explored. Instead, he had Edith Chester.

And yet it wasn't her fault. It was his, and he ought to be shot.

"Look—" he said, "you don't want to see that phony Egyptian thing." He nodded across the street to where one of the expensive, quality movie houses was showing a European picture. "How about going to see that, instead?"

"If you want to, I'd like that."

And she was so damned ready to follow his lead! He almost tested her by changing his mind again, but all he did was to say "Let's go, then," and start across the street. She followed him immediately, as though she hadn't expected him to wait for her.

She waited at the lobby doors as he bought the tickets, and

sat quietly beside him throughout the picture. He made no move to hold her hand or put his arm on the back of her seat, and halfway through the picture he suddenly realized that he wouldn't know what to do with her after it was over. It would be too early to take her home and thank her for the lovely evening, and yet too late to simply leave her adrift, even if he could think of some graceful way of doing it. He was tempted to simply excuse himself, get up, and walk out of the theater. Somehow, for all its clumsiness and cruelty, that seemed like the best thing to do. But he held the thought for only a few seconds before he realized he couldn't do it.

Why not? he thought. Am I such a wonderful fellow that it'd blight her life forever?

But it wasn't that. It wasn't what he was, it was what she was. He could have been the hunchback of Notre Dame and this same situation would still exist. He had put her in it, and it was up to him to see she wasn't hurt as the result of something he'd done.

But what was he going to do with her? He chain-smoked angrily through the rest of the picture, shifting back and forth in his seat.

The picture reached the scene where they'd come in, and she leaned over. "Do you want to go now?"

Her voice, after ninety minutes of silence, startled him. It was as gentle as it had been when he first spoke to her—before the realization of what was happening had quite come home to her. Now, he supposed, she'd had time to grow calm again.

"All right." He found himself reluctant to leave. Once out on the street, the awkward, inevitable "What'll we do now?" would come, and he had no answer. But he stood up and they left the theater.

Standing under the marquee, she said, "It was a good picture, wasn't it?"

He pushed the end of a cigarette into his mouth, preoccupied. "Do you have to go home now, or anything?" he mumbled around it.

She shook her head. "No, I live by myself. But you've probably got something to do tonight. I'll just catch a bus here. Thank you for taking me to the movie."

"No—no, that's all right," he said quickly. Damn it, she'd

been *expecting* him to try and get rid of her. "Don't do that."
And now he had to propose something for them to do. "Are
you hungry?"

"A little."

"All right, then, let's go find some place to eat."

"There's a very good delicatessen just around the corner."

"All right." For some reason, he took her hand. It was small,
but not fragile. She seemed neither surprised nor shocked.
Wondering what the devil had made him do that, he walked
with her down to the delicatessen.

The place was still fairly empty, and he led her to a booth in the
back. They sat down facing each other, and a waiter came and
took their orders. When he left, Lucas realized he should have
thought of what would happen when he came in here with her.

They were cut off. The high plywood back behind him separated them from the rest of the room. On one side of them
was a wall, and on the other, barely leaving people clearance to
slide in and out of the booth's far seat, was an air conditioner.
He had let himself and the girl be maneuvered into a pocket
where they had nothing to do but sit and stare at each other
while they waited for their food.

What was there to do or say? Looking at that hair-do and
the metallic pink polish on her nails, he couldn't imagine what
she could possibly talk about, or like, that he could find the
faintest interest in.

"Have you been in the city long?" he asked.

She shook her head. "No, I haven't."

That seemed to be that.

He'd thrown his cigarette away, somewhere. He knocked a
fresh one out of the pack in his shirt pocket and lit it, wishing
the waiter would hurry up so they could at least eat. He stole a
glance at his watch. It was only six o'clock.

"Could—could I have a cigarette, please?" she asked, her
voice and expression uncertain, and he jumped.

"What?" He thrust the pack out clumsily. "Oh—gee, Edith,
I'm sorry! Sure—here. I didn't . . ." Didn't what? Didn't even
offer her the courtesy of a cigarette. Didn't stop to wonder
whether she smoked or not. Treated her as if she was a pet dog.

He felt peculiarly embarrassed and guilty. Worse, now, than
ever before.

She took the cigarette and he lit it for her quickly.

She smiled a little nervously. "Thank you. I come from Connecticut, originally. Where're you from, Luke?"

She must've known how I felt about her, he was thinking. It must have been sticking out all over me. But she let me go on, because . . . Because why? Because I'm the man of her dreams?

"New Jersey," he said. "From a farm."

"I always wished I could live on a farm. Are you working here?"

Because I'm probably the first guy that's talked to her since she got here, that's why. I may not be much, but I'm all she's got.

"I am for the time being. I work for an espresso house down in the Village."

He realized he was starting to tell her things he hadn't intended to. But he had to talk, now, and besides, this wasn't what he'd planned—not at all.

"I've only been down there once or twice," she said. "It must be a fascinating place."

"I guess it is, in a way. I'm going to be starting school next year, though, and I won't be seeing much of it."

"Oh—what're you going to study, Luke?"

So it came out, bit by bit, more and more fluently. They talked while they ate, and words seemed to jump out of him. He told her about the farm, and about high school, and about the espresso house.

They finished eating and went for a walk, up Central Park South and then turning uptown, and he continued to talk. She walked beside him, her feet in their slippers making soft, padding sounds on the asphalt pavement.

After a while, it was time to take her home. She lived on the West Side, near the gas plant in the Sixties, on the third floor of a tenement. He walked her upstairs, to her door, and suddenly he was out of talk.

He stopped, as abruptly as he'd started, and stood looking down at her, wondering what the devil had gotten into him. The roots of her hair were very dark, he saw.

"I've been bending your ear," he said uncomfortably.

She shook her head. "No. No, you're a very interesting

person. I didn't mind at all. It's—" She looked up at him, and dropped even the minimum of pretense that she had managed to keep throughout the afternoon and evening. "It's nice to have somebody talk to me."

He had nothing to say to that. They stood in front of her door, and the silence grew between them.

"I had a very good time," she said at last.

No, you didn't, he thought. You had a miserable time. The worst thing that ever happened to you was when I spoke to you in front of the lion cages. And now I'm going to walk down those stairs and never call you up or see you again, and that'll be worse, I guess. I've really messed things up. "Look— have you got a phone?" he found himself saying.

She nodded quickly. "Yes, I do. Would you like the number?"

"I'll write it down." He found a piece of paper in his wallet and a pencil in his shirt pocket. He wrote the number down, put his wallet and his pencil back, and once again they simply stood there.

"Monday's my day off," he said. "I'll call you."

"All right, Luke."

He looked down at her, thinking, No, no, God damn it, I'm not going to try and kiss her good night. This isn't like that. This is a crazy thing. She's not like that.

"Good night, Edith."

"Good night, Luke."

He reached out and touched her shoulder, feeling as though he had a stupid expression on his face. She put her hand up and covered his. Then he turned away and went quickly down the stairs, feeling like a fool, and a savage, and an idiot, and like almost anything but an eighteen-year-old boy.

5.

When he went to work the next day, he was all mixed up. No matter how much he thought about it, he couldn't make sense out of what had happened yesterday. He went about his work in an abstracted daze, his mind so knotted that his face was completely blank. He avoided Barbara's eyes, and tried to keep from talking to her.

Finally, in the middle of the afternoon, she trapped him

behind the counter. He stood there hopelessly, caught between the espresso machine and the cash register, an emptied cup dangling from his hand.

Barbara smiled at him pleasantly. "Hey, there, Tedesco, thinking about your money?" There was an anxious tightness in the skin at the corners of her eyes.

"Money?"

"Well—you know. When somebody goes around in a fog, people usually ask him if he's thinking about his money."

"Oh! No—no, it's not anything like that."

"What'd you do yesterday? Fall in love?"

His face turned hot. The cup almost dropped out of his hand, as though he were an automatic machine and Barbara had struck a button. And then he was astonished at his reaction to the word. He stood gaping, completely off-stride.

"I'll be damned," Barbara said. "I hit it."

Lucas had no clear idea of what to say. Fall in love? *No!* "Look—Barbara—it's not . . . *that* way . . ."

"What way?" Her cheekbones were splotched with red.

"I don't know. I'm just trying to explain . . ."

"Look, *I* don't care what way it is. If it's giving you trouble, I hope you get it straightened out. But I've got a fellow who gives *me* troubles, now and then."

As she thought about it, she realized she was being perfectly honest. She remembered that Tommy was a very nice guy, and interesting, too. It was a shame about Lucas, because she'd always thought he'd be nice to go out with, but that was the way things worked out: you got a certain fair share of good breaks from life, and you had no right to expect things your way every time.

She was already closing down her mind to any possibility that there might have been more than a few friendly dates between them. She was a girl with a great deal of common sense, and she had learned that there was nothing to be gained in life from idle second thoughts.

"Well, rush hour's coming up," she said pointedly, got the sugar can out from under the counter, and went to refill the bowls on her tables. Her heels tapped rapidly on the wooden floor.

For a long moment, Lucas was only beginning to get his thoughts in order. The whole business had happened so fast.

He looked toward where Barbara was busy with her tables, and it was obvious to him that as far as she was concerned, the whole episode was over.

Not for him. It was barely beginning. Now it had to be analyzed—gone over, dissected, thoroughly examined for every possible reason why things had worked out this way. Only yesterday morning he had been a man with a definite course of action in mind, based on a concrete and obvious situation.

Now everything was changed, in such a short space of time, and it was unthinkable that anyone could simply leave it at that, without asking how, and why.

And yet Barbara was obviously doing just that—accepting a new state of affairs without question or investigation.

Lucas frowned at the problem. It was an interesting thing to think over.

It was even more than that, though he was at best partially aware of it. It was a perfect problem to consider if he didn't want to think about the way he felt toward Edith.

He stood behind the counter, thinking that all the people he had ever known—even people fully as quick-minded as Barbara —consistently took things as they came. And it struck him that if so many people were that way, then there must be value in it. It was actually a far simpler way of living—less wasteful of time, more efficient in its use of emotional energy, more direct.

Then, it followed that there was something inefficient and basically wrong with his whole approach to living among other people. It was no surprise he'd fallen into this emotional labyrinth with Barbara and Edith.

Now his mind had brought him back to that. How *did* he feel about Edith? He couldn't just forget about it. He'd asked for her phone number. She'd be expecting him to call. He could see her, quite plainly, waiting at night for the phone to ring. He had a responsibility there.

And Barbara. Well—Barbara was tough-fibered. But he must have hurt her at least a little bit.

But how had this whole business come about? In one day,

he'd made a mess of everything. It might be easy to simply forget it and start fresh, but could he do that? Could he let something like this stay in the back of his mind forever, unre-solved?

I'm all fouled up, he thought.

He had thought he understood himself, and had shaped himself to live most efficiently in his world. He had made plans on that basis, and seen no flaws in them. But now he had to re-learn almost everything before a new and better Lucas Martino could emerge.

For one more moment before he had to get to work, he tried to decide how he could puzzle it all out and still learn not to waste his time analyzing things that couldn't be changed. But rush hour was coming. People were already starting to trickle into the store, and his tables weren't set up yet.

He had to leave it at that, but not permanently. He pushed it to the back of his mind, where he could bring it out and worry at it when he had time—where it could stay forever, unchanging and waiting to be solved.

6.

Circumstances trapped him. Soon he was in school. There he had to learn to give precisely the answers expected of him, and no others. He learned, and there was no difficulty about the scholarship to Massachusetts Tech. But that demanded a great deal of his attention.

He saw Edith fairly often. Whenever he called her, it was al-ways with the hope that *this* time something would happen—they'd fight, or elope, or do something dramatic enough to solve things at one stroke. Their dates were always nerve-racking for that reason, and they were never casual with each other. He noticed that she gradually let her hair grow out dark brown, and that she stopped living on her parents' checks. But he had no idea of what that might mean. She found work in a store on Fourteenth Street, and moved into a nearby cold-water flat where they sometimes visited together. But he had maneuvered himself into a position where every step he made to solve one problem only made the other worse. So he wavered between them. He and Edith rarely even kissed. They never made love.

He stayed on at *Espresso Maggiore* until his studies began taking up too much of his time. He often talked to Barbara through slack times in the day. But they were just two people working in the same place and helping each other fight boredom. The only things they could talk about were the work, his studies, or what would happen to her fiancé now that the Allied Nations Government had been formed and American men might well find themselves as replacements at Australian technical installations. Never, with anyone, could he talk about anything important.

In the fall of 1968 he left New York for Boston. He had not been working since January, and had fallen out of touch with his uncle and Barbara. His relationship with Edith was such that he had nothing to write letters about. They exchanged Christmas cards for a few years.

The work at Tech was exhausting. Fifty per cent of every freshman class was not expected to graduate, and those who intended to stay found themselves with barely enough time to sleep. Lucas rarely left the campus. He went through three years of undergraduate work, and then continued toward his Master's and his Doctorate. For seven years he lived in exactly the same pocket universe.

Before he ever even got his Master's degree, he saw the beginning of the logic chain that was to end in the K-88. When he received his Doctorate, he was immediately assigned to an American government research project and lived for years on one research reservation after another, none of them substantially different from an academic campus. He was consistently deferred from military service. When he submitted his preliminary paper on the K-88 field effect, he was transferred to an identical A.N.G. installation. When his experimental results proved to be worth further work, he was given his own staff and laboratory, and, again, he was not free of schedules, routines, and restricted areas. Though he was free to think, he had only one world to grow in.

While still at M.I.T., he had been sent Edith's wedding announcement. He added the fact to the buried problem, and, with that one change, it lay carefully safeguarded by his perfect memory, waiting, through twenty years, for his first free time to think.

Chapter Nine

IT WAS almost eight o'clock at night. Rogers put down his office phone and looked over toward Finchley. "He stopped for a hamburger and coffee at a Nedick's on the corner of Eighth Street and Sixth Avenue. But he still hasn't talked to anybody, been anywhere in particular, or looked for a place to stay. He's still walking. Still wandering."

Rogers thought to himself that at least the man had eaten. Rogers and Finchley hadn't. On the other hand, the two of them were sitting down, while, with every step the man took on the concrete sidewalks, two hundred sixty-eight pounds fell on his already ruined feet. Then, why was he walking? Why didn't he stop? He'd been up since before dawn in Europe, and yet he kept going.

Finchley shook his head. "I wonder why he's doing that? What could he be after? Is he looking for somebody—hoping to run across someone?"

Rogers sighed. "Maybe he's trying to wear us out." He opened the Martino dossier in front of him, turned to the proper page, and ran his finger down the scant list of names. "Martino had exactly one relative in New York, and no close friends. There's this woman who sent him the wedding announcement. He seems to have gone with her for a while, while he was at C.C.N.Y. Maybe that's a possibility."

"You're saying this man might be Martino."

"I'm saying no such thing. He hasn't made a move toward her place, and it's no more than five blocks outside the area he's been covering. If anything, I'm saying he's not Martino."

"Would you want to visit an old girl friend that's been married fifteen years?"

"Maybe."

"It doesn't prove anything one way or another."

"I believe that's what we've been saying right along."

Finchley's mouth quirked. His eyes were expressionless. "What about that relative?"

"His uncle? Martino used to work in his coffee house, right down in that area. The coffee house is a barbershop now. The uncle married a widow when he was sixty-three, moved to California with her, and died ten years ago. So that cleans it up. Martino didn't make friends, and had no relatives. He wasn't a joiner, and he didn't keep a diary. If there was ever anyone made for this kind of thing, Martino's the one." Rogers clawed at his scalp.

"And yet," Finchley said, "he came straight to New York, and straight down into the Village. He must have had a reason. But, whatever it was, all he's doing is walking. Around and around. In circles. It doesn't tie in. It doesn't make sense—not for a man of this caliber." Finchley's voice was troubled, and Rogers, remembering the episode between them earlier in the afternoon, gave him a sharp look. Rogers was still ashamed of his part in it, and didn't care to have it revived.

He picked up his phone. "I'll order some food sent up."

2.

The drugstore on the corner of Sixth Avenue and West Seventh Street was small, with one narrow, twisting space of clear floor between the crowded counters. Like all small druggists, the owner had been forced to nail uprights to the counters and put shelves between them. Even so, there was barely room to display everything he had to carry in competition with the chain store up the street.

Salesmen had piled their display racks on every inch of eye-level surface, and tacked their advertising cards wherever they could. There was only one overhead cluster of fluorescent tubes, and the tight space behind the counters was always dark. There was one break in the wall of merchandise on the counters. There, behind an opening walled by two stands of cosmetics and roofed by a razor-blade card, the druggist sat behind his cash register, reading a newspaper.

He looked up as he heard the door open and close. His eyes went automatically to the metal side of the display case across from him, which he used for a mirror. The case was scuffed, and a little dirty. The druggist saw the vague outlines of a man's large silhouette, but the creaking of the floorboards had already told him as much. He peered for a look at the face, and brought one hand up to the temple bar of his glasses. He got out of his chair, still holding his paper in his other hand, and thrust his head and shoulders out over the counter.

"Something I can do for—"

The man who'd come in turned his glittering face toward him. "Where're your telephone books, please?" he asked quietly.

The druggist had no idea of what he might have done in another minute. But the matter-of-fact words gave him an easy response. "Back through there," he said, pointing to a narrow opening between two counters.

"Thank you." The man squeezed himself through, and the druggist heard him turning pages. There was a faint rustle as he pulled a sheet out of the telephone company's notepaper dispenser. The druggist heard him take out a pencil with a faint click of its clip. Then the telephone book thudded back into its slot, and the man came out, folding the note and putting it in his breast pocket. "Thank you very much," he said. "Good night."

"Good night," the druggist answered.

The man left the store. The druggist sat back on his chair, folding the paper on his knee.

It was a peculiar thing, the druggist thought, looking blankly down at his paper. But the man hadn't seemed to be conscious of anything peculiar about himself. He hadn't offered any explanations; he hadn't done anything except ask a perfectly reasonable question. People came in here twenty times a day and asked the same thing.

So it couldn't really be anything worth getting excited about. Well—yes, of course it was, but the metal-headed man hadn't seemed to think so. And it would be his business, wouldn't it?

The druggist decided that it was something to think about, and to mention to his wife when he got home. But it wasn't anything to be panicked by.

In a very brief space of time, his eyes were automatically following print. Soon he was reading again. When Rogers' man came in a minute later, that was the way he found him.

Rogers' man was one of a team of two. His partner had stayed with their man, following him up the street.

He looked around the drugstore. "Anybody here?"

The druggist's head and shoulders came into sight behind the counter. "Yes, mister?"

The Security man fished in his pocket. "Got a pack of Chesterfields?"

The druggist nodded and slipped the cigarettes out of the rack behind the counter. He picked up the half dollar the Security man put down.

"Say," the Security man said with a puzzled frown, "did I just see a guy wearing a tin mask walk out of here?"

The druggist nodded. "That's right. It didn't seem to be a mask, though."

"I'll be damned. I *thought* I saw this fellow, but it's kind of a hard thing to believe."

"That's what happened."

The Security man shook his head. "Well, I guess you see all kinds of people in this part of town. You figure he was dressed up to advertise a play, or something?"

"Don't ask me. He wasn't carrying a sign or anything."

"What'd he do—buy a can of metal polish?" The Security man grinned.

"Just looked in a phone book, that's all. Didn't even make a call." The druggist scratched his head. "I guess he was just looking up an address."

"Boy, I wonder who *he's* visiting! Well"—and he shrugged— "you sure do run into funny people down here."

"Oh, I don't know," the druggist said a little testily, "I've seen some crazy-looking things in other parts of town, too."

"Yeah, sure. I guess so. Say—speakin' of phones, I guess I might as well call this girl. Where's it at?"

"Back there," the druggist said, pointing.

"O.K., thanks." The Security man pushed through the space between the two counters. He stood looking sourly down at the stand of phone books. He pulled the top sheet out of the note dispenser, looked at it for impressions, and saw none that made any sense. He slipped the paper into his pocket, looked at the books again—six of them, counting the Manhattan

Classified—and shook his head. Then he stepped into the booth, dropped coins into the slot, and dialed Rogers' office.

3.

The clock on Rogers' desk read a few minutes past nine. Rogers still sat behind his desk, and Finchley waited in the chair beside it.

Rogers felt tired. He'd been up some twenty-two hours, and the fact that Finchley and their man had done the same was no help.

It's piled up on me, he thought. Day after day without enough sleep, and tension all the time. I should have been in bed hours ago.

But Finchley had gone through it all with him. And their man must feel infinitely worse. And what was a little lost sleep compared to what the man had lost? Still Rogers was feeling sick to his stomach. His eyes were burning. His scalp was numb with exhaustion, and he had a vile taste in his mouth. He wondered if his sticking to the job was made any the less because Finchley was younger and could take it, or because the metal-faced man was still following his ghost up and down the city streets. He decided it was.

"I hate to ask you to stay here so late, Finch," he said.

Finchley shrugged. "That's the job, isn't it?" He picked up the piece of Danish pastry left over from supper, swirled his cold half-container of old coffee, and took a swallow. "I've got to admit I hope this doesn't happen every night. But I can't understand what he's doing."

Rogers toyed with the blotter on his desk, pushing it back and forth with his fingertips. "We ought to be getting another report fairly soon. Maybe he's done something."

"Maybe he's going to sleep in the park."

"The city police'll pick him up if he tries to."

"What about that? What's the procedure if he's arrested for a civil crime?"

"One more complication." Rogers shook his head hopelessly, drugged by fatigue. "I briefed the Commissioner's office, and we've got cooperation on the administrative level. It'd be a poor move to issue a general order for all patrolmen to leave him alone. Somebody'd let it slip. The theory is that beat patrolmen will call in to their precinct houses if they spot a metal-headed man. The precinct captains have instructions that he's to be left alone. But if a patrolman arrests him for vagrancy before he calls in, then all kinds of things could go wrong. It'll be straightened out in a hurry, but it might get on record somewhere. Then, a few years from now, somebody doing a book or something might come across the record, and that'll be that. We can't keep the publishers bottled up forever." Rogers sighed. "I only hope it'd be a few years from now." He looked down at his desktop. "It's a mess. This world was never organized to include a faceless man."

It's true, he thought. Just by being alive, he's made me stumble from the very start. Look at us all—Security, the whole A.N.G.—handcuffed because we couldn't simply shoot him and get him out of the way. Going around in circles, trying to find an answer. And he hasn't yet *done* anything.

For some reason, Rogers found himself thinking, "Commit a crime and the world is made of glass." Emerson. Rogers grunted.

The telephone rang.

He picked it up and listened.

"All right," he said finally, "get back to your partner. I'll have somebody intercept and pick that paper up from you. Call in when your man gets to wherever he's going." He hung up. "He's made a move," he told Finchley. "He looked up an address in a phone book."

"Any idea of whose?"

"I'm not sure . . ." Rogers flipped the Martino dossier open.

"The girl," Finchley said. "The one he used to know."

"Maybe. If he thinks they're still close enough for her to do him any good. Why did he have to look up the address? It's the same as the one on the wedding announcement."

"It's been fifteen years, Shawn. He could have forgotten it."

"He may never have known it." And there was no guarantee the man was going to the address he'd copied. He might have looked it up for some future purpose. They couldn't take chances. Everything had to be covered. The phone books had to be examined. There might be some mark—some oily fingerprint, wet with perspiration, some pencil mark; some trace—

Six New York City phone books. God knew how many pages, each to be checked.

"Finch, your people'll have to furnish a current set of New York phone books. Worn ones. We're going to switch 'em for a set I want to run through your labs. Got to have 'em right away."

Finchley nodded and reached for the phone.

4.

A travel-worn young man, lugging a scuffed cardboard suitcase, came into the drugstore on the corner of Sixth Avenue and West Seventh Street.

"Like to make a phone call," he said to the druggist. "Where is it?"

The druggist told him, and the young man just managed to get his suitcase through the narrow gap between the counters. He bumped it about clumsily for a few moments, and shifted it back and forth, annoying the druggist at his cash register, while he made his call.

When he left, the druggist's original books went to the F.B.I. laboratory, where the top sheet of notepaper had already checked out useless.

The Manhattan book was run through first, on the assumption that it was the likeliest. The technicians did not work page by page. They had a book with all Manhattan phones listed by subscribers' addresses, and they laid out a square search pattern centering on the drugstore. An IBM machine arranged the nearest subscribers' addresses in alphabetical order, and then the technicians began to work on the book taken from the store, using their new list to skip whole columns of numbers that had a low probability under this system.

Rogers hadn't supplied the technicians with Edith Chester's name. It would have done no good. By the time the results came through, the man would have reached there. If that was where he was going. Furthermore, there was no proof he'd only looked up one address. Eventually, all six books would be checked out, and probably show nothing. But the check would be made, and no one knew how many others afterward.

Commit a crime and the world is made of glass.

5.

Edith Chester Hayes lived in the back apartment on the second floor of a house off Sullivan Street. The soot of eighty years had settled into every brick, and industrial fumes had gnawed the paint into flakes. A narrow doorway opened into the street, and a dim yellow bulb glowed in the foyer. Battered garbage cans stood in front of the ground floor windows.

Rogers looked out at it from his seat in an F.B.I. special car. "You always expect them to have torn these places down," he said.

"They do," Finchley answered. "But other houses grow old faster than these get condemned." His voice was distracted as though he were thinking of something else, and thinking of it so intently that he barely heard what he was saying. He hunched in his corner of the back seat, his hand slowly rubbing the side of his face. He paid no attention when one of the A.N.G. team that had followed the man here came up to the car and leaned in Rogers' window.

"He's upstairs, on the second floor landing, Mr. Rogers," the man said. "He's been there for fifteen minutes, ever since we got here. He hasn't knocked on any door. He's just up there, leaning against a wall."

"Didn't he even ring a doorbell?" Rogers asked. "How'd he get into the building?"

"They never lock the front doors in these places, Mr. Rogers. Anybody can get into the halls any time they want to."

"Well, how long can he stay up there? Some tenant's bound to come along and see him. That'll start a fuss. And what's the point of his just staying in the hall?"

"I couldn't say, Mr. Rogers. Nothing he's done all day makes sense. But he's got to make a move pretty soon, even if it's just coming back down and starting this walking around business again."

Rogers leaned over the front seat and tapped the shoulder of the F.B.I. technician, wearing headphones, who was bent over a small receiving set. "What's going on?"

The technician slipped one phone. "All I'm getting is breathing. And he's shuffling his feet once in a while."

"Will you be able to follow him if he moves?"

"If he stays in a narrow hall, or stands near a wall in a room, yes, sir. These induction microphones're pretty sensitive, and I've got it flat against a riser halfway up the first floor stairs. I can move it in behind him, if he goes into an apartment."

"Won't he see it?"

"Probably not unless it's in motion when he looks. And we can tell if anyone's facing toward it by the volume of the sounds they make. It looks just like a matchbook, and it's got little sticky plastic treads it crawls on. It doesn't make any noise, and the wires it trails are only hairlines. We've never had any trouble with one of these gadgets."

"I see. Let me know if he does anyth—"

"He's moving." The technician snapped a switch, and Rogers heard the sound of heavy footsteps on the sagging hall floorboards. Then the man knocked softly on a door, his knuckles barely rapping the wood before he stopped.

"I'm going to get a little closer," the technician said. They heard the microphone scrape quietly up the stairs. Then the speaker was full of the man's heavy breathing.

"What's he upset about?" Rogers wondered.

They heard the man knock hesitantly again. His feet moved nervously.

Someone was coming toward the door. They heard it open, and then heard a gasp of indrawn breath. There was no way of telling whether their man had made the sound or not.

"Yes?" It was a woman, taken by surprise.

"Edith?" The man's voice was low and abashed.

Finchley straightened out of his slump. "That's it—that explains it. He spent all day working up his nerve."

"Nerve for what? Proves nothing," Rogers growled.

"I'm Edith Hayes," the woman's voice said cautiously.

"Edith—I'm Luke. Lucas Martino."

"Luke!"

"I was in an accident, Edith. I just left the hospital a few weeks ago. I've been retired."

Rogers grunted. "Got his story all straight, hasn't he?"

"He's had all day to think of how to put it," Finchley said. "What do you expect him to do? Tell her the history of twenty years while he stands in her doorway?"

"Maybe."

"For Pete's sake, Shawn, if this isn't Martino how'd he know about her?"

"I can think of lots of ways Azarin could get this kind of detail out of a man."

"It's not likely."

"Nothing's likely. It's not likely any one particular germ cell would grow up to be Lucas Martino. I've got to remember Azarin's a thorough man."

"Edith—" the man's voice said, "may—may I come in for a moment?"

The woman hesitated for a second. Then she said, "Yes, of course."

The man sighed. "Thank you."

He stepped into the apartment and the door closed. The F.B.I. technician moved the microphone forward and jammed it tightly against the panels.

"Sit down, Luke."

"Thank you." They sat in silence for a few moments. "You have a very nice-looking apartment, Edith. It's been fixed up very comfortably."

"Sam—my husband—liked to work with his hands," the woman said awkwardly. "He did it. He spent a long time over it. He's dead now. He fell from a building he was working on."

There was another pause. The man said, "I'm sorry I was never able to come down and see you after I left college."

"I think you and Sam would have liked each other. He was a good deal like you, orderly."

"I didn't think I ever showed much of that with you."

"I could see it."

The man cleared his throat nervously. "You're looking very well, Edith. Have you been getting along all right?"

"I'm fine. I work. Susan stays at a friend's house after school until I pick her up on my way home at night."

"I didn't know you had children."

"Susan's eleven. She's a very bright little girl. I'm quite proud of her."

"Is she asleep now?"

"Oh, yes—it's well past her bedtime."

"I'm sorry I came so late. I'll keep my voice down."

"I wasn't hinting, Luke."

"I—I know. But it is late. I'll be going in a minute."

"You don't have to rush. I never go to bed before midnight."

"But I'm sure you have things to do—clothes to iron, Susan's lunch to pack."

"That only takes a few minutes. Luke—" Now the woman seemed steadier. "We were always so uncomfortable around each other. Let's not keep to that old habit."

"I'm sorry. Edith. You're right. But—do you know, I couldn't even call you and ask if I could come see you? I tried, and I found myself imagining you'd refuse to see me. I spent all day nerving myself to do this." The man was still uncomfortable. And as far as anyone listening could tell, he hadn't yet taken off his coat.

"What's the matter, Luke?"

"It's complicated. When I was in their—in the—hospital, I spent a long time thinking about us. Not as lovers, you understand, but as people—as friends. We never knew each other at all, did we? At least, I never knew you. I was too wrapped up in what I was doing and wanted to do. I never paid any real attention to you. I thought of you as a problem, not as a person. And I think I'm here tonight to apologize for that."

"Luke—" The woman's voice started and stopped. She moved in her creaking chair. "Would you like a cup of coffee?"

"I know I'm embarrassing you, Edith. I would have liked to handle this more gracefully. But I don't have much time. And it's almost impossible to be graceful when I have to come here looking like this."

"That's not important," she said quickly. "And it doesn't matter what you look like, as long as I know it's you. *Would* you like some coffee?"

The man's voice was troubled. "All right, Edith. Thank you. We can't seem to stop being strangers, somehow, can we?"

"What makes you say that— No. You're right. I'm trying

very hard, but I can't even fool myself. I'll start the water boiling." Her footsteps, quick and erratic, faded into the kitchen.

The man sighed, sitting by himself in the living room.

"Well, *now* do you think?" Finchley demanded. "Does that sound like Secret Operative X-Eight hatching a plan to blow up Geneva?"

"It sounds like a high school boy," Rogers answered.

"He's lived behind walls all his life. They all sound like this. They know enough to split the world open like a rotten orange, and they've been allowed to mature to the age of sixteen."

"We aren't here to set up new rules for handling scientists. We're here to find out if this man's Lucas Martino."

"And we've found out."

"We've found out, maybe, that a clever man can take a few bits of specific information, add what he's learned about some kinds of people being a great deal alike, talk generalities, and fool a woman who hasn't seen the original in twenty years."

"You sound like a man backing into the last ditch with a lost argument."

"Never mind what *I* sound like."

"Just what do you suppose he's doing this for, if he isn't Martino?"

"A place to stay. Someone to run errands for him while he stays under cover. A base of operations."

"Jesus Christ, man, don't you *ever* give up?"

"Finch, I'm dealing with a man who's smarter than I am."

"Maybe a man with deeper emotions, too."

"You think so?"

"No. No—sorry, Shawn."

The woman's footsteps came back from the kitchen. She seemed to have used the time to gather herself. Her voice was firmer when she spoke once more.

"Lucas, is this your first day in New York?"

"Yes."

"And the first thing you thought of was to come here. Why?"

"I'm not sure," the man said, sounding more as if he didn't want to answer her. "I told you I thought a great deal about us. Perhaps it became an obsession with me. I don't know. I shouldn't have done it, I suppose."

"Why not? I must be the only person you know in New York, by now. You've been badly hurt, and you want someone to talk to. Why shouldn't you have come here?"

"I don't know." The man sounded helpless. "They're going to investigate you now, you know. They'll scrape through your past to find out where I belong. I hope you won't feel bad about that—I wouldn't have done it if I thought they'd find something to hurt you. I thought about it. But that wouldn't have stopped me from coming. That didn't seem as important as something else."

"As what, Lucas?"

"I don't know."

"Were you afraid I'd hate you? For what? For the way you look?"

"No! I don't think that little of you. You haven't even stared at me, or asked sneaking questions. And I knew you wouldn't."

"Then—" The woman's voice was gentle, and calm, as though nothing could shake her for long. "Then, did you think I'd hate you because you broke my heart?"

The man didn't answer.

"I was in love with you," the woman said. "If you thought I was, you were right. And when nothing ever came of it, you hurt me."

Down in the car, Rogers grimaced with discomfort. The F.B.I. technician turned his head briefly. "Don't let this kind of stuff throw you, Mr. Rogers," he said. "We hear it all the time. It bothered me when I started, too. But after a while you come to realize that people shouldn't be ashamed to have this kind of thing listened to. It's honest, isn't it? It's what people talk about all over the world. They're not ashamed when they say it to each other, so you shouldn't feel funny about listening."

"All right," Finchley said, "then suppose we all shut up and listen."

"That's O.K., Mr. Finchley," the technician said. "It's all going down on tape. We can play it back as often as we want to." He turned back to his instruments. "Besides, the man hasn't answered her yet. He's still thinking it over."

"I'm sorry, Edith."

"You've already apologized once tonight, Lucas." The woman's chair scraped as she stood up. "I don't want to see you crawling. I don't want you to feel you have to. I don't hate you—I never did. I loved you. I had found somebody to come alive to. When I met Sam, I knew how."

"If you feel that way, Edith, I'm very glad for you."

Her voice had a rueful smile in it. "I didn't always feel that way about it. But you can do a great deal of thinking in twenty years."

"Yes, you can."

"It's odd. When you play the past over and over in your head, you can begin to see things in it that you missed when you were living it. You come to realize that there were moments when one word said differently, or one thing done at just the right time, would have changed everything."

"That's true."

"Of course, you have to remind yourself that you might be seeing things that were never there. You might be maneuvering your memories to bring them into line with what you'd want them to be. You can't be sure you're not just daydreaming."

"I suppose so."

"A memory can be that way. It can become a perfect thing. The people in it become the people you'd like best, and never grow old—never change, never live twenty years away from you that turn them into somebody you can't recognize. The people in a memory are always just as you want them, and you can always go back to them and start exactly where you stopped, except that now you know where the mistakes were, and what should have been done. No friend is as good as the friend in a memory. No love is quite as wonderful."

"Yes."

"The—the water's boiling in the kitchen. I'll bring the coffee."

"All right."

"You're still wearing your coat, Lucas."

"I'll take it off."

"I'll be right back."

Rogers looked at Finchley. "What do you suppose she's leading up to?"

Finchley shook his head.

The woman came back from the kitchen. There was a clink

of cups. "I remembered not to put any cream or sugar in yours, Lucas."

The man hesitated. "That's very good of you, Edith. But—As a matter of fact, I can't stand it black any more. I'm sorry."

"For what? For changing? Here—let me take that in the kitchen and do it right."

"Just a little cream, please, Edith. And two spoons of sugar."

Finchley asked, "What do we know about Martino's recent coffee-drinking habits?"

"They can be checked," Rogers answered.

"We'll have to be sure and do that."

The woman brought the man's coffee. "I hope this is all right, Lucas."

"It's very good. I—I hope it doesn't upset you to watch me drink."

"Should it? I have no trouble remembering you, Luke."

They sat quietly for a few moments. Then the woman asked, "Are you feeling better now?"

"Better?"

"You hadn't relaxed at all. You were as tense as you were that day you first spoke to me. In the zoo."

"I can't help it, Edith."

"I know. You came here hoping for something, but you can't even put it in words to yourself. You were always that way, Luke."

"I've come to realize that," the man said with a strained chuckle.

"Does laughing at it help you any, Luke?"

His voice fell again. "I'm not sure."

"Luke, if you want to go back to where we stopped, and begin it again, it's all right with me."

"Edith?"

"If you want to court me."

The man was deathly quiet for a moment. Then he heaved to his feet with a twang of the chair springs. "Edith—*look* at me. Think of the men that'll follow you and me until I die. And I am going to die. Not soon, but you'd be alone again just when people depend on each other most. I can't work. I couldn't even ask you to go anywhere with me. I can't do that, Edith. That's not what I came here for."

"Isn't it what you thought of when you were lying in the hospital? Didn't you think of all these things against it, and still hope?"

"Edith—"

"Nothing could ever have come of it, the first time. And I loved Sam when I met him, and was happy to be his wife. But it's a different time, now, and I've been remembering, too."

In the car, Finchley muttered softly and with savage intensity, "Don't mess it up, man. Don't foul up. Do it right. Take your chance." Then he realized Rogers was looking at him and went abruptly quiet.

In the apartment, all the man's tension exploded out of his throat. "I *can't* do it!"

"You can if I want you to," the woman said gently.

The man sighed for one last time, and Rogers could see him in his mind's eye—the straight, set shoulders loosening a little, the fingers uncurling; the man standing there and opening the clenched fist of himself. Martino or not, traitor or spy, the man had won—or found—a haven.

A door opened inside the apartment. A child's voice said sleepily, "Mommy—I woke up. I heard a man talking. *Mommy —what's that?*"

The woman caught her breath. "This is Luke, Susan," she said quickly. "He's an old friend of mine, and he just came back to town. I was going to tell you about him in the morning." She crossed the room and her voice was lower, as if she were holding the child and speaking softly. But she was still talking very rapidly. "Lucas is a very nice man, honey. He's been in an accident—a very bad accident—and the doctor had to do that to cure him. But it's not anything important."

"He's just standing there, Mommy. He's *looking* at me!"

The man made a sound in his throat.

"Don't be afraid of me, Susan—I won't hurt you. Really, I won't." The floor thudded to his weight as he moved clumsily toward the child. "See? I'm really a very funny man. Look at me blink my eyes. See all the colors they turn? Aren't they funny?" He was breathing loudly. It was a continuous, unearthly noise in the microphone. "Now, you're not afraid of me, are you?"

"Yes! Yes, I am. Get away from me! Mommy, Mommy, don't let him!"

"But he's a nice man, Susan. He wants to be your friend."

"I can do other tricks, Susan. See? See my hand spin? Isn't that a funny trick? See me close my eyes?" The man's voice was urgent, now, and trembling under the nervous joviality.

"I don't like you! I don't like you! If you're a nice man, why don't you smile?"

They heard the man step back.

The woman said clumsily, "He's smiling inside, honey," but the man was saying "I'd—I'd better go, Edith. I'll only upset her more if I stay."

"Please—Luke—"

"I'll come back some other time. I'll call you." He fumbled at the door latches.

"Luke—oh, here's your coat—Luke, I'll talk to her. I'll explain. She just woke up—she may have been having a nightmare. . . ." Her voice trailed away.

"Yes." He opened the door, and the F.B.I. technician barely remembered to pull his microphone away.

"You *will* come back?"

"Of course, Edith." He hesitated. "I'll be in touch with you."

"Luke—"

The man was on the stairs, coming down quickly. The crash of his footsteps was loud, then fading as he passed the microphone blindly. Rogers signaled frantically from the car, and the two waiting A.N.G. men began walking briskly in opposite directions away from the building. The man came out, tugging his hat onto his head. As he walked, his footsteps quickened. He turned up his coat collar. He was almost running. He passed one of the A.N.G. men, and the other cut quickly around a corner, circling the block to fall in with his partner.

The man disappeared into the night, with the surveillance team trying to keep up behind him.

The microphone, left on the stairs, was still listening.

"Mommy—Mommy—who's Lucas?"

The woman's voice was very low. "It doesn't matter, honey. Not any more."

6.

"All right," Rogers said harshly, "let's get going before he gets away from us." He braced himself as the technician yanked his microphone back on its spring reel, thumbed the starter, and lurched the car forward.

Rogers was busy on his own radio, dispatching cover teams to cross the man's path and pick up the surveillance before he could outwalk the team behind him. Finchley had nothing to say as the car moved up the street. His face, as they passed under a light, was haggard.

The car rolled past the nearest A.N.G. man. He looked upset, trying to walk fast enough to keep the hurrying man in sight and still not walk so fast as to attract attention. He threw a quick glance toward the car. His mouth was set, and his nostrils were flared.

Their headlights touched the bulky figure of their man. He was taking short, quick steps, his shoulders hunched and his hands in his pockets. He kept his face down.

"Where's he going now?" Rogers said unnecessarily. He didn't need Finchley to tell him.

"I don't think he knows," Finchley said.

In the darkness, the man was walking uptown on Mac-Dougal Street. The lights of the coffee shops above Bleecker lay waiting for him. He saw them and turned abruptly toward an alley.

A girl had come down the steps of the house beside him, and he brushed by her. He stopped, suddenly, and turned. He raised his head, his mouth falling open. He was frozen in a pantomime of surprise. He said something. The car lights splashed against his face.

The girl screamed. Her throat opened and she clapped her hands to her eyes. The hideous sound she made was trapped in the narrow street.

The man began to run. He swerved into the alley, and even in the car, the sound of his feet was like someone pounding on a hollow box. The girl stood quiet now, bent forward, holding herself as though she were embarrassed.

"Get after him!" Rogers, in turn, was startled by the note his voice had struck. He dug his hands into the back of the front seat as the driver yanked the car into the alley.

The man was running well ahead of them. Their headlights shone on the back of his neck, and the glare of reflected light winked in the rippling shadows thrown by the flapping skirt of his trailing coat. He was running clumsily, like an exhausted man, and yet he was moving at fantastic speed.

"My God!" Finchley said. "Look at him!"

"No human being can run like that," Rogers said. "He doesn't have to drive his lungs. He won't feel oxygen starvation as much. He'll push himself as fast as his heart can stand."

"Or faster."

The man threw himself against a wall, breaking his momentum. He thrust himself away, down a cross street, headed back downtown.

"*Come* on!" Rogers barked at the driver. "Goose this hack."

They screamed around the corner. The man was still far ahead, running without looking back. The street was lined with loading platforms at the backs of warehouses. There were no house lights, and street lamps only at the corners. A row of traffic lights stretched down toward Canal Street, changing from green to red in a pre-set rhythm that rippled along the length of the street in waves. The man careered down among them like something flapping, driven by a giant wind.

"Jesus, Jesus, Jesus!" Finchley muttered urgently. "He'll kill himself."

The driver jammed speed into the car, flinging them over the truck-broken street. The man was already well past the next corner. Now he turned his head back for an instant and saw them. He threw himself forward even faster, came to a cross street, and flailed around the corner, running toward Sixth Avenue now.

"That's a one-way street against us!" the driver yelled.

"Take it anyway, you idiot!" Finchley shouted back, and the car plunged west with the driver working frantically at the wheel. "Now, *catch* him!" Finchley raged. "We can't let him run to death!"

The street was lined with cars parked at the crowded curbs.

The clear space was just wide enough for a single car to squeeze through, and somewhere a few blocks ahead of them another set of headlights was coming toward them, growing closer.

The man was running desperately now. As the car began to catch him, Rogers could see his head turning from side to side, looking for some narrow alleyway between buildings, or some escape of any kind.

When they pulled even with him, Finchley cranked his window down. "Martino! Stop! It's all right. Stop!"

The man turned his head, looked, and suddenly reversed his stride, squeezing between two parked cars with a rip of his coat and running across the street behind them.

The driver locked his brakes and threw the gear lever into reverse. The transmission broke up, but it held the driveshaft rigid. The car slid on motionless wheels, leaving a plume of smoke upon the street, the tires bursting into flame. Rogers' face snapped forward into the seat back, and his teeth clicked together. Finchley tore his door open and jumped out.

"Martino!"

The man had reached the opposite sidewalk. Still running west, he did not stop or look behind. Finchley began to run along the street.

As Rogers cleared the doorway on his side, he saw the oncoming car just on the other side of the next street, no more than sixty feet away.

"Finch! Get off the street!"

Their man had reached the corner. Finchley was almost there, still in the street, not daring to waste time and fight his way between the bumper-to-bumper parked cars.

"Martino! Stop! You can't keep it up—Martino—you'll die!"

The oncoming car saw them and twisted frantically into the cross street. But another car came around the corner from MacDougal and caught Finchley with its pointed fender. It spun him violently away, his chest already crumpled, and threw him against the side of a parked car.

For one second, everything stopped. The car with the crushed fender stood rocking at the mouth of the street. Rogers kept one hand on the side of the F.B.I. car, the stench of burnt rubber swirling around him.

Then Rogers heard the man, far down a street, still running, and wondered if the man had really understood anything he'd heard since the girl screamed at him.

"Call in," he snapped to the F.B.I. driver. "Tell your headquarters to get in touch with my people. Tell them which way he's going, and to pick up the tail on him." Then he ran across the street to Finchley, who was dead.

7.

The hotel on Bleecker Street had a desk on the ground floor and narrow stairs going up to the rooms. The entrance was a narrow doorway between two stores. The clerk sat behind his desk, his chair tipped back against the stairs, and sleepily drooped his chin on his chest. He was an old, worn-out man with gray stubble on his face, and he was waiting for morning so he could go to bed.

The front door opened. The clerk did not look up. If somebody wanted a room, they'd come to him. When he heard the shuffling footsteps come to a stop in front of him, he opened his eyes.

The clerk was used to seeing cripples. The rooms upstairs were full of one kind or another. And the clerk was used to seeing new things all the time. When he was younger, he'd followed things in the paper. It had been no surprise to him when the Third Avenue El was torn down, or cars came out with four headlights. But now that he was older, things just drifted by him. So he never was surprised at anything he hadn't seen before. If doctors were putting metal heads on people, it wasn't much different from the aluminum artificial legs that often stumped up and down the stairs behind him.

The man in front of the desk was trying to talk to him. But for a long while, the only sound he made was a series of long, hollow, sucking sounds as air rushed into his mouth. He held onto the front edge of the desk for a moment. He touched the left side of his chest. Finally he said, laboring over the words, "How much for a room?"

"Five bucks," the clerk said, reaching behind him for a key. "Cash in advance."

The man fumbled with a wallet, took out a bill, and dropped

it on the desk. He did not look directly at the clerk, and seemed to be trying to hide his face.

"Room number's on the key," the clerk said, putting the money in the slot of a steel box bolted through the floor.

The man nodded quickly. "All right." He gestured self-consciously toward his face. "I had an accident," he said. "An industrial accident. An explosion."

"Buddy," the clerk said, "I don't give a damn. No drinking in your room and be out by eight o'clock, or it's another five bucks."

8.

It was almost nine o'clock in the morning. Rogers sat in his cold, blank office, listening to the telephone ring. After a time, he picked it up.

"Rogers."

"This is Avery, sir. The subject is still in the hotel on Bleecker. He came down a little before eight, paid another day's rent, and went back to his room."

"Thank you. Stay on it."

He pushed the receiver back on the cradle and bent until his face was almost touching the desk. He clasped his hands behind his neck.

The interoffice buzzer made him straighten up again. He moved the switch over. "Yes?"

"We have Miss DiFillipo here, sir."

"Would you send her in, please."

He waited until the girl came in, and then let his hand fall away from the switch. "Come in, please. Here's—here's a chair for you."

Angela DiFillipo was an attractive young brunette, a trifle on the thin side. Rogers judged her to be about eighteen. She came in confidently, and sat down without any trace of nervousness. Rogers imagined that in ordinary circumstances she was a calm, self-assured type, largely lacking in the little guilts that made even the most harmless people turn a bit nervous in this building.

"I'm Shawn Rogers," he said, putting on a smile and holding out his hand.

She shook it firmly, almost mannishly, and smiled back without giving him the feeling that she was trying to make an impression on him. "Hello."

"I know you have to get to work, so I won't keep you here long." He turned the recorder on. "I'd just like to ask you a few questions about last night."

"I'll be glad to help out."

"Thank you. Now—your name is Angela DiFillipo, and you live at thirty-three MacDougal Street, here in New York, is that right?"

"Yes."

"Last night—that would be the twelfth—at about ten-thirty P.M., you were at the corner of MacDougal and an alley between Bleecker and Houston Streets. Is that correct?"

"Yes."

"Would you tell me how you got there and what happened?"

"Well, I'd just left the house to go to the delicatessen for some milk. The alley's right next to the door. I didn't particularly notice anybody, but I did know somebody was coming up MacDougal, because I could hear his footsteps."

"Coming toward Bleecker? On the west side of the street?"

"Yes."

"Go on, Miss DiFillipo. I may interrupt you again, to clarify the record, but you're doing fine." And the record's piling up, he thought. For all the good it does.

"Well, I knew somebody was coming, but I didn't take any special notice of it, of course. I noticed he was walking fast. Then he changed direction, as if he was going to go into the alley. I looked at him then, because I wanted to get out of his way. There was a streetlight behind him, so all I could see was that it was a man—a big man—but I couldn't see his face. From the way he was walking, I didn't think he saw me at all. He was headed straight for me, though, and I guess I got a little tensed up.

"Anyhow, I took a short step back, and he just brushed my sleeve. That made him look up, and I saw there was something odd about his face."

"How do you mean 'odd,' Miss DiFillipo?"

"Just odd. I didn't see what it was, then. But I got the feeling it had something wrong with it. And I guess that made me a little bit more nervous."

"I see."

"Then I saw his face. He stopped, and he opened his mouth —well, his face was metal, like one of those robot things in the Sunday paper, and it was where a mouth would be—and he looked surprised. And he said, in a very peculiar voice, 'Barbara—it's I—the German.'"

Rogers leaned forward in surprise. "Barbara—it's I—the German? Are you sure of that?"

"Yes, sir. He sounded very surprised, and—"

"What is it, Miss DiFillipo?"

"I just realized what made me scream—I mean, what *really* did it."

"Yes?"

"He said it in Italian." She looked at Rogers with astonishment. "I just realized that."

Rogers frowned. "He said it in Italian. And what he said was 'Barbara—it's I—the German.' That doesn't make sense, does it? Does it mean anything to you?"

The girl shook her head.

"Well." Rogers looked down at the desk, where his hands were tapping a pencil on the blotter. "How good is your Italian, Miss DiFillipo?"

"I speak it at home all the time."

Rogers nodded. Then something else occurred to him. "Tell me—I understand there are a number of regional Italian dialects. Could you tell which one he was using?"

"It sounded pretty usual. You might call it American Italian."

"As if he'd been in the country a long time?"

"I guess so. He sounded pretty much like anybody around here. But I'm no expert. I just talk it."

"I see. You don't know anyone named Barbara? I mean—a Barbara who looks a little like you, say?"

"No . . . no, I'm sure I don't."

"All right, Miss DiFillipo. When he spoke to you, you screamed. Did anything else happen?"

"No. He turned around and ran into the alley. And then a

car followed him in there. After that, one of your F.B.I. men came up to me and asked if I was all right. I told him I was, and he took me home. I guess you know all that."

"Yes. And thank you, Miss DiFillipo. You've been very helpful. I don't think we'll need you again, but if we do we'll be in touch with you."

"I'll be glad to help if I can, Mr. Rogers. Good-bye."

"Good-bye, Miss DiFillipo." He shook her hand again, and watched her leave.

Damn, he thought, there's a kind of girl who wouldn't get upset if her man was in my kind of business.

Then he sat frowning. "Barbara—it's I—the German." Well, that was one more thing to check out.

He wondered how Martino was feeling, holed up in his room. And he wondered how soon—or how long—it would be before they came upon the kind of evidence you could put on record and have stand up.

The interoffice buzzer broke in on him again.

"Yes?"

"Mr. Rogers? This is Reed. I've been running down some of the people on the Martino acquaintance list."

"And?"

"This man, Francis Heywood, who was Lucas Martino's roommate at M.I.T."

"The one who got to be a big gun in the A.N.G. Technical Personnel Allocations Bureau? He's dead. Died in a plane crash. What about him?"

"The F.B.I. just got a package on him. They pulled in a net of Soviet people in Washington. A really top-notch bunch, that'd been getting away with it for years. Sleepers, mostly. When Heywood was in Washington for the American government, he was one of them."

"The same Francis Heywood?"

"Fingerprints and photos check with our file, sir."

Rogers let the air seep out between his lips. "All right. Bring it here and let's have a look at it." He hung up slowly.

When the F.B.I. file came in, the pattern it made was perfect, with no holes anyone couldn't fill with a little experienced conjecture, if he wanted to.

Francis Heywood had attended M.I.T. with Lucas Martino,

sharing a room with him in one of the small dormitory apartments. Whether he was a Soviet sleeper even that far back was problematic. It made no significant difference. He was definitely one of them by the time he was transferred out of the American government into the A.N.G. Working for the A.N.G., he was hired to assign key technical personnel to the best working facilities for their specific purposes. He had been trained for this same kind of work in the American government, and was considered the best expert in the specialty. At some point near this period, he could have turned active. The natural conclusion was that he had been able to maneuver things so that the Soviets could get hold of Martino. Heywood, in effect, had been a talent scout.

He might, or might not, have known what K-88 was. He was supposed to have only a rough idea of the projects he found space for, but it would certainly have been easier for him to make specific guesses than for most people. Or, if it was felt he ought to take the risk, he could have taken steps to find out. In any case, he had known what kind of man, and how important a project, he could deliver over the border.

That, again, was secondary. What mattered most was this:

A month after Lucas Martino had disappeared over the border, Francis Heywood had taken a transatlantic plane from Washington, where he had been on a liaison mission that might actually have been a cover for almost anything. The plane had reported engine explosions in mid-ocean, sent out a crash distress call, and fallen into the sea. Air rescue teams found some floating wreckage and recovered a few bodies, Francis Heywood's not among them. The plane *had* crashed—sonar mapping found its pieces on the bottom. And, at the time, that had been that. Simple engine trouble of some kind. No report whatsoever of Soviet fighter planes sent out to create an incident, and the radio operator sending calm, well-trained messages to the last.

But now Rogers thought of the old business of dropping a man into the water at a prearranged spot, and having a submarine stand by to pick him up.

If you wanted to vary that so the man wouldn't be missed, then you could crash a whole commercial flight—who'd think it strange to miss one body?—and the submarine could make sure only that one man didn't drown. It was a little risky, but with the right kind of prearranged crash, and your man set for it, it was well within the kind of chance you took in this business.

He looked at Heywood's dossier statistics:

Height: 6 feet. Weight: 220. He'd been a heavy-set man, with a dark complexion. His age was almost exactly the same as Martino's. While in Europe, he had learned to speak Italian —presumably with an American accent.

And Rogers wondered just how much Lucas Martino had told him, through three years in the same room. How much the lonely boy from New Jersey had talked about himself. Whether he might not have had a picture of his girl, Edith, on his desk. Or even of a girl called Barbara, for Heywood to have seen every day until it was completely soaked into his memory. Maybe Heywood could have explained what Angela DiFillipo had heard last night on MacDougal Street.

How good an actor was their man? Rogers wondered. How good an actor do you believe a man can be?

God help us, Finch, he thought.

Chapter Ten

YOUNG LUCAS MARTINO came to Massachusetts Tech convinced there was something wrong with him, determined to repair it if he could. But as he went through registration, drew his classroom assignments, and struggled to fit himself into a study routine like nothing he had ever met before, he began to realize how difficult that might be.

Tech students were already handpicked on the day they entered. Tech graduates were expected to fill positions at the top. A thousand projects were piled up on the Allied world's schedules, waiting for men to staff them. Once they were implemented, each project had a thousand other schedules waiting for its completion. Plans made a dozen years ahead of time were ready, each timed, each meshed to another, each dependent on the successful completion of each schedule. If a man were to some day endanger that structure in any way, his weakness had to be located as early as possible.

So Tech instructors were people who never gave a doubtful answer the benefit of the doubt. They did not drive their classes, or waste time in giving any particular student more attention than the next. Tech students were presumed capable of digesting as much of the text as was assigned to them, and of knowing exactly what it meant. The instructors lectured quietly, competently, and ruthlessly, never going back to review a point or, in tests, to shade a mark because an otherwise good student had slipped once.

Lucas admired it as the ideal system for its purpose. The facts were presented, and those who could not grasp them, use them, and fit themselves to the class's progress, had to be eliminated before they slowed everyone down. It was a natural approach for him, and he had a tendency to be mildly incredulous when someone in the next chair turned to him helplessly, already far behind and with no hope of catching up. In the first few weeks of school, he established himself among his classmates as a cold, unfriendly brain, who acted as if he were somehow better than the rest of them.

His instructors, in that first year, took no notice of him. It was the potential failures that they were paid to pay attention to.

Lucas thought no more of that than he had at C.C.N.Y., where his teachers had been something close to overenthusiastic. He plunged into the work, not so much attracted to it as to the discovery that he *could* work—that it was expected of him, that he was given every opportunity to do so, and that the school was organized for people who could think in terms of work and nothing else.

It was almost two months before he became accustomed to it enough to lose the first edge of his enthusiasm. Then he could settle down and develop a routine. Then he had time for other things.

But he found that he was isolated. Somehow—he could not quite decide how—he had no friends. When he tried to approach some of his classmates, he found that they either resented him or were too busy. He discovered that most of them took at least half again as long at their assignments as he did, and that none of them were as sure of themselves as he. He puzzled over that—these were *Tech* students, after all—and learned that most people could be content to know what they were doing only eighty-five per cent of the time. But that did nothing to help him.

It only confused him more. He had expected, without question, that here at Tech he would meet a different breed of people. And, as a matter of fact, he had. There were plenty of students who abandoned every other concern when they came here. They slept little, ate hurriedly, and did nothing but study. In classes, they took notes at incredible length, took them back to their rooms at night, and pored over them. Letters from home went unanswered, and side trips into town at night were completely out of the question. Their conversation was a series of discussions about their work, and if any of them had personal problems, these were buried and left to take care of themselves while the grind of study went remorselessly on.

But, Lucas discovered, this did not mean that any of them were either happy or outstandingly familiar with their subjects. It only meant that they were temporary monomaniacs.

He wondered, for a while, if he might not be one, too. But that idea didn't seem to fit the facts. So, once again, he was forced to the conclusion that he was a sort of freak—someone who had, somewhere, missed a step most people took so naturally that they never noticed it. He found himself deeply worried by it, at those odd moments when his mind would let him. Through most of the day, he was completely absorbed in work. But, at night, when he sat in his room with the day's notes completed and the assignments read, when the current project was completed and he closed his books, then he sat staring blankly at the wall behind his desk and wondered what to do about the botch he'd made of Lucas Martino.

The only progress he ever made was in that brief time when he almost literally discovered his roommate.

Frank Heywood was the ideal person to share a small room with Lucas Martino. A quiet, calm type who never spoke except when it was absolutely necessary, he seemed to fit his movements about the room so that they never interfered with Lucas'. He used the room only to sleep and study in, slipping out whenever he had any free time. When Lucas thought about it, some weeks after the year began, he decided that Frank, like himself, had been too busy for friendship or anything more than enough politeness to let them live in peace. But, evidently, Frank also settled down and began to find a little leisure, because it was his roommate, and not Lucas, who initiated the short friendship between them.

"You know," Frank astonished him by saying one night, "you are without a doubt the big gun in this student body."

Lucas looked over from his desk, where he had been sitting with his chin in his hands. "Who, me?"

"Yes, you." Heywood's expression was completely serious. "I mean it. The word around the campus is you're a grind. That's a lot of bushwah. I've watched you, and you don't hit the books half as hard as most of these monkeys. You don't have to. One look and it's in your head for keeps."

"So?"

"So you've got brains."

"Not many morons get into a school like this."

"Morons?" Frank gestured scornfully. "Hell, no! This place is the cradle of next generation's good old American know-how, the hope of the future, the repository of all our finest young technical minds. And most of them couldn't give you the square of plus one without scratching their behinds and thinking about it for an hour. Why? Because they've been taught what book to look it up in, not how to use it. But not you."

Lucas looked at him in amazement. For one thing, this was by far the longest thing Frank had ever said to him. For another, here was a completely new viewpoint—an attitude toward Tech and everything it represented that he had never heard before, and never considered.

"How do you mean that?" he asked, curious to learn as much about it as he could.

"Like this: the way things are taught around here, the only way most people can get through is by memorizing what they're told. I've been talking to some of these jokers. I'll bet you I can find ten guys right on this floor who can repeat their texts back word for word, right down to the last comma, and do it like somebody pulling a tapeworm up his throat hand over hand. I will also bet you that if it turns out, fifteen years from now, that some Commie typesetter deliberately fouled up the words in the text, Allied science is going to be shot to hell because nobody'll have initiative enough to figure out what should have been there. Particularly not those ten guys. They'd keep on forever designing missile control systems that tuned in WBZ, because that was the way the book said to do it."

"I still don't follow you," Lucas said, frowning.

"Look—these guys aren't morons. They're pretty damned bright, or they wouldn't be here. But the only way they've ever been taught to learn something is to memorize it. If you throw a lot of new stuff at them in a hurry, they'll still memorize it —but they haven't got time to *think*. They just stuff in words, and when it comes time to show what they know, they unroll a piece. Yard goods.

"I say that's a hell of a dangerous thing to have going on. I say anybody with brains ought to realize what he's doing to himself and the whole Allied effort when he stuffs facts down indiscriminately. I say anybody who *did* realize it would want to do something about it. But these clucks aren't even both-ered by it enough to wrinkle their foreheads. So, considering everything, I say they may have brains, but they don't have brains *enough.*

"Now, you I've watched. When I sit here looking at you doing up your notes, it's a pleasure. Here's a guy with a look on his face as if he's looking at a love letter, for Christ's sake, when he's reading an electronics text. Here's a guy who fills out project reports like a man building a good watch. Here's a guy that's chewing before he swallows—here's a guy who's doing something with what they give them. Here, when you come right down to it, is a guy this place was *really* set up to produce."

Lucas raised his eyebrows. "Me?"

"You. I get around. I guess I've at least taken a look at every bird on this campus. There's a few like you on the faculty, but none in the student body. A few come close, but nobody touches you. That's why I say out of all the students here, all four classes, you're the guy to watch. You're the guy who's going to be really big in his field, I don't give a damn if it's civil engineering or nuclear dynamics."

"Electronic physics, I think."

"O.K., electronic physics. My money's on the Commies to be really worried about you in a few years' time."

Lucas blinked. He was completely overwhelmed. "I'm the illegitimate son of Guglielmo Marconi," he said in reply. "You notice the similarity in names." But he couldn't do more with that defense than to put a temporary stop to Heywood's trend of conversation. He had to think it over—think hard, to arrange all this new data in its proper order.

In the first place, here was the brand-new notion that a difference from other people was not necessarily bad. Then, there was the idea that somebody actually thought enough of him to observe his behavior and analyze it. That was not something he expected from people other than his parents. And, of course, the second conclusion led to a third. If Frank Heywood was thinking along lines like these, and if he could see what other people couldn't, then Frank, too, was a person different from most.

That could mean a great deal. It could mean that he and Frank could at least talk to each other. Certainly it meant that Frank, despite his disclaimer, was just as capable as he—perhaps more so, since Frank had seen it and he had not.

In many ways, Lucas found this an attractive train of thought. If he accepted any part of it, it automatically meant he also accepted the idea that he was some kind of genius. That in itself made him look at the whole hypothesis suspiciously. But he had very little or no real evidence to refute it. In fact, it was the kind of hypothesis that made it possible to reinterpret his whole life, and thus reinterpret every piece of evidence that might have stood against it.

For several more weeks, he went through a period of great emotional intoxication, convinced that he had finally come to understand himself. In those weeks, he and Frank talked about whatever interested Lucas at the moment, and carried on serious discussions long into the night. But the feeling of being two geniuses together was an essential part of it, and one night Lucas thought to ask Frank how he was doing at his studies.

"Me? I'm doing fine. Half a point over passing grade, steady as a chalkline."

"*Half* a point?"

Heywood grinned. "You go to your church and I'll go to

mine. I'll get a sheepskin that says Massachusetts Institute of Technology on it, the same as yours."

"Yes, but it's not the diploma—"

"—it's what you know? Sure, if you're planning to go on from there. I could, to be completely honest, give even you a run for the money when it comes to that. But why the hell should I? I'm not going to sweat my caliones off at Yucca Flat for the next forty years, draw my pension, and retire. Uh-uh. I'm going to take that B.S. from M.I.T. and make it my entrance ticket into some government bureau, where I'll spend the next forty years sitting behind a desk, freezing my caliones off in an air-conditioned office, and some day I'll retire on a bigger pension."

"And—and that's all?"

Heywood chuckled. "That's all, paisan."

"It sounds so God-damned empty I could spit. A guy with your brains, planning a life like that."

Heywood grinned and spread his hands. "There it is, though. So why should I kill myself here? This way I get by, and I've got lots of free time." He grinned again. "I get to have long talks with my roommate, I get to run around and see other people—hell, amico, there's no sweat this way. And it takes a guy with brains to pull it in a grind house like Tech, I might add."

It was the total waste of those brains that appalled Lucas. He found it impossible to understand and difficult to like. Certainly, it destroyed the mood of the past month.

He drew back into his shell after that. He was not hostile to Heywood, or anything like it, but he let the friendship die quickly. He lost, with it, any idea of being a genius. In time he even forgot that he had ever come close to making a fool of himself over it, though occasionally, when something went especially well for him in his later life, the idle thought would crop up to be instantly, and embarrassedly, suppressed.

He and Heywood finished their undergraduate work, still roommates. Heywood was once more the perfect person for one small room with Lucas Martino, and seemed not to mind Lucas' long periods of complete silence. Sometimes Lucas saw him sitting and watching him.

After they graduated, Heywood left Boston and, as far as

Lucas was concerned, disappeared. And it was only some years later that one of his graduate instructors came to him and said, "This hypothesis you were talking about, Martino—it might be worth your doing a paper on it."

So Heywood missed the birth of the K-88 completely, and Lucas Martino, for his part, once again had something to claim all his attention and keep him from thinking about the unanswered problems in his mind.

Chapter Eleven

EDMUND STARKE had become an old man, living alone in a rented four-room bungalow on the edge of Bridgetown. He had dried to leathery hardness, his muscles turning into strings beneath his brittle skin, his veins thick and blue. The hair was gone from the top of his skull, revealing the hollows and ridges in the bone. His glasses were thick, and clumsy in their cheap frames. His jaw was set, thrust forward past his upper teeth, and his eyes were habitually narrowed. Like most old men, he slept little, resting in short naps rather than for very long at any one time. He spent his waking hours reading technical journals and working on an elementary physics textbook which, he felt suspiciously, was turning out to resemble every elementary physics text written before it.

Today he was sitting in the front room, twisting the spine of a journal in his fingers and peering across the room at the opposite wall. He heard footsteps on the dark porch outside and waited for the sound of the bell. When it came, he got up in his night robe and slippers, walked slowly to the door and opened it.

A big man stood in the doorway, his face bandaged bulkily, the collar of his coat pulled up and his hat low over his eyes. The light from the room glittered blankly on dark glasses.

"Well?" Starke rasped in his high, dry-throated voice.

The man wagged his head indecisively. The bandages over his jaw parted once, showing a dark slit, before he said anything. When he did speak, his voice was indistinct. "Professor Starke."

"Mister Starke. What is it?"

"I . . . don't know if you remember me. I was one of your students. Class of sixty-six at Bridgetown High School. I'm Lucas Martino."

"Yes, I remember you. Come in." Starke moved aside and held the door, pushing it shut carefully behind the man, disgusted at having to be so careful of drafts. "Sit down. No, that's my chair. Take the one opposite."

The chief impression his visitor was giving was one of embarrassment. He sat down gingerly, unsure of himself, and opened his coat with clumsy, gloved fingers.

"Take off your hat." Starke lowered himself back into his chair and peered at the man. "Ashamed of yourself?"

The man pulled the hat off, dragging it slowly. His entire skull was bandaged, the white gauze running down under his collar. He gestured toward it. "An accident. An industrial accident," he mumbled.

"That's none of my concern. What can I do for you?"

"I—I don't know," the man said in a shocked voice, as though his plans had extended only to Starke's front door and he had never thought, till now, of what to do after that.

"What did you expect? Did you think I'd be surprised to see you? Or see you all wrapped up like the invisible man? I'm not. I know all about you. A man named Rogers was here and said you were on your way." Starke cocked his head. "So now you're caught flatfooted. Well—think. What're you going to do now?"

"I was afraid Rogers would find out about you. Did he bother you?"

"Not a bit."

"What did he tell you?"

"He told me you might not be who you say you are. He wanted my opinion."

"Didn't he tell you not to let me know that?"

"He did. I told him I'd do this my way."

"You haven't changed."

"How would you know?"

The man sighed. "Then you don't think I'm Lucas Martino."

"I don't care. It's no longer important whether you used to be in my class or not. If you're here for help of any kind, you've wasted your time."

"I see." The man began putting his hat back on.

"You'll wait and hear my reasons."

"What reasons?" the man asked with dull bitterness. "You don't trust me. That's a good reason."

"If that's what you think, you'd better listen."

The man sank back. "All right." He seemed not to care. His emotional responses seemed to reach him slowly and indistinctly, as if traveling through cotton wool.

"What would you want me to do?" Starke rasped. "Take you in here to live with me? How long would that last—a month or two, a year? You'd have a corpse on your hands, and you'd still have no place to go. I'm an old man, Martino or whoever you are, and you ought to have taken that into account if you were making plans."

The man shook his head.

"And if that's not what you wanted, then you wanted me to help you with some kind of work. Rogers said it might be that. Was that it?"

The man raised his hands helplessly.

Starke nodded. "What made you think I was qualified? What made you think I could work on something forty years advanced over what I was taught at school? What made you think I could have kept up with new work in the field? I don't have access to classified publications. Where did you think we'd get the equipment? What did you think would pay for it and—"

"I have some money."

"—what did you think you'd gain by it if you did think you could answer those objections? This nation is effectively at war, and wouldn't tolerate unauthorized work for a moment. Or weren't you planning to work on anything important? Were you planning to drop corks into mousetraps?"

The man sat dumbly, his hands trailing over his thighs.

"Think, man."

The man raised his hands and dropped them. He hunched forward. "I thought I was."

"You weren't." Starke closed the subject. "Now—where're you going to go from here?"

The man shook his head. "I don't know. You know, I had decided you were my last chance."

"Don't your parents live near here? If you are Martino?"

"They're both dead." The man looked up. "They didn't live to be as old as you."

"Don't hate me for that. I'm sorry they're dead. Life wasn't meant to be given up gladly."

"They left me the farm."

"All right, then you've got a place to stay. Do you have a car?"

"No. I took the train down."

"Muffled in your winding sheet, eh? Well, if you don't want to sleep in the hotel, take my car. It's in the garage. You can return it tomorrow. That'll get you there. The keys are on the mantelpiece."

"Thank you."

"Return the car, but don't visit me again. Lucas Martino was the one student whose brains I admired."

2.

"So you're not sure," Rogers said heavily, sitting in the chair where the man had sat the night before.

"No."

"Can you take an educated guess?"

"I think in facts. It's not a fact that he recognized me. He might have been bluffing. I saw no purpose in laying little traps for him, so I answered to my name. My picture has appeared in the local newspaper several times. 'Local Educator Retires After Long Service' was the most recent caption. He had my name to begin with. Am I to judge him incapable of elementary research?"

"He didn't visit the newspaper office, Mr. Starke."

"Mr. Rogers, police work is your occupation, not mine. But if this man is a Soviet agent, he could easily have had the way prepared for him."

"That's occurred to us, Mr. Starke. We've found no conclusive proof of anything like that."

"Lack of contrary proof does not establish the existence of a fact. Mr. Rogers, you sound like a man trying to push someone into a decision you want."

Rogers rubbed his hand along the back of his neck. "All right, Mr. Starke. Thank you very much for your cooperation."

"I was a good deal more satisfied with my life before you and this man came into it."

Rogers sighed. "There's nothing very much any of us could do about that, is there?"

He left, made sure his surveillance teams were properly located, and went back to New York, driving up the turnpike at a slow and cautious rate.

3.

Matteo Martino's old farm had stood abandoned for eight years. The fences were down, and the fields overgrown. The barn had lost its doors long ago, and all the windows of the house were broken. There was no paint left on the barn, and very little on the house. What there was, was cracked, peeling, and useless. The inside of the house was littered, water-soaked, and filthy. Children had broken in often, despite the county police patrol, and scrawled messages on the walls. Someone had stolen the sinks, and someone else had hacked the few pieces of furniture left in it with a knife, at random.

The ground was ditched by gullies and flooded with rain-washed sand. Weeds had spread their tough roots into the soil. Someone had begun a trash pile along the remains of the back fence. The apple trees along the road were gnarled and grown out, their branches broken.

The first thing the man did was to have a telephone installed. He began ordering supplies from Bridgetown: food, clothes—overalls and work shirts, and heavy shoes—and then tools. No one questioned the legality of what he was doing—only Rogers could have raised the issue at all.

The surveillance teams watched him work. They saw him get up before dawn each morning, cook his meal in the improvised kitchen, and go out with his hammer and saw and nails while it was still too dark for anyone else to see what he was doing. They watched him drive fence posts and unroll wire, tearing the weeds aside. They watched him set new beams into the barn, working alone, working slowly at first, and then more and more insistently, until the sound of the hammer never seemed to stop throughout the day.

He burned the old furniture and the old linoleum from the

house. He ordered a bed, a kitchen table, and a chair, put them in the house, and did nothing more with it except to gradually set new panes in the windows as he found spare moments from re-shingling the barn. When that was done, he bought a tractor and a plow. He began to clear the land again.

He never left the farm. He spoke to none of the neighbors who tried to satisfy their curiosity. He did no trading at the general store. When the delivery trucks from Bridgetown filled his telephone orders, he gave unloading instructions with his order and never came out of the house while the trucks were in the yard.

Chapter Twelve

LUCAS MARTINO stood looking up at the overhead maze of bus bars that fed power to the K-88. Down in the pit below his catwalk, he heard his technicians working around the thick, spherical, alloy tank. One of them cursed peevishly as he snagged his coveralls on a protruding bolt head. The tank bristled with them. The production models would no doubt be streamlined and neatly painted, but here in this experimental installation, no one had seen any necessity for superfluous finishing. Except perhaps that technician.

As he watched, the technicians climbed out of the pit. The telephone rang beside him, and when he answered it the pit crew supervisor told him the tank area was cleared.

"All right. Thank you, Will. I'm starting the coolant pumps now."

The outside of the tank began to frost. Martino dialed the power gang foreman. "Ready for test, Allan."

"I'll wind 'em up," the foreman answered. "You'll have full power any time you want it after thirty seconds from . . . now. Good luck, Doctor Martino."

"Thank you, Allan."

He put the phone down and stood looking at the old brick wall across the enormous room. Plenty of space here, he thought. Not the way it was back in the States, when I was working with the undersized configurations because Kroenn's equations showed

I could. I knew he was wrong, somewhere, but I couldn't prove it—I ought to know more mathematics, damn it. I do, but who can keep up with Kroenn? I remember, he was raving angry at himself for weeks when he found his own mistake.

It happens. The best of us slip a cog now and then. Well, it took Kroenn to see Kroenn's mistake. . . . Well, here we go . . .

He picked up the public address microphone and thumbed the button. "Test," his voice rumbled through the building. He put the microphone down and started the tape recorder.

"Test Number One, experimental K-Eighty-eight configuration two." He gave the date. "Applying power at—" he looked at his watch "—twenty-one hundred hours, thirty-two minutes." He threw the switch and leaned over the railing to look down into the pit. The tank exploded.

Chapter Thirteen

IT WAS, once again, a rainy summer in New York. Gray day followed gray day, and even when the sun was out, the clouds waited at the edge of the horizon. The weather seemed to have gone bad all over the world. Hot winds scoured the great mid-continental plains of the north, and below the equator there was snow, and thaw, and snow, and thaw again. The oceans were never still, and from one seaboard to another the waves cracked against breakwaters with the hard, incessant slapping of high-velocity artillery. Icebergs prowled down out of the polar caps, and migratory birds flew closer to the land. There were riots in Asia, and violent homicides in London.

Shawn Rogers left New York on a teeming day, the tires of his car singing on wet blacktop, and for all his windscreen cleaner could do, the world seemed blurred, shifting, and impermanent. His car whined almost alone down the freeway, swaying in sharp lurches as the gusty wind struck it, and all the way down into the end of New Jersey the rain pursued him.

The secondary road to the farm surprised him by being wide, well graded, and smoothly surfaced. He was able to drive with only half his attention.

Five years, he thought, since I saw him last. Almost five since that night he came over the line. I wonder how he feels about things?

Rogers had his folders of daily reports, for the surveillance team still followed the man faithfully. A.N.G. men delivered his milk, A.N.G. men brought his rolls of fencing, and A.N.G. men sweated in the fields across from his farm. And every month, Rogers' secretary brought him a neatly typed résumé of everything the man did. But even though he always read them, Rogers had learned how little was ever accurately abstracted from a man and successfully transferred to paper.

Rogers moved his mouth into a strained smile, his face tired and growing old. But what else was anyone to go by?

I wonder how he'll take the news I'm bringing?

Rogers swung the car around the curve, and saw the farm the surveillance team had so often photographed for him.

Set in one corner of the farm, the house was a freshly-painted white building with green shutters. There was a lawn, carefully mowed and bordered by hedges, and across the yard from the house stood a solidly built barn, with a pickup truck parked in front of it, with no name lettered on its doors. There was a kitchen garden beside the house, laid out with geometrical exactness, the earth black, freshly weeded, and without a stone, textured like chocolate cream. A row of apple trees marched beside the road, every limb pruned, the foliage glistening with spray. The fence beside them shone with new wire, each post set exactly upright, every strand stretched perfectly parallel to the others. The fields lay green in the rain, furrows deep to carry off the excess water, and at the far end of the property, shrubs marked the edge of a small brook. As Rogers drove into the yard and stopped, a dog trotted out from behind the barn and stood in the rain, barking at him.

Rogers buttoned his raincoat and turned his collar up. He jumped out of the car, giving the door a hasty push shut, and ran across the yard to the back porch. As he reached its shelter, the door directly in front of him opened, and he found himself standing less than a foot away from the overalled man in the doorway.

There was change visible in the face. The metal had acquired a patina of microscopic scratches and scuffs, softening its machine-turned lustre and fogging the sharpness with which it reflected light. The eyes were the same, but the voice was different. It was duller, drier, and seemed to come out more slowly.

"Mr. Rogers."

"Hello, Mr. Martino."

"Come in." The man stepped aside, out of the doorway.

"Thank you. I should have called first, but I wanted to be sure we had a chance to talk at length." Rogers stopped uncomfortably, just inside the door. "There's something rather important to talk about, if you'll spare me the time . . ."

The man nodded. "All right. I've got work to do, but you can come along and talk, I guess. I just cooked some lunch. There's enough for two."

"Thank you." Rogers took off his raincoat, and the man hung it up on a hook beside the kitchen door. "I—how've you been?"

"All right. Chair over there. Sit down, and I'll get the food." The man walked over to a cupboard and took down two plates.

Rogers sat down at the kitchen table, looking around stiffly for lack of something else to do.

The kitchen was neat and clean. There were curtains up over the sink, and there was fresh linoleum on the floor. There were no dishes left over on the drainboard, the sink itself had been scrubbed clean, and everything was put away, carefully and systematically. Rogers tried to picture the man washing, ironing, and hanging curtains—doing it all according to a logically thought-out system, with not a move wasted, taking a minimum of time, as carefully as he'd ever set up a test series or checked the face of an oscilloscope. Day after day, for five years.

The man set a plate down in front of Rogers: boiled potatoes, beets, and a thick slice of pork tenderloin. "Coffee? Just made some fresh."

"Thanks. I'll take it black, please."

"Suit yourself." There was a faint grinding noise as the man put the cup down with his metal hand. Then he sat opposite Rogers and began to eat silently, without lifting his head or stopping. He was obviously impatient to get the necessary meal over and done with so he could get back to his work. Rogers had no choice but to eat as quickly as possible, and no opening to start talking. The meal was cooked well.

When they finished, the man stood up and silently gathered the plates and silverware, stacking them in the sink and running water over them. He handed Rogers a dish towel. "I'd appreciate your drying these. We'll get done sooner."

"Certainly." They stood together at the sink, and as the man handed him each washed plate and cup, Rogers dried it carefully and put it in the drainboard rack. When they were through, the man put the dishes back in the cupboard, and Rogers started to put on his raincoat.

"Be with you in a minute," the man said. He opened a drawer and took out a roll of bandaging. He held one end between the fingers of his metal hand and carefully wound a loose spiral up his arm, pushing his shirtsleeve out of the way. Taking safety pins out of his overall pocket, he fastened the two ends. Then he took a can of oil out of the drawer and carefully soaked the bandage before putting everything back and pushing the drawer shut. "Got to do it," he explained to Rogers. "Dust and grit gets in there, and it wears."

"Of course."

"Well, let's go."

Rogers followed the man out into the yard, and they walked across to the barn. The dog ran up beside them, and the man reached down to pet his neck. "Get back in your house, stupe. You'll get wet. Go on, Prince. Go on, boy." The dog sniffed uncertainly at Rogers, trotted along with them for a few steps, and turned back.

"Prince? Is that his name? Nice-looking dog. What breed is he?"

"Mongrel. He's got a barrel he sleeps in, back of the barn."

"You don't keep him in the house, then?"

"He's a watchdog. He's got to be outside. And he's not housebroken." The man looked at Rogers. "A dog's a dog, you know. If the only friend a man had was a dog, it'd mean he couldn't get along with his own kind, wouldn't it?"

"I wouldn't exactly say that. You like the dog, don't you?"

"Yes."

"Ashamed of it?"

"You're pushing again, Rogers."

Rogers dropped his eyes. "I suppose I was."

They went into the barn, and the man switched on the

lights. There was a tractor sitting in the middle of the barn, with a can full of drained transmission oil beside it. The man unrolled an oily tarpaulin, pulled it over beside the tractor, and laid out the tools that had been rolled inside it. "I have to fix this transmission today," he said. "I bought this tractor second-hand, and the fellow that had it before chipped the gears. They've got to be replaced today, because I've got a field to harrow tomorrow." He selected a wrench and slid under the tractor, on his back. He began loosening the nuts around the rim of the gearbox cover, paying no further attention to Rogers.

Rogers stood uncertainly beside the tractor, looking down at the man working under it. Finally, he looked around for something to sit on. There was a box set against the barn wall, and he went over, got it, and sat down beside the tractor, bending forward until he could see the man's face. But that did him little good. Even though the gearbox had been drained during the morning, there was still oil dripping out of it. The man was working by touch, his eyes and mouth tightly shuttered, deaf, with dirty oil running in narrow streaks down across his skull.

Rogers sat and waited for ten minutes, watching the man's hands working deftly at the cover, right hand guiding left, right hand, with its wrench, breaking the nuts loose from their lugs, then left hand taking the nuts off with its hard fingers. Finally, the man put the wrench aside, locating the tool tarpaulin without difficulty, and lifted the cover down, dropping the nuts inside it. The left hand probed inside the gearbox, and a retaining slide dropped out, into the waiting right hand. The slide, too, went into the up-ended gearbox cover, and the left hand popped the gears out of their mounts. The man wriggled out from under the tractor and opened his eyes.

"I was going to ask you—" Rogers began.

"Minute." He stood up and took the worn gears over to a workbench, where he held them up to the light, cursing bitterly. "A man has no business buying machinery if he won't treat it right. That's a damned good design, that transmission. No reason in the world for anybody to have trouble with it." His voice was almost querulous. "A machine won't ever let you down, if you'll only take the trouble to use it right—use it the way you're supposed to, for the jobs it's built to do. That's all.

All you have to do is understand it. And no machine's that
complicated an average man can't understand it. But nobody
tries. Nobody thinks a machine's worth understanding.
What's a machine, after all? Just a few pieces of metal. One's
exactly like another, and you can always get another one just
like it.

"But I'll tell you something, Mr. Rogers—" He turned suddenly, and faced across the barn. The light was behind him,
and Rogers saw only his silhouette—the body lost in the
shapeless, angular drape of the overalls, the shoulders square,
and the head round and featureless. "Even so, people don't
like machines. Machines don't talk and tell you their troubles.
Machines don't do anything but what they're made for. They
sit there, doing their jobs, and one looks like another—but it
may be breaking up inside. It may be getting ready to not plow
your field, or not pump your water, or throw a piston into
your lap. It might be getting ready to do *anything*—so people
are afraid of them, a little bit, and won't take the trouble to
understand them, and they treat them badly. So the machines
break down more quickly, and people trust them less, and
mistreat them more. So the manufacturers say, 'What's the use
of building good machines? The clucks'll only wreck 'em anyway,' and build flimsy stuff, so there're very few good machines
being made any more. And that's a shame."

He dropped the gears on the bench and picked up a box
holding the replacement set. Still angry, he ripped the top off
the box, took out the gears, and brought them back to the
tractor.

"Mr. Martino—" Rogers said again.

"Yes?" he asked, laying the gears out in sequence on the
tarpaulin.

Now that he'd come to the point of saying it, Rogers didn't
know how. He thought of the man, trapped in the casque of
himself through these five years, and Rogers didn't know how
to put it.

"Mr. Martino, I'm here as the official representative of the
Allied Nations Government, empowered to make you an offer."

The man grunted, picking up the first gear and reaching up
under the tractor to slip it in place.

"Frankly," Rogers stumbled on, "I don't think they quite

knew how to say it, so they chose me to do it, thinking I knew you best." He shrugged wryly. "But I don't know you."

"Nobody does," the man said. "What's the A.N.G. want?"

"Well, the point I was trying to make was that I probably won't phrase this properly. I don't want my fumbling to prejudice your decision."

The man made an impatient sound. "Get to it, man." Then, with infinite gentleness, he slipped the gear into place and reached for the next.

"Well—you know things all over the world're getting tense again."

"Yes." He wriggled further under the tractor, reached over with his right hand, and helped his left locate the second gear exactly in place. "What's that got to do with me?" He took the last gear, mounted it, and forced the tight retaining slide into position, moving the closely machined part only as firmly as needed and no more. He scooped the nuts out of the gearbox cover and began hand-tightening it back in place.

"Mr. Martino—the A.N.G. has re-instituted the K-Eighty-eight program. They'd like you to work on it."

The man under the tractor reached for his wrench, and his fingers slipped on the oily metal. He twisted around and reached with his left arm. There was a faint click as his fingers closed over it firmly, and then he turned back and began taking up the gearbox lugs.

Rogers waited, and after a while the man said, "So Besser failed."

"I wouldn't know about that, Mr. Martino."

"He must have. I'm sorry for him—he really believed he was right. It's funny with scientists, you know—they're supposed to be objective and detached, and formulate theories according to the evidence. But a man's baby is a man's baby, and sometimes they feel it very badly when an idea of theirs is proved wrong." He finished tightening the cover, and screwed the drain plug in firmly. He crawled out from under the tractor, put the wrench down, and carefully rolled up the tarpaulin. "Well, that's done," he said. He put the tarpaulin under his arm, bent to pick up the can of old oil, and went over to the work bench, where he put the tools down and carefully poured the can out into a waste drum.

He took a new half-gallon can from a rack, punched a pouring spout into its top, and brought it back to the tractor, where he took off the filler cap and up-ended the can over the transmission. "Now I can get that field done tomorrow. The ground's got to be loosened up, you know, or it'll get crusty and cake."

"Aren't you going to say anything about whether you'll accept the offer or not?"

The man lifted the pouring spout of the filler and replaced the cap. He put the empty can down and climbed up into the driver's saddle, where he began going carefully through the gears, testing them for engagement and smoothness, without looking at Rogers until he was satisfied he'd done a good job. Then he turned his head. "They decide I was Martino?"

"I think," Rogers said slowly, "they simply needed someone very badly. They felt, I think, that even if you weren't Lucas Martino, you'd have been trained to replace him. It—seems to be very important to them to get the K-Eighty-eight program working again as quickly as possible. They have plenty of competent technicians. But geniuses don't appear often."

The man climbed down off the tractor, picked up the empty oil can, and took it over to the bench. His arm bandage was black with floor dust, and he pulled a five-gallon can out from under the bench, uncapped it, and began taking the bandage off. The sharp smell of gasoline burned into Rogers' nostrils.

"I was wonderin' how they'd come to decide for sure. I can't see any way of doing it." He dropped the bandage into the gasoline. Plunging both arms into the can, he washed the bandage clean and hung it over a nail to dry.

"You'd be watched very closely, of course. And probably kept under guard."

"I wouldn't mind. I don't mind your people being around here all of the time." He took a tin cup out of the bottom of the gasoline can and sluiced down his arm, twisting and turning it to make sure every working part was washed out thoroughly. He took a stiff, fine-bristled brush from a rack and began cleaning his arm with methodical care, following an obviously old routine. Rogers watched him, wondering, once again, just what kind of brain lived behind that mask and was neither angry, nor bitter, nor triumphant that they'd had to come to him at last. "But I can't do it," the man said. He picked up an oil can and began lubricating his arm.

"Why not?" Rogers thought he saw the man's composure wavering.

The man shrugged uncomfortably. "I can't do that stuff any more." The bandage was dry, and he wrapped his arm again. He didn't meet Rogers' eyes.

"What're you ashamed of?" Rogers asked.

The man walked over to the tractor, as though he thought it was safer there.

"What's the matter, Martino?"

The man put his left arm over the tractor's hood and stood facing out through the open barn doors. "It's a pretty good life, here. I work my land, get it in shape; I fix up the place—I guess you know what it was like when I moved in. It's been a lot of work. A lot of rebuildin'. Ten more years and I'll have it right in the shape I want."

"You'll be dead."

"I know. I don't care. I don't think about it. The thing is—" His hand beat lightly on the tractor's hood. "The thing is, I'm working all the time. A farm—everything on a farm—is so close to the edge between growing and rotting. You work the land, you grow crops, and when you do that, you're robbing the land. You're going to fertilize, and irrigate, and lime, and drain, but the land doesn't know that. It's got to get back what you took out of it. Your fenceposts rot, your building foundations crumble, the rain comes down and your paint peels, your crops get beaten down and start to rot—you've got to work hard, every day, all day, just to stay a little bit better than even. You get up in the morning, and you have to make up for what's happened during the night. You can't do anything else. You don't think about anything else. Now you want me to go work on the K-Eighty-eight again." Suddenly, his hand beat down on the tractor, and the barn echoed to the clang of metal. His voice was agonized. "I'm not a physicist. I'm a farmer. I can't *do* that stuff any more!"

Rogers took a slow breath. "All right—I'll go back and tell them."

The man was quiet again. "What're you going to do after that? Your men going to keep watching me?"

Rogers nodded. "It has to be that way. I'll see you to your grave. I'm sorry."

The man shrugged. "I'm used to it. I haven't got anything that people watching is going to hurt."

No, Rogers thought, you're harmless now. And I'm watching you, so I'm useless. I wonder if I'll end up living on a farm down the road?

Or is it just that you don't dare take the chance of going on the K-Eighty-eight project? Did they risk it, after all, with somebody who couldn't fool us there?

Rogers' mouth twisted. One more—once more and for the thousandth time, he'd raise the old, pointless question. Something bubbled through his blood, and he shivered slightly. I'll be an old man, he thought, and I'll always think I knew, but I'll never get an answer.

"Martino," he blurted. "*Are* you Martino?"

The man moved his head, and the metal glowed with a dull nimbus under its film of oil. He said nothing for a moment, his head moving from side to side as though he were looking for something lost. Then he tightened his grip on the tractor, and his shoulders came back. For a moment his voice had depth in it, as though he remembered something difficult and prideful he had done in his youth. "No."

Chapter Fourteen

ANASTAS AZARIN lifted the glass of lukewarm tea, pressed the spoon out of the way with his index finger, and drank it down without stopping until the glass was empty. He thumped it down in a circle of old stains on the end of his desk, and the spoon rattled. His orderly came in from the outer office, took the glass, refilled it, and set it down on the desk in easy reach. Azarin nodded shortly. The orderly clicked his heels, about-faced, and left the room.

Azarin watched him go, his mouth hooking deeply at one corner in a grimace of amusement that wrinkled all his face before it died as abruptly as it came. During that short moment, he had been transformed—his face had been open, frank, and friendly. But when his features smoothed again, all trace of the peasant, Azarin, left them. It was possible to see what Azarin had taught himself to become during his years of rising through the system: impersonal, efficient, wooden.

He went back to reading the weekly sector situation report, his blunt, nicotine-stained forefinger following the words, his lips muttering inaudibly.

He knew they laughed at him for his old-fashioned samovar. But the orderly knew what would happen to him if the glass ever remained empty. He knew they joked about the way he read. But they knew what would happen to them if he found errors in their reports.

Anastas Azarin had never graduated from their academies. He had never scribbled on their blackboards or filled their copybooks. While they were polishing the seats of their school uniforms on classroom benches, he had been out with his father, hefting an axe and dragging the great balks of timber through the dark forest. While they took their civil service examinations, he was supervising labor gangs on the taiga. While they hunched over their desks, he was in Mandjuria, eating bad rice with the little brown men. While they sat at home with their wives, reading their newspapers and dreaming of promotion, he was in a dressing station, dying of typhus.

And now he had a desk of his own, and an office of his own, and a pink-cheeked, wide-eyed orderly who brought him tea and clicked his heels. It was not their joke—it was his. It was he who could laugh—not they. They were nothing, and he was sector commandant—Anastas Azarin, Colonel, S.I.B. Gospodin Polkovnik Azarin, if you please!

He bent over the reports, muttering. Nothing new. As usual, the Allieds kept their sector tight. There was this American scientist, Martino. What was he doing, in his laboratory?

The American, Heywood, could not tell. From his post with the Allied Nations Government, Heywood had managed to arrange things so that Martino's laboratory was placed close to Azarin's sector. But that was the best he had been able to do. He had known Martino, knew Martino was engaged in something important that required a room with a twenty-foot ceiling and eight hundred square feet of floor space, and was called Project K-88.

Azarin scowled. It was all very well and good to have such faith in Martino's importance, but *what* was K-88? What good was an empty name? The American, Heywood, was very glib with his data, but the fact was that there was no data. The A.N.G. internal security system was such that no one, even Heywood, could know much of what was going on. That in itself was quite normal—the Soviet system was the same. But the fact was that in the end it would not be some cloak-and-dagger secret agent, with his flabby white skin and his little cameras who would deliver the K-88 to them. It would be Azarin—simple Anastas Azarin, the peasant—who would pull this thing apart as a bear destroys a dead tree to find the honey.

Martino would have to be interrogated. There was no other method of doing it. But for all Novoya Moskva wasted its air on the telephone, there was no quick way of doing it. There was no getting people into Martino's laboratory. He had to be waited for. Men had to be ready at all times, prepared to pluck him from some dark street on the day he wandered too close to the line, if that lucky accident ever did occur. Then—one, two, three, he would be here, he would be questioned, he would be released, all in a matter of a few days before the Allieds could do anything, and the Allieds would have lost the K-88. And that devil, the American Rogers, no matter how clever he was, would have been taught at last that Anastas Azarin was a better man. But until that time, everyone—Azarin, Novoya Moskva—everyone—would have to wait. All in good time, if ever.

The telephone on his desk began to ring. Azarin swept up the receiver. "Polkovnik Azarin," he growled.

"Gospodin Polkovnik—" It was one of his staff assistants. Azarin recognized the voice and fumbled for the name. He found it.

"Well, Yung?"

"There has been an explosion in the American scientist's laboratory."

"Get men in there. Get the American."

"They are already on their way. What shall we do next?"

"Next? Bring him here. No—one moment. An explosion, you say? Take him to the military hospital."

"Yes, sir. I very much hope he is alive, because this, of course, is the opportunity we have been waiting for."

"Is it? Go give your orders."

Azarin dropped the receiver on its cradle. This was bad. This was the worst possible thing. If Martino was dead, or so badly damaged as to be useless for weeks, Novoya Moskva would become intolerable.

2.

As soon as his car had come to a stop in front of the hospital, Azarin jumped out and climbed quickly up the steps. He marched through the main doors and strode into the lobby, where a doctor was waiting for him.

"Colonel Azarin?" the wiry little doctor asked, bowing slightly from the waist. "I am Medical Doctor Kothu. You will forgive me—I do not speak your language fluently."

"I do well enough in yours," Azarin said pleasantly, anticipating the gratifying surprise on the little man's face. When it came, it made him even more well disposed toward the doctor. "Now, then—where is the man?"

"This way, please." Kothu bowed again and led the way to the elevator. A brief smile touched Azarin's face as he followed him. It always gave him pleasure when simple-looking Anastas Azarin proved to be as learned as anyone who had spent years in the universities. It was something to be proud of, too, that he had learned the language while burning leeches off his legs in a jungle swamp, instead of out of some professor's book.

"How badly is the man injured?" he asked Kothu as they stepped out into another hall.

"Very badly. He was dead for a few moments."

Azarin jerked his head toward the doctor.

Kothu nodded with a certain pride of his own. "He died in the ambulance. Fortunately, death is no longer permanent, under certain circumstances." He led Azarin to a plate glass window set in the wall of a white-tiled room. Inside, still wearing the torn remnants of his clothes, incredibly bloodied, a man lay in the midst of a welter of apparatus.

"He is quite safe now," Kothu explained. "You see the autojector there, pumping his blood, and the artificial kidney that purifies it. On this side are the artificial lungs." The machines were bunched together haphazardly, where they had quickly been brought from their usual positions against the walls. Doctors and nurses were clustered around them, carefully supervising their workings, and other doctors were busy on the man himself, clamping torn blood vessels and applying compression to his armless left shoulder. As Azarin watched, orderlies began shifting the machines into systematic order. The emergency was over. Things were assuming a routine. A nurse glanced at her watch, looked over at a rack where a bottle was draining of whole blood, and substituted a fresh one.

Azarin scowled to hide his nervousness. He was having a certain amount of difficulty in keeping his glance on the monstrous scene. A man, after all, was made with his insides decently hidden under his skin. To look at a man, you did not see the slimy organs doing their revolting work of keeping him alive and real. To see a man like this, ripped open, with mysteriously knowledgeable, yes—frightening—men like this Kothu pushing and pulling at the moist things that stuffed the smooth and handsome skin . . .

Azarin risked a sidelong glance at the little brown doctor. Kothu could do these abominable things just as easily to him. Anastas Azarin could lie there like that, hideously exposed, with men like this Kothu desecrating him at his pleasure.

"That's very good," Azarin barked, "but he's useless to me. Or can he speak?"

Kothu shook his head. "His head is crushed, and he has lost a number of his sensory organs. But this is only emergency equipment, such as you will find in any accident ward. Inside of two months, he'll be as good as new."

"Two *months*?"

"Colonel Azarin, I ask you to look at what lies on that table and is barely a man."

"Yes—yes, of course, I'm lucky to have him at all. He can't be moved, I suppose? To the great hospital in Novoya Moskva, for example?"

"It would kill him."

Azarin nodded. Well, with every bad, some good. There would be no question, now, of Martino being taken away from him. It would be Anastas Azarin who did it—Anastas Azarin who tore the honey from the tree.

"Very well—do your best. And quickly."

"Of course, Colonel."

"If there is anything you need, come to me. I will give it to you."

"Yes, sir. Thank you."

"There's nothing to thank me for. I want this man. You will do your best work to see that I get him."

"Yes, Colonel." Medical Doctor Kothu bowed slightly from the waist. Azarin nodded and walked away, down the hall to the elevator, his booted feet thudding against the floor.

Downstairs, he found Yung just driving up with a squad of S.I.B. soldiers. Azarin gave detailed instructions for a guard, and ordered the accident floor of the hospital sealed off. Already, he was busy thinking of ways this story might be spreading. The ambulance crew had to be kept quiet, the hospital personnel might talk, and even some of the patients here might have gathered an idea of what was going on. All these leaks had to be plugged. Azarin went back to his car, conscious of how complex his work was, how much ability a man needed to do it properly, and of how, inevitably, the American, Rogers, would sooner or later bring it all to nothing.

Five weeks went by. Five weeks during which Azarin was unable to accomplish anything, and of which Martino knew nothing.

3.

Every time Martino tried to focus his eyes, something whirred very softly in his frontal sinuses. He tried to understand that, but he felt very weak and boneless, and the sensation was so disconcerting that he was awake for an hour before he could see.

For that hour he lay motionless, listening, and noticing that his ears, too, were not serving him properly. Sounds advanced and receded much too quickly; were suddenly here and then there. His face ached slightly as each new vibration struck his ears, almost as if it were resonating to the sounds he heard.

There was some kind of apparatus in his mouth. His tongue felt the hard sleekness of metal, and the slipperiness of plastic. A splint, he thought. My jaw's broken. He tried it, and it worked very well. It must be some kind of traction splint, he thought.

Whatever it was, it kept his teeth from meeting. When he closed his jaws, he felt only pressure and resistance, instead of the mesh and grind of teeth coming together.

The sheets felt hot and rough, and his chest was constricted. The bandaging felt lumpy across his back. His right shoulder was painful when he tried to move it, but it moved. He opened and closed the fingers of his right hand. Good. He tried his left arm. Nothing. Bad.

He lay quietly for a while, and at the end of it he had accepted the fact that his arm was gone. He was right-handed, after all, and if the arm was the only thing, he was lucky. He set about testing, elevating his hips cautiously, flexing his thighs and calves, curling his toes. No paralysis.

He had been lucky, and now he felt much better. He tried his eyes again, and though the whirring came and jarred him, he kept focus this time. He looked up and saw a blue ceiling, with a blue light burning in its center. The light bothered him, and after a moment he realized he wasn't blinking, so he blinked deliberately. The ceiling and the light turned yellow.

There had been a peculiar shifting across his field of vision. He looked down toward his feet. Yellow sheets, yellowish-white bedstead, yellow walls with a brown strip from floor to shoulder height. He blinked again, and the room went dark. He looked up toward the ceiling and barely saw a faint glow where the light had been, as though he were looking through leaded glass.

He couldn't feel the texture of the pillow against the back of his neck. He couldn't smell the smell of a hospital. He blinked again and the room was clear. He looked from side to side, and at the edges of his vision, just barely in sight and very close to his eyes, he saw two incurving cuts in what seemed to be metal plating. It was as though his face were pressed up to the door slit of a solitary confinement cell. He inched his right hand up to touch his face.

4.

Five weeks—of which Martino knew nothing and during which Azarin had been unable to accomplish anything.

Azarin held the telephone headpiece in one hand and opened the inlaid sandalwood box on his desk with the other. He selected a gold-tipped papyros and put the tip in one corner of his mouth where it would be out of the way. There was a perpetual matchbox on his desk, and he jerked at the protruding match. It came free, but the pull had been too uneven to draw a proper spark out of the flint in the box. The match wick failed to catch light, and he thrust the match back into the box, jerked it out again, and once more failed to get a light. He swept the matchbox off his desk and into the wastebasket, pulled open his desk drawer, found real matches, and lit the papyros. His lip curled tightly to hold the cigarette and let him talk at the same time.

"Yes, sir. I appreciate that the Allieds are putting great pressure on us for the return of this man." The connection from Novoya Moskva was thin, but he did not raise his voice. Instead, he tightened it, giving it a hard, mechanical quality, as though he were driving it over the wires by force of will. He cursed silently at the speed with which Rogers had located Martino. It was one thing, negotiating with the Allieds when it was possible to say there was no knowledge of such a man. It was quite another when they could reply with the name of a specific hospital. It meant time lost that might have been stolen, and they were short of time to begin with. But there had never been any hiding anything important from Rogers for very long.

Very well, then that was the way it was. Meanwhile, however, there were these telephone calls.

"The surgeons will not have completed their final operation until tomorrow, at the earliest. I shall not be able to interrogate the man for perhaps two days thereafter. Yes, sir. I suggest the delay is the surgeons' responsibility. They say we are lucky to have the man alive at all, and that everything they are doing is absolutely necessary. Martino's condition was most serious. Every one of the operations was extremely delicate, and I am informed that nervous tissue regenerates very slowly, even with the most modern methods. Yes, sir. In my opinion, Medical Doctor Kothu is highly skilled. I am confirmed in this by my file copy of his certification from your headquarters."

Azarin was gambling a little there, he knew. Central Headquarters might decide to step in whether it had an ostensible reason or not. But he thought they would wait for a time. Their own staff had passed on Kothu and the rest of the medical team in the local hospital, since it was a military establishment. They would hesitate to belie themselves. And they knew Azarin was one of their best men. At Central Headquarters, they did not laugh at him. They knew his record.

No, he could afford to gamble with his superiors. It was a valuable thing to practice, for a man who would some day be among the superiors and was readying himself for it.

"Yes, sir. Two weeks more." Azarin bit down on the end of the papyros, and the hollow filter tube of gilt-wrapped pasteboard crumpled. He began chewing it lightly, sucking the smoke in between his teeth. "Yes, sir. I am aware of the already long delay. I will bear the international situation in mind."

Good. They were going to let him go ahead. For a moment, Azarin was happy.

Then the edge of his mind nibbled at the fact that he still had no idea of where to begin in his interrogation—that not the first shred of the earliest groundwork had been done.

Azarin scowled. Preoccupied, he said, "Good bye, sir," put the telephone down, and sat with his elbows on the desk, leaning forward, the papyros held between the thumb and forefinger of his right hand.

He was very good at his work, he knew. But he had never before encountered precisely these conditions. Neither had Novoya Moskva, and that was a help, but it was no help on the direct problem.

These temporary detentions were normally quite cut-and-dried. The man was diplomatically pumped of whatever he would yield in a short space of time. Usually, this was little. Occasionally, it was more. But always the man was returned as quickly as possible. Except in cases where it was desirable to stir the Allieds up, for some larger purpose, it was always best not to annoy them. The Allieds, upset by something like this, could go to quite extraordinary lengths of retaliation, and no one could tell what other strategies they might not cripple with their countermoves. Similarly, there were certain methods it was best not to use on their people. Returning a man in bad condition invariably made things difficult for months afterward.

So, usually it was a day or two at most before a man was returned to the Allieds. There, Rogers would take a day or two in discovering how much Azarin had found out. And that was the sum of it. If, at times, Azarin learned something useful, Rogers neutralized it at once. In Azarin's opinion, the entire business was a pitiful waste of time and energy.

But now, with this Martino, what did he have? He had a man who had invented something called a K-88, a man of high but undocumented reputation. Once more, Azarin cursed the circumstances of the times in which he lived. Once more he was angrily conscious of the fact that it was being left for the working professional—for Anastas Azarin—to clean up the work done by such fumbling amateurs as Heywood.

Azarin stared down at his desk in blank fury. And, of course, Novoya Moskva refused to act as though such a thing was basically its own fault. They simply pressed Azarin for results. Was he not an intelligence officer, after all? What could possibly be so difficult? What could possibly have taken him five weeks?

It was always this way in dealing with clerks. They had books, after all. The books had taught them how things were done. So things were done as they had been done in 1914 and in 1941, when the books were written.

No one knew anything about this man, except that he'd invented something. They had no file on him except for his undergraduate period at the technical academy in Cambridge, Massachusetts. Cursing, Azarin wished that the S.I.B. had, in actuality, some of the super-ferrets with which it was credited by the kino studios—the daring and supernally intelligent operatives who somehow passed through concrete walls and into vaults stuffed with alphabetically arranged Allied secrets conveniently shapirographed in Cyrillic print. He would have enjoyed having one or two of these on his staff, knowing that any information they brought back was completely accurate, correctly interpreted, did not have to be confirmed by other operatives, was up to date, had not been planted, and, furthermore, that these operatives had not meanwhile been subverted by Rogers. Such people did occur, of course. They immediately became instructors and staff officers, because they were altogether too few.

So there he had been, this Martino, protected by the usual security safeguards common to both sides. Azarin had planned to some day add the K-88 to the always incomplete and usually obsolescent jigsaw puzzle of information that was the best anyone could do. But he had not planned to have it happen like this.

Now he had him. He'd had him five useless weeks already. He had him almost fatally injured, bedridden, the makings of a good *cause célèbre* if he wasn't back in Allied hands soon—a man who looked extremely valuable, though he might turn out not to be—a man who, therefore, ought to be returned as soon as possible and kept as long as possible, and with whom, peculiarly, neither thing could be done at once.

It was a situation which verged on the comic in some of its aspects.

Azarin finished his papyros and shredded it to bits in the ashtray. It was all far from hopeless. He already had the rough outline of a plan, and he was acting on it. He would get results.

But Azarin knew Rogers was almost inhumanly clever. He knew Rogers must be fully aware of the situation here. And Azarin did not like the thought that Rogers must be laughing at him.

5.

A nurse put her head in the door of Martino's room. He slowly lowered his hand back to his side. The nurse disappeared, and in a moment a man in a white smock and skullcap came in.

He was a wiry, curly-haired little man with olive skin, broad, chisel-shaped teeth and a knobby jaw, who smiled down cheerfully as he took Martino's pulse.

"I'm very glad to see you awake. My name is Kothu, I am a medical doctor, how do you feel?"

Martino moved his head slowly from side to side.

"I see. There was no help for it, it had to be done. There was very little cranial structure remaining, the sensory organs were largely obliterated. Fortunately, the nature of the damage-inflicting agency was severe flashburns which did not expose your brain tissue to prolonged heat, and followed by a slow concussive shockwave crushing your cranium without splintering. Not pleasant to hear, I know, but of all possible damages the best. The arm, I am afraid, was severed by a metallic fragment. Would you speak, please?"

Martino looked up at him. He was still ashamed of the scream that had brought the nurse. He tried to picture what he must look like—to visualize the mechanisms that evidently were replacing so many of his organs—and he could not recall exactly how he had produced the scream. He tried to gather air in his lungs for the expected effort of speech, but there was only a rolling sensation under his ribs, as though a wheel or turbine impeller were spinning there.

"Effort is unnecessary," Dr. Kothu said. "Simply speak."

"I—" It felt no different in his throat. He had thought to find his words trembling through the vibrator of an artificial larynx. Instead, it was his old voice. But his rib cage did not sink over deflating lungs, and his diaphragm did not push out air. It was effortless, as speech in a dream can be, and he had the feeling he could babble on and on without stopping, for paragraphs, for days, for ever. "I— One, two, three, four. One, two, three, four. Do, re, mi, fa, sol, la, ti, do."

"Thank you, that is very helpful. Tell me, do you see me clearly? As I step back and move about, do your eyes follow and focus easily?"

"Yes." But the servomotors hummed in his face, and he wanted to reach up and massage the bridge of his nose.

"Very good. Well, do you know you have been here over a month?"

Martino shook his head. Wasn't anyone trying to get him back? Or did they think he was dead?

"It was necessary to keep you under sedation. You realize, I hope, the extent of the work we had to do?"

Martino moved his chest and shoulders. He felt clumsy and unbalanced, and somehow awkward inside, as though his chest were a bag that had been filled with stones.

"A great deal was done." Dr. Kothu seemed justifiably proud.

"I would say that Medical Doctor Verstoff did very well in substituting the prosthetic cranium. And of course, Medical Doctors Ho and Jansky were responsible for the connection of the prosthetic sensory organs to the proper brain centers, as Medical Technicians Debrett, Fonten, and Wassil were for the renal and respiratory complexes. I, myself, am in charge, having the honor to have developed the method of nervous tissue regeneration." His voice dropped a bit. "You would do us the kindness, perhaps, to mention our names when you return to the other side? I do not know your name," he added quickly, "nor am I intended to know your origin, but, you see, there are certain things a medical professional can perceive. On our side, we give three smallpox inoculations on the right arm. In any case—" Kothu seemed definitely embarrassed now. "What we have done here is quite new, and quite outstanding. And on our side, in these days, they do not publish such things."

"I'll try."

"Thank you. There are so many great things being done on our side, by so many people. And your side does not know. If you knew, your people would so much more quickly come to us."

Martino said nothing. An uncomfortable moment dragged by, and then Dr. Kothu said, "We must get you ready. One thing remains to be done, and we will have accomplished our best. That is the arm." He smiled as he had when he first came in. "I will call the nurses, and they will prepare you. I shall see you again in the operating theatre, and when we are finished, you will be as good as new."

"Thank you, Doctor."

Kothu left, and the nurses came in. They were two women dressed in heavily starched, thick white uniforms with headdresses that were banded tightly across their foreheads and draped back to their shoulders, completely covering their hair. Their faces were a little rough-skinned, but clear, and expressionless. Their lips were compressed, as they had been taught to keep them by the traditions of their nursing academies, and they wore no cosmetics. Because none of the standard cues common to women of the Allied cultures were present, it was impossible to guess at their ages and arrive at an accurate answer. They undressed him and washed him without speaking to each other or to him. They removed the pad from his left shoulder, painted the area with a colored germicide, loosely taped a new sterile pad in place, and moved him to an operating cart which one of them brought into the room.

They worked with complete competence, wasting no motion and dividing the work perfectly; they were a team that had risen above the flesh and beyond all skills but their one, completely-mastered own, who had so far advanced in the perfect practice of their art that it did not matter whether Martino was there or not.

Martino remained passively silent, watching them without getting in their way, and they handled him as though he were a practice mannikin.

6.

Azarin strode down the corridor toward Martino's room, with Kothu chattering beside him.

"Yes, Colonel, although he is not yet really strong, it is only a matter now of sufficient rest. All the operations were a great success."

"He can talk at length?"

"Not today, perhaps. It depends on the subject of discussion, of course. Too much strain would be bad."

"That will be largely his choice. He is in here?"

"Yes, Colonel." The little doctor opened the door wide, and Azarin marched through.

He stopped as though someone had sunk a bayonet in his belly. He stared at the unholy thing in the bed.

Martino was looking at him, with the sheets around his chest. Azarin could see the dark hole where his eyes were, lurking out from the metal. The good arm was under the covers. The left lay across his lap, like the claw of something from the Moon. The creature said nothing, did nothing. It lay in its bed and looked at him.

Azarin glared at Kothu. "You did not tell me he would look like this."

The doctor was thunderstruck. "But, I did! I very carefully

described the prosthetic appliances. I assured you they were perfectly functional—engineering marvels—if, regrettably, not especially cosmetic. You approved!"

"You did not tell me he would look like this," Azarin growled. "You will now introduce me."

"Of course," Doctor Kothu said nervously. He turned hastily toward Martino. "Sir, this is Colonel Azarin. He has come to see about your condition."

Azarin forced himself to go over to the bed. His face crinkled into its smile. "How do you do?" he said in English, holding out his hand.

The thing in the bed reached out its good hand. "I'm feeling better, thank you," it said neutrally. "How do you do?" Its hand, at least, was human. Azarin gripped it warmly. "I am well, thank you. Would you like to talk? Doctor Kothu, you will bring me a chair, please. I will sit here, and we will talk." He waited for Kothu to place the chair. "Thank you. You will go now. I will call you when I wish to leave."

"Of course, Colonel. Good afternoon, sir," Kothu said to the thing in the bed, and left.

"Now, Doctor of Science Martino, we will talk," Azarin said pleasantly, settling himself in his chair. "I have been waiting for you to recover. I hope I am not inconveniencing you, sir, but you understand there are things that have waited—records to be completed, forms to fill in, and the like." He shook his head. "Paperwork, sir. Always paperwork."

"Of course," Martino said. Azarin had difficulty fitting the perfectly normal voice to the ugly face. "I suppose our people have been annoying your people to get me back, and that always means a great deal of writing back and forth, doesn't it?"

Here is a clever one, Azarin thought. Within the first minute, he was trying to find out if his people were pressing hard. Well, they were, God knew, they were, if Novoya Moskva's tone of voice meant anything.

"There is always paperwork," he said, smiling. "You understand, I am responsible for this sector, and my people wish reports." So, now you may guess as much as you wish. "Are you comfortable? I hope everything is as it should be. You understand that as colonel in command of this sector, I ordered that you be given the best of all medical attention."

"Quite comfortable, thank you."

"I am sure that you, as a Doctor of Science, must be even more impressed with the work than I, as a simple soldier."

"My specialty is electronics, Colonel, not servomechanics."

Ah. So now we are even.

Less than even, Azarin thought angrily, for Martino had yet to give him any sign of being helpful. It did not matter, after all, how much Martino did not find out.

These first talks were seldom very productive in themselves. But they set the tone of everything that followed. It was now that Azarin had to decide what tactics to use against this man. It was now that the lines would be drawn, and Azarin measured against Martino.

But how could anyone see what this man thought when his face was the face of a metal beast—a carved thing, unmoving, with no sign of anything? No anger, no fear, no indecision—no weakness!

Azarin scowled. Still, in the end, he would win. He would rip behind that mask, and secrets would come spilling out.

If there is time, he reminded himself. Six weeks, now. Six weeks. How far would the Allieds stretch their patience? How far would the Allieds let Novoya Moskva stretch theirs?

He almost glared at the man. It was his fault this incredible affair had ever taken place. "Tell me, Doctor Martino," he said, "don't you wonder why you are here, in one of our hospitals?"

"I assume you got the jump on our rescue teams."

It was becoming clear to Azarin that this Martino intended to leave him no openings. "Yes," he smiled, "but would you not expect your Allied government to take better safety precautions? Should they not have had teams close by?"

"I'm afraid I never thought about it very much."

So. The man refused to tell him whether the K-88 was normally considered an explosion hazard or not.

"And what *have* you thought about, Doctor of Science?"

The figure in the bed shrugged. "Nothing much. I'm waiting to get out of here. It's been quite a while, hasn't it? I don't imagine you'll be able to keep me very long."

Now the thing was deliberately trying to get him angry. Azarin did not like being reminded of the wasted weeks. "My dear Doctor of Science, you are free to go almost as soon as you wish."

"Yes—exactly. Almost."

So. The thing understood the situation perfectly, and would not yield—no more than its face could break out into fearful sweat.

Azarin realized his own palms were damp.

Abruptly, Azarin stood up. There was no good in pursuing this further. The lines were clearly drawn, the purpose of the talk was accomplished, nothing more could be done, and it was becoming more than he could stand to remain any longer with this monster. "I must go. We will talk again." Azarin bowed. "Good afternoon, Doctor of Science Martino."

"Good afternoon, Colonel Azarin."

Azarin pushed the chair back against the wall and strode out. "I am finished for today," he growled to the waiting Doctor Kothu, and went back to his office, where he sat drinking tea and frowning at the telephone.

7.

Doctor Kothu came in, examined him, and left. Martino lay back in his bed, thinking.

Azarin was going to be bad, he thought, if he was given the chance to build up his temper over any period of time. He wondered how much longer the A.N.G. would take to get him out of this.

But Martino's greatest preoccupation, at the moment, was the K-88. He had already decided what unlikely combination of factors had produced the explosion. Now, as he had been doing for the past several hours, he worked toward a new means of absorbing the terrific heat wastage that the K-88 developed.

He found his thoughts drifting away from it and toward what had happened to him. He raised his new arm and looked at it in fascination before he forced himself off the subject. He flung the arm down on the bed beside him, out of his field of vision, and felt the shock against the mattress.

How long am I going to stay in this place? he thought. Kothu had told him he could be getting out of bed soon. How much good is that going to do me if they keep me on this side of the line indefinitely?

He wondered how much the Soviets knew about the K-88. Probably just enough so they'd do their best to keep him and pump it out of him. If they hadn't known anything, they'd never have come after him. If they knew enough to use, again, they wouldn't have bothered.

He wondered how far the Soviets would go before they were ready to give up. You heard all kinds of stories. Probably the same stories the Soviets heard about the A.N.G.

He was frightened, he suddenly realized. Frightened by what had happened to him, by what Kothu had done to save him, by the thought of having the Soviets somehow get the K-88 out of him, by the sudden feeling of complete helplessness that came over him.

He wondered if he might be a coward. It was something he had not considered since the age when he learned the difference between physical bravery and courage. The possibility that he might do something irrational out of simple fear was new to him.

He lay in the bed, searching his mind for evidence, pro or con.

8.

It was now two months, and still Azarin did not even know whether the K-88 was a bomb, a death ray, or a new means of sharpening bayonets.

He had had several totally unsatisfactory talks with that thing, Martino, who would not give in. It was all very polite, and it told him nothing. A man—any man—he could have fought. But a blank-faced nothing like some nightmare in the dark forests, that sat in its wheelchair looking like the gods they worshiped in jungle temples, that knew if it waited long enough Azarin would be beaten—that was more than could be tolerated.

Azarin remembered this morning's call from Novoya Moskva, and suddenly he crashed his fist down upon his desk.

Their best man. They knew he was their best man, they knew he was Anastas Azarin, and yet they talked to him like that! *Clerks* talked to him like *that!*

It was all because they wanted to give Martino back to the

Allieds as quickly as they could. If they would give Azarin time, it would be another matter. If Martino did not have to be returned at all, if certain methods could be used, then something might really be done.

Azarin sat behind his desk, searching for the answer. Something must be thought of to satisfy Novoya Moskva—to delay things until, inevitably, a way was found to handle this Martino. But nothing would satisfy Central Headquarters unless they could in turn satisfy the Allieds. And the Allieds would be satisfied with nothing less than Martino.

Azarin's eyes opened wide. His thick eyebrows rose into perfect semicircles. Then he reached for his telephone and called Doctor Kothu's number. He sat listening to the telephone ring. He made one, Azarin thought. Perhaps he can make two.

His upper lip drew back from his teeth at the thought that the American, Heywood, was the best choice for the assignment. He would have much preferred to send someone solid— one of his own people, whose capabilities he knew and whose weaknesses he could allow for. But Heywood was the only choice. Probably he would fail sooner or later. But the important thing was that Novoya Moskva would not think so. They were very proud of their foreigners at Central Headquarters, and of the whole overcomplicated and inefficient system that supported them. They had it in their heads that a man could be a traitor to his own people and still not be crippled by the weaknesses that had driven him to treachery. Their repeated failures had done nothing to enlighten them, and for once Azarin was glad of it.

"Medical Doctor Kothu? This is Azarin. If I were to send you a suitable man—a whole man this time—could you do with him what you did with Martino?" He slapped the ends of his fingers against the edge of his desk, listening. "That is correct. A whole man. I wish you to make me a brother for the monster. A twin."

When he was through speaking to Kothu, Azarin called Novoya Moskva, hunching forward over his desk, his papyros jutting straight out from his hand. His jaw was firmly set, his lower teeth thrust forward past his upper jaw. His lips were stretched. His face lost its wooden blankness. It was a different sort of a grin, this, from the one he usually showed the world.

Like his habitual reticent mask, it had been forged in the years since he left his father's forest. Its lines on his face had been baked in by foreign suns and scoured by the sand of alien deserts. It came to him as easily, now, as the somewhat boyish smile he'd always had. The difference was that Azarin was not aware he possessed this third expression.

It took some little time to convince Central Headquarters, but Azarin felt no impatience. He hammered his plan forward like a man hewing through a tree, steadily and with measured blows, knowing that he has only to swing often enough and the tree must fall.

He hung up, finally, and drained his tea glass in a few gulps. The orderly brought more. Azarin's eyes crinkled pleasantly at the corners as he thought that once again it had been Anastas Azarin who found solutions while the clerks at Central Headquarters twittered with indecision.

He put his hands on the edge of his desk and unhurriedly pushed himself to his feet. He walked into his outer office. "I am on my way downstairs. You will have the car waiting for me," he told his chief clerk.

It would take the courier several days to reach Washington with Heywood's orders, but that part of the system, at least, was foolproof. Heywood would arrive here in a week. Meanwhile, there was no reason to wait for him. The cover plan was functioning automatically as of this moment. The Allieds would find Novoya Moskva much different to deal with, now that Azarin had stiffened some of the pliant spines at Central Headquarters. And, in consequence, Azarin would find his telephone much more silent, and much less peremptory.

So. Everything was arranged. By the simple, uneducated peasant, Anastas Azarin. By the dolt who moved his lips when he read. By the tea drinker. By the ignorant man from the dark forest, who worked while Novoya Moskva talked.

Azarin's eyes twinkled as he came into Martino's room, stopped, and looked at the man. "We will talk more," he said. "Now we have plenty of time to find out about the K-Eighty-eight." It was the first time he had been able to bring the term out into the open. He saw the man's body twitch.

9.

The first thing lost under these conditions, Martino discovered, was the sense of time. He was not particularly surprised, since a completely foreign experience could not possibly contain any of the usual cues by which a human being learned his chronology. The room had no windows, and no clocks or calendars. These were the simplest and most obvious lacks. Then, there was no change in his routine. There was no stopping to sit down to a meal, or lying down to rest, and hunger or sleepiness furnish no help when they are constant. This room itself, somewhere in Azarin's sector headquarters, was so constructed as to offer no signposts. It was rectangular, cast in unpainted cement from floor to ceiling. Martino's route of passage was from one end to the other, and one of the walls toward which he walked was almost exactly the same as the other, even in such details as the grain of the gray surface. As he walked, he passed between two identical oak desks, facing each other, and each desk had a man in a gray-green uniform behind it. The men contrived to look alike, and a similar door entered the room behind each of them. The light fixture was exactly in the center of the ceiling. Martino had no idea of which door he had originally used to come into the room, or toward which wall he had first marched.

As he passed the desks, it was always the man on his right who asked the first question. It might be anything: "What is your middle name?" or "How many inches in a foot?" The questions were meaningless, and no record was kept of his answers. The men behind the desks, who changed shifts at what might have been irregular intervals but who nevertheless always looked somehow alike, did not even care if he answered or not. If he remembered correctly, for some time at the beginning he had not answered. Somewhat later, he had irritatedly taken to giving nonsense replies: "Newton," or "eight." But now it was much less exhausting to simply tell the truth.

He knew what was happening to him. In the end, the brain in effect began manufacturing its own truth drugs in self defense against the fatigue poisons that were flooding it. The equation was: Correct replies = relief. There was none of the saving adrenalin of pain. There was only this walking through a meaningless world.

It was that last which was affecting him most strongly. The men behind the desks paid him no attention, unless he tried to stop walking. The remainder of the time they simply asked their questions, looking not at him but at each other. He suspected they neither knew who he was nor cared why he was here. Lately, he had become certain of it. They were practicing their trade on each other, not on him. They used him only because most two-handed games require a ball. It meant nothing to them when he began giving correct answers, because they were not here to pass judgment on his answers.

He knew they were here simply to soften him up, and that eventually Azarin would take over. But meanwhile he felt a mounting, querulous sense of terrible injustice. He was near to pouting as he walked.

He knew why that was, too. His brain, after all, had solved the problem. He was fulfilling the equation—he was doing what they wanted him to. He was giving correct answers, and by all that was reasonable, they ought to respond by giving him relief. But they ignored him; they showed no sign of understanding that he was doing what they wanted. And if he was doing what they wanted, and they ignored him, the brain could only decide somehow it was not transmitting its signals through his actions to them. If there had been only one of them, the brain could have decided that one was deaf and blind, reciting his questions by idiotic rote. But there were two of them, always, and there must be a dozen in all. So the brain could only decide that it was he who was incapable of making himself heard—that it was Lucas Martino who was nothing.

At the same time, he knew what was happening to him.

10.

Azarin sat patiently behind his desk, waiting for word to come from the interrogation room. It was three days, now, since Martino had been brought from the hospital, and Azarin knew, as a man knows his trade, that the word would come sometime today.

It was quite a simple business, Azarin thought. One took a

man and peeled things away from him—more vital things than skin, though he had seen that technique work at the hands of men who had not learned the subtler phases of their trade. In effect, it was much the same, though the result was cleaner. A man carries very little excess baggage in his head. Even a clerk, and a man like Martino was not a clerk. The more intelligent the man, the less excess baggage and the quicker the results. For once you exposed the man underneath, he was raw and tender—a touch here and there, and he gave up what he knew.

Of course, having done that and knowing he had done that, the man was empty thereafter. He had found himself to be pliable, and after that anyone could use him—could do anything he wanted with him. He bore the mark of whoever touched him last. He did what you wanted of him. He was a living nothing.

Ordinarily, Azarin drew only a normal measure of satisfaction from having done this to a man while he himself remained, forever and imperishable, Anastas Azarin. But in this case—

Azarin growled at something invisible across the room.

Chapter Fifteen

EDDIE BATES was a sleeper. He was a wiry, flat-bellied, ugly man with a face that had been grotesquely scarred by acne. His youth had been miserable, for all that he faithfully lifted weights a half-hour every day in his bedroom. Toward the end of his teens he had spent six months in a reformatory for assault and battery. It should have been assault with intent to kill, but only Eddie knew how far he had planned to go when he first began hitting the other boy—a flashily good-looking youngster who had made a remark about a girl Eddie never had found the courage to speak to.

When he was twenty, he found a job in a garage. He worked in a mood of perpetual sullen resentment that made most of the customers dislike him. Only one of them—a casually like-able man who drove an expensive car—had taken pains to cultivate his friendship. Eddie ran a few errands for him after work, and assumed he was a criminal of some kind, since he paid quite well and had Eddie deliver his cryptic messages by roundabout methods.

Eddie did his work well and faithfully, tied to the man by something more than money. The man was the only respectable friend he had in the world, and when the man made him another offer, Eddie accepted.

So, Eddie Bates had become a sleeper. His friend now paid him not to run messages, and to stay out of trouble. He found him a job as an airlines mechanic. Every month that Eddie continued to be a respectable citizen, and drew his pay from the airline, an envelope with additional pay reached him by means as devious as those in which Eddie had once been employed. By now, Eddie knew who his friend was working for. But the man was his friend, and he was never asked to do anything else to earn the extra money.

Eddie avoided considering the realities of his position. As time went by, this became progressively easier.

He grew older, and continued to work for the airline. Several things happened to him. For one thing, he had a natural talent for machinery. He understood it, respected it, and was willing to work with infinite patience until it was functioning properly. He found that very few of the people he worked with turned away from his face once they had seen him work on an engine. For another, he had found a girl.

Alice worked in the diner where Eddie ate his lunch every day. She was a hard-working girl who knew that the only kind of man worth bothering with was a steady man with a good trade. Looks were not particularly important to her—she distrusted handsome men on principle. It was an accepted thing between her and Eddie that they would be married as soon as they had enough money saved for the down payment on a house near the airport.

But now Eddie Bates, the sleeper, had been activated. He crouched near the plane's inboard engine nacelle, up on the high wing far above the dark hangar floor, and wondered what he was going to do.

He had his orders. He had more—he had the thing his friend had given him. It was a metal cartridge the size of a pint milk bottle, one end of which was a knob with time calibrations marked off on it. His friend had preset it and given it to him, and told him to put it in an engine. He had not explained that it was only intended to force the plane down into the water at a pre-calculated point. Eddie assumed it was meant to blow the wing off in flight. He was a mechanic, not an explosives expert. Like most people, he had no accurate idea of the power of a given weight of charge, and no idea how much of the cartridge's actual bulk was taken up by timing mechanisms.

He wavered for a long time, hidden by himself in the darkness near the hangar roof. He added things up time after time, growing more desperate and more indecisive.

He had never quite expected that he would be asked to do something like this. He gradually admitted to himself that as time had gone by, he had come to believe that he would never be asked to do anything. But the man was his friend, and Eddie had taken his money.

But he had other friends, now, and he had worked on this engine himself this afternoon, tuning it patiently.

But the money was important. It was helping his savings a great deal. The more he saved, the sooner he could marry Alice. But if he didn't plant the bomb, the money would stop.

Other things might happen if he didn't plant the bomb. His friend might turn him in somehow, and then he would lose the respect of his friends here in the shop, and never marry Alice.

He had to do something.

He drew a quick breath and thrust the bomb through the opened inspection plate into the space between the engine and the inner surface of the nacelle. He hastily bolted the plate back down and ran out of the hangar.

He had done only one thing to offset the complete helplessness he felt. As he slipped the cartridge through the opened inspection plate, his fingers closed on it convulsively, almost as though by reflex, almost as though clutching at some hope of salvation, or almost as though thrusting away something precious to him. And he knew as he was doing it that it was only an empty gesture, because what did it matter when the plane crashed?

He had re-set the timer, but no one—certainly not Eddie Bates—could have said by how much.

Chapter Sixteen

I MUST remember, Martino thought, looking across the office at Colonel Azarin, that the K-Eighty-eight is not meant to be a bribe. Some people buy the attention of other people by telling them things. No man is so drab as not to have some personal detail that will intrigue others. I must remember that I can tell Azarin about the time I played hookey from grammar school because I was ashamed to raise my hand to go to the washroom. That is intriguing enough, and will attract enough attention to me. Or I can tell him some back fence gossip—about Johnson, the astrophysicist, for instance, who looks at figure studies in his room at night. That will hold his attention at least until I have exhausted all the details of the story. I can tell him all these things, and as many more as I can remember, but I must not try to hold his attention by telling him about the K-Eighty-eight because that is not a proper use of it.

I must remember, he thought with infinite patience for clarity's sake, never to admit I know anything about the K-Eighty-eight. That is the greatest defense against the urge to gossip —to look surprised or pretend disinterest when someone comes to you for further details.

"Sit down, Doctor of Science Martino," Azarin said, smiling pleasantly. "Please be so good."

Martino felt the answering smile well up through his entire body. He felt the traitor joy begin as a faint surprise that someone had spoken to him at last, and then spread into a great warmth at this man who had called him by name.

Not thinking that nothing would show on his face, he trembled with panic at the thought of how easily Azarin was breaking through his defenses. He had hoped to be stronger than this.

I must remember to say *nothing*, he thought, urgently now. If ever I begin, my friendship for this man won't let me stop. I have to fight to say nothing at all.

"Would you care for a cigarette?" Azarin extended the sandalwood box across the desk.

Martino's right hand was trembling. He reached with his

left. The metal fingertips, badly controlled, broke the papyros to shreds.

He saw Azarin frown for a moment, and in that moment Martino almost cried out, he was so upset by what he had done to offend this man. But it took an effort to activate the proper vocal affectors in his brain, and his brain detected it and stopped it.

I must remember I have other friends, he thought. I must remember that Edith and Barbara will be killed if I please this friend.

He realized in a panic that Edith and Barbara were not his friends any longer—that they probably did not remember him—that no one remembered or noticed him or cared about him except Azarin.

I must remember, he thought. I must remember to apologize to Edith and Barbara if I ever leave here. I must remember I will leave here.

Azarin was smiling again. "A glass of tea?"

I must think about that, he thought. If I take tea, I will have to open my mouth. If I do that, will I be able to close it again?

"Don't be afraid, Doctor of Science Martino. Everything is all right now. We will sit, and we will talk, and I will listen to you."

He felt himself beginning to do it. I must remember not going to school—and Johnson, he thought frantically.

Why? he wondered.

Because the K-Eighty-eight is not meant to be a bribe.

What does that mean?

He listened to himself think in fascination, absorbed by this phenomenon of two opposing drives in a single mechanism, and wondered just exactly how his mind did the trick—what kind of circuits were involved, and were they actually in operation simultaneously or did they use the same components alternately?

"Are you playing with me?" Azarin shouted. "What are you doing, behind that face? Are you *laughing* at me?"

Martino stared at Azarin in surprise. What? What had he done?

He could not wonder how long it might take him to complete a train of thought. It did not seem to him that a very long time at all had gone by since Azarin's last question, or that a man looking at him might see nothing but an implacable, graven-faced figure with a deadly metal arm lying quiet but always ready to crush.

"Martino, I did not bring you here for comedies!" Azarin's eyes suddenly narrowed. Martino thought he saw fear under the anger, and it puzzled him greatly. "Did Rogers plan this? Did he *deliberately* send you?"

Martino began to shake his head, to try to explain. But he caught himself. The thought began to come to him that there was no need to talk to this man—that he had already attracted all of Azarin's attention.

The telephone rang, with the hard, shrill insistence that always came when the switchboard operator was relaying a call from Novoya Moskva.

Azarin picked it up and listened.

Martino watched him with no curiosity while Azarin's eyes opened wide. After a time, Azarin put the phone down, and Martino still took no notice. Even when Azarin's shrunken voice muttered, "Your college friend, Heywood, drowned six hundred miles too soon," Martino had no notion of what it meant.

2.

Martino sat motionless in the Tatra as it drew near the border. The S.I.B. man beside him—an Asiatic named Yung—was too quick to interpret every movement as an opening to practice his conversational English.

Three months wasted, Martino was thinking. The whole program must be bogged down. I only hope they haven't tried to rebuild that particular configuration.

He searched his mind for the modified system he was almost certain he had thought of in their hospital. He had been trying to bring it back for the past two weeks, while Kothu and a therapist worked on him. But he had not been able to quite grasp it. Several times he thought he had it, but the memory was patchy and useless.

Well, he thought as the car stopped, the therapist told me

there was bound to be some trouble for a while. But it'll come to me.

"Here you are, Doctor Martino," Yung said brightly, unsnapping the door.

"Yes." He looked out at the gateway, with its Soviet guards. Beyond it, he could see the Allied soldiers, and a car with two men getting out of it.

He began to walk toward them. There'll be problems, he reminded himself. These people aren't used to my looks. It'll take a while to overcome that.

But it can be done. A man is something more than just a collection of features. And I'll get to work soon. That'll keep me busy. If I can't remember that idea I had in the hospital, I can always work out something else.

It's been a bad time, he thought, stepping through the gate. But I haven't lost anything.

THE BIG TIME

Fritz Leiber

1

When shall we three meet again
In thunder, lightning, or in rain?

When the hurlyburly's done.
When the battle's lost and won.
　　　　　　　　　　　—Macbeth

ENTER THREE HUSSARS

MY NAME is Greta Forzane. Twenty-nine and a party girl would describe me. I was born in Chicago, of Scandinavian parents, but now I operate chiefly outside space and time —not in Heaven or Hell, if there are such places, but not in the cosmos or universe you know either.

I am not as romantically entrancing as the immortal film star who also bears my first name, but I have a rough-and-ready charm of my own. I need it, for my job is to nurse back to health and kid back to sanity Soldiers badly roughed up in the biggest war going. This war is the Change War, a war of time travelers—in fact, our private name for being in this war is being on the Big Time. Our Soldiers fight by going back to change the past, or even ahead to change the future, in ways to help our side win the final victory a billion or more years from now. A long killing business, believe me.

You don't know about the Change War, but it's influencing your lives all the time and maybe you've had hints of it without realizing.

Have you ever worried about your memory, because it doesn't seem to be bringing you exactly the same picture of the past from one day to the next? Have you ever been afraid that your personality was changing because of forces beyond your knowledge or control? Have you ever felt sure that sudden death was about to jump you from nowhere? Have you ever been scared of Ghosts—not the story-book kind, but the billions of beings who were once so real and strong it's hard to believe they'll just sleep harmlessly forever? Have you ever wondered about those things you may call devils or Demons—spirits able to range through all time and space, through the hot hearts of stars and the cold skeleton of space between the galaxies? Have you ever thought that the whole universe might be a crazy, mixed-up dream? If you have, you've had hints of the Change War.

How I got recruited into the Change War, how it's conducted, what the two sides are, why you don't consciously know about it, what I really think about it—you'll learn in due course.

The place outside the cosmos where I and my pals do our nursing job I simply call the Place. A lot of my nursing consists of amusing and humanizing Soldiers fresh back from raids into time. In fact, my formal title is Entertainer and I've got my silly side, as you'll find out.

My pals are two other gals and three guys from quite an assortment of times and places. We're a pretty good team, and with Sid bossing, we run a pretty good Recuperation Station, though we have our family troubles. But most of our troubles come slamming into the Place with the beat-up Soldiers, who've generally just been going through hell and want to raise some of their own. As a matter of fact, it was three newly arrived Soldiers who started this thing I'm going to tell you about, this thing that showed me so much about myself and everything.

When it started, I had been on the Big Time for a thousand sleeps and two thousand nightmares, and working in the Place for five hundred-one thousand. This two-nightmares routine every time you lay down your dizzy little head is rough, but you pretend to get used to it because being on the Big Time is supposed to be worth it.

The Place is midway in size and atmosphere between a large nightclub where the Entertainers sleep in and a small Zeppelin hangar decorated for a party, though a Zeppelin is one thing we haven't had yet. You go out of the Place, but not often if you have any sense and if you are an Entertainer like me, into the cold light of a morning filled with anything from the earlier dinosaurs to the later spacemen, who look strangely similar except for size.

Solely on doctor's orders, I have been on cosmic leave six times since coming to work at the Place, meaning I have had six brief vacations, if you care to call them that, for believe me they are busman's holidays, considering what goes on in the Place all the time. The last one I spent in Renaissance Rome, where I got a crush on Cesare Borgia, but I got over it. Vacations are for the birds, anyway, because they have to be fitted by the Spiders into serious operations of the Change War, and you can imagine how restful that makes them.

"See those Soldiers changing the past? You stick along with them. Don't go too far up front, though, but don't wander off either. Relax and enjoy yourself."

Ha! Now the kind of recuperation Soldiers get when they come to the Place is a horse of a far brighter color, simply dazzling by comparison. Entertainment is our business and we give them a bang-up time and send them staggering happily back into action, though once in a great while something may happen to throw a wee shadow on the party.

I am dead in some ways, but don't let that bother you—I am lively enough in others. If you met me in the cosmos, you would be more apt to yak with me or try to pick me up than to ask a cop to do same or a father to douse me with holy water, unless you are one of those hard-boiled reformer types. But you are not likely to meet me in the cosmos, because (bar Basin Street and the Prater) 15th Century Italy and Augustan Rome—until they spoiled it—are my favorite (Ha!) vacation spots and, as I have said, I stick as close to the Place as I can. It is really the nicest Place in the whole Change World. (Crisis! I even *think* of it capitalized!)

Anyhoo, when this thing started, I was twiddling my thumbs on the couch nearest the piano and thinking it was too late to do my fingernails and whoever came in probably wouldn't notice them anyway.

The Place was jumpy like it always is on an approach and the gray velvet of the Void around us was curdled with the uneasy lights you see when you close your eyes in the dark.

Sid was tuning the Maintainers for the pickup and the right shoulder of his gold-worked gray doublet was streaked where he'd been wiping his face on it with quick ducks of his head.

Beauregard was leaning as close as he could over Sid's other shoulder, one white-trousered knee neatly indenting the rose plush of the control divan, and he wasn't missing a single flicker of Sid's old fingers on the dials; Beau's copilot besides piano player. Beau's face had that dead blank look it must have had when every double eagle he owned and more he didn't were riding on the next card to be turned in the gambling saloon on one of those wedding-cake Mississippi steamboats.

Doc was soused as usual, sitting at the bar with his top hat pushed back and his knitted shawl pulled around him, his wide eyes seeing whatever horrors a life in Nazi-occupied Czarist Russia can add to being a drunk Demon in the Change World.

Maud, who is the Old Girl, and Lili—the New Girl, of course—were telling the big beads of their identical pearl necklaces.

You might say that all us Entertainers were a bit edgy; being Demons doesn't automatically make us brave.

Then the red telltale on the Major Maintainer went out and the Door began to darken in the Void facing Sid and Beau, and I felt Change Winds blowing hard and my heart missed a couple of beats, and the next thing three Soldiers had stepped out of the cosmos and into the Place, their first three steps hitting the floor hard as they changed times and weights.

They were dressed as officers of hussars, as we'd been advised, and—praise the Bonny Dew!—I saw that the first of them was Erich, my own dear little commandant, the pride of the von Hohenwalds and the Terror of the Snakes. Behind him was some hard-faced Roman or other, and beside Erich and shouldering into him as they stamped forward was a new boy, blond, with a face like a Greek god who's just been touring a Christian hell.

They were uniformed exactly alike in black—shakos, fur-edged pelisses, boots, and so forth—with white skull emblems on the shakos. The only difference between them was that Erich had a Caller on his wrist and the New Boy had a black-gauntleted glove on his left hand and was clenching the mate in it, his right hand being bare like both of Erich's and the Roman's.

"You've made it, lads, hearts of gold," Sid boomed at them, and Beau twitched a smile and murmured something courtly and Maud began to chant, "Shut the Door!" and the New Girl copied her and I joined in because the Change Winds do blow like crazy when the Door is open, even though it can't ever be shut tight enough to keep them from leaking through.

"Shut it before it blows wrinkles in our faces," Maud called in her gamin voice to break the ice, looking like a skinny teen-ager in the tight, knee-length frock she'd copied from the New Girl.

But the three Soldiers weren't paying attention. The Roman —I remembered his name was Mark—was blundering forward stiffly as if there were something wrong with his eyes, while Erich and the New Boy were yelling at each other about a kid and Einstein and a summer palace and a bloody glove and the Snakes having booby-trapped Saint Petersburg. Erich had that taut sadistic smile he gets when he wants to hit me.

The New Boy was in a tearing rage. "Why'd you pull us out so bloody fast? We fair chewed the Nevsky Prospekt to pieces galloping away."

"Didn't you feel their stun guns, *Dummkopf*, when they sprung the trap—too soon, *Gott sei Dank?*" Erich demanded.

"I did," the New Boy told him. "Not enough to numb a cat. Why didn't you show us action?"

"Shut up. I'm your leader. I'll show you action enough."

"You won't. You're a filthy Nazi coward."

"Weibischer Engländer!"

"Bloody Hun!"

"Schlange!"

The blond lad knew enough German to understand that last crack. He threw back his sable-edged pelisse to clear his sword arm and swung away from Erich, which bumped him into Beau. At the first sign of the quarrel, Beau had raised himself from the divan as quickly and silently as a—no, I won't use that word—and slithered over to them.

"Sirs, you forget yourselves," he said sharply, off balance, supporting himself on the New Boy's upraised arm. "This is Sidney Lessingham's Place of Entertainment and Recupera-tion. There are ladies—"

With a contemptuous snarl, the New Boy shoved him off and snatched with his bare hand for his saber. Beau reeled against the divan, it caught him in the shins and he fell toward the Maintainers. Sid whisked them out of the way as if they were a couple of beach radios—simply nothing in the Place is nailed down—and had them back on the coffee table before Beau hit the floor. Meanwhile, Erich had his saber out and had parried the New Boy's first wild slash and lunged in return, and I heard the scream of steel and the rutch of his boot on the diamond-studded pavement.

Beau rolled over and came up pulling from the ruffles of his shirt bosom a derringer I knew was some other weapon in disguise—a stun gun or even an Atropos. Besides scaring me damp for Erich and everybody, that brought me up short: us Entertainers' nerves must be getting as naked as the Soldiers', probably starting when the Spiders canceled all cosmic leaves twenty sleeps back.

Sid shot Beau his look of command, rapped out, "I'll handle this, you whoreson firebrand," and turned to the Minor Maintainer. I noticed that the telltale on the Major was glowing a reassuring red again, and I found a moment to thank Mamma Devi that the Door was shut.

Maud was jumping up and down, cheering I don't know which—nor did she, I bet—and the New Girl was white and I saw that the sabers were working more businesslike. Erich's flicked, flicked, flicked again and came away from the blond lad's cheek spilling a couple of red drops. The blond lad lunged fiercely, Erich jumped back, and the next moment they were both floating helplessly in the air, twisting like they had cramps.

I realized quick enough that Sid had shut off gravity in the Door and Stores sectors of the Place, leaving the rest of us firm on our feet in the Refresher and Surgery sectors. The Place has sectional gravity to suit our Extraterrestrial buddies—those crazy ETs sometimes come whooping in for recuperation in very mixed batches.

From his central position, Sid called out, kindly enough but taking no nonsense, "All right, lads, you've had your fun. Now sheathe those swords."

For a second or so, the two black hussars drifted and contorted. Erich laughed harshly and neatly obeyed—the commandant is used to free fall. The blond lad stopped writhing, hesitated while he glared upside down at Erich and managed to get his saber into its scabbard, although he turned a slow somersault doing it. Then Sid switched on their gravity, slow enough so they wouldn't get sprained landing.

Erich laughed, lightly this time, and stepped out briskly

toward us. He stopped to clap the New Boy firmly on the shoulder and look him in the face.

"So, now you get a good scar," he said.

The other didn't pull away, but he didn't look up and Erich came on. Sid was hurrying toward the New Boy, and as he passed Erich, he wagged a finger at him and gayly said, "You rogue." Next thing I was giving Erich my "Man, you're home" hug and he was kissing me and cracking my ribs and saying, "*Liebchen! Doppchen!*"—which was fine with me because I do love him and I'm a good lover and as much a Doubleganger as he is.

We had just pulled back from each other to get a breath—his blue eyes looked so sweet in his worn face—when there was a thud behind us. With the snapping of the tension, Doc had fallen off his bar stool and his top hat was over his eyes. As we turned to chuckle at him, Maud squeaked and we saw that the Roman had walked straight up against the Void and was marching along there steadily without gaining a foot, like it does happen, his black uniform melting into that inside-your-head gray.

Maud and Beau rushed over to fish him back, which can be tricky. The thin gambler was all courtly efficiency again. Sid supervised from a distance.

"What's wrong with him?" I asked Erich.

He shrugged. "Overdue for Change Shock. And he was nearest the stun guns. His horse almost threw him. *Mein Gott*, you should have seen Saint Petersburg, *Liebchen*: the Nevsky Prospekt, the canals flying by like reception carpets of blue sky, a cavalry troop in blue and gold that blundered across our escape, fine women in furs and ostrich plumes, a monk with a big tripod and his head under a hood—it gave me the horrors seeing all those Zombies flashing past and staring at me in that sick unawakened way they have, and knowing that some of them, say the photographer, might be Snakes."

Our side in the Change War is the Spiders, the other side is the Snakes, though all of us—Spiders and Snakes alike—are Doublegangers and Demons too, because we're cut out of our lifelines in the cosmos. Your lifeline is all of you from birth to death. We're Doublegangers because we can operate both in the cosmos and outside of it, and Demons because we act reasonably alive while doing so—which the Ghosts don't. Entertainers

and Soldiers are all Demon-Doublegangers, whichever side
they're on—though they say the Snake Places are simply
ghastly. Zombies are dead people whose lifelines lie in the so-
called past.

"What were you doing in Saint Petersburg before the am-
bush?" I asked Erich. "That is, if you can talk about it."

"Why not? We were kidnapping the infant Einstein back
from the Snakes in 1883. Yes, the Snakes got him, *Liebchen*,
only a few sleeps back, endangering the West's whole victory
over Russia—"

"—which gave your dear little Hitler the world on a platter
for fifty years and got me loved to death by your sterling troops
in the Liberation of Chicago—"

"—but which leads to the ultimate victory of the Spiders
and the West over the Snakes and Communism, *Liebchen*, remember that. Anyway, our counter-snatch didn't work. The
Snakes had guards posted—most unusual and we weren't
warned. The whole thing was a great mess. No wonder Bruce
lost his head—not that it excuses him."

"The New Boy?" I asked. Sid hadn't got to him and he was
still standing with hooded eyes where Erich had left him, a
dark pillar of shame and rage.

"*Ja*, a lieutenant from World War One. An Englishman."

"I gathered that," I told Erich. "Is he really effeminate?"

"*Weibischer?*" He smiled. "I had to call him something when
he said I was a coward. He'll make a fine Soldier—only needs a
little more shaping."

"You men are so original when you spat." I lowered my
voice. "But you shouldn't have gone on and called him a Snake,
Erich mine."

"*Schlange?*" The smile got crooked. "Who knows—about
any of us? As Saint Petersburg showed me, the Snakes' spies
are getting cleverer than ours." The blue eyes didn't look sweet
now. "Are you, *Liebchen*, really nothing more than a good loyal
Spider?"

"Erich!"

"All right, I went too far—with Bruce and with you too.
We're all hacked over these days, riding with one leg over the
breaking edge."

Maud and Beau were supporting the Roman to a couch,

Maud taking most of his weight, with Sid still supervising and the New Boy still sulking by himself. The New Girl should have been with him, of course, but I couldn't see her anywhere and I decided she was probably having a nervous breakdown in the Refresher, the little jerk.

"The Roman looks pretty bad, Erich," I said.

"Ah, Mark's tough. Got virtue, as his people say. And our little starship girl will bring him back to life if anybody can and if . . ."

". . . you call this living," I filled in dutifully.

He was right. Maud had fifty-odd years of psychomedical experience, 23rd Century at that. It should have been Doc's job, but that was fifty drunks back.

"Maud and Mark, that will be an interesting experiment," Erich said. "Reminiscent of Goering's with the frozen men and the naked gypsy girls."

"You are a filthy Nazi. She'll be using electrophoresis and deep suggestion, if I know anything."

"How will you be able to know anything, *Liebchen*, if she switches on the couch curtains, as I perceive she is preparing to do?"

"Filthy Nazi I said and meant."

"Precisely." He clicked his heels and bowed a millimeter. "Erich Friederich von Hohenwald, *Oberleutnant* in the army of the Third Reich. Fell at Narvik, where he was Recruited by the Spiders. Lifeline lengthened by a Big Change after his first death and at latest report Commandant of Toronto, where he maintains extensive baby farms to provide him with breakfast meat, if you believe the handbills of the *voyageurs* underground. At your service."

"Oh, Erich, it's all so lousy," I said, touching his hand, reminded that he was one of the unfortunates Resurrected from a point in their lifelines well before their deaths—in his case, because the date of his death had been shifted forward by a Big Change after his Resurrection. And as every Demon finds out, if he can't imagine it beforehand, it is pure hell to remember your future, and the shorter the time between your Resurrection and your death back in the cosmos, the better. Mine, bless Bab-ed-Din, was only an action-packed ten minutes on North Clark Street.

Erich put his other hand lightly over mine. "Fortunes of the Change War, *Liebchen*. At least I'm a Soldier and sometimes assigned to future operations—though why we should have this monomania about our future personalities back there, I don't know. Mine is a stupid *Oberst*, thin as paper—and frightfully indignant at the *voyageurs!* But it helps me a little if I see him in perspective and at least I get back to the cosmos pretty regularly, *Gott sei Dank*, so I'm better off than you Entertainers."

I didn't say aloud that a Changing cosmos is worse than none, but I found myself sending a prayer to the Bonny Dew for my father's repose, that the Change Winds would blow lightly across the lifeline of Anton A. Forzane, professor of physiology, born in Norway and buried in Chicago. Woodlawn Cemetery is a nice gray spot.

"That's all right, Erich," I said. "We Entertainers Got Mittens too."

He scowled around at me suspiciously, as if he were wondering whether I had all my buttons on.

"Mittens?" he said. "What do you mean? I'm not wearing any. Are you trying to say something about Bruce's gloves—which incidentally seem to annoy him for some reason. No, seriously, Greta, why do you Entertainers need mittens?"

"Because we get cold feet sometimes. At least I do. Got Mittens, as I say."

A sickly light dawned in his Prussian puss. He muttered, "Got mittens . . . *Gott mit uns* . . . God with us," and roared softly, "Greta, I don't know how I put up with you the way you murder a great language for cheap laughs."

"You've got to take me as I am," I told him, "mittens and all, thank the Bonny Dew—" and hastily explained, "That's French—*le bon Dieu*—the good God—don't hit me. I'm not going to tell you any more of my secrets."

He laughed feebly, like he was dying.

"Cheer up," I said. "I won't be here forever, and there are worse places than the Place."

He nodded grudgingly, looking around. "You know what, Greta, if you'll promise not to make some dreadful joke out of it: on operations, I pretend I'll soon be going backstage to court the world-famous ballerina Greta Forzane."

He was right about the backstage part. The Place is a regular theater-in-the-round with the Void for an audience, the Void's gray hardly disturbed by the screens masking Surgery (Ugh!), Refresher and Stores. Between the last two are the bar and kitchen and Beau's piano. Between Surgery and the sector where the Door usually appears are the shelves and taborets of the Art Gallery. The control divan is stage center. Spaced around at a fair distance are six big low couches—one with its curtains now shooting us into the gray—and a few small tables. It is like a ballet set and the crazy costumes and characters that turn up don't ruin the illusion. By no means. Diaghilev would have hired most of them for the Ballet Russe on first sight, without even asking them whether they could keep time to music.

2

Last week in Babylon,
Last night in Rome,
            —Hodgson

A RIGHT-HAND GLOVE

BEAU HAD gone behind the bar and was talking quietly at Doc, but with his eyes elsewhere, looking very sallow and professional in his white, and I thought—Damballa!—I'm in the French Quarter. I couldn't see the New Girl. Sid was at last getting to the New Boy after the fuss about Mark. He threw me a sign and I started over with Erich in tow.

"Welcome, sweet lad. Sidney Lessingham's your host, and a fellow Englishman. Born in King's Lynn, 1564, schooled at Cambridge, but London was the life and death of me, though I outlasted Bessie, Jimmie, Charlie, and Ollie almost. And what a life! By turns a clerk, a spy, a bawd—the two trades are hand in glove—a poet of no account, a beggar, and a peddler of resurrection tracts. Beau Lassiter, our throats are tinder!"

At the word "poet," the New Boy looked up, but resentfully, as if he had been tricked into it.

"And to spare your throat for drinking, sweet gallant, I'll be so bold as to guess and answer one of your questions," Sid rattled on. "Yes, I knew Will Shakespeare—we were of an age —and he was such a modest, mind-your-business rogue that we all wondered whether he really did write those plays. Your pardon, faith, but that scratch might be looked to."

Then I saw that the New Girl hadn't lost her head, but gone to Surgery (Ugh!) for a first-aid tray. She reached a swab toward the New Boy's sticky cheek, saying rather shrilly, "If I might . . ."

Her timing was bad. Sid's last words and Erich's approach had darkened the look in the young Soldier's face and he angrily swept her arm aside without even glancing at her. Erich squeezed my arm. The tray clattered to the floor—and one of the drinks that Beau was bringing almost followed it. Ever since the New Girl's arrival, Beau had been figuring that she was his responsibility, though I don't think the two of them had reached an agreement yet. Beau was especially set on it because I was thick with Sid at the time and Maud with Doc, she loving tough cases.

"Easy now, lad, and you love me!" Sid thundered, again shooting Beau the "Hold it" look. "She's just a poor pagan trying to comfort you. Swallow your bile, you black villain, and perchance it will turn to poetry. Ah, did I touch you there? Confess, you are a poet."

There isn't much gets by Sid, though for a second I forgot my psychology and wondered if he knew what he was doing with his insights.

"Yes, I'm a poet, all right," the New Boy roared. "I'm Bruce Marchant, you bloody Zombies. I'm a poet in a world where even the lines of the King James and your precious Will whom you use for laughs aren't safe from Snakes' slime and the Spiders' dirty legs. Changing our history, stealing our certainties, claiming to be so blasted all-knowing and best intentioned and efficient, and what does it lead to? This bloody SI glove!"

He held up his black-gloved left hand which still held the mate and he shook it.

"What's wrong with the Spider Issue gauntlet, heart of gold?" Sid demanded. "And you love us, tell us." While Erich laughed, "Consider yourself lucky, *Kamerad*. Mark and I didn't draw any gloves at all."

"What's wrong with it?" Bruce yelled. "The bloody things are both lefts!" He slammed it down on the floor.

We all howled, we couldn't help it. He turned his back on us and stamped off, though I guessed he would keep out of the Void. Erich squeezed my arm and said between gasps, "*Mein Gott, Liebchen*, what have I always told you about Soldiers? The bigger the gripe, the smaller the cause! It is infallible!"

One of us didn't laugh. Ever since the New Girl heard the name Bruce Marchant, she'd had a look in her eyes like she'd been given the sacrament. I was glad she'd got interested in something, because she'd been pretty much of a snoot and a wet blanket up until now, although she'd come to the Place with the recommendation of having been a real whoopee girl in London and New York in the Twenties. She looked disapprovingly at us as she gathered up the tray and stuff, not forgetting the glove, which she placed on the center of the tray like a holy relic.

Beau cut over and tried to talk to her, but she ghosted past him and once again he couldn't do anything because of the tray in his hands. He came over and got rid of the drinks quick. I took a big gulp right away because I saw the New Girl stepping through the screen into Surgery and I hate to be reminded we have it and I'm glad Doc is too drunk to use it, some of the Arachnoid surgical techniques being very sickening as I know only too well from a personal experience that is number one on my list of things to be forgotten.

By that time, Bruce had come back to us, saying in a carefully hard voice, "Look here, it's not the dashed glove itself, as you very well know, you howling Demons."

"What is it then, noble heart?" Sid asked, his grizzled gold beard heightening the effect of innocent receptivity.

"It's the principle of the thing," Bruce said, looking around sharply, but none of us cracked a smile. "It's this mucking inefficiency and death of the cosmos—and don't tell me that isn't in the cards!—masquerading as benign omniscient authority. The Spiders—and we don't know who they are ultimately; it's just a name; we see only agents like ourselves—the Spiders pluck us from the quiet graves of our lifelines—"

"Is that bad, lad?" Sid murmured, innocently straight-faced.

"—and Resurrect us if they can and then tell us we must

fight another time-traveling power called the Snakes—just a name, too—which is bent on perverting and enslaving the whole cosmos, past, present and future."

"And isn't it, lad?"

"Before we're properly awake, we're Recruited into the Big Time and hustled into tunnels and burrows outside our space-time, these miserable closets, gray sacks, puss pockets—no offense to this Place—that the Spiders have created, maybe by gigantic implosions, but no one knows for certain, and then we're sent off on all sorts of missions into the past and future to change history in ways that are supposed to thwart the Snakes."

"True, lad."

"And from then on, the pace is so flaming hot and heavy, the shocks come so fast, our emotions are wrenched in so many directions, our public and private metaphysics distorted so insanely, the deepest thread of reality we cling to tied in such bloody knots, that we never can get things straight."

"We've all felt that way, lad," Sid said soberly; Beau nodded his sleek death's head; "You should have seen me, *Kamerad*, my first fifty sleeps," Erich put in; while I added, "Us girls, too, Bruce."

"Oh, I know I'll get hardened to it, and don't think I can't. It's not that," Bruce said harshly. "And I wouldn't mind the personal confusion, the mess it's made of my spirit, I wouldn't even mind remaking history and destroying priceless, once-called imperishable beauties of the past, if I felt it were for the best. The Spiders assure us that, to thwart the Snakes, it is all-important that the West ultimately defeat the East. But what have they done to achieve this? I'll give you some beautiful examples. To stabilize power in the early Mediterranean world, they have built up Crete at the expense of Greece, making Athens a ghost city, Plato a trivial fabulist, and putting all Greek culture in a minor key."

"You got time for culture?" I heard myself say and I clapped my hand over my mouth in gentle reproof.

"But *you* remember the dialogues, lad," Sid observed. "And rail not at Crete—I have a sweet Keftian friend."

"For how long will I remember Plato's dialogues? And who after me?" Bruce challenged. "Here's another. The Spiders want

Rome powerful and, to date, they've helped Rome so much that she collapses in a blaze of German and Parthian invasions a few years after the death of Julius Caesar."

This time it was Beau who butted in. Most everybody in the Place loves these bull sessions. "You omit to mention, sir, that Rome's newest downfall is directly due to the Unholy Triple Alliance the Snakes have fomented between the Eastern Classical World, Mohammedanized Christianity, and Marxist Communism, trying to pass the torch of power futurewards by way of Byzantium and the Eastern Church, without ever letting it pass into the hands of the Spider West. That, sir, is the Snakes' Three-Thousand-Year Plan which we are fighting against, striving to revive Rome's glories."

"Striving is the word for it," Bruce snapped. "Here's yet another example. To beat Russia, the Spiders kept England and America out of World War Two, thereby ensuring a German invasion of the New World and creating a Nazi empire stretching from the salt mines of Siberia to the plantations of Iowa, from Nizhni Novgorod to Kansas City!"

He stopped and my short hairs prickled. Behind me, someone was chanting in a weird spiritless voice, like footsteps in hard snow.

"*Salz, Salz, bringe Salz. Kein' Peitsch', gnädige Herren. Salz, Salz, Salz.*"

I turned and there was Doc waltzing toward us with little tiny steps, bent over so low that the ends of his shawl touched the floor, his head crooked up sideways and looking through us.

I knew then, but Erich translated softly. " 'Salt, salt, I bring salt. No whip, merciful sirs.' He is speaking to my countrymen in their language." Doc had spent his last months in a Nazi-operated salt mine.

He saw us and got up, straightening his top hat very carefully. He frowned hard while my heart thumped half a dozen times. Then his face slackened, he shrugged his shoulders and muttered, " *Nichevo.*"

"And it does not matter, sir," Beau translated, but directing his remark at Bruce. "True, great civilizations have been dwarfed or broken by the Change War. But others, once crushed in the bud, have bloomed. In the I870's, I traveled a Mississippi that had never known Grant's gunboats. I studied

piano, languages, and the laws of chance under the greatest
European masters at the University of Vicksburg."

"And you think your pipsqueak steamboat culture is
compensation for—" Bruce began but, "Prithee none of that,
lad," Sid interrupted smartly. "Nations are as equal as so many
madmen or drunkards, and I'll drink dead drunk the man who
disputes me. Hear reason: nations are not so puny as to shrivel
and vanish at the first tampering with their past, no, nor with
the tenth. Nations are monsters, boy, with guts of iron and
nerves of brass. Waste not your pity on them."

"True indeed, sir," Beau pressed, cooler and keener for the
attack on his Greater South. "Most of us enter the Change
World with the false metaphysic that the slightest change in the
past—a grain of dust misplaced—will transform the whole future. It is a long while before we accept with our minds as well
as our intellects the law of the Conservation of Reality: that
when the past is changed, the future changes barely enough to
adjust, barely enough to admit the new data. The Change Winds
meet maximum resistance always. Otherwise the first operation
in Babylonia would have wiped out New Orleans, Sheffield,
Stuttgart, and Maud Davies' birthplace on Ganymede!

"Note how the gap left by Rome's collapse was filled by the
imperialistic and Christianized Germans. Only an expert
Demon historian can tell the difference in most ages between
the former Latin and the present Gothic Catholic Church. As
you yourself, sir, said of Greece, it is as if an old melody were
shifted into a slightly different key. In the wake of a Big Change,
cultures and individuals are transposed, it's true, yet in the main
they continue much as they were, except for the usual scattering of unfortunate but statistically meaningless accidents."

"All right, you bloody savants—maybe I pushed my point
too far," Bruce growled. "But if you want variety, give a
thought to the rotten methods we use in our wonderful
Change War. Poisoning Churchill and Cleopatra. Kidnapping
Einstein when he's a baby."

"The Snakes did it first," I reminded him.

"Yes, and we copied them. How resourceful does that make
us?" he retorted, arguing like a woman. "If we need Einstein,
why don't we Resurrect him, deal with him as a man?"

Beau said, serving his culture in slightly thicker slices, "*Par-*

donnez-moi, but when you have enjoyed your status as Double-ganger a *soupçon* longer, you will understand that great men can rarely be Resurrected. Their beings are too crystalized, sir, their lifelines too tough."

"Pardon me, but I think that's rot. I believe that most great men refuse to make the bargain with the Snakes, or with us Spiders either. They scorn Resurrection at the price demanded."

"Brother, they ain't that great," I whispered, while Beau glided on with, "However that may be, you have accepted Resurrection, sir, and so incurred an obligation which you as a gentleman must honor."

"I accepted Resurrection all right," Bruce said, a glare coming into his eyes. "When they pulled me out of my line at Passchendaele in '17 ten minutes before I died, I grabbed at the offer of life like a drunkard grabs at a drink the morning after. But even then I thought I was also seizing a chance to undo historic wrongs, work for peace." His voice was getting wilder all the time. Just beyond our circle, I noticed the New Girl watching him worshipfully. "But what did I find the Spiders wanted me for? Only to fight more wars, over and over again, make them crueler and stinkinger, cut the swath of death a little wider with each Big Change, work our way a little closer to the death of the cosmos."

Sid touched my wrist and, as Bruce raved on, he whispered to me, "What kind of ball, think you, will please and so quench this fire-brained rogue? And you love me, discover it."

I whispered back without taking my eyes off Bruce either, "I know somebody who'll be happy to put on any kind of ball he wants, if he'll just notice her."

"The New Girl, sweetling? 'Tis well. This rogue speaks like an angry angel. It touches my heart and I like it not."

Bruce was saying hoarsely but loudly, "And so we're sent on operations in the past and from each of those operations the Change Winds blow futurewards, swiftly or slowly according to the opposition they breast, sometimes rippling into each other, and any one of those Winds may shift the date of our own death ahead of the date of our Resurrection, so that in an instant—even here, outside the cosmos—we may molder and rot or crumble to dust and vanish away. The wind with our name in it may leak through the Door."

Faces hardened at that, because it's bad form to mention Change Death, and Erich flared out with, "*Halt's Maul, Kamerad!* There's always another Resurrection."

But Bruce didn't keep his mouth shut. He said, "Is there? I know the Spiders promise it, but even if they do go back and cut another Doubleganger from my lifeline, is he me?" He slapped his chest with his bare hand. "I don't think so. And even if he is me, with unbroken consciousness, why's he been Resurrected again? Just to refight more wars and face more Change Death for the sake of an almighty power—" his voice was rising to a climax—"an almighty power so bloody ineffectual, it can't furnish one poor Soldier pulled out of the mud of Passchendaele, one miserable Change Commando, one God-forsaken Recuperee a proper issue of equipment!"

And he held out his bare right hand toward us, fingers spread a little, as if it were the most amazing object and most deserving of outraged sympathy in the whole world.

The New Girl's timing was perfect. She whisked through us, and before he could so much as wiggle the fingers, she whipped a black gauntleted glove on it and anyone could see that it fitted his hand perfectly.

This time our laughing beat the other. We collapsed and slopped our drinks and pounded each other on the back and then started all over.

"*Ach, der Handschuh, Liebchen!* Where'd she get it?" Erich gasped in my ear.

"Probably just turned the other one inside out—that turns a left into a right—I've done it myself," I wheezed, collapsing again at the idea.

"That would put the lining outside," he objected.

"Then I don't know," I said. "We got all sorts of junk in Stores."

"It doesn't matter, *Liebchen*," he assured me. "*Ach, der Handschuh!*"

All through it, Bruce just stood there admiring the glove, moving the fingers a little now and then, and the New Girl stood watching him as if he were eating a cake she'd baked.

When the hysteria quieted down, he looked up at her with a big smile. "What did you say your name was?"

"Lili," she said, and believe you me, she was Lili to me even in my thoughts from then on, for the way she'd handled that lunatic.

"Lilian Foster," she explained. "I'm English also. Mr. Marchant, I've read *A Young Man's Fancy* I don't know how many times."

"You have? It's wretched stuff. From the Dark Ages—I mean my Cambridge days. In the trenches, I was working up some poems that were rather better."

"I won't hear you say that. But I'd be terribly thrilled to hear the new ones. Oh, Mr. Marchant, it was so strange to hear you call it Passiondale."

"Why, if I may ask?"

"Because that's the way I pronounce it to myself. But I looked it up and it's more like Pas-ken-DA-luh."

"Bless you! All the Tommies called it Passiondale, just as they called Ypres Wipers."

"How interesting. You know, Mr. Marchant, I'll wager we were Recruited in the same operation, summer of 1917. I'd got to France as a Red Cross nurse, but they found out my age and were going to send me back."

"How old were you—are you? Same thing, I mean to say."

"Seventeen."

"Seventeen in '17," Bruce murmured, his blue eyes glassy.

It was real corny dialogue and I couldn't resent the humorous leer Erich gave me as we listened to them, as if to say, "Ain't it nice, *Liebchen*, Bruce has a silly little English schoolgirl to occupy him between operations?"

Just the same, as I watched Lili in her dark bangs and pearl necklace and tight little gray dress that reached barely to her knees, and Bruce hulking over her tenderly in his snazzy hussar's rig, I knew that I was seeing the start of something that hadn't been part of me since Dave died fighting Franco years before I got on the Big Time, the sort of thing that almost made me wish there could be children in the Change World. I wondered why I'd never thought of trying to work things so that Dave got Resurrected and I told myself: no, it's all changed, I've changed, better the Change Winds don't disturb Dave or I know about it.

"No, I didn't die in 1917—I was merely Recruited then," Lili was telling Bruce. "I lived all through the Twenties, as you can see from the way I dress. But let's not talk about that, shall we? Oh, Mr. Marchant, do you think you can possibly remember any of those poems you started in the trenches? I can't fancy them bettering your sonnet that concludes with, 'The bough swings in the wind, the night is deep; Look at the stars, poor little ape, and sleep.'"

That one almost made me whoop—what monkeys we are, I thought—though I'd be the first to admit that the best line to use on a poet is one of his own—in fact as many as possible. I decided I could safely forget our little Britons and devote myself to Erich or whatever needed me.

3

Hell is the place for me. For to Hell go the fine churchmen, and the fine knights, killed in the tourney or in some grand war, the brave soldiers and the gallant gentlemen. With them will I go. There go also the fair gracious ladies who have lovers two or three beside their lord. There go the gold and the silver, the sables and ermine. There go the harpers and the minstrels and the kings of the earth.

—Aucassin

NINE FOR A PARTY

I EXCHANGED my drink for a new one from another tray Beau was bringing around. The gray of the Void was beginning to look real pleasant, like warm thick mist with millions of tiny diamonds floating in it. Doc was sitting grandly at the bar with a steaming tumbler of tea—a chaser, I guess, since he was just putting down a shot glass. Sid was talking to Erich and laughing at the same time and I said to myself it begins to feel like a party, but something's lacking.

It wasn't anything to do with the Major Maintainer; its telltale was glowing a steady red like a nice little home fire amid the tight cluster of dials that included all the controls except the lonely and frightening Introversion switch that was never touched. Then Maud's couch curtains winked out and there were she and the Roman sitting quietly side by side.

He looked down at his shiny boots and the rest of his black duds like he was just waking up and couldn't believe it all, and he said, "*Omnia mutantur, nos et mutamur in illis*," and I raised my eyebrows at Beau, who was taking the tray back, and he did proud by old Vicksburg by translating: "All things change and we change with them."

Then Mark slowly looked around at us, and I can testify that a Roman smile is just as warm as any other nationality, and he finally said, "We are nine, the proper number for a party. The couches, too. It is good."

Maud chuckled proudly and Erich shouted, "Welcome back from the Void, *Kamerad*," and then, because he's German and thinks all parties have to be noisy and satirically pompous, he jumped on a couch and announced, "*Herren und Damen*, permit me to introduce the noblest Roman of them all, Marcus Vipsaius Niger, legate to Nero Claudius (called Germanicus in a former time stream) and who in 763 A.U.C. (Correct, Mark? It means 10 A.D., you meatheads!) died bravely fighting the Parthians and the Snakes in the Battle of Alexandria. *Hoch, hoch, hoch!*"

We all swung our glasses and cheered with him and Sid yelled at Erich, "Keep your feet off the furniture, you un-schooled rogue," and grinned and boomed at all three hussars, "Take your ease, Recuperees," and Maud and Mark got their drinks, the Roman paining Beau by refusing Falernian wine in favor of scotch and soda, and right away everyone was talking a mile a minute.

We had a lot to catch up on. There was the usual yak about the war—"The Snakes are laying mine fields in the Void," "I don't believe it, how can you mine nothing?"—and the shortages —bourbon, bobby pins, and the stabilitin that would have brought Mark out of it faster—and what had become of people—"Marcia? Oh, she's not around any more," (She'd been caught in a Change Gale and green and stinking in five seconds, but I wasn't going to say that)—and Mark had to be told about Bruce's glove, which convulsed us all over again, and the Roman remembered a legionary who had carried a gripe all the way to Octavius because he'd accidentally been issued the unbelievable luxury item sugar instead of the usual salt, and Erich asked Sid if he had any new Ghost-girls in stock and Sid sucked his beard like the old goat he is. "Dost thou ask me, lusty Allemand? Nay, there are several great beauties, amongst them an Austrian countess from Strauss's Vienna, and if it were not for sweetling here . . . Mnnnn."

I poked a finger in Erich's chest between two of the bright buttons with their tiny death's heads. "You, my little von Hohenwald, are a menace to us real girls. You have too much of a thing about the unawakened, ghost kind."

He called me his little Demon and hugged me a bit too hard to prove it wasn't so, and then he suggested we show Bruce the Art Gallery. I thought this was a real brilliant idea, but when I tried to argue him out of it, he got stubborn. Bruce and Lili were willing to do anything anyone wanted them to, though not so willing to pay any attention while doing it. The saber cut was just a thin red line on his cheek; she'd washed away all the dried blood.

The Gallery gets you, though. It's a bunch of paintings and sculptures and especially odd knickknacks, all made by Soldiers recuperating here, and a lot of them telling about the Change War from the stuff they're made of—brass cartridges, flaked flint, bits of ancient pottery glued into futuristic shapes, mashed-up Incan gold rebeaten by a Martian, whorls of beady Lunan wire, a picture in tempera on a crinkle-cracked thick round of quartz that had filled a starship porthole, a Sumerian inscription chiseled into a brick from an atomic oven.

There are a lot of things in the Gallery and I can always find some I haven't ever seen before. It gets you, as I say, thinking about the guys that made them and their thoughts, and the far times and places they came from, and sometimes, when I'm feeling low, I'll come and look at them so I'll feel still lower and get inspired to kick myself back into a good temper. It's the only history of the Place there is and it doesn't change a great deal, because the things in it and the feelings that went into them resist the Change Winds better than anything else.

Right now, Erich's witty lecture was bouncing off the big ears I hide under my pageboy bob and I was thinking how awful it is that for us there's not only change but Change. You don't know from one minute to the next whether a mood or idea you've got is really new or just welling up into you because the past has been altered by the Spiders or Snakes.

Change Winds can blow not only death but anything short of it, down to the featheriest fancy. They blow thousands of times faster than time moves, but no one can say how much faster or how far one of them will travel or what damage it'll do or how soon it'll damp out. The Big Time isn't the little time.

And then, for the Demons, there's the fear that our personality will just fade and someone else climb into the driver's seat and us not even know. Of course, we Demons are supposed to be able to remember through Change and in spite of it; that's why we are Demons and not Ghosts like the other Doublegangers, or merely Zombies or Unborn and nothing more, and as Beau truly said, there aren't any great men among us— and blamed few of the masses, either—we're a rare sort of people and that's why the Spiders have to Recruit us where they find us without caring about our previous knowledge and background, a Foreign Legion of time, a strange kind of folk, bright but always in the background, with built-in nostalgia and cynicism, as adaptable as Centaurian shape-changers but with memories as long as a Lunan's six arms, a kind of Change People, you might say, the cream of the damned.

But sometimes I wonder if our memories are as good as we think they are and if the whole past wasn't once entirely different from anything we remember, and we've forgotten that we forgot.

As I say, the Gallery gets you feeling real low, and so now I said to myself, "Back to your lousy little commandant, kid," and gave myself a stiff boot.

Erich was holding up a green bowl with gold dolphins or spaceships on it and saying, "And, to my mind, this proves that Etruscan art is derived from Egyptian. Don't you agree, Bruce?"

Bruce looked up, all smiles from Lili, and said, "What was that, dear chap?"

Erich's forehead got dark as the Door and I was glad the hussars had parked their sabers along with their shakos, but before he could even get out a Jerry cuss-word, Doc breezed up in that plateau-state of drunkenness so like hypnotized sobriety, moving as if he were on a dolly, ghosted the bowl out of Erich's hand, said, "A beautiful specimen of Middle Systemic

Venusian. When Eightaitch finished it, he told me you couldn't look at it and not feel the waves of the Northern Venusian Shallows rippling around your hoofs. But it might look better inverted. I wonder. Who are you, young officer? *Nichevo*," and he carefully put the bowl back on its shelf and rolled on.

It's a fact that Doc knows the Art Gallery better than any of us, really by heart, he being the oldest inhabitant, though he maybe picked a bad time to show off his knowledge. Erich was going to take out after him, but I said, "Nix, *Kamerad*, remember gloves and sugar," and he contented himself with complaining, "That *nichevo*—it's so gloomy and hopeless, *ungeheuerlich*. I tell you, *Liebchen*, they shouldn't have Russians working for the Spiders, not even as Entertainers."

I grinned at him and squeezed his hand. "Not much entertainment in Doc these days, is there?" I agreed.

He grinned back at me a shade sheepishly and his face smoothed and his blue eyes looked sweet again for a second and he said, "I shouldn't want to claw out at people that way, Greta, but at times I am just a jealous old man," which is not entirely true, as he isn't a day over thirty-three, although his hair is nearly white.

Our lovers had drifted on a few steps until they were almost fading into the Surgery screen. It was the last spot I would have picked for the formal preliminaries to a little British smootching, but Lili probably didn't share my prejudices, though I remembered she'd told me she'd served a brief hitch in an Arachnoid Field Hospital before she'd transferred to the Place.

But she couldn't have had anything like the experience I'd had during my short and sour career as a Spider nurse, when I'd acquired my best-hated nightmare and flopped completely (jobwise, but on the floor, too) at seeing a doctor flick a switch and a being, badly injured but human, turn into a long cluster of glistening strange fruit—ugh, it always makes me want to toss my cookies and my buttons. And to think that dear old Daddy Anton wanted his Greta chile to be a doctor.

Well, I could see this wasn't getting me anywhere I wanted to go, and after all there was a party going on.

Doc was babbling something at a great rate to Sid—I just hoped Doc wouldn't get inspired to go into his animal imitations, which sound pretty fierce and once seriously offended some recuperating ETs.

Maud was demonstrating to Mark a 23rd Century two-step and Beau sat down at the piano and improvised softly on her rhythm.

As the deep-thrumming relaxing notes hit us, Erich's face brightened and he dragged me over. Pleasantly soon I had my feet off the diamond-rough floor, which we don't carpet because most of the ETs, the dear boys, like it hard, and I was shouldering back deep into the couch nearest the piano, with cushions all around me and a fresh drink in my hand, while my Nazi boy friend was getting ready to discharge his *Weltschmerz* as song, which didn't alarm me too much, as his baritone is passable.

Things felt real good, like the Maintainer was just idling to keep the Place in existence and moored to the cosmos, not exerting itself at all or at most taking an occasional lazy paddle stroke. At times the Place's loneliness can be happy and comfortable.

Then Beau raised an eyebrow at Erich, who nodded, and next thing they were launched into a song we all know, though I've never found out where it originally came from. This time it made me think of Lili, and I wondered why—and why it's a tradition at Recuperation Stations to call the new Lili, though in this case it happened to be her real name.

> *Standing in the Doorway just*
> *outside of space,*
> *Winds of Change blow 'round*
> *you but don't touch your face;*
> *You smile as you whisper*
> *tenderly,*
> *"Please cross to me, Recuperee;*
> *"The operation's over, come*
> *in and close the Door."*

4

De Bailhache, Fresca, Mrs. Cammel, whirled
Beyond the circuit of the shuddering Bear
In fractured atoms.
—Eliot

S O S FROM NOWHERE

I REALIZED the piano had deserted Erich and I cranked my
head up and saw Beau, Maud and Sid streaking for the
control divan. The Major Maintainer was blinking emergency-
green and fast, but the mode was plain enough for even me to
recognize the Spider distress call and for a second I felt just
sick. Then Erich blew out his reserve breath in the middle of
"Door" and I gave myself another of these helpful mental
boots at the base of the spine and we hurried after them toward the center of the Place along with Mark.

The blinks faded as we got there and Sid told us not to move
because we were making shadows. He glued an eye to the
telltale and we held still as statues as he caressed the dials like
he was making love.

One sensitive hand flicked out past the Introversion switch
over to the Minor Maintainer and right away the Place was
dark as your soul and there was nothing for me but Erich's arm
and the knowledge that Sid was nursing a green light I couldn't
even see, although my eyes had plenty time to accommodate.

Then the green light finally came back very slowly and I
could see the dear reliable old face—the green-gold making
him look like a merman—and then the telltale flared bright
and Sid flicked on the Place lights and I leaned back.

"That nails them, lads, whoever and whenever they may be.
Get ready for a pick-up."

Beau, who was closest of course, looked at him sharply. Sid
shrugged uneasily. "Meseemed at first it was from our own
globe a thousand years before our Lord, but that indication
flickered and faded like witchfire. As it is, the call comes from
something smaller than the Place and certes adrift from the

cosmos. Meseemed too at one point I knew the first of the caller—an antipodean atomicist named Benson-Carter—but that likewise changed."

Beau said, "We're not in the right phase of the cosmos-Places rhythm for a pick-up, are we, sir?"

Sid answered, "Ordinarily not, boy."

Beau continued, "I didn't think we had any pick-ups scheduled. Or stand-by orders."

Sid said, "We haven't."

Mark's eyes glowed. He tapped Erich on the shoulder. "An octavian denarius against ten Reichsmarks it is a Snake trap."

Erich's grin showed his teeth. "Make it first through the Door next operation and I'm on."

It didn't take that to tell me things were serious, or the thought that there's always a first time for bumping into something from really outside the cosmos. The Snakes have broken our code more than once. Maud was quietly serving out weapons and Doc was helping her. Only Bruce and Lili stood off. But they were watching.

The telltale brightened. Sid reached toward the Maintainer, saying, "All right, my hearties. Remember, through this Doorway pass the fishiest finaglers in and out of the cosmos."

The Door appeared to the left and above where it should be and darkened much too fast. There was a gust of stale salt sea-wind, if that makes sense, but no stepped-up Change Winds I could tell—and I had been bracing myself against them. The Door got inky and there was a flicker of gray fur whips and a flash of copper flesh and gilt and something dark and a clump of hoofs and Erich was sighting a stun gun across his left forearm, and then the Door had vanished like that and a tentacled silvery Lunan and a Venusian satyr were coming straight toward us.

The Lunan was hugging a pile of clothes and weapons. The satyr was helping a wasp-waisted woman carry a heavy-looking bronze chest. The woman was wearing a short skirt and high-collared bolero jacket of leather so dark brown it was almost black. She had a two-horned *petsofa* hairdress and she was boldly gilded here and there and wore sandals and copper anklets and wristlets—one of them a copper-plated Caller—and from her wide copper belt hung a short-handled double-headed

ax. She was dark-complexioned and her forehead and chin receded, but the effect was anything but weak; she had a face like
a beautiful arrowhead—and a familiar one, by golly!

But before I could say, "Kabysia Labrys," Maud shrilly beat
me to it with, "It's Kaby with two friends. Break out a couple
of Ghostgirls."

And then I saw it really was old-home week because I recognized my Lunan boy friend Ilhilihis, and in the midst of all the
confusion I got a nice kick out of knowing I was getting so I
could tell the personality of one silver-furred muzzle from another.

They reached the control divan and Illy dumped his load and
the others let down the chest, and Kaby staggered but shook off
the two ETs when they started to support her, and she looked
daggers at Sid when he tried to do the same, although she's his
"sweet Keftian friend" he'd mentioned to Bruce.

She leaned straight-armed on the divan and took two gasping breaths so deep that the ridges of her spine showed through
her brown-skinned waist, and then she threw up her head and
commanded, "Wine!"

While Beau was rushing it, Sid tried to take her hand again,
saying, "Sweetling, I'd never heard you call before and knew
not this pretty little first," but she ripped out, "Save your comfort for the Lunan," and I looked and saw—Hey, Zeus!—that
one of Ilhilihis' six tentacles was lopped off halfway.

That was for me, and, going to him, I fast briefed myself:
"Remember, he only weighs fifty pounds for all he's seven feet
high; he doesn't like low sounds or to be grabbed; the two legs
aren't tentacles and don't act the same; uses them for long walks,
tentacles for leaps; uses tentacles for close vision too and for manipulation, of course; extended, they mean he's at ease; retracted,
on guard or nervous; sharply retracted, disgusted; greeting—"

Just then, one of them swept across my face like a sweet-
smelling feather duster and I said, "Illy, man, it's been a lot of
sleeps," and brushed my fingers across his muzzle. It still took
a little self-control not to hug him, and I did reach a little
cluckingly for his lopped tentacle, but he wafted it away from
me and the little voicebox belted to his side squeaked,
"Naughty, naughty. Papa will fix his little old self. Greta girl,
ever bandaged even a Terra octopus?"

I had, an intelligent one from around a quarter billion A.D., but I didn't tell him so. I stood and let him talk to the palm of my hand with one of his tentacles—I don't savvy feather-talk but it feels good, though I've often wondered who taught him English—and watched him use a couple others to whisk a sort of Lunan band-aid out of his pouch and cap his wound with it.

Meanwhile, the satyr knelt over the bronze chest, which was decorated with little death's heads and crosses with hoops at the top and swastikas, but looking much older than Nazi, and the satyr said to Sid, "Quick thinkin, Gov, when ya saw the Door comin in high n soffened up gravty unner it, but cud I hav sum hep now?"

Sid touched the Minor Maintainer and we all got very light and my stomach did a flip-flop while the satyr piled on the chest the clothes and weapons that Illy had been carrying and pranced off with it all and carefully put it down at the end of the bar. I decided the satyr's English instructor must have been quite a character, too. Wish I'd met him—her—it.

Sid thought to ask Illy if he wanted Moon-normal gravity in one sector, but my boy likes to mix, and being such a light-weight, Earth-normal gravity doesn't bother him. As he said to me once, "Would Jovian gravity bother a beetle, Greta girl?"

I asked Illy about the satyr and he squeaked that his name was Sevensee and that he'd never met him before this operation. I knew the satyrs were from a billion years in the future, just as the Loonies were from a billion in the past, and I thought—Kreesed us!—but it must have been a real big or emergency-like operation to have the Spiders using those two for it, with two billion years between them—a time-difference that gives you a feeling of awe for a second, you know.

I started to ask Illy about it, but just then Beau came scampering back from the bar with a big red-and-black earthenware goblet of wine—we try to keep a variety of drinking tools in stock so folks will feel more at home. Kaby grabbed it from him and drained most of it in one swallow and then smashed it on the floor. She does things like that, though Sid's tried to teach her better. Then she stared at what she was thinking about until the whites showed all around her eyes and her lips pulled way back from her teeth and she looked a lot less human than the two ETs, just like a fury. Only a time traveler knows how like the wild murals and engravings of them some of the ancients can look.

My hair stood up at the screech she let out. She smashed a fist into the divan and cried, "Goddess! Must I see Crete destroyed, revived, and now destroyed again? It is too much for your servant."

Personally, I thought she could stand anything.

There was a rush of questions at what she said about Crete—I asked one of them, for the news certainly frightened me—but she shot up her arm straight for silence and took a deep breath and began.

"In the balance hung the battle. Rowing like black centipedes, the Dorian hulls bore down on our outnumbered ships. On the bright beach, masked by rocks, Sevensee and I stood by the needle gun, ready to give the black hulls silent wounds. Beside us was Ilhilihis, suited as a sea monster. But then . . . then . . ."

Then I saw she wasn't altogether the iron babe, for her voice broke and she started to shake and to sob rackingly, although her face was still a mask of rage, and she threw up the wine. Sid stepped in and made her stop, which I think he'd been wanting to do all along.

5

When I take up a newspaper and read it, I fancy I see ghosts creeping between the lines. There must be ghosts all over the world. They must be as countless as the grains of the sands, it seems to me.

—Ibsen

SID INSISTS ON GHOSTGIRLS

My Elizabethan boy friend put his fists on his hips and laid down the law to us as if we were a lot of nervous children who'd been playing too hard.

"Look you, masters, this is a Recuperation Station and I am running it as such. A plague of all operations! I care not if the frame of things disjoints and the whole Change World goes to ruin, but you, warrior maid, are going to rest and drink more wine slowly before you tell your tale and your colleagues are going to be properly companioned. No questions, anyone. Beau, and you love us, give us a lively tune."

Kaby relaxed a little and let him put his hand carefully against her back in token of support and she said grudgingly, "All right, Fat Belly."

Then, so help me, to the tune of the Muskrat Ramble, which I'd taught Beau, we got girls for those two ETs and everybody properly paired up.

Right here I want to point out that a lot of the things they say in the Change World about Recuperation Stations simply aren't so—and anyway they always leave out nine-tenths of it. The Soldiers that come through the Door are looking for a good time, sure, but they're hurt real bad too, every one of them, deep down in their minds and hearts, if not always in their bodies or so you can see it right away.

Believe me, a temporal operation is no joke, and to start with, there isn't one person in a hundred who can endure to be cut from his lifeline and become a really wide-awake Doubleganger —a Demon, that is—let alone a Soldier. What does a badly hurt and mixed-up creature need who's been fighting hard? One *individual* to look out for him and feel for him and patch him up, and it helps if the one is of the opposite sex—that's something that goes beyond species.

There's your basis for the Place and the wild way it goes about its work, and also for most other Recuperation Stations or Entertainment Spots. The name Entertainer can be misleading, but I like it. She's got to be a lot more than a good party girl—or boy— though she's got to be that too. She's got to be a nurse and a psychologist and an actress and a mother and a practical ethnologist and a lot of things with longer names—and a reliable friend.

None of us are all those things perfectly or even near it. We just try. But when the call comes, Entertainers have to forget grudges and gripes and envies and jealousies—and remember, they're lively people with sharp emotions—because there isn't any time then for anything but *help and don't ask who!*

And, deep inside her, a good Entertainer doesn't care who. Take the way it shaped up this time. It was pretty clear to me I ought to shift to Illy, although I wasn't quite easy in my mind about leaving Erich, because the Lunan was a long time from home and, after all, Erich was among anthropoids. Ilhilihis needed someone who was *simpatico.*

I like Illy and not just because he is a sort of tall cross between a spider monkey and a persian cat—though that is a handsome combo when you come to think of it. I like him for himself. So when he came in all lopped and shaky after a mean operation, I was the right person to look out for him. Now I've made my little speech and know-nothings in the Change World can go on making their bum jokes. But I ask you, how could an arrangement between Illy and me be anything but Platonic?

We might have had some octopoid girls and nymphs in stock —Sid couldn't be sure until he checked—but Ilhilihis and Sevensee voted for real people and I knew Sid saw it their way. Maud squeezed Mark's hand and tripped over to Sevensee ("Those are sharp hoofs you got, man"—she's picked up some of my language, like she has everything else), though Beau did frown over his shoulder at Lili from the piano, maybe to argue that she ought to take on the ET, as Mark had been a real casualty and could use live nursing. But it was plain as day to anybody but Beau that Bruce and Lili were a big thing and the last to be disturbed.

Erich acted stiffly hurt at losing me, but I knew he wasn't. He thinks he has a great technique with Ghostgirls and he likes to show it off, and he really is pretty slick at it, if you go for that sort of thing and—yang my yin!—who doesn't at times?

And when Sid formally wafted the Countess out of Stores— a real blonde stunner in a white satin hobble skirt with a white egret swaying up from her tiny hat, way ahead of Maud and Lili and me when it came to looks, though transparent as cigarette smoke—and when Erich clicked his heels and bowed over her hand and proudly conducted her to a couch, black Svengali to her Trilby, and started to German-talk some life into her with much head cocking and toothy smiling and a flow of witty flattery, and when she began to flirt back and the dream look in her eyes sharpened hungrily and focused on him—well, then

I knew that Erich was happy and felt he was doing proud by the *Reichswehr*. No, my little commandant wasn't worrying me on that score.

Mark had drawn a Greek hetaera name of Phryne; I suppose not the one who maybe still does the famous courtroom strip-tease back in Athens, and he was waking her up with little sips of his scotch and soda, though, from some looks he'd flashed, I got the idea Kaby was the kid he really went for. Sid was coaxing the fighting gal to take some high-energy bread and olives along with the wine, and, for a wonder, Doc seemed to be carrying on an animated and rational conversation with Sevensee and Maud, maybe comparing notes on the Northern Venusian Shallows, and Beau had got on to Panther Rag, and Bruce and Lili were leaning on the piano, smiling very appreciatively, but talking to each other a mile a minute.

Illy turned back from inspecting them all and squeaked, "Animals with clothes are so refreshing, dahling! Like you're all carrying banners!"

Maybe he had something there, though my banners were kind of Ash Wednesday, a charcoal gray sweater and skirt. He looked at my mouth with a tentacle to see how I was smiling and he squeaked softly, "Do I seem dull and commonplace to you, Greta girl, because I haven't got banners? Just another Zombie from a billion years in your past, as gray and lifeless as Luna is today, not as when she was a real dreamy sister planet simply bursting with air and water and feather forests. Or am I as strangely interesting to you as you are to me, girl from a billion years in my future?"

"Illy, you're sweet," I told him, giving him a little pat. I noticed his fur was still vibrating nervously and I decided to heck with Sid's orders, I'm going to pump him about what he was doing with Kaby and the satyr. Couldn't have him a billion years from home and bottled up, too. Besides, I was curious.

6

Maiden, Nymph, and Mother are the eternal royal Trinity of the island, and the Goddess, who is worshipped there in each of these aspects, as New Moon, Full Moon, and Old Moon, is the sovereign Deity.

—Graves

CRETE CIRCA 1300 B.C.

KABY PUSHED back at Sid some seconds of bread and olives, and, when he raised his bushy eyebrows, gave him a curt nod that meant she knew what she was doing. She stood up and sort of took a position. All the talk quieted down fast, even Bruce's and Lili's. Kaby's face and voice weren't strained now, but they weren't relaxed either.

"Woe to Spider! Woe to Cretan! Heavy is the news I bring you. Bear it bravely, like strong women. When we got the gun unlimbered, I heard seaweed fry and crackle. We three leaped behind the rock wall, saw our gun grow white as sunlight in a heat-ray of the Serpents! Natch, we feared we were outnumbered and I called upon my Caller."

I don't know how she does it, but she does—in English too. That is, when she figures she's got something important to report, and maybe she needs a little time to get ready.

Beau claims that all the ancients fit their thoughts into measured lines as naturally as we pick a word that will do, but I'm not sure how good the Vicksburg language department is. Though why I should wonder about things like that when I've got Kaby spouting the stuff right in front of me, I don't know.

"But I didn't die there, kiddos. I still hoped to hurt the Greek ships, maybe with the Snake's own heat gun. So I quick tried to outflank them. My two comrades crawled beside me—they are males, but they have courage. Soon we spied the ambush-setters. They were Snakes and they were many, filthily disguised as Cretans."

There was an indignant murmur at this, for our cutthroat

Change War has its code, the Soldiers tell me. Being an Entertainer, I don't have to say what I think.

"They had seen us when we saw them," Kaby swept on, "and they loosed a killing volley. Heat- and knife-rays struck about us in a storm of wind and fire, and the Lunan lost a feeler, fighting for Crete's Triple Goddess. So we dodged behind a sand hill, steered our flight back toward the water. It was awful, what we saw there; Crete's brave ships all sunk or sinking, blue sky sullied by their death-smoke. Once again the Greeks had licked us!—aided by the filthy Serpents.

"Round our wrecks, their black ships scurried, like black beetles, filth their diet, yet this day they dine on heroes. On the quiet sun-lit beach there, I could feel a Change Gale blowing, working changes deep inside me, aches and pains that were a stranger's. Half my memories were doubled, half my lifeline crooked and twisted, three new moles upon my sword-hand. Goddess, Goddess, Triple Goddess—"

Her voice wavered and Sid reached out a hand, but she straightened her back.

"Triple Goddess, give me courage to tell everything that happened. We ran down into the water, hoping to escape by diving. We had hardly gotten under when the heat-rays hit above us, turning all the cool green surface to a roaring white inferno. But as I believe I told you, I was calling on my Caller, and a Door now opened to us, deep below the deadly steam-clouds. We dived in like frightened minnows and a lot of water with us."

Off Chicago's Gold Coast, Dave once gave me a lesson in skindiving and, remembering it, I got a flash of Kaby's Door in the dark depths.

"For a moment all was chaos. Then the Door slammed shut behind us. We'd been picked up in time's nick by—an Express Room of our Spiders!—sloshing two feet deep in water, much more cramped for space than this Place. It was manned by a magician, an old coot named Benson-Carter. He dispelled the water quickly and reported on his Caller. We'd got dry, were feeling human, Illy here had shed his swimsuit, when we looked at the Maintainer. It was glowing, changing, melting! And when Benson-Carter touched it, he fell backward—death was in him. Then the Void began to darken, narrow, shrink and close around us, so I called upon my Caller—without wasting time, let me tell you!

"We can't say for sure what was it slowly squeezed that sweet Express Room, but we fear the dirty Snakes have found a way to find our Places and attack outside the cosmos!—found the Spiderweb that links us in the Void's gray less-than-nothing."

No murmur this time. This reaction was genuine; we'd been hit where we lived and I could see everybody was scared as sick as I was. Except maybe Bruce and Lili, who were still holding hands and beaming gently. I decided they were the kind that love makes brave, which it doesn't do to me. It just gives me two people to worry about.

"I can see you dig our feeling," Kaby continued. "This thing scared the pants off of us. If we could have, we'd have even Introverted the Maintainer, broken all the ties that bind us, chanced it incommunicado. But the little old Maintainer was a seething red-hot puddle filled with bubbles big as handballs. We sat tight and watched the Void close. I kept calling on my Caller."

I squeezed my eyes shut, but that made it easier to see the three of them with the Void shutting down on them. (Was ours still behaving? Yes, Bibi Miriam.) Poetry or no poetry, it got me.

"Benson-Carter, lying dying, also thought the Snakes had done it. And he knew that death was in him, so he whispered me his mission, giving me precise instructions: how to press the seven death's hands, starting lockside counterclockwise, one, three, five, six, two, four, seven, then you have a half an hour; after you have pressed the seven, do not monkey with the buttons—get out fast and don't stop moving."

I wasn't getting this part and I couldn't see that anyone else was, though Bruce was whispering to Lili. I remembered seeing skulls engraved on the bronze chest. I looked at Illy and he nodded a tentacle and spread two to say, I guessed, that yes, Benson-Carter had said something like that, but no, Illy didn't know much about it.

"All these things and more he whispered," Kaby went on, "with the last gasps of his life-force, telling all his secret orders—for he'd not been sent to get us, he was on a separate mission, when he heard my SOSs. Sid, it's you he was to contact, as the first leg of his mission, pick up from you three black hussars, death's-head Demons, daring Soldiers, then to wait until the Places next match rhythm with the cosmos—matter of two mealtimes, barely—and to tune in northern Egypt in the age of the last Caesar, in the year of Rome's swift downfall, there to start on operation in a battle near a city named for Thrace's Alexander, there to change the course of battle, blow sky-high the stinking Serpents, all their agents, all their Zombies!

"Goddess, pardon, now I savvy how you've guided my least foot-step, when I thought you'd gone and left me—for I flubbed your three-mole signal. We've found Sid's Place, that's the first leg, and I see the three black hussars, and we've brought with us the weapon and the Parthian disguises, salvaged from the doomed Express Room when your Door appeared in time's nick, and the Room around us closing spewed us through before it vanished with the corpse of Benson-Carter. Triple Goddess, draw the milk now from the womanhood I flaunt here and inject the blackest hatred! Vengeance now upon the Serpents, vengeance sweet in northern Egypt, for your island, Crete, Goddess!—and a victory for the Spiders! Goddess, Goddess, we can swing it!"

The roar that made me try to stop my ears with my shoulders didn't come from Kaby—she'd spoken her piece—but from Sid. The dear boy was purple enough to make me want to remind him you can die of high blood pressure just as easy in the Change World.

"Dump me with ops! 'Sblood, I'll not endure it! Is this a battle post? They'll be mounting operations from field hospitals next. Kabysia Labrys, thou art mad to suggest it. And what's this prattle of locks, clocks, and death's heads, buttons and monkeys? This brabble, this farrago, this hocus-pocus! And where's the weapon you prate of? In that whoreson bronze casket, I suppose."

She nodded, looking blank and almost a little shy as poetic possession faded from her. Her answer came like its faltering last echo.

"It is nothing but a tiny tactical atomic bomb."

7

After about 0.1 millisecond (one ten-thousandth part of a second) has elapsed, the radius of the ball of fire is some 45 feet, and the temperature is then in the vicinity of 300,000 degrees Centigrade. At this instant, the luminosity, as observed at a distance of 100,000 yards (5.7 miles), is approximately 100 times that of the sun as seen at the earth's surface. . . . the ball of fire expands very rapidly to its maximum radius of 450 feet within less than a second from the explosion.

—Los Alamos

TIME TO THINK

BROTHER, THAT was all we needed to make everybody but Kaby and the two ETs start yelping at once, me included. It may seem strange that Change People, able to whiz through time and space and roust around outside the cosmos and knowing at least by hearsay of weapons a billion years in the future, like the Mindbomb, should panic at being shut in with a little primitive mid-20th Century gadget. Well, they feel the same as atomic scientists would feel if a Bengal tiger were brought into their laboratory, neither more nor less scared.

I'm a moron at physics, but I do know the Fireball is bigger than the Place. Remember that, besides the bomb, we'd recently been presented with a lot of other fears we hadn't had time to cope with, especially the business of the Snakes having learned how to get at our Places and melt the Maintainers and collapse them. Not to mention the general impression—first Saint Petersburg, then Crete—that the whole Change War was going against the Spiders.

Yet, in a free corner of my mind, I was shocked at how badly we were all panicking. It made me admit what I didn't like to: that we were all in pretty much the same state as Doc, except that the bottle didn't happen to be our out.

And had the rest of us been controlling our drinking so well lately?

Maud yelled, "Jettison it!" and pulled away from the satyr

and ran from the bronze chest. Beau, harking back to what they'd thought of doing in the Express Room when it was too late, hissed, "Sirs, we must Introvert," and vaulted over the piano bench and legged it for the control divan. Erich seconded him with a white-faced "*Gott im Himmel, ja!*" from beside the surly, forgotten Countess, holding, by its slim stem, an empty, rose-stained wine glass.

I felt my mind flinch, because Introverting a Place is several degrees worse than foxholing. It's supposed not only to keep the Door tight shut, but also to lock it so even the Change Winds can't get through—cut the Place loose from the cosmos altogether.

I'd never talked with anyone from a Place that had been Introverted.

Mark dumped Phryne off his lap and ran after Maud. The Greek Ghostgirl, quite solid now, looked around with sleepy fear and fumbled her apple-green chiton together at the throat. She wrenched my attention away from everyone else for a moment, and I couldn't help wondering whether the person or Zombie back in the cosmos, from whose lifeline the Ghost has been taken, doesn't at least have strange dreams or thoughts when something like this happens.

Sid stopped Beau, though he almost got bowled over doing it, and he held the gambler away from the Maintainer in a bear hug and bellowed over his shoulders, "Masters, are you mad? Have you lost your wits? Maud! Mark! Marcus! Magdalene! On your lives, unhand that casket!"

Maud had swept the clothes and bows and quivers and stuff off it and was dragging it out from the bar toward the Door sector, so as to dump it through fast when we got one, I guess, while Mark acted as if he were trying to help her and wrestle it away from her at the same time.

They kept on as if they hadn't heard a word Sid said, with Mark yelling, "Let go, *meretrix!* This holds Rome's answer to Parthia on the Nile."

Kaby watched them as if she wanted to help Mark but scorned to scuffle with a mere—well, Mark had said it in Latin, I guess—call girl.

Then, on the top of the bronze chest, I saw those seven lousy skulls starting at the lock as plain as if they'd been under a magnifying glass, though ordinarily they'd have been a vague circle to my eyes at the distance, and I lost my mind and started to run in the opposite direction, but Illy whipped three tentacles around me, gentle-like, and squeaked, "Easy now, Greta girl, don't you be doing it, too. Hold still or Papa spank. My, my, but you two-leggers can whirl about when you have a mind to."

My stampede had carried his featherweight body a couple of yards, but it stopped me and I got my mind back, partly.

"Unhand it, I say!" Sid repeated without accomplishing anything, and he released Beau, though he kept a hand near the gambler's shoulder.

Then my fat friend from Lynn Regis looked real distraught at the Void and blustered at no one in particular, "'Sdeath, think you I'd mutiny against my masters, desert the Spiders, go to ground like a spent fox and pull my hole in after me? A plague of such cowardice! Who suggests it? Introversion's no mere last-ditch device. Unless ordered, supervised and sanctioned, it means the end. And what if I'd Introverted 'ere we got Kaby's call for succor, hey?"

His warrior maid nodded with harsh approval and he noticed it and shook his free hand at her and scolded her, "Not that I say yea to your mad plan for that Devil's casket, you half-clad clack-wit. And yet to jettison . . . Oh, ye gods, ye gods—" he wiped his hand across his face—"grant me a minute in which I may think!"

Thinking time wasn't an item even on the strictly limited list at the moment, although Sevensee, squatting dourly on his hairy haunches where Maud had left him threw in a dead-pan "Thas tellin em, Gov."

Then Doc at the bar stood up tall as Abe Lincoln in his top hat and shawl and 19th Century duds and raised an unwavering arm for silence and said something that sounded like: "Introversh, inversh, glovsh," and then his enunciation switched to better than perfect as he continued, "I know to an absolute certainty what we must do."

It showed me how rabbity we were that the Place got quiet as a church while we all stopped whatever we were doing and waited breathless for a poor drunk to tell us how to save ourselves.

He said something like, "Inversh . . . bosh . . ." and held

our eyes for a moment longer. Then the light went out of his and he slobbered out a "*Nichevo*" and slid an arm far along the bar for a bottle and started to pour it down his throat without stopping sliding.

Before he completed his collapse to the floor, in the split second while our attention was still focused on the bar, Bruce vaulted up on top of it, so fast it was almost like he'd popped up from nowhere, though I'd seen him start from behind the piano.

"I've a question. Has anyone here triggered that bomb?" he said in a voice that was very clear and just loud enough. "So it can't go off," he went on after just the right pause, his easy grin and brisk manner putting more heart into me all the time. "What's more, if it were to be triggered, we'd still have half an hour. I believe you said it had that long a fuse?"

He stabbed a finger at Kaby. She nodded.

"Right," he said. "It'd have to be that long for whoever plants it in the Parthian camp to get away. There's another safety margin.

"Second question. Is there a locksmith in the house?"

For all Bruce's easiness, he was watching us like a golden eagle and he caught Beau's and Maud's affirmatives before they had a chance to explain or hedge them and said, "That's very good. Under certain circumstances, you two'd be the ones to go to work on the chest. But before we consider that, there's Question Three: Is anyone here an atomics technician?"

That one took a little conversation to straighten out, Illy having to explain that, yes, the Early Lunans had atomic power —hadn't they blasted the life off their planet with it and made all those ghastly craters?—but no, he wasn't a technician exactly, he was a "thinger" (I thought at first his squeakbox was lisping); what was a thinger?—well, a thinger was someone who manipulated things in a way that was truly impossible to describe, but no, you couldn't possibly thing atomics; the idea was quite ridiculous, so he couldn't be an atomics thinger; the term was worse than a contradiction, well, really!—while Sevensee, from his two-thousand-millennia advantage of the Lunan, grunted to the effect that his culture didn't rightly use any kind of power, but just sort of moved satyrs and stuff by wrastling spacetime around, "or think em roun ef we hafta.

Can't think em in the Void, tho, wus luck. Hafta have—I dunno wut. Dun havvit anyhow."

"So we don't have an A-tech," Bruce summed up, "which makes it worse than useless, downright dangerous, to tamper with the chest. We wouldn't know what to do if we did get inside safely. One more question." He directed it toward Sid. "How long before we can jettison anything?"

Sid, looking a shade jealous, yet mostly grateful for the way Bruce had calmed his chickens, started to explain, but Bruce didn't seem to be taking any chance of losing his audience, and as soon as Sid got to the word "rhythm," he pulled the answer away from him.

"In brief, not until we can effectively tune in on the cosmos again. Thank you, Master Lessingham. That's at least five hours—two mealtimes, as the Cretan officer put it," and he threw Kaby a quick soldierly smile. "So, whether the bomb goes to Egypt or elsewhere, there's not a thing we can do about it for five hours. All right then!"

His smile blinked out like a light and he took a couple of steps up and down the bar, as if measuring the space he had. Two or three cocktail glasses sailed off and popped, but he didn't seem to notice them and we hardly did either. It was creepy the way he kept staring from one to another of us. We had to look up. Behind his face, with the straight golden hair flirting around it, was only the Void.

"All right then," he repeated suddenly. "We're twelve Spiders and two Ghosts, and we've time for a bit of a talk, and we're all in the same bloody boat, fighting the same bloody war, so we'll all know what we're talking about. I raised the subject a while back, but I was steamed up about a glove, and it was a big jest. All right! But now the gloves are off!"

Bruce ripped them out of his belt where they'd been tucked and slammed them down on the bar, to be kicked off the next time he paced back and forth, and it wasn't funny.

"Because," he went right on, "I've been getting a completely new picture of what this Spiders' war has been doing to each one of us. Oh, it's jolly good sport to slam around in space and time and then have a rugged little party outside both of them when the operation's over. It's sweet to know there's no cranny of reality so narrow, no privacy so intimate or sacred, no wall of was or will be strong enough, that we can't shoulder in. Knowledge is a glamorous thing, sweeter than lust or gluttony or the passion of fighting and including all three, the ultimate insatiable hunger, and it's great to be Faust, even in a pack of other Fausts.

"It's sweet to jigger reality, to twist the whole course of a man's life or a culture's, to ink out his or its past and scribble in a new one, and be the only one to know and gloat over the changes—hah! killing men or carrying off women isn't in it for glutting the sense of power. It's sweet to feel the Change Winds blowing through you and know the pasts that were and the past that is and the pasts that may be. It's sweet to wield the Atropos and cut a Zombie or Unborn out of his lifeline and look the Doubleganger in the face and see the Resurrection-glow in it and Recruit a brother, welcome a newborn fellow Demon into our ranks and decide whether he'll best fit as Soldier, Entertainer, or what.

"Or he can't stand Resurrection, it fries or freezes him, and you've got to decide whether to return him to his lifeline and his Zombie dreams, only they'll be a little grayer and horrider than they were before, or whether, if she's got that tantalizing something, to bring her shell along for a Ghostgirl—that's sweet, too. It's even sweet to have Change Death poised over your neck, to know that the past isn't the precious indestructible thing you've been taught it was, to know that there's no certainty about the future either, whether there'll even be one, to know that no part of reality is holy, that the cosmos itself may wink out like a flicked switch and God be not and nothing left but nothing."

He threw out his arms against the Void. "And knowing all that, it's doubly sweet to come through the Door into the Place and be out of the worst of the Change Winds and enjoy a well-earned Recuperation and share the memories of all these sweetnesses I've been talking about, and work out all the fascinating feelings you've been accumulating back in the cosmos, layer by black layer, in the company of and with the help of the best bloody little band of fellow Fausts and Faustines going!

"Oh, it's a sweet life, all right, but I'm asking you—" and here his eyes stabbed us again, one by one, fast—"I'm asking you what it's done to us. I've been getting a completely new picture, as I said, of what my life was and what it could have been if there'd been changes of the sort that even we Demons can't make, and what my life is. I've been watching how we've all been responding to things just now, to the news of Saint Petersburg and to what the Cretan officer told beautifully— only it wasn't beautiful what she had to tell—and mostly to that bloody box of bomb. And I'm simply asking each one of you, what's happened to you?"

He stopped his pacing and stuck his thumbs in his belt and seemed to be listening to the wheels turning in at least eleven other heads—only I stopped mine pretty quick, with Dave and Father and the Rape of Chicago coming up out of the dark on the turn and Mother and the Indiana Dunes and Jazz Limited just behind them, followed by the unthinkable thing the Spider doctor had flicked into existence when I flopped as a nurse, because I can't stand that to be done to my mind by anybody but myself.

I stopped them by using the old infallible Entertainers' gimmick, a fast survey of the most interesting topic there is—other people's troubles.

Offhand, Beau looked as if he had most troubles, shamed by his boss and his girl given her heart to a Soldier; he was hugging them to himself very quiet.

I didn't stop for the two ETs—they're too hard to figure— or for Doc; nobody can tell whether a fallen-down drunk's at the black or bright end of his cycle; you just know it's cycling.

Maud ought to be suffering as much as Beau, called names and caught out in a panic, which always hurts her because she's plus three hundred years more future than the rest of us and figures she ought to be that much wiser, which she isn't always —not to mention she's over fifty years old, though her home-century cosmetic science keeps her looking and acting teen-age most of the time. She'd backed away from the bronze chest so as not to stand out, and now Lili came from behind the piano and stood beside her.

Lili had the opposite of troubles, a great big glow for Bruce, proud as a promised princess watching her betrothed. Erich frowned when he saw her, for he seemed proud too, proud of the way his *Kamerad* had taken command of us panicky whacks

Führer-fashion. Sid still looked mostly grateful and inclined to let Bruce keep on talking.

Even Kaby and Mark, those two dragons hot for battle, standing a little in front and to one side of us by the bronze chest, like its guardians, seemed willing to listen. They made me realize one reason Sid had for letting Bruce run on, although the path his talk was leading us down was flashing with danger signals: When it was over, there'd still be the problem of what to do with the bomb, and a real opposition shaping up between Soldiers and Entertainers, and Sid was hoping a solution would turn up in the meantime or at least was willing to put off the evil day.

But beyond all that, and like the rest of us, I could tell from the way Sid was squinting his browy eyes and chewing his beardy lip that he was shaken and moved by what Bruce had said. This New Boy had dipped into our hearts and counted our kicks so beautifully, better than most of us could have done, and then somehow turned them around so that we had to think of what messes and heels and black sheep and lost lambs we were—well, we wanted to keep on listening.

8

Give me a place to stand, and I will move the world.
                                                    —Archimedes

A PLACE TO STAND

BRUCE'S VOICE had a faraway touch and he was looking up left at the Void as he said, "Have you ever really wondered why the two sides of this war are called the Snakes and the Spiders? Snakes may be clear enough—you always call the enemy something dirty. But Spiders—our name for ourselves? Bear with me, Ilhilihis; I know that no being is created dirty or malignant by Nature, but this is a matter of anthropoid feelings and folkways. Yes, Mark, I know that some of your legions have nicknames like the Drunken Lions and the Snails, and that's about as insulting as calling the British Expeditionary Force the Old Contemptibles.

"No, you'd have to go to bands of vicious youths in cities slated for ruin to find a habit of naming like ours, and even they would try to brighten up the black a bit. But simply— Spiders. And Snakes, for that's their name for themselves too, you know. Spiders and Snakes. What are our masters, that we give them names like that?"

It gave me the shivers and set my mind working in a dozen directions and I couldn't stop it, although it made the shivers worse.

Illy beside me now—I'd never given it a thought before, but he did have eight legs of a sort, and I remembered thinking of him as a spider monkey, and hadn't the Lunans had wisdom and atomic power and a billion years in which to get the Change War rolling?

Or suppose, in the far future, Terra's own spiders evolved intelligence and a cruel cannibal culture. They'd be able to keep their existence secret. I had no idea of who or what would be on Earth in Sevensee's day, and wouldn't it be perfect black hairy poisoned spider-mentality to spin webs secretly through the world of thought and all of space and time?

And Beau—wasn't there something real Snaky about him, the way he moved and all?

Spiders and Snakes. *Spinne und Schlange*, as Erich called them. S & S. But SS stood for the Nazi *Schutzstaffel*, the Black Shirts, and what if some of those cruel, crazy Jerries had discovered time travel and—I brought myself up with a jerk and asked myself, "Greta, how nuts can you get?"

From where he was on the floor, the front of the bar his sounding board, Doc shrieked up at Bruce like one of the damned from the pit, "Don't speak against the Spiders! Don't blaspheme! They can hear the Unborn whisper. Others whip only the skin, but they whip the naked brain and heart," and Erich called out, "That's enough, Bruce!"

But Bruce didn't spare him a look and said, "But whatever the Spiders are and no matter how much they use, it's plain as the telltale on the Maintainer that the Change War is not only going against them, but getting away from them. Dwell for a bit on the current flurry of stupid slugging and panicky anachronism, when we all know that anachronism is what gets the Change Winds out of control. This punch-drunk pounding on the Cretan-Dorian fracas as if it were the only battle going and the only way to work things. Whisking Constantine from Britain to the Bosporus by rocket, sending a pocket submarine back to sail with the Armada against Drake's woodensides—I'll wager you hadn't heard those! And now, to save Rome, an atomic bomb.

"Ye gods, they could have used Greek fire or even dynamite, but a fission weapon . . . I leave you to imagine what gaps and scars that will make in what's left of history—the smothering of Greece and the vanishment of Provence and the troubadours and the Papacy's Irish Captivity won't be in it!"

The cut on his cheek had opened again and was oozing a little, but he didn't pay any attention to it, and neither did we, as his lips thinned in irony and he said, "But I'm forgetting that this is a cosmic war and that the Spiders are conducting operations on billions, trillions of planets and inhabited gas clouds through millions of ages and that we're just one little world—one little solar system, Sevensee—and we can hardly expect our inscrutable masters, with all their pressing preoccupations and far-flung responsibilities, to be especially understanding or tender in their treatment of our pet books and centuries, our favorite prophets and periods, or unduly concerned about preserving any of the trifles that we just happen to hold dear.

"Perhaps there are some sentimentalists who would rather die forever than go on living in a world without the *Summa*, the Field Equations, *Process and Reality*, *Hamlet*, Matthew, Keats, and the *Odyssey*, but our masters are practical creatures, ministering to the needs of those ragged souls who want to go on living no matter what."

Erich's "Bruce, I'm telling you that's enough," was lost in the quickening flow of the New Boy's words. "I won't spend much time on the minor signs of our major crack-up—the canceling of leaves, the sharper shortages, the loss of the Express Room, the use of Recuperation Stations for ops and all the other frantic patchwork—last operation but one, we were saddled with three Soldiers from outside the Galaxy and, no fault of theirs, they were no earthly use. Such little things might happen at a bad spot in any war and are perhaps only local. But there's a big thing."

He paused again, to let us wonder, I guess. Maud must have worked her way over to me, for I felt her dry little hand on my arm and she whispered out of the side of her mouth, "What do we do now?"

"We listen," I told her the same way. I felt a little impatient with her need to be doing something about things.

She cocked a gold-dusted eyebrow at me and murmured, "You, too?"

I didn't get to ask her me, too, what? Crush on Bruce? Nuts!—because just then Bruce's voice took up again in the faraway range.

"Have you ever asked yourself how many operations the fabric of history can stand before it's all stitches, whether too much Change won't one day wear out the past? And the present and the future, too, the whole bleeding business. Is the law of the Conservation of Reality any more than a thin hope given a long name, a prayer of theoreticians? Change Death is as certain as Heat Death, and far faster. Every operation leaves reality a bit cruder, a bit uglier, a bit more makeshift, and a whole lot less rich in those details and feelings that are our heritage, like the crude penciled sketch on canvas when you've stripped off the paint.

"If that goes on, won't the cosmos collapse into an outline of itself, then nothing? How much thinning can reality stand, having more and more Doublegangers cut out of it? And there's another thing about every operation—it wakes up the Zombies a little more, and as its Change Winds die, it leaves them a little more disturbed and nightmare-ridden and frazzled. Those of you who have been on operations in heavily worked-over temporal areas will know what I mean—that look they give you out of the sides of their eyes as if to say, 'You again? For Christ's sake, go away. We're the dead. We're the ones who don't want to wake up, who don't want to be Demons and hate to be Ghosts. Stop torturing us.'"

I looked around at the Ghostgirls; I couldn't help it. They'd somehow got together on the control divan, facing us, their backs to the Maintainers. The Countess had dragged along the bottle of wine Erich had fetched her earlier and they were passing it back and forth. The Countess had a big rose splotch across the ruffled white lace of her blouse.

Bruce said, "There'll come a day when all the Zombies and all the Unborn wake up and go crazy together and figuratively come marching at us in their numberless hordes, saying, 'We've had enough.'"

But I didn't turn back to Bruce right away. Phryne's chiton had slipped off one shoulder and she and the Countess were sitting sagged forward, elbows on knees, legs spread—at least, as far as the Countess's hobble skirt would let her—and swayed toward each other a little. They were still surprisingly solid, although they hadn't had any personal attention for a half hour, and they were looking up over my head with half-shut eyes and they seemed, so help me, to be listening to what Bruce was saying and maybe hearing some of it.

"We make a careful distinction between Zombies and Unborn, between those troubled by our operations whose lifelines lie in the past and those whose lifelines lie in the future. But is there any distinction any longer? Can we tell the difference between the past and the future? Can we any longer locate the now, the real now of the cosmos? The Places have their own nows, the now of the Big Time we're on, but that's different and it's not made for real living.

"The Spiders tell us that the real now is somewhere in the last half of the 20th Century, which means that several of us here are also alive in the cosmos, have lifelines along which the now is traveling. But do you swallow that story quite so easily, Ilhilihis, Sevensee? How does it strike the servants of the Triple Goddess? The Spiders of Octavian Rome? The Demons of Good Queen Bess? The gentlemen Zombies of the Greater South? Do the Unborn man the starships, Maud?

"The Spiders also tell us that, although the fog of battle makes the now hard to pin down precisely, it will return with the unconditional surrender of the Snakes and the establishment of cosmic peace, and roll on as majestically toward the future as before, quickening the continuum with its passage. Do you really believe that? Or do you believe, as I do, that we've used up all the future as well as the past, wasted it in premature experience, and that we've had the real now smudged out of existence, stolen from us forever, the precious now of true growth, the child-moment in which all life lies, the moment like a newborn baby that is the only home for hope there is?"

He let that start to sink in, then took a couple of quick steps and went on, his voice rising over Erich's "Bruce, for the last time—" and seeming to pick up a note of hope from the very word he had used, "But although things look terrifyingly black, there remains a chance—the slimmest chance, but still a chance—of saving the cosmos from Change Death and restoring reality's richness and giving the Ghosts good sleep and perhaps even regaining the real now. We have the means right at hand. What if the power of time traveling were used not for war and destruction, but for healing, for the mutual enrichment of the ages, for quiet communication and growth, in brief, to bring a peace message—"

But my little commandant is quite an actor himself and knows a wee bit about the principles of scene-stealing and he was not going to let Bruce drown him out as if he were just another extra playing a Voice from the Mob. He darted across our front, between us and the bar, took a running leap, and landed bang on the bloody box of bomb.

A bit later, Maud was silently showing me the white ring above her elbow where I'd grabbed her and Illy was teasing a clutch of his tentacles out of my other hand and squeaking reproachfully, "Greta girl, don't ever do that."

Erich was standing on the chest and I noticed that his boots carefully straddled the circle of skulls, and I should have known anyway you could hardly push them in the right order by jumping on them, and he was pointing at Bruce and saying, "—and that means mutiny, my young sir. *Um Gottes willen*, Bruce, listen to me and step down before you say anything worse. I'm older than you, Bruce. Mark's older. Trust in your *Kameraden*. Guide yourself by their knowledge."

He had got my attention, but I had much rather have him black my eye.

"You older than me?" Bruce was grinning. "When your twelve-years' advantage was spent in soaking up the wisdom of a race of sadistic dreamers gone paranoid, in a world whose thought-stream had already been muddied by one total war? Mark older than me? When all his ideas and loyalties are those of a wolf pack of unimaginative sluggers two thousand years younger than I am? Either of you older because you have more of the killing cynicism that is all the wisdom the Change World ever gives you? Don't make me laugh!

"I'm an Englishman, and I come from an epoch when total war was still a desecration and the flowers and buds of thoughts not yet whacked off or blighted. I'm a poet and poets are wiser than anyone because they're the only people who have the guts to think and feel at the same time. Right, Sid? When I talk to all of you about a peace message, I want you to think about it concretely in teams of using the Places to bring help across the mountains of time when help is really needed, not to bring help that's undeserved or knowledge that's premature or contaminating, sometimes not to bring anything at all, but just to check with infinite tenderness and concern that everything's safe and the glories of the universe unfolding as they were intended to—"

"Yes, you are a poet, Bruce," Erich broke in. "You can tootle soulfully on the flute and make us drip tears. You can let out the stops on the big organ pipes and make us tremble as if at Jehovah's footsteps. For the last twenty minutes, you have been giving us some very *charmante* poetry. But what are you? An Entertainer? Or are you a Soldier?"

Right then—I don't know what it was, maybe Sid clearing his throat—I could sense our feelings beginning to turn against Bruce. I got the strangest feeling of reality clamping down and bright colors going dull and dreams vanishing. Yet it was only then I also realized how much Bruce had moved us, maybe some of us to the verge of mutiny, even. I was mad at Erich for what he was doing, but I couldn't help admiring his cockiness.

I was still under the spell of Bruce's words and the more-than-words behind them, but then Erich would shift around a bit and one of his heels would kick near the death's head push-buttons and I wanted to stamp with spike heels on every death's-head button on his uniform. I didn't know exactly what I felt yet.

"Yes, I'm a Soldier," Bruce told him, "and I hope you won't ever have to worry about my courage, because it's going to take more courage than any operation we've ever planned, ever dreamed of, to carry the peace message to the other Places and to the wound-spots of the cosmos. Perhaps it will be a fast wicket and we'll be bowled down before we score a single run, but who cares? We may at least see our real masters when they come to smash us, and for me that will be a deep satisfaction. And we may do some smashing of our own."

"So you're a Soldier," Erich said, his smile showing his teeth. "Bruce, I'll admit that the half-dozen operations you've been on were rougher than anything I drew in my first hundred sleeps. For that, I am all honest sympathy. But that you should let them get you into such a state that love and a girl can turn you upside down and start you babbling about peace messages—"

"Yes, by God, love and a girl have changed me!" Bruce shouted at him, and I looked around at Lili and I remembered Dave saying, "I'm going to Spain," and I wondered if anything would ever again make my face flame like that. "Or, rather, they've made me stand up for what I've believed in all along. They've made me—"

"*Wunderbar*," Erich called and began to do a little sissy dance on the bomb that set my teeth on edge. He bent his wrists and elbows at arty angles and stuck out a hip and ducked his head simperingly and blinked his eyes very fast. "Will you invite me to the wedding, Bruce? You'll have to get another best man, but I will be the flower girl and throw pretty little posies to all the distinguished guests. Here, Mark. Catch, Kaby. One for you, Greta. *Danke schön. Ach, zwei Herzen im drei-vierteltakt . . . ta-ta . . . ta-ta . . . ta-ta-ta-ta-ta . . .*"

"What the hell do you think a woman is?" Bruce raged. "Something to mess around with in your spare time?"

Erich kept on humming "Two Hearts in Waltz Time"—and jigging around to it, damn him—but he slipped in a nod to Bruce and a "Precisely." So I knew where I stood, but it was no news to me.

"Very well," Bruce said, "let's leave this Brown Shirt *maricón* to amuse himself and get down to business. I made all of you a proposal and I don't have to tell you how serious it is or how serious Lili and I are about it. We not only must infiltrate and subvert other Places, which luckily for us are made for infiltration, we also must make contact with the Snakes and establish working relationships with their Demons at our level as one of our first steps."

That stopped Erich's jig and got enough of a gasp from some of us to make it seem to come from practically everybody. Erich used it to work a change of pace.

"Bruce! We've let you carry this foolery further than we should. You seem to have the idea that because anything goes in the Place—dueling, drunkenness, *und so weiter*—you can say what you have and it will all be forgotten with the hangover. Not so. It is true that among such a set of monsters and free spirits as ourselves, and working as secret agents to boot, there cannot be the obvious military discipline that would obtain in a Terran army.

"But let me tell you, Bruce, let me grind it home into you— Sid and Kaby and Mark will bear me out in this, as officers of equivalent rank—that the Spider line of command stretches into and through this Place just as surely as the word of *der Führer* rules Chicago. And as I shouldn't have to emphasize to you, Bruce, the Spiders have punishments that would make my countrymen in Belsen and Buchenwald—well, pale a little. So while there is still a shadow of justification for our interpreting your remarks as utterly tasteless clowning—"

"Babble on," Bruce said, giving him a loose downward wave of his hand without looking. "I made you people a proposal." He paused. "How do you stand, Sidney Lessingham?"

Then I felt my legs getting weak, because Sid didn't answer right away. The old boy swallowed and started to look around at the rest of us. Then the feeling of reality clamping down got something awful, because he didn't look around, but straightened his back a little. Just then, Mark cut in fast.

"It grieves me, Bruce, but I think you are possessed. Erich, he must be confined."

Kaby nodded, almost absently. "Confine or kill the coward, whichever is easier, whip the woman, and let's get on to the Egyptian battle."

"Indeed, yes," Mark said. "I died in it. But now perhaps no longer."

Kaby said to him, "I like you, Roman."

Bruce was smiling, barely, and his eyes were moving and fixing. "You, Ilhilihis?"

Illy's squeak box had never sounded mechanical to me before, but it did as he answered, "I'm a lot deeper into borrowed time than the rest of you, tra-la-la, but Papa still loves living. Include me very much out, Brucie."

"Miss Davies?"

Beside me, Maud said flatly, "Do you think I'm a fool?" Beyond her, I saw Lili and I thought, "My God, I might look as proud if I were in her shoes, but I sure as hell wouldn't look as confident."

Bruce's eyes hadn't quite come to Beau when the gambler spoke up. "I have no cause to like you, sir, rather the opposite. But this Place has come to bore me more than Boston and I have always found it difficult to resist a long shot. A very long one, I fear. I am with you, sir."

There was a pain in my chest and a roaring in my ears and through it I heard Sevensee grunting, "sicka these lousy Spiders. Deal me in."

And then Doc reared up in front of the bar and he'd lost his hat and his hair was wild and he grabbed an empty fifth by the neck and broke the bottom of it all jagged against the bar and he waved it and screeched, "*Ubivaytye Pauki—i Nyemetzi!*"

And right behind his words, Beau sang out fast the English of it, "Kill the Spiders—and the Germans!"

And Doc didn't collapse then, though I could see he was hanging onto the bar tight with his other hand, and the Place got stiller, inside and out, than I've ever known it, and Bruce's eyes were finally moving back toward Sid.

But the eyes stopped short of Sid and I heard Bruce say, "Miss Forzane?" and I thought, "That's funny," and I started to look around at the Countess, and felt all the eyes and I realized, "Hey, that's me! But this can't happen to me. To the others, yes, but not to me. I just work here. Not to Greta, no, no, no!"

But it had, and the eyes didn't let go, and the silence and the feeling of reality were Godawful, and I said to myself, "Greta, you've got to say something, if only a suitable four-letter word," and then suddenly I knew what the silence was like. It was like that of a big city if there were some way of shutting off all the noise in one second. It was like Erich's singing when the piano had deserted him. It was as if the Change Winds should ever die completely . . . and I knew beforehand what had happened when I turned my back on them all.

The Ghostgirls were gone. The Major Maintainer hadn't merely been switched to Introvert. It was gone, too.

9

"We examined the moss between the bricks, and found it undisturbed."

"You looked among D——'s papers, of course, and into the books of the library?"

"Certainly; we opened every package and parcel; we not only opened every book, but we turned over every leaf in each volume . . ."

—Poe

A LOCKED ROOM

THREE HOURS later, Sid and I plumped down on the couch nearest the kitchen, though too tired to want to eat for a while yet. A tighter search that I could ever have cooked up had shown that the Maintainer was not in the Place.

Of course it had to be in the Place, as we kept telling each other for the first two hours. It had to be, if circumstances and the theories we lived by in the Change World meant anything. A Maintainer is what maintains a Place. The Minor Maintainer takes care of oxygen, temperature, humidity, gravity, and other little life-cycle and matter-cycle things generally, but it's the Major Maintainer that keeps the walls from buckling and the ceiling from falling in. It is little, but oh my, it does so much.

It doesn't work by wires or radio or anything complicated like that. It just hooks into local space-time.

I have been told that its inside working part is made up of vastly tough, vastly hard giant molecules, each one of which is practically a vest-pocket cosmos in itself. Outside, it looks like a portable radio with a few more dials and some telltales and switches and plug-ins for earphones and a lot of other sensory thingumajigs.

But the Maintainer was gone and the Void hadn't closed in, yet. By this time, I was so fagged, I didn't care much whether it did or not.

One thing for sure, the Maintainer had been switched to Introvert before it was spirited away or else its disappearance automatically produced Introversion, take your choice, because we sure were Introverted—real nasty martinet-schoolmaster grip of reality on my thoughts that I knew, without trying, liquor wouldn't soften, not a breath of Change Wind, absolutely stifling, and the gray of the Void seeming so much inside my head that I think I got a glimmering of what the science boys mean when they explain to me that the Place is a kind of interweaving of the material and the mental—a Giant Monad, one of them called it.

Anyway, I said to myself, "Greta, if this is Introversion, I want no part of it. It is not nice to be cut adrift from the cosmos and know it. A lifeboat in the middle of the Pacific and a starship between galaxies are not in it for loneliness."

I asked myself why the Spiders had ever equipped Maintainers with Introversion switches anyway, when we couldn't drill with them and weren't supposed to use them except in an emergency so tight that it was either Introvert or surrender to the Snakes, and for the first time the obvious explanation came to me:

Introversion must be the same as scuttling, its main purpose to withhold secrets and materiel from the enemy. It put a place into a situation from which even the Spider high command couldn't rescue it, and there was nothing left but to sink down, down (out? up?), down into the Void.

If that was the case, our chances of getting back were about those of my being a kid again playing in the Dunes on the Small Time.

I edged a little closer to Sid and sort of squunched under his shoulder and rubbed my cheek against the smudged, gold-worked gray velvet. He looked down and I said, "A long way to Lynn Regis, eh, Siddy?"

"Sweetling, thou spokest a mouthful," he said. He knows

very well what he is doing when he mixes his language that way, the wicked old darling.

"Siddy," I said, "why this goldwork? It'd be a lot smoother without it."

"Marry, men must prick themselves out and, 'faith I know not, but it helps if there's metal in it."

"And girls get scratched." I took a little sniff. "But don't put this doublet through the cleaner yet. Until we get out of the woods, I want as much around as possible."

"Marry, and why should I?" he asked blankly, and I think he wasn't fooling me. The last thing time travelers find out is how they do or don't smell. Then his face clouded and he looked as though he wanted to squunch under my shoulder. "But 'faith, sweetling, your forest has a few more trees than Sherwood."

"Thou saidst it," I agreed, and wondered about the look. He oughtn't to be interested in my girlishness now. I knew I was a mess, but he had stuck pretty close to me during the hunt and you never can tell. Then I remembered that he was the other one who hadn't declared himself when Bruce was putting it to us, and it probably troubled his male vanity. Not me, though— I was still grateful to the Maintainer for getting me out of that spot, whatever other it had got us all into. It seemed ages ago.

We'd all jumped to the conclusion that the two Ghostgirls had run away with the Maintainer, I don't know where or why, but it looked so much that way. Maud had started yiping about how she'd never trusted Ghosts and always known that some day they'd start doing things on their own, and Kaby had got it firmly fixed in her head, right between the horns, that Phryne, being a Greek, was the ringleader and was going to wreak havoc on us all.

But when we were checking Stores the first time, I had noticed that the Ghostgirl envelopes looked flat. Ectoplasm doesn't take up much space when it's folded, but I had opened one anyway, then another, and then called for help.

Every last envelope was empty. We had lost over a thousand Ghostgirls, Sid's whole stock.

Well, at least it proved what none of us had ever seen or heard of being demonstrated: that there is a spooky link—a sort of Change Wind contact—between a Ghost and its lifeline;

and when that umbilicus, I've heard it called, is cut, the part away from the lifeline dies.

Interesting, but what had bothered me was whether we Demons were going to evaporate too, because we are as much Doublegangers as the Ghosts and our apron strings had been cut just as surely. We're more solid, of course, but that would only mean we'd take a little longer. Very logical.

I remember I had looked up at Lili and Maud—us girls had been checking the envelopes; it's one of the proprieties we frequently maintain and anyway, if men check them, they're apt to trot out that old wheeze about "instant women" which I'm sick to death of hearing, thank you.

Anyway, I had looked up and said, "It's been nice knowing you," and Lili had said, "Twenty-three, skiddoo," and Maud had said, "Here goes nothing," and we had shook hands all around.

We figured that Phryne and the Countess had faded at the same time as the other Ghostgirls, but an idea had been nibbling at me and I said, "Siddy, do you suppose it's just barely possible that, while we were all looking at Bruce, those two Ghostgirls would have been able to work the Maintainer and get a Door and lam out of here with the thing?"

"Thou speakst my thoughts, sweetling. All weighs against it: Imprimis, 'tis well known that Ghosts cannot lay plots or act on them. Secundo, the time forbade getting a Door. Tercio— and here's the real meat of it—the Place folds without the Maintainer. Quadro, 'twere folly to depend on not one of—how many of us? ten, elf—not looking around in all the time it would have taken them—"

"I looked around once, Siddy. They were drinking and they had got to the control divan under their own power. Now when was that? Oh, yes, when Bruce was talking about Zombies."

"Yes, sweetling. And as I was about to cap my argument with quinquo when you 'gan prattle, I could have sworne none could touch the Maintainer, much less work it and purloin it, without my certain knowledge. Yet . . ."

"Eftsoons yet," I seconded him.

Somebody must have got a door and walked out with the thing. It certainly wasn't in the Place. The hunt had been a lulu. Something the size of a portable typewriter is not easy to hide and we had been inside everything from Beau's piano to the renewer link of the Refresher.

We had even fluoroscoped everybody, though it had made Illy writhe like a box of worms, as he'd warned us; he said it tickled terribly and I insisted on smoothing his fur for five minutes afterward, although he was a little standoffish toward me.

Some areas, like the bar, kitchen and Stores, took a long while, but we were thorough. Kaby helped Doc check Surgery: since she last made the Place, she has been stationed in a Field Hospital (it turns out the Spiders actually are mounting operations from them) and learned a few nice new wrinkles.

However, Doc put in some honest work on his own, though, of course, every check was observed by at least three people, not including Bruce or Lili. When the Maintainer vanished, Doc had pulled out of his glassy-eyed drunk in a way that would have surprised me if I hadn't seen it happen to him before, but when we finished Surgery and got on to the Art Gallery, he had started to putter and I noticed him hold out his coat and duck his head and whip out a flask and take a swig and by now he was well on his way toward another peak.

The Art Gallery had taken time too, because there's such a jumble of strange stuff, and it broke my heart but Kaby took her ax and split a beautiful blue woodcarving of a Venusian medusa because, although there wasn't a mark in the paw-polished surface, she claimed it was just big enough. Doc cried a little and we left him fitting the pieces together and mooning over the other stuff.

After we'd finished everything else, Mark had insisted on tackling the floor. Beau and Sid both tried to explain to him how this is a one-sided Place, that there is nothing, but nothing, under the floor; it just gets a lot harder than the diamonds crusting it as soon as you get a quarter inch down—that being the solid equivalent of the Void. But Mark was knuckleheaded (like all Romans, Sid assured me on the q.t.) and broke four diamond-plus drills before he was satisfied.

Except for some trick hiding places, that left the Void, and things don't vanish if you throw them at the Void—they half melt and freeze forever unless you can fish them out. Back of the Refresher, at about eye-level, are three Venusian coconuts that a Hittite strongman threw there during a major brawl. I try not to look at them because they are so much like witch heads they give me the woolies. The parts of the Place right up against the Void have strange spatial properties which one of the gadgets in Surgery makes use of in a way that gives me the worse woolies, but that's beside the point.

During the hunt, Kaby and Erich had used their Callers as direction finders to point out the Maintainer, just as they're used in the cosmos to locate the Door—and sometimes in the Big Places, people tell me. But the Callers only went wild—like a compass needle whirling around without stopping—and nobody knew what that meant.

The trick hiding places were the Minor Maintainer, a cute idea, but it is no bigger than the Major and has its own mysterious insides and had obviously kept on doing its own work, so that was out for several reasons, and the bomb chest, though it seemed impossible for anyone to have opened it, granting they know the secret of its lock, even before Erich jumped on it and put it in the limelight double. But when you've ruled out everything else, the word impossible changes meaning.

Since time travel is our business, a person might think of all sorts of tricks for sending the Maintainer into the past or future, permanently or temporarily. But the Place is strictly on the Big Time and everybody that should know tells me that time traveling *through* the Big Time is out. It's this way: the Big Time is a train, and the Little Time is the countryside and we're on the train, unless we go out a Door, and as Gertie Stein might put it, you can't time travel through the time you time travel in when you time travel.

I'd also played around with the idea of some fantastically obvious hiding place, maybe something that several people could pass back and forth between them, which could mean a conspiracy, and, of course, if you assume a big enough conspiracy, you can explain anything, including the cosmos itself. Still, I'd got a sort of shell-game idea about the Soldiers' three big black shakos and I hadn't been satisfied until I'd got the three together and looked in them all at the same time.

"Wake up, Greta, and take something, I can't stand here forever." Maud had brought us a tray of hearty snacks from then and yon, and I must say they were tempting; she whips up a mean hors d'oeuvre.

I looked them over and said, "Siddy, I want a hot dog."

"And I want a venison pasty! Out upon you, you finical jill, you o'erscrupulous jade, you whimsic and tyrannous poppet!"

I grabbed a handful and snuggled back against him.

"Go on, call me some more, Siddy," I told him. "Real juicy ones."

10

> My thought, whose murder yet is but fantastical,
> Shakes so my single state of man that function
> Is smother'd in surmise, and nothing is
> But what is not.
>
> —Macbeth

MOTIVES AND OPPORTUNITIES

MY BIG bad waif from King's Lynn had set the tray on his knees and started to wolf the food down. The others were finishing up. Erich, Mark and Kaby were having a quietly furious argument I couldn't overhear at the end of the bar nearest the bronze chest, and Illy was draped over the piano like a real octopus, listening in.

Beau and Sevensee were pacing up and down near the control divan and throwing each other a word now and then. Beyond them, Bruce and Lili were sitting on the opposite couch from us, talking earnestly about something. Maud had sat down at the other end of the bar and was knitting—it's one of the habits like chess and quiet drinking, or learning to talk by squeak box, that we pick up to pass the time in the Place in the long stretches between parties. Doc was fiddling around the Gallery, picking things up and setting them down, still managing to stay on his feet at any rate.

Lili and Bruce stood up, still gabbing intensely at each other, and Illy began to pick out with one tentacle a little tune in the high keys that didn't sound like anything on God's earth. "Where do they get all the energy?" I wondered.

As soon as I asked myself that, I knew the answer and I began to feel the same way myself. It wasn't energy; it was nerves, pure and simple.

Change is like a drug, I realized—you get used to the facts never staying the same, and one picture of the past and future dissolving into another maybe not very different but still different, and your mind being constantly goosed by strange moods and notions, like nightclub lights of shifting color with weird shadows between shining right on your brain.

The endless swaying and jogging is restful, like riding on a train.

You soon get to like the movement and to need it without knowing, and when it suddenly stops and you're just you and the facts you think from and feel from are exactly the same when you go back to them—boy, that's rough, as I found out now.

The instant we got Introverted, everything that ordinarily leaks into the Place, wake or sleep, had stopped coming, and we were nothing but ourselves and what we meant to each other and what we could make of that, an awfully lonely, scratchy situation.

I decided I felt like I'd been dropped into a swimming pool full of cement and held under until it hardened.

I could understand the others bouncing around a bit. It was a wonder they didn't hit the Void. Maud seemed to be standing it the best, maybe she'd got a little preparation from the long watches between stars; and then she is older than all of us, even Sid, though with a small "o" in "older."

The restless work of the search for the Maintainer had masked the feeling, but now it was beginning to come full force. Before the search, Bruce's speech and Erich's interruptions had done a passable masking job too. I tried to remember when I'd first got the feeling and decided it was after Erich had jumped on the bomb, about the time he mentioned poetry. Though I couldn't be sure. Maybe the Maintainer had been Introverted even earlier, when I'd turned to look at the Ghostgirls. I wouldn't have known. Nuts!

Believe me, I could feel that hardened cement on every inch of me. I remembered Bruce's beautiful picture of a universe without Big Change and decided it was about the worst idea going. I went on eating, though I wasn't so sure now it was a good idea to keep myself strong.

"Does the Maintainer have an Introversion telltale? Siddy!"

" 'Sdeath, chit, and you love me, speak lower. Of a sudden, I feel not well, as if I'd drunk a butt of Rhenish and slept inside it. Marry yes, blue. In short flashes, saith the manual. Why ask'st thou?"

"No reason. God, Siddy, what I'd give for a breath of Change Wind."

"Thou can'st say that eftsoons," he groaned. I must have looked pretty miserable myself, for he put his arm around my shoulders and whispered gruffly, "Comfort thyself sweetling, that while we suffer thus sorely, we yet cannot die the Change Death."

"What's that?" I asked him.

I didn't want to bounce around like the others. I had a suspicion I'd carry it too far. So, to keep myself from going batty, I started to rework the business of who had done what to the Maintainer.

During the hunt, there had been some pretty wild suggestions tossed around as to its disappearance or at least its Introversion: a feat of Snake science amounting to sorcery; the Spider high command bunkering the Places from above, perhaps in reaction to the loss of the Express Room, in such a hurry that they hadn't even time to transmit warnings; the hand of the Late Cosmicians, those mysterious hypothetical beings who are supposed to have successfully resisted the extension of the Change War into the future much beyond Sevensee's epoch—unless the Late Cosmicians are the ones fighting the Change War.

One thing these suggestions had steered very clear of was naming any one of us as a suspect, whether acting as Snake spy, Spider political police, agent of—who knows, after Bruce?—a secret Change World Committee of Public Safety or Spider revolutionary underground, or strictly on our own. Just as no one had piped a word, since the Maintainer had been palmed, about the split between Erich's and Bruce's factions.

Good group thinking probably, to sink differences in the emergency, but that didn't apply to what I did with my own thoughts.

Who wanted to escape so bad they'd Introvert the Place, cutting off all possible contact and communication either way with the cosmos and running the very big risk of not getting back to the cosmos at all?

Leaving out what had happened since Bruce had arrived and stirred things up, Doc seemed to me to have the strongest motive. He knew that Sid couldn't keep covering up for him forever and that Spider punishments for derelictions of duty are not just the clink of a firing squad, as Erich had reminded us. But Doc had been flat on the floor in front of the bar from the time Bruce had jumped on top of it, though I certainly hadn't had my eye on him every second.

Beau? Beau had said he was bored with the Place at a time when what he said counted, so he'd hardly lock himself in it maybe forever, not to mention locking Bruce in with himself and the babe he had a yen for.

Sid loves reality, Changing or not, and every least thing in it, people especially, more than any man or woman I've ever known—he's like a big-eyed baby who wants to grab every object and put it in his mouth—and it was hard to imagine him ever cutting himself off from the cosmos.

Maud, Kaby, Mark and the two ETs? None of them had any motive I knew of, though Sevensee's being from the very far future did tie in with that idea about the Late Cosmicians, and there did seem to be something developing between the Cretan and the Roman that could make them want to be Introverted together.

"Stick to the facts, Greta," I reminded myself with a private groan.

That left Erich, Bruce, Lili and myself.

Erich, I thought—now we're getting somewhere. The little commandant has the nervous system of a coyote and the courage of a crazy tomcat, and if he thought it would help him settle his battle with Bruce better to be locked in with him, he'd do it in a second.

But even before Erich had danced on the bomb, he'd been

heckling Bruce from the crowd. Still, there would have been time between heckles for him to step quietly back from us, Introvert the Maintainer and . . . well, that was nine-tenths of the problem.

If I was the guilty party, I was nuts and that was the best explanation of all. Gr-r-r!

Bruce's motives seemed so obvious, especially the mortal (or was it immortal?) danger he'd put himself in by inciting mutiny, that it seemed a shame he'd been in full view on the bar so long. Surely, if the Maintainer had been Introverted before he jumped on the bar, we'd all have noticed the flashing blue telltale. For that matter, I'd have noticed it when I looked back at the Ghostgirls—if it worked as Sid claimed, and he said he had never seen it in operation, just read in the manual—oh, 'sdeath!

But Bruce didn't need opportunity, as I'm sure all the males in the Place would have told me right off, because he had Lili to pull the job for him and she had as much opportunity as any of the rest of us. Myself, I have large reservations to this woman-is-putty-in-the-hands-of-the-man-she-loves-madly theory, but I had to admit there was something to be said for it in this case, and it had seemed quite natural to me when the rest of us had decided, by unspoken agreement, that neither Lili's nor Bruce's checks counted when we were hunting for the Maintainer.

That took care of all of us and left only the mysterious stranger, intruding somehow through a Door (how'd he get it without using our Maintainer?) or from an unimaginable hiding place or straight out of the Void itself. I know that last is impossible—nothing can step out of nothing—but if anything ever looked like it was specially built for something not at all nice to come looming out of, it's the Void—misty, foggily churning, slimy gray . . .

"Wait a second," I told myself, "and hang onto this, Greta. It should have smacked you in the face at the start."

Whatever came out of the Void, or, more to the point, whoever slipped back from our crowd to the Maintainer, Bruce would have seen them. He was looking at the Maintainer past our heads the whole time, and whatever happened to it, he saw it.

Erich wouldn't have, even after he was on the bomb, because
he'd been stagewise enough to face Bruce most of the time to
build up his role as tribune of the people.

But Bruce would have—unless he got so caught up in what
he was saying . . .

No, kid, a Demon is always an actor, no matter how much
he believes in what he's saying, and there never was an actor
yet who wouldn't instantly notice a member of the audience
starting to walk out on his big scene.

So Bruce knew, which made him a better actor than I'd have
been willing to grant, since it didn't look as if anyone else had
thought of what had just occurred to me, or they'd have gone
over and put it to him.

Not me, though—I don't work that way. Besides, I didn't
feel up to it—Nervy Anna enfold me, I felt like pure hell.

"Maybe," I told myself encouragingly, "the Place is Hell,"
but added, "Be your age, Greta—be a real rootless, ruleless,
ruthless twenty-nine."

11

The barrage roars and lifts. Then, clumsily bowed
With bombs and guns and shovels and battle gear,
Men jostle and climb to meet the bristling fire.
Lines of gray, muttering faces, masked with fear,
They leave their trenches, going over the top,
While time ticks blank and busy on their wrists,
                                                —Sassoon

THE WESTERN FRONT, 1917

"PLEASE DON'T LILI."
        "I shall, my love."
    "Sweetling, wake up! Hast the shakes?"
    I opened my eyes a little and lied to Siddy with a smile,
locked my hands together tight and watched Bruce and Lili
quarrel nobly near the control divan and wished I had a great

love to blur my misery and provide me with a passable substitute for Change Winds.

Lili won the argument, judging from the way she threw her head back and stepped away from Bruce's arms while giving him a proud, tender smile. He walked off a few steps; praise be, he didn't shrug his shoulders at us like an old husband, though his nerves were showing and he didn't seem to be standing Introversion well at all, as who of us were?

Lili rested a hand on the head of the control divan and pressed her lips together and looked around us, mostly with her eyes. She'd wound a gray silk bandeau around her bangs. Her short gray silk dress without a waistline made her look, not so much like a flapper, though she looked like that all right, as like a little girl, except the neckline was scooped low enough to show she wasn't.

Her gaze hesitated and then stopped at me and I got a sunk feeling of what was coming, because women are always picking on me for an audience. Besides, Sid and I were the centrist party of two in our fresh-out-of-the-shell Place politics.

She took a deep breath and stuck out her chin and said in a voice that was even a little higher and Britisher than she usually uses, "We girls have often cried, 'Shut the Door!' But now the Door is jolly well shut for keeps!"

I knew I'd guessed right and I felt crawly with embarrassment, because I know about this love business of thinking you're the other person and trying to live their life—and grab their glory, though you don't know that—and carry their message for them, and how it can foul things up. Still, I couldn't help admitting what she said wasn't too bad a start—unpleasantly apt to be true, at any rate.

"My fiance believes we may yet be able to open the Door. I do not. He thinks it is a bit premature to discuss the peculiar pickle in which we all find ourselves. I do not."

There was a rasp of laughter from the bar. The militarists were reacting. Erich stepped out, looking very happy. "So now we have to listen to women making speeches," he called. "What is this Place, anyhow? Sidney Lessingham's Saturday Evening Sewing Circle?"

Beau and Sevensee, who'd stopped their pacing halfway between the bar and the control divan, turned toward Erich, and

Sevensee looked a little burlier, a little more like half a horse, than satyrs in mythology book illustrations. He stamped—medium hard, I'd say—and said, "Ahh, go flya kite." I'd found out he'd learned English from a Demon who'd been a longshoreman with syndicalist-anarchist sympathies. Erich shut up for a moment and stood there grinning, his hands on his hips.

Lili nodded to the satyr and cleared her throat, looking scared. But she didn't speak; I could see she was thinking and feeling something, and her face got ugly and haggard, as if she were in a Change Wind that hadn't reached me yet, and her mouth went into a snarl to fight tears, but some spurted out, and when she did speak her voice was an octave lower and it wasn't just London talking but New York too.

"I don't know how Resurrection felt to you people, because I'm new and I loathe asking questions, but to me it was pure torture and I wished only I'd had the courage to tell Suzaku, 'I wish to remain a Zombie, if you don't mind. I'd rather the nightmares.' But I accepted Resurrection because I've been taught to be polite and because there is the Demon in me I don't understand that always wishes to live, and I found that I still felt like a Zombie, although I could flit about, and that I still had the nightmares, except they'd grown a deal vivider.

"I was a young girl again, seventeen, and I suppose every woman wishes to be seventeen, but I wasn't seventeen inside my head—I was a woman who had died of Bright's disease in New York in 1929 and also, because a Big Change blew my lifeline into a new drift, a woman who had died of the same disease in Nazi-occupied London in 1955, but rather more slowly because, as you can fancy, the liquor was in far shorter supply. I had to live with both those sets of memories and the Change World didn't blot them out any more than I'm told it does those of any Demon, and it didn't even push them into the background as I'd hoped it would.

"When some Change Fellow would say to me, 'Hallo, beautiful, how about a smile?' or 'That's a posh frock, kiddo,' I'd be back at Bellevue looking down at my swollen figure and the light getting like spokes of ice, or in that dreadful gin-steeped Stepney bedroom with Phyllis coughing herself to death beside me, or at best, for a moment, a little girl in Glamorgan looking at the Roman road and wondering about the wonderful life that lay ahead."

I looked at Erich, remembering he had a long nasty future back in the cosmos himself, and at any rate he wasn't smiling, and I thought maybe he's getting a little humility, knowing someone else has two of those futures, but I doubted it.

"Because, you see," Lili kept forcing it out, "all my three lives I'd been a girl who fell in love with a great young poet she'd never met, the voice of the new youth and all youth, and she'd told her first big lie to get in the Red Cross and across to France to be nearer him, and it was all danger and dark magics and a knight in armor, and she pictured how she'd find him wounded but not seriously, with a little bandage around his head, and she'd light a fag for him and smile lightly, never letting him guess what she felt, but only being her best self and watching to see if that made something happen to him . . .

"And then the Boche machine guns cut him down at Passchendaele and there couldn't ever have been bandages big enough and the girl stayed seventeen inside and messed about and tried to be wicked, though she wasn't very good at that, and to drink, and she had a bit more talent there, though drinking yourself to death is not nearly as easy as it sounds, even with a kidney weakness to help. But she turned the trick.

"Then a cock crows. She wakes with a tearing start from the gray dreams of death that fill her lifeline. It's cold daybreak. There's the smell of a French farm. She feels her ankles and they're not at all like huge rubber boots filled with water. They're not swollen the least bit. They're young legs.

"There's a little window and the tops of a row of trees that may be poplars when there's more light, and what there is shows cots like her own and heads under blankets, and hanging uniforms make large shadows and a girl is snoring. There's a very distant rumble and it moves the window a bit. Then she remembers they're Red Cross girls many, many kilometers from Passchendaele and that Bruce Marchant is going to die at dawn today.

"In a few more minutes, he's going over the top where there's a crop-headed machine-gunner in the sights and swinging the gun a bit. But she isn't going to die today. She's going to die in 1929 and 1955.

"And just as she's going mad, there's a creaking and out of the shadows tiptoes a Jap with a woman's hairdo and the whitest face and the blackest eyebrows. He's wearing a rose robe and a black sash which belts to his sides two samurai swords, but in his right hand he has a strange silver pistol. And he smiles at her as if they were brother and sister and lovers at the same time and he says, *'Voulez-vous vivre, mademoiselle?'* and she stares and he bobs his head and says, 'Missy wish live, yes, no?'"

Sid's paw closed quietly around my shaking hands. It always gets me to hear about anyone's Resurrection, and although mine was crazier, it also had the Krauts in it. I hoped she wouldn't go through the rest of the formula and she didn't.

"Five minutes later, he's gone down a stairs more like a ladder to wait below and she's dressing in a rush. Her clothes resist a little, as if they were lightly gummed to the hook and the stained wall, and she hates to touch them. It's getting lighter and her cot looks as if someone were still sleeping there, although it's empty, and she couldn't bring herself to put her hand on the place if her new life depended on it.

"She climbs down and her long skirt doesn't bother her because she knows how to swing it. Suzaku conducts her past a sentry who doesn't see them and a puffy-faced farmer in a smock coughing and spitting the night out of his throat. They cross the farmyard and it's filled with rose light and she sees the sun is up and she knows that Bruce Marchant has just bled to death.

"There's an empty open touring car chugging loudly, waiting for someone; it has huge muddy wheels with wooden spokes and a brass radiator that says 'Simplex.' But Suzaku leads her past it to a dunghill and bows apologetically and she steps through a Door."

I heard Erich say to the others at the bar, "How touching! Now shall I tell everyone about my operation?" But he didn't get much of a laugh.

"That's how Lilian Foster came into the Change World with its steel-engraved nightmares and its deadly pace and deadlier lassitudes. I was more alive than I ever had been before, but it was the kind of life a corpse might get from unending electrical shocks and I couldn't summon any purpose or hope and Bruce Marchant seemed farther away than ever.

"Then, not six hours ago, a Soldier in a black uniform came through the Door and I thought, 'It can't be, but it does look like his photographs,' and then I thought I heard someone say the name Bruce, and then he shouted as if to all the world that he was Bruce Marchant, and I knew there was a Resurrection beyond Resurrection, a true resurrection. Oh, Bruce—"

She looked at him and he was crying and smiling and all the young beauty flooded back into her face, and I thought, "It has to be Change Winds, but it can't be. Face it without slobbering, Greta—there's something that works bigger miracles than Change."

And she went on, "And then the Change Winds died when the Snakes vaporized the Maintainer or the Ghostgirls Introverted it and all three of them vanished so swiftly and silently that even Bruce didn't notice—those are the best explanations I can summon and I fancy one of them is true. At all events, the Change Winds died and my past and even my futures became something I could bear lightly, because I have someone to bear them with me, and because at last I have a true future stretching out ahead of me, an unknown future which I shall create by living. Oh, don't you see that all of us have it now, this big opportunity?"

"*Hussa* for Sidney's suffragettes and the W.C.T.U.!" Erich cheered. "Beau, will you play us a medley of 'Hearts and Flowers' and 'Onward Christian Soldiers'? I'm deeply moved, Lili. Where do the rest of us queue up for the Great Love Affair of the Century?"

12

Now is a bearable burden. What buckles the back is the added weight of the past's mistakes and the future's fears.

I had to learn to close the front door to tomorrow and the back door to yesterday and settle down to here and now.

—Anonymous

A BIG OPPORTUNITY

NOBODY LAUGHED at Erich's screwball sarcasms and still I thought, "Yes, perish his hysterical little gray head, but he's half right—Lili's got the big thing now and she wants to serve it up to the rest of us on a platter, only love doesn't cook and cut that way."

Those weren't bad ideas she had about the Maintainer, though, especially the one about the Ghostgirls doing the Introverting—it would explain why there couldn't be Introversion drill, the manual stuff about blue flashes being window-dressing, and something disappearing without movement or transition is the sort of thing that might not catch the attention—and I guess they gave the others something to think about too, for there wasn't any follow-up to Erich's frantic sniping.

But I honestly didn't see where there was this big opportunity being stuck away in a gray sack in the Void and I began to wonder and I got the strangest feeling and I said to myself, "Hang onto your hat, Greta. It's hope."

"The dreadful thing about being a Demon is that you have all time to range through," Lili was saying with a smile. "You can never shut the back door to yesterday or the front door to tomorrow and simply live in the present. But now that's been done for us: the Door is shut, we need never again rehash the past or the future. The Spiders and Snakes can never find us, for who ever heard of a Place that was truly lost being rescued? And as those in the know have told me, Introversion is the end as far as those outside are concerned. So we're safe from the Spiders and Snakes, we need never be slaves or enemies again, and we have a Place in which to live our new lives, the Place prepared for us from the beginning."

She paused. "Surely you understand what I mean? Sidney and Beauregard and Dr. Pyeshkov are the ones who explained it to me. The Place is a balanced aquarium, just like the cosmos. No one knows how many ages of Big Time it has been in use, without a bit of new material being brought in—only luxuries and people—and not a bit of waste cast off. No one knows how many more ages it may not sustain life. I never heard of Minor

Maintainers wearing out. We have all the future, all the security, anyone can hope for. We have a Place to live together."

You know, she was dead right and I realized that all the time I'd had the conviction in the back of my mind that we were going to suffocate or something if we didn't get a Door open pretty quick. I should have known differently, if anybody should, because I'd once been in the Place without a Door for as long as a hundred sleeps during a foxhole stretch of the Change War and we'd had to start cycling our food and it had been okay.

And then, because it is also the way my mind works, I started to picture in a flash the consequences of our living together all by ourselves like Lili said.

I began to pair people off; I couldn't help it. Let's see, four women, six men, two ETs.

"Greta," I said, "you're going to be Miss Polly Andry for sure. We'll have a daily newspaper and folk-dancing classes, we'll shut the bar except evenings, Bruce'll keep a rhymed history of the Place."

I even thought, though I knew this part was strictly silly, about schools and children. I wondered what Siddy's would look like, or my little commandant's. "Don't go near the Void, dears." Of course that would be specially hard on the two ETs, but Sevensee at least wasn't so different and the genetics boys had made some wonderful advances and Maud ought to know about them and there were some amazing gadgets in Surgery when Doc sobered up. The patter of little hoofs . . .

"My fiance spoke to you about carrying a peace message to the rest of the cosmos," Lili added, "and bringing an end to the Big Change, and healing all the wounds that have been made in the Little Time."

I looked at Bruce. His face was set and strained, as will happen to the best of them when a girl starts talking about her man's business, and I don't know why, but I said to myself, "She's crucifying him, she's nailing him to his purpose as a woman will, even when there's not much point to it, as now."

And Lili went on, "It was a wonderful thought, but now we cannot carry or send any message and I believe it is too late in any event for a peace message to do any good. The cosmos is too raveled by change, too far gone. It will dissolve, fade, 'leave not a rack behind.' We're the survivors. The torch of existence has been put in our hands.

"We may already be all that's left in the cosmos, for have you thought that the Change Winds may have died at their source? We may never reach another cosmos, we may drift forever in the Void, but who of us has been Introverted before and who knows what we can or cannot do? We're a seed for a new future to grow from. Perhaps all doomed universes cast off seeds like this Place. It's a seed, it's an embryo, let it grow."

She looked swiftly at Bruce and then at Sid and she quoted, " 'Come, my friends, 'tis not too late to seek a newer world'."

I squeezed Sid's hand and I started to say something to him, but he didn't know I was there; he was listening to Lili quote Tennyson with his eyes entranced and his mouth open, as if he were imagining new things to put into it—oh, Siddy!

And then I saw the others were looking at her the same way. Ilhilihis was seeing finer feather forests than long-dead Luna's grow. The greenhouse child Maud ap-Ares Davies was stowing away on a starship bound for another galaxy, or thinking how different her life might have been, the children she might have had, if she'd stayed on the planets and out of the Change World. Even Erich looked as though he might be blitzing new universes, and Mark subduing them, for an eight-legged *Führer-imperator*. Beau was throbbing up a wider Mississippi in a bigger-than-life sidewheeler.

Even I—well, I wasn't dreaming of a Greater Chicago. "Let's not go hog-wild on this sort of thing," I told myself, but I did look up at the Void and I got a shiver because I imagined it drawing away and the whole Place starting to grow.

"I truly meant what I said about a seed," Lili went on slowly. "I know, as you all do, that there are no children in the Change World, that there cannot be, that we all become instantly sterile, that what they call a curse is lifted from us girls and we are no longer bondage to the moon."

She was right, all right—if there's one thing that's been proved a million times in the Change World, it's that.

"But we are no longer in the Change World," Lili said softly, "and its limitations should no longer apply to us, including that one. I feel deeply certain of it, but—" she looked around slowly—"we are four women here and I thought one of us might have a surer indication."

My eyes followed hers around like anybody's would. In fact, everybody was looking around except Maud, and she had the silliest look of surprise on her face and it stayed there, and then, very carefully, she got down from the bar stool with her knitting. She looked at the half-finished pink bra with the long white needles stuck in it and her eyes bugged bigger yet, as if she were expecting it to turn into a baby sweater right then and there. Then she walked across the Place to Lili and stood beside her. While she was walking, the look of surprise changed to a quiet smile. The only other thing she did was throw her shoulders back a little.

I was jealous of her for a second, but it was a double miracle for her, considering her age, and I couldn't grudge her that. And to tell the truth, I was a little frightened, too. Even with Dave, I'd been bothered about this business of having babies.

Yet I stood up with Siddy—I couldn't stop myself and I guess he couldn't either—and hand in hand we walked to the control divan. Beau and Sevensee were there with Bruce, of course, and then, so help me, those Soldiers to the death, Kaby and Mark, started over from the bar and I couldn't see anything in their eyes about the greater glory of Crete and Rome, but something, I think, about each other, and after a moment Illy slowly detached himself from the piano and followed, lightly trailing his tentacles on the floor.

I couldn't exactly see him hoping for little Illies in this company, unless it was true what the jokes said about Lunans, but maybe he was being really disinterested and maybe he wasn't; maybe he was simply figuring that Illy ought to be on the side with the biggest battalions.

I heard dragging footsteps behind us and here came Doc from the Gallery, carrying in his folded arms an abstract sculpture as big as a newborn baby. It was an agglomeration of perfect shiny gray spheres the size of golfballs, shaping up to something like a large brain, but with holes showing through here and there. He held it out to us like an infant to be admired and worked his lips and tongue as if he were trying very hard to say something, though not a word came out that you could understand, and I thought, "Maxey Aleksevich may be speechless drunk and have all sorts of holes in his head, but he's got the right instincts, bless his soulful little Russian heart."

We were all crowded around the control divan like a football team huddling. The Peace Packers, it came to me. Sevensee would be fullback or center and Illy left end—what a receiver! The right number, too. Erich was alone at the bar, but now even he—"Oh, no, this can't be," I thought—even he came toward us. Then I saw that his face was working the worst ever. He stopped halfway and managed to force a smile, but it was the worst, too. "That's my little commandant," I thought, "no team spirit."

"So now Lili and Bruce—yes, and *Grossmutterchen* Maud—have their little nest," he said, and he wouldn't have had to push his voice very hard to get a screech. "But what are the rest of us supposed to be—cowbirds?"

He crooked his neck and flapped his hands and croaked, "Cuc-koo! Cuc-koo!" And I said to myself, "I often thought you were crazy, boy, but now I know."

"*Teufelsdreck!*—yes, Devil's dirt—but you all seem to be infected with this dream of children. Can't you see that the Change World is the natural and proper end of evolution?—a period of enjoyment and measuring, an ultimate working out of things, which women call destruction—'Help, I'm being raped!' 'Oh, what are they doing to my children?'—but which men know as fulfillment.

"You're given good parts in *Götterdämmerung* and you go up to the author and tap him on the shoulder and say, 'Excuse me, Herr Wagner, but this Twilight of the Gods is just a bit morbid. Why don't you write an opera for me about the little ones, the dear little blue-eyed curly-tops? A plot? Oh, boy meets girl and they settle down to breed, something like that.'

"Devil's dirt doubled and damned! Have you thought what life will be like without a Door to go out of to find freedom and adventure, to measure your courage and keenness? Do you want to grow long gray beards hobbling around this asteroid turned inside out? Putter around indoors to the end of your days, mooning about little baby cosmoses?—incidentally, with a live bomb for company. The cave, the womb, the little gray home in the nest—is that what you want? It'll grow? Oh, yes, like the city engulfing the wild wood, a proliferation of *Kinder, Kirche, Küche*—I should live so long!

"Women!—how I hate their bright eyes as they look at me from the fireside, bent-shouldered, rocking, deeply happy to be old, and say, 'He's getting weak, he's giving out, soon I'll have to put him to bed and do the simplest things for him.' Your filthy Triple Goddess, Kaby, the birther, bride, and burier of man! Woman, the enfeebler, the fetterer, the crippler! Woman! —and the curly-headed little cancers she wants!"

He lurched toward us, pointing at Lili. "I never knew one who didn't want to cripple a man if you gave her the chance. Cripple him, swaddle him, clip his wings, grind him to sausage to mold another man, hers, a doll man. You hid the Maintainer, you little smother-hen, so you could have your nest and your Brucie!"

He stopped, gasping and I expected someone to bop him one on the schnozzle, and I think he did, too. I turned to Bruce and he was looking. I don't know how, sorry, guilty, anxious, angry, shaken, inspired, all at once, and I wished people sometimes had simple suburban reactions like magazine stories.

Then Erich made the mistake, if it was one, of turning toward Bruce and slowly staggering toward him, pawing the air with his hands as if he were going to collapse into his arms, and saying "Don't let them get you, Bruce. Don't let them tie you down. Don't let them clip you—your words or your deeds. You're a Soldier. Even when you talked about a peace message, you talked about doing some smashing of your own. No matter what you think and feel, Bruce, no matter how much lying you do and how much you hide, you're really not on their side."

That did it.

It didn't come soon enough or, I think, in the right spirit to please me, but I will say it for Bruce that he didn't muck it up by tipping or softening his punch. He took one step forward and his shoulders spun and his fist connected sweet and clean.

As he did it, he said only one word, "Loki!" and darn if that didn't switch me back to a campfire in the Indiana Dunes and my mother telling me out of the Elder Saga about the malicious, sneering, all-spoiling Norse god and how, when the other gods came to trap him in his hideaway by the river, he was on the point of finishing knotting a mysterious net big enough, I had imagined, to snare the whole universe, and that if they'd come a minute later, he would have.

Erich was stretched on the floor, his head hitched up, rubbing his jaw and glaring at Bruce. Mark, who was standing beside me, moved a little and I thought he was going to do something, maybe even clobber Bruce in the old spirit of you can't do that to my buddy, but he just shook his head and said, "*Omnia vincit amor.*" I nudged him and said, "Meaning?" and he said, "Love licks everything."

I'd never have expected it from a Roman, but he was half right at any rate. Lili had her victory: marriage by laying out the woman-hating boy friend who would be trying to get him to go out nights. At that moment, I think Bruce wanted Lili and a life with her more than he wanted to reform the Change World. Sure, us women have our little victories—until the legions come or the Little Corporal draws up his artillery or the Panzers roar down the road.

Erich scrambled to his feet and stood there in a half-slump, half-crouch, still rubbing his jaw and glaring at Bruce over his hand, but making no move to continue the fight, and I studied his face and said to myself, "If he can get a gun, he's going to shoot himself, I know."

Bruce started to say something and hesitated, like I would have in his shoes, and just then Doc got one of his unpredictable inspirations and went weaving out toward Erich, holding out the sculpture and making deaf-and-dumb noises like he had to us. Erich looked at him as if he were going to kill him, and then grabbed the sculpture and swung it up over his head and smashed it down on the floor, and for a wonder, it didn't shatter. It just skidded along in one piece and stopped inches from my feet.

That thing not breaking must have been the last straw for Erich. I swear I could see the red surge up through his eyes toward his brain. He swung around into the Stores sector and ran the few steps between him and the bronze bomb chest.

Everything got very slow motion for me, though I didn't do any moving. Almost every man started out after Erich. Bruce didn't, though, and Siddy turned back after the first surge forward, while Illy squunched down for a leap, and it was between Sevensee's hairy shanks and Beau's scissoring white pants that I saw that under-the-microscope circle of death's heads and watched Erich's finger go down on them in the order Kaby had given: one, three, five, six, two, four, seven. I was able to pray seven distinct times that he'd make a mistake.

He straightened up. Illy landed by the box like a huge silver spider and his tentacles whipped futilely across its top. The others surged to a frightened halt around them.

Erich's chest was heaving, but his voice was cool and collected as he said, "You mentioned something about our having a future, Miss Foster. Now you can make that more specific. Unless we get back to the cosmos and dump this box, or find a Spider A-tech, or manage to call headquarters for guidance on disarming the bomb, we have a future exactly thirty minutes long."

13

> But whence he was, or of what wombe ybore,
> Of beasts, or of the earth, I have not red:
> But certes was with milke of wolves and tygres fed.
> —Spenser

THE TIGER IS LOOSE

I GUESS when they really push the button or throw the switch or spring the trap or focus the beam or what have you, you don't faint or go crazy or anything else convenient. I didn't. Everything, everybody, every move that was made, every word that was spoken, was painfully real to me, like a hand twisting and squeezing things deep inside me, and I saw every last detail spotlighted and magnified like I had the seven skulls.

Erich was standing beyond the bomb chest; little smiles were ruffling his lips. I'd never seen him look so sharp. Illy was beside him, but not on his side, you understand. Mark, Sevensee and Beau were around the chest to the nearer side. Beau had dropped to a knee and was scanning the chest minutely, terror-under-control making him bend his head a little closer than he needed to for clear vision, but with his hands locked together behind his back, I guess to restrain the impulse to push any and everything that looked like a disarming button.

Doc was sprawled face down on the nearest couch, out like a light, I suppose.

Us four girls were still by the control divan. With Kaby, that surprised me, because she didn't look scared or frozen, but almost as intensely alive as Erich.

Sid had turned back, as I'd said, and had one hand stretched out toward but not touching the Minor Maintainer, and a look on his beardy face as if he were calling down death and destruction on every boozy rogue who had ever gone up from King's Lynn to Cambridge and London, and I realized why: if he'd thought of the Minor Maintainer a second sooner, he could have pinned Erich down with heavy gravity before he could touch the buttons.

Bruce was resting one hand on the head of the control divan and was looking toward the group around the chest, toward Erich, I think, as if Erich had done something rather wonderful for him, though I can't imagine myself being tickled at being included in anybody's suicide surprise party. Bruce looked altogether too dreamy, Brahma blast him, for someone who must have the same steel-spiked thought in his head that I know darn well the rest of us had: that in twenty-nine minutes or so, the Place would be a sun in a bag.

Erich was the first to get down to business, as I'd have laid any odds he would be. He had the jump on us and he wasn't going to lose it.

"Well, when are you going to start getting Lili to tell us where she hid the Maintainer? It has to be her—she was too certain it was gone forever when she talked. And Bruce must have seen from the bar who took the Maintainer, and who would he cover up for but his girl?"

There he was plagiarizing my ideas, but I guess I was willing to sign them over to him in full if he got the right pail of water for that time-bomb.

He glanced at his wrist. "According to my Caller, you have twenty-nine and a half minutes, including the time it will take to get a Door or contact headquarters. When are you going to get busy on the girl?"

Bruce laughed a little—deprecatingly, so help me—and started toward him. "Look here, old man," he said, "there's no need to trouble Lili or to fuss with headquarters, even if you could. Really not at all. Not to mention that your surmises are quite unfounded, old chap, and I'm a bit surprised at your advancing them. But that's quite all right because, as it happens, I'm an atomics technician and I even worked on that very bomb. To disarm it, you just have to fiddle a bit with some of the ankhs, those hoopy little crosses. Here, let me—"

Allah il allah, but it must have struck everybody as it did me as being just too incredible an assertion, too bloody British a barefaced bluff, for Erich didn't have to say a word; Mark and Sevensee grabbed Bruce by the arms, one on each side, as he stooped toward the bronze chest, and they weren't gentle about it. Then Erich spoke.

"Oh, no, Bruce. Very sporting of you to try to cover up for your girl friend, but we aren't going to let ourselves be blown to stripped atoms twenty-eight minutes too soon while you monkey with the buttons, the very thing Benson-Carter warned against, and pray for a guesswork miracle. It's too thin, Bruce, when you come from 1917 and haven't been on the Big Time for a hundred sleeps and were calling for an A-tech yourself a few hours ago. Much too thin. Bruce, something is going to happen that I'm afraid you won't like, but you're going to have to put up with it. That is, unless Miss Foster decides to be cooperative."

"I say, you fellows, let me go," Bruce demanded, struggling experimentally. "I know it's a bit thick to swallow and I did give you the wrong impression calling for an A-tech, but I just wanted to capture your attention then; I didn't want to have to work on the bomb. Really, Erich, would they have ordered Benson-Carter to pick us up unless one of us were an A-tech? They'd be sure to include one in the bally operation."

"When they're using patchwork tactics?" Erich grinningly quoted back at him.

Kaby spoke up beside me and said, "Benson-Carter was a magician of matter and he was going on the operation disguised as an old woman. We have the cloak and hood with the other garments," and I wondered how this cold fish of a she-officer could be the same girl who was giving Mark slurpy looks not ten minutes ago.

"Well?" Erich asked, glancing at his Caller and then swinging his eyes around at us as if there must be some of the old *Wehrmacht* iron somewhere. We all found ourselves looking at Lili and she was looking so sharp herself, so ready to jump and so at bay, that it was all *I* needed, at any rate, to make Erich's theory about the Maintainer a rock-bottom certainty.

Bruce must have realized the way our minds were working, for he started to struggle in earnest and at the same time called, "For God's sake, don't do anything to Lili! Let me loose, you idiots! Everything's true I told you—I can save you from that bomb. Sevensee, you took my side against the Spiders; you've nothing to lose. Sid, you're an Englishman. Beau, you're a gentleman and you love her, too—for God's sake, stop them!"

Beau glanced up over his shoulder at Bruce and the others surging around close to his ankles and he had on his poker face. Sid I could tell was once more going through the purgatory of decision. Beau reached his own decision first and I'll say it for him that he acted on it fast and intelligently. Right from his kneeling position and before he'd even turned his head quite back, he jumped Erich.

But other things in this cosmos besides Man can pick sides and act fast. Illy landed on Beau midway and whipped his tentacles around him tight and they went wobbling around like a drunken white-and-silver barber pole. Beau got his hands each around a tentacle, and at the same time his face began to get purple, and I winced at what they were both going through.

Maybe Sevensee had a hoof in Sid's purgatory, because Bruce shook loose from the satyr and tried to knock out Mark, but the Roman twisted his arm and kept him from getting in a good punch.

Erich didn't make a move to mix into either fight, which is my little commandant all over. Using his fists on anybody but me is beneath him.

Then Sid made his choice, but there was no way for me to tell what it was, for, as he reached for the Minor Maintainer, Kaby contemptuously snatched it away from his hands and gave him a knee in the belly that doubled me up in sympathy and sent him sprawling on his knees toward the fighters. On the return, Kaby gave Lili, who'd started to grab too, an effortless backhand smash that set her down on the divan.

Erich's face lit up like an electric sign and he kept his eyes fixed on Kaby.

She crouched a little, carrying her weight on the balls of her feet and firmly cradling the Minor Maintainer in her left arm, like a basketball captain planning an offensive. Then she waved her free hand decisively to the right. I didn't get it, but Erich did and Mark too, for Erich jumped for the Refresher sector and Mark let go of Bruce and followed him, ducking around Sevensee's arms, who was coming back into the fight on which side I don't know. Illy unwhipped from Beau and copied Erich and Mark with one big spring.

Then Kaby twisted a dial as far as it would go and Bruce, Beau, Sevensee and poor Siddy were slammed down and pinned to the floor by about eight gravities.

It should have been lighter near us—I hoped it was, but you couldn't tell from watching Siddy; he went flat on his face, spread-eagled, one hand stretched toward me so close, I could have touched it (but not let go!), and his mouth was open against the floor and he was gasping through a corner of it and I could see his spine trying to sink through his belly. Bruce just managed to get his head and one shoulder up a bit, and they all made me think of a Doré illustration of the *Inferno* where the cream of the damned are frozen up to their necks in ice in the innermost circle of Hell.

The gravity didn't catch me, although I could feel it in my left arm. I was mostly in the Refresher sector, but I dropped down flat too, partly out of a crazy compassion I have, but mostly because I didn't want to take a chance of having Kaby knock me down.

Erich, Mark and Illy had got clear and they headed toward us. Maud picked the moment to make her play; she hadn't much choice of times, if she wanted to make one. The Old Girl was looking it for once, but I guess the thought of her miracle must have survived alongside the fear of sacked sun and must have meant a lot to her, for she launched out fast, all set to straight-arm Kaby into the heavy gravity and grab the Minor Maintainer with the other hand.

14

Like diamonds, we are cut with our own dust.
—Webster

"NOW WILL YOU TALK?"

CRETANS HAVE eyes under their back hair, or let's face it, Entertainers aren't Soldiers. Kaby waved to one side and flicked a helpful hand and poor old Maud went where she'd been going to send Kaby. It sickened me to see the gravity take hold and yank her down.

I could have jumped up and made it four in a row for Kaby, but I'm not a bit brave when things like my life are at stake.

Lili was starting to get up, acting a little dazed. Kaby gently pushed her down again and quietly said, "Where is it?" and then hauled off and slapped her across the face. What got me was the matter-of-fact way Kaby did it. I can understand somebody getting mad and socking someone, or even deliberately working up a rage so as to be able to do something nasty, but this cold-blooded way turns my stomach.

Lili looked as if half her face were about to start bleeding, but she didn't look dazed any more and her jaw set. Kaby gabbed Lili's pearl necklace and twisted it around her neck and it broke and the pearls went bouncing around like ping-pong balls, so Kaby yanked down Lili's gray silk bandeau until it was around the neck and tightened that. Lili started to choke through her tight-pressed lips. Erich, Mark and Illy had come up and crowded around, but they seemed to be content with the job Kaby was doing.

"Listen, slut," she said, "we have no time. You have a healing room in this place. I can work the things."

"Here it comes," I thought, wishing I could faint. On top of everything, on top of death even, they had to drag in the nightmare personally stylized for me, the horror with my name on it. I wasn't going to be allowed to blow up peacefully. They weren't satisfied with an A-bomb. They had to write my private hell into the script.

"There is a thing called an Invertor," Kaby said exactly as I'd known she would, but as I didn't really hear it just then—a mental split I'll explain in a moment. "It opens you up so they can cure your insides without cutting your skin or making you bleed anywhere. It turns the big parts of you inside out, but not the blood tubes. All your skin—your eyes, ears, nose, toes, all of it—becoming the lining of a little hole that's half-filled with your hair.

"Meantime, your insides are exposed for whatever the healer wants to do to them. You live for a while on the air inside the hole. First the healer gives you an air that makes you sleep, or you go mad in about fifty heartbeats. We'll see what ten heartbeats do to you without the sleepy air. Now will you talk?"

I hadn't been listening to her, though, not the real me, or I'd have gone mad without getting the treatment. I once heard Doc say your liver is more mysterious and farther away from you than the stars, because although you live with your liver all your life, you never see it or learn to point to it instinctively, and the thought of someone messing around with that intimate yet unknown part of you is just too awful.

I knew I had to do something quick. Hell, at the first hint of Introversion, before Kaby had even named it, Illy winced so that his tentacles were all drawn up like fat feather-sausages. Erich had looked at him questioningly, but that lousy Looney had un-endeared himself to me by squeaking, "Don't mind me, I'm just sensitive. Get on with the girl. Make her tell."

Yes, I knew I had to do something, and here on the floor that meant thinking hard and in high gear about something else. The screwball sculpture Erich had tried to smash was a foot from my nose and I saw a faint trail of white stuff where it had skidded. I reached out and touched the trail; it was finely gritty, like powdered glass. I tipped up the sculpture and the part on which it had skidded wasn't marred at all, not even dulled; the gray spheres were as glisteningly bright as ever. So I knew the trail was diamond dust rubbed off the diamonds in the floor by something even harder.

That told me the sculpture was something special and maybe Doc had had a real idea in his pickled brain when he'd been pushing the thing at all of us and trying to tell us something. He hadn't managed to say anything then, but he had earlier when he'd been going to tell us what to do about the bomb, and maybe there was a connection.

I twisted my memory hard and let it spring back and I got "Inversh . . . bosh . . ." Bosh, indeed! Bosh and inverse bosh to all boozers, Russki or otherwise.

So I quick tried the memory trick again and this time I got "glovsh" and then I grasped and almost sneezed on diamond dust as I watched the pieces fit themselves together in my mind like a speeded-up movie reel.

It all hung on that black right-hand hussar's glove Lili had produced for Bruce. Only she couldn't have found it in Stores, because we'd searched every fractional pigeonhole later on and there hadn't been any gloves there, not even the left-hand mate there would have been. Also, Bruce had had two left-hand gloves to start with, and we had been through the whole Place with a fine-tooth comb, and there had been only the two black gloves on the floor where Bruce had kicked them off the bar—those two and those two only, the left-hand glove he'd brought from outside and the right-hand glove Lili had produced for him.

So a left-hand glove had disappeared—the last I'd seen of it, Lili had been putting it on her tray—and a right-hand glove had appeared. Which could only add up to one thing: Lili had turned the left-hand glove into an identical right. She couldn't have done it by turning it inside out the ordinary way, because the lining was different.

But as I knew only too sickeningly well, there was an extraordinary way to turn things inside out, things like human beings. You merely had to put them on the Invertor in Surgery and flick the switch for full Inversion.

Or you could flick it for partial Inversion and turn something into a perfect three-dimensional mirror image of itself, just what a right-hand glove is of a left. Rotation through the fourth dimension, the science boys call it; I've heard of it being used in surgery on the highly asymmetric Martians, and even to give a socially impeccable right hand to a man who'd lost one, by turning an amputated right arm into an amputated left.

Ordinarily, nothing but live things are ever Inverted in Surgery and you wouldn't think of doing it to an inanimate object, especially in a Place where the Doc's a drunk and the Surgery hasn't been used for hundreds of sleeps.

But when you've just fallen in love, you think of wonderful crazy things to do for people. Drunk with love, Lili had taken Bruce's extra left-hand glove into Surgery, partially Inverted it, and got a right-hand glove to give him.

What Doc had been trying to say with his "Inversh . . . bosh . . ." was "Invert the box," meaning we should put the bronze chest through full Inversion to get at the bomb inside to disarm it. Doc too had got the idea from Lili's trick with the glove. What an inside-out tactical atomic bomb would look like, I could not imagine and did not particularly care to see. I might have to, though, I realized.

But the fast-motion film was still running in my head. Later on, Lili had decided like I had that her lover was going to lose out in his plea for mutiny unless she could give him a really captive audience—and maybe, even then, she had been figuring on creating the nest for Bruce's chicks and . . . all those other things we'd believed in for a while. So she'd taken the Major Maintainer and remembered the glove, and not many seconds later, she had set down on a shelf of the Art Gallery an object that no one would think of questioning—except someone who knew the Gallery by heart.

I looked at the abstract sculpture a foot from my nose, at the clustered gray spheres the size of golfballs. I had known that the inside of the Maintainer was made up of vastly tough, vastly hard giant molecules, but I hadn't realized they were quite *that* big.

I said to myself, "Greta, this is going to give you a major psychosis, but you're the one who has to do it, because no one is going to listen to your deductions when they're all practically living on negative time already."

I got up as quietly as if I were getting out of a bed I shouldn't have been in—there are some things Entertainers are good at—and Kaby was just saying "you go mad in about fifty heartbeats." Everybody on their feet was looking at Lili. Sid seemed to have moved, but I had no time for him except to hope he hadn't done anything that might attract attention to me.

I stepped out of my shoes and walked rapidly to Surgery—there's one good thing about this hardest floor anywhere, it doesn't creak. I walked through the Surgery screen that is like a wall of opaque, odorless cigarette smoke and I concentrated on remembering my snafued nurse's training, and before I had time to panic, I had the sculpture positioned on the gleaming table of the Invertor.

I froze for a moment when I reached for the Inversion switch, thinking of the other time and trying to remember what it had been that bothered me so much about an inside-out brain being bigger and not having eyes, but then I either thumbed my nose at my nightmare or kissed my sanity goodby, I don't know which, and twisted the switch all the way over, and there was the Major Maintainer winking blue about three times a second as nice as you could want it.

It must have been working as sweet and steady as ever, all the time it was Inverted, except that, being inside out, it had hocused the direction finders.

15

black legged spiders with red hearts of hell
—Marquis

LORD SPIDER

"JESUS!" I turned and Sid's face was sticking through the screen like a tinted bas-relief hanging on a gray wall and I got the impression he had peered unexpectedly through a slit in an arras into Queen Elizabeth's bedroom.

He didn't have any time to linger on the sensation even if he'd wanted to, for an elbow with a copper band thrust through the screen and dug his ribs and Kaby marched Lili in by the neck. Erich, Mark and Illy were right behind. They caught the blue flashes and stopped dead, staring at the long-lost. Erich spared me one look which seemed to say, so you did it, not that it matters. Then he stepped forward and picked it up and held it solidly to his left side in the double right-angle made by fingers, forearm and chest, and reached for the Introversion switch with a look on his face as if he were opening a fifth of whisky.

The blue light died and Change Winds hit me like a stiff drink that had been a long, long time in coming, like a hot trumpet note out of nowhere.

I felt the changing pasts blowing through me, and the uncertainties whistling past, and ice-stiff reality softening with all its duties and necessities, and the little memories shredding away and dancing off like autumn leaves, leaving maybe not even ghosts behind, and all the crazy moods like Mardi Gras dancers pouring down an evening street, and something inside me had the nerve to say it didn't care whether Greta Forzane's death was riding in those Winds because they felt so good.

I could tell it was hitting the others the same way. Even battered, tight-lipped Lili seemed to be saying, you're making me drink the stuff and I hate you for it, but I do love it. I guess we'd all had the worry that even finding and Extroverting the Maintainer wouldn't put us back in touch with the cosmos and give us those Winds we hate and love.

The thing that cut through to us as we stood there glowing was not the thought of the bomb, though that would have come in a few seconds more, but Sid's voice. He was still standing in the screen, except that now his face was out the other side and we could just see parts of his gray-doubleted back, but, of course, his "Jesu!" came through the screen as if it weren't there.

At first I couldn't figure out who he could be talking to, but I swear I never heard his voice so courtly obsequious before, so strong and yet so filled with awe and an undernote of, yes, sheer terror.

"Lord, I am filled from top to toe with confusion that you should so honor my poor Place," he said. "Poor say I and mine, when I mean that I have ever busked it faithfully for you, not dreaming that you would ever condescend . . . yet knowing that your eye was certes ever upon me . . . though I am but as a poor pinch of dust adrift between the suns . . . I base myself. Prithee, how may I serve thee, sir? I know not e'en how most suitably to address thee, Lord . . . King . . . Emperor Spider!"

I felt like I was getting very small, but not a bit less visible, worse luck, and even with the Change Winds inside me to give me courage, I thought this was really too much, coming on top of everything else; it was simply unfair.

At the same time, I realized it was to be expected that the big bosses would have been watching us with their unblinking beady black eyes ever since we had Introverted waiting to pounce if we should ever come out of it. I tried to picture what was on the other side of the screen and I didn't like the assignment.

But in spite of being petrified, I had a hard time not giggling, like the zany at graduation exercises, at the way the other ones in Surgery were taking it.

I mean the Soldiers. They each stiffened up like they had the old ramrod inside them, and their faces got that important look, and they glanced at each other and the floor without lowering their heads, as if they were measuring the distance between their feet and mentally chalking alternate sets of footprints to step into. The way Erich and Kaby held the Major and Minor Maintainers became formal; the way they checked their Callers and nodded reassuringly was positively esoteric. Even Illy somehow managed to look as if he were on parade.

Then from beyond the screen came what was, under the circumstances, the worst noise I've ever heard, a seemingly wordless distant-sounding howling and wailing, with a note of menace that made me shake, although it also had a nasty familiarity about it I couldn't place. Sid's voice broke into it, loud, fast and frightened.

"Your pardon, Lord, I did not think . . . certes, the gravity . . . I'll attend to it on the instant." He whipped a hand and half a head back through the screen, but without looking back and snapped his fingers, and before I could blink, Kaby had put the Minor Maintainer in his hand.

Sid went completely out of sight then and the howling stopped, and I thought that if that was the way a Lord Spider expressed his annoyance at being subjected to incorrect gravity, I hoped the bosses wouldn't start any conversations with me.

Erich pursed his lips and threw the other Soldiers a nod and the four of them marched through the screen as if they'd drilled a lifetime for this moment. I had the wild idea that Erich might give me his arm, but he strode past me as if I were . . . an Entertainer.

I hesitated a moment then, but I had to see what was happening outside, even if I got eaten up for it. Besides, I had a bit of the thought that if these formalities went on much longer, even a Lord Spider was going to discover just how immune he was to confined atomic blast.

I walked through the screen with Lili beside me.

The Soldiers had stopped a few feet in front of it. I looked around ahead for whatever it was going to turn out to be, prepared to drop a curtsy or whatever else, bar nothing, that seemed expected of me.

I had a hard time spotting the beast. Some of the others seemed to be having trouble too. I saw Doc weaving around foolishly by the control divan, and Bruce and Beau and Sevensee and Maud on their feet beyond it, and I wondered whether we were dealing with an invisible monster; ought to be easy enough for the bosses to turn a simple trick like invisibility.

Then I looked sharply left where everyone else, even glassy-eyed Doc, was coming to look, into the Door sector, only there wasn't any monster there or even a Door, but just Siddy holding a Minor Maintainer and grinning like when he is threatening to tickle me, only more fiendishly.

"Not a move, masters," he cried his eyes dancing, "or I'll pin the pack of you down, marry and amen I will. It is my firm purpose to see the Place blasted before I let this instrument out of my hands again."

My first thought was, " 'Sblood but Siddy is a real actor! I don't care if he didn't study under anyone later than Burbage, that just proves how Burbage is."

Sid had convinced us not only that the real Spiders had arrived, but earlier that the gravity in the edge of Stores had been a lot heavier than it actually was. He completely fooled all those Soldiers, including my swelled-headed victorious little commandant, and I kind of filed away the timing of that business of reaching out the hand and snapping the fingers without looking, it was so good.

"Beauregard!" Sid called. "Get to the Major Maintainer and call headquarters. But don't come through Door, marry go by Refresher. I'll not trust a single Demon of you in this sector with me until much more has been shown and settled."

"Siddy, you're wonderful," I said, starting toward him. "As soon as I got the Maintainer unsnarled and looked around and saw your sweet old face—"

"Back, tricksy trull! Not the breadth of one scarlet toenail nearer me, you Queen of Sleights and High Priestess of Deception!" he bellowed. "You least of all do I trust. Why you hid the Maintainer, I know not, 'faith, but later you'll discover the truth to me or I'll have your gizzard."

I could see there was going to have to be a little explaining.

Doc, touched off, I guess, by Sid waving his hand at me, threw back his head and let off one of those shuddery Siberian wolf-howls he does so blamed well. Sid waved toward him sharply and he shut up, beaming toothily, but at least I knew who was responsible for the Spider wail of displeasure that Sid had either called for or more likely got as a gift of the gods and used in his act.

Beau came circling around fast and Erich shoved the Major Maintainer into his hands without making any fuss. The four Soldiers were looking pretty glum after losing their grand review.

Beau dumped some junk off one of the Art Gallery's sturdy taborets and set the Major Maintainer on it carefully but fast, and quickly knelt in front of it and whipped on some earphones and started to tune. The way he did it snatched away from me my inward glory at my big Inversion brainwave so fast, I might never have had it, and there was nothing in my mind again but the bronze bomb chest.

I wondered if I should suggest Inverting the thing, but I said to myself, "Uh-uh, Great, you got no diploma to show them and there probably isn't time to try two things, anyway."

Then Erich for once did something I wanted him to, though I didn't care for its effect on my nerves, by looking at his Caller and saying quietly, "Nine minutes to go, if Place time and cosmic time are synching."

Beau was steady as a rock and working adjustments so fine that I couldn't even see his fingers move.

Then, at the other end of the Place, Bruce took a few steps toward us. Sevensee and Maud followed a bit behind him. I remembered Bruce was another of our nuts with a private program for blowing up the place.

"Sidney," he called, and then, when he'd got Sid's attention, "Remember, Sidney, you and I both came down to London from Peterhouse."

I didn't get it. Then Bruce looked toward Erich with a devil-may-care challenge and toward Lili as if he were asking her forgiveness for something. I couldn't read her expression; the bruises were blue on her throat and her cheek was puffy.

Then Bruce once more shot Erich that look of challenge and he spun and grabbed Sevensee by a wrist and stuck out a foot—even half-horses aren't too sharp about infighting, I guess, and the satyr had every right to feel at least as confused as I felt—and sent him stumbling into Maud, and the two of them tumbled to the floor in a jumble of hairy legs and pearl-gray frock. Bruce raced to the bomb chest.

Most of us yelled, "Stop him, Sid, pin him down," or something like that—I know I did because I was suddenly sure that he'd been asking Lili's pardon for blowing the two of them up—and all the rest of us too, the love-blinded stinker.

Sid had been watching him all the time and now he lifted his hand to the Minor Maintainer, but then he didn't touch any of the dials, just watched and waited, and I thought, "Shaitan shave us! Does Siddy want in on death, too? Ain't he satisfied with all he knows about life?"

Bruce had knelt and was twisting some things on the front of the chest, and it was all as bright as if he were under a bank of Klieg lights, and I was telling myself I wouldn't know anything when the fireball fired, and not believing it, and Sevensee and Maud had got unscrambled and were starting for Bruce, and the rest of us were yelling at Sid, except that Erich was just looking at Bruce very happily, and Sid was still not doing anything, and it was unbearable except just then I felt the little arteries start to burst in my brain like a string of firecrackers and the old aorta pop, and for good measure, a couple of valves come unhinged in my ticker, and I was thinking, "Well, now I know what it's like to die of heart failure and high blood pressure," and having a last quiet smile at having cheated the bomb, when Bruce jumped up and back from the chest.

"That does it!" he announced cheerily. "She's as safe as the Bank of England."

Sevensee and Maud stopped themselves just short of knocking him down and I said to myself, "Hey, let's get a move on! I thought heart attacks were fast."

Before anyone else could speak, Beau did. He had turned around from the Major Maintainer and pulled aside one of the earphones.

"I got headquarters," he said crisply. "They told me how to disarm the bomb—I merely said I thought we ought to know. What did you do, sir?" he called to Bruce.

"There's a row of four ankhs just below the lock. The first to your left you give a quarter turn to the right, the second a quarter turn to the left, same for the fourth, and you don't touch the third."

"That is it, sir," Beau confirmed.

The long silence was too much for me; I guess I must have the shortest span for unspoken relief going. I drew some nourishment out of my restored arteries into my brain cells and yelled, "Siddy, I know I'm a tricksy trull and the High Vixen of all Foxes, but what the Hell is Peterhouse?"

"The oldest college at Cambridge," he told me rather coolly.

16

"Familiar with infinite universe sheafs and open-ended postulate systems?—the notion that everything is possible—and I mean everything—and everything has happened. *Everything*."

—Heinlein

THE POSSIBILITY-BINDERS

AN HOUR later, I was nursing a weak highball and a black eye in the sleepy-time darkness on the couch farthest from the piano, half watching the highlighted party going on around it and the bar, while the Place waited for rendezvous with Egypt and the Battle of Alexandria.

Sid had swept all our outstanding problems into one big bundle and, since his hand held the joker of the Minor Maintainer, he had settled them all as high-handedly as if they'd been those of a bunch of schoolkids.

It amounted to this:

We'd been Introverted when most of the damning things had happened, so presumably only we knew about them, and we were all in so deep one way or another that we'd all have to keep quiet to protect our delicate complexions.

Well, Erich's triggering the bomb did balance rather neatly Bruce's incitement to mutiny, and there was Doc's drinking, while everybody who had declared for the peace message had something to hide. Mark and Kaby I felt inclined to trust anywhere, Maud for sure, and Erich in this particular matter, damn him. Illy I didn't feel at all easy about, but I told myself there always has to be a fly in the ointment—a darn big one this time, and furry.

Sid didn't mention his own dirty linen, but he knew we knew he'd flopped badly as boss of the Place and only recouped himself by that last-minute flimflam.

Remembering Sid's trick made me think for a moment about the real Spiders. Just before I snuck out of Surgery, I'd had a vivid picture of what they must look like, but now I couldn't get it again. It depressed me, not being able to remember—oh, I probably just imagined I'd had a picture, like a hophead on a secret-of-the-universe kick. Me ever find out anything about the Spiders?—except for nervous notions like I'd had during the recent fracas?—what a laugh!

The funniest thing (ha-ha!) was that I had ended up the least-trusted person. Sid wouldn't give me time to explain how I'd deduced what had happened to the Maintainer, and even when Lili spoke up and admitted hiding it, she acted so bored I don't think everybody believed her—although she did spill the realistic detail that she hadn't used partial Inversion on the glove; she'd just turned it inside out to make it a right and then done a full Inversion to get the lining back inside.

I tried to get Doc to confirm that he'd reasoned the thing out the same way I had, but he said he had been blacked out the whole time, except during the first part of the hunt, and he didn't remember having any bright ideas at all. Right now, he was having Maud explain to him twice, in detail, everything that had happened. I decided that it was going to take a little more work before my reputation as a great detective was established.

I looked over the edge of the couch and just made out in the gloom one of Bruce's black gloves. It must have been kicked there. I fished it up. It was the right-hand one. My big clue, and was I sick of it! Got mittens, God forbid! I slung it away and, like a lurking octopus, Illy shot up a tentacle from the next couch, where I hadn't known he was resting, and snatched the glove like it was a morsel of underwater garbage. These ETs can seem pretty shuddery nonhuman at times.

I thought of what a cold-blooded, skin-saving louse Illy had been, and about Sid and his easy suspicions, and Erich and my black eye, and how, as usual, I'd got left alone in the end. My men!

Bruce had explained about being an A-tech. Like a lot of us, he'd had several widely different jobs during his first weeks in the Change World and one of them had been as secretary to a group of the minor atomics boys from the Manhattan-Project-Earth-Satellite days. I gathered he'd also absorbed some of his bothersome ideas from them. I hadn't quite decided yet what species of heroic heel he belonged to, but he was thick with Mark and Erich again. Everybody's men!

Sid didn't have to argue with anybody; all the wild compulsions and mighty resolves were dead now, anyway until they'd had a good long rest. I sure could use one myself, I knew.

The party at the piano was getting wilder. Lili had been dancing the black bottom on top of it and now she jumped down into Sid's and Sevensee's arms, taking a long time about it. She'd been drinking a lot and her little gray dress looked about as innocent on her as diapers would on Nell Gwyn. She continued her dance, distributing her marks of favor equally between Sid, Erich and the satyr. Beau didn't mind a bit, but serenely pounded out "Tonight's the Night"—which she'd practically shouted to him not two minutes ago.

I was glad to be out of the party. Who can compete with a

highly experienced, utterly disillusioned seventeen-year-old really throwing herself away for the first time?

Something touched my hand. Illy had stretched a tentacle into a furry wire to return me the black glove, although he ought to have known I didn't want it. I pushed it away, privately calling Illy a washed-out moronic tarantula, and right away I felt a little guilty. What right had I to be critical of Illy? Would my own character have shown to advantage if I'd been locked in with eleven octopoids a billion years away? For that matter, where did I get off being critical of anyone?

Still, I was glad to be out of the party, though I kept on watching it. Bruce was drinking alone at the bar. Once Sid had gone over to him and they'd had one together and I'd heard Bruce reciting from Rupert Brooke those deliberately corny lines, "For England's the one land, I know, Where men with Splendid Hearts may go; and Cambridgeshire, of all England, The Shire for Men who Understand"; and I'd remembered that Brooke too had died young in World War One and my ideas had got fuzzy. But mostly Bruce was just calmly drinking by himself. Every once in a while Lili would look at him and stop dead in her dancing and laugh.

I'd figured out this Bruce-Lili-Erich business as well as I cared to. Lili had wanted the nest with all her heart and nothing else would ever satisfy her, and now she'd go to hell her own way and probably die of Bright's disease for a third time in the Change World. Bruce hadn't wanted the nest or Lili as much as he wanted the Change World and the chances it gave for Soldierly cavorting and poetic drunks; Lili's seed wasn't his idea of healing the cosmos; maybe he'd make a real mutiny some day, but more likely he'd stick to barroom epics.

His and Lili's infatuation wouldn't die completely, no matter how rancid it looked right now. The real-love angle might go, but Change would magnify the romance angle and it might seem to them like a big thing of a sort if they met again.

Erich had his *Kamerad*, shaped to suit him, who'd had the guts and cleverness to disarm the bomb he'd had the guts to trigger. You have to hand it to Erich for having the nerve to put us all in a situation where we'd have to find the Maintainer or fry, but I don't know anything disgusting enough to hand to him.

I had tried a while back. I had gone up behind him and said, "Hey, how's my wicked little commandant? Forgotten your *und so weiter?*" and as he turned, I clawed my nails and slammed him across the cheek. That's how I got the black eye. Maud wanted to put an electronic leech on it, but I took the old handkerchief in ice water. Well, at any rate Erich had his scratches to match Bruce's not as deep, but four of them, and I told myself maybe they'd get infected—I hadn't washed my hands since the hunt. Not that Erich doesn't love scars.

Mark was the one who helped me up after Erich knocked me down.

"You got any omnias for that?" I snapped at him.

"For what?" Mark asked.

"Oh, for everything that's been happening to us," I told him disgustedly.

He seemed to actually think for a moment and then he said, "*Omnia mutantur, nihil interit.*"

"Meaning?" I asked him.

He said, "All things change, but nothing is really lost."

It would be a wonderful philosophy to stand with against the Change Winds. Also damn silly. I wondered if Mark really believed it. I wished I could. Sometimes I come close to thinking it's a lot of baloney trying to be any decent kind of Demon, even a good Entertainer. Then I tell myself, "That's life, Greta. You've got to love through it somehow." But there are times when some of these cookies are not too easy to love.

Something brushed the palm of my hand again. It was Illy's tentacle, with the tendrils of the tip spread out like a little bush. I started to pull my hand away, but then I realized the Loon was simply lonely. I surrendered my hand to the patterned gossamer pressures of feather-talk.

Right away I got the words, "Feeling lonely, Greta girl?"

It almost floored me, I tell you. Here I was understanding feather-talk, which I just didn't, and I was understanding it in English, which didn't make sense at all.

For a second, I thought Illy must have spoken, but I knew he hadn't and for a couple more seconds I thought he was working telepathy on me, using the feather-talk as cues. Then I tumbled to what was happening: he was playing English on my palm like on the keyboard of his squeakbox, and since I could play English on a squeakbox myself, my mind translated automatically.

Realizing this almost gave my mind stage fright, but I was too fagged to be hocused by self-consciousness. I just lay back and let the thoughts come through. It's good to have someone talk to you, even an underweight octopus, and without the squeaks Illy didn't sound so silly; his phrasing was soberer.

"Feeling sad, Greta girl, because you'll never understand what's happening to us all," Illy asked me, "because you'll never be anything but a shadow fighting shadows—and trying to love shadows in between the battles? It's time you understood we're not really fighting a war at all, although it looks that way, but going through a kind of evolution, though not exactly the kind Erich had in mind.

"Your Terran thought has a word for it and a theory for it —a theory that recurs on many worlds. It's about the four orders of life: Plants, Animals, Men and Demons. Plants are energy-binders—they can't move through space or time, but they can clutch energy and transform it. Animals are space-binders— they can move through space. Man (Terran or ET, Lunan or non-Lunan) is a time-binder—he has memory.

"Demons are the fourth order of evolution, possibility-binders—they can make all of what might be part of what is, and that is their evolutionary function. Resurrection is like the metamorphosis of a caterpillar into a butterfly: a third-order being breaks out of the chrysalis of its lifeline into fourth-order life. The leap from the ripped cocoon of an unchanging reality is like the first animal's leap when he ceases to be a plant, and the Change World is the core of meaning behind the many myths of immortality.

"All evolution looks like a war at first—octopoids against monopoids, mammals against reptiles. And it has a necessary dialectic: there must be the thesis—we call it Snake—and the antithesis—Spider—before there can be the ultimate synthesis, when all possibilities are fully realized in one ultimate universe. The Change War isn't the blind destruction it seems.

"Remember that the Serpent is your symbol of wisdom and the Spider your sign for patience. The two names are rightly frightening to you, for all high existence is a mixture of horror and delight. And don't be surprised, Greta girl, at the range of my words and thoughts; in a way, I've had a billion years to study Terra and learn her languages and myths.

"Who are the real Spiders and Snakes, meaning who were the first possibility-binders? Who was Adam, Greta girl? Who was Cain? Who were Eve and Lilith?

"In binding all possibility, the Demons also bind the mental with the material. All fourth-order beings live inside and outside all minds, throughout the whole cosmos. Even this Place is, after its fashion, a giant brain: its floor is the brainpan, the boundary of the Void is the cortex of gray matter—yes, even the Major and Minor Maintainers are analogues of the pineal and pituitary glands, which in some form sustain all nervous systems.

"There's the real picture, Greta girl."

The feather-talk faded out and Illy's tendril tips merged into a soft pad on which I fingered, "Thanks, Daddy Long-legs."

Chewing over in my mind what Illy had just told me, I looked back at the gang around the piano. The party seemed to be breaking up; at least some of them were chopping away at it. Sid had gone to the control divan and was getting set to tune in Egypt. Mark and Kaby were there with him, all bursting with eagerness and the vision of ranks on ranks of mounted Zombie bowmen going up in a mushroom cloud; I thought of what Illy had told me and I managed a smile—seems we've got to win and lose all the battles, every which way.

Mark had just put on his Parthian costume, groaning cheerfully, "Trousers again!" and was striding around under a hat like a fur-lined ice-cream cone and with the sleeves of his metal-stuffed candys flapping over his hands. He waved a short sword with a heart-shaped guard at Bruce and Erich and told them to get a move on.

Kaby was going along on the operation wearing the old-woman disguise intended for Benson-Carter. I got a half-hearted kick out of knowing she was going to have to cover that chest and hobble.

Bruce and Erich weren't taking orders from Mark just yet. Erich went over and said something to Bruce at the bar, and Bruce got down and went over with Erich to the piano, and Erich tapped Beau on the shoulder and leaned over and said something to him, and Beau nodded and yanked "Limehouse

Blues" to a fast close and started another piece, something slow and nostalgic.

Erich and Bruce waved to Mark and smiled, as if to show him that whether he came over and stood with them or not, the legate and the lieutenant and the commandant were very much together. And while Sevensee hugged Lili with a simple enthusiasm that made me wonder why I've wasted so much imagination on genetic treatments for him, Erich and Bruce sang:

"To the legion of the lost ones, to the cohort of the damned,
To our brothers in the tunnels outside time,
Sing three Change-resistant Zombies, raised from death and
  robot-crammed,
And Commandos of the Spiders—
Here's to crime!
We're three blind mice on the wrong time-track,
  Hush—hush—hush!
We've lost our now and will never get back,
  Hush—hush—hush!
Change Commandos out on the spree,
Damned through all possibility,
Ghostgirls, think kindly on such as we,
  Hush—hush—hush!"

While they were singing, I looked down at my charcoal skirt and over at Maud and Lili and I thought, "Three gray hustlers for three black hussars, that's our speed." Well, I'd never thought of myself as a high-speed job, winning all the races—I wouldn't feel comfortable that way. Come to think of it, we've got to lose and win all the races in the long run, the way the course is laid out.

I fingered to Illy, "That's the picture, all right, Spider boy."

BIOGRAPHICAL NOTES

NOTE ON THE TEXTS

NOTES

Biographical Notes

Robert A. Heinlein   Born Robert Anson Heinlein in Butler, Missouri, on July 7, 1907, the third child of Rex Ivar Heinlein, an accountant, and Bam Lyle Heinlein. Moved to Kansas City as an infant; attended Central High School and Kansas City Junior College. In 1925 entered the United States Naval Academy in Annapolis, Maryland. Served as a midshipman on the U.S.S. *Lexington* (1929–32) and on the U.S.S. *Roper*, later promoted to lieutenant, but was forced to retire in 1934 after contracting tuberculosis. Married Leslyn MacDonald in 1932 (his first marriage, to Elinor Curry in 1929, ending quickly in divorce). Moved to Los Angeles in 1934 and became involved in Upton Sinclair's End Poverty in California movement; ran unsuccessfully for California State Assembly as an EPIC candidate in 1938. Published his first story, "Life-Line," in *Astounding Science Fiction* in 1939 (also completed a novel, *For Us, the Living*, published posthumously in 2003). Joined the Los Angeles Science Fiction League, and began hosting gatherings of the Mañana Literary Society—an informal group of science fiction writers including Leigh Brackett, Ray Bradbury, L. Sprague de Camp, Henry Kuttner, and C. L. Moore. Traveled to New York in 1940, meeting John W. Campbell Jr., L. Ron Hubbard, and others, and in 1941—already established as a leading writer for *Astounding*—was guest of honor at World Science Fiction Convention in Denver. Volunteered for active duty after Pearl Harbor but was turned down; worked as a civil service engineer in the Aeronautical Materials Lab at the Philadelphia Navy Yard (1942–45), recruiting Isaac Asimov and others as coworkers. Returned to Los Angeles and to writing after the war, selling stories to *The Saturday Evening Post* and beginning a series of juvenile novels for Scribner's with *Rocket Ship Galileo* (1947), followed by *Space Cadet* (1948), *Red Planet* (1949), and others. Moved to Colorado Springs, Colorado, in 1948, after a divorce; married engineer Virginia Gerstenfeld. (Their jointly designed ultramodern house was featured in *Popular Mechanics* in 1952.) Began work with Alford Van Ronkel on screenplay for *Destination Moon* (loosely based on *Rocket Ship Galileo*), filmed in 1949–50. Reworked earlier magazine serials into such novels as *Beyond This Horizon* (1948) and *Sixth Column* (1949), and wrote new novels *The Puppet Masters* (1951), *Double Star* (1956), *The Door into Summer* (1957), and *Starship Troopers* (1959), initially rejected as a juvenile because of its violence. Concentrated exclusively on novels after 1959.

Gained cult following beyond the science fiction community with *Stranger in a Strange Land* (1961). Final juvenile *Podkayne of Mars* (1963) was followed by *Glory Road* (1963), *Farnham's Freehold* (1964), and *The Moon Is a Harsh Mistress* (1966). Moved to Santa Cruz, California, in 1966. Later novels included *I Will Fear No Evil* (1970), *Time Enough for Love* (1973), *The Number of the Beast* (1980), *Friday* (1982), *Job: A Comedy of Justice* (1984), *The Cat Who Walks Through Walls: A Comedy of Manners* (1985), and *To Sail Beyond the Sunset* (1987). Moved for last time to Carmel, California, in 1987; died there on May 8, 1988, of emphysema and congestive heart failure. Was posthumously inducted into the Science Fiction Hall of Fame in 1998.

Alfred Bester   Born Alfred M. Bester in New York City on December 18, 1913, the second child of James J. Bester, who owned a shoe store, and Belle Bester (née Silverman), a Russian immigrant. Graduated from the University of Pennsylvania, where he played on the football team, in 1935; studied law at Columbia for two years. In 1936 married Rolly Goulko, an actress and later advertising executive. Published his first story, "The Broken Axiom," in *Thrilling Wonder Stories* in 1939, winning a prize for best amateur contribution. Wrote thirteen more stories for the magazine by 1942, when he followed his editors Jack Schiff and Mort Weisinger to DC Comics; contributed scripts and outlines for *Superman*, *Batman*, *Green Lantern*, and *Captain Marvel*, also working on the Lee Falk comic strips *The Phantom* and *Mandrake the Magician*. In 1946, began writing radio scripts for *The Shadow*, *Charlie Chan*, *Nick Carter*, *Nero Wolfe*, and other programs, shifting to television in 1948, most notably with *Tom Corbett: Space Cadet*. Returned to science fiction beginning in 1950, publishing stories in *Astounding Science Fiction* and *The Magazine of Fantasy and Science Fiction* and his first novel, *The Demolished Man*, in *Galaxy* magazine in 1952 (book, 1953); it won the first Hugo Award. Attended gatherings of the Hydra Club, meeting Isaac Asimov, James Blish, Anthony Boucher, Avram Davidson, Judith Merril, Theodore Sturgeon, and others. In 1953 published "*Who He?*" (later reprinted as *The Rat Race*), a novel about the television industry. With the proceeds of the film rights, moved with Rolly to England and then Italy, where he wrote articles on European television for *Holiday* magazine, and finished *The Stars My Destination*, his third novel (first published in England as *Tiger! Tiger!*, 1956, then in the U.S. in 1957; adapted as a graphic novel in 1979 and 1992). In 1957, delivered lecture "Science Fiction and the Renaissance Man" at the University of Chicago. Published *Starburst*, a collection of stories, in 1958 (later collections included *The Dark Side of the Earth*, 1964, and *Starlight*, 1976). Adapted his story "Fondly Fahrenheit" for television as *Murder and* *the Android* (1959). Became a regular contributor to *Holiday* and then senior editor from 1963 to 1971, when the magazine folded. Went on to write novels *The Computer Connection* (1975; serialized as *The Indian Giver* and published in the United Kingdom as *Extro*), *Golem*[100] (1980), and *The Deceivers* (1981). Moved to Ottsville, Pennsylvania, in the early 1980s; died of complications from a broken hip on September 30, 1987, in nearby Doylestown. His unpublished early thriller *Tender Loving Rage* appeared posthumously in 1991, followed in 1998 by an unfinished novel, *Psychoshop* (completed by Roger Zelazny). In 2001 he was inducted into the Science Fiction Hall of Fame.

James Blish   Born James Benjamin Blish in East Orange, New Jersey, on May 23, 1921, the only child of Asa Rhodes Blish, an advertising manager, and Dorothea Schneewind Blish, a pianist. While still in high school edited fanzine *The Planeteer* (six issues, 1935–36) and began attending meetings of the Futurian Society in New York, where he met Isaac Asimov, Cyril Kornbluth, Frederik Pohl, and others. Published first science fiction story, "Emergency Refueling," in *Super Science Stories* in 1940. Majored in zoology at Rutgers, graduating in 1942. Drafted into the army, he served as a medical technician at Fort Dix, New Jersey. Started at Columbia University in 1944, switching from zoology to literature; did not complete his M.A. degree, but later revised his thesis on Ezra Pound and sold it to *The Sewanee Review*, where it appeared in 1950. After the war, wrote stories for *Western Action*, *Crack Detective Stories*, and *Super Sports* along with science fiction, trying to earn a living as a freelance writer; worked for trade magazines, including *Frosted Food Field* and *Drug Trade News*, and as a reader for a literary agency. Edited little magazines *Renascence* (1945–46) and *Tumbrils* (1945–50). Married literary agent Virginia Kidd in 1947; they would have two children. Published novels *Jack of Eagles* (1952), *The Duplicated Man* (1953, with Robert Lowndes, as a magazine serial), and *The Warriors of Day* (1953, originally serialized as *Sword of Xota*, 1951), and the first of his "Okie" stories (1950–53), later much expanded in the "Cities in Flight" series of novels: *Earthman, Come Home* (1955), *They Shall Have Stars* (1956), *The Triumph of Time* (1958), *A Life for the Stars* (1962), and *Cities in Flight* (omnibus, 1970). In 1953 moved with Virginia to Milford, Pennsylvania, where he would cofound the Milford Science Fiction Writers' Conference; wrote fifteen scripts for the television series *Captain Video*. In 1955 learned to fly and joined the Civil Air Patrol; took job as science editor and public relations counsel for drug company Pfizer. Published story collections *The Seedling Stars* (1957), *Galactic Cluster* (1959), and *So Close to Home* (1961), and novels *The Frozen Year* (1957), *VOR* (1958), and *A Case of Conscience* (1958), the latter winning a Hugo

Award and earning him an invitation as guest of honor at the eighteenth World Science Fiction Convention (Pittsburgh, 1960). From
1962 to 1968 worked in public relations for the tobacco industry.
Wrote novels *Titan's Daughter* (1961), *The Star Dwellers* (1961), and
The Night Shapes (1962). In 1964 married Judith Ann Lawrence;
published historical novel *Doctor Mirabilis* and essay collection *The
Issue at Hand* (both 1964). Underwent major surgery after a diagnosis of tongue cancer. Published novels *Mission to the Heart Stars*
(1965), *A Torrent of Faces* (1967, with Norman L. Knight), *Welcome to
Mars* (1967), *The Vanished Jet* (1968), and *Black Easter* (1968); also
produced a dozen lucrative volumes of *Star Trek* episode adaptations
(1967–75) and a *Star Trek* novel, *Spock Must Die!* (1970). Moved to
England in 1969. During the 1970s, published new story collections,
including *Anywhen* (1970), and novels *The Day After Judgment*
(1971), *And All the Stars a Stage* (1971), *Midsummer Century* (1972),
and *The Quincunx of Time* (1973). A special issue of *The Magazine of
Fantasy and Science Fiction* devoted to Blish appeared in 1972. Died
from lung cancer at Henley-on-Thames on July 30, 1975.

Algis Budrys   Born Algirdas Jonas Budrys on January 9, 1931, in
Königsberg, East Prussia (now Kaliningrad, Russia), the only child of
Jonas Budrys, a Lithuanian diplomat, and Regina Kashuba Budrys,
who had worked in the Lithuanian intelligence service. Moved to
New York in 1936, his father serving as Lithuanian consul-general.
With the Soviet annexation of Lithuania in 1940, the family was ren-
dered stateless; his father became consul-general of the Lithuanian
government-in-exile. (Budrys finally took U.S. citizenship in 1996.)
Published a fanzine, *Slantasy*, in 1946, while still in high school. Attended the University of Miami (1947–49) and Columbia (1951–52),
interrupting his schooling briefly to work as an investigations clerk for
American Express. Published his first story, "The High Purpose," in
Astounding Science Fiction in 1952. Began a career as a science fiction
editor, working for Gnome Press (assistant editor, 1952), *Galaxy* (assistant editor, 1953–54), *Venture* (associate editor, 1957), and Royal
Publications (editor, 1958–61). Married Edna F. Duna in 1954; they
would have four sons. The same year, published his first novel, *False
Night* (later republished as *Some Will Not Die* in 1961, restoring material cut from the original edition), followed by *Who?* (1958; film version 1973), *Man of Earth* (1958), *The Falling Torch* (1959), and *Rogue
Moon* (1960). *The Unexpected Dimension* (1960) gathered some of
almost one hundred stories he published during the 1950s. In 1961,
moved to Evanston, Illinois, where he became editor-in-chief of Regency Books. Later worked as editorial director for Playboy Press
(1963–65), president of Commander Publications (1965–66), reviewer

for *Galaxy* magazine (1965–71), public relations account executive at Young & Rubicam (1969–74), reviewer for *The Magazine of Fantasy and Science Fiction* (1975–93), and editor and later publisher for *Tomorrow Speculative Fiction* (1993–2000; beginning in 1997, one of the first online science fiction magazines). Edited eighteen anthologies for the *L. Ron Hubbard Presents Writers of the Future* series (1985–2007). Along with novels *The Iron Thorn* (1967), *Michaelmas* (1977), and *Hard Landing* (1993), published criticism and other nonfiction in *Benchmarks: Galaxy Bookshelf* (1985), *Writing to the Point* (1994), and *Outposts: Literatures of Milieux* (1996), and several collections of short fiction. Died in Evanston, Illinois, on June 9, 2008.

Fritz Leiber Jr. Born Fritz Reuter Leiber Jr. in Chicago, Illinois, on December 24, 1910, to Fritz Leiber Sr. and Virginia Bronson Leiber, both Shakespearean actors. Toured with father's repertory company in 1928 before entering the University of Chicago, from which he graduated in 1932; went on to study at General Theological Seminary in New York, and was briefly a candidate for ordination in the Episcopal Church. Toured intermittently with father's company and appeared with him in films *Camille* (1936) and *The Great Garrick* (1937). Married Jonquil Stephens in 1936 and moved to Hollywood; they soon had a son. Corresponded with horror writer H. P. Lovecraft, who encouraged and influenced his literary development; wrote a supernatural novella, *The Dealings of Daniel Kesserich* (1936; published posthumously in 1997), and showed Lovecraft early stories. Returning to Chicago, took job as staff writer for Consolidated Book Publishing (1937–41), contributing to the *Standard American Encyclopedia*. His first publication as a professional writer, "Two Sought Adventure" (in John W. Campbell Jr.'s *Unknown* in 1939), introduced popular characters Fafhrd and the Gray Mouser, developed with his friend Harry Fischer and modeled on their relationship; the story inaugurated a series he would continue for more than fifty years, helping to define the subgenre he labeled "Sword and Sorcery." (Fafhrd and the Gray Mouser stories were later collected in *Two Sought Adventure*, 1957; *Swords in the Mist*, 1968; *Swords Against Wizardry*, 1968; *The Swords of Lankhmar*, 1968; *Swords and Deviltry*, 1970; *Swords and Ice Magic*, 1977; *The Knight and Knave of Swords*, 1988; and other volumes.) Worked as a drama and speech instructor at Occidental College in 1941, and during the war as an inspector at Douglas Aircraft. His first novel, *Conjure Wife*—about secret witchcraft on a college campus—appeared in *Unknown* in 1943 (but not as a book until 1952; it was filmed three times). His first science fiction novel, *Gather, Darkness!*, was also serialized in 1943 (book version, 1950). From 1945 to 1956, he worked as an editor at *Science Digest* in Chicago. Published science fiction novels *Destiny Times Three* (in *Astounding*, 1945; as book, 1957); *The Green Millennium* (1953); and *The Big Time* (in *Galaxy*, 1958; as book, 1961), the last winning a Hugo Award and inaugurating his popular "Change War" series. Moved back to Los Angeles in 1958, and turned to writing full-time; published science fiction novels *The Silver Eggheads* (1961), *The Wanderer* (1964), and *A Specter Is Haunting Texas* (1969). Lived in San Francisco after the death of his wife in 1969; the city forms the setting of his fantasy novel *Our Lady of Darkness* (1977). In 1976, he received a World Fantasy Award for Life Achievement, and in 1981 a Grand Master Award from Science Fiction Writers of America. Married Margo Skinner in May 1992; died on September 5, 1992, in San Francisco, of an apparent stroke. In 2001 he was inducted posthumously into the Science Fiction Hall of Fame.

Note on the Texts

This volume collects five American science fiction novels of the 1950s: *Double Star* (1956) by Robert A. Heinlein, *The Stars My Destination* (1957) by Alfred Bester, *A Case of Conscience* (1958) by James Blish, *Who?* (1958) by Algis Budrys, and *The Big Time* (1961) by Fritz Leiber. A companion volume in the Library of America series, *American Science Fiction: Four Classic Novels, 1953–1956*, includes four earlier works: *The Space Merchants* (1953) by Frederik Pohl and C. M. Kornbluth, *More Than Human* (1953) by Theodore Sturgeon, *The Long Tomorrow* (1955) by Leigh Brackett, and *The Shrinking Man* (1956) by Richard Matheson. The texts of all of these novels have been taken from the first American book editions, to which the dates in the preceding list refer. (Though not published in book form until after the decade had ended, *The Big Time* was completed in 1957 and published in its entirety in *Galaxy* magazine in 1958. *The Stars My Destination* was first published in England in 1956 as *Tiger! Tiger!*)

Double Star. Robert A. Heinlein finished a draft of *Double Star* toward the end of March 1955. "Its present title is *Star Role*," he wrote his agent Lurton Blassingame; other titles he considered (from a list at the beginning of an early revised typescript, now at the University of California, Santa Cruz) included *Star Path*, *False Star*, *Star Orbit*, *Command Performance*, *Guest Star*, *Understudy*, *Star Billing*, and *Devil's Dilemma*. Heinlein deliberately kept the novel short and avoided "sexy scenes" and "taboo monosyllables" in order to make it more attractive to publishers. "I hope this one will finally crack Collier's, the Post, or some other adult & not-SF-specialized market," he explained to Blassingame, also wondering if the novel might be placed with Ballantine Books rather than Doubleday, whose prior contractual and royalty arrangements had disappointed him. Ultimately, however, it was Doubleday that published the novel, in April 1956, after a first serial appearance in *Astounding Science Fiction* in February, March, and April of the same year. Heinlein's papers at Santa Cruz show that he saw his manuscript through the press at Doubleday with considerable care and control. He did not alter the novel thereafter, though it appeared in several subsequent editions during his lifetime. In 2006, a corrected text of the novel was published by Meisha Merlin in Decatur, Georgia, as part of the Virginia Edition of Heinlein's works. (The editor acknowledges the kind assistance of Jeffrey E. Cook, who

copyedited the text of *Double Star* for the Virginia Edition, in checking the text in the present volume.) The text of *Double Star* has been
taken from the 1956 Doubleday first printing.

The Stars My Destination. Alfred Bester began *The Stars My Destination* in England, in "a romantic white cottage down in Surrey." Having sold the film and reprint rights to his previous novel, "*Who He?*"
(1953), he had decided with his wife to "blow the loot on a few years
abroad"; they took little with them, but he did bring "an idea for
another science fiction novel," inspired by an account in *National
Geographic* about a cook's helper who had endured four months adrift
on an open raft (see Samuel F. Harby, "They Survived at Sea," May
1945). In November 1955, after a frustrated attempt to start writing,
he relocated with his wife to Rome, where he finished the novel, once
he had settled into the task, in about three months. It was first published in August 1956, by Sidgwick & Jackson in London, as *Tiger!
Tiger!* (Earlier in the year, *The Magazine of Fantasy and Science Fiction* had announced it would publish the novel as a serial, *The Burning
Man*, beginning in June, but Bester is said to have withdrawn from
this arrangement, either because he was still revising or because Horace Gold of *Galaxy* magazine had asserted a prior right to first serial
publication. Another working title for the novel, reportedly, was *Hell's
My Destination.*) Returning to the U.S., Bester found "there was
some competition for the book," and he saw it published as *The Stars
My Destination*, first as a four-part serial in *Galaxy* magazine (October
1956–January 1957), and then in March 1957 as a Signet paperback
(New York: New American Library).

The texts of these three initial printings of the novel vary significantly, and Bester's original typescript, along with correspondence and
other documents associated with the novel's early publication history,
is not known to have survived. A comparison of the three texts suggests that each was prepared separately—probably from carbon copies
of the typescript—and each varies uniquely at many points. The Sidgwick & Jackson text shows considerable evidence of nonauthorial revision: Bester's American references and usages are altered throughout,
and his diction is made plainer (in one frequently cited instance, the
presumably authorial "'Vorga,' I kill you filthy" becomes "Vorga, I
kill you deadly"). Along with many such local verbal revisions, the
text of *Tiger! Tiger!* entirely omits a number of passages present in
some form in both later texts, and it only minimally attempts the experiments in typography that in the later texts illustrate Gully Foyle's
experience of synesthesia. (Initially uncredited, the synesthetic images
in the novel have since been attributed to Jack Gaughan. Some are

identical in both *Galaxy* and the Signet edition, but others vary slightly.)

Notwithstanding the evidence of nonauthorial revision to the text of *Tiger! Tiger!*, it is possible that Bester read and revised *Tiger! Tiger!* after he had submitted his novel, making changes not subsequently included in either American text. The *Galaxy* text, of the three, contains the greatest number of unique variants and is the least likely—given Horace Gold's reputation as an editor who often rewrote the manuscripts he published without his authors' advice or consent—to represent Bester's particular intentions. The Signet *Stars My Destination* probably reflects the text of Bester's original version with the least editorial revision of the three, though it too may contain nonauthorial changes, and it is conceivable that it was prepared for publication without Bester's direct involvement. Bester did not revise the text of the novel after these initial printings; in England it was subsequently published on a number of occasions during his lifetime as *Tiger! Tiger!* following the Sidgwick & Jackson first edition and in the United States as *The Stars My Destination* following the Signet text. In 1996, after Bester's death, a new edition containing a "special restored text" compiled and edited by Alex and Phyllis Eisenstein was published by Random House in New York; this text, presented without a stated editorial rationale or textual apparatus, is principally derived from the Signet edition but also occasionally adds or omits material following the Sidgwick & Jackson or *Galaxy* texts. The text of *The Stars My Destination* in the present volume has been taken from the 1957 Signet first printing.

A Case of Conscience. James Blish began *A Case of Conscience* as a long story or novella rather than a novel. He had been invited by Fletcher Pratt to be one of three contributors, along with Pratt, to a "Twayne Science-Fiction Triplet" titled *Lithia*, whose stories would share a common setting. The proposed collection was never published, but working from an initial description of the planet Lithia by John D. Clark and Willy Ley (later included as an appendix in the novel), Blish completed what would ultimately become Book One of *A Case of Conscience* and published it (as "A Case of Conscience") in *If: Worlds of Science Fiction* in September 1953. In 1955 "A Case of Conscience" was anthologized by Faber & Faber in *Best SF: Science Fiction Stories*, edited by Edmund Crispin. Around the beginning of 1957, at the suggestion of Blish's agent Frederik Pohl, Ballantine Books solicited an extended version of "A Case of Conscience," and Blish returned to the work, thoroughly revising his original novella and adding the novel's second half. He corresponded often and at length with Pohl in the course of this writing and rewriting, and he was also guided by an initial reader's report from Ballantine. *A Case of Conscience* was published by Ballantine Books in New York in March 1958 and won a Hugo Award for best science fiction novel the following year. A subsequent British edition (London: Faber & Faber, 1959) included a new introduction and a few possibly authorial revisions, such as a new epigraph, along with many changes in spelling, punctuation, and vocabulary introduced to bring the novel into conformity with British usage. Blish did not revise the text of the novel for subsequent editions published during his lifetime, though he referred to it, along with *Doctor Mirabilis* (1964) and two novellas, *Black Easter* (1968) and *The Day After Judgment* (1971), as part of a trilogy, *After Such Knowledge*, first collected in a single volume in 1991, after his death. The text of *A Case of Conscience* in the present volume has been taken from the 1958 Ballantine Books first printing.

Who? Algis Budrys's novel *Who?* was initially written as a short story, also titled "Who?" and published in the April 1955 issue of *Fantastic Universe* magazine. Budrys had been inspired by a painting of Kelly Freas's that he had seen in the offices of *Fantastic Universe*, showing a man with a metal-domed head and a mechanical arm: "It just immediately captured my imagination entirely," he recalled in a 1981 interview, "and I had to write a story around it." The painting later appeared on the cover of the magazine along with his story. About six months after "Who?" was published, Budrys returned to the story: "I realized I could build a novel around that character." Much revised and expanded, *Who?* was published by Pyramid Books in New York in June 1958. (The cover art, by Robert V. Engel, adapted Freas's original image.) *Who?* was subsequently published in several distinct editions in both England and the United States, without evidently authorial changes to the text. In 1975, for a Ballantine Books edition published in New York, Budrys revised some references in the novel for contemporary readers because he worried it was "dating to some extent." He felt particularly that he "had to find some way to get the Chinese back into the story, even though the Chinese and the Russians had split since the book had been written." The text in the present volume has been taken from the June 1958 Pyramid Books first printing.

The Big Time. Fritz Leiber wrote *The Big Time* in late 1956 and early 1957, "in exactly a hundred days from first note to final typing finished," he later recalled. He sent it to Horace Gold at *Galaxy*, who initially declined to publish it, thinking it too confusing for his readers. Gold later reconsidered, and the novel was printed in its entirety in *Galaxy* in March and April 1958. Though it won the 1958 Hugo Award on the basis of its inclusion in the magazine, the novel did not appear in book form until February 1961, when it was published by Ace Books in New York both as a separate paperback and as an "Ace Double," with his thematically related collection *The Mind Spider and Other Stories.* Aside from some minor adjustments in layout and paragraphing, the text of the book editions is identical to the *Galaxy* text. Leiber wrote a new introduction to the novel for an edition published by Collier in New York in 1982, and he grouped it, with a number of other separately published works, as part of his "Change War" series, but he did not otherwise revise it. The text in the present volume has been taken from the first book edition of 1961. Leiber's introduction is printed in the notes.

This volume presents the texts of the original printings chosen for inclusion here, but it does not attempt to reproduce nontextual features of their typographic design. The texts are reprinted without change, except for the correction of typographical errors. Spelling, punctuation, and capitalization are often expressive features and are not altered, even when inconsistent or irregular. The following is a list of typographical errors corrected, cited by page and line number: 12.13, Doc Scortia; 12.16, Scortia himself; 27.6, 'Griil'; 47.31, have no; 54.38, Mitsubushi; 95.23, learned); 95.39, business! Then; 96.22, party; 96.25, party; 104.27, sides the; 121.27, stars; 132.20, imposter!; 158.25, citrous; 159.15, planets; 162.26, AS-128/127:006.; 165.29, your's; 172.20, "Choose."; 174.8, girl."; 181.33, Not I rot; 185.34, Gillet,; 196.24–25, twenty-fourth; 204.27, salvagable."; 209.37, No on; 213.9, become; 219.29, millenia; 220.3, girl,"; 225.12, "But; 227.8, threestory; 234.19, folly.; 247.38, Gully,"; 260.26, represion's; 261.27, *Fidelis.*; 267.22, Pallos,; 269.39, *you*; 272.2, twenty-fourth; 279.11, 'Vorga',"; 282.8, 'Vorga,'; 282.13, "But; 282.14, AS-128/127:006,; 285.29, then——; 289.27, wave lengths; 291.8, an pistol.'; 292.36, 'Vorga'."; 305.30, panic-stiken; 317.18, Michele (and *passim*); 332.28, Presteign,"; 334.4, It's; 341.5, 'Nomad'."; 341.16, 'Nomad'."; 344.33, Jaunte Watch; 354.24, star-bubbles:; 364.14, choses; 369.33, Aldeberan; 370.1, Aldeberan; 384.9–10, van de Graaf; 387.18, Dali; 459.32, decades; 460.4, shelter (and *passim*); 474.9, slumps.); 496.33, thousand fold; 506.34, lhashin'."); 510.22, know; 530.17, Tannhauser; 544.3, simultaniety; 548.36, 2047).; 551.3, earth,; 551.4, it [line space] did; 551.13, earth,; 552.32, appetite.); 553.14, Pleistocene.); 566.33, either—or; 582.13, "Damn it."; 582.13, savagely,; 588.38, effected.; 590.31–32, everythng; 594.8, ino the; 595.15, seemd; 596.23, you.; 598.30, gas—fired; 601.19, It'll; 602.17, over world; 602.33, voice,; 604.23, detroyed; 605.33, that wasn't; 618.4, know; 628.27, doing.; 629.23, right,

he; 629.25, up."; 642.26, urgently,; 645.3, key."; 645.25, DeFillipo;
657.11, Bridegton; 661.36, of hammer; 663.13, "twenty-one; 679.8,
match-box; 687.25, "Don't; 692.4, possible; 696.1, told to; 707.14,
when,; 709.26, *Leibchen*:; 710.15, *Leibchen*,; 715.9, Merchant,; 719.2,
soupcon; 720.11. —an; 722.15, and and; 722.17, the the; 723.16, "*Heren*;
723.40, to way; 724.39, us that; 726.27, before transferred; 730.24,
Luan,; 731.17, instructor,; 739.7, year the; 739.22, Serpants,; 741.5, *in
Himmel*,; 741.9, degress; 742.4, Gretta; 742.17, Intorversion's; 743.19,
saftey; 747.1, *Fuhrer*-fashion.; 747.22, world; 754.29, *Herzen in*; 756.8,
Besides; 756.23, " " *Ubivaytye*; 767.5, was best; 768.31–32, smile locked;
770.35, 'Thats; 776.1, fade 'leave; 777.38, if her; 780.37, thought I;
781.12, Foster Now; 781.20, Spencer; 785.27, Dore; 785.31, secor;
786.8, Entainers; 787.6, know; 787.8, you skin; 787.24, unknow;
787.36, powered; 788.39, Martains; 789.32, mysef,; 796.22, trulland;
799.17, Undertand;"; 800.28, a a.

Notes

In the notes below, the reference numbers denote page and line of the present volume; the line count includes titles and headings but not blank lines. No note is made for material found in standard desk-reference books. Quotations from the Bible are keyed to the King James Version. Quotations from Shakespeare are keyed to *The Riverside Shakespeare*, ed. G. Blakemore Evans (Boston: Houghton Mifflin, 1974). For additional information and references to other studies, see *Hell's Cartographers: Some Personal Histories of Science Fiction Writers*, ed. Brian W. Aldiss and Harry Harrison (New York: Harper & Row, 1975); Mike Ashley, *Transformations: The Story of Science Fiction Magazines from 1950 to 1970* (Liverpool: Liverpool University Press, 2005); James Gifford, *Robert A. Heinlein: A Reader's Companion* (Sacramento, CA: Nitrosyncretic Press, 2000); David Ketterer, *Imprisoned in a Tesseract: The Life and Work of James Blish* (Kent, OH: Kent State University Press, 1987); Barry N. Malzberg, *Breakfast in the Ruins: Science Fiction in the Last Millennium* (Riverdale, NY: Baen Publishing, 2007); William H. Patterson, *Robert A. Heinlein: In Dialogue with His Century*, Vol. 1 (New York: Tor, 2011); Robert Silverberg, *Musings and Meditations: Reflections on Science Fiction, Science, and Other Matters* (New York: Nonstop Press, 2011); *Fritz Leiber: Critical Essays*, ed. Benjamin Szumskyj (Jefferson, NC: McFarland & Company, 2007); and Carolyn Wendell, *Alfred Bester* (Mercer Island, WA: Starmont House, 1982).

DOUBLE STAR

2.1   Henry and Catherine Kuttner] Henry Kuttner (1915–1958) and his wife Catherine (1911–1987) were both science fiction and fantasy writers, Catherine publishing mainly as C. L. Moore. After their marriage in 1940 they frequently collaborated.

3.12   Omar the Tentmaker] Colloquially, a maker of oversized clothes; originally a nickname for the Persian poet Omar Khayyám (1048–1131), and later the title of a novel (1899), a play (1914), and a movie (1922).

9.23   The Lambs Club] Club for theatrical professionals, established in New York City in 1874 after being founded in London in 1868 in honor of Charles and Mary Lamb.

12.13–16   Capek . . . Capek] Heinlein had originally named his character

"Doc Scortia," after his friend Thomas N. Scortia, but later changed the name to Capek throughout the novel. He neglected to do so in these two instances, so the text of the first edition has been emended.

12.27   Burbage and Booth]   Richard Burbage (1568–1619), English actor and associate of Shakespeare, and Edwin Booth (1833–1893), American Shakespearean actor.

14.23–24   true face . . . Alec Guinness.]   Guinness (1914–2000) was known for altering his appearance for different roles, notably for the multiple roles in the film *Kind Hearts and Coronets* (1949).

15.10–11   *Huey Long*]   Huey Pierce Long (1893–1935), governor of Louisiana from 1928 to 1932, was assassinated in 1935.

15.18   Factor's #5 sallow]   Max Factor (1872–1938) founded a cosmetics company known for its theatrical and film makeup, still in operation.

15.35   a punkin' doin's]   A small rural fair or carnival.

23.35   *Evangeline . . . Gabriel*]   Evangeline Bellefontaine and Gabriel Lajeunesse are tragically separated lovers in Henry Wadsworth Longfellow's epic poem *Evangeline, A Tale of Acadie* (1847).

34.14   the lead in *L'Aiglon*]   Play (1900) by Edmond Rostand whose protagonist is Napoleon's son.

34.17–18   how a man could go . . . in another man's place]   The reference is to Sydney Carton in Charles Dickens's *A Tale of Two Cities* (1859).

39.26–27   *giri* and *gimu*]   Japanese: duty and obligation.

39.33   *Le Grand Guignol*]   Parisian theater, founded in 1897, specializing in realistically staged horror plays.

52.14   Goddard City]   Likely named for American physicist and engineer Robert H. Goddard (1882–1945), a pioneer in early rocket design in the 1920s.

58.29–30   I. G. Farbenindustrie]   German chemical and industrial conglomerate founded in 1925.

89.1–2   'Include me *Out.*']   The phrase is attributed to film producer Samuel Goldwyn (1879–1974), though he denied having said it.

92.16   Farley]   James A. Farley (1888–1976) was Franklin D. Roosevelt's campaign manager in 1932 and 1936, and also served Roosevelt as postmaster general.

94.33   House of Orange]   Royal family central to Netherlands history since its founding by Willem I, Prince of Orange (1533–1584); more precisely the House of Orange-Nassau.

97.19–21   'Government . . . words of Lincoln.]   See the conclusion of Lincoln's Gettysburg Address of November 19, 1863.

97.28   Uncle Remus]   Storyteller invented by American journalist Joel Chandler Harris (1845–1908) for a popular series of tales from African American oral tradition, first collected in book form in 1881.

99.3–4   "Never give a sucker an even break"]   Catchphrase of American comic actor W. C. Fields (1880–1946), who first used the line in the 1936 film *Poppy* and made it the title of his last major film in 1941.

105.15   "Kong Christian"]   The Danish royal anthem, adopted in 1780.

105.23   "*Ave, Imperator!*"]   Latin: Hail, emperor!

106.21–22   Habsburg lips and the Windsor nose]   Thought to be identifying familial characteristics of the European House of Habsburg and the British House of Windsor.

114.12   "Weary Willie"]   Sad-clown persona created by the circus performer Emmett Kelly (1898–1979).

114.26   the King's Touch]   The belief, in medieval England and France, that the king's touch could cure scrofula ("the King's Evil").

129.30–31   "the cloud-capp'd . . . palaces,"]   See Shakespeare, *The Tempest*, IV.i.152.

133.29   the Birkenhead Drill]   H.M.S. *Birkenhead*, a British troopship, was wrecked off the coast of South Africa in 1852. The soldiers on board stood at attention as the ship sank, allowing women and children to board the lifeboats. The phrase "Birkenhead drill" was coined by Rudyard Kipling in his dialect poem "Soldier an' Sailor Too" (1896).

137.26–27   wounded Lion of Lucerne]   Sculpture in Lucerne, Switzerland, commemorating the Swiss Guards massacred at the Tuileries Palace during the French Revolution in 1792.

137.28   "The guard dies, but never surrenders."]   Phrase attributed to French general Pierre Cambronne (1770–1842), a commander of Napoleon's Imperial Guard, at the battle of Waterloo. Cambronne denied saying it.

138.33   *Cyrano*]   *Cyrano de Bergerac*, play (1897) by Edmond Rostand.

142.37   "Murder most foul"]   See Shakespeare, *Hamlet*, I.v.27.

THE STARS MY DESTINATION

150.2   *Truman M. Talley*]   Truman Macdonald Talley (b. 1925) was an editor at New American Library in New York during the 1950s, and would later publish books under his own imprint in association with St. Martin's Press.

151.2–6   Tiger! Tiger! . . . Blake] See "The Tyger" in William Blake's *Songs of Experience* (1794).

154.36   Charles Fort Jaunte] Charles Fort (1874–1932) was an American writer who compiled instances of anomalous phenomena in *The Book of the Damned* (1919) and other volumes.

156.15–16   Descartes . . . *sum*] René Descartes (1596–1650), French philosopher and mathematician, first proposed the formula "Je pense, donc je suis" ("I think, therefore I am") in his *Discourse on the Method* (1637).

176.12–13   *Etre entre . . . l'enclume.*] French: Between the hammer and the anvil.

192.14   Louis Quinze] In the baroque style associated with the French King Louis XV (1710–1774).

192.30   Mencius] Meng Tzu, Confucian philosopher born in the fourth century BCE, now commonly spelled Mengzi.

193.15   Shan-tung] A Chinese coastal province, now usually transliterated as Shandong.

196.24–25   twenty-fifth century] In both the British and American first editions of Bester's novel, the text here reads "twenty-fourth century." It has been emended to fit the date given elsewhere (on page 274 of the present volume) for *Vorga*'s encounter with *Nomad*, and other internal evidence.

199.26   Eumenides] Goddesses of vengeance in ancient Greek religion.

206.26   Gouffre Martel] Also known as Gouffre de Padirac; French cave in the department of Lot first explored by Édouard-Alfred Martel (1859–1938).

234.18–19   medieval ruin known as Fisher's Folly.] Attempting to make Montauk the "Miami Beach of the North," property developer Carl G. Fisher (1874–1939) constructed Montauk Manor (a Tudor-style resort hotel) and the Montauk Improvement Building (an office tower), beginning in 1926; the project went bankrupt in 1932.

251.2–10   With a heart . . . Tom-a-Bedlam] From "Tom o'Bedlam's Song," an anonymous poem originally preserved in a manuscript commonplace book (c. 1615) and later published with many variations; see, for instance, *Westminster-drollery* (1671–72). "Tom O'Bedlam" was a generic term for lunatic.

253.31   Mason & Dixon] Charles Mason (1728–1786) and Jeremiah Dixon (1733–1779), British surveyors best known for surveying a line that came to represent the demarcation between northern and southern states in the United States.

255.4   "Friends, Romans, Countrymen,"] Opening lines of Marc Antony's funeral oration in Shakespeare's *Julius Caesar* (c. 1599).

255.37   *Le roi est mort*]   French: "The king is dead."

256.19   Bloch's "*Das Sexual Leben*"]   *Das Sexualleben unserer Zeit in seinen Beziehungen zur modernen Kultur* (1906, translated as *The Sexual Life of Our Time in Its Relations to Modern Civilization*), an early cultural study of sexuality by German dermatologist Iwan Bloch (1872–1922).

261.31   *bourgeois gentilhomme*]   Molière's comedy *Le Bourgeois gentilhomme* (1670) concerns a prosperous merchant seeking social acceptance in aristocratic circles.

268.35   *Toujours de l'audace!*]   Saying of French revolutionary leader Georges-Jacques Danton (1759–1794): "We need audacity, and yet more audacity, and always audacity!"

270.39–40   Rockne . . . Thorpe]   Knute Rockne (1888–1931), football player and later coach at the University of Notre Dame; Jim Thorpe (1888–1953), football player and later Olympic medalist.

272.2   twenty-fifth]   See note 196.24–25.

273.27   Sinbad . . . Old Man of the Sea.]   In the *Thousand and One Nights*, Sinbad on his fifth voyage is enslaved by the Old Man of the Sea, whom he must carry on his shoulders.

276.22–23   Dürer's "Death and the Maiden"]   Albrecht Dürer's engraving "Young Woman Attacked by Death" (c. 1495) is one example of the "death and the maiden" motif in Renaissance art, but Dürer's student Hans Baldung (1484–1545) produced several better-known examples, including the 1517 painting "Death and the Maiden."

281.10–11   the view . . . Keats's house]   The poet John Keats (1795–1821), suffering from tuberculosis, moved into a villa beside the Spanish Steps in November 1820.

281.25–26   Cesare . . . Borgia]   Cesare Borgia (c. 1476–1507) and Lucrezia Borgia (1480–1519) were scions of the powerful and notoriously corrupt house of Borgia.

354.24   star-bubbles.]   In both the British and American first editions of Bester's novel and probably also in Bester's now-missing original typescript, "star-bubbles" is followed by a colon, prompting the expectation that Foyle's exclamation will be presented as a typographic image. No such image appears, however, in any extant version of the text. In the present volume the colon has been replaced with a period.

A CASE OF CONSCIENCE

373.1   A CASE OF CONSCIENCE]   Blish's title refers to the *casus conscientiae* or "cases of conscience" found in classical textbooks of casuistry: case histories illustrating ethical issues, used in the education of confessors.

When his novel was published in England (London: Faber & Faber, 1959), Blish added the following foreword:

> This novel is not about Catholicism, but since its hero is a Catholic theologian it inevitably contains certain sticking points for those who subscribe to the doctrines of the Roman and to a lesser extent the Anglican churches. Readers who have no doctrinal preconceptions should not find these points even noticeable, let alone troublesome.
>
> It was my assumption that the Roman Catholic Church of a century beyond our time will have undergone changes of custom and of doctrine, some minor and some major. The publication of this novel in America showed that Catholics were quite willing to allow me my Diet of Basra, my revival of the elegant argument from the navel to the geological record, and my jettisoning of the tonsure; but on two points they would not allow me to depart from what one may find in the *Catholic Encyclopedia* of 1945. (No scientist thus far has protested my jettisoning of special relativity in the year 2050.) These were:
>
> (1) My assumption that by 2050 the rite of exorcism will be so thoroughly buried in the medieval past that even the Church will teach it to its priests only perfunctorily—so perfunctorily that even a Jesuit might overlook it in a situation which in any event hardly suggests that exorcism would be even minimally appropriate. Yet even today non-Catholics generally do not believe that exorcism survives in the Church; it seems even more primitive and *outré* than habits and tonsures, which were frozen into Church usage at about the same time, i.e. the thirteenth century. In that period, too, it was commonplace to ring blessed bells to dispel thunderstorms; that has not survived; I think it is reasonable to assume that exorcism will be, officially, only a vestige by 2050.
>
> (2) My assumption that by 2050 a lay person who knows how may administer Extreme Unction, as today he may administer Baptism. Of course, this is not true today, and I can perhaps be excused my impatience with critics who thought me so lazy as to think it was. These amateur theologians forget that in the beginning none of the Sacraments could be administered by anyone but a priest, and that the fact that priests still have reserved Extreme Unction is the result of a bitterly fought holding action which lasted many centuries. The battle to reserve Baptism similarly was lost almost immediately, as was inevitable in an age where the population was small, subject to plagues and other catastrophes about which exactly nothing could be done, and so had to hold every soul precious at the moment of birth. Today, and (I greatly fear) tomorrow, our jammed neo-Malthusian world with its unselective wingless faceless angel of death who may reach us all in twenty minutes from the other side of the planet, confronts us with the probability of deaths in such great masses that no population of priests could minister to all the victims; and since I give the Church credit (against all appear-

ances, sometimes) for being basically a merciful institution, I have assumed that by 2050 Extreme Unction will no longer be reserved.

Anyone, of course, is at liberty to find my reasoning at fault, but I hope they will not quote 1945 doctrine to me as if it were sufficient in itself for 2050.

A number of people who wrote to me felt that my hero's conclusion as to the nature of Lithia was far from inevitable; but I was gratified to receive also several letters from theologians who knew the *present* Church position on the problem of the "plurality of worlds," as most of my correspondents obviously did not. (As usual, the Church, as an institution, is far ahead of most of its communicants.) Rather than justify my hero's irruption of Manichaeism in any words but his own, I will quote Mr. Gerald Heard, who has summarized the position best of all (as one would expect of so gifted a writer trained as a theologian):

"If there are many planets inhabited by sentient creatures, as most astronomers (including Jesuits), now suspect, then each one of such planets (solar or non-solar) must fall into one of three categories:

(*a*) Inhabited by sentient creatures, but without souls; so to be treated with compassion but extra-evangelically.

(*b*) Inhabited by sentient creatures with fallen souls, through an original but not inevitable ancestral sin; so to be evangelized with urgent missionary charity.

(*c*) Inhabited by sentient soul-endowed creatures that have not fallen, who therefore:

(1) inhabit an unfallen, sinless paradisal world;

(2) who therefore we must contact not to propagandize, but in order that we may learn from them the conditions (about which we can only speculate) of creatures living in perpetual grace, endowed with all the virtues in perfection, and both immortal and in complete happiness for always possessed of and with the knowledge of God."

The reader will observe with Ruiz-Sanchez, I think, that the Lithians fit none of these categories; hence all that follows.

The author, I should like to add, is an agnostic with no position at all in these matters. It was my intention to write about a man, not a body of doctrine.

373.8 *John Capgrave . . .* Pilgrims] Capgrave (1393–1464) was an English Augustinian friar and historian; his *Solace of Pilgrims* (c. 1451) largely consists of accounts of various religious sites.

374.1 LARRY SHAW] Lawrence Taylor Shaw (1924–1985), a science fiction author and literary agent who encouraged Blish to turn his 1953 novella "A Case of Conscience" into a novel.

377.17   the novel which had proposed the case]   James Joyce's *Finnegans Wake* (1939).

377.17–18   Index Expurgatorius]   Roman Catholic index of books to be censored before being read by Catholics, later incorporated into the *Index Librorum Prohibitorum*, or Index of Prohibited Books, until the latter was discontinued in 1966.

377.23   Magravius threatens . . . Jeremias and Eugenius]   See *Finnegans Wake* (1939), part III (page 573 of the first edition).

382.5–6   Berkefeld-filtered]   A Berkefeld filter removes bacterial and other impurities using diatomaceous earth.

384.9–10   van de Graaff generators]   Electrostatic generators invented in 1929 by Robert J. Van de Graaff (1901–1967).

385.11   pteropsid]   One of a large taxonomic group of vascular plants including all flowering plants and ferns.

385.21–23   ancient custom . . . half-century]   Pope Boniface VIII (c. 1235–1303) declared 1300 a "Jubilee" year, during which pilgrims could seek universal pardon; Jubilees were subsequently celebrated every twenty-five or fifty years.

387.17–18   the dream constructions . . . boiled beans.]   See *Soft Construction with Boiled Beans (Premonition of Civil War)*, a painting (1936) by Spanish surrealist Salvador Dalí (1904–1989).

390.6–7   Bois-d'Averoigne]   Averoigne was a medieval French province invented by the American writer Clark Ashton Smith (1893–1961) for a series of fantasy tales.

390.31–32   conspicuous consumption]   A phrase coined by sociologist Thorstein Veblen (1857–1929) in *The Theory of the Leisure Class* (1899) and earlier articles.

391.32–33   the Encke division]   Now known as the Encke Gap: a space within Saturn's A Ring caused by the presence of the moon Pan.

392.1   Crape ring]   Also known as the Crepe Ring: Saturn's C Ring, so called because of the opacity of its materials.

396.12   St. Simon Stylites]   Simeon Stylites, fifth-century Syrian ascetic who spent some four decades on top of a pillar.

407.23   "Only upon this . . . safely built."]   See the essay "A Free Man's Worship" (1903), by British philosopher Bertrand Russell (1872–1970).

415.21–416.3   the dark blue book . . . leading to nullity."]   See note 377.23.

428.18   Pecksniffian]   In the manner of Seth Pecksniff, archetypal hypocrite in Charles Dickens's *Martin Chuzzlewit* (1843–44).

430.24–25   Occam's Razor]   Principle developed by the English logician William of Ockham (1285–1349) that "entities should not be multiplied without necessity" and that the simplest explanation tends to be the most plausible.

433.23–25   *The groggy old . . . croziers*]   See Canto LII, first published in 1940, of Ezra Pound's *Cantos.*

439.34–35   theosophism and Hollywood Vedanta]   The Theosophical Society was founded by Helena Blavatsky in 1875. The Vedanta Society of Southern California was established in Hollywood in 1930 by Swami Prabhavananda, of the order of Sri Ramakrishna.

440.20–21   This has been willed . . . must be."]   See Dante, *Inferno,* canto 3, lines 95–96: "*vuolsi così colà dove si puote / ciò che si vuole.*"

441.13   Cantor]   Georg Cantor (1845–1918), German mathematician and inventor of set theory.

443.12–13   Kick a stone . . . Bishop Berkeley.']   See James Boswell's *Life of Samuel Johnson* (1791): "After we came out of the church, we stood talking for some time together of Bishop Berkeley's ingenious sophistry to prove the non-existence of matter, and that every thing in the universe is merely ideal. I observed, that though we are satisfied his doctrine is not true, it is impossible to refute it. I shall never forget the alacrity with which Johnson answered, striking his foot with mighty force against a large stone, till he rebounded from it, 'I refute it *thus.*'"

447.21   *Retro me, Sathanas.*]   Latin: Get thee behind me, Satan; see Matthew 16:23.

448.13–14   Haeckel . . . faking the evidence]   Ernst Haeckel (1834–1919), German biologist and philosopher, author of *General Morphology of Organisms* (1866), *The Riddle of the Universe* (1899), and many other works. While Haeckel was accused of fraud in connection with some of the illustrations in his books, the case remains controversial.

449.32–33   Mephistopheles himself . . . *doloris*]   Latin: Misery loves company. The proverbial phrase is spoken by Mephistophilis in Marlowe's play *Doctor Faustus* (1604).

455.28   Minerva from the brow of Jove]   See Hesiod, *Theogony:* "Then from his head he himself bore gray-eyed Athena."

458.38   Venus Callipygous]   Or Aphrodite Kallypygos, "Venus of the Beautiful Buttocks": an ancient Roman statue copied from a lost Greek original.

462.25   *Ah-so-deska*]   Japanese: *Ah, so desu ka*? Is that so?

466.4–5   eastward of Eden in 4004 B.C.]   In 1650, English cleric James

Ussher (1581–1656) published calculations regarding the chronology of the Old Testament that dated the creation at 4004 BCE.

468.33–34   the *Principia*]   *Principia Mathematica* (1910–13), by Alfred North Whitehead and Bertrand Russell.

470.28   *hnau*]   A term invented for sentient, reasoning beings in C. S. Lewis's science fiction novel *Out of the Silent Planet* (1938).

472.30   such comforters as Job had]   See Job 16:2: "Miserable comforters are ye all."

481.19   ataraxic]   Tranquilizer.

481.26   Belsen]   Bergen-Belsen, Nazi concentration camp in northwestern Germany established in 1943.

484.37   Ulysses stopped his men's ears with wax]   See *The Odyssey*, book 12.

486.20   Adlai E. Stevenson and Oliver J. Dragon]   Adlai E. Stevenson II (1900–1965), Democratic politician who ran for president in 1952 and 1956; Oliver J. Dragon or "Ollie," puppet featured on the children's television show *Kukla, Fran and Ollie* (1947–57).

501.19–20   an enterprise . . . a wolf child]   According to legend, Rome was founded by wolf-suckled twins Romulus and Remus; the date was assigned by Roman historians.

501.23   *udienza speciale*]   Italian: special audience.

501.37   Burchard]   Johann Burchard, papal master of ceremonies from 1483 to 1506.

504.12–13   *Perche mi . . . alcuno?*]   See Dante, *Inferno*, canto 13.

504.18–19   Schopenhauer's vicious *Rules for Debate*]   *Eristische Dialektik: Die Kunst, Recht zu Behalten* (1831).

507.3–4   Paul Klee's "Caprice in February"]   1938 oil painting (also titled *Capriccio im Februar*).

516.9   Kierkegaard]   Søren Kierkegaard (1813–1855), Danish philosopher.

516.9–10   the Grand Inquisitor]   Central figure of a parable recounted by Ivan Karamazov to his brother Alyosha in Dostoevsky's *The Brothers Karamazov* (1879–80).

517.6   Colin Wilson called an Outsider]   Wilson (b. 1931) published *The Outsider* in 1956.

519.26   *Into your hand are they delivered*]   See Genesis 9:2.

530.17–18   Tannhäuser . . . blossoming of the pilgrim's staff]   According to the German legend on which Wagner's opera is based, the pope's staff breaks into blossom after the departure of Tannhäuser, who is then sent for but never found.

530.34   *I believe . . . unbelief.*]   See Mark 9:24.

541.6   von Braun]   Wernher von Braun (1912–1977) was a Nazi rocket scientist who, after developing the V-2 missile, joined NASA to design the Saturn boosters for the U.S. space program.

542.10   *O felix culpa!*]   Latin: O happy fall!

542.12   Yggdrasil]   In Norse mythology, a vast tree at the center of the cosmos.

542.18   Dis]   City comprising the sixth through ninth circles of Hell in Dante's *Divine Comedy* (1321).

546.9–13   "AND THOU GREAT . . . INFERNAL KITCHEN]   Ruiz-Sanchez's curses come from Latin manuals of exorcism. See M. H. Dziweicki, "Exorcizo Te," *Nineteenth Century*, October 1888, which presents a cento of quotations from the 1626 *Thesaurus exorcismorum atque conjurationum terribilium*, an anthology of these manuals. Dziweicki translates the Latin curses "scrofa stercorate" and "porcarie pedicose" as "filthy sow" and "lousy swineherd."

WHO?

587.24   Young Tom Edison]   Film (1940) starring Mickey Rooney.

596.20–21   *Bello nipotino! . . . portano*?"]   Italian: Handsome nephew! And mama and papa, how are they?

629.18–19   "Commit a crime . . . Emerson.]   See "Compensation" in Emerson's *Essays: First Series* (1841).

644.24   when the Third Avenue El was torn down]   The demolition of the Third Avenue elevated railroad took place from August 1955 to February 1956.

654.6   WBZ]   Originating in Springfield, Massachusetts, and subsequently based in Boston, WBZ was the first commercial radio station in the United States.

655.4   Guglielmo Marconi]   Marconi (1874–1937), Italian inventor who pioneered the development of radio transmission.

656.7   Yucca Flat]   Region of southern Nevada established in 1951 as a United States government nuclear test site.

658.23   wrapped up like the invisible man?]   See chapter 1 of H. G. Wells's novel *The Invisible Man* (1897): "He was wrapped up from head to foot, and the brim of his soft felt hat hid every inch of his face but the shiny tip of his nose."

673.20   Mandjuria]   Archaic spelling of Manchuria.

673.28   S.I.B.]   Special Investigation Branch.

673.28–29   Gospodin Polkovnik]   Gospodin is a Russian honorific, like
Mister or Esquire; Polkovnik is a military rank equivalent to Colonel.

THE BIG TIME

701.1   THE BIG TIME]   Leiber added the following introduction to his
novel for an edition published by Collier Books in 1982:

> The remaining interior wall of the demolished building had on it the
> pattern of what had been destroyed: three floors and a stairway; grimy
> but with lighter rectangles where pictures had been hung on it or fur-
> niture set against it; a commanding and haunted flat expanse.
>   My friend Art Kuhl, author of *Royal Road* and the still more impres-
> sive novel *Obit.* (as far as I know never published) said, "What a chal-
> lenge to Gully Jimson!" He was surprised to find I'd never read Joyce
> Cary's *The Horse's Mouth* and so knew nothing of the rapscallion old
> painter who could never see a big empty wall without feeling the irre-
> sistible urge to paint a mural on it, whether it was coming down to-
> morrow or not.
>   I respected Art. I read the book at once and also the two other novels
> in the trilogy, *Herself Surprised* and *To Be a Pilgrim*, which cover the
> same events from three different viewpoints, and was struck by their
> style of what can be called intensified and embellished first person: not
> only is each story told by one person, but he or she has a unique and
> highly colorful way of speaking, with all sorts of vivid little eccentrici-
> ties of language—they even *think* to themselves differently.
>   So (although I didn't know it at once) Greta Forzane was born, with
> her punning religious ejaculations and her frank, cool, deliberately cute
> way of speaking—always the little girl putting on an ingratiating com-
> edy act.
>   I hadn't written anything for four years, my longest dry spell. I knew
> from experience that at such times a first-person story is the easiest way
> to break silence—it solves the problem of what you can tell and what
> you can't, whereas in a third-person story you can bring in anything, an
> embarrassment of riches, and I determined that my next story would
> be in the intensified first person of Joyce Cary.
>   I've always been fascinated by time-travel tales in which soldiers are
> recruited from different ages to serve side by side in one war—there's
> something irresistible about putting a Doughboy, a Hussar, a Lands-
> knecht and a Roman Legionary in one tent—and it's also exciting to
> think of a war fought in and across time, where battles can actually
> change the past (one of the truly impossibles, but who knows? Olaf
> Stapledon wrote about swinging it)—it's an old minor theme in science
> fiction; I remember stories by Ed Hamilton and, I think, Jack Wil-

liamson. I determined to write such a story and to put the emphasis on the soldiers rather than on the two (or More?) warring powers. Those would be big and shadowy, so you couldn't be altogether sure which side you were fighting on and at the very best you'd have only the feeling that you were defending something bad against something worse—the familiar predicament of man.

To keep the focus on a few individuals, I put the story in one setting, a small rest and recreation center staffed by entertainers who were also therapists—some of them sex therapists, a concept that had rather more novelty back in 1956 and early 1957, which was when I wrote this rather short novel (in exactly a hundred days from first note to final typing finished, it counted out). The words got to flowing rather fast and fluently for me—when I start to type phonetically ("I" for "eye," "to" and "too" and "two" interchangeable) I know I'm hot—though I rarely did more than a thousand a day. I tried the experiment of playing music to start myself off each day and this time it worked. The pieces were Beethoven's Ninth Symphony and Pathetique piano sonata and the Schubert Unfinished. The book is also keyed to the two songs "Gentlemen Rankers" and "Lili Marlene" and I sometimes played those two. (The only quotation haunting me that *didn't* get into the book was from a Noel Coward song, "We're all of us just rotten to the core, Maud.")

My plot was ready made. My disillusioned soldiers would try to resign from the war and set up a little utopia, like Spartacus and his gladiators, and then find out that they couldn't, "for there's no discharge from the war"—another familiar human predicament.

To dramatize the effects of time travel, science fiction usually asumes that if you could go back and change one crucial event, the entire future would be drastically altered—as in Ward Moore's great novel *Bring the Jubilee* where the Southrons seize the Round Tops at the start and win the Battle of Gettysburg and the Civil War (and then lose it again, heartbreakingly, when the hero goes back and unintentionally changes that same circumstance). But that wouldn't have suited my purposes, so I assumed a Law of the Conservation of Reality, meaning that the past would resist change (temporal reluctance) and tend to work back quickly into its old course, and you'd have to go back and make many little changes, sometimes over and over again, before you could get a really big change going—perhaps the equivalent of an atomic chain reaction. It still seems to me a plausible assumption, reflecting the tenacity of events and the difficulty of achieving anything of real significance in this cosmos—a measure of the strength of the powers that be.

The energy I generated writing this novel of the Change War of the Spiders and Snakes (as I called the two sides, to keep them mysterious and unpleasant, as major powers always are, inscrutable and nasty) overflowed at once into two related short stories, "Try and Change the

Past" and "Damnation Morning," and later into two others, "The Oldest Soldier" and "Knight to Move," but it wasn't until 1963 that I did a short novelette with most of the same characters, "No Great Magic," where my entertainers have become a travelling theatrical repertory company putting on performances, mostly one-night-stands, across space and time, and under that cover working their little changes in the fabric of history, nibbling like mice at the foundations of the universe—now they were becoming soldiers themselves as well as entertainers. An anachronistic performance of *Macbeth* for Elizabeth the First and for Shakespeare himself tied the story together and gave it dramatic unity, while I had to give Greta Fontane amnesia, so she could learn about the Change War all over again.

The story allowed me to draw on my own Shakespearean experiences and (once planned—it began as a modern tale of an agoraphobic young woman who literally lived in a dressing room, no Change War or science fantasy at all as first conceived) was remarkably quick in being written—ten days as I recall.

I'm *still* trying to write the sequel to that one—and still hope to do so one day; at least it's one of my penultimate projects.

703.2–6   When shall we three . . . Macbeth]   See Shakespeare, *Macbeth*, I.i.1–4.

703.13   immortal film star]   Greta Garbo (1905–1990).

707.15   *Gott sei Dank?*]   German: Thank God?

707.20   *Weibischer Engländer!*]   German: Sissy Englishman!

707.22   *Schlange!*]   German: Snake!

712.5   *Oberst*]   German military rank equivalent to Colonel.

713.10–11   Diaghilev . . . Ballet Russe]   Sergei Diaghilev (1872–1929), known as Serge, founded the Ballets Russes in 1909.

713.14–16   Last week in Babylon . . . Hodgson]   From the poem "Time, you Old Gipsy Man" in Ralph Hodgson's 1917 *Poems*.

717.35   *Nichevo*]   Russian: "Nothing," or "it can't be helped."

719.14   Passchendaele in '17]   Campaign fought in July–November 1917 near Ypres, Belgium, between Allied and German forces and ending with the capture of the village of Passchendaele.

720.2   *Halt's Maul*]   German: Shut up.

722.13–20   Hell is the place . . . Aucassin]   From the anonymous medieval romance *Aucassin and Nicolette* (c. late twelfth or early thirteenth century).

723.5   *"Omnia mutantur . . . illis,"*]   A version of the Latin adage *Tempora mutantur, nos et mutamur in illis*, meaning, "Times change, and we change with them," first published in the anthology *Delitiæ Poetarum Germanorum* (1612) by Matthias Borbonius (1566–1629), who presents it as a saying of Emperor Lothair I.

726.11–12   *ungeheuerlich*]   German: monstrous.

728.2–5   De Bailhache . . . Eliot]   See T. S. Eliot, "Gerontion" (1920), lines 67–69.

729.36   *petsofa*]   In the manner of Minoan figurines (c. 2700–1450 BCE) from the Petsofas or Petsofa hill sanctuary in eastern Crete.

732.25–29   When I take up a newspaper . . . Ibsen]   From act 2 of the play *Ghosts* (1881), by Henrik Ibsen (1828–1906).

733.11   Muskrat Ramble]   Jazz composition (1926) by Edward "Kid" Ory (1886–1973).

734.36–37   Svengali to her Trilby]   Characters from novel *Trilby* (1894) by George du Maurier (1834–1896).

735.2   *Reichswehr*]   German national defense force, 1919–35. In 1935 it was renamed the Wehrmacht.

735.4   hetaera]   Courtesan.

735.13   Panther Rag]   Jazz composition (1928) by Earl "Fatha" Hines (1903–1983).

736.2–6   Maiden, Nymph, and Mother . . . Graves]   See Robert Graves's novel *The Golden Fleece* (1944), published in the United States as *Hercules, My Shipmate* (1945).

740.2–10   After about 0.1 millisecond . . . Los Alamos]   From *A Program for the Nonmilitary Defense of the United States*, published by the National Planning Association in 1955.

741.33   *meretrix*]   Latin: prostitute.

747.22–23   Give me a place . . . Archimedes]   Archimedes's comment on the lever, as quoted by Pappus of Alexandria in *Synagoge*, book VIII (c. 340 CE).

749.11   Greek fire]   An incendiary substance used in Byzantine naval battles.

749.30–31   the *Summa* . . . *Process and Reality*]   The *Summa Theologica* (c. 1265–74) of Thomas Aquinas (c. 1225–1274); the Einstein field equations (1915) describing the curvature of spacetime; and *Process and Reality: An Essay in Cosmology* (1929), by English mathematician and philosopher Alfred North Whitehead (1861–1947).

752.33   *Um Gottes willen*]   German: For heaven's sake.

754.29–30   *zwei Herzen im dreivierteltakt*] "Zwei Herzen im Dreiviertel Takt" ("Two Hearts in Three-Quarter Time") was a song in the 1930 German screen operetta of the same name; Géza von Bolváry (1897–1961) directed the film, and Robert Stolz (1880–1975) wrote the music.

754.37   *maricón*] Spanish: homosexual (pejorative).

757.8–15   "We examined the moss . . . Poe] See "The Purloined Letter" (1844), by Edgar Allan Poe (1809–1849).

763.10–14   My thought . . . Macbeth] See Shakespeare, *Macbeth*, I.iii. 139–142.

768.20–26   The barrage roars . . . Sassoon] From the poem "Attack," in *Counter-Attack and Other Poems* (1918), by Siegfried Sassoon (1886–1967).

773.25   W.C.T.U.] Woman's Christian Temperance Union.

773.31–35   Now is a bearable burden . . . Anonymous] A quotation probably of Leiber's invention.

776.1–2   'leave not a rack behind.'] See Shakespeare, *The Tempest*, IV.i.156.

776.12   'Come, my friends . . . world'] See Alfred Tennyson, "Ulysses" (1833), lines 56–57.

778.27   *Götterdämmerung*] Opera (1876) by Richard Wagner, the last of the four operas in the *Ring* cycle.

779.2   *Kinder, Kirche, Küche*] German: Children, Church, Kitchen. A late nineteenth-century slogan defining the limits of women's social roles.

779.35   "Loki!"] Norse trickster deity described in the thirteenth-century *Poetic Edda*, sometimes termed the Elder Edda.

780.9   "*Omnia vincit amor.*"] Latin: Love conquers all. See Virgil, *Eclogues*, X.69 (c. 39–38 BCE).

781.16–19   But whence he was . . . Spenser] See Edmund Spenser's epic poem *The Faerie Queene* (1590–96), IV.7.7.

785.28   Doré illustration of the *Inferno*] Gustave Doré (1832–1883) published his engraved illustrations of Dante's *Inferno* in 1857. The *Purgatorio* and *Paradiso* followed in 1867.

786.4–5   Like diamonds . . . Webster] From John Webster's play *The Duchess of Malfi* (1613), V.v.87.

790.22–23   black legged spiders . . . Marquis] From the poem "archy declares war," in *archy and mehitabel* (1927), by Don Marquis (1878–1937).

793.32   Burbage] See note 12.27.

796.27–30   "Familiar with infinite universe . . . Heinlein] From Robert A. Heinlein's novel *Between Planets* (1951).

798.35   Nell Gwyn] Eleanor Gwyn (1650–1687), English actress and mistress of Charles II.

798.38   "Tonight's the Night"] Rock 'n' roll song recorded by Bill Haley & His Comets in 1956.

799.14–17   Rupert Brooke . . . Men who Understand;"] See lines 74–77 of Rupert Brooke's poem "The Old Vicarage, Grantchester," written in 1912.

800.17   "*Omnia mutantur, nihil interit.*"] See Ovid's *Metamorphoses*, book XV (8 CE).

801.16–23   four orders of life . . . possibility-binders] In his *Manhood of Humanity: The Science and Art of Human Engineering* (1921), Polish-American philosopher Alfred Korzybski (1879–1950) describes the first three of these orders; the fourth is Leiber's invention.

802.40–803.1   "Limehouse Blues"] Popular song (1922) by Douglas Furber (1885–1961) and Philip Braham (1881–1934).

*This book is set in 10 point Linotron Galliard,
a face designed for photocomposition by Matthew Carter
and based on the sixteenth-century face Granjon. The paper
is acid-free lightweight opaque and meets the requirements
for permanence of the American National Standards Institute.
The binding material is Brillianta, a woven rayon cloth made
by Van Heek-Scholco Textielfabrieken, Holland. Composition by Dedicated Book Services. Printing by
Malloy Incorporated. Binding by Dekker Book-
binding. Designed by Bruce Campbell.*

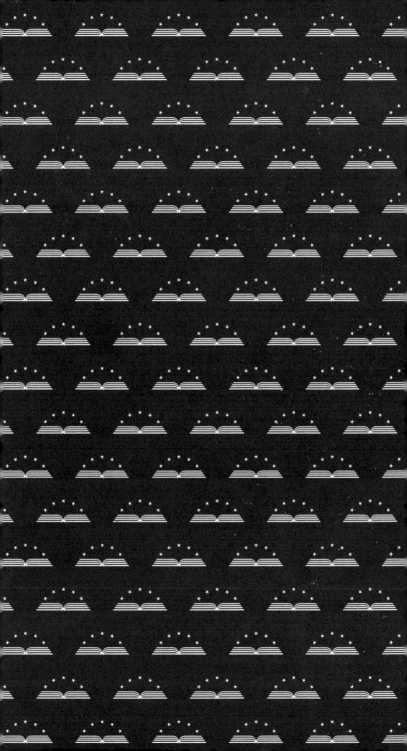